THE CULT OF SERENDEE

COMPLETE SERIES

ANGEL LAWSON

FOREWORD

Readers!

Welcome to Serendee. It's a peaceful utopia designed for living the perfect, sustainable, off-the-grid life. It's also a place where darkness and manipulation fester under the shiny surface. Greed and corruption.There's worse stuff too. That's what we need to talk about.

If you're a fan of the Royal's series...understand this book is a different kind of dark. Sam brings out my inner demon. But this series explores the fictional world of cults based on too much research and years of obsessive interest. Are there triggers? I think so. Will they send you hiding under the bed like Lords? Probably not, but here they are...

During the three book series you will encounter the following content: dub-con, arranged marriage, religious manipulation and high control, sex training, drug use, physical punishment, mental and emotional abuse, self-harm, manipulation, blood play, occult activities, sex trafficking and captivity. Oh, don't forget general mindfuckery.

Enjoy!

Angel

PROLOGUE

Before I step off the path, I glance behind me, making sure that no one else is around. The trail marker is nothing but a gash in the wood—nothing noticeable, unless it was pointed out. Which it was for me, by my mother.

Once I'm past the tree line, and starting up the hill, the trail is more noticeable. The terrain rocky, and less overgrown, although with every step I feel the sharp slap of weeds against my bare calves and relish every one.

Starting tomorrow, my legs will be covered when I go outside. Clothing requirements for females over the age of twelve require modest dress. Tomorrow is my birthday and I'll move into the domum with the other girls. But tonight, I'm still eleven—a child—and although physically I don't feel different, the teachings of the community say otherwise. Tonight is my last night of this kind of freedom, and I'm willing to make the risk because of it.

I see the outcropping up ahead and scramble up the swollen granite rock that provides a flat ledge and a view out at the community below. It's dusk, and soft light glows from the windows of the houses that dot the horizon. I can see the Main House and the dot of blue that marks the swimming pool. Beyond that is the fencing that surrounds our lands, and even further the small town just outside.

On the eve of my birthday, I should be at home celebrating with my family, but now it's just me and my father—my mother has been gone for a while. This was our special place—somewhere she told me she found while surveying the property before Anex bought it. It's on the edge of the property, the highest point and unfettered by a boundary line. It's quiet. Peaceful. And mine.

Or that's what she told me the night she left.

I wait for the sun to drop in the distance, offering a blessing for its warmth and light before the moon rises behind it. I'm focused on this, trying not to think about the changes coming tomorrow—the clothing and the lessons. The rules and preparation. Too focused, because by the time I realize I'm not alone.

Someone is already here.

"What the hell are you doing here?" he asks, standing before me, tall and lanky. I blink at the boy. I know him. *Everyone* knows him. Even at fifteen his cheekbones are sharp and defined and his shoulders unusually broad. I glance around, searching for the friends that are notoriously glued to his side, but after a beat I realize he's alone.

That makes it worse.

"I-I'll go," I stutter, knowing I shouldn't even speak to him.

"Why?" he asks bitterly, "so you can tell everyone you saw me up here? Tell my dad." He picks up a rock and tosses it over the ledge. The fading sunlight makes his pale hair shine like a halo. "Don't worry, he won't care."

I don't have to guess why he's here. I can see the dark smudges under his eyes. He looks tired. I know the look. I see it every time I look in the mirror.

"I'm sorry," I offer. What else is there to say to someone's whose mother has just died? His died a week ago. Unlike when mine left, there was a big ceremony for Beatrice, wife of Anex, mother of Rex. A parade through the center of the community. A celebration of her life and service.

"Shut up." He scowls, lip curled up. "I don't want pity. Especially from someone like you."

"Like me?" I clamp my mouth shut. My mouth. It gets me in trouble. I never know when to stop. Even now, alone with a dangerous boy, on top of a hill where neither of us should be. I will be the one in trouble if we're found. I will be the one scorned and shamed.

"I know who you are," his eyes flick over me with dark anger. "Imogene Montgomery. Your mother was the Regressive. A scar on this community."

I don't deny it.

"She's the one that should have died."

The word land like a punch. He's right. My mother betrayed us, Anex most of all, while his mother was devoted and true. I take a step back. I need to get out of here. I've heard the rumors about him and his friends. He senses that I am about to run and lunges at me, grabbing me by the wrist.

"Are you going to hurt me?" I ask, knowing he could destroy me.

His grip tightens, digging into my flesh. "Does it ever get better?" he asks. When I don't answer he adds, "Knowing they won't come back."

Oh. "No," I tell him truthfully. "Not really."

He nods, like it was what he wanted to hear and sits down on the rock. His back is to me and I should take the opportunity to run, but there's something about the slouch in his shoulders that glues my feet to the rock, knowing how much trouble I could get in for being alone with him like this. He's older than me, and I am almost twelve —old enough to know better than to be with a boy like this.

"It was so sudden, you know?" he says, picking up another stone and throwing it in the distance. "One minute she was there. The next gone."

"You father teaches us that when someone dies...The Way has determined that they are fully Integrated. Their work here is done. It's an honor."

His expression darkens. It doesn't make him less attractive. "Yes, I know what my father says. Which is why I'm up here on this rock, talking to the daughter of a Regressive. Everyone down there thinks we should be celebrating." He looks up at me with watery blue eyes and whispers. "I just want her to come back."

"I know."

I stare down at his hand for a long time until an urge overwhelms me. I pick it up and slide my fingers through his, feeling the warmth of his skin next to mine. It's wrong. Deceitful. But I understand what he's going through. How painful it feels and how much he must crave the touch of someone kind.

His fingers lock with mine and we sit on top of that rock until the sun vanishes completely and the moon shines high above. I know that tomorrow I will be a different person—a woman—but tonight it's just the two of us: Imogene and Rex.

Two kids, one powerful, one not, bound together because of what we've lost.

1

I mogene
    Six Years Later

"It doesn't work, you know."

I've just stepped out of the building, canvas bag gripped in my hand. I cut my eyes to the guy speaking to me, while definitely not making eye contact. He leans against the wall—a friend next to him, scrolling on a device in his hand. They're both in jeans and a T-shirt.

I keep walking.

"Hiding under that frumpy skirt and sweater," he continues from behind me. "It just makes us want to know what's under there even more."

My skin prickles at his insinuation. I also feel shame for being out on the street so late. I'd stayed late to help clean up after the meeting, volunteering to stay long after everyone else had left. That was foolish of me. Walking back and forth from my neighborhood to the strip of shops a few blocks away is normally not an issue, but with the University students back at school, the odds of running into someone that doesn't understand our lifestyle is amplified.

"She's one of those freaks, isn't she?" a second voice says. I guess his friend decided to join in. "Do they make you wear those skirts?"

I push past a line of people waiting to get into a popular restaurant. There are outdoor tables and people milling around. Rock music blares from speakers and the chaos makes it a good place to slip away. A small part of me wants to call out to the patrons for help and ask them to make these guys go away, but I don't. First, we're not supposed to talk to anyone outside of Serendee if we can help it. Second, I can see the judgement in their eyes. They think the same thing as the men following me; that I'm a freak.

I cut through the crowd, ignoring the looks and stares about my long, braided hair and plain clothes. I'm used to it. I grew up this way —with the locals thinking that those of us that live in Serendee are different. We are *different*, that's the whole point, but that doesn't mean we're freaks.

At the end of the building, I cut down the alley toward Serendee. The building is on one side of me and a short, picket fence on the other. My skirt swishes at my ankles and I use one hand to lift it high enough that I don't trip. The iron gate of the community comes into sight and I exhale, the feeling of safety coming back over me.

A shadow steps out from behind the building. No, two.

"Thought you could get away?" It's the man that spoke to me first. I catch the scent of stale cigarettes on his clothes. "We just want to know more about you." He jerks his head in the direction of the community. "Know more about what you people do in there."

"We don't do anything," I say defensively. Then press my teeth down on my tongue. A punishment. "Leave me alone."

"She speaks!" The second guy says, eyes bright with amusement. "I heard you aren't allowed to talk to men—or anyone really— outside your little cult. If you do, they'll kick you out."

"It's not a—" I clamp my mouth shut again.

"I heard they're not allowed to watch TV or have the internet."

"Huh," the second guy says, rubbing his scruffy chin, "then how do they watch porn?"

Despite my will, my cheeks burn at his statement—at the scrutiny of my lifestyle. I take a deep breath and conjure up an image of Anex and his intelligent, kind, face. He warned us over and over about people like this. It's why he stared Serendee in the first place.

"Tell me," the first man says, stepping closer, "do you have big orgies?"

"Nah, they only have sex with their hippie guru in charge." His brown eyes sweep over me. "That's what I heard."

I grip the handle on my bag, and I blink back hot tears at the corners of my eyes. The books inside are at least eight pounds. I could crack a head if I swung it hard enough. *A head. Not two. But I* don't want to do that. I just want to go home.

"Do you all have sex with him? I mean, isn't that what cults are really always about? Sex?" Again, I don't answer, but that just encourages him more. "You think you're better than us, don't you? With your weird outfits and innocent vibe." He continues. I follow his hand as it drops to his belt. "What would happen to you if you weren't so innocent? Would they kick you out?"

"Stop," I whisper.

His hand lowers to his crotch, cupping his manhood. "Maybe a little taste of what it's like out in the real world is exactly what you need."

A true flicker of fear rolls in my belly. I've been harassed before. So many times. But never have I been trapped alone like this. "Please," I finally say. "Please stop."

The first guy grins. "Oh, I like the way that word sounds coming out of your mouth. Say it again." His tongue darts out. "Beg me."

A heartbeat. That's how quickly things escalate. With a twisted smirk on his mouth, he closes the gap between us, and I act on instinct, rearing back, swinging the bag filled with books with all my strength. He blocks it easily, but I don't wait around, darting toward the gate. If I can just get behind it, I know they won't follow. I'm almost there when strong hands grab me by the shoulders. Fear drops into the pit of my stomach.

"Don't hurt me," I whisper.

"I'm not going to hurt you," the voice says harshly. I'm spun around. I look up and it's not one of the men in front of me. It's someone else. A member of my community. I know him. His name is Elon.

Behind him there are others—three more men, dressed more casually than is typically allowed Serendee, but these men aren't typical. Not at all. Two of them stand with clenched fists, easily separating my harassers. They're broad shouldered and intimidating. It's not a show, it's a fact. Silas and Levi. My eyes flick to the last one, and the instant I see his pale hair and blue eyes, I suck in a breath.

Rex.

"You dare speak to one of our women against her will?" Rex says, pushing up his sleeves. I can't see his face in the dark shadows of the alley, but I do see the familiar mark inked on the inside of his forearm. "Threaten her?"

The man with the scuff snorts. "At least I think she has free will. What about you? You think she's a possession, don't you? A belonging."

"Elon, get her out of here," Rex snaps, not looking our way. "Take her home."

Elon reaches around me and unlatches the gate. He doesn't touch me, as that is forbidden, but he doesn't need to. Everything about him is imposing, and I fear him almost as much as the men on the street. As I step through, the sound of flesh against flesh echoes in my ear. I glance back, looking around the man, and watch Rex punch the first guy and the other two quickly jump in.

"That is not for you to see," Elon says, ushering me forward. Soon whatever is happening is behind us and we're back in Serendee. Home.

Once I'm safe, I pause and say, "Thank you."

Dark anger clouds his expression. "If you hadn't been so foolish, you wouldn't need to thank me. If it had been up to me, I would have left you out there with the vultures."

His words hit like a slap. "Wha—"

"You should be home. Preparing for the ceremony tomorrow, not flaunting yourself to the men in town."

"I wasn—" The dark flicker in his eyes cuts me short. I know that look—the accusation behind it.

"Are you like her?" he asks suddenly. "Is that why you were out there alone? Trying to run away, too?"

That I understand. 'Her.' I'm well aware of who he's speaking about. It also means he knows exactly who I am. "I was working late at The Center so that the others could leave early to prepare. *For* the ceremony tomorrow." I lift my chin. "And I am nothing like her. Nothing."

He studies me like he's trying to assess if I'm telling the truth. I don't know what he determines, but he heads down the road toward my domum. We walk in uncomfortable silence. Men, they are allowed in and out of the community with no consequence. And men like Elon have even more freedom. The women, because of our nature—our value—we follow more complicated rules. I didn't exactly break them tonight, but it puts my motivations into question. My family's history doesn't afford much leeway.

I'm thankful when I see the building ahead. At the driveway, Elon pauses in the street, hands in his pockets, obviously waiting for me to make it safely inside. I'm still shaking as I take the path to the front door. A nagging question makes me stop.

"Why did he step in?" I ask. The 'he' is understood. A man like Rex shouldn't even spare a glance in my direction.

His eyes narrow. "You really don't know?"

I shake my head. Rex and his friends are an enigma to me. They're different from the rest of the community. Chosen.

"Don't worry, Imogene," he says, my name rolling bitterly off his tongue, "you'll find out soon enough."

2
———

Imogene

If today is a disaster, it's my mother's fault. What she did—how she abandoned us—those consequences have followed me for years. But today, I'll know exactly how much.

It's a big day. I can feel it from the instant I wake to the fluttering in my belly, in the current of energy running through the dormitory.

Today is the day we receive our Order.

"I think I may be sick."

I glance over at Maria. Her dark, wavy hair is a rumpled mess. Everything about her is familiar. Safe. We've been roommates since we both turned twelve and entered the girl's domum together. Now we're eighteen and it's the first day of spring and that's why she feels nauseous. I do, too. By noon, we'll have our Order and everything in our lives will change.

I reach over and squeeze her hand. "It'll be fine. The Orders are a direction of The Way. Anex will make a perfect match."

It's something I have to believe. That despite my mother's betrayal, I have done enough. I'm worthy enough for Anex to bless me like the others. Maria smiles gratefully, and together, along with the other eighteen-year-olds, we dress and get ready for the cere-mony. The dresses that we painstakingly made in sewing class are hung at the ends of our beds. The fabric is made of soft, white, cotton, with a high collar and long sleeves. I slide the dress over my head, and Maria and I help one another with the zipper in the back.

Hers is a little tight, and she sucks in her stomach. "I shouldn't have had that extra bread last night."

"Hold on." I wiggle the zipper, easing it up. Normally, our dresses are loose and covering, but not today. The dresses for the ceremony are special, and we're instructed to make the dresses a size smaller— to our ideal weight. Maria is thin, but she struggles with her food logs. There are always slip-ups, which lead to corrections. It's all part of the philosophy. Cravings of any kind are disrespectful to the body and a sign of a weak mind.

"Got it," I declare, pushing the zipper to the top. "See? It's perfect."

"Thank you, Imogene. You're a lifesaver." She spins and holds up a pair of new black shoes with a strap across the ridge of the foot and a slight heel. "I hope I don't trip and make a fool of myself."

"You won't," I promise. "It's a blessed day. Only good things will happen."

I almost tell her about the night before, about the altercation and the men that came to my rescue, but now isn't the time. Maybe Maria will think the same thing they did or already does. That I went out looking for trouble. That I'd asked for it in some way. Maybe, I consider now, I had.

The warning bell rings downstairs, and Maria and I finish up, heading downstairs to meet the others. There are nine of us that are of age, and we've known one another since we were children. Lived with one another since we were twelve—the year Anex thinks a child becomes an adolescent. Once you cross that thresh-old, he thinks males and females should separate entirely, from housing to education to spiritual services. Boys, I grew up with, played with and went to school and services with, were suddenly off-limits, segregated to a completely different world. At first, I was sad, but I trusted Anex to make the right decisions for the community as a whole. Everything he does is for a well-thought-out reason.

Dressed in white, the nine of us leave our domum at the back of a cul-de-sac surrounded by trees. The house next door is for the girls an age level below us, the one next to that the level below. The homes, or domum's, are nice. For a long time, people lived in their own homes, scattered across the city. People had their jobs; working in banks and schools or even at the University, but Anex had a bigger vision for people. An idea that spread like wildfire. He used some of his wealth to purchase acres of property just outside the city. A place with lots of space and room for gardens and hiking trails, meeting houses, businesses and homes. He and the other leaders created this amazing community. They decided to call it Serendee, after the word serendipity.

Community leaders will tell you that although the idea was great, Anex was the one that made it happen. He's blessed with wealth; financial and spiritual, and he used it to make Serendee come to fruition. In return, the residents give him our loyalty. Our trust. We protect one another from the darkness that festers outside our community. Out there, people don't understand what we're trying to do here—what we want to accomplish. They think it's a cult. We know they're wrong.

The nervous energy building among the girls only increases as we walk down the road toward Anex's home. That's where the ceremony will be held. The "Main House" is a mansion that sits at the top of a hill overlooking all of our community. It's white with a wide staircase to the front door and massive pillars along the front. It's a palace. A home fit for a king. For a man like Anex.

"Do you think we'll get to go inside?" Maria asks, nodding up at the house.

The butterflies swirl in my stomach. "I hope so."

During our education classes, we learned that Anex started this life as a regular man. He had two parents, went to public school, graduated with honors and entered the University. That's where he realized he was different. Smarter. Better than the other students. His

IQ is off the charts. His brain operates on a whole different level than those around him. Anex was blessed with gifts and one of those was creating The Way; a philosophy for life and success. At the beginning, it was just a bunch of college and graduate students sitting around, talking about how to live their best lives, but it emerged into something more. A philosophy that includes the body, mind, and soul.

My parents met at one of those early meetings. They saw the brilliance of Anex early on and admired his discontentment. How he always wanted more, and slowly, guided by energies deeper than I can comprehend, he built this world—our world. The one I was born into.

Clarissa, the woman that runs our house, stops at the iron gates in front of the house. She presses the intercom and announces our arrival. A moment later, the gates swing open, admitting us, and we start the climb up the hill. It's warm outside and sweat trickles down my back.

"Ouch," Maria mutters, slowing her gait.

"What?"

"It's just these shoes. They're rubbing my heel."

"Pain justifies the sacrifice," I remind her. "The reward will be worth it."

Her nose wrinkles, but she nods, holding back any other complaints. Today is not the day for complaints. It's a celebration.

As we walk past the side door, Clarissa approaches me and says, "Imogene, please come with me."

"Now?" I ask, glancing at Maria. Her eyes are wide with concern. I have no real idea about the process of today's events, but being pulled away from the others can't be good.

"Yes," she says, instructing the others to continue to the white tent up ahead. Another House Mother is waiting, waving at the girls to continue walking.

"Am I in trouble?" I ask, mind racing. Did someone hear about the night before? About the boys in town? Did Elon, or god forbid, Rex, say something to his father?

Sweat builds on my neck and I struggle to breathe.

"You're not in trouble," she says, giving me a reassuring smile while leading me into the house. I'm so anxious I can't even take in the fact that I'm in the main house. There's no time to get it together either, because Clarissa quickly leads me into a sparse white room.

The only other person inside is a female—Anex's personal healer, and a medical table.

I gape at the scene, looking to Clarissa for help. "Wha—"

"It's just a physical," she says, facing me head on and bracing my upper arms with her hands. "A formality."

"I didn't do anything. I swear."

"I know, honey. It's a formality. Everything is fine." She gives me a stern look. "This is Healer Bloom."

I've lived with Clarissa since I was twelve years old. The look in her eye does not imply that anything is 'fine.'

"Remove your dress," the healer says curtly. I've only seen her with Anex—she's his personal and private healer. Why is she examining me?

"My dress?" I repeat, slightly more upset because I spent so much time getting ready and now, right before the ceremony, she wants me to disrobe. I glance at Clarissa, and she nods reassuringly. My fingers unbutton the tiny pearl buttons I'd just fastened a short time before and I slowly, trying not to wrinkle the linen, step out of it. Underneath, I'm wearing approved undergarments, a cotton tank and shorts. They are the kind that do not encourage the male eye to gaze upon us.

"Those too," Clarissa says.

"Of course." I jump to oblige.

I curse myself as my cheeks bloom red. Embarrassment is a signal of shame, and I know I haven't done anything shameful. But I feel the healer's assessing eyes on me as I remove the undergarments, handing them over to Clarissa. My nipples harden from the cool air, and goosebumps travel down my skin. I've been to see one of the healers many times, but usually there is a robe or a barrier of some sort. I take a deep breath and remind myself that it's another reminder today is different.

The healer whips out a cloth tape measurer. "Are you following your caloric goals?"

"Yes, ma'am. Less than 800 a day." She nods and jots something down in a book resting on a tray attached to the table.

She then wraps the tape around my waist, hips and each thigh, taking a moment to pinch the skin at the base of my behind. "Every day?" she repeats, the question mark hanging in the air. I turn and look at my backside. There's some pesky flab that just won't go away no matter how little I eat.

"Yes. I log everything in my journals."

She raises the tape and circles it around my chest, at the highest point of my breasts. "32 D," she remarks, noting it in her book. She rests her pen on top and cups me with both hands. "Firm, but soft." Thumbs roll over the peaks before lowering her hands. "Sit on the table."

I do as I'm told; the paper crinkling underneath me as I arrange myself.

"It is important as we go into this day that your truth is known," the healer says, standing over me. "Every potential Ordering must be pure. Do you understand?"

"I do," I tell her, even though I'm not completely sure. I've spent my life honoring The Way. Probably more than the others.

She swings a bright light directly over my face, shocking my vision and causing the rest of the room to vanish in a dark haze. "The body doesn't lie, Imogene," she says, although I can no longer see her face. I just feel the weight of her hands and she begins her examination. "Is there anything you want to confess?"

As I search for the answer—she wouldn't be asking if there wasn't some Regression I've been hiding, I hear the soft snick of a door closing shut. Did Clarissa just leave? I blurt the first thing I think of, "Last night, on the street, a secular man and his friend tried to accost me on the way home from The Center." Her gloved fingers run down my throat, pausing to check my pulse. "They harassed me and made threats. Three men from Serendee were there to protect me, but it was my fault for being out alone at that time. I should have asked for a chaperone."

I jump with a start when she moves down to my breasts, fondling them gently with bare hands.

"Sorry," she says, with a small laugh, "I can exam you more thoroughly without the gloves." Her fingers are surprisingly firm and thick. Warm. "Am I the first to touch you here?"

"Y-yes," I say, stuttering over the feel of her circling my nipple. "I am pure. Devoted to The Way."

Her hands travel down my belly, soft yet methodical. Feeling me inch by inch. "You have let no male or female explore your body?"

I shake my head, embarrassed by my physical reaction. Can she tell that my stomach flutters from her touch? That my lower belly feels strange and full of heat? My insides twist with confusion. No one has touched or explored me like this. I gasp as she pushes my legs so that my knees are up and then taps the inside of each one. When she speaks again, her voice is further away—down near my feet. "Spread for your legs for me, Imogene. I need to check your barrier."

The barrier. Every girl has one. It is sacred and should only be broken when Anex decides. I allow my legs to drop to the side and feel the warm hands running up my inner thighs. I've been checked before—we all have—the last time a few weeks ago as we prepared for this day, but only externally. "You're going to feel a little pressure," she says. Pressure? I have no idea what this means, but it's not the soft brush against a sensitive spot, and I don't anticipate the jolt of electricity that shoots from my pelvis to my nipples.

"Oh," I gasp.

"How did that feel?"

I am unsure how to answer, so I go for the truth. "Exhilarating."

"Good. It should." After a pause, she adds, "You're sure no one has done this to you before?"

"No," I shake my head. "Never."

She touches me there again, but this time doesn't stop with one brief brush. The warm fingers roll around the nerves, coaxing and drawing me into a sense of bliss. I grip the edges of the table, trying to keep my hips still, but it's almost impossible. I stare so hard at the light that when I close my eyes all I see is spots. The sounds of the room float to me, the movement of the healer's hand, the repetitive sound of clothing shifting.

"That's right," the healer encourages, before I feel something lower, sharper. The pressure she'd warned me about.

"Oh," I gasp, jerking up, but hands hold me down. Something firm and intentional pushes between my legs. A piercing pain shoots through me, and I feel myself stretch. At the same time, warmth rushes up and down my limbs. Pleasure and pain, confusion and bliss. They're all wound up together in this moment and I don't know which direction to go. The pressure is removed as quickly as it happened, and my breath catches, a wave rushing over me as tiny pulses of release ripple across my skin. I exhale loudly, chest heaving, and feel myself slowly returning to the room.

"She's intact," the healer says. To herself? Did Clarissa return? Her comment is followed by a low strangled groan, as though someone stuffed a fist in their mouth. The light is still glaring in my eyes, blinding me from the rest of the room.

"Are we done?" I ask, feeling shaky and sweaty, not sure if I can handle much more. Is this what every female experiences before the ceremony? It feels like I've been in here forever.

"Yes." I hear that same soft snick of the door, and when I get to a sitting position, Clarissa has her hand on the knob. She smiles at me softly, eyes tense.

"Did I pass?"

The healer's eyebrows knit together. "That is for Anex to determine."

"Of course." Clarissa rushes to my side, ceremonial clothing in hand. As my eyes adjust, I notice something at the bottom of the table, down near where my feet had just been.

A pile of sticky, white, fluid.

Clarissa helps me off the table, my knees wobbly and a strange, hollow feeling at the crux of my body. I turn to look back at the fluid again, wondering with slight panic if it had come from me, but the sound of crinkling paper fills the room as the healer yanks it off the table and carries it over to the trash bin. It's the next thing that she does that makes my stomach twist uneasily.

Standing over the trash can, she peels off one glove and then the other.

I can't be sure, but a weird feeling in the pit of my stomach tells me that she never took them off.

3

———————

E^{lon}

"IT'S TIME," I say, banging on the door. The sound is matched from the opposite side of the door, dueling rhythmic grunts, each a little louder than the one before. "Rex. Man. We're going to be late."

"Give me a minute," he calls out, followed by, "you're so tight, you know that, baby?"

I roll my eyes. Leave it to Rex to get one last fuck in before a sacred event.

"Is he coming?" Silas asks. He's standing in the lobby of The Center. Levi is over on the couch, flipping through one of Anex's books, as though he hasn't memorized it by heart.

"Oh, he's coming alright." I glance back at the closed door of the instructional room and hear a female cry out in ecstasy. "I suspect about right... now."

Silas shakes his head, checking his reflection in the glass front door. We're all dressed in all black ceremonial attire chosen specifically for Anex's inner circle. Our leader is lenient with the four of us, but late to the Ordering? Rex's Ordering? That may push him too far, and I'm not interested in being on his bad side.

I walk back down the hall to the classroom door and don't knock this time. I open the door and see my best friend pounding into a redhead bent over the table. I recognized her from the night before. She'd slipped into the VIP section of the bar and glued herself to Rex pretty fast. Now, her tits bounce with every thrust, and her teeth bear down on her bottom lip as he relentlessly takes her. She's hot—they always are. Rex has a type. His eyes are closed as he chases release, his fingers pressing into the pale flesh of her ass.

"One minute," he grunts, picking up the pace. His nose wrinkles and he sputters to a stop, jerking twice more and groaning loudly. "Jesus Christ."

It's not blasphemy if you don't believe in it, right?

"Get dressed," I say to the both of them and walk back to the lobby. I shouldn't be surprised. Rex is taking every last minute before the ceremony to get his jollies off.

"Finally," Levi mumbles when the door opens and the redhead hops out, sliding a shoe on one foot. Her hair is a mess and her blouse buttoned wrong, but she doesn't look phased by the three of us.

"I assume you had a quality first lesson?" Levi asks, jumping off the couch. He grabs a schedule from the coffee table and thrusts it toward her. "We have classes every day this week."

She jerks her thumb back to the office. "Will he be there?"

Silas grins and leans against the door. "We have a rotation of instructors. It's better for you to get a firm grasp of The Way and how the system works from more than one member."

The woman sweeps her eyes over Silas—his handsome face, and easy demeanor and says, "Yeah, I'll think about it."

"Good," he says, swinging the door open and releasing her into the bright sunlight. "Have a beautiful day."

He shuts the door and Rex walks out, tugging his black linen pants over his hips. "Sorry about that, but you know how it is."

"No," I ask, leveling my oldest friend with a look. "Exactly how is it?"

His lips tug into a smile. "That girl wanted a deep and intensive understanding of The Way. I was just educating her."

"You had her bent over a table, with your dick buried so deep inside I'm pretty sure I heard her teeth clink together."

"So?" He buttons his shirt—his matching shirt to mine and the others. Anex likes uniformity. He says it creates authority. "I wanted to be thorough. Not just show her The Way, but let her feel it."

"Are you sure this doesn't have something to do with that incident last night—with the girl?"

The girl. Woman. *Imogene.* We all know who she is. What she is about to be.

Rex shoots me a glare. "No."

"Wait," Silas says, "are you calling your cock The Way now? Because that's too far for even me."

"You're not going to be able to do this forever," Levi says, his forehead creased. He doesn't like it when we joke about the rules and standards of our lifestyle. He believes in it. I mean, we all do... we just also like to have a little fun. "In fact, as of tonight—"

"Don't," Rex says, holding up his hand, revealing the scrapes from the fight the night before. "Please don't bring that up right now."

Levi exchanges a look with me and Silas. "But—"

"No 'buts.'" Rex walks toward the door. "Just because my father insists on me being part of the Ordering tonight doesn't mean my life has changed. I'll fuck who I want, when I want, how I want." He steps out on the sidewalk, looking deadly dressed in all back, and gives me a wink. "Even if it's on top of the conference room table."

4

I mogene

The lawn is emerald green, the grass thick under our shoes. There are rows of white chairs, nine on each side. Bunches of flowers are everywhere. At the back, behind a white rope, is open seating for the rest of the community. At the front, on a small stage, is a clear podium. That's where Anex will issue the Orders.

"Hurry along," Clarissa says, quickly ushering us to a tent on the left side of the stage, hiding us from the growing crowd. There's another tent opposite us, one for the men. We're not allowed to see one another until the ceremony begins.

I do manage to look out into the audience and spot my father on the front row. His hair is darker than mine, now flecked with gray. The hollow under his eyes is dark, and he looks tired, but when he sees me, he smiles. We've both suffered from my mother's betrayal. He lost his position on the leadership committee, and I carry around her sins like an albatross around my neck. Today is an opportunity for both of us to regain some credibility. I grin and wave in return before ducking beneath the flaps.

"How's my hair?" Renee asks, tugging a coil of her flame red hair. "I should have straightened it, right?"

"It looks great," Maria says, and I nod. Renee is the smartest in our group and was invited to a private meeting with Anex two weeks ago. Something only the most worthy girls accomplish while still in the domum. She didn't tell us what they spoke about—that is confidential—but when she returned, her eyes were glassy and her cheeks flushed. The most we could get out of her was that Anex is wiser than we could ever imagine, and it was the most eye-opening experience of her life.

"Settle down," Clarissa says, walking past and giving us each a small squeeze on the arm. Outside, the crowd grows quiet, which means Anex has arrived. I peek through the flap in the tent and see him up on the platform. He's dressed in his typical black. Shirt and pants. Round, small glasses perched on his nose. His fair hair glints in the sunlight, and his smile is warm and reassuring. His sleeves are rolled up over his elbows and dark ink is tattooed into the skin of his forearm. It's the same mark that I saw on Rex's arm the night before. Behind him are a group of men and women—all his confidants. One in particular catches my eye. Margaret—one of his Spiritual Mates. She's beautiful with dark, stylish hair and piercing blue eyes. She's special. She has to be, or Anex wouldn't have asked her to stand by his side.

Maria grabs my hand, threading our fingers together, and I draw my eyes away from Margaret. I cling back, overcome with the wild hammering of my heart. This is it. It's actually happening.

"Ready?" she whispers as the first name is called. Rebecca, with her white-blonde hair, exits the tent and crosses the yard. Through the narrow gap, I can see a boy—a man—stride from the other tent. His name is Paul, and I drink him in. Tall, lanky, a crooked nose, but kind eyes. He looks nervous as she does, but smiles when his eyes land on Rebecca. They meet in the middle and face the stage. Then they touch their foreheads and bow. Satisfied, Anex gives his Order.

Maria is still looking at me with expectation, her question still hanging in the air. *Ready?* I am, but I'm not. I have no idea what to expect, no clue who is on the other side of the Order. If Anex will punish me because of my mother's actions or why they needed to see me today. What I do know is that whoever he Orders me to be with, it is The Way, and there's no getting out of it.

I'll be betrothed to a man of Anex's choosing.

It didn't start like this, or so we're told. Anex didn't originally pick mates for members of the community. That happened later. It's not that he didn't think people shouldn't have free-will, of course we do. It's the twenty-first century. We live in America. But an unhappy marriage affects the whole community. Divorces are complicated. Messy and filled with toxic energy. And after a while, it seemed like a good idea to just give Anex the ability to arrange couples for the betterment of all of Serendee.

"Maria Castillo."

Her name sounds like honey on Anex's tongue. It's a thrill to get any of his attention, even if it's for only a moment. She gives me one last look and a squeeze of her hand before stepping through the flap into the bright sunlight. My breath catches as she trips over the grass, but she rights herself quickly. I exhale and watch my friend cross the yard. The tent opposite of ours opens, and a man comes out. His name is Elijah. I remember him from when we were kids. He has the same flat forehead and easy grin. Maria's smile falters for a second, but she regains it quickly. Elijah is a few years older than us, but that's expected. The rules are different for men. Women prepare for this day their whole lives. Men have to be trained to be good mates. Sometimes they have to wait until Anex decides they're ready.

One by one, the Order is given. Perfect couples, all hand-picked by Anex himself and betrothed to one another. We'll spend the next ninety days in courtship: learning about one another, preparing to be mates for life. Then we'll prepare for the bonding ceremony.

My adrenaline rises, inching up with each match, aware that my time is coming. Finally, it's just me and Clarissa in the tent alone. She gives me a reassuring look, but I see a crease in her forehead.

I'm still standing there, hands damp, when I hear Anex speak from the podium. He can't be finished, can he?

"I don't think people realize how much work goes into The Ordering. It's not an easy task, but you asked me to do it and I have tried to do my best." He smiles warmly out at his community. "These young men and women are the hope and future for our little Utopia. I am confident in their commitment to one another, to the community, and to Serendee."

I look at Clarissa and whisper, "What's happening? Why didn't he call my name?"

Her lips form a thin line, and she presses her finger against them, indicating I should listen.

"This year is special for me. Personal. After much consideration, my son, Rex, will also receive an Order. He's ready to take on the responsibility of a man—and mate."

The flaps of the tent part and Rex walks out, golden-haired and perfect, just as he was the night before when he came to my aid. My eyes drop to his hand. Sure enough, his knuckles are red and raw. Mirroring his father, he's also all in black, dressed fully in Serendee clothing today. It's hard to take my eyes off of him, but movement in the men's tent draws me away. Never alone, Rex's three best friends emerge. Are they to be Ordered as well? My gaze goes instantly to Elon, who looks just as intimidating and angry in the daylight as he did in the dark. Out here I can see the cool gray in his eyes. There's no kindness there.

Levi follows, with his flaming red hair and ivory skin. His coloring matches his sister, Renee, and I see her smile from her position in front of the stage. His green eyes are clear—his expression serious. He's well known around the center for being a dedicated student of

Anex's—one of the youngest—and a devout and a strict follower of The Way.

My eyes are drawn to the final man, Silas. He's known throughout Serendee for being a constant companion to both Rex and Anex. Even in a world where physical appearance isn't celebrated, there is no mistaking Silas' beauty. His features are almost feminine. Soft lips contrast sharp cheekbones. Long lashes and lean limbs. His smile is shy yet makes a funny tickle in my stomach. One look at the other females confirms they feel the same. Possibly some of the males. He is a very handsome, alluring person. People have wondered for years if he was going to ever be Ordered, but it seems his place is by Anex's side.

When all three are on the stage, Rex approaches his father, standing in the center of the stage. His features are more defined than Anex, more chiseled. Everyone—the newly Ordered—the crowd in the back gawks at the men on stage. This moment is very unusual, and my pulse quickens at the realization I'm a part of it.

"It took a great deal of consideration to determine Rex's Order, but in my heart, I already knew. I've been watching this young woman for years, blossoming into the perfect mate for my son..."

I feel the weight of Clarissa's hand on my shoulder, heavy and firm. When I look up at her stern expression, it all clicks.

"Imogene Montgomery," my name is called out, settling over the ceremony. Rex's eyes pin to me the instant Clarissa pushes me out of the tent. It's not just the heat of his eyes that I feel, or that of the crowd in the ceremony. It's from the other men on the platform, Silas, Levi and Elon, watching me with a careful eye. My skin prickles and my cheeks flush, but I walk across the grass anyway, the heels sinking into the dirt. Anex grins, lopsided and charming, gesturing for me to climb the small set of stairs at the front and as I do, Rex steps forward, offering me his hand.

"Here," he says softly. I take his hand, warm and strong, and a moment later I'm standing in front of the whole community.

Anex nods when he sees the two of us together. "Good. This is good." He faces the crowd. "In front of all of Serendee, I witness the

Order of each of these couples," he declares, hands up in blessing. "Today is the beginning of your courtship. Take this time to get to know one another, how to support and care for one another. To fulfill one another's needs." I may be mistaken, but I feel Anex's eyes flick toward his son when he says that last one. "The bonding ceremony will be on the first day of fall. You have been Ordered."

The audience stands and claps, cheering on the new couples. On the patio, volunteers have set up a celebration—sweets from the bakery, fresh food from the farm. I try to process everything, but I'm overwhelmed. Confused. Did Anex just Order me to his son? Me, the daughter of a Regressive, to the heir of Serendee?

"Congratulations," he says to the two of us, patting Rex on his shoulder, before striding off the platform, heading toward the festivities.

Out in the grass, the couples are shyly smiling at one another, excited about the prospect of their futures. I look over at Rex, the twist of anticipation warm in my chest.

I glance toward the party and say, "Should we—" That's when I realize he's not looking at me and is already halfway off the platform. "Where—"

He jerks his head at Elon. "Take her to her room," he says, "and get her settled. I'll deal with this later."

A moment later he's gone, and I'm being escorted off the stage, toward the massive home. In ninety days, it'll be my home, too. Mated to the second most powerful man in the community.

5

———

Imogene

I'm handed off three times before I get to my room. First by Elon, who walks me into the house and into the foyer. He doesn't acknowledge me, but I barely notice, too busy taking in the magnificence of the house. I've been to some of the public areas before, but I've never gone into the private quarters, and I'm struck by the opulence. Before I can get too invested in the inlaid floors and crystal chandeliers, I'm handed off to a member of the main house staff who leads me up two floors of the curved staircase. The hallways shoot off in every direction, wings inside of wings, each decorated with the same wood paneling and fine, but nondescript artwork. We pass multiple staircases, and by the time we reach the final handoff; I feel like I'm twisted in a maze. I'm given to Clarissa last, who waits by a set of thick double doors on the third floor.

"Imogene," she says, her smile genuine and proud, "congratulations on your Order, sweet girl. I always knew you'd do great things."

She opens the doors, revealing not just a room, but an entire suite. At the round table, just inside, are my belongings. A wooden trunk and a small suitcase. I walk over and open the case. Inside are my journals and logs, along with a few photos and my lesson books.

"Your clothes are there as well," she says. "Including the new outfits for the courtship."

I'd spent months sewing and creating a wardrobe to carry me up to the bonding ceremony. Now that I know that I've been arranged to Rex, the idea of wearing them for him sends a flurry of nerves in my stomach. Are they too simple? His clothing is always neatly tailored. I'm embarrassed for him to see my lack of ability.

"Did you know about this?" I ask, slowly closing the trunk. "That I was going to be Ordered to Rex?"

"Anex spoke to me about it, yes. I couldn't tell you."

I nod. It's understood that Anex speaks to the house mothers when he's making his decisions. There are other ways he learns about us; how we do in our studies. Are we attentive in lectures? Do we encompass The Way of Serendee? The extra physical makes a little more sense, in retrospect. The Heir of Serendee must have a pure mate, but that's also what creates my fear.

"Why," I finally say, "would Anex choose me for his son? I'm... the daughter of a Regressive. A runaway. An abandoner. Why would Anex want me to be with Rex, and how disappointed is Rex to have me as his betrothed?"

"It's not our place to question his Order," Clarissa replies, leading me deeper into the suite. "The only way this works is if we have faith. Don't you have faith in The Way?"

"Of course," I say quickly, feeling shame for even allowing the question to be asked.

"Then stop worrying," she says, "and let's take a look at your new home."

There is a living room and a well-appointed kitchen. There are two hallways going in opposite directions, and along the back wall is a wide window that overlooks all of Serendee. "There are bedrooms down each hall, including two masters. One for you and one for Rex." She gestures to the left. "Your room is this way."

She takes me down one of the hallways, passing two additional rooms, and leading me to another set of double doors that open into a large bedroom. The bed sits in the middle; the frame made of twisting iron. There's a quilt folded on top of the sheets. I step forward and see a note.

"The Women's Assembly?" I ask, reading their congratulations. "They made me a quilt?"

"You and Rex, yes. The bonding quilt. It's customary."

Me and Rex. In the same bed. It's something I've pushed out of my mind, as I've been instructed to my entire life. But here it is. Now that I'm Ordered the time has come to think about it; sex.

But not now, I think, feeling the heat in my cheeks. Not today. It's one reason for the courtship. Anex knows people develop intimacy at their own pace. I tuck the card, which includes an invitation to the next meeting, back inside the quilt.

"Imogene," Clarissa says, watching me carefully, "I know this is overwhelming, but you didn't just receive an Order today. You were *Chosen*. A position that many others would sacrifice to have."

True. There are many girls that would love to be in my position. And many girls are unhappy with the one they were given. But no one complained or questioned. That was the curse my mother left me with. Her obstinance and curious disposition. Her inability to just *accept*. It's like a disease running through me. I can't stop it no matter how much I try.

Being Chosen isn't something people know much about. It simply means that Anex has determined that you are worthy of being part of a higher circle in Serendee. Being Ordered to Rex elevates me to this level.

Clarissa clears her throat and sits on the end of the bed, patting the spot next to her. I take my place, feeling the soft give of the mattress underneath me. "You have spent the last seven years preparing for this moment. You know how to cook, clean, sew. You know how to maintain a home—"

"Even one this size?"

She nods. "That will be a challenge, but there will be assistance."

"I'm not worried about maintaining the home. I know I am ready." I tug at a thread on the quilt.

"Then what is on your mind?"

I want to push back my curiosity, the questions, but I can't. "At my job at The Center, I've had the opportunity to see Rex, and I know that he has lived differently than the rest of us. He often wears secular clothing and spends a lot of time around people outside of Serendee."

That's the nice way to put it and doesn't even include the gossip that swirls around Rex and his friends. Seeing him out the night before wasn't unexpected. Even in Serendee gossip flourishes, particularly about this group of men. That they go into town often and frequent the restaurants and bars filled with worldly college girls. Secular girls. That they are *experienced*.

"Imogene," she says, taking my hand, "I've taught you not to listen to petty rumors, haven't I?" I nod. "Rex was raised to be a leader, and leadership requires a different approach. His position at The Center requires him to straddle both our world and the secular world. There's no scandal there. Anex can't protect us from the outside world if he doesn't know what to protect us from, can he?"

"No."

"So yes, Rex and his companions have had access to that world so that they can lead Serendee in the best way possible. They are the ones that must bear the burdens of a fast-changing world—a sinful world." Her nose wrinkles and looks me in the eye. "You have been Ordered to be his mate, not to question his affairs. You are here to fulfill his needs as a partner, not as a confidant. That is not your place as his mate or as a member of Serendee. Do you understand?"

"Yes, ma'am."

"This will not be an easy transition for you, Imogene. You are going to be required to do things that feel foreign and strange. Subversive, even, but that is part of being given this honor. You will be the mate of the next leader of Serendee, and with that will come great sacrifice as well as rewards."

What she says makes sense. The pieces click into place. "I guess

I'm just overwhelmed by the honor of the arrangement. I never expected—"

"You deserve it. Anex sees something important in you. Something others have questioned." Her smile turns sympathetic. "From now on those questions will end."

Because no one will dare second guess Anex or Rex's judgement. It's a reprieve from the sins of my past and a second chance. One I will not squander.

~

I'm not the only one in a new home today. All of the Ordered are given a house to live in at the beginning of their courtship. Anex believes that during this time all areas should be explored together, making sure that by the time of the bonding ceremony the couple is ready. Outside of Serendee, a wedding is the start of a new life together, but not here. It all begins with the Order. It's another way that we are more advanced.

What I do have to wonder is if my friends are spending their first day alone like I am. Hours pass, and Rex has not made an appearance. I have no idea when or if he will. Anxious from waiting, I decide to take a shower and change, freshen up for if and when he does arrive.

The bathroom is luxurious with a big tub and a separate shower. There's a dressing table already supplied with toiletries. The idea of taking a shower in my own bathroom is a thrill. I've always had to share with strict time limits and limited hot water usage. Those habits die hard and even though I'm the only one here, I bathe quickly, still thinking about what happened the night before with those men in the alley.

It's well known that people think Serendee is a cult. The word is tossed around so frequently, so lightly, that it's something of a joke within the community. We don't prescribe to any specific religion other than a basic spirituality. The Way isn't about a higher deity. It's about living a responsible, accountable life. How can we be a cult? It's laughable. Anex tells us that people slight others when they're jealous or frightened. They're scared to take the risk that the founders did all those years ago. To have the belief that there's something more out there than how they've been conditioned.

The core concepts started with sustainability. Creating a community that relies on the government, the establishment, and corporate systems as little as possible. It was a bold plan, but Anex was an environmental engineer and his friends were skilled in other sciences and educated at the university and what they didn't know, they learned. One of these people was my mother, who was working on her master's degree in community development. Serendee was executed with a plan. We have gardens and livestock. We compost and reuse as much as possible. We use solar energy and limit our carbon footprint. We nurture the earth, and, in return, the earth nurtures us.

I know it all sounds hippie-dippy, but it's not just that. Anex is a brilliant thinker. He's prepared. He's gifted and our little community has been given awards and has been highlighted for how people should aspire to live. We have everything we need inside the walls of Serendee. Everyone has a role. A purpose. A job. There are farmers and builders, teachers and technicians. There's a bakery and a seamstress. A grocery and market. Each adult is given credits for their work and those credits are how we purchase what we need. Any supplies needed from outside the community are processed through the Main House. It's a perfect system, created by a perfect man.

That's what makes the Order today so intimidating.

Rex's purpose will be to take over for Anex one day.

My purpose will be to support him.

After I bathe, I take the time to brush and dry my long, thick hair. All the young girls and women have long hair—as we've been taught to downplay our physical appearance and focus on our inner value instead. Today is the first day I'll be viewed as more than just a girl. I'm a potential mate and I can't help but study myself in the mirror, wondering what he'll think of me. Is my hair too long? Too immature? I've seen secular women in town. They look... different. More sophisticated, exotic.

I braid my hair and change into one of the new dresses folded neatly in my trunk. The color is a soft blue, similar to Rex's eyes, and has a tighter bodice than I normally wear. Looking for hand lotion, I open one of the vanity drawers. I'm surprised to see a collection of makeup. None of the girls in the house wear makeup. It's considered secular—something done outside of Serendee. Nature gave us our looks. We don't need to accentuate it. Quickly, I shut the drawer and step away. Obviously, whoever stocked this room made a mistake.

When I enter the living room, I jolt to a stop, surprised to find Rex waiting for me in the living room. He's facing the window that overlooks Serendee. His golden hair shines in the afternoon light. My stomach flutters as I take in the tight fit of his black linen shirt across his wide shoulders. He has the body of a man, something I'm not accustomed to being around for more than a few seconds of time.

He's also alone.

The smile that spreads across my face isn't false. This is the moment I've been waiting for.

"Hello," I say when it's clear that he doesn't realize I've entered the room. He turns, and I'm struck with how he's even better looking than I realized. His eyes, they're so blue, like the reflection of the sky. His features, the line of his nose and the curve of his cheekbones, are startlingly strong. His hair shiny and pale. I can't help but look for the bruises on his knuckles. They're the only flaw I can see. Red, raw, and exposed.

"Imogene," he says, his voice curt. Jaw tight. "I wanted to stop by and speak to you."

Stop by... as in visit.

He gestures to the couch and I sit with my knees pressed together, hands folded on my lap. I wonder, as he takes the chair across from me and runs his thumb over his knuckles, if he remembers the last time we were alone together? That night when I was twelve, and he was a hurt, sad boy.

"Thank you for that," I say, staring at his hand. I'm not sure where to hold my gaze. "For defending me last night."

"No one should degrade our women." He chuckles darkly. "Or *my* woman in particular."

The statement causes a little thrill, something deep in my spine. It scares me, but also causes some excitement. I've waited so long for my Order, and now that it's here I feel so overwhelmed. I run my hands over my knees, smoothing my dress, daring a glance up at him and find him watching me.

"Would you like for me to cook dinner? Or would you prefer to show me how you want the house kept? Clarissa taught us to make sure everything was in order, but a home this size isn't what I was prepared for..." I trail off, aware that I'm rambling. "Please, tell me how we should proceed."

"That is what I came to talk to you about." He inhales deeply and then exhales. "We will not be proceeding in a typical fashion."

I frown. "What do you mean?"

"I mean that you and I will not participate in this farce created by my father. This life? Serendee... The Way? I don't believe in it. It's bullshit."

My gasp is audible. Everything he's said from the curse word to his statement throws me.

He shakes his head. "This is what I mean. What shocks you more? My vulgarity? Or my blasphemy?" I swallow the lump in my throat, but no words come out. He smirks. "It's both, right? I can see it on your face."

"I don't understand what you're saying."

He runs his thumb over his tattoo. It's a small circle depicting the sun and the moon. He got it when he was sixteen. There was a ceremony, and we all watched as the tattooist inked it on his forearm. It's the symbol of The Way and worn by the leader of Serendee to remind him to stay grounded. Or, in his case, the next leader.

"I've seen beneath the curtain and what lies on the other side. The good stuff. The real stuff; sex, drugs, alcohol, music, books. I may be forced into this role by my father, but I have no intention of settling down and abstaining."

Each admission is like a wrecking ball trying to knock me off my foundation. Although I understand the words he is saying, I do not understand why. Why would he feel this way? And why, if he did, would he— "If this is how you feel, why did you drag me into it? Why did you get Ordered?"

He laughs and narrows his eyes. "Why do you think?"

"I have no idea. I have no idea why you are saying such terrible, such despicable things."

"Do you think I have a choice? Any more than any of the others here?" He lifts his chin. "Than you? I don't believe, sweetheart, but there is no getting away from my father either. Not without paying for it dearly." He holds my eye. "I thought if anyone would understand it would be you."

"Me? Why me?" I'm dutiful and faithful. I work hard, study, and I follow all of the rules. But the set of his jaw and the lift of his eyebrow answers my question. "Oh. Because of my mother."

"When my father told me that I was to be Ordered this year, he did allow me one concession; the opportunity to choose my future mate. I could have anyone, obviously, but I didn't need the most beautiful girl or the most obedient." His eyes turn cold as the truth spills out. "I needed someone that no one else wanted—someone that was flawed and couldn't make demands. Someone that couldn't make a fuss when she learned the truth about the parameters of our relationship. He wasn't happy about it. He doesn't like the idea of having someone like you so close to our home, but I told him I would handle it, *you*, and ultimately he agreed."

A hot tear streaks down my cheek. There's no holding it back. I suck in a breath and ask, "What does that mean? For me?"

"It means you will live in this house, and we will pretend on the outside to have a perfect bonding. It will be a farce, but if we do not uphold it and convince the members of Serendee then we will both pay the price."

"Wait," I say, hopping out of my seat. All of this is moving so fast.

"If we pretend on the outside, why can't we just try to make it work. Even if you don't..." I swallow, "believe in your father's teachings, I am ready to be whatever you need me to be. I can make you happy."

Laughter rumbles from his chest, this time genuine and pure. "No, sweet Imogene, you cannot make me happy."

"Why?"

"Because...I want things that you can't give me." He stands inches away and rakes his eyes down my body. "Things I require to live like a man. Gluttonous, sinful, secular things." He reaches out and grazes those raw knuckles across my cheek, wiping away a tear. "Things a girl like you, no matter how much you're like your mother, could never provide me."

"That's not true. I've prepared my whole life for this. I can do—be, whatever you want."

He laughs, demoralizing and cruel. "Sorry, but no. I don't want home-cooked meals and a tidy house. I want a woman with meat on her bones, who doesn't look like she'll break when I bend her over the nearest surface and bury myself inside of her." His eyes narrow. "Do you even know what that means?"

I want to say yes, but it's a lie. Everything he says is confusing, but I know the tone. It's mean. He's mocking me. "No."

His fingers trail down my neck. "Figure out how to use that body of yours, and how to please me, and maybe we can talk."

My body reacts from the way he looks at me; embarrassment, humiliation, horror... but there's something else. Something deep inside that flickers like a hot, dangerous flame.

"So what do I do now? Everything I've prepared for is worthless."

The look he gives me is sympathetic—or maybe pitying. "You'll continue on as normal, going to your position at The Center, attending meetings, and we'll present as a couple when it's required. We'll go through the ceremonies and get bonded in the fall. Outside of this house, no one will know the difference." He takes a step back, and I think he's going to leave. I *hope*. But he stops and says, "You know this isn't the end of the world for you, Imogene. If it hadn't been for me, my father wouldn't have Ordered you with anyone at all. Not with your reputation." His words are cold and harsh. True. "I've given you a gift. This way, you've entered the most powerful home in Serendee. You're not just Ordered, you've been Chosen, and there are perks to being in this position even if it isn't what you expected."

With that, he walks out of the living room. I hop up and follow him to the front door. "Where are you going?"

"I'm not staying here. I have my own suite. You'll remain here."

"But—" I start, panic starting to rise. He vanishes, closing the door behind him. I'm left alone for the first time since I was twelve, in a strange house with nothing but my disgrace.

6

R ex

The look on Imogene's face when I leave the suite is exactly why I don't play with the females in Serendee. They're wound up so tight, caught in the layers upon layers of my father's manipulations, that they don't even know what's real and what's not.

Which is exactly the point.

I stride down the hall, pushing aside the image of those big blue eyes looking as though I had snakes coming out of my eyes. How dare I say I don't believe in The Way, or even worse, the teachings of Anex? *Blasphemy!* I knew she would struggle to even hear it, which is exactly why I told her. Imogene Montgomery is nothing but a sheep, but that doesn't mean she shouldn't know the truth about what's about to transpire between us. We are Ordered, after all. And if she needs to understand one thing up front, it's that I am not giving up my freedom for some innocent little virgin my father thinks will keep me latched to this bullshit society forever.

I enter my personal rooms, along the opposite wing of the house. I should be moving into the suite with Imogene today and beginning our courtship, but that's not happening. I walk into the den and see my best friends lounging on the couch. Silas and Elon are playing video games. Levi has his nose shoved in a book.

"So," Silas asks, "how did she take it?"

"Well enough. I didn't give her much choice." I pick up the controller but after a few movements toss it aside after the throbbing pain in my knuckles makes it too hard to play.

"I feel a little bad for her," Silas says. "She spent the last seven years preparing for this day and you completely crushed her dreams."

"Yeah," I admit. "She seemed ready to fulfill her role. She asked if she could make me dinner."

"I don't know why you have to push back on this," Elon says, striking a match. Sulfur fills the room, and he lights a rolled joint and takes a drag. He hands it off to me. "You're not leaving Serendee. Why does it matter?"

Because I'm not getting attached, I want to say. "Because my father Ordered me this season because he's trying to control me. He's the one that opened the door and showed us that there's a bigger life outside of Serendee. He taught us how to straddle the line. He thinks that if I get Bonded to one of his devoted; a damaged, needy, desperate little girl, then I'll come back to the fold."

"But why not just take her as your mate? She's cute. A little too skinny for my taste, but her tits are nice." Silas asks. "She'll probably make a good lay once she figures it out."

"Yeah," I snort. "They are pretty nice. Perky." I may not want to be Ordered to her, but I'm still a man. I'd felt it the other night in the alley when those men were harassing her. I may not want to Bond with her, but that doesn't mean someone else can have her. Especially some asshole from town.

"So you do like her?" Levi asks, glancing up from his books. I can tell from the spine it's one of my father's. Levi's the only one that doesn't game with us. Or smoke, or drink, or fuck around. Despite having more leniency with the standards in Serendee, he does his best to stay on track, unless it's for work. I think my father approved him as one of my confidants because he'll report back. What dad doesn't get is that he's more loyal to me than him. "It's understandable to be wary. Her mother was Regressive."

Regressive. It's the term we, no Anex, coined for the people that challenge him. The ones that are no longer welcome inside his sacred little walls.

"I'm not wary. She's just not my type."

Silas snorts. "You mean she's a virgin and not some skank at the bar. Think about it, Rex, I bet she's tighter than Levi's tie."

Levi frowns and touches his neck, shooting Silas a dirty look.

I push his arm, making his hand slip off the controller. "I'm not getting tied up with an emotionally stunted, devotee of my father's. No matter how fuckable her tits look or tight her pussy is."

When I turned eighteen, my father began showing me and the guys the other side of Serendee. The business and money and the methods he uses to keep his perfect little town under control. Learning that truth had been Earth shattering. I'd been like everyone else in the community—a sheep—believing all of Anex's manipulations and lies about the evil that resides outside Serendee's walls. About the roles of men and women—about sex and desire. I believed all of it. That if you followed The Way—followed him—happiness and contentment would follow.

I think, for a brief time, that it was true that Serendee had all of those things. The problem for Anex is that he always wants more, and to have more he had to spread his wings. Silas, Elon, and Levi, and I were the wings. We each have our own positions; mine is primary as a recruiter. Levi's is teaching classes down at the Center. Elon's task is quiet—working in the shadows doing whatever it is my father wants or needs. And Silas? My father capitalizes on his best feature; his ability to seduce people in and outside of Serendee.

My connection to The Center is how I knew about Imogene—the daughter of the betrayer. When Anex told me it was time to get Ordered, I already knew who I wanted. I chose the girl that was pretty enough, completely compliant and totally desperate. Someone I can control.

Because there is no leaving. No getting out. There is just... finding pleasure in one world and tolerating the other. My father is too dangerous to walk away from. The consequences... well, I'd seen what had happened to those that questioned him publicly. The people who had doubts. And he's made sure that I can't leave. I rely on him for everything: money, housing, support. He's sullied my hands. He has leverage. Even if I risked it, where would I go? Even with a foot in the secular world, I don't know how to exist there. Not the way I do here.

My father created my world, a world that one day will be mine. Even if I think every single word out of my father's mouth is a lie, I have to pretend otherwise. We all do. Now we're just four fucked up, directionless men, straddling two very different worlds.

And that's how it will continue—except in ninety days I'll have a woman by my side that needs to understand the truth. My truth. I will never be the mate she wants or needs, nor will I use her for my pleasure, because I refuse to put her in that kind of danger.

The sooner she understands that, the better.

7
____

I mogene

My mother wasn't always an embarrassment. She'd actually been one of the original members of Serendee, one of the innovators. She'd studied urban and community planning. She loved horticulture and advocated for the gardens that feed and nourish the members. For many years, Anex, along with everyone else in Serendee, relied on her intelligence and friendship. It's one reason her betrayal hit so hard.

As a mother, she'd been kind and fun. Strong. She took me with her to work as often as possible, showing me how to tend to the gardens. She told me all about her long-term plans to grow more vegetables, herbs and fruits. There would be a bigger greenhouse and the backfield would eventually be cleared and plowed. She advocated for less housing and more green space. That was something she and Anex disagreed on. It may not be why she ultimately left, but it was part of it. The real reason was her ego and pride, her lack of faith. But mostly, her questions.

Anex's vision is to continue to grow Serendee in land and population. Two years after my mother left, one of his dreams came to fruition. The Center—a three story building on Main Street—a visible spot in the middle of town for people to stop in and learn more about The Way. He could have built it inside the gates of our community, but that's not what he wanted. He wants the world to know about our way of life. We can't do that by hiding.

It's another reason we laugh at the idea of our lifestyle being a cult. Do cults set up shop for any and everyone to enter? We have no secrets, Anex says, just opportunities. And the opportunity to explore The Way is for everyone. That is, if they're willing to do the work.

It flies in the face of our detractors, that and the fact they think women aren't allowed to hold positions, but they're wrong. Anex tells us often, females are the glue that binds the community together. I'm the perfect example. I was given the position of managing the front desk at the center a year ago, when I turned eighteen.

After spending the night alone, where I was caught in restless sleep about Rex and his whereabouts, I came in early to get my mind off the odd turn in my life. There are three floors of offices, all strictly used for Serendee business. Floor one is for seminars and meetings. The second floor is for real estate and the day-to-day management required for a community the size of a small town. The third is the private offices for Serendee Leadership. They aren't used that frequently, and when they are, people tend to come in and out of the back door that leads directly to the staircase. Anex rarely comes in at all. Everyone wants a moment of his time. He's in high demand with people in and outside of the community, but it's widely understood he doesn't like traditional meetings, preferring to have more casual interactions down by the lake or playing a game of basketball at the gym. Which is why, when I hear the chime on the front door and look up from my desk, I'm shocked to see him walk through the door.

I drop the pencil and quickly touch the spot in the center of my forehead while bowing slightly. "Good morning."

He smiles warmly. "Good morning to you as well, Imogene. I hope you slept well after the excitement of yesterday."

"I did, thank you." It's a lie. One I will jot down in my journal later.

"I wanted to speak to you."

"Oh, yes. Of course." I step away from the desk. "Would you like my seat?"

"Thank you, dear." He moves behind the desk and sits in the chair. I don't miss how he assesses everything in my workspace. I move quickly, anxiously. Anex has never given me a reason to be uncomfortable around him. It's the opposite. He's so kind and generous. So wise with his knowledge. To be in his presence is to feel blessed—favored. "It's my understanding that you met with my son yesterday after the ceremony."

"Yes, I did."

He leans back in the seat. "And he told you his feelings about Serendee and The Way."

"He did." I add quickly, "I made it very clear that I did not agree with his views."

"Of course not. You are a loyal member of this community, Imogene. It's why I trust you in this position at The Center. In fact, it's why I agreed to his request for you to be his mate." He smiles. "You know what it is like to be betrayed by a family member."

It always comes back to this. "I do."

"But you also know how important it is to not let them go—to fight to keep them close."

"Yes, I do understand that." My father and I failed Anex when we couldn't make my mother stay.

"Your father fought for her," he says, as though he can read my thoughts, "but she was too far gone. Too poisoned." Hearing this is surreal. No one discusses my mother and if she is ever brought up at all, it is as a warning. "You were too young to do anything when Alia made her decision, but that is not the case today."

I frown. "What do you mean?"

"My son needs you, Imogene. He needs your guidance and your support. To be nurtured like plants in the garden." His eyes are clear and determined. "But most of all, he must stay in Serendee and continue to work toward leadership." He tilts his head. "I need him, Imogene, as much as you do."

The statement comes out softly, but the threat is there. I need him to make me reputable again. This is my shot at redemption in the eyes of the community. Anex and I look at one another for a long time, but all the apprehension drifts from my body. If I felt lost last night talking to Rex, things are much clearer now.

"I am at your service," I tell him, "and will do whatever must happen to keep Serendee on its righteous path. Tell me how to help your son."

~

What he asks of me is startling. Shameful. Uncomfortable.

"I don't blame my son for his... needs. All men have them, but those of use that believe in The Way, do our best to channel them into more productive activities." He sighs. "It's my fault, really. I gave Rex too much access to the secular world. I wanted him to have the same education and opportunities that I did, assuming it would only bolster his abilities for leadership. Instead, he has been swayed by the pleasures of that society and he doesn't want to give it up."

"I know nothing about the outside world," I tell him. "I don't know what I can do to help him."

"You show him that you can be everything he needs to be happy and successful."

Rex told me himself that he wants sex and drugs and fun. "I'm sorry, but I don't know how to provide that."

"I'm sure you don't, but... well," he looks around the office, picking up a few things on my desk, "did you know how to manage an office when you first started working here?"

"No. Not at all." I point to a bookshelf. "I studied books on office management, and I asked for help when I could. But the best method is trial and error—" I clasp my hands together and my skin turns hot. "Oh."

"Like with any new skill, you will need to be taught—trained."

Anex stands and walks around the desk. The uneasiness in my stomach grows. "I believe in you, Imogene. You are resilient and determined. Like your mother, you are very smart, but unlike her, you are loyal and will give what is needed to protect this community for the future."

"When," I swallow back my heartbeat, "when does my training begin?"

"Tonight. At your suite in the main house. I have assembled a skilled team to teach you everything you need to know about pleasing a man like my son. And although there will be times where it seems confusing or trying, understand that everything asked of you has been approved by me and is part of The Way." He reaches out and glides a hand down my hair and rests it on my shoulder. My skin prickles from his touch. "I have faith in you, Imogene."

It's an honor to have Anex believe in me like this, but I still fear what comes next. I close my eyes and brace myself, but it's unnecessary. His hand is gone and when I reopen my eyes, so is he.

8

S ilas

I WALK DOWN the patio steps, toward the small cottage at the back of the main house property. It was built for guests, primarily new recruits, that Anex wants to ease into Serendee. Although I was raised here, and our way of life seems normal, I know enough about the secular world to understand that at first glance, things around here seem... different.

They're right.

Serendee is a haven compared to the outside world. It's quiet and peaceful, with fresh air and locally grown food. Our lives are controlled, days filled with meditation and self-improvement, seeking enlightenment, but what most people in the community don't understand is utopia comes with a price. One I pay as part of my duty to Serendee as part of Anex's inner circle.

I pass the pool, the crystal-clear water refreshing and clean. This area is sacred to residents of the main house and Anex's personal guests. Many are secular, which means they must be kept separate from the main community. My job is to help potential members get comfortable. Anex saw my gift when I was just a teenager and helped me cultivate it.

I enter the guest cottage, which seems small in comparison to the main house, but is a nice size. There's a living room and kitchen, two bedrooms. There's the room I will attend to our guest—a woman named Kayla—heiress to the Montclair publishing company. They specialize in books focused on health and nutrition, as well as sustainable living. Anex has worked very hard to get her attention.

I knock on the door. I'd asked Kayla to be ready for me when I arrived.

"Kayla, it's Silas, are you ready?"

"Yes," I hear, the words slightly muffled. I step inside the room, dimming the lights, as I take in Kayla on the massage table. She's on her stomach with a white sheet draped over her body. Her shoulders are bare and even in the faint light, I can see the emerging gray streaks in her hair.

I take a moment to light candles around the room and turn on some soft music. I stop in front of a mirror and try to see past my reflection to the other side. It's impossible. Approaching the table, I say, "Are you ready to take another step toward enlightenment?"

She cranes her neck slightly and looks at me. I see the surprise in her eyes when she sees my face. I'm not just handsome, but appealing. Calming. I have a kind face. I know this. Women like it and I work it to Serendee's advantage. "If that means you'll work the knot out of my shoulder, then yes, I'm so ready."

Laughing, I squeeze a liberal drop of oil into my hands. I warm them up and start to work on her shoulders. She's right about the tension. I feel the knot almost instantly and begin rubbing that spot gently.

I took my first massage therapy class when I was sixteen. Anex felt this would be a good place for me to focus my gifts. I enjoy making people feel better, helping them with their aches and pains. The best, though, is when I'm working with a woman like Kayla. She's seeking more in her life, or she wouldn't be here. She wants to unblock her mind and release what's holding her back.

I know exactly how to help her.

Carefully, I push the sheet down to her lower back and begin focusing on that area. Next, through the sheet, I work her glutes, then the back of her thighs, her hamstrings and calves. She groans softly and shifts a little on the table. The movement is enough to let the sheet fall. I let it and wait for her response. When there is none, I continue to make passes up and down her body, easing the tension from her muscles.

Incrementally, my fingers knead into her glutes, dipping between her cheeks, and then a slow sweep between her thighs until I 'accidentally' brush against the lips of her pussy. Her body jolts. I wait a beat and her legs widen just a bit, and I know she's ready for me. She's ready to take the step toward enlightenment.

I'm just here to guide her.

My tactics change slightly, moving to long, deliberate strokes. Occasionally, I'll touch her pussy again, dragging my fingers over the opening, but then spend the majority of my focus elsewhere. I feel her tense, straining, wanting me to touch her there again and when I finally do, she exhales and spreads her legs a bit wider, giving me more access.

There's nothing rushed about this process. It's all part of the higher awareness of following The Way. Patience will get you where you want. Faith will guide you to pure joy. Enlightenment is within reach. When I touch her again, she's slick and ready and I massage around her opening. I put in the tip of my finger in applying pressure. When she's ready, I push all the way in. I've developed my own technique—one that I know with release the tightly wound energy pent up inside of this magnificent woman.

Once she comes, there will be no obstacle to her pathway.

I slide in a second finger, then press both against her inner walls. She hums in approval, toes curling on the table.

"Does that feel good?" I ask, moving them in a circular motion.

"Yes, god, yes."

"Good. I want you to breathe deep and enjoy the sensation. Open your mind, heart, and body. Embrace the moment."

It's all a little woo-woo, but I believe in this. Anex believes in it and as I feel her walls quivering around me and the moan of pleasure crossing her lips, I know she will too. A pink flush spreads across her skin and her hips writhe as her hands grip the edge of the table.

When she regains control, she blinks up at me and I pick up the sheet and place it back over her body. "Thank you for sharing that moment with me. I'm going to leave you now so that you can change. Anex will be waiting for you in the next room. He'll continue your journey there."

"Thank you," she says, getting herself to a sitting position. "That was quite extraordinary."

"Not when you're part of Serendee," I tell her, reaching for the door, "Revelations like this happen every day."

I exit the room and shut the door. Anex walks out of the adjoining room, straightening his shirt, and smiles at me. I bow slightly, and he claps his hand on my shoulder. "You're truly gifted, Silas."

"Just using the talents given to me by The Way."

He nods and meets my eye. "You understand what you're to do next?"

He's made his directives clear, who and what we're supposed to focus on next. "Yes," I reply. "I understand completely."

9

———————

I mogene

My heart leaps when I open the door of the suite and hear someone in the living room. Maybe Rex has come to his senses, and he's ready to begin our courtship. Maybe all of this was confusion. Cold feet. He wouldn't be the first Ordered male that struggled with the decision. Jonas Baker was ordered to Catherine Stillwell two years ago. He completely panicked and vanished for three days, returning with a black eye and smelling of alcohol. He was corrected by Anex and he and Catherine were bonded six months later. Now, they have a child.

But it's not Rex in the living room. It's his three best friends and confidants; Silas, Levi, and Elon.

I pause in the doorway, not sure how to proceed. I've never been in the presence of three men my age at the same time, alone, even at work. The simple sight of them; their broad shoulders and sharp features, is unfamiliar, yet intriguing. I consider running, but no, this is my house, and these men are confidants of my betrothed. Still, I don't move, and they pay me no attention until Silas, with his shaggy brown hair and perfect chin, looks up at me and grins. "She's here."

Elon, who has been pacing back and forth in front of the large window, stops and faces me. His dark gray eyes assess me, and that hard expression that is always on his face doesn't fade. "Where have you been?"

"At The Center. My shift doesn't end until after the last session." I'm not sure why I have to answer to him. "Is Rex here?"

"No," Levi replies. He stands from where he was sitting on the couch, a book in his hand. I recognize the cover. It's one of Anex's about how to incorporate The Way into all of your daily activities. We read it in school, and it is suggested we read it several times a year for a reminder. "We were sent by Anex."

The uneasy, uncomfortable feeling I'd carried all afternoon blooms brighter in my chest.

Silas throws an arm over the back of the couch and says, "We've been sent to assist you into acclimating with your Ordering."

Elon clears his throat and pushes his hands in his pockets. "We're responsible for training and preparing you for mating with Rex in the fall."

Nausea rolls over me and I clutch my stomach. "You'll be the ones training me? The three of you?"

I'd expected Clarissa, or maybe one of the other older, bonded women in the community to instruct me. There are other knowledge-able people: healers, high leaders, educators.

I did not expect three handsome, young, intimidating men. I did not expect Rex's closest friends.

"This can't be right," I mutter, anxiety building in my chest. "What Anex wants of me... it would be improper." We are kept apart all through adolescence to maintain purity for our Bonding. This would throw all of that away. Just being in this room together, talking about these matters, is enough to cause a problem.

"What's improper is for you to question the will of our leader," Elon grinds out. "Did he not tell you he approved of this? That he is orchestrating it?"

I lower my eyes. "Yes. I just don't understand. Isn't Rex your friend?"

"Yes," Silas says, "but, despite our friendship, like everyone else in Serendee, our priority is adhering to The Way above everything else."

"You mean, like everyone but Rex." I look to Levi, notably the most devout of the three, for confirmation, but he refuses to meet my eye. My hands tremble as realization washes over me. These men will train me to be a good mate to a man like Rex. A restless, selfish, spoiled man, who does not believe in the world or standards we live in.

After all this time, all these years of waiting, I realize it's happened.

I'm finally, truly, being punished for my mother's betrayal. *This* is the punishment.

And I have no choice but to let it happen.

~

They moved in while I was at work, taking the additional bedrooms, leaving the right-side master for Rex, although it remains empty. They don't have many belongings, just the loose cotton clothing all the men wear in Serendee, although they seem to prefer darker fabrics.

While they settle in, I shift into motion, forcing myself into the role I'd been trained for. The only difference is that my actions aren't for my mate. When I step into the kitchen to prepare dinner, one look in the refrigerator reveals that it's already stocked for this number of inhabitants. Obviously, I was the last to know about the assignment from Anex. Even the house managers were aware. It's an unsettling feeling, but what about the last twenty-four hours haven't been? This is my new life. One I must accept.

To people outside of Serendee, the gender roles of our community seem archaic. It's not that men can't cook. Or that women must take on the household. Anex is a historian and believes there are many reasons these roles have been upheld throughout time. It's not always about what people can do, but what brings them closer to The Way. Men feel stronger when they are using their bodies and minds. They are less likely to lose focus if they are protecting and providing for those they love. Whereas women feel more secure and less prone to anxiety when they are nurturing their families and creating a safe, functional, home. Efforts in the secular world to undermine these positions are one reason why there is so much strife and pain. Serendee is about harmony. Mental and physical. At home and at work. Balance is important. As are sacrifices for the greater good.

It's something I am forced to think about when we are all sitting around the table, a full meal plated before us. The roasted chicken turned out well, but the vegetables are a little mushy. I want to apologize as I set the dishes on the table, but I'm too stubborn. I didn't invite them here, although they certainly have no problem making themselves at home.

Silas comes to the table last, carrying a bottle of wine. He uncorks it and pours it into each of our glasses. I stare at the dark red liquid while the others pick theirs up.

"Lift your glass," Silas instructs.

"Using substances is not part of The Way," I refute, "unless it is part of the ceremonies."

"Well," he says, lips quirking, "consider this a ceremony."

Again, I glance to Levi for help. Even from a distance, it was obvious he was always studying and following Anex's words carefully. He is well regarded at The Center, but he too lifts his glass. I must have been wrong about his dedication.

"I would rather not," I say.

"Pick up your glass, Imogene," Elon growls from two seats away. "Or would you rather me force it down your throat?"

The dark spark in his eye makes me think that even if that's not what I want, he wouldn't mind. With a shaky hand, I pick up my glass and hold it level with the others.

"The next few months are going to be a challenge," Levi says, taking over for Silas, "but I have faith in Anex and The Way. He is guiding us down the righteous path, toward the road to retribution and certainty." He looks at me. "Silas is correct. This is a ceremony, one confirming our devotion to the future of Serendee."

The others murmur their toasts, then clink their glasses together. I follow their moves, not wanting to be reprimanded again. The wine is bitter at first, but after I swallow, I taste the tang of sweetness on my tongue. The men move on to their meals, eating ravenously, and I feel pride that they are pleased with what I prepared, even the vegetables. I'm not a complete fool when it comes to serving the needs of men.

Conversation is light while we eat—they speak of business— something I don't completely follow. Selling and trading; things that take place outside the walls. I know that most of the harvest from our garden stays inside Serendee to feed the community. What isn't used is sold at the local farmer's market. Nothing as complex as what they are talking about. They refer to measurements and weights. Dollar amounts. I pay it little mind, feeling the warmth of the wine spread through me. Midway through dinner, I notice Silas watching me.

"Is something wrong?" I ask.

He nods at my plate. "Why aren't you eating?"

"I'm eating," I say, looking down at the modest amount of food on my plate. I'd actually measured it out before cooking—taking into account how many grams of fat, protein, carbohydrates and overall calories I am consuming. "I just don't eat as much as you do."

"That's barely enough food to survive on," Silas adds. "A tiny piece of meat. Six green beans. No bread."

Typically, I pride myself on my control. Anex's teachings are very specific. It's not about weight—but about health and keeping oneself away from toxins. I glance at the wine and feel a conflicting twinge of guilt.

"She's following the standards," Levi says. "Imogene is faithful to the teachings she learned while living in the girl's domum." He scoops chocolate up on his fork and nods at me. "Do you maintain your logs?"

"Yes. Faithfully." Females are taught from a young age to document every morsel of food that goes into our bodies. These, along with our daily journals, guide us through The Way.

Silas' mouth opens and closes like he wants to argue, but Levi holds him off with a glare. I'm thankful for his defense. At least one person around here seems to understand.

I continue drinking, the warmth now buzzing in my head. When his plate is clean, Elon drapes his arm over the back of a chair and watches me with narrowed eyes.

"What?" I ask, not feeling as self-conscious as I should.

"I think we should begin our lessons."

"Tonight?"

"Why not?" He takes the last swallow of wine. "Come here."

I glance at the dishes and say, "I probably should—"

"Lesson number one: don't make me ask you to do something twice."

His voice is hard. Mean. His eyes filled with wicked intent. I stand, pushing my chair out behind me. I pass Levi, who chews a bite of food, and Silas, who takes a sip of wine, both watching me like an animal in the zoo. I approach Elon. He pushes back his own chair but remains seated, running a hand down his thigh. "Come. Sit on my lap."

"Excuse me?"

His jaw clenches, and he grabs my arm, yanking me down. When he speaks, his breath is hot in my ear. "Lesson number two: Rex can get his needs met by other women at any time. He probably is right now." From across the table, Silas snorts. "Which means that you do not want to give him any reason to turn away. The goal is to keep him interested in his home, in Serendee. Defiance isn't appealing." He pushes the hair off my shoulder, sending a wave of cool air across my neck. "Well, to most men, at least." I tremble as his fingers run down my arm. Goosebumps popping up in a shiver. "I know this is new, but you need to get used to the touch of a man."

I sit silently as he runs his hands along the bare skin of my arms and the column of my neck. His hands are big, and although he uses a gentle touch, I'm frozen in fear. I feel the eyes of Silas and Levi on me as Elon explores my body, each stroke taking a bit more liberty, moving up and down my sides, flattening over my belly. Despite my efforts, my breath becomes labored and my skin tingles as though it's on fire. I feel heat in places I didn't know could grow so warm. Damp.

"She's pretty," he says while exploring. "Don't you think?"

"Elon," Levi says. His voice is stern, but his eyes follow his friend's movements.

Elon's hands make a pass over my belly and then up to cup my breasts. I gasp, fighting the intrusion, but he holds firm. "She's skinny, but we were right, her tits are nice."

"Stop." I say, squirming against him. His body is like a wall, blocking me from moving. "This is wrong."

He ignores me, pulling at the neckline. His warm hands meet my skin and a rush of heat courses through my veins. "They fit perfectly. Right in my hands." He squeezes, pushing them together. I cry out in protest, but just laughs. "Silas, feel them yourself. You know you want to."

I'm thrust toward Silas who catches me by my breasts. To be fair, he drops his hands quickly with a look of pity on his face.

"Anex made it clear you are to do as you're told. To listen to us. To be trained," Elon says as I try to cover myself. "Why do you disobey the words of our leader? Are you truly like your mother?"

Anger and humiliation rush through me and my reaction is impulsive—my palm flattens across Elon's cheek. The slap echoes through the room and the look on Elon's face morphs from shocked to murderous. He takes a step toward me, but Silas slides between us.

"Go," he commands.

"I'm—" An apology stalls on my tongue. I'm not sorry. I'm raging.

"Imogene," Silas repeats, "go."

I spin on my heel and run down the hall, locking the bedroom door behind me, hating the sobs that heave out of me. I catch sight of myself in the bathroom mirror, and I walk into the room, making an effort to fix the top of my dress. The neck gapes, and there are streaks of red down my chest. I don't miss the hard points that press against the fabric, a clear sign of my arousal. I face my reflection and see my splotchy cheeks and red eyes. I see something else that I haven't noticed before.

My mother. I look very much like her during those last days before she left, when she always looked as though she'd just been crying. Like she was hiding something.

"Are you truly like your mother?"

Am I?

Am I disloyal?

A betrayer?

Am I defiant?

Do I not believe in Anex's guidance and The Way?

I don't want to be any of those things. I want to be good. Pure. Faithful to the end. I want to please Anex and help him with this complicated problem. I want to be a force for Serendee, not a destroyer.

I want redemption.

Is this how I get it?

Tomorrow, I'll figure out how to manage this. Maybe Clarissa knows. Maybe I'll have to speak to Anex again. But tonight, there is nothing to do but hide in my room, hoping none of these men decide to come to my door overnight.

10

L evi

"Was that really necessary?" I ask, leaning against the back of my chair. The last sound was Imogene's door slamming down the hall. Silas and Elon still face one another, caught in a tense standoff.

"Yes," Elon says, shoulders easing. "She needs to be tested."

"By you mauling her?" Silas asks.

"Sorry if I haven't been trained in the art of seduction," Elon snaps, shaking his head at Silas. He's right. We haven't been trained the way that our friend has. "I wanted to know what she would do if I treated her like one of the women outside of the community."

"She rebuffed you," Silas says. "Does that mean she passed?"

"No," I reply. "No, it doesn't. We don't know what she is capable of. What her motives truly are."

"Her motives are to mate, have babies and further The Way," Silas says. Suddenly, he's the most trusting of us all. You'd think with the women he's been with, manipulated, he'd have clearer eyes. "She's not a Regressive."

"How do you know?" I ask.

"I just do," he replies, sitting back at the table and pouring another glass of wine. "She's a normal girl."

"She's a sheep," Elon adds. There's no kindness in the title.

"Or a lamb on the way to slaughter," Silas points out.

"I'm with Elon," I tell him. They both look at me in surprise. Siding with Elon is rare for me. He's a brute and I'm an intellectual, but not in this situation. My gut tells me to be wary. "Imogene Montgomery is dangerous. Her blood is tainted. Her motives unclear. Rex and his father are playing a game that could catch us all on fire."

Elon runs his hand through his dark hair and narrows his eyes at me. He's always suspicious—even when I'm agreeing with him. It's one reason he makes a good bodyguard for Rex. "You're saying you're ready to test her? Really test her?"

I nod, swallowing back the apprehension. On the outside, testing and training Imogene goes against my nature. But according to The Way and the literature, this is what I have been preparing for my entire life. I'm protecting our community, potentially ferreting out a Regressive, and securing Rex's position as heir.

I've been given an honor by Anex, albeit an uncomfortable one. That's what makes it all the more important and prestigious.

Despite the fact that the dark glint in Elon's eye makes me nervous, and Rex's behavior is questionable, I will do as I'm told, and I will not let Serendee down.

11

Imogene

My sleep is fitful. I dream that Elon breaks through the door and drags me from the bed. His hands are all over me. Silas and Levi sit by and watch. I wake breathing heavy with a strange feeling in the pit of my stomach and a pounding headache. My tongue is dried out and tastes of old, bitter wine. A knock at the door forces me to sit up, and I hold back the swell of bile in the back of my throat.

"Imogene?" It's Silas. "Are you okay?"

My whole body is clammy and hot. "Go away, please."

"Imogene." The doorknob rattles. "Will you open the door?"

With every word, I think of the few moments his hands cupped my breasts. Oh god.

I take a deep breath and walk over to the door. I open it but only a crack. He looks relieved to see me in one piece.

"Can I come in?" he asks.

"I'm not presentable."

"I don't care." His eyes hold mine. "We need to talk about last night—to make sure that doesn't happen again."

Slowly I open the door, while walking to the closet and grabbing a robe to cover myself. Silas stands in the doorway, the strap of a slim bag hung over his shoulder. He runs a hand through his shaggy hair.

"I want to apologize for last night. It was never my intention to touch you like that."

"No?" I ask, crossing my arms over my chest. "I have a hard time believing that. Isn't that all part of my training?"

"Well, yes, but...this is complicated for us as well. You need to understand that."

I laugh darkly. "I doubt that. You have all the power here. All the knowledge."

"True, but that experience is a gift for you. This is a test for all of us, Imogene, one set up by Anex. If we all pass, then we will go on to glorious things in Serendee. But we have to pass. All of us."

"How can I pass a test I don't know the answers to?"

"Are you implying that you don't trust Anex to make the right decisions concerning you or his son?"

"No, I just—"

"Your questions say more about you than anyone else, Imogene. You need to dig deep into why you're fighting back."

He's right, of course. This is my flaw, not his.

"That is where we can help you, but you have to trust us."

I shake my head. "There is no way I can trust Elon. Not after last night."

His hand grips the strap of his bag. "Can I give you an important lesson?"

"Does it involve someone groping me?"

He dares a grin. "No, groping. Promise."

I exhale. "I'm listening."

"Not all men are the same. We don't have the same personalities, the same habits, or the same desires. I have no interest in forcing a woman into things she's uncomfortable doing. It makes *me* uncomfortable. Last night... I felt terrible. It's not how I would have handled this situation. I almost came to apologize a dozen times, but it seemed better to leave you alone."

"Smart."

"I have my moments." He laughs. "Levi? He is devoted to Anex and will do anything and everything he asks. He truly believes in Serendee and The Way."

"Does that mean you don't?"

He shrugs. "It means I've seen enough to understand why Rex struggles, but this is my home. My life. I have no intention of giving it up."

"And Elon?" I ask, swallowing back a lump of fear. "What about him?"

"It's important that you not test Elon. Do as he says, and things will be easier."

"You think I should just let him... do things like that to me?"

"I think that he knows better than anyone what Rex wants in a woman."

That answer turns my already tumultuous stomach. I push my hair out of my face while I try to hold back tears. It's pointless. "I don't understand what I'm supposed to do. All of this is foreign to me. It goes against everything I've been taught."

"Which is what I want to help you with." He reaches out and gently wipes a tear off my face with his thumb. "If you'll let me."

His touch is warm—gentle—nothing like the manhandling the night before. I don't imagine that I have many options and if Silas is throwing me a lifeline, I should take it.

12

———

Silas

"I think I calmed her down," I say, walking into the living room, "and hopefully did a little damage control for last night."

"I'm thinking it's time to stop treating her like a baby bird. She's out of the nest, Silas," Elon says, "it's time to fly."

"Yeah, well, what does that make you? The cat waiting at the base of the tree, ready to eat her?"

He grins. "Something like that."

I glance at Levi, who has said little this morning. "And you? You still think his tactics were the right decision?

"I think that Anex chose us with intention. He knows Elon's ways, just like he knows yours and mine. Together we'll create the perfect mate for Rex."

"So, he'll smash her into pieces, and I'll pick them back up? What will you do?" I ask, honestly wondering. "Report everything back to Anex?"

"Yes. I'm here to make sure that she stays on track and doesn't reveal anything that goes on here to others in the community. I'll monitor her journals and logs. I'll document her comings and goings as well as her progress." His mouth sets in a hard line. "This is a very delicate situation, if anything should go wrong—"

"It won't," Elon says, walking to the kitchen and opening the refrigerator door. He stares inside for a long moment before shutting it again. "Honestly, she's a good choice. Innocent and pure, yet very willing to please Anex. She wants redemption, and that makes her more pliable than most."

"She asks a lot of questions," I point out. Which is something I like about her. There's a spirit in her that seems unbreakable. That is hard to find in some of the women in the community. After being around secular women, the females in Serendee often seem a little robotic. That's not the impression I get from Imogene. She seems genuine. *Beautiful* and genuine.

"She won't for long," Elon says, taking a sip from his glass. "Give me one night and I'll shut that down."

I sigh and run my hand through my hair. That is what I'm most afraid of. To what length with Anex have us manipulate this girl? And how willing will she be to change?

It all feels risky to me—something Anex should know firsthand.

When he told us that we were chosen to help him with this task, I felt a sense of pride. Being singled out by him is a great honor. We're already in his inner circle, with a strong understanding of the inner working of Serendee, from business holdings to his visions for the whole of the community. It's much more complex than what is visible to the residents. Anex has created not just a utopia inside Serendee, but an empire.

Joining Anex's inner circle can be dangerous. It requires sacrifice, and it's a burden of information. At first, it's a bit of a mindfuck. Sometimes, his behavior and what he asks of us seems to go against the spirit of The Way.

But once I truly understood what we were doing—what Anex was doing, I realized that he truly is a genius working on a higher level than the rest of the community. Leadership isn't easy—neither is being a visionary. That's why he's in charge and it's why everyone follows.

What I told Imogene about this being a test for all of us... it's true. We all want to rise to our next level. Doing this together may be our only chance.

13

Imogene

The next morning I stand outside the Beatrice House in one of my new dresses, preparing myself to go in. Once a woman is Ordered, things change. One of the changes is an invitation to the weekly women's meeting. It's for bonded and ordered women only. A club every young girl inside Serendee wants to belong to. It's always seemed exclusive and secretive. Now that I'm finally here, under my circumstances, I feel less excited and more nervous. Will they be able to tell my Order is a sham? Do they know that Rex doesn't want a mate, and that I have to degrade myself to keep him in Serendee?

Faking contentment is something I'm used to—I learned how to do it after my mother abandoned us. I had to pretend like I didn't care about her anymore and that I was as disgusted as everyone else. In my heart, I missed her and had so many questions. Questions that I wasn't allowed to be asked.

"Imogene!"

Maria waves from the sidewalk. I lunge forward and pull her into a tight hug. "I've missed you," I tell her.

"I've missed you, too. It's weird not waking up from you talking in your sleep every night."

"I do not," I laugh. But it's an ongoing joke. Apparently, when I'm overwhelmed, I yammer along. I can only imagine what I've been saying the last few nights. It's a blessing no one is around to hear it.

"Can you believe we're finally here?" She looks up at the house and back at me. "Is it weirder because of Rex?"

Beatrice House It's named after Anex's former wife, Rex's mother. She died when he was a child, and the family couldn't bear to live in the house any longer, so they donated it to the women of Serendee— as a place to gather in her honor.

"Everything about this week has been a little weird," I confess. "I guess this is no different."

"True."

"How have you been?" I ask. "How is Elijah?"

She grins, and there's no mistaking the warm glow in her complexion. "Better than I ever thought. He's sweet and kind. Very attentive. I've enjoyed getting to know him."

"That's wonderful."

"And you? What's it like being Ordered to the most important single man in Serendee?"

The truth sits on my tongue, but I swallow it back. "It has been full of surprises. Every day I learn something new about the man that will be my mate."

"I bet," she says. "He's always been an enigma."

I nod. Enigma is putting it lightly. I haven't even seen him since the day of the Ordering and after last night...I am not sure I could ever face him again. That morning, I told the men that I wasn't going to fight them anymore. I was committed to the training Anex had requested. Silas looked relieved, while Levi just scribbled notes in his journal. Elon... well he looked at me as though I'd just issued him a challenge.

"What about his friends?" Maria asks, as though she can read my mind. "Are they around?"

"Yes, they are still thick as thieves. I get the feeling they can't breathe without the other in the same room."

She laughs and opens the gate. "Be careful or you may end up with four mates instead of just the one."

My eyes widen and I glance around, hoping none of the other women walking up to the house heard her. "Maria!"

She tries to stifle her giggles with her hand. "I'm just kidding." She rolls her eyes. "Can you imagine handling four men?"

"No." I smooth the front of my dress. "That sounds like a nightmare."

"I can barely figure out one," she agrees. "I've spent the last few days trying to figure out as much as I can about him; his favorite foods, how he likes his shirts ironed, what color he prefers me to wear. All of those little things."

This conversation only proves how different my situation is from the others. No one else is being asked to do something like this—to be trained to meet a man's subversive needs.

"I kind of feel bad for his friends," she says, as we enter the house. The first thing I see is a large portrait of a family. Anex is young, looking more like Rex now than I could imagine. Beatrice is beautiful, her golden hair shining like a halo. And Rex? He's a small, fair-haired toddler, clinging to his mother's side.

"Why?" I ask, drawing my eyes away from the portrait. "Why do you feel bad for them?"

"Because Anex didn't give them their own Orders. They must want women and families of their own?"

I think of the dark glint in Elon's eye and the way Silas' hands felt on my breasts. They're wise to Rex's needs and seem to have experienced them themselves. "It's none of my concern what they want," I reply. "The only person out of the four that matters to me is Rex."

"Come," she says, directing us toward one of the round tables set up for tea, "I'm hopeful that some of these more experienced women will help us understand better how to serve our men's needs. I realize now that Clarissa was holding back on us on some of the finer details."

I grab her arm and lean in. "Have you done something with Elijah? Intimately?"

Her cheeks redden, and she glances around. Quietly she says, "He kissed me. Using his tongue."

My eyebrows raise. "With his tongue?"

"It sounds weird, but it felt good."

Silas' hands on my breasts felt nice, too.

"Has Rex not tried to kiss you?"

I shake my head. "No, not yet." He'd have to be around to try something like that.

"I'm sure he will soon, but it's also okay to take things slow. That's what the courtship is all about, getting to know one another." The door opens and shuts behind us and Maria looks over my shoulder. "Oh, Renee! We were just talking about your brother."

Hearing that Levi's sister is behind me brings about another wave of discomfort. I know they aren't close. No male and females remain close after age twelve, even siblings, so I shouldn't worry that she knows what has transpired in our house but it still makes me uneasy. Renee's eyebrows rise in question.

I quickly reply, "Only because he's one of Rex's closest confidants."

"Ah, of course. They have always been thick as thieves—the four of them."

"Still seems that way," I reply.

"Imogene," a soft voice calls from behind me. I turn and see Margaret, Anex's Spiritual wife. Instinctively, me, Maria and Renee drop to a slight bow. "I was hoping to get a chance to meet you today. I'm Margaret."

"Yes," I reply. "I know." I blush at how stupid I sound, but Maria giggles next to me, which seems worse. "This is Maria."

She greets Maria and Renee but quickly shifts her attention back to me. "Can I speak to you for a moment?"

"Of course." I turn to my friend. "Talk soon?"

Maria still looks a little in awe as she and Renee walk toward the tea tables. I'm sure my expression is the same. Getting an audience with Margaret is almost like being in Anex's presence.

"I'm excited that you are joining our family," she says, once we're alone. "I'm sure you are feeling overwhelmed by the events of the past few days."

"Overwhelmed is an accurate description." I wonder how much she knows. Is she aware of what Rex told me? Or the training suggested by Anex? My skin prickles at the thought, but I don't give that away. "I'm definitely ready to serve the needs of the community."

She reaches for my hand, and squeezes it with hers. "I know you are. Anex wouldn't have chosen you if he didn't think you and Rex weren't perfect for one another."

"Thank you for the vote of confidence."

She leans in a little. "You're not alone, Imogene." Her voice is soft. "I host a small, exclusive, group of women in similar arrangements, and I would love for you to join us."

There are others like me? "That would be wonderful."

Her expression turns serious. "It's a place where we explore our personal growth and how to become better women and mates. Sometimes it takes a deeper introspection to find our truth, The Way, and the first step is to stop focusing on our own selfish desires."

"Yes," I say, both mesmerized by her words and the sound of her voice. "I would love to belong to that group."

"Ladies!" a voice calls from the front of the room. "Please find a seat!"

Margaret releases my hand and with one last small we're ushered to different tables. We're served tea and small cakes made down at the bakery. I'm introduced to the other women at the table, all bonded and mated. They talk about laundry and recipes and juggling home and their work to Serendee. None mention sex or a mate that's uninterested. None mention training. But none of these women are me. They don't have a scarred family past or a tarnished reputation that follows them. They aren't betrothed to the next leader of Serendee. None are Chosen.

In a room filled with women, and even my best friend, it has never been clearer exactly how alone I am. Except, just when I feel even more lost, I lock eyes with Margaret across the room, reminding me that maybe I'm not as isolated as I think I am.

I'M thankful that when I arrive back at the main house that no one is home. The men do have jobs—whatever they'd discussed the night before. Something that requires them to come and go from Serendee on Anex's orders.

Their absence gives me time to build up my courage. I have questions, and I want answers.

I'm thinking about what to cook for dinner when Silas comes through the front door. I pause when I see him. His clothing isn't exactly secular, but lines of his jacket reveal the broadness of his shoulders and the linen of his shirt is a purplish blue, that looks nice against his olive skin. Men here mostly wear black, white or tan and the burst of color is surprisingly appealing. I look away when I catch sight of his hands.

All I can think about is how they felt on my body the night before.

"Good evening, Silas," I say. "Do you know if the others will be home soon?"

"Actually, no," he says, shrugging out of his jacket. "They won't be home for dinner. I came back to change and then I'm going to meet them."

"Oh," I say, not sure how to feel. They make me so uneasy that the thought of a night alone isn't unappealing. On the other hand, I should be deep in my courtship during this time, or at least receive the lessons. I suck up my disappointment. "Thank you for telling me."

He nods and walks down the hallway toward his room. As he reaches the door, I blurt out something that has been on my mind all day. "Do you think what Elon said last night is true? That Rex is getting his needs met by someone else?"

He walks back toward me, his expression careful. "Yes. Most likely."

My stomach drops and a wave of sickness rolls over me. But I don't stop. "What does he do with them? Does he kiss them with his tongue?"

His lips quirk and I wonder briefly if they are as soft as they appear. "I would assume so, among other things."

"What other things?"

"Things you'll learn in your training."

The flicker of apprehension fills my chest. "But that's what I want to know. What will my training involve? Until last night, I'd never been touched by a man in such a...intimate way. Until today, at the women's meeting, I didn't know a man kissed with his tongue." I clasp my hands together. "I need to know what to expect from these lessons. What you want from me."

He studies me closely for a moment and abruptly walks to his bedroom door. He opens it and looks over at me. "Come with me."

He enters his room, and I follow, stopping at the door. His room is large, although not as big as my own. There's a king-sized bed and a small sitting area with a couch and two chairs. A desk sits against the wall. He lays the bag from his shoulder on the surface and pulls out a thin, silver device.

My pulse quickens. "What is that doing here?"

"It's mine. For work."

"Devices like that are not allowed in homes. You know that." Computers, phones, televisions... they're all forbidden outside of a regulated work environment. Anex doesn't want our daily lives swayed by the outside world.

"There are exceptions for everything, Imogene. You must know that."

"I didn't. Not until the last few days. I'd been raised to think that there was no leeway, and if you bent the rules, there will be consequences. How do I know I won't get in trouble from having this kind of contraband in my home?"

"It's my contraband," he says, laughing at me. "I assure you, Anex is well aware that I have this device. He's the one that gave it to me."

He did? I swallow. "Then I shouldn't be here. If it's part of your work, then I should leave you alone."

"No." He sits on the couch and rests the laptop on the coffee table. "Didn't you just ask me to explain more about what you should expect?"

"I did."

"Then let me do that—by using the resources provided to me by *Anex*."

When he puts it that way, it's hard to argue. I just can't imagine what he wants to show me on the computer that is relevant to my questions.

Silas pats the cushion next to him. "Sit next to me."

I do as I'm told, circling the table and sitting on the firm cushion. It's strange being so close to him. He smells good, manly, although I get the slightest hint of something flowery—feminine. I watch his face, the slope of his nose and the length of his eyelashes as he works. He pays me no attention, focused on the computer. It's not the first time I've seen one. In fact, we have an entire class dedicated to the evils of technology. How they seem like useful, yet benign devices. Things that make life easier— but an easy life can be deceiving. It makes a person lazy and compliant.

Like everything else, Anex thinks it's important that segments of the community maintain knowledge of dangerous things and certain people in the community are given that burden. Silas, and I assume the other men in our shared home, have been chosen to lift that weight off the rest of us.

A renewed sense of respect swells inside of me. Anex must truly find him to be an outstanding member of the community. Even so, as he presses buttons and the screen comes to life, I twist my hands in the fabric of my dress, trying to soothe my nerves. His fingers move quickly, confidently, and I'm in awe of his knowledge as much as the machine itself.

"You use this for work?" I ask, feeling the need to fill the air.

"Yes—all the time, actually."

"What kind of work do you and the others do?"

"Well, I work closely with the new recruits, making sure they are comfortable and ready for their decision to join the community. And, as you know, Levi works at The Center. Rex and Elon are involved with another side of Serendee. They distribute some of the local products to the secular world—things that don't have much use in the community but are valuable out there."

"What kind of product?" The community is prolific. Besides the garden there is the bakery, tailors, and other artisans. There are also skilled workers in farming, carpentry and welding. Everything that makes our little world run smoothly without outside intervention.

Silas draws his eyes from the screen and gives me a small smile. "Nothing for you to worry about. It's not very interesting."

I nod. "And this... product distribution... Rex works with you?"

"He does. We've always made a good team."

Obviously, or why else would they be trusted with training me? "I'm glad to hear you all are so close and have jobs Anex deems important."

"Very important," he agrees, taking a final swipe at the computer keyboard. He tilts the screen in my direction and it's frozen on a picture of a group of people. They're all young and strange looking. Pretty by secular standards. I've seen men and women like this in town near the University. Shiny hair and heavily made-up eyes and red lips. The men have clean-shaven faces and hair that swoops artfully away from their faces.

I can't take my eyes off of it.

"What is that?"

"It's a TV show. Have you ever seen one before?"

"No, but I've heard Anex speak of them in his lectures. Not positively," I add.

He shifts on the couch, turning to face me, and our thighs touch, sending a current of energy up my leg. "It's basically a story told in pictures. Moving pictures, obviously. And there are a million different kinds of stories, but one of the most popular types is a romance or love story. I think it may help answer some of your questions about what to expect."

"This is the kind of show that Rex watches?"

He laughs. "No. Not exactly, but the men and women, how they interact with one another, that is what a man expects from a secular woman."

Although the method makes me uncomfortable, it is better than being manhandled by Elon again. "Thank you. I will watch this and see if things make a little more sense."

"You can use the computer whenever you want."

I eye the machine. We were taught that computers have the ability to track and collect data. "Can I keep it in here? I don't feel comfortable taking it into my room."

"Sure," he says, his lips twisted in amusement. "I know this is moving fast for you. Believe it or not, I felt the same way at one point, but it's important that you try to make progress. There are obligations coming up, including the summer solstice, where you will need to be ready."

His hand rests on top of mine, and he squeezes it gently. It's the kind of touch that Maria and I would have shared, but the feeling behind it is very different. Sparks shoot through my body, igniting a million different emotions. I glance over at him, wondering if he feels it too, or is it just me and my naivety. His dark eyes hold mine and then dart down to my mouth. I yank my hand back and turn away.

I stay that way as he goes into the bathroom and changes. It's only after he leaves that I move, leaning toward the computer and pressing play.

14

R^{ex}

The house is big and ornate, sitting on the edge of the lake. Just outside of town is a quiet, but expensive, vacation area that draws in wealthy families. The house buzzes with life—a full-blown party is going on just past the large front porch. It's the kind of event nearly everyone in Serendee would feel uncomfortable attending, but not us.

I'm the one that gets us in the door. I inherited my father's easy smile and ability to lure people in. It's a gift. Of course, that's not all. It's the expensive car and clothes, the gold watch, but it's more than that. There's something mysterious about the three of us—members of this exclusive community. Good looking and rich. Entitlement oozes off us and people want that. They want what we have, even if they don't know exactly what that is. And they, unknowingly, have what we want.

They just don't know it yet.

"You came!" I hear, turning toward a pretty blonde. Her name is Jasmine West, heir of the Cobra tequila company. We'd met at the country club gym a few days before, and she'd extended the invitation. She approaches me and gives me a kiss on both cheeks, leaving a wake of her perfume in the air. "I didn't think you would."

"Why?" I ask, sliding my arm around her waist. "You think they lock us in after dark?"

Joking about the community is the first way to lower outsider's guards. She laughs and shakes her head. "I figured you'd be too busy. I told all my friends about the fascinating man I met from Serendee. They didn't believe me."

"I'm here for proof." I tilt my head toward the guys. "I hope it's okay that I brought a few friends."

Her eyes flit over each of them, lingering on Elon. She laughs. "You didn't need to bring me a gift—much less three."

"I never attend a party without bringing something for the hostess."

She drops her hand on my ass and gives it a playful squeeze. "Just make sure you save one for me, okay?"

"You got it." I reach into my pocket and pull out a small box. It's custom made in the Serendee workshop. "Oh, here's a little something else for you, too."

She opens it and takes a deep sniff. "I'm inviting you guys to all of my parties."

She walks off, tucking the box into her pocket and turning back to give Elon one last flirty grin.

Elon's eyes are zeroed in on her. "I call dibs."

Silas claps his hand on Elon's back and gazes into the room of beautiful women. "She's all yours, brother. I think there's plenty of fun for us all to have here."

He vanishes into the group, the mask already slipped into place. Between the four of us, by the end of the night, at least one of us will get laid, we'll have a list of names to pass on to my father, and I have no doubt we'll have secured new business for Serendee.

Tonight isn't about fun, it's about community; it's about building a future.

One that gets me as far away from here as possible.

15

E lon

While the guys attend to business, I follow Jasmine through the crowded living room. My only job is to keep Rex safe, and at a party like this, he needs a little space. We have a lot of product to sell—acres of it—and a high end party like this is the perfect place to make new connections. The sway of Jasmine's hips leads me into the state-of-the-art kitchen. It's less crowded in here. Most people are out on the deck or down by the lake.

I'm not going to deny that I want one thing from this woman. I've been horny as fuck for days. It's not that I'm not always horny, but a flip switched in me when I was messing with Imogene that first night. Dragging her light little body on my lap and feeling her tits. It wasn't just her body that got me hard—it was the way she fought back. The stinging slap on my cheek. I almost followed her into her room, pushed her down on the bed and showed her what happened to women that rebelled against me or Anex's rule.

But she's not mine to have. So I lay in bed at night, thinking of the Little Lamb a few rooms away, pretending to be all innocent and naïve, while I rub myself raw.

"You're following me," Jasmine says, cutting into my thoughts. She leans against the marble countertop, a little smile on her lips. My eyes are drawn to her blonde hair. Soft like a lamb.

"Just looking for some water."

"Follow me." She walks over to a door, and I follow her into a large pantry. It's immaculate and well stocked. She bends, opening a small refrigerator under the cabinet and pulls out a glass bottle. Looking back at me, she slowly screws off the top. Her nails are manicured into sharp points, and they drag against my hand as she gives me the bottle. This woman is everything that the women in Serendee aren't. Sleek, poised, confident. She eyes me with curiosity.

"What's it like in there?"

I take a sip of the bubbly water. "Can you be more specific?"

"In your compound or whatever. That place. Serendee."

"It's beautiful," I tell her truthfully. "Clean, self-sustaining, all organic and natural food. I'm lucky to call it home."

"What about the culty-stuff?"

Heat warms the back of my neck. I try not to get defensive about Serendee. Anex has taught us how to deal with people like this. We speak with honesty. Truth. A woman like Jasmine has the kind of wealth that Anex likes to get his hands on, but it's not always a good fit.

"If you think maximizing and understanding personal growth is culty, then I guess we're guilty as charged."

She steps forward, leaning over to give me a view of her cleavage. "I heard there are some kinky sex things going on in there."

I laugh. "Kinky?"

"Yeah, like, big orgies out in some field. People say they can hear the drumbeats from miles away during them."

"Hmm." I finish off the bottle and screw back on the cap. "Do you think I'd be at a party here if there were orgies going on in there? It's much less exciting than you think. It's just a bunch of people seeking enlightenment."

Her fingers tuck over the waist of my pants, her nails pressing against my stomach. "I know a really good path to enlightenment."

I tilt my head. Now that we're this close, I can't help but notice how much makeup she's wearing. How much perfume. I wrinkle my nose and suddenly my desire wanes. There's no thrill here. No chase. When did I stop wanting it so easy?

I place my hand over hers to remove it, but her thumb loosens the button. A moment later, my cock is in her hand and she's on her knees. Any other night, and I'd be down for some easy head, but again... there's that word. Easy. Is this what I want?

I look down to nudge her away, but I get a glimpse of the top of her head—the shiny blonde that's more yellow than white but still... close enough. Exhaling, I shove my fingers in her hair and pull, eliciting a gasp from the woman on her knees. She tries to look up at me, but I force her eyes down, and twist my fingers in her hair, "Don't," I tell her, allowing my own lids to fall, "don't look up and take me deep."

It may not be what I want, who I want, or the way I want it, but when do I get any of those things?

I'm at the mercy of a dictator, living in a paradox of gluttony and deprivation. As Jasmine's mouth closes around my cock, warm and wet, I think of a different blonde and remember that this is The Way. It's what Anex wants for me. My sacrifice for the greater whole.

16

I mogene

Hours pass. *Hours.* And I understand more than ever why Anex discourages technology. It's addictive. Consuming. Distracting.

I can't stop.

These people and their lives; I had no idea. It's flashy and bright and moves so fast that sometimes I have to press the button again to make it slow down, to repeat over again, so I can try to understand their words. It's so much talking and laughing and drinking coffee and wine. There are men and women, but it's the women I can't stop watching. With their shirts that show their flat, smooth stomachs, and strain across their breasts. Their pants are tight, and the skirts are short, revealing long, exposed legs. But it's not just their looks I'm obsessed with. It's the way they speak first, and take control, and have their own lives.

Then there's the kissing. With tongues. And all the hands. And the sex. So much sex. In jokes, in reality, it's in everything. It's not hidden or forbidden. It makes them laugh. Cry. Moan. My cheeks burn red.

It's terrifying.

I don't look away until the door opens, and I glance over and blink. Silas has returned. I fumble forward, jabbing the button with my finger. "You're back," I say, feeling like I got caught with my hand in the cookie jar. "What time is it?"

"Late," he says, easing off his coat. "After midnight. Have you been watching this the whole time?"

"Yes," I admit. "I couldn't stop."

He laughs. "I bet. It's called binge watching for a reason."

I frown. "Binge watching?"

"Yeah, when you start a show and can't stop. That's what they call it. A binge." He then kicks off his shoes, revealing dark socks. "How did you like it?"

"It was...overwhelming."

"I'm sure. I found all of this overwhelming at first too."

He'd said that before. "You did?"

He shrugs. "Sure. I was raised like you. It wasn't until Anex came to me and I started my own training that I understood the power of intimacy and that I had a gift to share with the community."

"How old were you?"

"Sixteen."

"But you still believe in Anex and The Way."

"I do. It took a while, but I understand my place in both worlds."

"But Rex doesn't. He wants to be in that world." I point to the laptop. "All the time."

He grimaces. "He's struggling. I believe with our help—your help —he can find his way back."

It's weird that for Rex to find his way back, I have to lose a little bit of myself, but I've already accepted this is my fate. "So, the women he is attracted to, they are like the ones on the show?"

"Sort of. Not specifically, but it's a good example." He sits next to me. "Did you learn anything useful?"

"Useful may not be the right word. I'm not sure any of them do anything useful other than talk too much."

He laughs. "You're funny, Imogene."

"I am?"

"Different." He takes my hand again and this time I force myself not to panic.

"Being different has always caused me problems."

He tucks a piece of hair behind my ear. The soft pads of his fingertips elicit a shiver as they trail down my cheek to my chin. "Are you ready to show me some of what you learned?"

My heart pounds wildly, banging against my ribcage. I want to escape, but his hand is on mine and I know there's no more running. I can learn this lesson from Silas or from Elon. Silas seems the better option. I don't want to fail Anex and his son and I realize that is what this whole night has been about.

"I don't know what to do."

"I doubt that, Imogene." He bends, brushing his lips across mine. They're warm and soft. A tingling sensation buzzes on my mouth. Silas grins. "See?"

He's not finished coming in for another kiss. This time it's harder, his mouth applying more pressure, his lips blistering and hungry. Panic builds in my chest—this is wrong, he is not my mate—but his hand moves to my back, keeping me in place. I open my mouth to suck in air and his tongue sweeps in, licking against mine. It feels like an explosion in my mouth and I lean into him, wanting more, taking more, until we're both breathing heavy.

"I'm sorry," I say, pulling back. "That was—"

"Perfect," he says, moving his hand behind my neck. "Are you sure you haven't done that before?"

"Of course not!" If possible, my cheeks burn hotter. I struggle to my feet and see his grin. "Don't make fun of me."

"I'm not," he says sincerely. "That was a very nice kiss. With tongue even."

Now I know he's mocking me. "Stop."

He grabs me and yanks me close, nose grazing mine. "I'm not making fun of you. That was a very good kiss. One, with a little practice, Rex will definitely approve of."

"You really think so?"

He nods. "I know so."

I exhale. "Good. And thank you for the lesson. The expectations, although way out of my wheelhouse, seem a little clearer now."

"I have no doubt you can do what you need to do to win Rex over." He smooths my hair and once again his lips brush against mine, and although it's not as shocking as the first one, when he releases me, it still leaves me feeling lightheaded. "You should go to bed. Get some sleep."

I nod and exit his room, feeling wobbly on my feet. Later, I lie on the bed, running my fingers over my lips. If this is what all of my lessons are like, then I may have something to look forward to.

SINCE I WAS TWELVE, my daily logs and journals have been filled with repetitive, neat documentation. What I consumed that day. How much I exercised. The hours I volunteered. The minutes spent studying, meditating, and giving to Serendee. There were occasional notes about celebrations or something unique; on March third, I saw a rainbow. On September ninth, we harvested the garden. On December twenty-first, we brought the gifts that we'd created to Anex, honoring him for his sacrifice and leadership. But mostly it was the mundane—something, after my mother disrupted my world, that I cherished. Watching those calories and grams add up to nice, appropriate numbers. Seeing my thoughts smooth into acceptable conformity, while internally chanting, *"I'm not my mother. I'm not my mother..."*

The peace I received from documenting the details of my life has slowly faded since moving into the main house. Sure, my food goals are still on target. Actually, I may be ahead of target, having skipped dinner last night. But that food was replaced by binge watching a TV show, which I dutifully record. That was followed by me kissing a man that is not my future mate. I know all of it was for the better good, but still...

I'm more aware than most that these logs... they aren't exactly private. Members of Anex's leadership council have the right to review them. After my mother betrayed Serendee, I was required to turn them into Clarissa so that they could assess my state of mind, my loyalty.

It's with that knowledge that I speak the truth about what happened. Lying...it never ends well. Anex has a way of knowing. Plus, this was his idea. The lessons are what he wanted. Despite my concerns, I have faith in my actions.

I place the journal in the wooden box on my desk and take one last look in the mirror. I'm in one of the dresses I made for my courtship. It's long, grazing my ankles as is required. My arms and collarbones are covered. It's fitted at the breast and waist—an offering to my betrothed. The fabric is pale gray. Nothing flashy. Nature provides the color and vibrancy to Serendee.

It took a while to get used to the clothing changes that began when we entered the domum. Before age twelve, females are allowed a more casual dress, shorts or pants. Boys could wear jeans or sweats. Whatever was made for play.

But Anex noticed that as members of Serendee reach adolescence, the boys and girls are driven to distraction by one another. He blames hormones—the desire to show off to one another for attention. Outlandish colors, skin revealing outfits. It's just another weakness that falls in the same category as food, and Anex was convinced that it is something that can be controlled if a person is dedicated. That's when the mandates for clothing came down. Girls over twelve must wear loose fitting, ankle-length dresses. Boys, cotton pants with a button-down shirt. Neutral colors only.

What I'm about to do will be in exact defiance of Anex's mandate.

As I secure my hair in a low ponytail, there's a knock on the door. Silas stands in the hallway, and his eyes dart immediately to my lips. They tingled all night, and it starts again when I see him.

"Am I late?" I ask.

"No. I just wanted to see you before you left for the day. To make sure you're okay about last night."

It's impossible for me not to watch his mouth as he speaks. My heart thrums, wanting to taste him again. "I'm fine."

I glance down, afraid that he can tell him I tossed and turned, thinking about him. His fingers press against the underside of my chin, lifting my face. His head is tilted and before I can think, his hand is on my lower back and his lips cover mine.

He tastes spicy, like mint, and there's less fumbling this time. I know to follow his pace, to try to anticipate his moves. My body explodes like someone has set fireworks off under my skin and I clutch the fabric of his shirt. The move forces his hips to brush against mine and that sends another, different tremor through me. I'm still clinging to him when he pulls away, hair flopped in his eyes and smiling down at me.

"Better than last time."

"Do you think?" I ask, knowing it's true. I feel unsteady on my feet.

"Absolutely." He tucks my hair back. "You're close to being proficient."

"That seems like a stretch." A cough from the living room draws both of our attention. "Is he waiting?"

"Yes."

Elon. That is who I am to spend the day with. I take a deep breath and start toward the living room. Silas's hand circles my wrist before I get there, drawing me back.

"Any lesson you've learned for Rex, you can apply to Elon," he says, grazing his fingers down my cheek. "Understand?"

I nod, but I don't. Elon is mean and angry. He clearly doesn't like me or the assignment he's been given. Which is probably why he's agreed to take me somewhere that will push me completely outside my boundaries.

"Good luck," Silas says.

"Thanks," I reply, knowing how much I'm going to need it.

～

It's not the first time I've been in a car, but it's the first time I've been in one this nice. I'd gaped when I saw it in the garage beneath the main house—a garage, along with the extensive fleet of vehicles I had no idea existed. Elon walks past each one, shiny and clean, to a black one at the end. Everything about this man is dark. His hair, his eyes, his complexion. He's the opposite of Rex, who is pale and fair. I'm reminded of the symbol of The Way, the sun and moon. These two encompass it, at least in looks. He presses a button that makes the lights blink. I don't know the type, but it looks too small for his large frame. Too extravagant for someone at Serendee.

"We're driving?" I ask.

"Obviously."

"But shouldn't we just walk? There's no reason to waste the resources a vehicle like this must expend and Anex..."

He sighs loud enough to cut me off and rubs his forehead. "How many times do I have to explain to you that all of this is approved by Anex?"

I swallow but don't respond and he starts to the driver's side door. He glances back, noticing I'm still in the middle of the garage. His exhale is deeper this time, but he circles around and opens the opposite door. "Get in, Imogene."

I glance at his face, and the directive is unmistakable.

Don't make me ask twice.

I hurry past him, getting a strong whiff of his spicy scent. The seats are low, and I gather the hem of my dress to get in properly. Once I'm settled, Elon slams the door and walks around to the other side. His big body fills the seat, but he doesn't look out of place. He looks comfortable—commanding. The stylish clothing and his dark looks make my heart stutter. His hand grips the knob between the seats, and he seems very much at ease.

"We can't walk," he explains, starting the engine. It sounds like a big cat purring. "Because we're not shopping in town."

"Oh," I reply. Of course. I can't be seen in town with Elon. If someone from Serendee saw us there would be too many questions. "Right."

He reaches up and presses another button, which opens a door in front of us. The car glides smoothly through the door and down the back driveway of the main house. I've seen this driveway from a distance, but never wondered too much about where it led. Elon approaches a tall gate and to my surprise, two men emerge to open it. Although they're dressed in black, it's not the standard male outfit. It's a more utilitarian fit. I notice their thick-soled boots and clunky jackets. They give Elon a curt nod, one he returns, and he exits the driveway. A moment later, Serendee is behind us.

"Do those men always stand there?" I ask, glancing behind me.

"Them or a few others." Elon cuts his eyes in my direction. "Anex has guards placed around the property. Just to keep everyone safe."

I look out the window, seeing the countryside flash by. "I had no idea."

"I suspect," he says, shifting the knob again, "that there are many things about Serendee that you have no idea about."

He says it with bite, like I should feel guilty or stupid about this, but how would I know? I've followed all the rules and directives, not asking questions. I'm doing my part.

He takes a sharp turn and I grab hold of the door to keep from sliding over. Truthfully, I don't want to be any closer to him than I have to. Whatever dislike he has for me, I have as much for him. I ignore him, fascinated by the interior of the car, the knobs and buttons, the little computer in the console. Every day in this new world of mine, I learn that what I thought was off limits, maybe really isn't.

Soon we enter the city, with more cars and taller buildings. I've been before—once or twice with my parents to take care of some business or to visit a doctor, but ever since my mother betrayed us, visits outside Serendee are few and far between other than the small town adjacent to the community.

Elon seems completely unbothered by the traffic and crowds. He pulls the car over to the curb in front of a store with big windows and mannequins posed in bright clothes. Even though they aren't real people, the amount of skin they're showing seems improper. I'm gawking at them, at the people on the street, at everything when Elon opens the car door and holds out his hand.

I stare at it and remember what Silas told me. To remember my lessons. I don't know much yet, but from the TV show, I know that casual touches are common in the secular world. I extend my hand. He takes it, pulling me out of the car. I trip over the hem of my dress and fall into him.

"Sorry," I say, feeling awkward and out of place. "I'm so sorry."

"Don't apologize," he replies, his voice tight. "Just hurry up. People are watching."

I look around. He's right. People are watching me, staring at my dress and my lack of makeup and plain hair. Maybe I should have used some of the makeup in my bathroom drawer. Elon probably feels as out of place by my appearance as I do—his black clothing fits in with everyone else. He yanks me forward, off of the street and into the shop. Inside I'm accosted by an explosion of color and thumping music.

"It looks like a flower garden in here," I exclaim, reaching for the fabrics. Everything is pink and red and orange. Some glitter with sequins or shiny thread.

"Pick a few things out." He looks me up and down. "Attractive things."

I haven't the faintest idea of where to begin. Everything is too much. Too bright. Too revealing. Elon must sense my problem because he approaches a shop girl and flashes her a lopsided, brilliant grin.

God. I had no idea he was even capable of that.

"Excuse me," he says, as though he speaks to women like this every day.

Maybe he does.

"How can I—" Her entire demeanor changes when she faces him. Her shoulders square and her breasts lift perkily. Her chin tilts while she looks under her long, black lashes. I think I'm more enthralled than he is. "Help you?"

"My cousin," he says, nodding over at me, "is in dire need of some new clothes."

She glances over and her eyes widen. I'm used to feeling self-conscious in town, but the people there are used to us. I've never experienced anything like this. "Oh, you poor thing." She keeps her attention on Elon. "I assume you want something a little more... fashionable?"

"Yes," he says, looking the shop girl up and down. There's a glint in his eye that makes my stomach twist anxiously. "Something like you're wearing would be good."

It's my turn to stare. The shop girl is wearing a skirt that barely covers her thighs along with a top with no sleeves, just straps that crisscross over the shoulders. The neckline plunges, revealing the swell of her breasts. I can't stop staring at the smooth, soft looking skin. I force my eyes upward to the large gold hoop earrings dangle from her lobes, then down to the spikes coming out of the heels of her shoes. I can't imagine going to these lengths for beauty.

"Head back to the changing room," she says, placing her hand on Elon's forearm. "I'll gather a few things and bring it back."

"Perfect," he says, giving her another grin. "Oh, and make sure you add in a few bra and panty sets. If my suspicions are correct, hers definitely need an upgrade."

My cheeks, no, my entire body, burns with humiliation. Our undergarments are made for functionality, nothing else. The seamstress creates them specifically for the women in Serendee and the accusation that they aren't acceptable for some reason bothers me. I fume as I follow Elon to the back of the store and into a back room. There are several stalls with curtains and a sitting area outside. There's an expanse of floor to ceiling mirrors along the wall, and I see multiples of myself. Compared to the shop girl, the contrast is alarming. I look like a frumpy child in my long dress and plain hair and face.

Elon sits in the comfy chair and says, "Undress. Let's see what we're really working with here."

"Undress?"

"It's time to shed the innocent image, Imogene. Rex wants to mate with a woman, not a little lamb."

"But why do you need to see me?" My arms wrap around my middle. "Anex makes this clear. No one should see a woman undressed unless they are Ordered."

"Undress, Imogene, or I'll do it for you."

The intent in his eyes is clear. I have no doubt if I don't follow his directions, he'll do as he says, and then some. My hands tremble as I reach behind my back, struggling to unbutton the top button. He watches my every move with an aloof, cold stare, and frays my nerves. Finally, he sighs and stands.

"I'm doing it," I promise him. "I just...my zipper..."

"Turn around."

I turn and expose my back. I wouldn't think his big hands could move so swiftly, but they do, pushing aside my hair and loosening the button with a gentle touch. I inhale a breath of air as he pulls the zipper down to my lower back. Cool air hits my skin, sending goosebumps along every inch.

He stands behind me for a moment and then runs a warm finger down my spine. "You're too thin."

I glance back and see that same look of annoyance. "Sorry my appearance doesn't please you."

He moves back to the seat and I reluctantly undress, still futilely trying to cover myself. "You're not unappealing," he says, "but you could use a little meat on your bones. Something to hold on to."

I frown and glance at the mirror. My undergarments are a standard two piece, supplied by the seamstress. A white, full coverage tank and loose shorts. "Why on earth would you need to hold on to me?"

A slow grin reveals his teeth. "Sometimes I think you play coy on purpose, Little Lamb, but then I remember how you've been raised."

"The same way as you."

"To an extent, but when I reached manhood, we were assigned to be Rex's confidants, and the veil dropped. It's dropping for you as well. Serendee is more than what you've always known. It's bigger and more complex, and part of that is embracing that knowledge."

"And that means I need to go against the rules Anex imposed to make us all better?" I ask. "Like my nutrition and food intake? Like my clothing and undergarments?"

"It means that you are now one of the Chosen. The few that get to see Serendee for what it really is." He doesn't say this with pride or awe, but as though it's a burden.

"And what is it?"

"For you? It's whatever Rex wants it to be."

"He made it very clear he does not want me."

"He doesn't want the you that grew up in Serendee, but the one we are making—creating—that is one he will not only accept but desire. Then he and Anex will be happy. If they are both happy, then all of Serendee will benefit."

The shop girl enters the room, and I tighten my arms over my chest. She holds out a stack of clothing; dresses, skirts, blouses, and yes, several pairs of thin, lacy undergarments. I blush just seeing them.

"Now, I brought you a few sizes, although you're obviously a small or extra small. The good thing is that means that—"

"Thank you," Elon says, cutting her off. He reaches into his pocket and removes a thick roll of money—twenty-dollar bills. I have never seen so much currency. Where would he even get that? He peels several off and hands them to her. "I think we're good, but make sure no one interrupts us."

She gives me a strange look, but grips the money in her hand and shrugs. "You got it."

A moment later, she's gone, and she's pulled another curtain across the main doorway. It's just me and Elon and a stack of clothing for me to try on. He flips through the outfits, quickly assessing each one. He stops and pulls out a bright blue dress. "Try this one," he says, thrusting it out. He's focused on the lingerie, fingering the straps, before handing it over, too. It's a set, black and lacy. "With this."

My heart pounds just looking at them. Even after all the justifications, the explanations, the confirming that this is what Anex wants me to do, it feels wrong. Like, a test I'm about to fail. I've worked so hard to reestablish my reputation. I can sense it slipping through my fingers.

But...

If Elon's right, and I am one of the chosen to help usher Rex into his position of leadership, then I must do everything to make that happen. Even if that means going against my own beliefs.

"Do you want me to change here or behind the curtain?" I ask, clutching the soft fabric to my body.

Elon's eyes flick over me, his mouth twists in approval. "Since you asked, you may go behind the curtain."

I nod and carry the clothing into the stall and begin the process of removing my undergarments. I've never exposed myself like this in a public space. Not even in front of the girls in the domum. To his credit, Elon says nothing on the other side of the curtain, although I feel his presence. I do my best to ignore him, focusing on the straps and clasps and adjusting the lace. I face myself in the mirror to check to see if I have it on correctly. The bra cups make my breasts look larger than normal. The low cut of the panties extends the length of my stomach. The lace does little to hide the dark-colored flesh of my nipples or the thatch of hair at the crux of my body. My skin is both hot and cold, prickling with sensation. The curtain opens with a jerk behind me, and my eyes meet Elon's in the mirror.

Forcing my arms to remain at my side, I lift my chin, pretending to be brave.

His gaze rakes over me, and he swallows thickly, his Adam's apple bobbing in this throat. The look in his eye is familiar—hungry like the night before. I take a step back, hitting the cool surface of the mirror.

"Hold still."

I don't dare disobey, but my heart pounds and my stomach twists with nerves. He steps forward until we're inches apart. His fingers run down the side of my breast, then graze over my nipple.

His eyebrow arches. "No man has ever touched you before, correct?"

I suck in a breath. "Correct."

He dips beneath the fabric and circles my nipple, forcing it to pebble and harden. "How does this make you feel?"

Dirty. Disloyal. Confused. Warm heat builds in my lower belly. I stare at the curly chest hair peeking out from under the collar of his shirt. "I don't know."

"Are you wet between your legs? Have you soiled those new panties before you even got them out of the store?"

My eyes flick to his. *How did he know?* "Stop. This is inappropriate."

He leans to whisper in my ear. "This is your world now, Imogene." He tugs at my nipple, pinching hard, and pain shoots through me. "It's better if you accept that. It'll go easier." His breath hot. "Do you understand?"

My fingers coil into a fist and that instinct, the one I try to drive out of my system, starts to rear its head but this time, before I can move, Elon's hand cinches around my wrist. "Hit me again and you'll regret it. I'm serious."

I nod.

"Say it, Imogene. Tell me you understand."

"I understand." My words are shaky but clear. I meet his eyes when I say it, holding them longer than necessary. "I will not raise my hand to you again."

Finally, he steps back, tweaking my nipple one last time and says, "I'll go settle with the girl up front. Put on the blue dress and the heels, then meet me at the car."

"You don't want me to try on the other clothes?"

"It's unnecessary. Rex will approve." His aloofness is back, cold and distant. The dark anger from moments before, gone. I can't keep track of this man's emotions. He repeats, "Get dressed and meet me at the car, we have somewhere to be."

"Where are we going?" I ask, reaching for the blue dress.

"To meet Anex."

17

———————

E lon

After paying, I ask the clerk to point me in the direction of the bathroom. The minute I get inside and lock the door, I lean against the sink and unzip my pants. Two seconds later I've got my hand wrapped around the base of my cock. I'd been rock hard all morning, but that little reveal of Imogene in a black lace bra and panties almost made me come in my shorts.

The Little Lamb... she has no fucking idea.

I made it worse by touching her. That hadn't been my plan, but seeing her barely covered in lace... I lost control.

Despite being too skinny, her tits are incredible, and her lips look puffy and soft. I think about how they felt, how aroused she became. I stroke up and down my cock, tugging and working myself to the brink. Underneath all that innocence is a woman that needs to be broken in. Fucked. I'd do it myself if it wouldn't violate Anex's orders. I close my eyes and think of her naked and splayed on my bed, eyes wide as she takes in my manhood for the first time. As sweet as she seems, underneath there's a fighter. I can smell it. The thought of battling her, dominating her as I claim her, ignites a rumble in my chest. It doesn't take me long to reach my peak, and I shudder through my orgasm, teeth clenched, and unload in the sink.

"Christ," I mutter, pushing and pulling until there's nothing left. I hold on to the counter and catch my breath. Getting hard over Imogene wasn't a surprise, but the ferocity of my orgasm was unexpected.

Jerking off is something boys learn to do efficiently at Serendee. Taking care of our needs quickly and without delay is encouraged. Anex understands there is nothing more inefficient and distracted than a pent-up male. These lessons start at age twelve, when we're separated from the girls. We're taught that males have less control over their physical desires, and that can lead to aggression, anger, and violence. Females have powerful attributes and are born with more self-control. It's their duty to maintain decorum with their appearances and behavior because males can't be held accountable for the flaws nature gave to us—the urge to fuck and procreate. The need to spread our seed. Anex demands that we do the best we can, treating women with honor and respect is important. One way to do that is to rid ourselves of the all-consuming tension to keep us from doing something stupid.

For most, what just happened with Imogene would fall into the realm of stupid, but I'm not like other people in Serendee. I'm one of the Chosen. I have a duty and breaking down Imogene's sexual resistance is part of it. If anything, I held back.

When my breathing is even and my cheeks return to normal color, I clean up myself and the sink, then exit the bathroom to pick up my packages at the counter.

"Everything okay?" the clerk asks. "Your cousin is still in the back." She leans over the counter, giving me an eyeful of her cleavage. "Sure, there's nothing else I can assist you with?"

She's been eye fucking me since I walked in. Any other day, I may have taken her into the back room, but things have changed over the last week. I've been given a mission.

"No thank you. Just tell her that I'll be in the car."

"Of course. Come back—any time."

I smile and push out the door, stepping onto the street. The BMW is parked right out front. I know seeing it had been a shock for Imogene. Hell, the first time I walked into the garage at the main house, I was shocked too. Fancy cars? High tech? My world turned upside down, but Anex was there to right me, to help me understand.

I load up the trunk with the packages and get in the front seat of the car, hoping she doesn't take long. Forcing Imogene to undress like that hadn't been for my own pleasure. Everything I do is with specific intent—that's one reason Anex chose me for this job. She needs to get comfortable with her body and learn how to use it. I know that Silas wants to ease her into it, but Anex isn't known for his patience. He'll want to see results. He's worried about Rex straying too far from Serendee. Understandably so. Every day he gets closer and closer to leaving and if that happens... well, the questions will start and Anex loathes questions.

That is another reason I've been so harsh with Imogene. She's inquisitive. Nosey. It's in her best interest to do as she's told. It's in *all* our best interests. The right girl had to be chosen to fill the role of Rex's mate, but the right girl also comes with risks.

It's my job, along with Silas and Levi, to make sure those risks are minimized.

Anex spent a lifetime breaking Imogene down.

It's our turn to build her into something new.

18

___

I mogene

After parking the car, Elon leads me back into the house, up a different staircase and down a narrow hall. I try to pretend like he hadn't just seen me—touched me. I feel violated and raw—shamed. Every nerve is frayed wire that I'm terrified he'll expose or ignite. It's a valid concern considering the blue dress I'm wearing.

As we walk the endless maze of hallways, I run my hands down my arms, seeking the comfort of sleeves, but instead feeling smooth, bare skin. The sensation is weird and jarring. I'm cold, even though the apprehension in my chest makes me sticky with heat. I keep my eyes on Elon's jet black hair and broad shoulders as we walk toward our destination—toward Anex—thinking they look less tense than before, wondering what changed since he left the dressing room.

"Can you tell me where we're going?" I ask. The hallway is strange, cutoff with no windows or doors.

"To Anex's private chambers. It's an area not accessible to members of Serendee. Only his inner-circle is invited here. No one from the community will see you dressed like that, if that's what you're worried about."

I am worried about it, but I hear the mocking in his voice. "An outfit like this is a symbol of regressive behavior—a punishable offense. After all my hard work, my sacrifices and dedication, if Anex disapproves..." I swallow and heat blooms in my cheeks. "What if he knows what you did to me?"

His gaze flicks to my breasts, making my nipples instantly hard. His smirk is cruel and indicates that he notices. "He won't disapprove, and he won't care that I touched you. It's my job, Little Lamb. How many times do I need to tell you that?"

A million, I think, because I can't process the sudden change in my life. This is not who I am, who *we* are as a community. Elon continues down the hall and I have no choice but to chase after him, clumsy in the unfamiliar heels. When he stops at a wooden door and he looks down at me with those cold, assessing eyes. They settle on my hair. I draw back as he reaches for me, but his hand moves to the back of my neck and yanks out the band holding my hair in a ponytail. Long waves tumble over my shoulders and down my back. "It's not great but it'll do."

Wow, he knows how to make a girl feel special.

He lifts his hand to knock on the door.

"Wait," I grab his arm, "What will be expected of me in there? What does Anex want?"

"He wants to see that we have made progress turning you into the kind of woman Rex will accept." His jaw tightens. "Otherwise behave as normal."

Normal.

Whatever that is.

He knocks and a moment later ,another man dressed in all black appears. Same pants with pockets down the legs, same black boots. More security. How have I never noticed these men before? Elon strides into the room and I follow, knowing now isn't the time to ask questions. Elon definitely knows more about this situation than I do. I've only truly been in Anex's presence independently a handful of times.

Whatever my worries are, they are pushed aside as we walk into the private quarters. It's a large additional wing of the house, with its own foyer and living areas. The room we're in is decorated in expensive looking art and warm rugs on the floor. The walls are painted in rich, bright colors.

I'm mesmerized by all of this—outside of nature, Serendee is a world of neutrals and earth tones, but here, everything is different. When I stop gazing at the rainbow of colors, I realize that we're not alone. A handful of people congregate around the room, settled on plush pillows arranged on the floor. Men *and* women dressed more like the people in town than at home. I want to touch the beads on one woman's dress, or the red paint on another's lips.

Elon stops so abruptly I almost run into him.

Anex sits in the middle of the room on a soft looking plush chair. Women, including Margaret, cluster around him on large pillows. It's not a completely unusual scene—Anex is typically surrounded by his confidants—but the colors, the clothes, the room. It's not the same at all. Even Margaret is wearing a soft pink dress with thin straps instead of sleeves.

There's a young woman standing in front of him, back straight, with her hands flat against her sides. I can tell immediately that she didn't grow up here. I recognize almost everyone, but there's also just a vibe from recruited members. It's radiating off of her.

"Charlotte," Anex says, his tone easy, yet tinged with something sharp, "it's come to my attention you went into town. Alone. Is that true?"

She hesitates, like she's considering her answer, but ultimately says, "Yes. I did."

"And if that wasn't violation enough, you went to a place of business and asked to use their phone?"

"Yes." Her chin drops and her hands twist together. "I was trying to call my sister."

Anex lounges back in his seat, elbow propped on the arm of the chair. "The sister who does not believe in the values of our community and has encouraged you to leave Serendee?"

"Yes."

The tension in the room is palpable. Deadly silent. My heart goes out to this girl, knowing what it's like to be on the wrong side of Anex's judgement. But even as a recruit, she should know better. Outsiders will always try to tear down what they don't understand, and it is clear her sister does not understand Serendee.

I look up at Elon to see what he thinks about this scene, but he stares straight ahead, seemingly unbothered.

"Is there a reason you called her?" Anex asks.

"She asked me to call once a month, to make sure I'm okay." She looks up at Anex. "She's just worried. It's her nature."

"Because she doesn't have faith," he replies. "She doesn't have the care and concern of a tight community like ours. One that builds one another up, instead of tearing each other down."

"Yes. She has none of that," she says, nodding. I can see a fat tear running down her cheek. "It was a mistake. One I won't make again."

He holds out his hand, palm facing Charlotte. "I can sense the internal struggle you have with this. Your genetic family versus your chosen one. It's a dark space."

"Please, help me get back. I want to be at peace with The Way."

"You chose this life, Charlotte, and I want to be here to help you be better. This isn't about me. It's about you." He nods, eyes flicking to one of the guards near the door. The man walks over and stands behind the girl. "You need to spend some time alone, considering what you've done. What you want to happen in the future."

"Yes, Anex."

"And I will be using your collateral."

Her eyes snap up and her body shudders. "No. Please don't."

"You've given me no choice," he says, voice tinged with sympathy. "It seems to be the only way to get you back on the right path."

He nods at the guard who leads the woman out of the room. Our eyes meet as she passes, and an uncomfortable feeling rises up my spine. I don't want to be associated with her, yet I pity her. I know what it's like to want to talk to someone outside the community.

When she and the guard have left, Elon steps forward. I follow, and we both go through the process of touching our forehead and bowing. Anex turns his attention to me and I wait until he speaks, until he finishes assessing me. I've never felt as *seen* as I have in the past few days. These men, they're always looking, watching, studying. Today is different ,though. I'm more exposed than I ever have been before. Physically and emotionally.

"Elon," he says, shifting his gaze, "tell me, how is Imogene progressing?"

I'm slightly taken aback that he's addressing Elon instead of me.

"She's doing well," Elon says. "She's eager to fulfill your Order and to please her mate and it shows in her willingness to make necessary changes."

"Good, good," Anex says, tenting his fingers and refocusing on me. "I wasn't sure if you could manage what was being asked of you, but as usual, you surprise me."

I'm both mesmerized by his blue eyes and trying to figure out if this is a compliment or not when Elon jabs me in the side. "T-thank you, Anex. It's an honor to please you."

He waves this off and picks up a bundle of books. The leather covers are familiar, and although it shouldn't, my stomach drops when I realize it is my logs and journals.

"As you can see, I have access to your books. Levi brought them to me." He nods across the room and for the first time I see that Levi is here, standing against the wall. He went through my things? Read my journals? I swallow back the strange feeling of knowing he knows my deepest thoughts and face Anex, who casually flips through the pages, stopping occasionally to study something I've thoughtfully written. "I'm happy to see that you've provided thorough documentation."

"I try to be diligent in my writings—as you suggest."

He smiles and then glances down again at the book. "I see you experienced your first kiss with Silas."

The kiss? That's what he wants to talk about? Not my food logs? Not my sewing? Not the work in The Center?

"Yes." I search for the right response. "He's a very thoughtful instructor."

He leans back in the chair. "Show me."

My eyebrows raise. "Show you?"

"If you're going to mate with my son, I need to be sure that the training I've directed is adequate." He holds up the journal. "Not that I don't believe you, Imogene, but I've always needed my own confirmation on important matters." He nods at Elon. "Kiss *him*."

I turn and face Elon, a man that has made it undeniably clear that he doesn't like me in the least. A man who violated me earlier in the day and the night before. He towers over me and I don't miss that despite the impassive expression on his face. His jaw clenches tight with disgust. He has no choice here—no more than I do.

My pulse quickens in warning, telling me this is not the man I am supposed to be intimate with, but my mind steels itself against emotion. We've both been Chosen, and this is an opportunity to prove our worth in Anex's eyes.

Elon reaches for me, his large hand sliding beneath my hair to cup the back of my neck. Silas had done something similar, and I sink into him the way I knew was pleasing. The pressure on the back of my neck lifts my chin and I stare at Elon's mouth and the way his tongue wets his lips. I mimic his motions and close my eyes. A moment later, his mouth is slanted over mine, lips parted. His breath enters my mouth, and his tongue flicks, slow and seductive. I gasp in surprise, and his other hand presses against my lower back, dragging me close, not letting me get away. The kiss is warm, deep, and penetrative. Elon's jaw is hard and hungry and over the pounding heartbeat in my ears, I hear a rumble in his chest. An inferno builds in my belly and I'm vaguely aware of his hand sliding lower down my backside, cupping my—

"Enough!"

Elon's hands drop, splitting us apart. He steps aside, looking forward, and other than the red mouth, you'd never know what we'd just done. He's calm and collected. Me? Well, I'm using every ounce of strength that I possess to hold myself upright. My heart slams against my ribcage, my lips tingle like they've been electrocuted, my limbs wobble like gelatin. I face Anex as though everything is normal, like my skin isn't on fire. Like I haven't just violated the sanctity of my courtship.

Anex stares between us, eyes roaming over my face. An apology sits on my tongue, but still tastes like Elon and I can't force it out.

"Acceptable," he says. "Obviously, there is a lot of progress that still needs to be made." he snaps the journal shut. "You're halfway there, which isn't enough to convince my son of your worth." His assessment turns clinical, and he nods to Margaret. "Schedule time to visit with Imogene. Do something with her hair and face."

My face? I lift my hand to touch my cheek, but drop it quickly. "Thank you, Anex," I say, remembering my place. "I want to do everything I can to make your Order go through smoothly."

He lifts his hand, and motions for me to come forward. I do as he commands, approaching his chair. He leans forward and takes my hand. "I appreciate your dedication to The Way and my family. Although we try to maintain other appearances, this has been a trying time for us. Everything about the future of our community hinges on this mating." His fingers wrap around my hand, tightening his grip. "You're a beautiful woman, Imogene. Don't be afraid to use the natural gifts you've been given." His eyes slide down my face, lingering on my neck and collarbone before settling on my breasts. "The Way has always encouraged us to use those gifts to make Serendee a better place."

"That's all I want," I tell him truthfully. "I feel it in my heart and soul. Serendee is my home, and The Way is my compass. Together they will keep me on track."

"Good girl," he says, lifting his hand to cup my cheek. "I knew you wouldn't disappoint me."

He dismisses us, and Elon leads me back the way we came. Levi falls in line, his expression impassive and difficult to read. Despite the emotional rollercoaster, I'm buoyed by the elation I feel from being in Anex's presence. I'd passed the test, all of us had, and that is the most important thing of all.

19

———————

L^{evi}

THE ROOM IS LOCATED in the basement of The Center with a door to the outside for coming and going. It's windowless and the walls are painted a dark blue and the floors a cream tile. A single desk with one chair sits in the middle of the room. It's utilitarian—as is the business done in here.

I've been in here before—many times—but never as a Guide. Usually, I am the one on the other side of the table, but this is my new role, one given to me by Anex, to ensure that Imogene is who she says she is.

"Oh," Imogene says, pausing in the doorway. She's surprised to see me but recovers quickly. I don't rise. Here I am, the authority. She will stand while I sit. The heavy door shuts behind her, locking from the outside. She can leave at any time, but it would be improper for someone to walk in on us during a session. What transpires in these walls is private. Sacred. The only one that will have access to the recordings is Anex himself.

She stands before me in a pale blue dress that buttons from mid-waist to her throat. The buttons are tiny, mother-of-pearl, and look like they would take small fingers to fasten. The hem of her dress skirts against her ankles. I know she went shopping with Elon the day before and purchased secular clothing. Her eyes go to the leather-bound journal sitting on the desk. I took it from her room earlier and read the latest entries.

That is why we are here today. For me to Guide her through her Lapses.

"I didn't expect you," she says, approaching the desk.

"No, I would think not. Usually, at this phase of your Ordering, you would have a female to lead you through the early stages of your betrothal, but Anex thought it would be best to have someone in the inner circle as you Guide. Someone that understands the intricacies of what you're being asked to do."

"I understand," she says. I notice a flicker of worry in her eyes. Fear? Guilt? Both probably. Her journals have gone from the mundane of Domum life, calorie counting and roommate annoyances, to a flurry of emotions she's never experienced before. "Before we start, can I ask you a question?"

"You can ask. I won't agree to answer."

"What is collateral? Like Anex spoke of yesterday?"

"Ah." This I can answer. "Recruits must offer collateral when they join the community. It's a way to firm up their commitment to Serendee since they do not have ties inside. People offer up something important to them that they do not want the rest of the world to know—something embarrassing or shameful, just for Anex to hold on to. It helps them stay on the path."

Her eyes flick to the book on the desk. "Sort of like our journals."

"Yes, but Anex requires more from recruits. It's risky that he allows them in at all." She seems satisfied with this answer, and I jerk my chin upward. "Are you ready?"

She exhales. "Yes."

I open the journal and my eyes skim the page from the day before, settling on the details of her trip to the store with Elon. She wrote a thorough description of the entire trip; riding in the extravagant car, the brightly lit shop, the clothes she tried on and purchased. She goes into exact detail about the lacy undergarments and Elon's behavior. I'm only focused on one thing.

"You wanted to strike him." It's not a question. She'd written down that when Elon pushed her boundaries, she'd wanted to lash out at him physically again.

She swallows, regret and shame written on her face. "I did."

"And you only stopped because he forced you."

"Correct." She shifts on her feet. "I know my defiance is wrong. I just... I get angry. It surges through me and although I try to control it, I don't always succeed."

She's honest to a fault. It makes it easier to do what I'm here for. The look in her eye. She's almost begging for it.

I close the journal. It's enough. More than enough. Imogene stares at her hands and quietly says, "I'm sorry."

"You do not need to apologize to me," I say, turning to face her. "These doubts imply a weakness. A lack of faith."

"I know, I just... I don't know how to rid myself of it."

"When we are confused, it's best to go back to the teachings. What does the literature say about doubt and fear?"

She lifts her chin slightly, but not enough for me to see her eyes. "It says that it's where evil has taken root and allowed to spread throughout a person. To rid ourselves, we must eradicate it, like a gardener with an invasive weed."

Every person in Serendee struggles with these concerns and must determine their own Correction. Some people meditate. Others throw themselves into working in the community. Others fast. But Imogene, her shame and guilt run deep. I've seen the red stains in her journal. She chooses a more physical form of Correction.

She swallows thickly and reaches for the journal, running her hand over the cover. She pushes her nail into the spine, and slides out something silver. It's a long, sharp piece of metal.

"I have spent years fighting against my mother's Regressiveness. Proving that I am not the same, but I fail. Often."

I nod. "These things push you to Correction?"

She nods.

"Show me."

Her fingers tremble as she reaches for the top button of her dress, high against her throat. Slowly, she pushes each one through until I see the pale expanse of her chest and the shadows that lead between her breasts. The edge of lace surprises me and it's my turn to be startled when she reveals a white lacy bra and not the standard undergarments.

"I was trying to get used to them," she says. "I was going to mark it in my journal."

"Of course," I say, forcing the words out past the lump in my throat. An unexpected rush of heat travels below my belt. I say a blessing to The Way, willing my body to behave. I arrange my face as though seeing this much female flesh is something I'm familiar with. I'm not.

She continues down until she's pushed the bodice of her dress down to her narrow hips. Her thumb rubs just above her hipbone. That's when I see the dark lines. They aren't open wounds, more like deep scratches. Her eyes glance at the tool on the table and I understand that is how she made them. She inhales and says, "One mark is for my mother's Lapse. Another is to quell my strong-will. Any others are for current Lapses, like defying Elon." She runs her fingers over them. "So five today."

I sigh and approach her, tentatively reaching out to touch the wounds. There are thick scars under the fresh scrapes, and I feel the pulse of heat against my thumb. "Rex will disapprove of the cuts—he will view them as another weakness, a sign of his father's control. Personally, I understand the need to find a release for the pain, but we'll have to find another way."

"You want me to stop cutting." The expression on her face tells me this isn't something she's ready or wants to do. Correction can become addictive. Pleasurable even. "I'm not sure I can."

"You must face your fears. Challenge and expose them to the light."

Her hands cover her face, and she whispers, "It's too much. It's wrong."

I stand and circle the table, wrestling her hands away from her face and cinching my fingers around her wrists. "Exploring this is the only way to move past it, Imogene. Shame lives in dark spaces. You must bring it to the light. Embrace these emotions and own them."

She finally looks up. "Will you help me?"

"Of course. That's why I'm here." I position us to face one another and force her to look at me. Her eyes are so blue in the light—so clear. "I will be taking over your correction."

She blinks. "Isn't that highly unusual?"

"It is, but you are no longer a typical woman in Serendee. You are Chosen. Part of the inner circle, and neither Anex nor Rex can have the slightest concern about your motivations."

"I want them to trust me."

"Good. Then you can start by trusting me." I nod in front of her. "Place your hands on the table."

Her jaw drops and I can see the defiance coming—the question— the argument. I raise an eyebrow, daring her to add fuel to the fire. She's already in enough trouble. After a moment of hesitation, she bites down on her bottom lip and swallows it back.

"Good girl," I tell her, moving behind her. I reach for the hem of her skirts and lift them up. I expect the white, chaste panties the women of Serendee notoriously wear. Instead, I get a glimpse of more lace and a scant amount of fabric covering the round curves of her ass. My cock twitches in response. I knew this was going to be hard, but I didn't expect this.

Her knees wobble, making her thighs shake, but her hands remain flat against the table, holding her upright. I don't give her notice before my palm comes down hard against the smooth flesh, her body lurching forward when I make contact, slapping hard.

"One," I tell her coldly, flexing my hand, "for your mother's lapse."

I spank her a second time, hearing a small cry come from her mouth. A coil of desire twists below my gut, something I've never felt before. I slap the flesh again, landing my palm on top of the red skin. "Two for striking Elon."

I continue on, giving her a spanking for each Lapse. The thought of slapping Elon in the dressing room. The urge to talk back. The constant questions. She falls forward on the third, down to her elbows, and a tear drops on the tabletop. Her knees shake furiously, and I tell her, "Don't you dare fall."

There are five in total, and I breathe heavily with the final one. My cock is rock hard, and something primal takes over. I stare at her for a long time, at the lace and red, blistering flesh. The desire to punish her further—mark her—surges through my veins.

"Straighten your legs," I tell her, annoyed at her slouching. I ignore the muffled grunt as she pushes herself back up. She moves too slowly, and I grab her hips, jerking her upright, while yanking her panties down at the same time. I haul back and spank her again, before dropping the lace on the table and saying, "This is for wearing those slut panties." I add one more. The sound of my palm meeting her ass, echoing through the bare room. There's no reason other than the fact I can't stop.

She falls over the table, her shiny ass red and exposed. Her breathing is fast-paced and shallow, while mine slows, struggling for control. I can see the dark folds of her pussy between her cheeks. I narrow my eyes and discover something else.

She's wet.

I'm not incredibly experienced with women's bodies, but I know the signs of arousal when I see them. I glance toward the famed image of the sun and moon on the wall, and back at the woman on the table.

"That's all," I tell her. "Get yourself together and we're done."

She pushes herself up and brushes the blonde hair off her forehead. Her cheeks are red and sweat dots her forehead. Her breasts are still exposed, and she quickly fastens them, pushing the buttons through the holes with shaky fingers. I walk over and grab the panties, balling them in my fist.

"Leave these. I will speak to Elon about the parameters of when and where you may wear this type of clothing."

"Yes," she says, her tone distant. "Thank you."

My eyebrow lifts. "For what?"

"Correcting me." She licks her lips and glances at me, making eye contact. "For showing me the path to enlightenment."

Something stirs inside of me, deep in my core. This woman. She is strong. Devoted. She takes on the challenge of four men, each determined to break her in one way or the other, to mold her into the perfect mate for our next leader, and she not only accepts every challenge, she thrives on them. The flash of her bare ass flickers in my mind again and the urge to bend her over the table and pound into her is compulsive and strong.

My response is quiet, but forceful. "Go."

She scrambles with the last buttons and leaves, going the way she came. The inner door opens moments after the door closes behind her, latching in place.

"That was excellent work," Anex says, leaning against the wall. "I wasn't sure you had it in you."

"You know I will do anything for Serendee," I say, remembering how she felt in my hands. "For you and Rex."

"The extra corrections were inspired." I feel his eyes on me. I know he was watching. Did he see her arousal as well? "You were right about the cuts. Rex won't like it." He steps back out of the room. "The marks you made on her will fade. Keep working with her. Break down those walls—rid her of all regressive traits. That is something we can't risk."

I nod, and once he's gone, I exhale, feeling like I've just gone through a battle. Like Anex, I didn't know if I had it in me to be so brutal. I also didn't expect to already want to do it again.

20

I mogene

I WAKE with my face smushed in the pillow, having slept on my stomach because of the lingering pain on my backside. Levi hadn't held back during my correction, but other than the sting from the spankings, I feel strangely refreshed. I'd known for a long time that my own Corrections weren't helping me progress, but having a Guide keep me accountable—one willing to push me to my limits? That changes things.

When he told me to bend over that table, a jolt of emotion ran through me. Fear, of course. I'd experienced being whipped with a leather strap as a child, but also the telltale defiance that brought me there in the first place. I loathe the hot streak that runs through me. It's not that I wanted Levi to Correct me, but I knew I deserved it.

The first slaps were sharp and jarring, more powerful than I imagined Levi could be. But his devotion to The Way runs deep. I accepted each strike, asking for strength and forgiveness. The pain stung, a physical reminder of what my Lapses do to the entire community. One member can weaken the whole. The first five were harsh and punishing. The final two? I've heard of the concept of Enlightenment my whole life. It wasn't until he jerked up my hips and yanked the panties down my legs that I felt it. Suddenly, it wasn't about pain and punishment—my body transcended that. Warm heat builds in my lower belly and every nerve sparked with life. My breath caught in my lungs and my skin ignited with fire.

I knew in that moment that I could truly experience enlightenment. I didn't quite reach it but it was there. So close. And Levi was the Guide that could take me there.

I'm still riding this high when I receive a message from Margaret announcing a visit after breakfast. Although I'm eager to have her assistance, when she arrives its surreal having her in my room. She's beautiful and poised—different from the girls I grew up with. But Margaret didn't grow up in Serendee. She was recruited from the outside—a late joiner, who was quickly embraced into Anex's inner spiritual circle, and joined him as a spiritual wife.

I'd carefully hung up the clothing from my shopping trip the day before and Margaret picks through them. Elon added a few things while I was in the changing room: jeans, tank tops, shoes, and a pile of silky lingerie.

"These are nice," she says, fingering the lace on a complicated-looking undergarment. "You have good taste."

"Oh, I didn't pick any of those out. Elon went with me. It's what he thinks Rex wants."

"He's probably very right." She gives me a little smirk. "Men have little patience and are focused on the flesh. Outfits like this force them to slow down a little."

I nod, pretending like I understand what she's talking about. Everything in my life has gone full speed the last few days. I can't imagine lace and sheer lingerie slowing anyone down. It made Levi angry. It makes Elon mean. For a man like Rex, who is used to getting exactly what he wants, when he wants it, I can't imagine what difference it will make.

"You have some makeup here, don't you?" she asks, folding the clothing neatly.

"In the bathroom," I reply. "How did you know?"

"I purchased it and had it sent up here when you moved in." We enter the bathroom and she opens the drawer. She bypasses the makeup and opens a small, rectangular compact. "I also had Healer Bloom prescribe these for you."

I take the rectangle and open it. Inside are rows of pills. "What is this?"

"Birth control. Take it every day at the same time. If there's an issue, talk to the healer, okay?"

Embarrassment heats my cheeks. Do I tell her that Rex has no interest in me? But she's already moved on and is pulling out the vanity chair. I take a seat, and she runs her fingers through my hair. "God, your hair is gorgeous."

"It's not as pretty as yours," I say. She wears it shorter than the girls I grew up with. Still long, but cut just above the shoulders. Anex feels that long hair is the most practical, requiring less upkeep and, ultimately, less vanity. He's right about it being easier. Pulling it back into a ponytail or just leaving it down takes very little time. I look at Margaret in the mirror's reflection. "Can I ask you a question?"

"Sure." She twists my hair into two ropes. She clamps one section to the top of my head.

"Is it weird having not grown up here? Not living like the rest of Serendee or getting Ordered?"

She laughs, showing her pretty, white teeth. "It took a while to adjust to the ways of the community, but not every female gets Ordered. Some are called for a higher purpose."

"What does that mean?"

"Do you know how Anex and I met?"

I shake my head and watch as she reaches for a pair of scissors in the drawer. "At a coffee shop in town. I overheard him talking about philosophy and his unique way of seeing life. I was working on a paper for school. His words drifted over to me, and it was exactly what I needed to hear. I pretended to work on that paper for an hour, while I absorbed everything he said. He must have noticed because when he parted from his friend, he approached me, and we started talking. I took my first lesson at The Center that weekend. Two weeks later, I had moved into Serendee. Anex told me that I wouldn't be living in the domums or any of the independent houses. I'd been called to The Way, to support Anex, as he guides the community." Her eyes flick to mine in the mirror. "Just like you've been called to support Rex."

My heart thrums from the beauty of her story and the declaration she'd made at the end. I was so enthralled by her words I didn't even notice the inches she cut off my hair until the tips grazed my collarbone. I looked so different.

"I'm going to show you how to use this makeup," she says, spinning me around. "The key is to use it to enhance your features, not overpower them."

I nod, and my skin tingles under her gentle touch as she applies makeup to my eyes and cheeks. She hands me a tube of lipstick and gestures for me to put it on. It's a pale pink and when I run it over my lips, I can only think about the burning heat I felt when kissing Elon earlier.

I look in the mirror again. It's like a different person stares back at me. Strangely, she looks older, more mature. "You're gorgeous," Margaret says, adjusting my hair. "No wonder Rex chose you."

"Rex doesn't want me," I admit. "He made it very clear that doesn't want to have anything to do with me."

"That's just his stubbornness talking. He and his father—they're two lions trying to figure out who runs the den. With your help, things should settle down soon." She puts away the makeup, arranging it neatly in the drawer. "Just keep up with your training. We're not like other females, Imogene. We're different. Chosen. We don't have the luxury of remaining passive. Men like Anex and Rex, they feed off the energy that we supply them. Their mood, their health, their abilities... it's tied back to us. We must always give them the fuel that they need to be the best leader possible."

"I've never considered it that way," I say. "I've been caught up in the strangeness of it all—how to straddle the values that I grew up with, with what I need to do now—but this? It helps."

"Good," Margaret says, giving me a tight hug. "Although it may seem like a sacrifice now, really, this is just another step toward the enlightenment of being a powerful woman."

Her words fill me with a surge of motivation—a purpose—and I vow to do everything that is asked of me to support the leadership of Serendee and fulfill my duty as one of the Chosen.

* * *

"Fuck," Silas mutters as I walk into the living room. He closes the laptop and sets it on the coffee table. "Sorry."

"Is something wrong?" I look down at my clothing, then back at his face. He's studying me closely. I thought I was home alone, but Silas may not like to see me in this clothing any more than Levi. "Is it too much? Should I change?"

"God no. You look..."

"Silly, I know." I changed from the dress I wore to Anex's chambers into a pair of tight-fitting jeans. They stick to me like a sheath. "I've never worn jeans before. They're kind of restrictive." I run my hands over my hips. I'm not used to the feeling of fabric so close to my skin. "I should put on something appropriate."

"No," he blurts. "Don't. It's exactly the kind of thing Rex would approve of. You should get used to it."

"You think?" I tuck my hair behind my ear.

"I know."

I smile. "Good. Elon picked it out, and Margaret did my hair and makeup. I just... it doesn't seem like it's enough."

"Well, you're right, that clothing is just one part of this," Silas says. "When Rex sees you in that he'll be interested and want more."

More. I'm not naïve enough to know this isn't about sex. It's all about sex, but Margaret taught me it's also about something else: a purpose.

"Then show me."

His eyes widen. "Show you?"

"Show me what he'll want. I'm ready." His lips form a line—

clearly doubtful that I'm truly ready, but I'm determined. "If our goal, my goal, is to bring Rex back into Serendee I will do whatever it takes. Anex has faith in me, and I have faith that The Way will get me through this."

He nods and picks up the laptop. "Come sit by me. I have an idea."

"More TV?" I'd binged the rest of the show he'd shown me, which is one reason I know this outfit is pleasing to men. I sit next to him and wait as he queues up a show.

"Something different," he says, scooting closer, leaving a small space between us. He places the computer on the table right in front of us. "A new lesson."

Flickers of energy spark through me at his closeness. He smells good. Soapy and warm. He presses play. I'm still enthralled at the way the screen comes to life, showing so many colors and pictures and—I gasp. "Oh."

A woman appears on screen wearing very little clothes. She's in a lacy red bra with matching panties. Her breasts are enormous and her hips curve with so much flesh I didn't even know a woman could possess. "What—what is she doing?" I ask, unable to keep my eyes off of her.

"Watch and see," Silas says, his voice a little rough. His hand moves to the gap between our legs, resting on the couch.

I do as I'm told, studying how this woman walks across the room, distracted by a tightening in my belly, something low and deep. She reaches a bed, and that's when I realize she isn't alone. A man waits for her. He's also wearing very few clothes, just a small pair of black shorts. His body is rippled with muscles, and the sensation in my stomach builds. It only increases when I feel Silas' pinky making sweeping strokes against the side of my leg.

I've seen people have sex on the other show he has me watch. They kissed and touched and then vanished under the covers or are shown the next day looking happy and refreshed. I know they had sex because the characters told me. What I'm witnessing on the screen is more than that. The couple meets at the edge of the bed and their hands are all over one another; grabbing, pulling, pushing. Their breathing is heavy, hypnotic. Their lips bite and their tongues lick. The man tears the bra off the woman, revealing her perfect breasts and round, brown nipples, and she pushes at the waist of his shorts, revealing paler skin and deep cut of muscles and a dark swirl of hair. I'd noticed the front of his shorts seemed lumpy, but when she removes them entirely, I'm struck dumb.

"What is that?" I ask quietly.

"It's his penis," Silas tells me. "His dick, cock, whatever."

I drag my eyes away from the bobbing, swollen appendage and look over at Silas' pants. "Are they always that big?"

He laughs and shrugs.

"And looks like that?" I point at the screen. The woman has his cock in her hands and makes a big show of running her fingers all over it. His jaw clenches and grabs her breasts with his hands, kneading them.

"Not exactly the same. They're all different, like how your tits look different from hers. But the function is the same."

"And what is that function?" I ask, no longer just feeling the warmth in my belly, but between my legs as well. "What does it do?"

"A couple of things," Silas says, placing his hand on my thigh. My nipples tighten, pushing against the thin fabric of my shirt. He leans close to my ear. "But the best one, the one that's in our lesson, is to fuck."

Fuck.

I've heard the word—Silas said it when he saw me. It's a curse, but obviously more. His hand runs down my leg. "Right now, he's going to fuck her mouth."

I watch as he does just that. The girl gets down on her knees, then takes the aggressive cock in her hands like a woman dying of hunger. She dotes on it, stroking, licking and lathing it with her tongue. She swallows it greedily, and the man, he thrusts his hips upward like he's keeping pace with a beating drum. My pulse maintains the same rhythm and Silas' hand continues to glide up and down my leg, fanning the flames of the fire burning inside of me.

"He's going to come," Silas says, licking his lips. "See how his body is all tense? He's about to come in her mouth."

I don't know what that means, but I see the man's body shift from erratic jerking motions to a stiff rigidity, his hips losing their pace. His hand moves to the back of her head and he shoves it down over his cock. A moment later, he jerks twice, and she breaks free of his grip, tilting her head back. Something white and slippery drips over her lips. She licks it and moans before grinning coyly at him.

Silas turns off the video and looks at me while continuing to touch me. My mind is still trying to process it all, but my body seems to understand. It's hot and flustered. Pulse beating in every part of my body, including between my legs. What those two did was natural. Animalistic. It was based on want and desire. It was raw and rough.

I can see why people, why Rex, would want that in his life.

"How did that make you feel?" Silas asks.

"Weird. Like it was wrong to watch such a private moment between two people, but..."

"But what?" he encourages.

"Like I wanted to do it too."

"It made you horny."

"What's that?"

"What you're feeling." He bends and plants a kiss on my neck, warm and lingering. My nipples grow even harder and all I want is for him to touch me like that man touched that woman. Like Levi touched me during our session. "It feels good, doesn't it?"

"Yes, but it also kind of hurts." I think about how bad the first slaps of Levi's palm felt against my skin, how bad they hurt, but then, how they started to feel different—good.

He looks up at me with those pretty green eyes. "I can take that hurt away if you want."

"You can?"

He nods, inching his hand up my side. He brushes the edge of my breast and then cups it with his palm. The feeling is overwhelming, so good, but so intense. These men, Silas, Elon, Levi, they've all been teasing me, taunting me and I feel like I'm going to explode.

His head tilts, and he kisses me, lips firm and hot, tongue licking against mine. My body feels like it's throbbing, all of it, every inch, and every bit of self-consciousness is gone when Silas' hand flattens over my belly and dips beneath my jeans. "Oh," I cry, when he reaches the crux of my legs. His thumb brushes hotly against a bundle of nerves, sending shivers up my spine. "Oh god."

"Does that feel good?" he asks, kissing along my neck.

"Y—yes."

He does it again, this time pressing down and rotating the pad of his thumb in a small circle.

"Silas," I breathe, burying my head into his chest.

"Almost there," he says, holding me to him. I'm so wound up—beyond wound up—I'm tight like a wire coil, and when he touches me one more time, it springs spreading through my body in pulsing, delicious waves.

I ride out the aftershocks tucked against his body. His hand strokes my hair. "How was that?"

"Unbelievable."

I draw away from him and accidentally brush against the front of his pants. He grimaces and shifts in his seat. I stare down at the bulge —at his cock—that I now understand a little better.

"Oh," I say, feeling foolish. "You're horny too."

He laughs. "A little."

"I'm not sure I can do what that woman did on the show. Not yet."

"I'm not asking you to."

"But I could do to you what you just did to me." I reach for the button on his pants. He doesn't stop me.

"Imogene—"

I don't listen to whatever argument he has. Silas has taught me something today—a true lesson about men and women, one that Anex has discussed before. Our bodies have needs. They have wants. And it hurts if we don't take care of it. I pull his cock out from under the fabric. At first glance, he doesn't seem as big as the man in the film, but he's still thick and warm. Harder along the shaft than I could imagine, but softer at the tip than seems possible. I run my thumb over the top and a small amount of fluid comes out.

"What is that?" I ask, rolling it between my fingers.

"Semen," he says, resting his head on the back of the seat. His chest rises and falls. "Like what was in the woman's mouth."

"Oh." I frown and dart my tongue out, swiping it over the rounded top. Silas grunts and I say, "It's salty."

"Mmhmm." His arm extends and his fingers thread through my hair. "Show me what you learned."

I make some fumbles, I can tell, because Silas grimaces and gives me little directions, like telling me to lick my palm first or to go slower or than faster, or to cup his balls in my hand. I lick and suck. I stroke and fondle. When he swells big and hard, I suddenly understand the urge to take him in my mouth, but I don't. He fucks my hand, hips rising, and jerking against my palm. I like the way he feels, soft but strong. I like the way Silas sounds right before he comes. His breathing is shallow, and his nose scrunches up and his fingers wind tight in my hair. He comes with a low groan, white, hot, fluid dripping down my hand.

"Oh," I say, realizing how much tidier this was in the movie. No mess. Silas pulls his shirt over the back of his head with one hand and uses it to wipe up my sticky hand.

"Did I do that right?" I ask.

He grins, contentment spread across his flushed face. "Perfect."

I smile back, feeling a strange sense of pride. "Thank you for showing me." I understand that this is my road to enlightenment, to a higher place, where I'll be ready to stand at Rex's side.

"It's my pleasure, Imogene," he says, "and my job."

"You're very good at your job."

"I know." He laughs and drops a kiss on my mouth, and I say a silent blessing to The Way for putting such a man in charge of my training.

21

L evi

I enter The Center at five 'til two. It's almost time for Imogene's break. Calling it lunch would be under the assumption she eats a mid-day meal. She doesn't. I checked her logs.

She's at the front desk when I walk in. Her new haircut is a drastic departure from the style of most women her age, but it's startlingly attractive. It's soft around her face and curls a little without so much weight. Her face lights up when she sees me.

"Hi. I didn't know you were coming in today." She checks the paper calendar on her desk. "Do you have an appointment? I don't see you on the list."

"No," I reply, leaning on the counter. "You go on a break in a few minutes, right?"

Her eyebrows furrow. "Is it time for another session?"

The session. It's all I've thought of for days. Obsessively. But since I can't lock her in a room and inflict Corrections on her each and every day, I've made it my job to know everything about Imogene. I've read through her journals—including the old ones—studied her food logs.

I know she's completely devoted to Anex and The Way. She also feels immense guilt about her mother's Regression. I know that this is why both Anex and Rex chose her. That guilt and shame makes her compliant. What they don't see is that she is strong. Very strong. The journals are meticulous. She documents every calorie she consumes, every thought that comes into her mind, every action she performs. Her Corrections are consistent, all part of her faith. That strength is also what fuels the defiant streak. The one I have been asked to eradicate.

"No session. Not yet. I just thought maybe we could talk."

"Oh, right." She seems surprised. "Well, yes. I do have a break coming up."

"Come outside with me," I suggest. "We can go for a walk."

I wait for Imogene outside and a few minutes later she walks out the front door of The Center. She's anxious, fussing with the waist of her gray dress. This is understandable. Until a few days ago, she'd never been alone with a male. Now she's Ordered, and I'm not her future mate. The difference, though, is that I'm one of Rex's confidants. That gives me leeway that most wouldn't have.

"How about we head over to Ash Park?"

She nods and I lead her to a quiet greenspace on the edge of the University. I notice the looks from the students passing by and I'm certain she does too, although she doesn't show it. Her lack of insecurity is another signal of her dedication. I know our hair and clothing seem odd, foreign to outsiders, but we're used to it. Anex has taught us not to fear this difference but to embrace it. It's all just another step toward The Way.

I point to a bench under a large tree, and we sit side by side. I reach into my backpack and pull out a container, and remove the lid. There is meat, cheese, and bread inside.

"Eat," I direct, handing it to her.

She shakes her head. "I can't eat that."

"You can and will."

"This is double my allotment for lunch." She glances around anxiously. "What if someone sees me? It's bad enough that I'm sitting with a man that I am not Ordered to, but this? They'll think I've gone full Regressive."

"No, they won't. I brought you here because no one is watching."

That's probably not true. Anex has eyes everywhere. But in this case, it doesn't matter. He knows I'm here and who I'm with.

"It's way over my calories. Too much fat. And bread? God." Her expression is one of horror. "You've seen my logs. I never cheat."

"I know you don't, and you shouldn't consider this cheating, at least not any more than that new haircut." I resist the urge to tug the ends of her hair. "The goal here is to win over Rex who is resistant to the methods of The Way. Controlling your calories is a way to reach enlightenment and breaking that is one sacrifice you will have to make to successfully draw him back in.

Imogene picks up the cheese and looks at it like its poison. "I can't."

No wonder Anex is obsessed with her. She's the poster child for The Way. I think about it for a moment and say, "What if we come up with some kind of balance. Eat the food that I supply you and in return you can do something that weighs out the actions."

"I like that idea."

"Good. What is something you think would be an appropriate trade off?"

She thinks it over. "How about for every meal I have, we add something to our sessions. Something to help me win over Rex."

"I think that's acceptable. Just make sure you continue to document and log everything—don't neglect that habit."

Imogene pops the piece of cheese in her mouth and slowly chews it as if she's savoring every bite. Fast or slow doesn't matter to me. If this is going to truly work, I need her to put some weight on her thin frame before she sees Rex again.

"This is because he likes women with bigger breasts, isn't it?" she asks suddenly.

"What?" I sputter, feeling the heat rise to my cheeks.

Her own skin is pink, but she continues anyway. "Silas showed me some film. The women in it were much more voluptuous than I am.

Breasts, hips, behind and thighs." She nibbles on bread. "Even Elon told me I was too skinny. I didn't understand it, since I've always followed Anex's policies, but now that I've seen some examples, it makes more sense."

I'm not privy to the film Silas showed her, but I can only imagine. I slowly form my response. "There are different features valued in the secular world. As with everything else, Rex finds them alluring."

She glances down at her chest and sighs. "I suspect that no matter how much bread I eat, it will never increase my bust size."

She looks so forlorn at this idea that I feel compelled to comfort her. "No, your... bust size is adequate. Pleasing even." Her cheeks redden even further, and I quickly add, "Rex will surely find you suitable once he actually pays attention."

"I'll do whatever it takes," she says dutifully. "And I trust you to Guide me."

"I will make it my priority," I tell her. "Rex's happiness is important to me, just as your journey to enlightenment. I think with some hard work, we can accomplish both."

The wind blows just as she takes another bite of her lunch, sending a strand of her hair into her eyes. Impulsively, I reach out and catch it with my finger, pushing it off her forehead and tucking it behind her ear. It's a gentle gesture that brings warmth in my chest and is at conflict with the role I played during our session. If I am going to fulfill my duties to Anex, I will need to make sure that my head and body are focused.

Now is not the time to get distracted.

* * *

Once Imogene's lunch break is over, we walk back to The Center. The longer we're out in the secular world, I can feel eyes following us. Men mostly. I think back to the night before the Order, when Imogene was harassed in the alley. We'd stumbled on her by accident. Thank The Way. Who knows what would have happened to her if we hadn't been there.

I'd heard what that man said to her, that the efforts of hiding her body didn't work. That it only appealed to men more—wondering what secrets lie beneath such modest clothing.

Never have I heard such truth.

"Thank you for bringing me lunch," Imogene says, when we're back at the office. "It was delicious."

"You're welcome." I glance at the schedule board over her head. "I think I'm going to take a meeting."

She smiles and says, "I'll mark you down."

Meetings are held constantly at The Center. I'm a member of the Men's Group; VRS. The letters stand for Viri Regum Sunt. Men Are Kings. There are daily meetings here and inside Serendee. Sometimes I even lead them, as it's a skill that has come easily to me as I grow and learn The Way. Anex says that my devotion and loyalty is my gift, but after the last week I'm feeling unsteady in my path. What we're doing to and with Imogene feels different. Altering this female—physically and mentally—seems to go against the teachings I've studied so thoroughly. Women are supposed to seek enlightenment and lose the need for vanity and for outside approval. The opposite of what I've spent the week doing.

But Anex asked me to do this. And I trust him. She trusts him.

I feel weak when I walk into the small room, and I hope that none of the men notice. I know them all. The only access to VRS is to be a long-term member of Serendee and pass through several stages of Anex's approval.

"Levi," Aaron greets me as I walk in. He's about ten years older and has been a mentor since I started coming to the meetings. "How are you today?"

"Feeling the need for a little reinforcement."

"You're working on a task for Anex, aren't you?"

"Yes, a challenging one."

"You need Refortification." His smile conveys sympathy, only confirming my weakness.

"Yes. I do."

Fortification is a process of The Way. Strengthening our mental and spiritual walls against attacks from the outside. It's how we are able to withstand assaults of gluttony, sex, greed, and the pleasures of secular men. Except, I don't always withstand those. Not in this job. I intentionally fed Imogene more food to make her body appear more pleasing to the male eye. Elon purchased her clothing to accentuate her figure. Silas taught her how to please a man using modern technology. Margaret showed her how to use tricks and paint to change her face.

All of these efforts have worked. Too well. I find myself... thinking of Imogene differently. I find my brain and body reacting differently as well. I can't stop thinking of her panties tucked in the back of a drawer in my room.

Hence the need for Refortification.

The room fills, and Aaron stands at the front. A big screen is behind him.

"All of you are here because you want to become stronger, more capable men. You want to be protectors. I know that each of you has that ability inside of you, but to get there, you have to dig past the influences that infiltrate us from the secular world. Past the innate emotions that cling to us biologically. The doubt. The worry. The fear. We must embrace our inner male. The true meaning of who we are."

Remotely, he lowers the lights and turns on the TV. It's a video of people on the street, in a bar. It's all smiles and radiance. Loud music. The women are all dressed provocatively. The camera lingers on one woman as man after man approaches. She rejects each one with a grin. Finally, a man of her pleasing draws her attention. He's handsome. Obviously strong. A winner's smile. She touches his hand, leans close, whispers in his ear.

Aaron stops the film. "This woman is a skilled predator—not because she wants to be, but because she has to be. Society has taught her to seek her own mate, because she doesn't trust these men to protect her. She must dress in revealing clothing, paint her face. She is forced into this position by society. The result is insecurity. Indulgency. A reduction in moral standards. It is why we allow Anex to pick our mates—and to determine when we, as men, are ready."

Aaron looks around the room. "The women are already there. It's innate. They are born with a need to be protected. And sure, men are raised to protect—in a greedy, self-absorbed way. It's nature, borne from the hormones that run through our systems—an overwhelming desire to fuck and spread our seed."

The men around me nod. This point has been repeated over and over. Our urge to not just have sex, but to fuck, to claim a woman or women, relentlessly, has been reinforced in every VRS meeting I've attended. It's not the women's fault. It's ours. And VRS is the reminder that we must be better. We shouldn't want a woman that shows her flesh easily or focuses on the outside. We should help them understand that their power comes from the inside. Anex took away that conflict between men and women by Ordering us with a mate of his choosing. If and when we're ready.

When the meeting is over, Aaron walks up and asks, "Do you feel better?"

"I'm more centered," I reply. "Prepared for the challenges ahead."

"Good," he says, resting his hand on my shoulder. "Anex chose you for a reason. Your walls are strong. Your foundation even more so. And when your task is complete, you will be rewarded by The Way."

His words reassure me even more and I walk out of the room, passing Imogene at her desk. She gives me a small wave and carries on with her work. She doesn't know it, but she needs me, and I will do my very best to keep her on the path to righteousness.

22

____

I mogene

    I've been on my new meal plan for several days when Elon enters my room. It's still weird to say that, my room. It's surreal. All of it. The room. The extra food. The clothes, oh and yeah, the handsome man who is not my mate, standing over my bed. That's surreal.

"Get dressed," he says, his voice curt. "And wear something from the new wardrobe. Jeans, a skirt, something secular. Sexy."

I flip the cover of my journal and place it on the bedside table. "Where are we going?"

"Out."

Beyond that, he doesn't clarify, leaving the room as abruptly as he entered. I pick through my closet for what I hope is an appropriate outfit. Sexy. I only have vague notions what that means. I assume it means all the parts of our body that we were told to hide from males because of their weakness for skin and flesh. After watching the video with Silas and feeling his hands on me, I understand that urge a little better.

Now that Silas has shown me what is between a man's legs, how it works and feels, I can't help but wonder about Elon and Levi. About

Rex. Even though I know I shouldn't, I have the desire to see them the same way; caught in the throes of euphoria. Warm and sticky on my hand. The sensation from that day—the burn—it hasn't left my belly. It's a low smolder all the time—ready to be stoked into flame.

I settle on a pair of tight black pants and a pale yellow top that clings against my body. There's a sweater to wear over it and a pair of boots with a slight heel. I take a minute to attend to my hair and face —attempting to replicate Margaret's designs. I'm not very good at it.

Elon waits in the living room, eyes glued to his phone. His gray shirt matches his eyes and is tucked into dark jeans. He doesn't see me at first and I study him; the muscle at the back of his jaw, like always, is clenched tight. He always seems angry and annoyed, like nothing I do is right, like I'm a complete nuisance. Maybe I am. Who wants to babysit a grown woman who has been rejected by her mate?

"I'm ready," I announce. "Is this outfit okay?"

He briefly glances up, then back down at his phone, then back again. Those gray eyes assess me with such intensity that I feel like I can't breathe.

"Take off the sweater," he demands. I slide my arms out of each sleeve. His gaze sweeps over my skin. "You can wear that outside, but indoors, take it off. You need to acclimate to people seeing your skin."

"Okay," I say. "Anything else?"

"Remove the bra. Show off those tits."

I blink. The shirt is so sheer I could see the pattern of lace beneath the fabric. Without it... "Are you sure?"

"Are you asking me to repeat myself, Little Lamb?"

I grimace at the nickname. I know he's mocking me—calling me a sheep. I reach under the back of my shirt and unhook the bra. Then drop the straps down my arms, removing it while keeping on the shirt. My nipples are already hard from the shifting around, and the tank has a slight rib in the fabric, creating friction that only makes it worse. Elon's eyes glide over me and he nods—granting me silent approval.

"Are the others coming?" I ask, balling up the bra and tucking it under a pillow on the couch.

"No. They had to work."

"At night?"

"Serendee's business doesn't end at sunset."

"Can you tell me where we're going?"

"To dinner." He opens the door that leads out of the suite. "At a restaurant downtown. You need to get used to being around more people."

I walk quickly to keep up, but as usual, he seems annoyed to be in my presence. It doesn't get any better when we get in the car. His hands wrapped around the steering wheel in a death grip. The longer we drive, the more uncomfortable I become. Spending time with this man is unbearable. He's rude and authoritative. He may have been sent by Anex to train me, but he has no right to treat me like dirt.

My irritation grows as he turns into a busy parking lot. He gets out and slams the door, walking around to open mine. His movements are jerky and curt. I've finally had enough of his attitude and when I stand, I ask, "What's your problem?"

"What?" He glares down at me and heaves the door shut.

"I said, what is your problem—with me?"

"I don't have a problem with you."

I blink and shake my head. "Okay, sure, just lie to me." I spot the door of what I assume is the restaurant we're going to and head that way.

"I don't have a problem," he says again, closing the gap in two long strides. "I don't give a shit about you." His words should hurt, but instead it's just a relief to hear the truth. "Anex gave me a job, a second job, because I already have one, but I'm doing it."

"I'm glad to know you're dedicated to The Way, Elon, but that doesn't mean you need to act petulant and rude. If you're teaching me how to behave in public settings, with my future mate, I should think you would cut the bad attitude and act civilized."

His eyes narrow, and I wait for a retort, but there isn't one. He simply pushes past me and walks into the restaurant. I follow, prepared to continue to push him, but two steps inside and I stop, unable to do anything but gape at the room in front of me. Music fills the entrance, along with the low murmur of conversation. There are people everywhere, clustered near the door and at all the tables. The phone rings at the pedestal just inside the door. My senses are on overload, visual, auditory, and god, it smells so good. My mouth waters and I try to take in everything at once.

Through it all, I sense Elon's imposing presence, and when my feet seem stuck to the floor, his arm loops through mine and he drags me forward to follow the woman from the pedestal.

"Are all restaurants like this?" I ask, leaning into his side. I'm aware of people watching us. It's a different sort of scrutiny than what I'm used to. Typically, people stare at my long dress and pinned up hair, but the man across from me won't stop staring at my chest. Two women around my age, who split their attention between smiling at Elon and glaring at my nipples. I tug the sweater tighter, but it's futile. "This loud and busy?"

"No," he says, "but you need to immerse yourself. It seems like a good choice. Plus, they have amazing steaks."

"Hope this suits your needs," the woman says when we reach a booth. She gives Elon a small smile. Why are these women always smiling at him? Can't they tell he's a terrible person?

I move to sit across from Elon, but he grabs me by the waist and pulls me down next to him.

"It does. Thank you," he says, ignoring her and glancing down at my sweater. Oh, right.

I remove it, tucking it next to me. If he approves of the gesture, he doesn't show it, instead calling over a waiter and ordering drinks. I'm overwhelmed by the menu—the list of foods I've never seen. Despite my work with Levi, I can't help but try to count the calories and feel a sense of guilt over the gluttony. When the waiter asks what I want and I'm unable to respond, Elon takes the menu from me and orders for the two of us. As annoyed as I am with him, I can't help but be fascinated by his actions. He moves with such ease and determination, like this world is just another layer of clothing.

"Now that we've clarified that I'm just a job to you, then let's get down to business," I say, breaking the silence. "How did you learn to do this? Leaving Serendee to do secular things like going to fancy restaurants and knowing what to wear and what to order?"

"Anex asked me to, and I did it."

I frown. "But what happened? What made you do this? Because it's not usual for the men in Serendee, any more than what I am being asked to do is normal for the women."

He takes a swallow of his drink and sighs. "When I turned eighteen, Anex asked me, Levi, and Silas to join him and Rex in his private quarters. He said that now that we were of age, he needed people he could trust to work for the businesses that fund Serendee."

"There's a business that funds the community? What about Anex's family money? And the classes at The Center? Or the profits from the farmer's market?"

The look he gives me is filled with superiority. It's been taught that the classes alone bring in enough income to support any needs we have on a cash basis. Obviously, that, along with so many other things I was raised to believe, is not entirely true.

"There are several businesses—all of which bring in substantial funds."

"Oh. And you just accepted your new role?"

"It was hard at first," he admits. "I was a little like you, wide-eyed and overwhelmed, but it also wasn't my first time in the secular world. Being friends with Rex allowed certain perks."

"Like what?"

He shrugs. "Vacations. Food. Access to technology."

"You've had that all along?"

"Not entirely. As we got older, Anex allowed more exposure and it felt normal. I'd known that Rex was special—he's Anex's son—but he realized that we were special too. He'd been teaching us individually long before we were of age. He knew that we had a calling and that exposing us to these small indulgences was a test of loyalty."

"You obviously passed."

The corners of his eyes tighten. "Enough that he trusted us with learning about the business, and now, to try to handle this situation with Rex."

"Do you feel bad about that? Going behind your friend's back and manipulating him?"

"Rex is like a brother—family—and sometimes you have to make hard decisions when it comes to family." Our food arrives, and he orders another drink. I stare at the pooling butter under my asparagus.

"Eat," he says, noticing my hesitation. He digs right in, cutting into his steak. "Anex taught us that the feeling you get when you're trying to decide if something is right or wrong—that's The Way nudging you in the right direction."

"I had to make a hard decision about my mother," I say. "When she was still here and was...acting Regressive, she tried to get me to leave with her."

With a knife and fork in each hand, he looks up at me in surprise. "She did?"

"Yes. She begged me to go with her when she ran. I didn't want to leave her, but I couldn't."

"Why not?"

"Serendee is all I've ever known. I was old enough to realize that if we left, we could never come back." He nods while popping a piece of meat in his mouth. I add, "But that wasn't all. Deep down, I have always believed in The Way and if I stayed, Anex would have an important position for me. At first, I thought it was working at The Center, but obviously it was much more than that."

"Way more," he agrees. "You think you're truly ready to do what it takes to bring Rex home?"

I don't need to think. I feel the little nudge that he was talking about, The Way, helping me make the right decision. Without hesitation, I reply, "Yes."

* * *

Of course, I didn't realize he meant immediately.

Elon paid for our dinner with his thick roll of cash and led us down the street to a club. More money exchanges hands between him and the guy at the door, then the bartender, and it's just another difference between here and Serendee that I don't fully understand.

"How did you learn to use money like that?" I ask, watching the roll disappear in his pocket. I know about money—and how secular society is ruled by their ever-loving desire to have more. I've never had any of my own. Just the credits we're given to spend in the community.

"We use cash only for the business, but you get used to it." He hands me a glass with a wide rim and red liquid inside the color of a ruby. He nods to a set of stairs. "Come on."

I follow close, not wanting to lose him. Not that it would be easy. His height and broad shoulders sets him apart. The further we get into the club, the more I notice people—men—watching me as I pass through the crowd. Can they tell it's my first time in a place like this?

"Stay close," he says, pulling me against his side. I can't help but inhale his warm, spicy scent. "I should have made you keep on the sweater."

"What? Why?"

"Because," he shoots a dark-haired guy at the bar a look of death, "because your tits are impossible to ignore and I'm not going to be able to leave your side all night."

"Stop," I say, my cheeks heating up. "They see some naïve little girl that shouldn't be here."

"Yeah, that they'd love to defile six different ways."

Now my entire body turns red. I'm sure of it. "I doubt it. You said it yourself, I'm too skinny for secular men."

"I also said you have nice tits." His eyes sweep over me. "You've put on a little weight. It looks good."

That may be the first and only nice thing he's said about me. Well, other than the tits one, and I'm not exactly sure that's a compliment.

"It doesn't matter," he says, resting his hand on my lower back, protectively. Warm tingles spread up my spine. "We won't be down here with the riff-raff."

"Where are we going?" Someone bumps into me and my drink sloshes.

He looks up the stairs. "Up there. To a private area."

I follow him up, high above the swarming crowd. There's another large man guarding the top, but he unlatches the rope the second he sees Elon, giving us access to the upper floor. The area is lofted with a second bar and raised platforms establishing distinct sections divided by wispy curtains and strung lights.

Elon steps up to one of the platforms and pushes aside the curtain. The first thing I notice is beautiful women sprawled about comfortable looking couches. The second? Rex.

My future mate is so handsome it hurts to look at him. Golden-haired and bright eyed. He sits on a leather chair with one of the women on his lap. She's got her nose nuzzled against his neck, under his ear, and her hand on his upper thigh. I stare at the two of them, stomach burning, as his finger strokes the outside of her breast.

No new outfits, no makeover, none of the upgrades I've been given in the last week will give me what I need to compete with that.

"I think I'm going to puke," I say, spinning around.

Elon grabs me with both hands. "No, you aren't. You're going to go in there and claim your mate."

"He doesn't want me. He wants... that."

"Then give it to him."

I peek over my shoulder at the sexy, gorgeous woman perched on top of Rex. She's smooth and sleek, dressed in a leather skirt and a top that shows more skin than it covers. She oozes confidence and experience. I can tell by the way she touches him, by how she reacts to his touch. She's a woman that can fulfill his every desire. I have no clue what to do.

"I'm not ready," I tell Elon, knowing that I'll never be ready.

He places two fingers under my chin and lifts my gaze upward. I can tell he wants to say something, but he struggles to find the words. Finally, he grinds out, "You're a beautiful woman, Imogene. You're smart and have intense perseverance. Anex believes in you. I believe in you. Don't be afraid to get what rightfully belongs to you."

Now that is a compliment. A strange compulsion runs through

me and I skim my fingers along Elon's strong jaw and say, "Thank you."

I don't falter this time, following Elon onto the platform. Rex's eyes light up when he sees his friend, but then narrow when he spots me. It's not anger, I don't think, it's confusion.

"Babe, move," he tells the woman, pushing her off his lap. She appears disgruntled, but shifts over. He stands and shakes hands with his friend. Then rakes his eyes over my body, lingering on my chest, and a small smile plays on his lips. "Well, aren't you a pretty little thing."

"Thank you." A little thrill runs through me.

"Elon brought you up here for me?"

"He did."

"I'm Rex." He thrusts his hand out. "What's your name?"

I stare at his hand, but years of programming kick in. I touch my forehead and bow slightly. "Imogene—your Ordered."

His eyes flick to Elon and then back to me, before he laughs loud and boisterous. "This is a joke, right?" Again, he looks at Elon. "Are you fucking with me? You dressed her up, took off her bra, and slapped some paint on her face. That doesn't change what she is inside." He glances at me again and barks out, "baaa, little sheep."

"This isn't a joke," Elon says, eyes narrowing in irritation. "And it's time for you to stop running from your responsibilities."

"Unlikely, but thanks for the laugh." He reaches out to slap Elon on the back, but his friend blocks his hand.

"Imogene is willing to do what it takes to get your approval."

"I sincerely doubt that," Rex says. "Nice try, though. Tell my father it'll take more than a slutty dress and a haircut to play his game."

He brushes past us, arm jostling my shoulder. I fall into Elon, who keeps me from totally wiping out. As he rights me, he says, "Let me go talk to him."

"No." I take a deep breath. "He's my Ordered. I'll talk to him."

Elon grimaces, but relents. "Don't remind him that you're his Ordered and don't use any terms associated with The Way. He wants secular, not a reminder of Serendee."

I nod and I walk across the loft to the bar. The bartender pushes a shot across to Rex and he drinks it quickly. Then orders another, paying for both with his own thick roll of cash.

When he spots me walking over, he laughs cruelly. "Don't you ever give up?"

"No. Not on you. I believe we're supposed to be together."

Rex knocks back the shot. "It's not going to happen, Imogene." He says my name with a sneer. "You're not my type." His hand shoots out and circles my arm. "Too skinny." He spins me around. "Flat ass. And you head is way too far up my father's prostate."

He walks away, but not back toward the platform, down a hallway. My eyes burn from his insults, but I know if he'll just give me a chance, I can win him over. Anex has faith in me and I have faith in The Way.

I follow him down the dark hallway, away from the music and crowd. He ducks through a door and when I step through, we're on an iron balcony that overlooks the alley below. Sulfur tickles my nostrils and Rex leans against the railing, smoking a rolled joint. The scent that wafts over is herbal, warm, the kind that wafts over the fields during Anex's birthday weekend, and when he looks up at me, he shakes his head.

"I know you're not this fucking stupid."

"I'm not stupid. Just determined."

"You don't want me, Imogene. I'm not who you think I am. I'm not some fucking savior." He takes a long drag and then blows out a cloud of smoke. "Sure, I'll play the role, convincing Serendee that I can continue my father's vision, but that person? You really won't like him." His words are hard—harsh—and I'm self-aware enough to hear the threat underneath, but Anex sent me here. I have no choice. "Leave while you have a chance, Imogene."

"I can't."

"Because my father said so?"

"Yes. He ordered it," I say, immediately regretting using the word.

"I assume he ordered those clothes and that haircut—the plumpness in your face." His fingers run down my cheek. He noticed that

I've gained weight? Rex may have been paying more attention than I realized. "Does that devotion transfer to me? Will you do anything I ask?"

"Yes."

His hand is still on my face, his thumb stroking up and down my cheek. His blue eyes are so distant, so cold, that I feel a chill run down my spine. He rubs the pad of this thumb over my bottom lip, and says, "Fine. Get on your knees."

His tone is so abrupt and his request so strange I blink and ask, "What?"

"Get on your knees, Imogene." His tongue darts out and his hand lands on my shoulder, pushing me down. My knees hit the metal balcony floor. "That's an order."

His hand cups his crotch and images from the video I watched with Silas pops in my head. I know what this is. What he wants. My eyes are level with his cock, and he doesn't hesitate to unzip his pants and reach inside, exposing his length. Oh god. I flinch at the size and look up. "Rex..."

"Shut up." His voice takes an even harder edge. "You're the one that wanted this. You pursued me. I told you to leave me the fuck alone, but you didn't. You want to be my mate? Well, open that hot little mouth and fulfill your goddam duties."

His fingers wind through my hair, rough and twisting. The action dashes any hope of getting out of this—that he's just messing with me. His cock swells, a sign that he's excited, that he likes it like this, and that's when it hits me. This is my mate. This is what he likes, and that means, by the applications of The Way, I will perform as he desires, no matter how uncomfortable or demeaning it is.

I exhale and conjure up the video, thankful that Silas had the foresight to show it to me. I mimic what Silas liked when I touched him with my hands, running them up and down the shaft. Rex is warm and heavy—wider than Silas. I feel him grow with my touch, getting impossibly bigger, and like before, heat explodes in my lower belly, burning with my own want.

"That's it, Imogene." He tilts my head upward. "Open that pretty mouth. Show me why my father picked you."

I blink, trying to understand that statement. Does he think I've done this before? With Anex? There's no time to ask—he doesn't want to know. He's pushing his cock against my lips before I can open them, smearing fluid. I lick my lips. He's saltier than Silas, his cum thicker. I close my mouth over the head, sucking the rest off with the twist of my tongue. His hand tightens in my hair and he leans back on one elbow. Groaning, he mumbles, "Goddamn. You're a greedy little bitch, aren't you? You like the way I taste?"

"Yes," I tell him, knowing that it's what he wants to hear.

I'm not sure how to handle his talk, the harsh words and name calling. It's shocking and unlike any way anyone has ever spoken to me before. It's not like it was with Silas. It's humiliating. Shameful. In contrast to his words, his movements are slow, precise, different from the video. Pushing the tip past my lips and slowing inching further down my throat. "Ah, mmmm... yeah..." he exhales. "Thatta girl."

It's a morsel of approval, and I grab onto it, willing to do anything to make this end. I use the moves I learned from the video, running my hand and tongue up and down his length. I fondle his balls. I lick the head. I refuse to look him in the eye as I take him deep and try not to gag, but he's not satisfied, and his big hand slides down to the back of my head holding it in place as he picks up the pace, pounding his cock into my mouth. I try to squirm away but he tightens his grip.

"Don't even think about it," he threatens, hips slamming into me, "don't stop. Don't you goddam stop. You want to play with the big kids, well suck it." He fucks harder, erratic and holding me by the neck. I don't think I can take it anymore, when it grows faster, and his movements turn erratic. I know that the clench of his jaw, and the loss of words, mean that it's almost over. I just want this over. Please let it be over.

My prayers are answered when a groan rumbles in his chest and his hips lurch forward, and hot, salty, come pools in my throat. I jerk back, nausea rolling over me. He glares down and says, "If you puke that up, I'll just do it again."

Closing my eyes, I force it down, fighting the urge to expel every drop of him. When it's settled and I look back at him again, he's tucking himself back in his pants. "I shouldn't be surprised daddy knew how to pick a girl that could service a man like that. How many times have you done that before?"

I cough and fight a wave of nausea. "None. Never. I swear."

His eyebrow arches skeptically. "Well, that's some outstanding beginner's luck." The sound of his zipper echoes in my ears, and he adds, "Get her the fuck out of here."

I turn as he passes me and spot Elon in the doorway. His eyes are dark, and his mouth set disapprovingly. How long has he been here? How much did he see? The humiliation I feel multiplies and the semen in my belly threatens to come back up. The tears I've held back this whole time let loose.

"Elon?" I say, my voice small. It was one thing to experience that embarrassment, the violation, with the person inflicting it. It's a whole other one to know that someone was watching. Especially, for some reason, Elon.

"He—" I start, but he strides over, lifting me off the ground with a jerk. I wiggle away. "Did you know that was going to happen? Is that why you brought me here?"

His lack of response is all I need to know the truth. He dressed me, fattened me up and delivered me like a lamb to slaughter.

23

R^{ex}

"My apartment is a few blocks away if you want a little privacy," the girl says, her breath tickling my ear. Her hand lays flat on my stomach, and her breasts press against my arm. I wait for the stir of arousal. It doesn't come, not like earlier when Imogene had me in her mouth, tongue gliding over my shaft, swallowing me whole.

That memory causes a twitch.

"How about you get me a fresh drink," I say, pushing her off my lap and shoving my glass at her. She frowns, and I give her a quick grin. "Thanks, babe."

She walks off, hips swinging, her skirt so short it gives me the barest hint of the curve of her ass cheeks underneath. I tilt my head to get a better glimpse, but a figure steps between us, blocking my view. I look up and see Elon glaring down at me.

"You're back," I say, making a show of looking behind him. "Come alone, or did you plan another ambush?"

"She's your Mate," he says, dropping into the leather seat across from mine. "I figured since you weren't coming home, I'd bring her to you."

"As unexpected as it was, I admit it did turn out pretty pleasurable." I throw my arm over the back of the chair. "She did better than expected."

"You had expectations?" he asks doubtfully.

"Although the submissive streak usually turns me off, with a pretty mouth like that, it was hard to resist." I shrug. "I needed to see what she would do."

Elon snorts. "A test. Father like son."

"A test she failed, Elon." My short-skirted friend returns with my drink. I take it from her, and she moves to perch back on my lap, but I wave her off. "You dressed her up like one of these bitches, but she's got no more spine than anyone else in Serendee."

"You mean like that girl you just brushed off? She'd let you fuck her right here, in front of the whole club." He cuts his eyes over to her, where she's dancing by the balcony railing. "You pretend like you want a strong, secular, female, but what you really want is to piss off your father."

I tip the glass back and consume the drink in one swallow and slam it on the table. "You're right. That girl over there will do anything I ask of her, but the difference is that she doesn't know Anex. She wouldn't be doing it for Anex or for some higher calling to The Way. She'd do it because she thinks I'm good looking, rich, well hung." She looks over and I wink, causing her to smile back. "With her it's just fun—not obligation."

"A Mate isn't an obligation," Elon says. "It's a gift—and Imogene..." he camps his mouth shut.

"Imogene what?" I ask, narrowing my eyes at him.

"She deserves better than you."

I laugh. "Ah, is that what this is about? You want to fuck her."

He shakes his head. "You're pathetic. Get your shit together, Rex. You can't run away from this, from her, or your father for much longer."

"No?" I ask, waving the girl over and making space for her to sit on my lap. "Despite what my father has implied, the end of the world isn't coming any time soon."

He stands. "No, but your world is. Your play time is up. It's up for all of us and the sooner you figure that out, the better."

He walks off, heading back down the stairs. The girl leans in but once he's gone; I push her aside. I don't care what Elon says. My father will not control my life—not the way he controlled my mother's and everyone else under his thumb. If he thinks a skinny little girl with puffy lips and shiny blonde hair is going to bring me back to the fold, Anex is dumber than I thought.

24

───────────

Imogene

"Oh my," Margaret says, opening the door to her suite. She's wearing all white and her blond hair curled just over the top of her shoulders. "What happened to your eyes?"

"Allergies," I lie, sniffing for good effect. "Stuck my nose in a bunch of flowers yesterday. I've been a mess ever since."

It's a lie, obviously. I'd tried to beg off when Levi appeared that morning with the handwritten invitation. Margaret wanted me to come to her rooms for tea. I almost blurted that I'm going to need something a lot stronger to wash the taste of Rex out of my mouth, but bit my tongue and said yes.

You don't say no to one of Anex's spiritual mates.

"Well, let's get something to ease that irritation."

I follow her through her apartment. It's in the main house, just like mine, only a floor beneath. I'm starting to think this place is filled with little suites, one for each of Anex's inner circle. It's obvious that Margaret decorated her own—the colors are light and breezy. Her back windows are open to let in the fresh spring air. I'd spent the night crying and trying to reconcile what'd happened between me and Rex. What he'd forced me to do in the cover of darkness. What Elon saw. Margaret's world, filled with brightness and light, is the opposite of that dark, gritty, confusing pain.

In the bright kitchen, I watch as Margaret opens the freezer and pulls out a few chunks of ice and places them in a bowl. "Fill that with water," she instructs. When I finish, she's standing at the island in the middle of the room, cucumber lying on the cutting board. Her hands move quickly, cutting the cucumber into slices. "Drop those into the ice." I do as I'm instructed, and she grins. "That should do the trick."

"Cucumbers?"

"For your eyes," she replies, strolling back into the living room. She crosses out to the balcony where there are lounge chairs and a table set up for tea. A plate of bakery cookies sits next to the tea service. "Lie back on that chair." She points to the one with the back that falls back. "Place the cucumbers on your eyelids. It'll take away the swelling and irritation."

It's an awkward position, lying out here with my eyes covered, but it feels good. I hear her sit in the chair next to mine, then filling our cups with tea. She asks if I like milk or sugar, offering honey from the hives down by the lake. Her voice is soothing and for the first time since I entered that club with Elon the night before, I start to feel better.

"How is your training going?" Margaret asks.

"It's... challenging," I admit, feeling the heat of tears building in my eyes again. Any fresh tears can be waved off as water from the cucumbers. "I'm definitely being tested."

"I'm sure you are."

I exhale and sit up, peeling off the cucumber. "May I speak freely?" I ask. "Confidentially?"

She nods. "Of course."

"I saw Rex last night."

Her eyebrow rises. "How did that go?"

"It was..." I have no idea how to even begin to describe what happened between us. He'd violated me. Used me. Made it very clear that he didn't want me. "It was complicated."

"Most powerful men are." She takes a sip of tea. "Did you try to make progress with him?"

"I tried. He was... aggressive. I don't think I was very effective."

"He's angry."

I sigh. "All the time. And distant. Even if I give him what he wants, he makes it very clear that he dislikes me and everything about me. Dislike is probably not a strong enough word. I'm doing my training —everything that's asked of me—but none of it seems to work."

"Anex would never set you on a journey without anticipating success. You know, it's my understanding that it was after Rex's mother died that he became so withdrawn and discontent. Over the years he rebelled against his father, and Anex gave him a little too much leeway in an attempt to soothe his pain."

I blink, stunned that Margaret would criticize Anex at all. "I doubt Anex could have managed it any differently. He was in pain, himself."

"True," Margaret says, tightening her finger around the handle of her cup, "but parenting children isn't the same thing as leading a flock." Her mouth forms a line. "If I may offer some advice—"

"Please," I reply, a bit too eagerly.

"Anex may think he knows what his son wants, but they've never seen eye to eye. I would focus on getting Rex to see you as a person— a mate—not just an obstacle. Rex is rebellious. Oppositional. He actively seeks the secular world and its women." She lifts her teacup to her mouth and says, "Giving him what he wants may not be the way to his spiritual truth."

"What does that mean?"

"Maybe you need to be a little less compliant. Maybe the way to win him over is by not being what his father wants, but by truly being what he wants."

"The clothes, the makeup and hair... I'm doing all that."

"It's not just the outside, Imogene. It's the attitude." She sets her cup on the table and picks up a cookie, nibbling on the edge. "Believe it or not, at first Anex and I didn't exactly get along."

"You didn't?"

"Nope. He totally rubbed me the wrong way. I thought he was pretentious and kind of full of it." My eyes widen in shock and she just laughs again. "I didn't understand him and, honestly, he didn't understand me. So, we started meeting up, taking these long walks and discussing—well, arguing—almost everything. Over time, we came to realize how charged the energy between us was. This difference fueled our relationship."

"That's amazing."

She reaches out and takes my hand. "I don't think the training you're being given is about just being able to meet Rex's secular desires. I think that there's more to it—something that will require you to dig deep and find your true self. Men like Anex and his son do not want the easy route."

I nod, finally understanding a little more. Going to Rex and giving in, caving to his demands and begging him to accept me. God. It was probably the exact thing he hates. Despite my clothing and hair, that was the behavior of a woman from Serendee. Not from the outside. No wonder he forced me into such humiliating submission. It was a test, and I failed.

"They seek strong women," Margaret continues. "They need that energy to balance them. They must be challenged to become better men, to be powerful leaders."

"I understand."

"You do?" she asks, head tilted in curiosity.

"Yes, I really think I do." She picks up the bowl of cucumbers and offers it to me, but I wave her off. "I'm good," I tell her.

If Rex wants a challenge, a woman that can meet his needs on a whole other level, I can be that person. I will be that person. I just need to figure out when and how.

As if she can see in my mind, Margaret says, "Anex's birthday celebration is next weekend. Rex should be there."

The birthday celebration. I'd forgotten. It's a full weekend of camping out in the back pasture. They put up tents and the adults spend the night. There are games and bonfires. Dancing and cake. Anex's birthday weekends are legendary, and it'll be my first year. "You think he'll come?"

"I know he will. Anex will demand it and since he's your Ordered, he will be required to stay in the tent with you." She grins. "All weekend."

"That gives me a week to prepare," I say, my mind already spinning with ideas. "I'm definitely going to be ready."

25

———————

Imogene

His fingers are somehow both delicate and strong. Firm but gentle. I watch, enthralled as he touches himself and then commands me to touch myself. I stare at him, confused, as warmth rushes across my skin.

"I can't do that."

"You can," Silas says propped up on his elbow and gazing down at me, his erect member hard between us, "because it is very important for you to understand what makes you feel good."

I'm lying next to him in his bed. I'd come to him for a lesson—something specific. Rex obviously doesn't respect a woman that simply obeys. That he made perfectly clear. He wants a woman of her own mind. I want to be that woman during the camping trip next weekend. I'd told Silas what happened at the bar. Every humiliating detail. He didn't seem surprised. Maybe he wasn't. Maybe Rex already told him or Elon.

God.

Silas just nodded his head and asked me to take off my dress, then instructed me to get on the bed. He'd then removed his own clothing, down to his shorts. I can't help but stare at his flesh—soft looking skin covering hard muscle. Silas' lean but fit body is a marvel of genetics. He's pretty, but handsome. Delicate but strong. It's his confidence that intrigues me the most.

"Touch yourself, Imogene," he repeats.

"Seeking pleasure is indulgent," I remind him—or maybe myself. "I'm happy to do whatever you need to feel good, but I can't do that to myself."

"What if watching you pleasure yourself makes me happy? What if you're being indulgent by not giving me what I need?"

These are common questions used to process The Way. What is the real meaning behind your thoughts and actions? Why are you hesitant to do something? Why do you resist?

"Do you know how often I touch myself?" he asks, running his hand down his shaft. It bobs lazily in response. "Daily."

"Daily?" I repeat, eyebrows shot up my forehead. "Once a day?"

"Several times," he says with a shrug. "Men's bodies want to spread its seed. We're always seeking a partner to thrust into, but that isn't always possible. We must find release and we do that by taking care of it on our own." He rolls his balls between his fingertips and swallows thickly. "That experience is how I know what makes me feel good and how it can make others feel. You need to do the same. Knowing yourself—your true self—will allow you to be a better mate to a man like Rex. A man that wants a partner, an equal."

It all sounds logical, and as Silas continues to fondle his cock, bringing himself closer and closer to release, I can see what he means. Silas knows what feels good. And he can show me. Seeing the pleasure on his beautiful face, watching the ecstasy undulate the ladder of muscles on his stomach—it's thrilling. It sparks the fire in my belly and ignites the heat between my legs. Just watching him makes me want him and I consider that if I can make Rex feel about me, the way I feel about Silas right now... well, that would make this practice worthwhile.

"Touch yourself," Silas commands. I place my hand on my belly and he shakes his head. "Start with your tits.

I reach for my breast, covered in the soft cotton of my tank, and run my palm over my nipple. Silas watches me, licking his lips, and continuing his own ministrations. Watching him has already pushed me closer to the edge. I'm already hot, horny, and touching my breasts only fans the flame.

"Now your pussy."

I swallow but obey, my other hand inching down my belly and between my legs, pushing aside my panties. I feel the cool air hit my core. It feels wrong to do these things to myself—the opposite of the self-control we'd strived for since entering the girl's domum. That's when we started learning that our bodies aren't our own. Aren't for our own indulgence. We were to save them for the Ordering and our mates.

That deep-seated notion is hard to shake, but Silas bends over and kisses me on the mouth. His tongue slips between my lips and my fingers explore, moving at the same slow pace as his kiss. I find the slow rhythm more appealing, and I lazily massage the bundle of nerves he'd helped me find. The motion shoots sparks of fire up my body. I groan into his mouth and his jaw slacks, breath panting in return.

"Take your time," he tells me. "Figure out how you like it. Hard. Soft. Gentle. Wet..." he continues, suggesting things I'd never thought about. I don't need any of it. Just his words and his closeness, the heat of his body and the sweet taste of his tongue, spurn the coil in my lower belly to twist tighter and tighter. My brain fogs and my resistance fades, leaving my body to take over.

"That's it," he says. "How does that feel?"

"Good," I blurt, then I open my eyes. I start to remove my hand. "This is wrong. I should save this—"

His fingers circle my wrist. "Don't you dare stop, Imogene. God gave you this body, these nerves and feelings. It's a dishonor not to learn the purpose of it." He forces my hand to move again, stroking against the heated, wet nerves. With his eyes holding mine, he asks again. "Tell me, how does that feel?"

"Amazing." I swallow back a sigh. "Heavenly."

"Then keep going." He releases me, watching to make sure I'm still pleasuring myself. He goes back to his own needs, resuming the lazy strokes up and down his shaft. My jaw slacks, and my breathing turns embarrassingly erratic. I don't stop, even though I still feel awkward and unsure. "That's right. God, you're beautiful."

My body reacts to his words and the urge for more propels me forward.

Silas' eyebrow arches and he says, "Climb on me. Ride me."

"I c-can't," I start, but he's pulled me onto his lap. His hard, slippery warmth glides against mine. "I can't let you enter me."

"I won't," he says, holding onto my hips. The position feels powerful—controlled. My tits rise and fall, and he captures a nipple between his teeth, biting down gently. I cry out from the feel of him—everywhere. Below, above, wet, sharp. He thrusts against me, friction building and it's not long before a spasm ripples through me. It's not fast or intense, it's slow and like riding a cresting wave. It feels good and warm, spreading through my limbs until I'm a puddle of goo.

Silas holds me upright, hips pounding against me, his eyes holding mine, until he jerks to a stop, a groan rumbling deep in his chest. He falls back, and the room filled with the two of us trying to catch our breath.

"How did that feel?" he asks, easing me to lie against his chest. "Pushing through your limits."

"Scary," I say. "But fulfilling. Powerful."

He nods and pulls my hand to his mouth, kissing the flat skin on the back. "You're very sexy, Imogene. And very powerful. Never underestimate that."

My cheeks are already flushed from the orgasm, but I feel them heat from the compliment. "How did you get so comfortable with this? Did it always come easily to you?"

"Not at first," he admits, rolling me off and settling us so that we're facing one another. "I had to work through some of my own hangups. Granted, I was sixteen when I started my training and a horny teenager, anyway. It wasn't a huge hardship."

"You were trained at sixteen?"

"I came into my gifts early. Anex saw my potential and encouraged me to start exploring them."

"Anex trained you?" This question makes me uneasy, but for some reason I need to know.

"No. Not directly." His lips form a line. "There are others in the inner circle that have gifts like I do. Together we explored these skills and learned how to use them to further the glory of The Way."

"What exactly is that gift? Sex?"

He grins, and it lights up his face. "Well, that's part of it, but only part. There are certain people that struggle to accept all aspects of The Way. They aren't like me and you. They didn't grow up here. They weren't raised within the walls of Serendee understanding the joy of this experience. They're caught up in the secular world, but Anex sees something in them—he can tell they want more. I, along with a few others, have the ability to reach them on that secular level. A physical level."

I nod, pretending I understand, but I'm not sure I do. Not completely. "So you connect with them and then..."

"And then once they have let down their guard and relax, they are ready to take the next steps toward following Anex and the visions of Serendee."

"So you're like a conduit of The Way." I've heard of these people. They're very special. And to learn there is one next to me now, teaching me his ways. I'm honored.

He smiles again. "A link between the outside and the inside."

"I bet you're good at your job."

"Oh, I'm very good." He runs his finger down the column of my neck. "Anex rewards me handsomely for my service." He kisses my shoulder, and it sends a cascade of butterflies down to my lower belly. "When he asked me to work with you, it was the highest honor."

It's hard to think clearly while Silas is touching me—or just near me in general. He's handsome, confident, charming. Sexy. He's like no other man I've ever met before. I can see why Anex would find him useful in easing the concerns of new members. Just talking to him has eased my worries.

"Thank you for the lesson," I tell him.

"I want you to continue practicing—really explore your desires."

"I will."

He kisses my forehead. "Rex is a lucky man. I know in my heart you'll please him and bring him back on the right path."

"He is lucky to have you as a devoted friend."

"He's lucky to have all of us," he says, allowing me a moment to curl into his side, "and one day he's going to realize it."

26

─────────

I mogene

I WAKE on the second note, the deep strains of classical music filling the air. Clair de Lune. It's the same song every time, although no one knows when it will come; morning, noon, or night. I grapple for the bedside clock and look. 2 AM.

I get up quickly, not taking the time to change or brush my hair. When the music plays, we are to go immediately to the community center. No questions asked. No dilly dallying. Once Clarissa had a cake baking in the oven. She shut it off and ruined the cake. It's a testament of faith, of obedience. When Anex calls, we come.

Elon, Silas, and Levi are in the living room when I walk out. Even the inner circle is required to attend. Well, except maybe one.

"He's not here," Elon says, answering my question before I ask it. He shoves his arms into his jacket and holds the door for everyone.

"Will he be?" I ask, already worried that walking into the meeting without my Ordered will look strange. People will notice. I know I would. We haven't been seen at a public event yet and gossip will start.

"Your guess is as good as ours, Little Lamb." The look exchanged between the men is an indicator they aren't happy about it either.

The meeting house is down the hill—and a cool breeze kicks up as we walk towards it with other residents of the Main House. I shiver in the thin nightgown. I see the healer that examined me before the ceremony, and a few of the women that clean the apartment. A drumbeat greets us as we enter. Anex thinks the sound of the drum mimics the heartbeat of the Earth and begins and ends each lecture with rousing music.

When I walk into the big room at the community center, I see Margaret on the platform, curled up by Anex's side. His other spiritual mates are there as well. Our leader is at center stage, sitting in a cushioned chair. Members of the community spill in, settling on the floor. I follow Elon, ignoring the eyes watching me, wondering about my mate. Maria catches my eye and waves. She sits with her Ordered, and they lean their shoulders together in support.

I wave back, but divert my eyes quickly, not wanting her to see the worry and grief I have over the failure to please Rex. Instead, I lock eyes with Anex. His gaze is critical, assessing, but jumps from my face to the space next to me. I sense him immediately, his figure eclipsing everyone and everything else in the room. Before I can look up, his fingers interlock with mine and he tugs me to a corner of the room where a second chair has been set up. The guys take their positions among the Chosen. Levi with the other Guides. Silas with the beautiful men and women, Anex surrounds himself with and Elon, just to the back of Rex's chair. Always on guard. Rex sits and just as I am about to take a cue from Margaret and sit on the floor, he pulls me onto his lap. I start to protest, but he holds me still. That's when I realize he managed to get the back of my nightgown pulled up and the bare backs of my thighs are against his.

"Play nice," he whispers in my ear. I'm frozen, unsure of how to act or even how to 'play nice' with this man I barely know—the man, that the last time I saw him had me down on my knees forcing me to pleasure him while he mocked me. "Unlike my father, I won't require my mate to sit on the floor."

"No, you'll just push them to their knees and force them to service you," I grind out.

His eyebrow raises, and a small, smug smile quirks at his lips. If he wants to say something back but his father's voice booms through the room, cutting across the drumbeat and forcing it to stop.

"Thank you for coming so quickly and efficiently," Anex says. "It's never my goal to wake you from your well-deserved sleep, but you know how I am when The Way speaks to me." He smiles, and the crowd smiles in return. "I have to share it with all of you because it's never about me. It's always about you."

"Here we go," Rex mutters, "get ready for a long one."

As always, his words catch me off guard. So full of contempt. Despite that, he settles in like the rest of us, adjusting his position so we sink closer together in the chair. I stiffen, not just because of the proximity, but because the focus of the crowd isn't just on Anex tonight. It's on me and Rex.

"You need to relax," he says in my ear.

"It's hard with everyone watching," I reply, keeping my eyes on his father. "And with your hand on my thigh."

"Does that distract you?" His fingers splay over the top of my leg. "Isn't this what you wanted? To be my mate?" His voice is low. I assume no one can hear him other than me. But, when I spare a glance at Elon, I gather from the tight set of his jaw that he can hear us as well. "That title comes with scrutiny."

With the hand above the folds of my dress, he takes my hand and rests them both on his lap, inches from his crotch. He rubs his thumb up and down the side of my hand. It's firm but soothing. I feel his breath on my neck and the strength of his body pressed against mine.

Heat boils under my skin.

"What are you doing?" I ask, unable to focus on Anex's lesson. I shift uncomfortably and am met with the hard press of his erection against my backside.

"Whatever I want, Little Lamb." He glances up at Elon. "Give me your coat."

With his dark eyes darting between us, Elon shrugs out of the jacket. It's heavy and black and I'm accosted by his scent when Rex drapes it over my lap.

"That's better."

Underneath the coat, his fingers move, dipping between my thighs. Warmth spreads at my core. It's not unfamiliar now. Silas has taught me how to understand my body, but the intensity is still surprising.

"Spread your legs for me."

"I should listen," I say weakly, trying to regain control, but he brushes his knuckles against the inside of my knee and they part like the Red Sea.

"Why?" he asks, brushing the pads of his fingers against the nub of nerves. My clit, Silas told me. The most sensitive place outside a woman's body. "You know why my father does these late-night lectures?"

"Because he's been given inspiration by The Way and he's excited to share it with us."

He chuckles softly in my ear and circles around my clit, sometimes too far away, sometimes dangerously close. I can't decide which I want more. "He does it to keep everyone off balance. Exhausted and tired. Sleep-deprivation keeps everyone in line."

"That's—" I start, but his finger pushes under my undergarments, touching my clit dead-on. I shudder and curl against him, biting down on the moan of pleasure. "Stop."

"I thought you liked being manipulated by men in power."

His tone is mocking and mean, the one I'm most familiar with. I lamely attempt to separate myself from him. "You're wet. You like this." He presses his fingers against my core and pushes past the entrance. "Tight, too," he says. "No man has entered you before, have they?"

"Of course not. I am yours and yours alone." My eyes flick to Elon as I say it, knowing I am skirting a line of truth.

He curls his finger inside, applying the most wonderful pressure. I want to plead for him to stop and beg him to keep going. At some point I shut out Anex and all I feel is Rex. I feel his hitched breathing against my ear, his heartbeat thrumming against my back, and his invasion inside. I feel him everywhere.

Across the stage, Anex pauses on stage and looks to the upper windows where the faint streaks of the sunrise brighten the sky. "Let's greet the new day with the song of The Way," he says, urging his musicians to start playing. Everyone around us rises, swaying to the beat, clapping and humming with song. But not us. Rex's hands hold me in place and under the cover of celebration he applies pressure against both my clit and something deep inside, causing my body to spasm with the growing drumbeat. It's not just an orgasm, it's so much more. Earth shatteringly more and I cry out, my voice just another in the cacophony praising his father.

I heave against him, hips rising and falling with the rush of euphoria. I tilt my chin upward and touch the side of his face. "That... that was incredible."

He scrapes his teeth against my ear and whispers, "Every time you think that man is a god, Little Lamb," he holds me against his chest and slowly removes his finger from inside, "you remember that I'm the one that made you feel like that."

He sits me up right and sets on wobbly legs, pawns me off on Elon, who catches me by the arms. Rex steps off the platform and vanishes into the crowd.

"Where is he going?" I ask, leaning into Elon's side.

He shakes his head, but his eyes dart over to Anex. I see that he's watching us, a twisted, knowing smile on his lips. Something just transpired—something deep and sensual and complicated and vindictive. Something between a father and son, and I'm right in the middle of it.

27

———————

S ilas

I'M WALKING down the road toward the market when I see a woman ahead. Her narrow shoulders taper down to a small waist, partially obscured by a baggy dress. Nevertheless, I recognize the swing of her hips and the pale blonde hair braided down her back. I jog to catch up, tugging her braid when I reach her.

"Hey!" she shouts, spinning in a circle. She grins when she sees me. "What are you doing out here?"

"Headed to the market. What about you?"

"Same." She lifts the empty basket in her hands. "I thought I'd find something for dinner tonight."

One of the perks of growing up in Serendee is the fresh food and natural products. All of the oils and lotions I use in my massages are locally made. "I thought you had to work today," I say. "Playing hooky?"

"Anex gave us the afternoon off." I raise an eyebrow. Afternoons off are not something that happens here—at least not spontaneously. She laughs. "I know, right? He had some kind of official meeting and didn't want anyone around."

"Well, that works out for my benefit. Now we can go together."

She hesitates. "Are you sure that's a good idea? For us to be alone?"

As much time as I spend with women up at the Main House, as a single, unordered man, walking with a female alone in the middle of Serendee is against the norm. "Do you think anyone would question me?" I ask, flexing a little. People are aware of my position in the inner circle.

"I'm less worried about you and a little more concerned with my reputation," she says. "You may be Rex's best friend, but I'm not sure that clears the way for us to be so familiar."

"I assure you, Little Lamb," I say quietly, as we pass a woman walking by with a small child, "they have no idea how familiar we've been at all."

The comment makes her cheeks flush pink, and it makes her even more beautiful. How Rex can turn this girl away is a mystery. To have her in my bed every night, waiting for me with those soft lips and her hungry mouth. Well, that is the kind of dream it's best not to have.

"You're bad," she mutters, entering the open-air market. "Terribly bad."

"You really have no idea," I reply, splitting apart. She's right. Walking around together in here would turn heads and elicit questions, less about me and more about her. The last thing I want to do is tarnish her reputation. I locate the woman that sells the oils. I purchase two and then add a bottle of lotion and lavender soap from another merchant. Imogene takes her time, looking through the organic fruit and vegetables. She's confident here, bartering with the other women or smelling and testing the skin of fruit. It's a different side of her from the woman I know at home. Less timid. More assured. She's trained for the life of a mate for years—I've only been training her to please a man in bed for just a few days.

While she pays, I linger by the fresh flowers, drawn to a bunch of daisies. Imogene would probably love these on the dining room table.

"Silas!"

I turn to the voice and see Kayla. I've had two more sessions with her since the first. Anex is pleased with her progress. I plaster on a warm smile and say, "I see you found our little market."

"It is adorable," she says, holding up a basket of items she's purchased. "My friends back home would die for this type of organic product."

"Well, your friend's back home aren't special like you." Unless they are. Wealthy. Impressionable. Anex will find out soon enough if it's worth pursuing. I spot Imogene walking our way over her shoulder and grab the bunch of flowers, paying for them quickly. "It was nice seeing you. I should let you get back to your shopping."

She digs into her basket and holds up a bottle of honeysuckle wine. She leans in and says, "I thought maybe you and I could crack this open tonight and spend a little more time together."

Imogene, who is now admiring the same daisies as the ones I just bought, flicks her eyes between us. Now I'm the one that has to play the part of living in two worlds. My job is to be available to the recruits as they need me, but none of the people around me have any idea. But a woman like Kayla is special. Even with Anex's directives for training Imogene, Kayla comes first.

"How about this?" I say, voice low. "I need to do a few more things, but you head back up to the house, slip into something comfortable, and I'll meet you in your room after dinner?"

"That sounds wonderful." Her hand lowers to my butt and squeezes. I step away, carrying my things and heading back to the road. A moment later, Imogene appears.

"I can explain—"

"There's no need," she says, walking past me. "I'm well aware that you and the others live by your own rules."

"It's not that." I feel the need to clear things up. "It's not something I want to do."

She looks back at the market—back at Kayla, who is standing by a table of strawberries. There's no doubt she's a beautiful woman; poised and cultured. She sticks out among the other women in the community—yet I know all she wants is to belong. She thinks she's found Utopia.

Imogene laughs and continues down the road. "You don't want to spend time with a woman like that? Drinking wine and... well, doing what I know you're very good at."

"That's not fair. It's my job."

She pauses. "I'm not judging you, Silas. And I don't expect exclusivity in this arrangement. We've been given a directive by Anex and it's our duty to fulfill it."

She hitches her basket in the crook of her elbow and starts back up the hill toward the Main House. Everything she said is true. I'm doing what Anex asked me to, the same way she is. The problem is that I'd rather spend the evening training her than Kayla.

Or, I realize, the further she gets away, I want to spend my time with Imogene over anyone at all.

28

———————

I mogene

"YOU KNOW why my father does these late-night lectures..."

The memory of Rex's voice draws me out of sleep.

"He does it to keep everyone off balance. Exhausted and tired. Sleep-deprivation keeps everyone in line."

I toss and turn, pushing the questions out of my mind. Rex is a liar. A troublemaker. He said it himself; he manipulates.

Then why does what he said make my stomach hurt? My chest pound with anxiousness? I know it's just my lack of faith talking. My Indulgence. My belief that I need to control everything. The Way will guide me. Anex is in control. I am nothing but a speck in the bigger plan. I repeat this to myself, over and over, hoping it quells my nerves, but it doesn't.

Only one thing will.

I sit up, feeling the cold sweat along my back, and open the drawer of my bedside table. I feel around in the dark for my journal and pull it out. I sit with it on my lap for a long time, feeling the heaviness of the leather and the weight of what's inside. Taking a stunted breath, I flip it open and search for the sharp metal tool shoved in the spine.

The end pierces my fingertip, giving me a sharp stab of pain. A small rush of release flows through me. Correction. That is what I need. To be corrected.

I stare at the tool and already know it's not enough.

Leaving the tool and journal on the bed, I step into the hallway, stopping at a closed door. I rest my hand on the doorknob. Do I knock? What if he doesn't hear? What if Elon or Silas do? Understanding that this is between me and Levi, my Guide, is what pushes me to twist the knob and enter his darkened room. The door shuts behind me with a soft click and I stand over the bed, shaking him by the arm.

He rouses slowly, rubbing his eyes. "Imogene? Is that you?"

"Yes," I say, my eyes adjusting to the dark. He shifts to a sitting position, and the faint light from under the door reveals he is shirtless. His upper body is exposed, down to the pooled sheet at his waist. He's lean with tight rows of muscles. A faint hair scatters over his chest.

"You should be in bed."

"I know." I wring my hands. "But I woke up, and I couldn't go back to sleep. My mind kept racing. All the things I've been doing, the extra calories, the urge to defy with questions and judgments... the Lapses." I still. "I was going to seek release."

"You were going to Correct yourself."

"I wanted to, but I stopped myself. I came to you for Guidance." As I talk, he sits up and turns on the light, giving me a better view of his body. Butterflies churn in my stomach. Not the kind of anxiety I was feeling in bed. Something different. I drag my eyes away from his flesh and blurt, "I'm sorry. This is inappropriate."

"No," he says, swinging his legs over the edge of the bed. "I'm your Guide, and you need my help. You did the right thing by coming to me."

I exhale in relief. "I'm ready."

He looks around the sparse room. Along with the bed, there is a dresser with a mirror and a small desk. He nods at the dresser. "I think that will work."

I face the dresser, getting a full view of myself in the mirror. I look a wreck. My braided hair is disheveled. Dark smudges mar the skin under my anxious, red eyes. I look tired. Exhausted. Levi is probably horrified to see me in such a state.

"Bend over," he says, placing a hand on my back.

I do as he says, flattening my palms on the wooden surface. My body tenses and tingles, knowing what is going to come. I want it. I need it. A strange flicker warms my lower belly. In the mirror, I watch as Levi opens a drawer and pulls out a white T-shirt. "You're going to have to be quiet, so the others don't hear." I nod in understanding. He holds up the shirt. "Bite down on this."

He pushes the cotton in my mouth, and I face the mirror, watching as he lifts up the back of my nightdress, pushing it to my waist. He stares at me for a long moment, so long that I think he's about to change his mind, but then he moves, hooking his fingers into my underwear and dropping them to the floor. I feel a tap on my inner knee, and he says, "Brace yourself."

Anticipation bubbles in my chest: fear combined with want. I want to rid myself of these Lapses. Of these Indulgences. I want to feel the pain of Correction. Levi and I make eye contact in the mirror, his jaw tight and determined. I'm looking into the grass-green of his eyes when his hand comes down hard on my backside, lurching me forward. The cry is trapped behind cotton.

He spanks me again, palm flat and stinging. The pain and heat shooting across my skin, building in my core. I know I should look at myself in the mirror—reconcile my Lapses—but I can't look away from him. Not away from the conviction on his face, and the fire burning in his eyes.

"It is not your place to question," he says quietly, between spankings. "It is your role to follow. To uplift. To reflect."

His hand comes down harder, and I fall on the dresser, landing on my elbows. I bite down on the cloth and shift to rise, but his hand comes down flat on my lower back, holding me in place. "It's my job to Correct the wildness out of you." Smack! "The Regression." Smack! "The doubt and distraction." Smack! The spankings come faster now and the pain spreads across my nerves. I feel it in the sharp points of my nipples, in the slick heat between my legs.

He reaches around and yanks the shirt out of my mouth.

"Confess, Imogene. Everything."

"I eat too much. Fatty foods. Even sugar. I let Rex get into my head, spreading doubt about this father." Levi grunts behind me and I catch his eye. He hasn't touched me again, but I sense him moving —hear him. The rustle of fabric, the jerk of his arm. "I let Silas touch me. I daydream of Elon's harsh hands, groping, pinching, and grabbing." I swallow, seeing Levi's jaw tighten, his nose wrinkle. "I fear that I Lapse so that I can come see you. To do this. Seeking this pain because no matter how bad it makes me feel, there's another side that makes me feel good. So good." The confession comes out in a rush and Levi's hand grabs my hip. His fingers dig into me, and I feel the brush of something wet hit my backside as his hand pumps up and down. I know the look on his face, the motion. Silas has done it in front of me. He's pleasuring himself to my pain.

"Spank me," I beg, catching his eye once more.

He releases my hip, and his hand comes down painfully hard, the slap of our skin against one another loud and raw. The ache between my legs throbs almost as much as the flesh of my backside.

"Again," I plead. "Please."

He does it again, and without the shirt in my mouth; I cry out.

"You're filthy. Dirty. Dangerous." His jaw slacks and his movements pick up, hand jacking up and down. "You're bad, Imogene. You're a bad girl." His assault is cut off by a deep groan rumbling in his throat, and he lurches forward, falling against me. I feel his breath on my neck as hot, sticky, fluid spills on my lower back, branding me with his come.

I'm frozen like this as he breathes heavily against me, his chest rising and falling. He reaches around me for the shirt and a moment later I feel him wiping the come from my back. Levi tosses the shirt toward the closet and lifts me up. My dress falls to my ankles. My backside burns.

"Do you feel better?" he asks, face stoic.

"Yes. Thank you for the Correction."

His head tilts, eyes narrowed, and assessing. "You're lying."

"I-I'm not."

He reaches for me, gathering the dress in his hand, exposing me. "You may have gotten what you came here for, but you don't feel better." His hand dips between my legs, brushing against my clit. "You're wet. Horny. You get off on feeling the pain."

I swallow. "And you get off on giving it."

He laughs. I'm not sure I've ever seen him laugh, although it's not filled with joy but derision. His next move is as surprising. He lifts me by my hips and places me on the dresser. He pushes aside my dress and yanks me to the edge. I wince at the pain.

"What are you—"

He drops to his knees and spreads my thighs wide, swiping his tongue along my folds. He flattens it at the apex, lathing my clit with hot, warm heat. Electricity runs up my spine.

"Oh my—Levi!"

Holding my legs apart, he kisses me down there once again, mixing intense pleasure with the slightest hint of pain. What he's doing lands somewhere in the middle—the good middle—the one I came to him for tonight, even if I didn't know this is where it would end.

The tension I woke up with melts away with each and every swipe of his tongue, every flick and suck. He's gentle in a way that's unexpected, the brutality of his Corrections not in this space. I sink my fingers into his thick, copper hair, and press my back against the cool mirror.

That diligence, the one that makes him a good teacher, a good student, keeps him focused and soon hard bursts of air push from my lungs, while my hips rise to meet his mouth. That tightly wound coil that started winding when I walked in his room, spins and spins and spins, until it snaps, unfurling in waves of spine melting pleasure. It feels so good, so very, very good, better than the spanking, better than the highest high. I reach the peak and float back down, loosening my grip in his hair. I sink against the mirror, breathing hard, and feeling warm all over.

"Where did you learn to do that?" I ask once I can speak again. It's unspoken, but unlike the others, I've had the distinct feeling Levi is not overly experienced with women.

He stands and wipes his mouth with the back of his hand. "I'm a student," he says quietly, "of everything. I make it my job to learn as much about everything as I can."

I ease myself off the dresser and wince. The pain in my backside throbs.

I want to say something, anything, but the cool, distant look that is so often on his face is back. He turns his back to me and says, "Good night, Imogene. I expect you to do better from now on."

I nod and exit his room, that same shame bubbling under the surface as I quietly go back to my own. I lie on the bed, flat on my stomach, too tired to focus on the heat radiating off my tender skin. The tension I'd been carrying has dissipated, leaving me relaxed, if not sore. I drift off quickly, easily, only waking when the light shines through my window the next morning. When I roll over, grunting at the pain, something soft and malleable falls off my still sore backside. I pick it up and blink at the object.

An ice pack.

29

E^{lon}

Th e f i r st pe r s on I see when I enter The Center is Imogene, standing behind her desk.

"Have you seen Rex?" I ask her.

"The last place he'd be is here," she says, collating sheets of paper lined up on the desk into a single packet, "he spends most of his time avoiding me."

I tap on her calendar. "Any idea then? Isn't it your job to keep up with the comings and goings of the community?"

She gathers the stack of packets and circles her desk. "No. He does what he wants, you know that. Maybe he's holed up with some girl right now." She pushes past me, arm grazing mine. "Maybe some other woman is taking care of his needs."

"We have an appointment, and we were supposed to meet at the Main House, but he never showed," I say, following her down the hall. My eyes travel the lines of her thin shoulders down to the narrowing of her hips. That's when I frown. Something is wrong with her gait. She's walking tenderly, as if she's injured.

I reach out and flatten a hand over her ass. She yelps, her whole body shudders, and comes to a stop.

"I don't think that was about me touching you, Little Lamb. What's wrong?"

"Nothing." She swallows. "You just surprised me."

I reach for the nearest doorknob, open it and drag her inside. It's the supply closet, musty and smelling of chemicals. I shut the door and stand in front of it, blocking her escape.

"Show me."

"There's nothing to show, Elon." She clutches the packets to her chest. "Please let me go so I can put these in the lesson room."

"Not until I see what has you walking like a hobbled old lady."

She eyes me. "You're not going to let this go, are you?"

"Nope."

She sighs and shoves the stack of papers at me. I grab them, and she slowly pulls up the hem of her dress until it's bundled around her waist. I look down at her pale legs and see nothing wrong, but her fingers hook into those godforsaken utilitarian panties, and she pulls them down.

Using my finger, I make a swirling motion, gesturing for her to turn. I need to see exactly what is causing her so much pain. Even in the dim light, when her back is to me, I can see the red, blistering flesh on her ass. "Holy shit," I say, resting the papers on a shelf. I crouch down and stare at the imprint of a hand. Gently, I run my fingers over the skin. She flinches, cheeks squeezing. "Was it Rex?"

"It's none of your business."

"Little Lamb, don't make me drag you door to door throughout Serendee and force the person that did this to you to step forward, because I will."

"They are corrections. Inflicted by my Guide."

I blink at the hand imprint. "Levi did this?"

"Yes."

"He marked you." I run the back of my hand over the heated welts. "He went too far. It's unacceptable."

"No. I asked him to do it," she confesses, looking over her shoulder. "He's helping me deal with my Lapses. He isn't doing anything to me that I don't deserve."

I narrow my eyes at her. "Nothing you are doing deserves this sort of Correction. You are obedient and devoted. I've seen it with my own eyes."

"I struggle with defiance. I have questions and judgements."

"You are human." I lift the undergarments from around her ankle and slowly drag them back up, being careful as I cover her swollen cheeks. Her dress falls and I stand, turning her around to face me.

"I'm bad," she whispers.

I touch her chin. "Because you have a brain? A mind of your own? Remember, this is who Rex wants."

"No," she says, turning her face away, "because I like it when he hurts me. I am not only getting Correction, I'm getting pleasure."

My eyebrow raises. I have a feeling she's not the only one getting off from these sessions.

"It's not wrong to want to feel something when you're having sex," I tell her, "even if it's rough and hard. But you don't need to punish yourself for it. Do you think Rex punishes himself? Silas? Or even me?"

"You're different."

I run my fingers down the side of her face. "You're one of us. Different rules. Different desires."

"But what about Levi?"

"Levi is fucked up. He buys into all of Anex's bullshit, and like you, he's twisting things up."

Her expression clouds with confusion and it strikes me how much mental endurance it must take to be in her position. She's got all four of us, plus Anex and herself, coming at her from all angles.

I open the door. "Come with me."

She grabs the packets off the shelf. "I have to work. A class is coming in and—"

"And someone else can deal with it. I'm overruling it. You're sick and you're coming with me."

She opens her mouth to argue, but I give her a stern look. One she knows means to shut up and follow directions. "Let me drop these off and get my things."

"I'll meet you out front."

I watch her walk down the hall, now fully aware of why her gait is so stilted. It's not my place to interfere with Levi's Guidance. That's his role in the community, but I can make sure she's taken care of. I wait for her outside and pull out my phone, sending a message to the one person that will know how to treat this kind of wound, and when she meets me outside, her blonde hair shining in the sun, I take her there.

30

I mogene

It was bad enough having Elon see the marks from Levi's spankings, but this was worse.

"Ouch," Silas says. "These do look painful."

Elon took me to the guest cottage behind the pool, apparently where Silas has a studio for work. Foolishly, I stood outside while the two spoke, no doubt discussing the wounds on my backside. I can't even describe the feeling I had when Elon left, handing me over like a child that needs supervision. Silas instructed me to remove my clothes and lie on a table in his studio, covered only with a sheet. I've never quite understood what he does for Serendee, other than working with recruits, and now that I'm in the small room filled with candles and incense, doesn't clear things up much.

"Are you a healer?" I'm naked and flat on my stomach on the table. It's not sterile like the healer's offices, but I understand now that things are different for The Chosen.

"Not exactly," he says, "although it's not totally wrong. I help people relax and get to know their bodies, using massage and other techniques." He walks over to a shelf and removes a small jar. "You know, like I've helped you understand your body better."

I bite back a laugh. "Then maybe you can let me know why I want Levi to Correct me like this. Elon says I shouldn't."

I hear the scrape of the jar lid as Silas unscrews it and a moment later, a cooling sensation spreads across my buttocks. "Oh," I exhale. "That feels good."

"I thought it would."

His fingers knead and glide over my skin, working away from the painful area to my lower back. The sensation is firm but gentle, and I sink into the table. "Do you know why?" I ask, serious now. "Why do I like it?"

"It's not wrong to want things a little rough," he says, continuing up my back. "People like things differently. You're a strong woman, Imogene, I'm not surprised you can handle more than most." He moves to my shoulders, working against my muscles. His moves aren't sexual but sensual. With every passing second, I'm putty in his very skilled hands. "You're one of the Chosen now. Correction is relative. You have permission to indulge more than you used to. You're still behaving like a normal member of the community."

"I don't understand."

His fingers prod at my neck, teasing out the knots. He leans close to my ear and says, "If you want to enjoy rough sex, go for it, but it doesn't have to be a punishment. Unless, of course, you want it that way."

What I want doesn't matter in the grand scheme of things. It's not part of the principals of The Way, and Rex certainly doesn't care. Everything in my mind is muddled. I feel less in control than I did when I was in the domum. Did I want Rex to shove me to my knees? Or Elon to touch me harshly. Did I go to Levi in the middle of the night to get what I wanted, or to do what was right?

"It's going to take time," Silas says, "but until then, we need to make sure you're healthy. Ultimately, our goal is to make you Rex's mate—one that can handle anything thrown at her."

"If that's the goal, then I guess you're training me correctly."

He squats down so that our faces are level. "From now on you come to me if you have any injuries, worries, or concerns about this, okay?"

"I will."

He leans forward, kissing me softly on the lips, tongue licking against the seam. I'm spun with a whole other kind of heat.

When he pulls away, I sit up. "I do have one thing to ask you. A favor." I grab the sheet and cover myself. "For Rex."

* * *

"As you know, this weekend is Anex's birthday party. Rex should be there, and I want to take the opportunity to show him I can be a good mate."

Silas' face brightens as we exit the cottage and step onto the deck that surrounds the pool. "What do you have in mind?"

"The things I was taught growing up about how to make my mate happy are not the things Rex wants. He doesn't just want a submissive, doting female from Serendee. He wants a strong companion, but I don't always know what that means and," I exhale, "I thought maybe a little insight into his private life could help me get a better grasp."

"You want me to tell you about him? Personal things?"

"I know nothing about the man, and he certainly isn't telling me. I don't even know where he lives."

He studies me closely, like he's trying to figure out a puzzle. "He lives in the Main House. With everyone else in Anex's inner circle."

"Obviously, but I thought maybe you could show me his quarters."

"You want to go to his suite?"

"I want to see how he lives. What he eats and drinks. How he arranges his furniture." We stand near the pool. The water is crystal blue and I wonder what it feels like to swim in it. "I think if I can understand him a little better, I can make things go a little more smoothly. Especially if we have no choice but to spend the weekend together. The last thing I want, and I assume Anex wants, is for him to run off and reject me. Again."

"None of us want that," he says, taking my hand in his. "I'll take you there."

He opens the back door that enters the house library. It's filled with books and papers—many penned by Anex. A few, I suspect, were written by my mother.

"Do you know why he rejects The Way?" I ask, as we go up the backstairs.

"I've heard his arguments," he says, slowing his gait. "He has a lot of anger directed at his father, and in all fairness, he has had his faith rocked more than once."

I nod, trying to process it all. I can understand that. When my mother was determined to be a Regressive and left Serendee my faith wavered as well. "But you don't think he's lost, do you?"

His mouth is set in a grim line. "I hope not, which is why I'll assist you in whatever way you need, even if it means violating my best friend's privacy." I hadn't thought of it that way. "Being Anex's son isn't easy. He's forced to share his father, his only parent, with the rest of the community."

"That had to be hard."

"It was, and it's one reason Anex encouraged him to become so close to me, Elon, and Levi. He needed support and over time we grew to be like brothers."

I grab his forearm and look into his eyes. "You're very devoted to him. It shows. And I appreciate how that devotion has spread to me. Once Rex and I are mated, I hope that you feel the same toward me—like family. Until you get your own mate, of course."

He looks down at my hand and then back up. His eyes are so clear, but they are filled with something deep inside that I can't reach. "That would be nice."

He continues forward, easing his arm out of my grasp, and I follow him through the maze of hallways and staircases. All I know is how to get from my room to the foyer, but generally it's not necessary. One of the guys usually escorts me to and from work, or someone from the house walks me up when I return. No areas of the house are barricaded or blocked off, but everything looks identical to the clean white paint and the modest décor. There are no identifying traits and more than once, I've gotten turned around. Silas confidently walks the halls until he stops at the door and unlocks it with a key, but I pause before I cross the threshold. "Are you sure he's not here?"

"He's with Elon, remember? They had business to take care of today outside of Serendee." His eyebrow arches. "Are you having second thoughts?"

"No," I say, as much for myself as him. Snooping into people's things isn't something I'm accustomed to. I've never had secrets and as far as I know, no one I've known has either. Well, other than my mother.

The layout is similar to my suite, but the contents are very much male. Secular male, from what I've learned during my TV watching.

The living room has comfy leather couches and a massive television. There are electronic devices that Silas explains belong to the video games Rex likes to play. He describes the games and they run through different themes; sports, mazes, battles, military. I don't understand any of it, but that's okay. At least I know.

I wander into the adjacent room—the kitchen—and feel more at ease. This is what I know about serving my mate. Feeding and nurturing him. I open the refrigerator and see well organized food, plenty of fruits and vegetables from the Serendee market, but I also notice the soda and sugary drinks. A box from the bakery is on the counter. Bags of chips and crackers are lined up against the backsplash.

"Did he do this himself? Buy these things?"

"There's a maid and a cook."

I nod. It makes sense. "Do they live here?"

"In the house, not the suite. There are servant quarters somewhere," he says, opening the box and taking out two cookies. He hands me one. "Eat."

I look at it guiltily, but he nods in encouragement. I take the bite and sugar rushes into my taste buds.

"How long has he lived here?" I ask.

"We all moved in when he turned sixteen."

It's a different journey than my own or the others in the domum. The non-chosen. Further proof Rex and his friends grew up in a totally different world. One I have to acclimate to.

Silas leads me through the suite, pointing out the different bedrooms; his, Elon's, Levi's. They're bare—empty, having moved their things to my suite instead. I stop in the doorway of Levi's room and stare at the empty walls and the neatly made bed. There are a few books on the shelf, but I know most of them are at my place.

"Do you miss living here?" I ask.

He glances in and shrugs. "Not really."

"But it's been your home for years."

"'Home' is a construct," he replies. "An emotional attachment to the physical. The Way teaches us to focus on spiritual growth. Who we are, not what we possess."

"Of course," I reply, knowing he's right. It's another reason for our simple clothing, our clean eating, our lack of materialism. It hammers home how much they sacrifice for Anex and Rex. They live in transition—their whole lives centered around these two important men. They aren't Ordered and they bear the weight of Serendee's secrets. Maybe I'm not the only one that struggles with following the right path.

"You're very strong for maintaining these values despite living in the center of opulence and a friend that insists on pushing the limits."

He looks down at me. "It's a gift to serve Rex and his father."

"I agree."

"I know, Imogene." His hand moves. Up, then down, finally tucking my hair behind my ear. He's so good at these intimate moments, so at ease. "I have no doubt you are perfectly Chosen for Rex."

He turns and continues down the hallway and I pause for a

moment, letting my heart slow its pace. His touch kicked it in gear. My body responds so differently now to the slightest affection. It's not satisfied with a simple touch. It wants more.

Rex's scent hits me before I even step into his room. It lands like a punch to my gut—the memory of him pushing me to the ground, the way he tasted in my mouth, comingled with the clean soapy scent and masculine cologne. The feel of him under me during the lecture, invading my body with his fingers, drawing me to the edge.

I push the emotions back—like we're taught with The Way. Females all too often let emotions rule, instead of accepting it like a man would. The incident was nothing more than a power play in an attempt to prove his father wrong. It had nothing to do with me.

His bedroom appears more lived-in than the others. There are a few things on the dresser. A couple of framed photos. I recognize his mother from the portrait at the Beatrice House. There are none of his father. Other items; a small carved wooden box. A jar with coins. A sleek tablet.

There's a stack of books on the bedside table. None authored by his father. The titles are in bold: Escape. Infidel. Educated. Witness.

Silas is silent as I comb the room, opening both closets. One for Serendee. One for the secular world. On the floor are sneakers. Sports equipment.

"He likes sports?" I ask, trying to glean something. "Does he play basketball like his father?"

Silas shifts in the doorway, arms crossed over his chest. "No. He likes to watch football. But he plays soccer."

I nod. There are sports teams in Serendee for the children. Athleticism is encouraged. A healthy body is a temple to The Way. Anex has frequent basketball games late at night. I've seen the hard lines of Rex's body. The broad shoulders. I'm not surprised he's athletic.

Even though it's overkill, I enter the bathroom and peer into the shower. Bottles of soaps and gels line the tiled shelf. A razor sits on top of a can of shaving cream next to the sink. I pull open the drawer and it glides out easily. A box of condoms sits on top. I know what they are. We have sex education. I also know that men prefer not to use them—it's best for women to take care of birth control on our own. Males are ruled by biological need. Seeing the box does make me wonder... does he bring women here?

I don't expect the twist of jealousy swirling in my gut.

That thought propels me out of the bathroom. I stare at the bed. It's comfortable looking, stacked with pillows and a soft, worn quilt. A T-shirt and sweatpants lay at the foot of the bed. On the small table I see a black leather journal—a thin cord is wrapped around it.

"He logs?" I ask him.

"I suppose. It's a hard habit to break, even for him."

What I'd give to read between those pages, but I don't dare. It would be unforgivable.

But I do open the drawer and see two things. A few other journals. One with a pink cover. Also, money. A lot of money. Curled into tight rolls. I pick it up and study it. There are dozens, if not hundreds, of bills tucked inside.

Glancing over at Silas, I find him staring back, stone faced. After a moment he says, "We should go."

I place the cash back in the drawer exactly how I found it and shut the drawer. We exit the suite quickly. In the hallway, Silas asks, "Did you find what you were looking for?"

"Maybe," I reply, still processing everything I saw. My mind is mostly on the money. Why does he have so much? What does he do with it? Does Anex know? Although I do feel like maybe I learned a little more about Rex today, I definitely feel like something is missing. Something about Rex that I just don't understand. There's one other person I want to talk to before I make my final plans for the weekend.

Elon.

31

I mogene

    It's dark when Elon returns home, his jacket smelling of smoke and his eyes rimmed red. I'm in the living room. Silas and Levi are on the basketball court with Anex.

"What are you doing up?" he asks, tossing the jacket on the chair. "Shouldn't you be in bed?"

"I'm waiting for you," I tell him. "There's something I need."

"Really?" His eyes rake over me, and I shift anxiously. Does he think I mean sex? He could be stoned or drunk enough to consider it. Would I consider it? Whatever brief desire I see in his eyes—or think I see—shutters and he says, "It'll have to wait until tomorrow. I'm beat."

"Wait." I hop from my seat and jump in front of him. If he wanted, he could pick me up and move me. Instead, he stares down at me impatiently. "I want to know what I'm really dealing with here."

His eyebrow rises. "Dealing with?"

"With Rex. You took me to him at the club, and he showed up that night for Anex's lesson—neither encounter did much to improve our relationship. You've taught me how to dress and act. Silas has attempted to teach me how to attend to his needs," his other eyebrow lifts and I quickly add, "at least on a basic level."

"Then you're good." He starts around me, but I hold my ground.

"I'm not." I hold. My. Ground.

He notices.

"I need to know about the business. What exactly does Rex do for Serendee? What does Anex pay him all that money for?"

He runs his hand through his dark hair. "That's not possible."

"Says who? You?"

"It doesn't matter. It's not happening."

"Make it happen, Elon." I rest my hands on my hips. It feels strong, even if I'm quaking inside.

"And if I don't?"

"I guess I go ask Anex on my own." I tap my finger on my chin. "Do you think he knows Rex has all those rolls of cash in his bedside table? He may be curious about that."

His steel-gray eyes pin mine, but I don't falter. Finally, he grimaces and says, "Fine." Then takes in my outfit. "Get out of that dress. Jeans. Black sweater. Sneakers."

"Sneakers?"

"I know I bought you some."

"You did."

"Well, put them on."

I don't hesitate, changing quickly, sliding on the stretchy but tight jeans and a dark sweater from the back of the closet. When I return to the living room, I see that he's in a similar outfit.

"Are you sure you want to do this?" he asks, zipping up his hoodie.

"Yes."

His head tilts slightly, like he's gearing up to talk me out of it, but he ultimately says nothing, and we head out of the suite. The Main House keeps a constant rhythm, open all day and night because Serendee runs on Anex's time. Basketball all night. Sleeping late. Courses and training go as long as needed. Even so, we don't pass anyone on the way out, and although I assumed we would go down to the garage, we don't. Elon takes me out one of the back doors, along the back driveway, until we reach a path that I know leads behind the school.

The gym lights glow a block away, and I notice Elon places himself on the outside of the path, blocking me from the street. We pass the playground and suddenly he announces, "That's where I first saw you."

I glance over and stumble over a root. His hand shoots out to catch me. "What did you say?"

"Remember when we were kids, and everyone would pile onto that merry-go-round and an older kid would come around and spin it really fast?"

"Yes," I say, the memory flooding back. A dozen kids would climb onto the flat surface and hang onto the bars for dear life. It was thrilling and exciting and even though it made my stomach twist anxiously, I always wanted more. "You were there?"

"I was the older kid."

I look up at his face and try to place this Elon with one that's much younger, although still strong and using that strength to make everyone on the playground happy. A flash of color bursts through and I see him. Bigger than everyone else, laughing and enjoying the game. "Wait. You always wore that soccer jersey, right?"

"Yeah," he smiles. It may be the only genuine one I've seen. "I loved that jersey. I had to give it up when we moved into the domum."

"Same, but mine was pink overalls. I loved all the pockets."

We walk a little further, veering away from the school and taking the path that leads to the agricultural sector. "You really remember me from back then?"

"Yes. You were small but always had a big smile. Bossy." He laughs. "You'd scream, 'go faster! Make it faster!'"

"And you'd do it." I can almost feel the wind on my face. "It felt like flying. Sorry I was so demanding."

"It was worth it to see you happy." That's a revelation I'm not sure how to handle and I stay quiet as we cut through the woods until straight ahead is the big red barn. Elon stops. "I miss those days," he says suddenly. "Just being a kid."

"It was easier," I agree. Of course, back then, my mother was still living at home. My family was intact, and I wasn't connected to a Regressive. And Elon, well, he hadn't started on the journey that led us here—out by the barn in the middle of the night. When he doesn't say anything else, I point to the building. "Is this what you're showing me? The barn?"

The tension returns, tugging at his eyes, and I regret breaking the spell. "Not the barn exactly." He starts down the hill and grabs my hand, pulling me along with him. He's quiet, and I try my hardest to be the same. We reach the storm door on the backside of the building. Flat doors that open outward. "We're not going in the barn, but under it."

There's a keypad, and he punches in the code. A moment later, the doors unlock, and a dark staircase is revealed. Apprehension rolls in my belly. Is this a trap? A trick? Suddenly, fluorescent lights flash on, illuminating the stairway. My steps falter when I see what is stretched out before us: rows and rows of tall, leafy plants.

"A nursery?" I ask, trying to process the enormity of what I'm seeing. It's clean, the rows are orderly. Complicated light and sprinkler systems are attached to the ceiling.

"Of sorts, yes."

I touch the plant closest to me and sniff the leaves. The odor is herbal, woodsy, and a little skunky. "Is this...?" I don't want to ask, but I have to. He's showing me for a reason.

"Three acres of specially cultivated marijuana." He nods down the row. "It's longer than the building."

I frown. "What does specially cultivated mean?"

He gives me a look. "You definitely don't want to know that."

I stare out at the rows of plants. "So this is the business Rex carries outside the community."

He walks over and tugs a leaf off and smells it. "Yep. The farmers grow it. We sell it and the money flows back to Serendee."

Pieces click together about my betrothed and his friend. The hours working outside Serendee. The mingling with secular people. Their secretive nature. And, of course, the money.

"Rex is a drug dealer."

His face twists up in displeasure. "Rex is a salesman. Of Serendee and the product that keeps the community running. He's the face of Anex's world."

"And you?"

"I'm his bodyguard. I protect his very lucrative face."

My mind spins. Anex believes in the healing qualities of natural supplements—or drugs. It's preferred to other toxins. Marijuana. Herbal extracts. Natural potions. It's common. I knew we even had products made of hemp. But to be involved in it to this extent—to this level of secrecy is shocking. There's so much I didn't know about Serendee and most of it conflicts with everything I've ever been taught.

"Isn't this illegal?" I ask.

Elon shrugs. "You know, Serendee does not always prescribe to the laws of the secular world. We don't believe in government bureaucracy and regulation. Marijuana is grown naturally."

I nod. I do know this. We're Ordered and mated. There's no official wedding or paperwork. Women have children at home. We work for ourselves, without the use of social security numbers or even identification. Anex thinks the government will want to shut us down if they know how efficiently, how sustained we are living.

I glance into the cavernous warehouse again and realize that Anex is more prepared, more serious, than I ever could have expected. Rex is an important leader in all of this. He is definitely not expendable. No wonder he has to keep him close.

I have more questions, like, what does Rex do with all the money besides stash it in his bedside table? Who knows about the farm? Has there ever been trouble? But the sound of footsteps and voices echo off the cement floor, cutting off my thoughts. I've barely processed that they're coming or that maybe we should hide, when Elon grabs me and pulls me into a dark corner behind oily smelling machinery. The people pass us, talking quietly to one another as they take their time walking down the rows.

My heart pounds, both in my chest and in my ears. It's hot back here, near the generators, and I'm tucked against Elon's large frame. His arms are wrapped around me like a shield, and my ear is pressed against his chest. My heart isn't the only one beating like a drum.

Neither of us speaks as the voices drift farther away, although Elon shifts out of discomfort. The space is cramped, and the movement pushes us chest to chest as his hips brush against my lower belly, revealing the hard bulge in his pants.

I suck in a gasp. Oh.

Elon has been more abrasive to me than Rex. He's insulted me, groped me, belittled and watched as his friend humiliated me. He doesn't like me. It must be the proximity. Men can't control their bodies, which is why we're taught it's up to us to take precaution. It's my fault for putting us in this situation. For demanding that we come here.

We're frozen like this, his cock drilling into me, and my body tunes in to the fact that on some primal level, he wants me. Heat spreads through my limbs and my pulse changes, thrumming in a steady beat; less fear, more desire. Just when I think I'm making it up, Elon's hand slides down and cups my backside. In one swift move, he's lifted me off the ground and spun us around. My back is against the wall and our bodies fit together. Nose to nose, he stares at me, eyes dark and hard.

An apology for being a woman, for pushing him to bring me here, for dragging him out in the night, sits on the tip of my tongue. "Elon, I—"

He cuts me off with a kiss. It's not our first that happened at Anex's will, but this—it's all him—us. There's no hesitation, only lust. I taste it on his tongue as he parts the seam of my lips. I feel it in my core, where he rocks his hips against mine. It burns in my belly, my spine, my ears. His breath is warm, his hands greedy. He holds me against the wall, like I'm light as a feather, and slips a hand up my sweater and palms my breast.

My legs hook around him, anchoring me in place. We're clothed. We're cramped. We're caught in this moment alone. The people we're hiding from are long gone, and it's dark enough that I can barely see his face. I'm glad, because I don't want him to know how good this feels, because is it any different from Levi's Corrections? Isn't this just me wanting something that hurts? A man that loathes me?

But I am that person—that woman—and I grind into him. He pushes back, a growl rumbling in his chest. It reveals that sensation I felt with Silas—power. Anex tells us that to get what we want, women need to be more like men. Less emotional. More demanding. I want what's happening right now as much as Elon. My body demands release. I push into him again, and he ruts against me in return. Back and forth we go, rubbing, grunting, allowing our needs to take control.

It hits me hard—harder than with Silas or on my own. As hard as it was when Levi placed his mouth on me, which seems crazy, with the barriers surrounding us. It comes down like rain, sweeping over my body with such intensity that I have to hold on to Elon. My teeth bite into his shoulder—holding my groan inside. His movements stop abruptly, hips jerking upward as he buries his face in my neck. "So good," he mutters. "So fucking good."

It's the only thing he's said since he dragged me back here. I almost think I made it up.

Elon shudders and exhales and steps back, slowly unpinning me from the wall. He grimaces down at his pants and mutters, "Jesus," while I straighten my shirt. My panties are wet and sticky, but I assume it's nothing compared to his.

He eases around the generator and then glances back. "It's clear," he says, jerking his head for me to follow. "We need to get back."

I nod and slip back up the staircase and out into the night.

Elon showed me a lot in a few hours. The truth about Serendee. The obligations of my mate. The ties that bind him here. The power that I hold.

He also revealed that he's a man that takes what he wants, even if it doesn't belong to him.

32

———————

R^{ex}

I toss a jacket into my bag and grab my journal and a roll of cash out of the bedside table. It's enough to get me through the weekend—which is how long I plan on staying away from Serendee. There's no way in hell I'm celebrating my father's birth with a three-day celebration. Fucking narcissist.

I'm not expecting company when I walk back into the living room.

"Going somewhere?" Silas asks. He's sprawled on the couch. His feet are propped on the coffee table. Levi is next to him, while Elon stands near the door peeling an apple with the blade of a knife.

"Out. Away. Anywhere but here."

"You're bailing on your dad's birthday weekend." Levi says it as a fact, not a question.

"Nailed it." I knock over Silas' legs and cut through the room. "Have a piece of coconut cake without me." Anex loves coconut cake. There will be at least twenty cakes, all in his preferred flavor. Just the thought of it makes me gag.

"Rex, put down the bag," Elon says mid-peel. I've been pissed at

Elon for weeks now. Ever since, he showed up with Imogene at the club. My goal had been to ignore her completely, but he pushed that altercation. I had to do what I had to do.

"And why would I do that?"

He doesn't bother with an explanation. "You're going camping with the rest of us."

It's not often that my friends stand up to me. I eye the three of them. "Why? Because it'll hurt daddy's feelings if I'm not there to fawn over him like the other minions?"

"Because your mate is expecting you there," Silas says matter-of-factly. It's exactly the answer I don't want to hear. "The final day is Solstice. You have to show."

Imogene. God, that woman is both expected and unexpected at the same time. I expect her to follow my father's rules. I expect her to be submissive and compliant. I expect her to behave like a sheep, even when she's being led to slaughter.

I did not anticipate her beauty, or the way she would look in secular clothing when she walked in that bar. A lethal combination of sexy and sweet. I wasn't prepared to see her on her knees, to feel her mouth around my cock, to watch her swallow even though I was the one that made her do it. I thought there would be tears. Anger. Humiliation. I thought she'd run long before we got to that place. But she didn't run, and I had to follow through. She made me do that. Anex made me.

And then the night she perched on my lap, when I'd pushed my way inside of her, making her come.

She needed to know what a man—a mate—from Serendee was truly like. We take. We demand. We possess.

I snort, brushing Silas off. "Imogene is not my concern."

Elon pushes off the wall and drops the spiral of skin on the kitchen counter. He then snaps the blade shut and tucks it in his pocket. "She is your concern. You agreed to the Ordering. You picked her. Now you have to fulfill your obligation and this weekend is one of them."

"I'm not obligated to anything or anyone—at least not yet. No one will notice if I'm not at Solstice."

Even I know that's a stretch.

Elon shakes his head. His whole attitude confuses me. None of these guys has ever cared what I do. We work, we party, we live by our own rules. Why is this suddenly a big deal? I narrow my eyes. "I'm missing something, aren't I?"

"You're missing out on hanging with a sweet, sexy girl that's willing to do whatever you want," Silas says with a shrug. "I know I'd stick around."

Silas calling Imogene sexy triggers my suspicions. "That's an awfully descriptive way to talk about another man's mate."

Elon takes a loud, crunching bite into his apple. "Two seconds ago, you didn't want her. Silas says she's sexy and you get territorial? Classic Rex."

I look at Levi. "What's this about?"

He spares a glance at the others and then says, "We've been working with her."

"Working with her. What does that mean?"

"Preparing her to be the mate of an entitled asshole that hates everything she believes in," Levi says. "Training. She wasn't ready for you."

"You did this on my father's orders?" I ask, avoiding the truth behind what they're saying. I know the kind of work my father would ask of them. The kind of training they would expose her to. If I could string them from the ceiling, I would. But I can't. I repeat, "You did this on my father's orders?"

"Yes," Levi says.

"Son of a—" I swallow it back. "You had no right."

"No," Elon says, stepping forward. He's got three inches on me, and I know for a fact he can kick my ass. "You had no right to lock this girl into being your mate and then abandoning her. If she shows up without you this weekend, she'll be ruined. You know that."

"Especially with her family history," Levi adds. "People will blame her for your absence. They'll ask questions she can't answer."

"And your father?" Silas says. "You think he'll just let her go back to the community? She knows too much. She's locked in now, whether you want her or not."

"Whose fault is that? Who showed her what goes on behind the curtain? It sure as hell wasn't me." I glare at the three of them. This is exactly what I didn't want to happen. I wanted to keep her—all of them out of this. I run my hand through my hair. "Fine. I'll go. I'll stand by her and pretend like everything is fine, but it doesn't change anything."

"Give her a chance," Silas says. Levi nods in agreement. Elon, well, he won't meet my eye. "I don't think you'll regret it."

I don't respond but turn and carry my bag back in my room, holding back a scream of rage. Giving Imogene a chance was never something I planned on doing. And regrets? Picking her to be my mate, even if just symbolically, was definitely going to be my biggest one yet.

* * *

I'm not sure when Anex's birthday became a three-day weekend. After my mother died, I think, but I could have that wrong since children aren't allowed in the encampment during the party. At sixteen, after we'd moved into the main house, we still weren't invited, but the continuous drumbeat lured me, Elon, Levi, and Silas through the pastures to get as close as we possibly could. During the day, the adults participated in field day—traditional races and matches. At night, it turned to dancing and feasting. Each day was a celebration of my father's existence—a way to show thanks for his sacrifice to Serendee and his devotion to The Way. There are birthday cakes, and musicians, drinks and the wafting of smoked herbs. Back then, I'd been enthralled by the mystique of my father. Only a man of extreme worth would deserve a celebration like this.

Now I know better.

This year it's even more of an event—the final day lands on the Summer Solstice and the Ordered will gather in front of Anex for a blessing, and the couples will gift their mates with a token of some kind. In the secular world, rings are the traditional gift, and that is acceptable here, but since material possessions are not coveted here, it can be almost anything. I walk through the campground, past the small tents and makeshift circles of friends and family. There's a hierarchy in Serendee. My father and his inner circle establish the order—the outside is filled with those who contribute less. Less skill. Less devotion. Less access. Less money. The next ring is for people diligently working their way through the lessons, whose logs are in order and their dedication clear. They attend late night basketball or sit at his side during lectures.

Then there is the ring of tents occupied by the Ordered. Each newly ordered couple gets a tent of their own—a gift from Anex in support of their mating. My tent isn't there. I am in the inner circle—usually in an encampment with my confidants. This year a volunteer points me in the direction of my lodgings and I see that it's an angular yurt perched on the edge of the circle. Imogene and I have been given privacy.

Another of my father's manipulations.

I push past the flap of the tent and step inside. I've come to this event for four years and not once have my accommodations been like this—even as a member of the inner circle. The yurt is draped in colorful fabric, and a mattress has been brought in and covered with soft quilts. Pillows are stacked on the bed, as well as on the floor, which is also covered in a thick rug. I'm taking it all in, spinning in a circle, when I see her standing in the doorway. She's in a loose white dress, the neck scooped out, revealing the hint of the soft flesh underneath. Her skin looks healthier than before—her cheeks plumper. The weight gain makes sense. Levi, or one of the guys, has been feeding her better.

"Hi," she says. It's the first time I've seen her up close since that night, and as much as I try not to, the first thing I look at is her mouth.

Jesus.

"Imogene." I clutch the strap of my bag over my shoulder. "I guess my father went all out this year."

"The tent, yes," she says, "but I brought most of the furnishings."

I eye the flickering lanterns hanging from the tent poles. "Did you?"

"I figured that if you showed, it would be our first weekend actually together. I should make it special."

And there it is. The need to make everything more. To push and manipulate. I hold back my criticism and nod at the door flap on the other side of the room. "Where does that go?"

"A separate room for Levi, Silas and Elon."

"You invited them?"

"Of course. They're your family."

A family of betrayers, I think, wondering how much they had to do with this. I know they mean well. I do. We've been through everything together. But we're talking about an outsider. She's not an outsider to Serendee—far from it. It's clear she's devoted to The Way, but she's an outsider to our tight group. They know how I feel about bringing in anyone new, particularly someone on my father's radar. There's a reason I only see women outside the community.

"Well, it's nice." I'm trying to be polite. "Far more comfortable than I expected. You better not let my father see this or he'll get jealous of my special treatment."

She smiles and blushes, pleased that I've complimented her. "I tried to remember everything we may need for the weekend, but I'm sure I've forgotten something. Don't hesitate to ask if there's something you want or need."

Irritation flickers under my skin and my response comes out harsh. "You're not my slave, Imogene."

"I know."

"Then stop acting like one."

"I'm just—"

"Behaving the way you were raised. I know that. I'm not my father. This isn't the kind of relationship that I want."

"Then what do you want?"

I laugh, and I know it sounds meaner than I intend. "What I want isn't an option. Not here. Here I live with what my father wants for us.

Everyone does. You know that." I tilt my head and study the woman next to me. "I doubt I was what you expected."

"No," she admits. "I never considered being ordered to someone of your position. Not with my family history. But then, I guess that explains a lot of what's happening here. If you wanted a true mate, you would have been Ordered to a more worthy female."

Her statement lands hard. Truthfully. We stand across from one another for an awkward beat. She's right. I chose her for her flaws.

"You can leave," she finally says. "Or I can. I don't want to ruin the weekend by forcing you to be around me if you find me so unappealing."

I drop my bag and step closer, reaching out to touch the side of her face. She flinches. I can't blame her. Not after what I've made her do the times, we've been together. She's trying. I can see that and although it doesn't make a difference, I do feel compelled to say, "Your appeal has nothing to do with this, Imogene. If you understand nothing else, understand that."

Her big eyes hold mine and again I can't help but look at her lips. They're pink and soft. I know what they feel like on my skin. Quickly, I drop my hand and say, "It's more of a hassle to deal with Anex's disapproval than to last the weekend. As long as we have to be here, I think we should make the most of it. Give the people what they want. Get my father off my back."

"If that's what you want."

I grimace. "What I want, Imogene, is for you to stop conceding everything to me."

"I know." She twists her hands. "It's hard to stop. My mind just snaps back to my lessons—to the things we've been taught. Even after the training with Levi, Elon and Silas, I find myself slipping back into it."

"If we have to spend the weekend together, maybe I know how we can make that a little better."

"How?"

"By doing my favorite thing." I grin cheekily. "Breaking the rules."

33

Imogene

I try to manage myself as I walk through the camp with Rex by my side. To pretend this situation is normal and that we've spent the last few weeks getting to know one another like the other Ordered mates. I hope no one can tell my heart races like a horse's hoofbeats, or that my palms are clammy with sweat. I hope no one can see that he loathes his father, Serendee, and The Way, or that his dislike of all those things trickles down to me. I desperately pray that no one knows that the last time he saw me, he forced me to take him in my mouth and swallow his seed out of spite and intimidation.

And that I let him.

"Where are we going?" I ask, keeping up with his long strides.

"To make an appearance—let my father know we're here."

I've underestimated Rex. He glides through the crowd, nodding at men he knows from meetings or other members of the community. He accepts their slight bows, their well wishes, the way the female's eyes absorb his good looks. He is respectful to me, making sure I'm by his side, and I find myself caught up in the game. These people have no idea who he truly is: a criminal, an abuser, a blasphemer. They see what he wants to show them, and he knows his role—or at the very least, how to perform it flawlessly. His behavior creates a gnawing feeling of confusion in my belly. One, I do my best to keep off my face.

"Are you ready?" he asks, as we approach the canvas gazebo in the center of the field. It's up on a circular platform, a chair in the middle, surrounded by pillows on the ground. There's a crowd bunched around the tent, but my eyes are on the man in the chair. Anex speaks in his quiet, consistent tone, captivating the crowd.

"What is the point of this beautiful life," he says, gazing down at his followers, "if you are living it inauthentically? How do you process what you hear and see and feel if you don't know how to manage that input? Authenticity is where you find the truth in yourself and in one another. It's how your soul can open up to mesh with the soul of another person. If you are inauthentic, you will never meet that other person's true self. Which is why you have to stop fighting yourself. Fighting others. You must dig deep for who you are so that you can become whole."

The group is mesmerized. I'm mesmerized, although once he stops speaking and someone asks a question, I become attuned to the vibrations rolling off of Rex. I glance over and see his profile—his jaw clenched tight and his hands balled into angry fists. I'd had him here with me for a moment, but seeing his father threatens to shatter any truce we'd come to in the tent. On instinct, I reach for his hand. Sliding my palm over the backside of his fist. He tenses further, but I don't stop. I push the pads of my fingers into the gaps of his and wind our hands together.

"Come on," I say. "We don't need to be here."

He glances down, blue eyes hard as glass. "He'll expect..."

"He'll survive." I can't believe I said that, but I tug him away. He doesn't relax as we work our way through the crowd, but he also doesn't let go. I lead him behind a portable trailer—a kitchen used to feed everyone over the weekend. There's a covered dining area filled with picnic tables and an entire counter is covered in the cakes for Anex's birthday.

"He really bothers you," I say, starting to understand this man a little better. Not much, but a little.

"You have no idea."

"Then forget him. He'll be busy all weekend, and as long as we're together, he can't complain too much. We can blame it on him—he's the one that made the Ordered."

"True." A smile tugs at his lips. "It's not our fault we're so focused on one another. We're betrothed after all." He looks at me hungrily and my belly flutters. Fear? Apprehension? I'm not sure. He glances back and forth, making sure no one is around and it builds, but he turns away from me.

"What are you doing?" I ask, trying to settle my breathing.

He sneaks over to the cake table and grabs a big one. "Hungry?"

Of course, that look wasn't for me.

"You're stealing a cake?" I whisper.

"Breaking the rules, Imogene. That's how I survive." He rolls his eyes. "Ugh, it's coconut. Of course."

Breaking the rules is something I've tried to never do. There's no leeway with my family's history. But it dawns on me that I have a new family—at least in theory. He stares down at the cake with disgust, and I wrinkle my nose. "I'm not a fan of coconut either. We can scrape it off."

"Yeah?" he asks, surprised. Not about the cake, but about my willingness to go along with him.

"Yes." I nod in the direction of our yurt. "I have a few other things that can go along with it. Come on."

This time, I lead the way, sneaking along the backside of the campground on the way back to our makeshift home. My plan for the weekend had been to feed him, ease his anger, gain his trust. I glance back at him, carrying the cake in one hand and licking an icing covered finger with the other. I may be able to accomplish that yet.

* * *

I make him stop by the tent to gather a few of the things I'd brought with me for the weekend. I have a picnic basket full of snacks, like I'd seen in his suite. I'd also added drinks and healthier foods like fruit and meat and cheese.

We settle on an area by the lake—far from the growing celebration in the center of the camp. "You sure this is a safe spot?" I ask. I'd been full of bravado near the kitchen, but the idea of being caught not participating in Anex's birthday makes me uncomfortable.

Rex watches me spread the blanket out. "Things get a little wild as the night progresses. My father will be so caught up in it all he won't notice."

From the sound of the music and laughter drifting our way, I assume he's right.

I unpack the basket, laying out a spread of food. Rex stretches out on the blanket, his legs so long his feet hang off the edge. He watches me, and I pretend not to notice the scrutiny. I know he's looking for flaws. Weaknesses. He's coming up with reasons to reject me further.

"This isn't local," he says, picking up a package of crackers. "Did you go shopping in town?"

"Levi took me," I reply. I didn't have actual money, but I suspected he did, and I was too flustered to ask Elon. I knew for certain he had cash, but after what happened between us under the barn... well, I was still processing that. The way he kissed and rubbed against me— that was not a lesson. It was not training. It just felt good and every time I look at him, my skin sets on fire and I want to do it again. I have no idea what he thinks or feels or wants.

It's easier to push all of that aside, because Rex is here and despite the intimacy I've had with his confidants, they must fit squarely in another box.

"Levi." He opens the box and shakes out a handful of crackers. "That must have been hard for him. He doesn't like to disobey the rules."

"No." I shrug and cut slices of meat and cheese on a board. "But he will do anything to support our Ordering, even if it means pushing me a little."

I arrange the food on a plate and hand it to him. Our fingers brush underneath and I wait for a spark—a flicker of something—but no, his walls are too high.

"Don't you see how fucked up that is?" he asks, taking the plate from me. "Levi shouldn't ask you to go against your values just because my father wants something. And those values never should exist in the first place."

"Following The Way means we have to challenge our notions of self every day, Rex. You know that."

"Is that why you're okay with my father having you trained? With my confidants touching you in a way only a mate should?"

My face heats. He knows. Of course he knows. They're his confidants. Did Silas tell him about how I touched myself while he did the same? Did Elon confess to what we did in the barn. And Levi... does he know about the Corrections? I can't answer his question and from the expression on his face, he doesn't need one. The flush in my skin tells him everything.

"He'll do anything to get in your head, you know that, right? To get in my head."

Everything Rex says is the kind of thing that would get a normal resident of Serendee removed for Regression. But he speaks freely, which means he's either not afraid or he wants to be caught.

"Can I ask you something?" I ask.

"Sure."

"What made you turn against The Way?"

His lips turn down. "Do you really want to know?"

"I do." Desperately.

"I was a believer—like everyone else that grows up here. I didn't just think my father was the light and the moon. I knew it. He was smart and fun. Innovative and generous." He swallows and sets his plate aside. "But when my mother died, my father changed. Everything I'd been raised to believe shifted. His ideas became more extreme, and his sense of superiority grew. You probably don't remember any of this because you were too young, but Serendee didn't used to be like this—Imogene." He lifts his chin up the hill toward the party. "It truly was a place that co-existed with the outside world. People weren't bound to this land—to him."

"I know what it's like to lose a mother—not one to death," I add quickly, "but she's gone all the same. Life changes when someone leaves. People change. Even your father."

He shakes his head and the blonde highlights glint in the light of our lantern. "You don't know him, Imogene. Not like I do."

"So your reaction is to rebel. Regardless of who you hurt."

He looks at me, eyes blazing. "I don't want to hurt anyone. That's the point. I work and I play—doing as much of it away from Serendee as possible. Bringing you and the guys into this—that is against my wishes. If anyone gets hurt—blame the one responsible. Anex."

Every response I have is tangled in the words of The Way. Indulgency. Regression. Integrated. I know it will just make him angry. So I rise to my feet, taking care not to step on the hem of my dress.

"Where are you going?" he asks.

"For a swim." I walk to the edge of the bank, the soft ground sinking between my toes. I've swum in this lake a million times— during hot summer days and long weekend retreats. There's a dock out in the middle. I lift the hem of my dress and take the first step in. It's chillingly cold, but it zaps the uncomfortable heat off my skin.

"You can't swim right now," he says, scrambling up. "It's dark. And cold. And someone may see you."

"I thought you were all about breaking the rules." I wade deeper, futilely holding the bottom of my dress in a tight fist. The cold water reaches my knees, then thighs, then I take the final step up to my waist. When I'm far enough out, I look back at the land. "What? You scared?"

The strongest compulsion comes over me, and I fling water at him. My aim is true, and the splash rains down on his face. He glares with his hands on his hips.

I do it again.

"So that's how you want to do this," he says, springing into action. He shucks off his shirt and pants. There's zero trace of self-consciousness as he strips to his shorts. I half-expect him to get completely naked. Why wouldn't he? I've already seen—and tasted—his most private parts.

But he keeps them on and lunges into the water, making waves with every step. I can't help but take in his body—mercy, he's beautiful. Hard, lean muscle ladders up his abdomen. Smooth skin stretches over his chest. It's difficult to find him threatening like this, but the wicked grin curving his lips isn't innocent.

"Where are you going?" he taunts as the threat of retaliation propels me deeper in the lake. I'm deep now, my feet no longer touching the ground. I'm closer to the deck than to the shore, so I continue deeper, even though my dress is dragging me down. It only takes him a few moments to catch up—his long arms cutting through the water. His hand grabs the back of my dress and drags me toward him.

"Wait!" I yelp. "I'm—"

He clutches me against his chest and whispers in my ear. "Not so brave with me right here, are you?"

My legs swirl beneath me, trying to tread water, but they keep getting tangled in the folds of my long dress. I reach behind me and grip his side. "My dress." I dip below the surface. "It's too heavy."

He believes me, thankfully, moving into action. With his arm around my stomach, he swims one armed to the dock, lifting me up on the wooden boards. Lake water rushes from the hem of my skirt, and he hoists himself next to me, and mutters, "I hate these fucking dresses. It shouldn't be a surprise it could kill you."

It feels like a fifty-pound weight hanging off my frame. Ignoring the chill on my skin, I gather the hem and twist, squeezing out as much water as I can. Sitting, I ask, "What are you talking about?"

He touches the lace around my neck and goosebumps rush across my skin. His eyes dart down to where I know the fabric clings against my breasts. My nipples are hard peaks, surely visible through the sheer, wet material.

"These dresses. It's basically a leash, Imogene. A fucking choker to keep you in line." He fingers the button at the top, loosening it and then the two below that. Air blows across my skin and his touch is so gentle, I'm not sure how to process it. Gentle isn't a word I associate with Rex, but here he is. Here we are. "My father wants you afraid of your body—afraid of the power that it wields. His group, VRS? It isn't about teaching men to be better. It's about teaching men to be animals. To take what they want. To cave to their primal instincts, while you've been raised to let men do what they want."

I swallow, burning at his touch—tentatively, I brush the wet hair off his forehead. "Is that so wrong? For men to get what they want."

"You should think so." He laughs darkly.

"What if I'm not afraid?" I trail my fingers down his neck and place my hand on his chest. I'm acting bold. I'm really terrified.

"You should be scared." He exhales as my hands explore his chest. His skin is surprisingly warm. "Of my father, of his inner circle, but most of all, me."

He keeps saying this. Threatening me. Hurting me. But something rings false. A different idea pops into my head and I blurt, "Maybe you're the one that's scared."

His entire body tensed with that accusation. He doesn't like the tables being flipped back on him. His response is physical. Moving quickly, his hand grips the back of my neck, pulling me to him, crashing our mouths together.

Startled, I rear back, but he doesn't let me go. His strong hands keep me in place, his lips controlling the pace. His tongue licks at my lips, parting them, invading my mouth. I fight, pushing with all my strength, and he only tightens his grip.

"This is what I want, Little Lamb." A wicked smile tugs at his mouth. "I want to bury myself inside of you. I want to feel you quiver around me. I want you to cry my name out—in pain or desire. I don't care. As long as it's my name on your lips and no one else'."

His words are mean. Terrifying. Far beyond what the men prepared me for. He's meaner than Elon. And the pain he inflicts when he touches me is harder than the ones Levi inflicts in secret.

"Stop," I tell him. "Stop!"

"I won't. You belong to me, Imogene. This is what you wanted, and I tried to warn you. I tried. But you wouldn't fucking listen." His lips drop to my neck, and he scrapes his teeth down the tender flesh.

His powerful hands lift my dress over my head and drop it on the wooden planks. His warm hand palms my breast, and he kisses me painfully. That ticking desire, the one that I've felt with Levi, surges through me, ebbing with every kiss, every touch. But there's no limit here. I can sense it—it does scare me. So much that when the swelling between his legs grows harder, more insistent, I try to fight him off. The rules about consummating an Ordered relationship are clear; once the Order has been given, couples can explore one another freely, but we should not have penetrative sex until after the mating ceremony at the fall equinox. After Anex gives his final blessing.

Rex is not a man bound by rules, and it becomes clear in the way his fingers pull and prod. I make a break, rushing to the opposite side of the platform, lake water sloshing on the floating dock. He grabs me before I get to the edge, arm wrapped around my waist and throwing me roughly to the platform. I cry out when I land with a thud, the hard planks scraping my backside. "Rex—"

"Shut up." He stands over me and removes his shorts. His cock is erect and stabbing at the air. He's a god, I know this, and I know then he's not going to take no for an answer. "You asked for this."

He bends before me and yanks away the lace panties I wore just for him.

"You're beautiful," he says, eyes roaming over my body. "I'll give you that, but you're not enough to bind me to this place, Little Lamb." He crawls over me, twice my size. When his face is above mine, his expression is cloaked in darkness, pain. "You need to understand who I really am. Who my father created me to be."

"You're a good man," I try to tell him, but his blue eyes glaze over and he wrenches my legs apart. "Don't do this, Rex, it's not The Way."

I never expected my first time to be good, or even gentle. Clarissa warned us that it was about a man's need over anything at all, but I thought it would be inside the realm of The Way. That it would be done right, with Anex's blessing, and at the very least in a bed with a man just as nervous as myself.

But I don't expect large hands holding me down, or strong knees pushing my thighs apart. "Tell me you didn't let them fuck you."

Them. His friends. Elon, Levi. Silas.

"N-no."

"But you let them do something, didn't you Little Lamb." His nose is inches from mine, and I feel the tip of his erection prodding at my entrance. "Did you let Silas con his way into your boring little panties? Or maybe Elon humiliated and belittled you until you caved, just to get him to stop?" He laughs darkly. "Levi? Did he guilt you into it? Telling you it's the road to Enlightenment?"

"It wasn't like that," I promise, but he doesn't believe me. I see it on his face. I see it when he wrenches my legs apart, barely giving me a moment to catch my breath before he stops nudging at my core and thrusts inside.

"Ungh," I cry, biting down on my bottom lip, the width of his cock tearing through the final barriers.

"If you fight, it'll be worse," he says, stilling for a single moment, before pulling out and punching in again.

"Please," I start, although I don't know why. He's already inside me—he's broken my barrier—he's claimed me, even if he doesn't want me.

This can't be happening, this can't be real. But the weight of him on top of me, the power of his body, there's no mistaking the invasion going on inside of me, or the man taking everything from me. I try to focus on anything else, the sound of the water sloshing against the dock, the drumbeats from up on the hill, the rising moon over his shoulder. But none of it works. Instead, because this is who I am, I narrow in on the pain, the biting grip of his fingers, the friction as he moves in and out of me. The tickle in my lower belly, the one that I feel when Levi's hand blisters against my flesh, flickers to life. When Silas pushes me to the edge or Elon pushes too hard.

The self-loathing I feel when I want it, bubbles under my skin and I seek more. My hips rise to meet his. Craving the burn of skin against skin, I fight against his hands. His brow furrows when he looks at me, confused by my actions. He should be. I'm sick and from the look in his eye, he sees it, knows it, and crashes our mouths together. I bite down on his bottom lip, and he groans with hunger. It ignites something in him, an intensity that makes his hips pound into me harder, his teeth scrape deeper and his hands bruise.

We fight like this—we fuck like this—hard and angry, until the pressure builds between my legs, in my lower belly, and his kisses swallow my desperate moans. He smirks down at me, knowing he brought me to orgasm, knowing he brought me down to his level. My muscles quiver around him and soon the movement of his hips grows erratic, and he grunts, deep and guttural, punching into me one last time.

His back arches as he spills into me, hot and wet. I stare up at this demon of a man—this hateful, terrible man, and know that he has ruined my life. Ruined me.

"Fuck," he mutters, rolling off me and lying flat on the dock, chest rising and falling from exertion. I wait, trying to separate the drumbeat on the hill from my racing heart, both intertwined—just like my desire for pleasure and pain. He blinks at me, like he's seeing me for the first time all night. Again, he says, "Fucking hell," but this time he stands, lurching forward and diving into the dark water.

The dock rocks from the wave, tossing me to the side. I should be happy to see him go—to be rid of him—but instead all I feel is cold and lost. I'd spent years as an outsider in this community, scrambling to hold my head up high. Rex just took that all away. He took everything.

34

———

S ilas

"They're not in the tent," Levi says, walking up to me and Elon. "Any luck in the dining pavilion?"

"No," Elon says, running his hand through his hair. I've noticed he's edgy when he doesn't know Imogene's location. It may be the bodyguard in him—or something else. He holds his emotions so close to the vest it's impossible to know. "Not in the crowd around Anex either."

We agree to walk around the edge of the campground. It's not that both Imogene and Rex being missing is a problem or even a concern, the whole weekend is a free-for-all, and they are Ordered to one another. They should be together, and Imogene had this whole thing planned out, but... it's just feels like something is off.

"Wait," Levi says, grabbing my arm and pointing down the hill toward the lake. "Is that Rex?"

Our friend emerges from the water like a monster from the deep. It's dark, but the moon is high, providing enough light to see that he's bare from the waist down. He grabs his clothing and heads up the hill.

"Rex!" I call, thinking he must not see us. His expression is stormy, and he doesn't stop. "Rex, hold up!"

He stops, but only to tug his pants on. The fabric snags on his wet legs and he curses under his breath.

"Where's Imogene?" Levi asks, getting to him first.

Rex tugs his shirt on, and it clings to his wet upper body. He jerks his thumb back at the water. "She's on the dock."

I look out at the dark water. It's hard to even see the dock from here. "On the dock? She was with you?"

"You left her there?" Levi asks, already starting down the hill. "It's pitch black."

"She can find her way back. There's a lantern on shore."

Elon steps forward and grabs him by the front of his shirt. "What did you do to her?"

Rex pushes him off with both hands. "None of your fucking business. She's my Ordered, not yours, no matter what my father convinced you to do."

"Are you mad about that?" I ask, noting the tight set of his jaw. "You are, you're mad we were working with her."

"We told you," Elon says, "we're training her. There's no way you would have accepted an innocent little virgin raised in the heart of Serendee."

He laughs darkly. "You're right, I wouldn't have, but—"

"But what?"

Water drips down his face and he flips his hair back. "She's not so innocent anymore."

There's no mistaking what that means. None. Tight, primal anger spreads across my chest and I barely notice Levi take off for the water's edge. "Did you hurt her?"

"Even if I did," he winks, "I think she liked it."

Before I can make a move, Elon lunges at him, grabbing him by the shirt. "What the fuck is wrong with you? She's innocent. Naïve."

"Isn't this what you wanted? For me to claim her?" His eyes narrow at Elon. "You had the chance to break her in brother, and you didn't. I took care of it—just like daddy wanted."

The way he says it, there's no doubt that it's the truth. Elon knows it, too. "You fucked her? On the dock? Outside of the ceremony? You know what that means!"

"I don't give a shit about what that means," Rex says, his voice cold. He holds Elon's gaze. "Get your hands off of me, brother, or I'll have to make you."

"Fuck you," Elon says, shoving Rex across the grass. His chest puffs out and his shoulders widen. "I'll ruin you the way you ruined her."

Rex is a big guy, but Elon? He's a beast. That doesn't stop Rex from taking a swing at him. Elon catches his hand before it hits his jaw and pushes him back. Rex isn't finished, rushing at Elon full force, catching him in the waist with both hands. They tumble to the ground and start to pummel one another. It's not the first fight they've had and I doubt it'll be the last. This is how they communicate—with their fists. Sometimes at the gym in the ring, other times on the basketball court—this is the first time it's been over a female. I glance down at the water and see Levi is waist deep, but his entire body is soaking wet. I jog toward him and as I get closer; I realize Imogene is clinging to his side, shivering from the cold.

"Get a blanket!" Levi calls and I dart down to where they'd set up a picnic and grab the blanket off the ground, scattering food and plates across the grass.

"Hurry," I say. Imogene's lips are blue. Levi gets her to the shore, and I wrap the blanket around her quaking frame. "Are you okay?"

"I just want to get warm."

"Come on," I say, lifting her in my arms. "I've got you."

She snuggles into my chest. Up close, I can tell she's been crying. Rage swells in me as I carry her back up the hill. Rex is gone, but Elon is still there, breathing heavily and sporting a blackening eye. His gaze goes instantly to Imogene, and he walks over, holding out his arms. "I'll carry her the rest of the way." He looks at me. "Go check on the tent. Grab some dry clothes for her when we get there."

There's a deeper instruction—make sure Rex isn't there. Reluctantly, I hand her over and run through the campground. People are at the evening session—one of the designated times Anex will be addressing the group. It's not mandatory, but everyone will be there. At least no one will see us bringing Imogene back to the tent.

I don't know if Rex was telling the truth about what happened out on the dock, but he's not a liar. Even though we've spent so much of our lives together, we've never been at odds like this and definitely never over a woman. It complicates things in a way I didn't know was possible.

I enter the tent and go straight to the wood-burning stove. The perks of being Anex's son. He always has been given the best—which is part of his problem. He doesn't realize what he has when it's right in front of him.

Once it's lit, I find Imogene's bag. I pick out a dry pair of panties and a T-shirt, but nothing else is warm enough, so I go to my own luggage and pull out a sweatshirt and a thick pair of socks. I dim the lights on the lanterns and bring in two extra blankets from our side of the tent to the big bed in the middle.

Making people comfortable is what I do best. My job is to ease the people Anex has deemed worthy in to Serendee so that they'll commit to our community. Dealing with Imogene isn't what I'm used to. The more I get to know her—the deeper entrenched we all have been in making sure Rex and Anex are both happy—the harder it gets. I like her. A lot. I like talking to her, laughing with her, making her come on my fingers.

But I also know my place. She's not mine. She never will be. My duty is to The Way. To Anex and ultimately Rex. For the first time in my life, all of that makes me angry. Furious.

The tent flap opens, and Elon ducks in, carrying Imogene in his arms. Levi follows, turning a little purple himself from the cold. I wave Elon over and say, "Bring her over by the fire. Levi, go change. I've got this."

She's still pale and her body quakes with chills. I have no idea where her clothes are—she'd been in a dress earlier and now she's in nothing but a sheer bra. Her panties are missing. I reach under the blanket and run my hands down her arms, trying to warm her up.

"Can I take off this wet stuff?" I ask. "I found some dry things in your bag."

She nods, lips quivering.

Elon hands me the pair of panties, and quickly I run them up each leg. Next, I pull the T-shirt over her head and then the sweatshirt. It hangs down to her thighs. Elon paces the room behind her, still furious about his altercation with Rex. He took a hard hit in the eye—it's already starting to swell. "You need some ice on that," I say over Imogene's head.

"I'm fine."

Levi rolls his eyes and Elon and just says, "Let's get you into bed."

I help her walk over and get under the covers. She balls up on her side, but doesn't stop shivering.

I sit on the edge of the bed, and her eyes open wide and she flinches. "Hey, I'm not going to hurt you."

"I-I know."

But it's clear she doesn't. Why should she? "You're going to need something else to help warm you up. Can I get under the cover with you?"

She swallows, and the shiver that runs down her spine seems to have nothing to do with how cold she is. Levi and I exchange a look. He noticed it, too. "Baby," I tell her, gently touching her shoulder. "I just want to warm you up. The best way I can do that is by sharing my body heat with you."

She stares at me, eyes guarded, and for a moment, I consider finding Rex and making him tell me exactly what he did to her. But this isn't about him. It's about getting her better. "Please?" I ask. "I promise, no one is going to hurt you."

Reluctantly, she nods, and I kick off my shoes and get under the covers. Her body wracks with cold. I wrap my arms around her and pull her tight against my chest. I look up at Levi who is also shivering, cold and wet from getting her out of the water.

"Baby, we need to let Levi in here, too. He's freezing." I whisper. "He'll be good. I promise."

"O-okay."

He hesitates—a flicker of emotion crossing his face. Imogene shudders again, and I shoot him a look. "Get in the bed Levi."

I know it's more of a testimony about how cold he is than anything else, but quickly gets under the covers. I reach underneath and wiggle the socks on her feet—they're cold as ice—and then look up at Elon who has been hovering by the door. "She's still freezing. Levi, too. Want to share some of that muscle mass?"

He glances over at us but gives a curt shake of his head. "I'm going to wait out here. Just to keep an eye out."

What he doesn't say is who he's keeping an eye out for. One thing is for certain, Imogene doesn't have to worry about dealing with Rex again tonight. Elon isn't going to let him back into this tent.

He steps outside and I refocus my attention on the woman next to me. She's gotten herself wrapped up in Levi's stiff arms—the baby spoon. I scoot as close as I can get and lift her head so that it's resting on my shoulder. I stroke her hair and lay a hand on her hip, rubbing it in circles, doing my best to generate warmth.

"Can you tell me what happened?" I ask her, when I see that her eyes are wide open and she's watching me.

"R-Rex happened." She takes a deep breath and reaches beneath my shirt. Her cold hands touch my stomach and I inhale in surprise. "We were getting along—kind of. W-we snuck off from Anex's talk, stole a cake, had a picnic, then went swimming."

"But something went wrong?"

"I don't know what happened." Her cheeks bloom a faint pink. "One minute we were fine, flirting a little. The next it was like someone else was out there with me. Someone that hates me."

Levi has been quiet this whole time. Overt affection isn't something he's used to. He has his kinks—I saw the welts on Imogene's backside, but that's not the same. I'm sure thought the first time he'd be in a bed with a woman was after Anex Ordered him. He certainly didn't expect me to be here.

"Did he hurt you?" Levi asks, breaking his silence.

"He…" She pinches her eyes shut. "He took what belongs to him."

Dread fills my belly, and I see the same emotion written on Levi's face. I knew Rex was a bastard, but I didn't know he was cruel. What he did to Imogene has consequences. Sex before the mating ceremony isn't acceptable, and Rex has made it clear he isn't mating with Imogene, anyway. He tarnished her. He made her vulnerable and now she's a target. That I understand—more than anyone else. Not only has Rex rejected her, but he stole her worth—the one thing she could give to another man. Anex will not Order her a second time and there will be nowhere for her to go. She will become Fallen and move directly under Anex's care.

A female as beautiful as Imogene? Well, Anex will not let that go to waste. He'll either put her to work, lock her up, or keep her for himself. Maybe all three.

As she slowly drifts to sleep and Levi and I continue to give her warmth, I promise myself that I won't let that happen. I won't let her become a slave for Anex's greed. I've accepted my fate, the role I play in Serendee, but that isn't what Imogene was made for and I'll do whatever it takes to keep her safe.

35

I mogene

I wake in a cocoon of strong arms, bundled in warmth.

It's early morning, the campground is silent. People must be sleeping off the late-night celebration from the night before. Levi's body curves against my back, his arm around my belly. For once, he isn't tense.

Silas faces me, and I'm tucked into him, my head resting in the crook of his shoulder. He smells good and with his eyes closed, his eyelashes are thick and shiny. His leg is wound around mine and I snuggle closer, not wanting the moment to end. It's the first time I've shared a bed with someone—make that someone's—and it feels nice.

That is until I feel the dull ache below my belly and remember what happened on the dock. The reason why they're in the bed with me. Rex.

Things had been going so good—at least comparatively. He talked to me. He flirted. He kissed me. And then... well, like I said, he took what belong to him. Forcefully.

That's not all I remember about the night before. I remember Levi swimming into the lake and helping me back to shore. Silas wrapping me in the blanket and carrying me up the hill to Elon. Elon's arms wrapping tighter around me with each chilled tremor. I recall the expression on his face as he checked to make sure Rex wasn't in the yurt before bringing me in. The tent was warm and cozy, and Silas gently dressed me in dry clothes and bundled me into bed.

For every cruel mark Rex left on my body, these men soothed the pain.

Levi shifts behind me, dragging me closer with the arm wrapped around my waist. My backside presses into him, and I feel the hard insistence of his manhood. My body reacts instantly with flutters of arousal in my lower belly, craving approval after Rex's rejection.

I arch back and I feel the rush of warm air on my neck. "Oh God," Levi mumbles, jumping out of the bed. "I'm sorry. I am so sorry."

Silas' eyes bolt open. He smiles, but it fades when he looks up at Levi, who I can sense pacing behind me. "What's wrong?"

"That was inappropriate," he continues. I turn and see his cheeks are as red as his hair. "I'm—" He starts, but then he just shakes his head and stalks out of the main tent and into the small adjacent room.

I face Silas again, and he's propped up on his elbow watching me. "Any idea what that was about?"

"It seems that the only way men want me is if they're inflicting pain."

He frowns. "What are you talking about?"

"Rex only wants me when he can humiliate and hurt me. Levi has only shown his own arousal in the midst of my Correction. Elon? He certainly doesn't show me tenderness."

Silas touches my cheek gently. "And what about me?"

"Your job is to make women feel safe and cared for. What we have isn't any more real than what I have with Rex."

His kind expression falls, shifting into something I can't quite read. "This isn't easy for us," he says. "To do what I do... there has to be a level of disconnection. You're right. Sex is a not just a job, but my calling. I provide something to the men and women that come into our society that I don't get in return. It's sex, not intimacy. The line is very clear." His chin lifts toward the flap Levi vanished behind. "He has spent his whole life focused on rules and order—maintaining the disciples of VRS. He believes in those philosophies as much as you do. He woke up with your sweet, sexy body next to his and he panicked. He's probably in there listing his Lapses in his journal right now."

I reach to push the covers back. "Maybe I should do the same. I'm the one leading him to a bad place."

Silas grabs my hand and pulls me back under the blankets. He then presses my palm against his lower belly. His cock is ramrod straight, thick, and tucked under his shorts. I curve my fingers around it. "Levi didn't break any rules," he says. "It's nature. Men wake up like this every day."

"Every day?"

"Yep. It's a constant, if there is a woman in the bed or not." He swallows, forcing the lump in his throat to bob. "Which is not something any of us are used to, by the way."

I frown, pulling my hand away. "What do you mean?"

"None of us wake up with a partner in bed. Not even Rex. We may all go to fulfill our needs in one way or the other, but the construct of Serendee is hard to shake. We're all waiting for our Order." He looks down. "It's just unlikely to happen. We're too valuable to Anex as we are. When he Ordered Rex, for a brief moment I thought maybe this meant it could happen, but I see now that this was all just a test. Anex knew Rex would fail and that failure would give him exactly what he wanted."

The way he speaks, it's soft but stern. He's telling me the truth, but I don't understand what he's saying.

"What does Anex really want?"

He looks up at me, his expression twisted in pain. "You."

36

I mogene

"Me?"

"I think so," he says. "It makes sense. You're beautiful. Smart. Dedicated. He's probably had his eye on you for a while."

"Then why not just claim me for his own. Make me into one of his Spiritual Mates? He can do that." He can do whatever he wants.

"Because nothing with Anex is easy, Imogene." His forehead creases. "He manipulates. Controls. He got us to break down your values, show you the dark side of Serendee. We made you complicit."

"But why? Why me? I'm devoted. I do my work. I ask for nothing. I submit to Corrections—"

"He holds grudges," Levi says, walking back into the main tent. "For a very long time."

I meet his eyes and I see the meaning behind his words. "My mother. This is about my mother."

"That's my guess," he says. "She rejected him and his ways,

causing doubt in the community. Along with the death of Rex's mother, your mother leaving is what pushed him into becoming more controlling."

"So you think he wants to punish me for her Regression?" Panic flutters in my chest. I think about the girl who made the phone call, Charlotte. That was a blip compared to this. I look between them. "What is he going to do to me?"

"I don't know," Silas says. "It could be service. A dangerous job." He takes my hand. "Or he could just keep you for his own."

"For sex?" Disgust churns in my stomach. I have no doubt that Anex is aware of my sick need for pain along with my pleasure. What he'll do with that information scares me most of all.

"I suspect that you'll find out tonight," Levi adds, "when Rex does not show up for the Solstice Ceremony."

"Oh god." I hop to my feet and pace the small room. My heart pounds with every step. "What do I do?"

Silas and Levi look at me with sympathy. The answer is clear. There is nothing I can do. I have no money. No formal education. No connections outside. Hot tears build in the corner of my eyes. I have no idea how to find my mother. And even if I wanted to, I shunned her like the rest of the community. I am truly all alone.

"Come here," Silas says, grabbing my hand as I pass by, and tugging me back on the bed. He tucks me into his side. I wrap my arms around him, grateful for the familiar warmth.

"I don't want to lose myself," I tell him. "I don't want to just become an object for him to exploit."

"I understand." He smooths my hair with his hand. "You're strong, Little Lamb. You can get through this."

I sit up and wipe a tear off my face. "Will you do something for me?"

Silas glances at Levi. "Anything."

"Show me what it's like to be loved. To have a man treat me... with care and respect." I sniff. "Treat me like the men and women you service. Just for pretend."

"Of course." Silas gives me a soft smile. "It would be my pleasure."

Levi starts to leave, but I call out. "Stay. Please."

He pauses, surprised. "Are you sure?"

"Yes."

He moves to the chair across the small space, but Silas stops him. "Levi, get in the bed. Sit behind Imogene. Support her."

It takes us a moment to get situated, but I like the feeling of being cradled against Levi's chest. He's strong. Authoritative. And I know that he is always devoted to The Way. Yes, I still care about that. Too much.

"Thank you," I say, craning my neck to see him. "I feel more secure with you here."

"I just want you to relax," Silas says, kneeling at the end of the bed.

I nod, but I'm still stiff. I can't help but think of the pain the night before. The rough intrusion of Rex's body.

"Lev," Silas says, looking at the man behind me, "rub her shoulders."

I sense Levi's hesitation, but he does as commanded and massages the blades of my shoulders. The pressure is deep in my muscles, and I finally feel the tension releasing. Silas lifts my foot. He kisses the top, then my ankle, then moves to the other side. His kisses are gentle, slow, and sweet. Although every move he makes is the opposite of the night before, when he parts my legs, they tremble in anticipation of pain.

"Don't be afraid," Silas says, ever aware of my emotions. "I'm not going to hurt you, Imogene. I'm going to make you feel good."

Levi shifts my body for me, so that I'm even more reclined. I feel the hard press of his arousal against my back. He glides his pale hands up and down my arms, gentle in a way I didn't know he had in him. Beneath the sweatshirt, my nipples harden to sharp peaks. My focus is split, partially on Levi's touch and then on the man between my legs. I bend my knees as Silas moves higher, removing my panties gently, carefully. Warm air heats my core, followed by the wet flick of his tongue.

"Oh, God—" My words are lost, caught behind a building moan.

It had felt good when Levi did this to me, but to have them both touching me at once, it is something otherworldly. Again, he lathes my clit with his tongue, flattening it before drawing back. The focusing on the tight bundle of nerves is nearly too much and I writhe against Levi while thrusting my hands into Silas' hair.

"Does that feel good?" Silas asks, grinning up at me with shiny lips. I nod and he goes back to work, alternating between the pad of his thumb and the wet heat of his mouth. He works in a rhythm, one that my hips chase. He groans against me, fingers digging into my thighs. I spread wider, lift higher, push for more, until he sits up, taking it all away and I cry out. "Don't. No."

"Don't what?" he asks. There's a playful glint in his eyes. "Stop? Keep going? More?"

"Just—" I'm overcome, pressing against Levi. I grab his hands and push them up my shirt. My whole body is on fire and nothing will quench it but the touch of these men. Unmoving, Levi palms my breasts. "Touch me," I say, looking up at his face. "Please."

His hands are big, firm, and I sense his reluctance. We've only done this under the cloak of Correction. I'm about to tell him to forget it—that it's okay, when his thumbs brush against my nipples. I exhale and see Silas watching us. His fingers make lazy turns around my clit, building my arousal.

"Can I kiss you?" he asks.

I nod fervently. His mouth meets mine, tongue sweeping into my parted lips. My heart bangs around in my chest, my stomach coils. I thought I understood pleasure, but I was wrong. There's so much more out there than I realized.

Silas leans back and says, "You're wet, ready. Fuck." He licks my lips and moves on top of me, cock pushing at my entrance. "Slow and gentle. You let me know if it's too much."

He pushes in and it's so different—so good. I'm slippery and ready and his movements are firm but kind. Even while he's inside of me, he keeps his thumb on the place that sends shudders up my spine. I feel the same deep pressure, but it's not bad. If anything, it's not enough.

"Is this okay?"

"Yes." My legs spread wider and Levi cradles me as I open up. "Keep going."

He pushes in all the way, inch by inch, stretching me as he goes. I lift my hips up to meet his and he grins down. "You want more."

It's not a question, but I nod anyway. He withdraws and goes back in again, this time stretching me further. It hurts a little, but the pain is good, lost under Levi's touch and Silas' sparking touch.

"I want you to relax all the way, baby," he says, kissing me on the stomach. "I'm going to fuck you now, and I want you to let go." He rises above me, his muscular arms holding me up. He pumps in and out of me, and while I'm caught up in the movement, he bends to kiss me, saying, "Take a deep breath."

I do as I'm told, but I'm slowly losing focus. Through the haze of desire, I feel Levi behind me, his hips rocking against my backside and his breath hot on my neck. His fingers pluck my nipples, sending electricity across my skin. It's the kind of pressure I need—want—but it isn't the harsh pain of our sessions. Having two men pleasure me all at once is a new high, one that strips away the worry that I'm not enough, that I'm not worthy.

"That's it," Silas says, coaxing me toward the orgasm. His jaw is clenched tight. I know him well enough by now that it won't take much to pull him to the edge. He pumps his cock inside and Levi breathes heavy in my ear.

Their need spurs on my own and "I—oh—" I buck upward, the coil of tension that had been winding up inside springs, sending shock waves from my belly through every other inch of my body. I shudder, clamping my thighs around Silas' body and grabbing onto his shoulders. He seizes, body rigid, as he punches into me.

"Fuck, fuck, fuck," Levi mutters in my ear, his body taking a final rock behind me. Beyond the warmth cascading through my limbs, I feel damp heat spreading across my lower back.

I look into Silas' eyes and smile. "That... thank you."

I look over my shoulder at Levi. His cheeks are flushed, and he opens his mouth to speak, but I lean in and kiss him, cutting whatever apology or excuse or anxiety off at the source. His mouth is frozen at first, but he loosens up and kisses me in return.

As we part, and the taste of Levi is strong on my lips, it comes to me that this may be the last time I feel this kind of contentment—this sort of happiness—and I curl up in these men, holding onto the feeling as long as I can.

* * *

The feeling of connection follows me to the dining tent. It even dampens some of the awkwardness of walking in with Elon as my escort and not my mate. He'd showed up after we had all cleaned up and dressed. There was no sign of what we'd just accomplished together—the bed was made. Our hair straight. But the deep crease on his forehead and the suspicious look in his eye made me think he knew that something had transpired between the three of us.

"I can go to breakfast on my own," I tell him. It's obvious he's in a bad mood. As usual.

"Rex doesn't want you walking around the campground alone."

"There's a solution to that." I glance up at him. He looks tired, like he barely slept, and his jaw is unshaved. "He could do it himself."

He grunts in reply and reaches into his pocket. "I have something for you." He hands me a small envelope. My name is across the front in even handwriting. Female handwriting. Any hopes it's from my future mate are dashed.

"You're my messenger now?"

His reply is curt. "Like everyone else here, I do as I'm told."

I pause outside the dining tent and open the envelope. It's an invitation for a women's meeting in Margaret's tent for breakfast.

"Do you know anything about this?" I ask.

He scans the details. "It's for women. Why would I know?"

"Imogene!"

I turn and find Maria a few steps away. She's dressed in an apron, with her hair tucked in a bandana.

"Hi!" I give her a hug. "What's with the apron?"

"They asked all the newly Ordered to help out in the kitchen. It's tradition. I've been looking for you."

"I had no idea." I glance at Elon, but his expression is blank. "Maybe I missed the memo."

"Or maybe the mate of Anex's son doesn't have to work the kitchens." She smiles good-naturedly and then winks. "I'm sure it's only one of the perks."

The first image that comes to my mind is Levi and Silas this morning in bed. I choke back a cough and say, "Nothing more than any new mate, I'm sure."

"Well, it's good to see you. I want to catch up. Will you be at the women's session this afternoon?"

"I'm going to try. I have a few obligations first."

She gives me another hug, and just smelling her apple scented shampoo makes me wistful for when we used to live together in the domum. Things were easier then. I knew who I was and what my role was in the community. Now I'm mixed up and turned around in a world of emotions and confusion.

Elon leads me through the campground toward the center tents. Although Anex speaks from the main gazebo, several smaller yurts have been set aside for groups to meet more privately. The closer we get to these tents, the further away I feel from the rest of the community.

"Is Maria right? Did they let me out of kitchen duty because I am Rex's ordered?"

"Probably," Elon says, sidestepping a tether. "Things are different in the inner circle. There are different expectations for you."

"Like eating breakfast with one of the spiritual mates."

"Like that," he agrees.

"Is it wrong that I'd rather be working with the others from my domum?" I don't really know why I ask Elon anything. His answers are always short and limited. His façade as hard as his muscles. "I don't feel like I'm anything special. Certainly not with how Rex treats me."

He stops at a tent but blocks the entrance. "Being in the inner circle is complicated. There are, like your friend said, perks. But it also comes with the burden of knowing how Serendee operates. Anex has determined that you are worthy of knowing these things."

To hold them over my head, I wonder. To force me into compliance? "Like how the community really is funded."

His eyes dart around. "Yes."

"Am I to assume that once I enter that tent, I'm going to become even more educated in the ways of Serendee."

"I told you, I don't know." But something in his gray eyes tells me that he knows more than he lets on. Is he protecting me or keeping me ignorant? Compliant?

Every day is something new—something that chips away at my core belief system yet requires me to have even more faith in Anex and The Way. All I've learned in the last day is that there is no escaping the game.

* * *

Once again, Margaret outshines the rest of the community. Her guests, five other women besides the two of us, sit on soft padding, drinking tea and eating pastries inside her cozy tent. The tea is served in real China, painted with delicate pink flowers and rimmed in gold. The pastries are from the Serendee bakery, light and flaky. The blackberry preserves inside come from the berry shrubs that line the fencing on the backside of the farm. I eat mine slowly, methodically, mostly to keep something to keep my mouth busy.

The other women are all Anex's spiritual mates. I've seen them around him when he makes presentations—or gone to them in a time of need. They're the buffer between the community and Anex—necessary because his time is so valuable, and people crave his attention and opinion. There are men too, like Levi, who teaches the VRS classes or other instructors or founding members. But these women are important. Not just to Anex, but to the whole of Serendee.

I'm introduced to everyone; Jane has been with Anex the longest —right after Rex's mother died. She's the oldest, but the gray hair and fine lines don't detract from her beauty. She's quiet and kind. Ansley sits next to her, small but full of life. Her blonde hair is in pigtails that hang in waves over her shoulders. Her pastry sits untouched on her plate. Her food logs are probably immaculate. I set mine down and wipe my fingers, feeling gluttonous.

"It's wonderful to have you here," the fourth, Bridget, says, passing me a tiny pitcher of milk for the tea. "We've all wanted to get to know you a little better. Moving into the main house can be a little isolating."

I smile and nod. She's right. Sort of. It would be isolating if I wasn't juggling the whims and schedules of three men. It's possible that these women, outside of Margaret are unaware of that. "It's been a big change from the domum and living with so many other females."

"Yes," Ansley says. "I lived in the donum, too, and it was weird going from having a million girls around and all their drama to the peace and quiet of the main house." She curls her finger around the handle of her teacup. "Don't get me wrong, I love it. It was just an adjustment."

"Yes," I reply with a knowing smile. "Exactly. I shared a room with several girls for years. We did everything together; eat, clean, lessons, play." I think about seeing Maria earlier that day and how far apart we seemed now. "I miss them."

"Well," Margaret says with a small grin, "that's why we're here. I noticed that some women were struggling with their roles once they entered a more mature phase of life—one outside the domum. We've all left things behind."

"Friends and family," Jane says. "The structure of the domum and the support of the housemothers."

Their words strike home. I have missed all of those things. Maria, Clarissa, and the consistency. It was so very consistent.

"We started a new group." Margaret looks at me. "It's very exclusive, and the goal is to form an empowering, supportive group of women that are dedicated to both Serendee and The Way. We'd like you to consider being a member."

"Oh." I'm flattered. Incredibly so. And it sounds like what I've been missing in all the recent chaos. I've been so lost in pleasing Rex and training with the guys, I've lost focus. "That sounds amazing."

"It's not something to take lightly," Bridget says, tucking her dark hair behind her ear. "It requires a significant commitment. Part of the problem is that once we leave the domum or our old lives, some of that automatic accountability is gone. Sure, we still have our logs, but we're more independent, and it's harder to stay on the path toward self-actualization when we're also focused on caring for someone else."

"Staying true to our inner female is important while also not succumbing to indulgency," Margaret says. All four women seem excited about this group and it's infectious. I want what they have. "There are some conditions for joining the group. It's incredibly exclusive. It's also a secret. No one can know about it."

"A secret?" I stumble over this admission. Our lives in Serendee are so exposed. Logs, journals, group meetings and public expressions. "From everyone?"

Margaret takes my hand. "I know that when you bond with someone, it feels like everything should be shared, but it's important to keep a few things for yourself. It's a select group of women and anything we share between us is in strict confidence." She tilts her head. "Don't you think Rex's confidants know things about him that you do not?"

"I'm sure they do. They're very close."

"Well, you can have the same."

"And Anex is okay with this?" I ask.

"Anex is not involved, but he's given his blessing. He knows how important it is for women to support one another, but," Ansley says, "this group is not for everyone. You have to have strong fortitude and a deep understanding of The Way. Only a few women are chosen."

"Think on it," Jane says. "Meditate and journal. Search your heart. Once you join there is no going back."

"When do you need to know?"

"The summer solstice," Margaret says. "It marks a new season."

As quickly as it's brought up, the subject changes, and Jane refills my tea. I already sense the bond between these women. The solidarity of their faith and determination. They aren't the sheep that Rex complains about. They're strong and true. This group could be another way to show him that I'm different; special. A way to show him that I'm worthy of being his mate.

37

____

E lon

Some things are certain in this life. Playing the annual basketball game for Anex's birthday is one of them. The entire party walks down to the gym and the spectators pack the stands. Back in the locker room, Peter, one of Anex's confidants, passes out shirts for the game. Purple, Anex's favorite color, marks his team. Orange is for the opposing. I pull the purple shirt over my head and listen to the guys talk about the weekend. Everyone seems to be in good spirits—why wouldn't they? They're having an amazing time—good food, fellowship, the honor of being chosen for the game. They haven't had to spend the past twenty-four hours dealing with Rex's mess, or carrying Imogene's shivering body back to the tent, or seeing her tear-stained face as she came to the realization her betrothed is a monster.

Something about my friend is broken, and I worry it is beyond repair. I've known it for some time, but he seemed content to take his energies out on the women in town or through the thrill of our business dealings. I figured he'd settle down once he agreed to an Order, and I assumed our efforts to make her less like the female sheep that fill Serendee's domums, would appease him. But I realize now he'll never be satisfied. Not until he has broken everyone inside this place, the same way he is.

There's a problem with his methods.

Anex may not have the guts to take out his own son, but he will punish everyone around him. Everyone that failed. Me. Silas. Levi. And especially Imogene.

I will never get a mate of my own.

Silas will never advance out of the position of a whore. Not until his looks fade and he's no longer useful.

Levi will never ascend to the higher levels of instruction.

And Imogene? She won't be let free if Rex truly rejects her. She'll be blamed for the failure. A final strike after what happened with her mother. If she is even allowed to stay in Serendee she'll end up at the whim of Anex. No mate. No home of her own. No job. Nothing.

It shouldn't bother me, and I shouldn't care, but I don't like the way all of this sits on my chest. The rest of us have had the dark side of Serendee's claws in us for a long time. Imogene? She didn't ask for this.

"Elon!" Anex calls. He's sitting on the bench tying his shoes. He eyes my bruised face. "You going to be okay for the game?"

I touch the bruised skin. "Yeah, it's nothing big. Just a little skirmish last night."

"Anything important?"

"Not enough to keep us from winning the game." I glance over at Silas, who is changing across the room. "What do you think, Silas? Twenty-point lead?"

"Twenty-five." He pulls his shirt over his head. He's a good player to have on the team. Lean but strong—fast. Levi is a quiet force. Peter is a killer center, hand-picked by Anex to fill out our team. The only weak spot? Anex. He's smart and surrounds himself with stronger, more skilled athletes. There are other second-stringers hanging around, just happy to bask in the glow of Anex's good will. No one that will outshine him. We all know our place. There's only one player in Serendee that doesn't follow those rules.

Rex.

Which is why he was kicked off the team a year ago. And why, as we walk into the gym to a packed crowd, seeing him standing with the opposing team dressed in an orange T-shirt is a complete shock. His jaw bears the brunt of my fist from the night before, and his lip is split. It just makes him look dangerous.

What the fuck is he doing here?

There are never 'big' moments in Serendee. Everything runs smoothly. If not? The fallout is not worth it. That is ingrained in us from childhood. But sometimes there are small, rippling disturbances. Rex is six foot four, with the wingspan of an Olympic swimmer. Him being here isn't a ripple. It's a fucking earthquake.

"I see my son has shown up to wish me a happy birthday." Anex's tone is light—jovial. I know better. So do Silas and Levi. "I wonder who gave him a spot on the team."

The other captain, Steve, looks across the court with apology. Anex created a complicated system. No one is to say no to his son. What was Steve to do? Tell him he can't play? Anex knows this and says nothing, but the firm set of his mouth reveals his anger. This is a fucking nightmare.

"Do you want me to talk to him?" I ask Anex quietly. "Tell him to get the fuck out of here?"

"No." He looks into the crowd. It only takes a moment to find his Spiritual Mates. Sitting with them is a new face—Imogene. She's noticed Rex as well and her eyes draw from him to mine. "Maybe he's here to impress his betrothed."

Levi grunts, but busies himself with stretching. Is Anex truly this clueless about what's happening between his son and Imogene? "Maybe, but still. There's no predicting what he'll do."

"It's fine," Anex replies with his jaw tight. "My son feels the need to test me today. It's a natural result of someone that feels weak and inferior."

The game starts off with an announcement from some of the members of Serendee. They present Anex with a new ball for his birthday—signed by Michael Jordan.

Anex grabs the microphone to a wave of cheers. "Thank you all for the touching gift. As you know, Jordan is a hero of mine. He is tough, competitive, ruthless. He doesn't worry about what others think. His goal is to win. He expects perfection from not only those around him but also himself. He never compromises." His eyes flick to Rex sitting on the bench. "I'm proud to have my son with me here today, Rex, come on over and give your old man a hug."

I cross my arms over my chest, waiting, watching. Levi shifts next to me, a tell of his apprehension. The audience has no comprehension of the animosity between these two. How close Rex is to walking away and shattering the illusion. Rex follows his father's command and jogs to center court. Imogene watches from the bleachers, conflict written on her face. She should be conflicted. Both men provide hope and a danger to her.

Rex and Anex hug in the middle of the gym, bringing a round of stomping feet and cheers. Although Rex has a foot of height on him, his father takes his face between his hands and draws his head down, whispering something in his ear. From my angle I can see that Rex responds, his features tense. It's too low to hear—it appears intimate and personal—and no one presses for more. It's just a father and son sharing a moment.

They part and go to their opposite sides of the gym. Levi, shockingly, is the one to ask. "What did you say to him?"

Equally surprising is the fact that Anex answers. "I told him that if he made a fool out of me, I would ruin everything he cares for in this life."

It's a pointed threat. For Rex as much as the three of us.

"What did he say in return?" I ask.

"Nothing," he lies, pulling a sweatband over his forehead as he steps onto the court.

We follow him onto the court and the referee, a guy named James, tosses the ball in his hands. The orange team is led by Rex, and they take their positions on the court. A moment later, the game starts with the screech of James' whistle and the ball being tossed in the air. Peter jumps, but Rex gets there first, tipping the ball forward.

It's an intentional move—one that makes it clear that he's not going to bow down to his father. Not in this game or anywhere else. More than ever, I'm determined to stop my friend. I can't let him take us all down. Not like this. Not over something so petty and false.

I run down the court, ignoring the cheering crowd, and throw my arms up in defense. I'm bigger than Rex, both of are still sporting injuries from the fight the night before. He dribbles the ball lazily, tongue darting out at his split lip. I lunge for the ball and he spins, jabbing his elbow into my side. Silas is on him in a heartbeat, slamming his chest into Rex's. Silas does his best to get the ball out of his hands, but his arms just aren't long enough. I regain my balance, joining in to block him from the net, but Rex finds the gap he needs to take a shot. The ball arcs through the air and swishes through the net.

The crowd isn't sure what to do. Cheer for Rex? Is that okay? Hell if I know. I don't even look at Anex as I throw the ball in his direction. Rex bumps into me on his way back to his side of the court. "You're playing like a pussy. You can't hold back for him and win against me. Pick a side, Elon."

The energy escalates from there. Every ball thrown to Anex is picked off by Rex. Our leader is down on his game and Rex is right. We can't help him win by boosting him up. It's total bullshit and an allegory of our entire life. Damned if you do, damned if you don't. I leap out in front of a ball, going from the orange guard to Rex, intercepting it. I pound the ball on the court, dribbling to the net. I set up the shot ball poised on my fingers. Rex charges at me, knocking me on the ground. The ball spins loose, picked up by his quick hands, but I don't give a fuck. I jump up and chase Rex down. Shouts from my teammates, the fans, everyone bounces off of me. At the opposite end of the court, I tackle him, landing hard on top of his body. Using all my weight, I pin him down and say, "Don't do this. Not now."

I punch him in the face, the sound of my fist crashing into his jaw echoing in my ears. Before I get the next strike in, hands grab me from behind. I hear Levi shout and Silas pulling me back. Rex grins at me and gets his hands on my chest, shoving me off.

"You're just here to fuck things up," I tell him. "Get out of here."

"Why? Because I'm winning?" His eyes dart around. "Because I'm not going to play this stupid little game anymore?"

"Stop!" Anex shouts, commanding the attention of the whole room. Everyone is silent. Everyone. Anex is a man of many things, but anger isn't one of them. "Get him out of here. Now."

Rex spits blood on the floor and says, "If you want me out of here so bad, Old Man, why don't you make me."

Anex cuts me a long, hard look and says quietly. "Now."

It's all the excuse I need, and I grab him from behind. He doesn't fight me, not as much as he could and when we get outside, I shove him against the brick wall of the gym.

"What the hell are you doing?"

He runs his hands through his hair, the temples dark with sweat. "I'm done, Elon. It's over. I'm leaving."

"Bullshit," I bark, done with his theatrics.

He holds my eye. "I'm serious."

"He won't let you come back," Levi says.

"I don't want to come back. That's the whole point."

"Well, I'm glad you have that choice," Silas says, voice rising with anger. "You're destroying us, you know that, right?"

"We're men now. Not boys," he says, and I hear the sincerity in his voice. He is serious. "It's time for you to live your own life."

Levi says. "We were always loyal to you."

"If you were loyal, you'd be happy that I'm walking out of the gates of this place or," he glances at the three of us, "you'd be walking out with me."

No one speaks. No one, because what Rex is talking about is dangerous. It's Regressive. It's the kind of talk that destroys lives for real, and none of us are willing to do that—not even for him.

"What about Imogene?" Silas asks.

"What about her?" Rex's eye twitches. "Imogene isn't your concern."

I laugh. For real, laugh. "The minute you agreed to get Ordered and handpicked her to be your mate, you made her part of our lives.

We can't pretend she doesn't exist or that you're not dooming her by leaving like this."

"You think she's safer with me here? Because I've seen what happens to the women I care about." He swallows. "She'll be fine."

"Are you pretending you care about her?" Levi asks. "After what you did to her last night? You just don't care about anyone, Rex. Not us, not her, not Serendee. You only care for yourself."

Rex's jaw clenches and I brace myself to stop him if he jumps on Levi. He just shakes his head and looks more exhausted than I've ever seen him. "You don't understand. You never will and I envy that." He looks between us. "I'm leaving at midnight. If you want to come with me, come. If not, this is goodbye."

Watching Rex walk off hits like a punch in the gut. We've been brothers our whole life. Groomed to serve as his confidants. He's bitched about Serendee, and wanting to leave for years, but I never thought he'd actually do it. Not until now.

38

———————

I mogene

"I'm leaving at midnight. If you want to come with me, come. If not, this is goodbye."

Rex's words ring in my ears long after he said them. Would he really leave Serendee? I, more than anyone, understand the ramifications of such an act. There is no coming back to Serendee if you leave.

I'd slipped out the back door of the gym just after they dragged Rex off the court and eavesdropped on their argument. I've never seen any of them this angry—or defeated.

After Rex walks off, I follow him. I keep my distance, taking the long walk from the campground back to the main house. He goes in the front door and although I'm not close enough to see him; I suspect he's going to his suite. His door is unlocked, and I can hear him in his room. My stomach sinks when I see him, tossing fat rolls of cash into a black bag, along with various personal items.

"So you're leaving," I blurt.

He doesn't look up, just continues to pick through his bedside drawer, picking and choosing items to toss in his luggage. "I am."

"But—the Solstice is tomorrow. We've been seen around the

campground. You chose to come and now you're just going to abandon me because... what? You want to run away? You hate your father? Or am I just not good enough for you? Even with all the sacrifices I've made for you."

He snorts. "I doubt having Silas teach you how to get off was a huge sacrifice."

I step into the room and close the distance between us. He looks up, but before he can react; I slap him hard across the side of his face that is already bruised from the night before. He doesn't recoil, not even an inch, but he clenches his jaw and closes his eyes, a sure sign he's holding back from retaliation.

I'm not finished. "I violated my beliefs for you. I went against The Way and the values instilled in me. I subscribed to the training requested of me for you, which put me in positions I never thought I'd be in. Not just sex outside my mating, but secular things. Dirty things." I glare at him, fighting the shame. "I know you may not care, but I do, and now I'm tarnished in the eyes of this community. In the eyes of your father. You've ruined me."

Now I'm finished and I spin on my heel. I'm stopped by his strong hand, clamping down on my upper arm and pulling me back with a hard yank.

"I told you up front my expectations for this relationship. I made my intentions perfectly clear. You are the one that conspired with my father and confidants. They are the ones that convinced you to go against your beliefs. Not me."

"You forced yourself on me." I say, hoping the accusation gets through to him.

His lip curls up. "You liked it. Don't pretend like you didn't." His fingers tighten around my bicep. "Did it ever—ever—cross your mind that my actions aren't selfish? That maybe I was trying to do the right thing?"

I shake him off and step back. "By assaulting me? By forcing me to my knees? By handing me off to your friends? Or do you mean when you raped me?"

"No, Imogene," his voice is a hiss, "That was to scare you off—to make you hate me. Yet here you are again, in my face, in my room, trying your damnedest to make this work." His eyes dart between my lips and my mouth. "Everything I did was for your own good."

"That's a lie, Rex, and you know it."

He steps forward, and I fear he's going to grab me again. But he just looks down at me. The anger dulls in his blue eyes and is replaced with another emotion. "My father killed my mother."

I frown. "What?" I search his face for any hint of humor. There is none. "What are you talking about?"

"My mother didn't get sick and die, Imogene. She didn't approve of the changes in my father or the direction he was taking Serendee. He wanted to open his marriage to other women—younger women who were more pliable to his manipulations. He started actively recruiting outside the community for wealthy, attractive females to become his spiritual mates and to line his bank account. He started the drug businesses, the illegal stuff." He swallows. "My mother was prepared to expose him for the fraud that he is—a charlatan."

I'd known Rex was struggling with The Way and the lifestyle at Serendee. I knew he hated his father, but I had no idea he was prone to delusions. "Rex, that's crazy."

He turns and reaches into his bag, pulling out a pink journal. "She documented everything. Hid it in a safe deposit box and left me information on how to find it all."

My knees threaten to buckle. Not because I believe him, but because all of this is insane. What will Anex do when he finds out that Rex is spreading lies about him? Or worse, what will he do to me if he finds out I know?

"I know you don't believe me." He says, returning to his packing. "Why would you?"

"It's not that I don't believe you..." The words ring hollow to both of us.

"I picked you, Imogene, because I knew your mother had similar feelings. Just like how I waited for you on the rock that night because I knew you would understand."

The rock? The memory of the night I found him on my rock, high above Serendee comes rushing back. Not only does he remember, he'd been there on purpose, waiting for me.

"What are you talking about?"

"Your mother got away. I thought maybe she had instilled some of that rebellion into you." He tosses the journal back in the bag. "Obviously not." He zips it up. "That's why I forced myself on you last night. Hoping to ruin you for my father so that you'd finally snap out of it."

"Excuse me?" I'm stunned. "You're justifying that as kindness? As pity?"

"I gave you an opportunity, and you're too ignorant to see it!"

"You didn't give me an opportunity—you gave me a life sentence. Silas told me what your father will do to me now that you've ruined me."

"There is one other option," he says, tossing the bag over his shoulder. "I told the others they can meet me at midnight and come with me. I doubt they will. They're too afraid." He touches my chin. "I know you think I did you wrong, Imogene, but I truly was trying to protect you. I lost someone I cared for once before, and I promised myself I would never let it happen again."

He's an abuser. A criminal. A blasphemer. I don't trust him, but there's something about Rex that still draws me to him. Maybe it's because I like being hurt. Maybe I feel like I deserve the pain these men inflict on me. There's a tug at my inner belly that makes me want to follow him. To see this other life he wants so badly. But I also have to consider that a small part of me wants to follow him because I think I deserve a man like him.

"No." I shake my head. "I'm not going with you. Serendee is my home, and I'll accept my fate."

He stops before me and cups my cheek. It's intimate—sweet—nothing like how he's touched me in the past.

"Good luck, Imogene," he says, stepping around me. He walks out the door, headed toward another life, while I stay here and faithfully await the fallout.

* * *

Hours later, Levi pops his head in the bedroom. I've been sitting here since Rex left.

"We've been looking for you," he says, stepping into the room. "Are you okay?"

"Rex is gone."

"I know."

I look up at him—at his red shock of hair and his handsome face. He tries so hard to be a good servant to the community. Losing Rex must cut him like a knife. "Are you leaving with him?"

He sighs and sits on the bed next to me. "No."

"Me neither." I stare down at my hands. They feel detached. Everything is numb. "Did you know about his mother? Or, what he thinks happened to her?"

He glances over at me, surprised I guess that Rex confided in me. "Yes. We were there when he got the information and a key to the safe deposit box. It was before we had free access to go into town, and we had to sneak out. I'd never been to a bank before. I was convinced the whole time we were going to get caught and dragged back home." He picks at his fingernail. "Nothing happened, of course. No one even noticed us other than giving us a few looks for our clothing. All Rex had to do was show them the key. Ten minutes later his whole world turned upside down."

"Do you believe him? That his mother was murdered?"

"I know he believes it, but other than the ramblings in her journals, there is no evidence. I've used my position at the Center to look into paperwork about her death, to try to ease his concerns, but I can't find anything. She has a death certificate, and it states she died from natural causes—an aneurysm, not murder."

"Is there anything we can do?"

He shakes his head. "He won't listen. I love Rex like a brother, but I believe in The Way. I want to help him, but it's not possible. I believe he's lost."

"You're a good friend." I take his hand in mine.

"Not good enough." He rubs his thumb against mine. A gentle, surprising gesture. "Anex wants to speak to you. In his tent."

I bolt to my feet. "Now?"

"Yes."

"Does he know about Rex leaving? Is he upset that I didn't get him to stay?" I pace the room. "I never meant to let him down. I did everything he asked."

Levi hops up and forces me to stop. "Hey, this is not your fault, and he knows it, and if for some reason he doesn't, I'll tell him."

I look up at him, heart pounding with fear. A nervous tear rolls down my cheek. Levi wipes it away. "This is such a mess."

"You're strong, Imogene. Whatever comes your way, I have faith that you can survive."

I don't tell Levi that I want more out of life than surviving.

I want to live.

* * *

Anex's tent isn't as big as I would expect, but he does spend most of his time outdoors, celebrating, and providing lessons at the gazebo. It is large enough for a soft chair, which is where he's sitting when Levi pulls back the flap. One of the guards, dressed in black, stands just inside. A large bed takes up most of the room. It's made neatly and covered in a thick comforter.

"Give us some privacy," he says to Levi and the guard, waving them off. Levi gives me one last look before heading back outside. I wish he could stay—to be witness to whatever is about to happen, but that isn't Anex's command.

My stomach rolls anxiously as I stand before our leader. I bow and touch the center of my forehead, honoring the gift of his presence. He looks tired—but it's been a few busy days of celebration and gluttony. He smiles gently at me and says, "Tell me what the status is on my son."

I feel he already knows the answer, and this is some sort of test. There's nothing I can do but lay myself bare and pray for his mercy.

"Rex is not interested in Mating with me," I admit. "He does not feel as though we are compatible. He has rejected me. I am so sorry I've failed you."

He nods, his expression revealing nothing about how he feels about this. "There's more you aren't telling me."

How does he know? Did Levi tell him? Or Rex? Are there other spies I don't know about?

My cheeks burn with humiliation, but I know it's useless not to confess. "Last night Rex and I... we consummated our relationship."

"Before my blessing."

"Yes." I nod, staring down at the carpet. I could blame Rex and tell his father what he did, but I know better. This is my fault. My weakness. Casting blame will only make me look worse.

"I see." He taps his ring on the arm of the chair. "Do you know where he is now?"

"I don't. The last time I saw him was hours ago."

"This is an unfortunate situation, Imogene. I'd hoped that you could convince him to stay on the righteous path, but my son is stubborn." He taps his fingers on the arm of the chair. "I'd hoped that this could be your retribution—a way to clear your name after your mother's extreme betrayal."

"I know. Thank you for the opportunity."

"You're aware this puts your reputation in a precarious situation?"

"I am, and I am willing to do whatever it is needed to remain in Serendee. I am devoted to The Way and I am at your service."

A dark light flickers in his eyes. "Come forward."

I step toward him, and he gestures to the rug at his feet. I kneel and stare at his ankles until his fingers gently touch my chin and force my eyes upward.

"I knew it was possible that my son would make this decision, which is another reason I put you in training. Serendee doesn't abandon our Fallen. There is a place for you here. A place where you can work toward redemption. I won't lie and pretend it is easy, but nothing about salvation ever is. I understand that all too well. After the solstice is over, you'll move into my wing of the Main House, to a special section of rooms for other people like you." His hand trails down my throat, to the base of my neck. His fingers are calloused. Wrong. "Tomorrow night you will not attend the Solstice celebration. You will wait in your tent until the following morning, and then you will go back to your suite and pack what you came into the house with. Someone will fetch you." He takes my hand and helps me off the ground. He moves close and runs his hand down my arm, stopping at my bicep. His fingertips graze the side of my breast. A shudder of repulsion rolls through me, but I fight to control it. "This isn't the end, Imogene, it's a new path, one that I will guide you down personally."

"Yes, Anex. Thank you." I bow once again, touching my forehead, and hastily exit the tent. I inhale the fresh air, hoping to fight back the nausea rising from the pit of my stomach. I should feel honored. Saved. But those are not the feelings consuming me right now.

I am afraid.

39

Silas

Levi and I split off from one another on the main floor as we search for Imogene. We'd gone back to the gym after the altercation with Rex and she was gone. He takes the front staircase and I go toward the back. Heavy footsteps echo off the hardwoods and I look up. Rex is coming down the stairs. He pauses when he sees me, clutching the bag hooked over his shoulder.

"You can't stop me, Silas."

"I'm not trying to stop you." I narrow my eyes. "I'm not here for you at all."

"Then you won't mind getting out of my way."

I step aside, and he moves past me.

Anger wells inside and I swing around. "You know what will happen to her, don't you?"

He pauses and sighs. "A letter will be delivered to my father in two days asking him to assign her to one of you." He glances back. "I can amend that. Do you want her as your mate? I can make it happen. He may be willing to make an exception under the circumstances."

The circumstance that he created when he took her virginity, abandoned her, and left her in ruins.

"No," I tell him, although it's not entirely true. I just know it isn't right. "You can't. I know you think you're aware of how Serendee functions—and for much of it, you do, but your father has secrets." I frown. "We all have secrets, Rex."

"If you're telling me, my father is deceitful, I'm not surprised. He did kill my mother after all."

I inhale deeply. Rex has often stood by his conviction that his father killed his mother, and of the three of us, I know more than anyone what Anex is willing to do with those that do not follow his lead. "What do you think he'll do to your rejected mate?"

For the first time, I see doubt in his eyes. "You think he'll kill her?"

"No," I reply. "I think he'll do something worse."

His hand grips his bag. "How much worse?"

I jerk my head toward the staircase. "I'll show you."

* * *

The hallway looks like all the others, just another in the never-ending maze running through the house. But to get to this one you have to have been here before and there's no doubt in my mind that Rex has never come down to this part of the house.

There are a dozen doorways, six on each side. A small window with a sliding cover is in the center of each one. Keypad locks secure the knobs.

"What is this?" Rex asks, staring down at the locks.

"This is where your father keeps the Fallen."

"Regressives?" he asks.

"No. The Fallen. They're believers—devoted usually, but they've also had some kind of infraction and are sent here for re-education." I slide open the window covering and look inside. A small redhead sits on the bed. Her eyes dart to the window and she stares at me until I step aside and let Rex peer in.

"Who is that?"

"Her name is Bethany."

"She looks young." He glances in again. "What is she doing in there?"

"She's fifteen. She violated The Way when she snuck out of her domum and met up with a boy. Your father sentenced her to come here for punishment."

"For meeting up with a boy?"

"For violating The Way and not waiting for her Ordering. Anex believed she needed personal intervention, isolation, and training. If she submits to these things and repents, she may ultimately be allowed back into the community."

Rex looks at me. "How long will that take?"

"As long as your father determines." I slide the cover shut. "A few people have been in here for years."

I walk to another door and open it. A different young woman is curled up asleep on the small bed. Her skin is pale and her hair stringy. Rex peers in and says, "I know her. That's Charlotte Bently. I recruited her."

"Me too."

He did the work to bring her in; I did the work to make her stay. We're both responsible for this woman's fate. "What did she do?" he asks.

"She tried to contact her family, who Anex knows have been looking for her. They have resources." He nods. Her family's wealth is one reason she was targeted. "She's been down here for a few weeks."

He steps back. "Why are you showing me this? I already know what my father is capable of. All you're doing is proving the point."

"I'm showing you this because this is Imogene's fate. One of these boxes."

"I gave her a choice. Just like I gave you."

I shake my head. "Losing everyone you love and to run off with the man that abused you? That doesn't sound like a choice to me."

"Then what about you?"

I look down the hall. The guilt I feel for my participation in bringing these women here threatens to drown me. "Not all of us can walk away, Rex. That is a privilege only you have."

"You won't make me feel bad about this." He exhales. "I can't stay here."

He turns to walk away and I call out to him. "You know, I think this is exactly what he's wanted this whole time."

He narrows his eyes. "What are you saying?"

"The people down here... they're all women, Rex. Young, beautiful, independent women. Your father brings them here to break them. To use them." I stare at Bethany's door. "He claims them, because he can, and calls it "training" or "reintegrating." Imogene was a test—one he knew you would fail. One that sends her straight to him."

"I don't believe you." He shakes his head. "This is just your way of trying to get me to stay, so that you'll continue to have my protection and my father's favor. I want you to come with me, but you won't. That's on you."

He turns to leave, but I grab his arm, fueled by more than my own anger. Fear rolls up my spine. "You don't believe me because you think you understand Serendee, but you don't. You've lived a charmed life. Your father gives you everything you want because you're goddamned royalty. Women, money, drugs, sex... there are no limits, but the rest of us... we've made our sacrifices."

"That's—"

"I'm your father's whore, Rex."

"Stop," he says. "He never—"

"Not for him, no." I look at the locked doors. "That is what these women are for. He trained me to whore myself out for the Community. For money and assets and power. I do whatever it takes to bring them in; I charm them, wine them, fuck them. Elon and Levi are tangled in similar strings. We've accepted that this is our role in Serendee, but once you walk out the door, Imogene will suffer the same fate."

In all these years, I've never been this truthful to Rex, but this isn't about me. It's about an innocent. Imogene deserves better than to be locked behind one of these doors because of his petty differences with his father.

"Don't do this to her," I say, hoping he'll do the right thing.

His jaw clenches, and his eyes dart to the ground. "I'm sorry, Silas, but the girl isn't my problem."

As he walks away, the emotion I feel isn't disappointment. It's resignation. Rex is his father's son, spoiled and entitled. Asking him to do something for someone else?

It was never going to happen.

40

———————

I mogene

I'm packing the tent when I hear the soft clearing of a throat in the doorway.

"Clarissa," I say, surprised to see my old house mother, "what are you doing here?"

The expression on her face says it all. "I heard about your Ordering."

"Yes," I go back to sorting, "I've been rejected. Rex didn't want me after all."

She walks over and brushes the hair off my cheek and gives me a hug. "I know it doesn't seem like it, but it's not the end for you."

"It certainly feels like it."

"I don't think you know about how I ended up being a house-mother, do you?"

"No." The girl's in the domum gossiped, wondering why she didn't have a mate of her own. "Whatever the reason, you're very good at it."

"Thank you." She smiles and sits on the bed next to my bag. "I came to Serendee from the outside, recruited. I was instantly intrigued by the community and wanted to follow The Way, but Anex has to make sure we are truly loyal. Have you ever heard of collateral?"

I shake my head.

"Some people offer up money, others land or valuables. I had none of that, so I had to offer up something different." Her smile is tight. "I had to earn my place in the community and once I did, he assigned me to house mother."

"What did you have to do?" I ask, because that's the question. What does a fallen have to do to earn her way back into the fold? "I'm scared."

She places her hand over mine. "You're strong, Imogene. Beautiful. You've spent these last few weeks learning how to provide pleasure to a man. I am confident you can give Anex what he needs to lead you down the path of redemption."

As usual, she doesn't speak with transparency, no one here does. Well, no one but Elon, Silas and Levi. They've never hidden the truth from me, but the truth is clear. She gave her body to Anex. Her greatest asset.

"What if I fail again? Then what happens?"

"You won't fail. You're a fighter, Imogene. It's in your blood."

Clarissa gives me another hug and walks out of the tent. Her final words linger, tickling at my spine. I've never considered myself a fighter. Everything I've done has been compliant, focused on immersing myself in The Way, and most of all, not being like my mother.

What would she say about this? About my failed Order. About my rejection. But most of all, my punishment.

She wouldn't have stood by and waited for Anex to control her future. She would have saved herself—run. I look at the door of the tent and think about Rex's invitation. He'd offered for me to go with him, but where? How? The thought of leaving my home and everything I've ever known for a man that resents me is terrifying.

More terrifying than what awaits me tomorrow?

Rex doesn't love me. He doesn't even care for me and the accusations he's made about his mother... well, both father and son are dangerous.

The question is... which one do I pick?

41

I mogene

THE SUN RISES in the east, casting the whole field in a warm pink glow. I sit on the bed in my tent. Other than the small box next to me, everything I bought is packed neatly by the door. I didn't go meet Rex. My future and my fate lie in Serendee. With Anex's command. I've seen the secular world and I don't want any part of it. Even if it means I'm Fallen.

Outside I hear the start of the day, eggs cooking in the dining tent, happy voices talking about the Solstice ceremony later in the day. I wait as I was told—when it's over, I'll settle into my new existence.

I don't know how long I sit, although it's enough time to chew my nail to the quick. Every time someone walks by the tent entrance, I look up, expecting someone to come for me. Elon? Levi? Or did they run with Rex? Will Anex send Clarissa or Margaret or will it be one of the guards dressed in black? The figures walk past, and no one enters. Eventually, I grow used to the foot traffic, which is why when the flap opens, I barely notice. It's not until he's standing right over me that I blink and take him in.

"What are you doing here?" I ask, rising to my feet. "Why?"

His jaw is made of marble—hard set and clenched. "Giving you up to my father means that I'm letting him win. I thought that by rejecting The Way, and leaving, I was protecting you. It seems my father anticipated that." He lifts his chin. "I thought that by accepting the Ordering I would be giving him control, but I realize it's the opposite. He wants me to fail—to leave you abandoned and Fallen. Vulnerable. I won't let that happen."

I look up into his stormy eyes. "So you want me to be your mate?"

"Yes." His answer is gruff. "But you must understand what I will require of you."

"Whatever you demand," I say quickly. Too quickly.

His hand slides behind my neck with a tight grip, forcing me to look up. "You will do everything I ask of you—whether it makes you uncomfortable or not. You will fulfill my every need and desire. You will keep my secrets and not betray me."

"I will do what you ask of me." I'm willing to give this man everything, even if it means violating my beliefs, but I do have one limitation. "But if you're my mate, it has to look real. I want you to come home at night. Every night."

He stares at me for a moment, but then his lips curve. "I can agree to that but understand that if I am not getting my needs met elsewhere, you will have to meet them instead."

I swallow back the rising emotions and nod. "I will."

"You will continue with your training," he continues. "The others will make sure you are prepared not just for me, but for the role of my Mate. I want you to know the truth about this community. I will not have a blind sheep standing by my side."

He wants them to continue training me? My skin burns at the memory of Silas and Levi's hands on me. Of Elon's kiss. "If that's what you want."

His fingers tighten their grip. "My brothers are all I have. I trust them with everything, including you. But they are as trapped here as much as you are. As much as I am. Together we will reveal to the rest of Serenedee that my father is a fraud and murderer. Are you capable of doing that?"

What he's asking is harder than anything else—worse than the training or agreeing to fulfilling his needs and desires. He wants me to betray my people, my community and, most of all, my leader.

I almost say no, but that vein of blood pumping through my system—my mother's blood—compels me to follow in her footsteps, to possibly find out what happened to her and to Rex's mother. Maybe I will prove him wrong and he will be satisfied. "I'm ready to be your partner, in all things."

He jerks his head toward the door. "We should go, the ceremony is starting."

"Wait." I return to the bed and pick up the box, handing it to him.

His eyebrow raises. "What is this?"

"It's your gift. For the Solstice."

"You were prepared for me to come back for you?"

"Not really." It hurts to admit that, but it's true. "I hoped."

He opens the box and pulls out the leather cord. Two beads are nestled next to one another. It's a symbol of a joined couple. He runs his fingers over the beads and then holds out the cord with one hand and then his wrist.

"Put it on," he demands.

I take the cord and wrap it around his wrist two times, then secure it with a knot. Once we leave this tent, there will be no mistaking our commitment to one another. Butterflies flutter in my belly. He holds my eye for a long moment and then pulls me to him, mouth crashing into mine. His tongue tastes sweet and his kiss is demanding—claiming. Fear skates across my skin, combined with the tickle I've come to recognize in my lower belly.

When he pulls away, I know that I have sealed my fate. There's no going back.

* * *

We're late, pushing our way through the crowd of witnesses. I hear the murmurs among the community as they take us in; Rex's fingers are wound with mine, leading us to the front of the Ordered, the cord wrapped around his wrist. I see Elon first, standing just to the side of the stage. His expression is blank, but his eyes follow us as we cut through the flock. Silas stands next to him, the hint of a smile on his mouth, as if he'd hoped we would appear. Levi just looks relieved. Like me, I know he wants to salvage this—return to normal.

Margaret is up on the stage and grins widely. She wanted this for me—for Serendee. Now that Rex has claimed me, I can join her group and do my best to serve the community.

Anex moves to the edge of the stage, his eyes sweeping over the couples, his smile warm and proud. When he reaches us, his expression falters—just for a beat—before he recovers quickly. It lasted long enough that I saw what was underneath; the look of a man that has lost something. Power, control, domination.

Me.

When he graces us with a false, warm smile, my reaction is physical, like someone dumped cold ice down my spine. I glance over my shoulder at the other Ordered, at the witnesses, at the sea of faces looking at the man commanding all of us. They are enthralled by his presence, by his words, but I know better. I know the truth and there is no turning back.

Bile rises to the back of my throat, and I force myself to look at Elon, Silas, and Levi. They are the strongest members of this community, and they too have no real power. We have nothing but one another. At that moment, everything becomes crystal clear. Rex was right. My mother was right. We should have run.

My mate's grip tightens around mine, and he holds me in place. "It's too late, Imogene," he mutters low enough that only I can hear. "Welcome to the family."

42

I mogene

"It's too late, Imogene," he mutters low enough that only I can hear. "Welcome to the family."

Those are the words that haunt me as I watch Rex undress.

The last forty-eight hours have been complicated—confusing—he'd threatened to leave Serendee for good. He'd asked me to go with him. But in the end, we'd both stayed, our bond to one another witnessed by the entire community and most of all, his father.

Elon, Silas and Levi... they'd supported me, but none of it eases my nerves at seeing Rex shrugging his shirt over his broad, muscular shoulders. The last time we were together like this he hurt me—forced his way inside. Rex had claimed me in the physical sense, and I let him because that's how I was raised, what Anex Ordered. And now that he's my Bonded Mate, I'll do whatever he demands, despite the potential for pain.

Pain, I suspect, that will run deeper than the feel of him inside of me.

Methodically, he drapes his shirt over the back of a chair. The Mating quilt gifted to us by the women of Serendee lies smooth and crisp on top of the mattress. I wrap my arms around my waist, desperately trying to ground myself.

This is The Way.

This is what Anex wants.

This is what *I* want.

I repeat the words like a mantra, willing myself to accept them. I'm not afraid of sex. Not anymore. Silas showed me how good it can feel. But we'd left him, Elon and Levi after the ceremony, and I followed Rex back to our suite in the main house. Rex isn't Silas, a man trained to please women with the barest of touches. Rex is a brute. He's angry. Vindictive. And if it wasn't for me—and some strange obligation—he'd be gone from this world for good.

Rex saved me from something tonight, something I'm not even sure I understand, and for that, I owe him.

"Take off your clothes," he says, voice adrift. He faces away from me and when he drops his pants, I see the hard-curved lines of his backside. He's molded of marble. Like all gods should be.

My fingers move to the long row of buttons that travels my sternum, up to my throat. We'd made this agreement. I do what he asks of me—*everything* he asks of me. No questions. No arguments. My hands shake as they fuss with the buttons, and he finally turns, frowning when he sees my struggle.

"Christ," he mutters, coming at me. I stare at his erection, swollen and swinging between his legs. My belly drops, sparking that confusing mix of arousal and fear. His fingers replace mine, pushing at the buttonholes, the tattoo on his forearm shifting as his muscles unfurling as he works. "They make these fucking things like this just to make us crazy," he says, jaw tensing in annoyance. I shiver when the pads of his fingertips brush against my skin. "You realize my father's wives don't wear this type of clothing. He doesn't have the patience."

Irritation flickers in his cool blue eyes, and he grabs the fabric with both hands and wrenches them apart. The sound of tearing fills the room followed by the ping of buttons falling across the hardwoods follows. It took me months to create this dress, sewing each stitch by hand, fastidiously placing every button. In one furious moment he destroyed it—*ruined* it.

I look up at Rex's angry face. I absorb his chiseled jaw, the bright halo of hair, the mean darkness in his eyes. It's in all of these that I see him—the real him. All shreds of the decent man that came to my side at the Ceremony have vanished.

Good, I understand *this* Rex better.

He hurts. He takes. He controls. All I have to do is survive.

He pushes the dress off my shoulders, allowing it to pool at my feet, while his finger runs under the strap of my bra—one Elon bought me—and he tugs that, too, until my breasts break free. His fingers ghost around my nipple—toying, teasing—until he tweaks it, forcing a cry from my lips.

He grins and says, "I love that sound, Little Lamb," scooping me up and tossing me on the bed. Not bothering with the covers, he climbs over me, his weapon sharp and pointed between his legs.

I've barely caught my breath, settled my eyes on his intimidating frame when he spreads my legs and presses the tip of his cock against my entrance. My fingers wrap in the quilt, bracing myself for the impact, but he just hovers there, eyes meeting mine.

"You're still taking the contraceptive?" he asks.

I blink, trying to process the words. Contraceptive. The pills Margaret gave me.

"Yes."

He nods and without another word, punches inside. I yelp, then suck in air, trying to work through the intrusion. It burns, the stretching of my inner walls, but pain isn't my enemy. Pain is something I crave to endure. His father taught me that with the hours of relentless lessons, the years of sacrifice, the intensity of Correction. Pain is something I understand, and I emit a whimper, wanting more.

A frown tugs at his mouth and rocks his hips into me. "Does it hurt?" he asks, not stopping.

"Do you want it to?" I ask, because I'm here to please him.

He expression shutters, and he grabs my inner thigh, pushing it wide. The sensation is different, deeper, and a moan builds in my chest. Silas showed me enough about my body to know what it likes. Levi taught me though Corrections what I crave. And Elon... under his darkness, I felt the true heat of passion—I understand *want*. I'm too scared of Rex to feel any of these things, too intimidated by his perfect body, by his cold stare, by the power he holds inside this bed and out. By his birthright.

I lay rigid while he thrusts into me, mute as he rocks his hips with rugged force.

"Jesus," he mutters, followed by a string of swear words. "It's nice that you're tight, but fuck, you need to let me in."

I don't know what that means, how to be what he wants.

"Unclench a little," he commands, pulling out before slamming back in.

He tears through me, a different sort of innocence stripped away. I smell his body, his scent. I feel the slick heat of his sweat as our bodies slap together. I close my eyes, floating away as he grows more erratic, the grunts coming faster, his hips pummeling into me.

My whole body is tense when he comes and I peek at him, at his clenched jaw, spine stiff, his manhood pulsing deep inside, filling me with his seed. I feel no more lonely when he pulls out than I did when he was inside of me, although when I move to close my legs, he holds them apart, one finger scooping up his seed and pushing it back inside.

I'm still lying there, sticky cum between my legs, pulse pounding from the lack of my own release, confused and conflicted. This is all I'd ever wanted. All I'd ever dreamed.

After all the trials and tribulations, that one act seals it.

Rex and I are officially Bonded Mates.

43

━━━━━━

S ilas

THE BEDROOM DOOR OPENS, and I look past Rex's frame to catch a glimpse at Imogene. All I see is a her naked on the bed before the door snaps shut.

My friend passes, and I reach for the knob.

"Don't you dare go in there."

"And why the fuck not?"

Rex sighs, running his hand through his hair. "Because you'll go in there and hover over her like some mama hen. She needs a minute, and I need to talk to you."

Rex is my best friend—one of them at least—but at all times he outranks us and although I've defied him before, I know now is not the time.

Elon and Levi are both in the living room. Elon sits in an armchair, his body almost too big for the space. His eyes search Rex's as he walks in the room. "You ready to tell us what the fuck is going on?"

"I changed my mind," he says, walking to the refrigerator. He skips the door, moving to the cabinet above where he unearths a bottle of whisky—contraband, but who is going to tell him no? He unscrews the top and takes a long swig. His shirt is untucked. His pants are wrinkled. His face has the pink flush of a man who'd just exerted himself. "We're Bonded. In the eyes of my father, there's no going back."

The last we knew Rex was leaving Serendee. He'd been threatening it for years and after his father's birthday weekend things reached a climax. None of us expected him to show up for the ceremony—or to claim Imogene as his mate.

"So you stayed," Levi says. "Why?"

He looks to me. I'd shown him exactly what happened to women that were not tied to a man in Serendee—women that held Anex's interest. "Does there have to be a reason?" Rex asks. Elon snorts. Even Levi rolls his eyes. He leans against the doorframe. "What?"

"You do nothing without a reason," Elon says. "It's either self-serving or to get back at your father."

"Maybe this time it's both."

It probably is.

"So what?" Levi asks. "You brought her back here immediately following the ceremony and staked your claim?"

"You don't get to tell me how to run my Bonding, Levi." Rex narrows his eyes. "She's mine. Not yours."

"You say that," Elon starts, "but you leave her to us to mold into the woman you want. Were you not happy with the way Levi put meat on her bones? Or the sexy lingerie I bought her before you tore them off? Or the fact Silas tended to her after you ripped her virginity from her so ruthlessly?"

"In the eyes of my father and all of Serendee, she is mine and mine alone," Rex says, crossing his legs at the ankle, "but you're right, this is less about me and more about exposing my son of a bitch father for being a fraud and a predator. I'm also not inclined to give him what he wants, which," his eyes dart to mine, "Silas pointed out to me before the ceremony, is Imogene."

Levi's eyes widen with alarm. "You want to expose him for what? Rex, I know you and Anex have years of problems. I know you think —well," Levi can't say it, '*You think your father killed your mother,*' but we all know it. "Does she know this is your plan?"

"Not that it's any of your business," Rex says, "but I made my demands clear to Imogene before we stepped into the ceremony. We made an agreement."

"What kind of agreement?" Levi asks. His devoutness to Serendee is being put to the test, and sometimes I wonder if he'll eventually break under Rex's Lapses.

"She's to be available to me and to meet my needs at all times. And in return I will play the part of her Mate in front of my father and the other residents of Serendee while I continue to collect evidence of his manipulations."

"What do you mean by play the part?" I ask. Everything about this made me uneasy. It was one thing when it was the four of us humoring Rex's ideas but dragging in an innocent like Imogene made me anxious.

"I've agreed to come home at night. Every night."

Elon's eyebrow raises. "You're abstaining from other women?"

He hesitates, which isn't a surprise. Rex has never denied himself of anything especially the excess found in the secular world. "She's right to want me to come home at night but... she's not ready to meet my needs." He pushes off the wall, eyes meeting each of ours. "She's too timid and unsure. She's still too fucking compliant." I think of her small frame and shiny blonde hair. "I want you to continue with her training."

"You're sure about that?" Elon asks. They're both still sporting the bruises from fighting over her. "You can handle the three of us being with her?"

"Yes. I'm asking you to do it this time—not Anex. That's the difference."

"I'm in," I say, unwilling to give up a chance to be close to her. To protect her from Anex's plans. "Whatever you need."

Rex looks at Elon. He nods. The hold out, of course, will be Levi. He may not be devoted to Anex, but he believes deeply in the tenants of Serendee. It's the foundation of his entire persona. Without it, I don't know who or what Levi would be.

Even so, it's not a surprise when he says, "I'll continue to offer my guidance," because I've seen the effect Imogene has had on him; body, mind, and soul. He wants her as much as the rest of us.

What isn't said aloud is that although Rex claims her as his own, Imogene is not the kind of woman that can be bound to one man. She belongs to all of us.

44

I mogene

THE MESSAGE COMES the next morning, before I leave for work. I have
an appointment at the healer. Even though the office is located downstairs, I still need an escort through the maze of hallways that crisscross their way through the main house.

"Is something wrong?" I ask before Healer Bloom can even speak.
The last time I saw her was the day of The Ordering, when she did a
physical to confirm my innocence.

"No," she replies, giving me a tight smile. "Standard procedure
after the Bonding Ceremony."

I frown. "But it was just yesterday, that seems very fast."

"Not if your Mate is Anex's son."

"Oh," I say, flattening my hand over my stomach. "His father
wants to know if we've consummated the Bonding."

"With their strained relationship, everything is over scrutinized."

"We have," I tell her, feeling the heat in my cheeks. "Bonded."

"I'm sure that is true, but an examination is mandatory." Just like last time she waits while I undress, taking forever to unbutton my dress. I feel her eyes on me as she assesses the non-approved undergarments. I'm to wear secular bras and panties for Rex. She whips out her measuring tape. "You've gained weight."

"At the request of my mate," I explain, knowing that with anyone other than Rex that would be a sign of disobedience. "He prefers a woman with more flesh."

She hums her disapproval. "I suppose he likes the lace undergarments as well."

He does, although Elon picked them out, and I've seen the way Silas has reacted to them. I'd venture to guess all men like them. I swallow. "Yes."

She catalogues my body, running her finger over a pale mark on my wrist. "These marks?"

"From Correction. Everything is documented in my logs." I don't tell her that I no longer give self-correction. Levi has taken over that duty.

Another hum, this one less negative. "Get on the table."

I lay back and once again the bright light shines in my face, making me unable to see anything else in the room. I hear Healer Bloom shuffling about, the roll of her instrument cart, the soft snick of a drawer opening and shutting. She directs me to place my feet in the stirrups, tapping the insides of my knees. "Spread apart, Imogene."

The room grows quiet under her examination, but this time something is different. I understand the touch of a man now. I know the parts of my body that provide pleasure and sometimes pain. The hot button of my clitoris and the deep canal of my vagina. As Healer Bloom examines my body, fingers brush against my clit sending a shuddering wave up my body. I jolt up, moving to shade my eyes from the light, but two hands pin me down by the shoulders.

"What—"

"Shhh, Imogene, settle down." Warm fingers stroke my inner thigh.

Bile rises in the back of my throat. There's no mistaking the voice. Anex.

"What are you doing?" I ask, pulling against the hands holding me down, but they are strong and powerful.

"It's my duty to make sure my son is following through with his commitment to you." I feel the pressure of a finger at my entrance, pushing at the barrier. "You know the problems that I've had with him, the sacrifices I've made to keep him part of Serendee." One finger pushes in, then a second. "It would be just like him to pretend he Bonded with you."

"Why would he do that?"

He chuckles. "To manipulate. Play mind games. To keep you from me." He curls his fingers and my body clenches, trying to expel the invasion. "If he hadn't stepped up at the Ceremony, Imogene, you would have become mine by default. You would have been Fallen and come under my care and training." He feels around for a moment longer and sighs. "It seems as though he staked his claim, didn't he?" He shifts and whispers close to my ear, "Was he gentle when he took you? Or did he barrel into you with the finesse of a bull on a rampage?"

I gasp at his crassness, but he just slips his fingers out of my body as quickly as they intruded. I feel hollow. Repulsed. The light swings away, and all I see are white spots. Blinking them away, I see him standing over the table, handsome. Powerful. Terrifying.

"I want you to understand that I'm watching you." He sniffs his fingers, inhaling my scent, before cleaning them with a cloth. "All of you, and if there's any sign that this relationship is a farce or worse, an attempt to usurp my position, all of you will suffer. Do you understand?"

I nod, wrapping an arm around my stomach, willing the contents of my breakfast to stay down. He isn't just threatening me and Rex. He's threatening the guys as well. "Yes. I understand."

"Good." He offers his hand and obediently, I take it. He leans forward, speaking right in my ear. "Now that he's tasted your tight little pussy, don't expect my son to remain interested. It's a novelty that he'll grow restless of soon."

"Rex and I are Bonded, Anex. In front of you and all of Serendee. I have faith that I can be a good mate and that he won't grow restless of me."

"I hope you're right." He steps back and lifts his hand, ghosting it over my hair. "But if you're wrong, don't worry. I'll always have a room reserved for you." His grin is dark. Wicked. "It's right next to the one I saved for your mother."

As I RUSH to the recruitment office for my shift, I'm forced to reconcile that Rex's indifferent Bonding the night before was more than him just getting off. He was protecting me from his father.

I wasn't a virgin—he'd taken that from me before the ceremony. And I'd had sex with Silas later. But Anex has made it clear he knows everything going on in Serendee. In our private quarters and in our beds. We can't be too careful. Our leader seems too eager for his son to fail.

I'm caught between two powerful men and it's my duty to try to keep the peace.

I manage to work the rest of the day, filing interest forms for potential recruits and organizing pamphlets for members to pass out on the college campus nearby. The upscale University allows a fertile recruiting ground, with so many young people seeking Enlightenment. I always believed I was doing good work by sitting at this desk; that I'd been chosen by Anex because of my character and proof of responsibility. Now, the twisting uneasiness in my stomach is a reality check. Anex has kept an eye on me because of my mother's betrayal—and has been looking for any opportunity to announce a claim on me for his own purposes.

I'm cleaning up my desk when the door opens. I sense his presence before I see him—broad and imposing. Rex appears before me, features tense.

"Rex," I say, smoothing down the front of my dress. His eyes sweep over me, and I wonder if he can tell that I'd been examined— that his father's fingers had been inside of me. "Are you teaching today?"

"No. I was just finishing up on campus and thought I'd stop by to see you home."

"Oh." I'm shocked, but we'd agreed to behave like a Bonded couple. I suppose that's what this looks like. "That would be wonderful. Let me get my things."

I hurry, not wanting to annoy him. His temper is sharp, less explosive, and more honed than the blade of a knife. He opens the door for me, allowing me to go first and when we step onto Main Street, he takes the position next to the sidewalk, protecting me from the passing traffic.

"So you worked on campus today?" I broach, hoping I don't sound lost and clueless. I am. Outside of stealing a cake from his father's birthday celebration and a disastrous picnic, we've barely had a normal conversation.

"I had a few deliveries," he says, eyes watchful as we pass a series of restaurants with seating on the sidewalk. I don't miss the judgment from the patrons as they take in my hand sewn dress. I'm accustomed to the looks, but what's unusual is the way the women's eyes slide right over me and straight to Rex. It's well known in our community how handsome he is, but clearly secular women really do find him as attractive. He seems completely unaware of that as he continues, "Then, I set up another transaction for one of the fraternity houses."

"Selling the product under the barn?" I ask quietly.

He frowns. "Elon shouldn't have shown you that."

"You're right," I say. "You should have been the one to tell me the truth about the businesses Serendee operates under our noses."

The muscle in the back of his jaw tenses and he grabs me by the bicep, pulling me away from a line of people waiting to be seated. He doesn't let go once we're past them, instead pushing me down the alley that leads to the entrance of our community. My breath is knocked out of me as he tosses me hard against the wall. "He shouldn't have told you because it's dangerous. It's not a place for a woman like you."

"Like me?" I ask. "What does that mean?" Does he think I'm untrustworthy, like my mother? A betrayer of Serendee?

His hand is flat against the wall next to my head and our eyes level. "An innocent. A follower of The Way. Someone that doesn't need the burden of Serendee's true weight on her shoulders."

"You don't trust me."

His eyes narrow. "Other than the feel of your pussy clenching around my cock when I'm inside of you, I don't know you, Imogene."

My jaw drops, the shock of his crassness overtaking any other emotion. It's not the first time he's treated me like this. He's a disgusting pig. He's assaulted me more than once. And here I am, Bound to him. God, I'm a fool.

Maybe I should have just let Anex have what he wants.

A hot tear burns at the corner of my eye. Humiliation—and not the first I've experienced today. "I'm no longer an innocent," I say, "You and your father took that option away from me the day you arranged to make me your mate. And the moment I accepted the Order, the weight of this community fell to my shoulders, because you and I are one. We are Bonded. In the eyes of Serendee, and it was sealed when you pushed past my barrier and left your seed inside of me." I place my hands on his hard, muscular chest. "If you don't think you know me, then figure out a way to find out, because I have no choice but to stand by your side."

His eyes narrow. "You spoke to him. Anex. When? Today?"

My cheeks burn. "Healer Bloom examined me." I can't bring myself to say that Anex had done the actual exam. "She gathered proof that we're truly Bonded. Your father," I swallow, "he was there."

His hand clenches around my arm. "Did he touch you?" Before I can answer he tightens his grip and repeats, "Did he?"

I see the dark, murderous, glint in his eye, and I understand then that Rex is hanging by a thread. He's looking for an excuse and he'll end his father if given the chance. I can't allow that. What if he fails?

What happens to me then? What happens to Elon, Silas, and Levi without the protection of their best friend?

"No," I tell him, wincing at the pain of his fingers digging into my skin. "No. He was just there for confirmation, but he's watching us. Closely."

He registers my pain and releases me. My arm throbs, but I take the chance to duck under his arm and hastily walk toward the gate. I fumble with the latch, and his hand comes down over mine, taking over. He stops me before I walk through.

"If he approaches you again, let me or Elon know."

"I will."

"I won't allow him to hurt you, Imogene."

"Why not?" I ask, pushing past him, exiting the secular world for the safety of Serendee, "Or is hurting me something reserved just for you and your friends?"

WE WALK IN SILENCE, the hostility growing between us like bricks in a wall. I regret telling him he has to come home every night. All it will do is create pain. My pain. I'd be better off if he was off in the city, getting his needs met by secular women.

Except that thought makes my stomach hurt.

At the fork in the road, he stops. The main house, where we'd both been living, although separately, looms up the hill.

"We won't be going back to my father's house." He looks down the other road. "We'll live in a cottage like all of the other couples that went through the ceremony yesterday."

"Why?" Mixed emotions swirl in my stomach. In the Main House there were always people around. Staff, guards, Anex's spiritual wives... but a cottage? That feels isolated.

"Because I need some space from him." He glances up at the imposing Main House. "He's a murderer. A criminal." His hand balls in a fist. "I can't be near him any longer, and I don't trust him with you."

His words should be comforting, but they just bring up conflict and turmoil. I've lived my whole life with Anex as my spiritual guide. I can admit things are confusing right now. Anex's behavior... it's discomforting, but he's told us many times that following him, and The Way, is not an easy path. Our own resistances will try to sway us. Our Regressive thoughts will creep in, trying to lure us away from the life he's built for us. I'm not ready to give that up because Rex is delusional and hurt because he lost his mother at a young age.

Join the club.

I follow him down the road, until he stops in front of a pale green house. I raise an eyebrow. "You think this is a cottage?"

He looks down at me, blue eyes cold as ice. "Compared to the mansion? Yes."

The house is a large, two-story, bungalow with a wrap-around porch. "It's quite big for the two of us."

He brushes his blonde hair out of his eyes. "Four bedrooms. One for us and one for each of the guys."

The big news here should be that he's suggesting we'll share a room and I assume a bed, but that's not what forces me to snap my eyes away from the house, toward him. "The guys?"

Elon, Levi, and Silas.

"They'll be living with us. Keeping an eye on you while I'm at work." 'Work' for Rex, means selling the drugs grown in secret underneath Serendee. The real funds Anex uses to bankroll his mission. It's the excuse Rex has to spend his time outside of Serendee around the gluttony of the secular world. He rests his hand on the porch railing and sweeps his eyes over me. "You'll continue with your job during the day at The Center, assuaging my father's suspicions, while I search for the truth about what really happened to my mother."

"And at night?" I ask, needing to be prepared for another round. "What are your expectations of me at night?"

His eyes sweep over me, and he steps close, tilting my chin up with a surprisingly gentle touch. "I expect you in my bed, ready for me."

My body trembles, remembering the ways he forcefully took me, claiming me hard and quick. The memory of pain flickers deep in my belly. Pain is something I've gotten used to, but not the shame that comes with it.

"Of course," I say, pushing the words past the lump in my throat. "Whatever you wish."

He holds my eye for a long moment, like maybe he wants to say more, but ultimately, he drops his hand and climbs the porch steps. There is no ceremony here. No happy couple crossing the threshold, no cake or champagne waiting on the kitchen table or homemade goods from members of the community.

It's just the two of us, both treading water, trying to cling to something that makes sense.

Unfortunately, in this scenario, neither of us can swim and in the end, we'll both drown under the weight of one another.

45

Elon

ALL OF MY belongings are already at the cottage when I arrive. They've been brought over, I assume, by some of the workers in the Main House. There's a whole hierarchy in Serendee. At the top are the Chosen, the inner circle. At the bottom... well, visibly they are people wanting Anex's favor. The minions that do the grunt work around the community. Less visibly? That would be the Fallen, or those who have gone against Anex and The Way. They are not even worthy of carrying my boxes from one house to the other. Their time is spent isolated and in penance.

I've never felt out of step with my place in Serendee. My friendship with Rex solidified my position years ago, but something shifted in the last twenty-four hours. Rex did the right thing by standing by Imogene, but I'm not sure that's what his father really wanted or how the fallout will affect all of us.

"Is anyone here?" I call out, walking down the hall. The bedrooms are on the second floor. Levi and Silas' are both empty, their beds stacked with moving boxes. The master bedroom door is closed, but the faint glow of light shines underneath the gap.

I knock and hear Imogene's soft voice from the other side. "Come in."

When I open the door, I'm not prepared for the sight of her. Not sitting in bed, wearing a little black negligee, made of more lace than silk. It's one of the ones that I bought for her and with the extra meat on her bones she has cleavage that wasn't there a month ago. Her eyes widen when she sees me, and she tugs at the blanket to cover her body. I start to shoot her a command, to tell her to put her hands down and let me see her like this, but I remember things have changed. She's now a Bonded female. Rex says he wants us to continue training her, but can I really still force her to my will?

"I thought you were Rex." The red burn of her cheeks travels down her neck to her chest, making it hard not to look. "He's not here, if you're looking for him. He brought me here, showed me the room and told me he was going out for a while."

Only Rex would leave a beautiful woman waiting half-naked in his bed out of some possibly misguided defiance to his father.

Despite his absence, he is still Imogene's betrothed. I shouldn't be standing here. I take a step back toward the hallway and she blurts, "He agreed to come home every night." I hesitate and raise an eyebrow. "That was the deal between us. He comes home every night and I..." she tries to pull the blanket up higher, "well, I have to do as he says. *Everything* he says."

I'm aware Rex took Imogene's virginity out on that dock in the lake. He and I got into a fight about it—a physical fight that left him with a black eye and me with a bruised fist. He felt like it was his right to claim her, but there are ways to do things in Serendee. Taking her like that, no matter how tempting it was, shouldn't have happened. He could have ruined her in the eyes of the community, or worse, the eyes of his father.

"If you're lucky," I say, thinking it's what she wants to hear, "he'll come home drunk and satisfied and leave you alone."

"You think he's with another woman?"

Oh *fuck*. Not what she wants to hear. Dammit. This is new to me, too.

I think a bit harder on how to respond to this. "I think he's spent a lifetime running away from his responsibilities and trying to dull the pain. Those habits are hard to break."

"Do you think his father killed his mother?"

I blink. I guess he told her his suspicions? That comes as a surprise. "I know Rex thinks that his father killed his mother. Are his suspicions real or delusions? I'm not sure." I walk back into the room and sit on the edge of the bed. "I know losing her almost broke him. Then later when he found the papers she left him, we were already starting to learn about the side of Serendee Anex keeps hidden from the rest of the community. He's struggled with his faith in The Way for a long time. That's why he runs wild when he's outside the walls."

"That kind of talk would get the rest of us tossed out of Serendee."

"Like your mother." Imogene's mother was a full-blown Regressive and had been banished when she was young. It's part of the reason Rex agreed to be Ordered to her. She knows what it's like to lose a mother and, no matter how hard she tries to be devout, defiance runs in her blood. "You won't get tossed out, Little Lamb." I take her hand, which causes the blanket to drop. I push my finger under the leather straps of her bracelet, feeling her warm skin. Rex wears a matching one, signaling their commitment. I stare at her mouth, remembering the kiss we shared when I showed her the secrets beneath the barn. "Rex claiming you made you legitimate. Chosen. Your loyalty won't be tested."

She bites down on her bottom lip and my eyes drop to the smooth skin between her breasts. She's not mine, I remind myself. No matter what liberties I took before. That had been commanded by Anex. I did my job. I made her ready. Bought her these lacy things—taught her how to wear them. Now she belongs to my best friend and is here for his needs, even if he's offered to share.

It's not what I really want. I want *her*, not scraps tossed to me by a friend.

"Somehow I doubt that," she says, quietly.

She may not be tested, but I know I will be. Just the sight of her cloaked in silk and lace... it would be so easy to push her against the pillows and take her right here. She wouldn't fight me. I know that from the pink in her cheeks and the way her chest rises and falls. If she did? There's part of me that knows why Rex did it—why he took her like that. Feeling this Little Lamb tremble beneath him?

It's tempting. Everything about her is tempting.

I look away and catch a glimpse of the two of us in the mirror. My dark hair hangs messily across my forehead and my eyes look wild. I'm exhausted from the weekend of celebration, of fighting, but none of that is what propels me to my feet. It's the way Imogene looks in the reflection—small and innocent. Sweet but sexy. Truly an innocent, vulnerable, little lamb.

And there's no doubt as I walk out of the room without another word, that I'm the big bad wolf.

It's NOT hard to find him. Like all other pack animals, he has a preferred hunting ground, and that's right where I find him. There are two rows of commercial business that surround the University. The Center took up one of these spots for our recruitment office, but otherwise, The Strip, as the college kids call it, is filled with restaurants, bars and other places to hang out. That's the first place Rex goes when he's looking for a quick hookup—and to fulfill his recruitment quota. Two birds, one stone—and hopefully an orgasm or two.

He's leaning against the brick wall just outside the bar towering over a cute redhead he's been putting the hardsell on for weeks now. Anex may be a conniving bastard but he knows how to sell his way of life—Serendee and The Way. Some people are already on a journey and seeking Enlightenment and walk in off the street. But a lot of these people need coaxing—and what better salesman than a guy who looks, and acts, like Rex.

The apple didn't fall far from the tree.

From the way his body is angled, his forearm resting on the wall, glass of alcohol in his fingertips, to the slight lean into the girl, the way he pushes a strand of hair off her shoulder, it's clear he's going in for the kill. Which is exactly why I need to stop him.

"Hey," I call, hands shoved in the pockets of my jacket. "Rex."

He looks up, eyes curious, but quickly shifting to annoyance. "Hey man."

"You need to come home."

He grins—it's for the girl. Cocky and sure. "I'm a little busy."

She glances over at me and does a double take. I don't have that golden boy thing going on like Rex, but I know I'm a good-looking guy. Built. Women are drawn to me.

"I'm sure," I reply. "But I need you back at the house."

His hand slides down her hip. "I'm sure you can handle it," he grins at the girl, "Katelyn and I were just going to go over some of the level one tenants, to see if she's interested in finding out more."

"Tenants, sure." I roll my eyes. I walk over and insert myself between the two of them. "Katelyn," I say, addressing her directly, "I hate to interfere, but do you think you can swing by the Center tomorrow? I'm sure someone, maybe even Rex, will be happy to discuss this further."

"Um..." she looks between us, eyes wide and confused. "I guess so."

"Thanks, sweetheart," I say, giving her my own persuasive grin. "I promise, whatever, um, *information*, my brother was about to give you, will be readily available at the Center during business hours."

Katelyn giggles, but walks off, engulfed by the group of students standing near the front of the bar. Once she's gone, Rex gives me the stink eye and says, "Seriously? What the fuck dude?"

"Your mate is waiting for you at home."

He scoffs. "Trust me, brother, she's better off with me here than at home." He looks wistfully toward the bar. "You realize I wasn't really going over Serendee info, right? I was about to get my dick sucked."

"Yeah, I'm aware, but unfortunately you're not a single guy anymore. You have obligations. At home."

His eyes narrow. "So, you're worried about the Little Lamb all the sudden? Really?"

"I am when I find her stressed and worried, waiting for you to come home."

"What the hell does she have to be stressed about?"

See that's the thing about Rex—or being Rex. He can just exist in his own reality. Sure, he has obligation to Serendee and Anex like the rest of us, but he has a long rope. No one has ever depended on him. "She's a fucking basket case. Totally unsure about her position, here. With you, with her dad, with her mother's history. She has no idea where she stands, which in my opinion, is exactly how your father wants it. I don't blame her for being nervous about it, because it feels like she's nothing but a pawn in a game being played by you and your father."

"If you're so worried about her, why don't you fuck her? I gave you permission."

Jesus. He'll never get it. Never. "You're a prick, you know that?"

"And you're overly invested in my life."

I laugh. God, this is rich. "You think I have a choice about that? You think I don't want to have my own life? My own options." I lunge forward, gripping the front of his shirt in my fist. "My own fucking mate?" I tilt my head, locking eyes. "That's not how our world works. So yeah, I did what I always do, what we all always do, follow up on the mess you leave behind." I nod to where Katelyn had just been pressed against the wall. "Who do you think is going to clean her up tomorrow? Smooth that over?"

Silas. We both know that. He'll be the one to meet her if she shows up tomorrow at the Center or track her down if she doesn't. He'll follow up, soothe her bruised ego and work his magic.

"Jesus, Elon. I'm just blowing off a little steam," he says, having the good sense to look a little guilty. I release him and he shakes his head. "Fucking Imogene... it's like screwing a plank. She just lies there, looking like she's waiting for it to be over."

I stare at him. "Then maybe you need to up your goddamn game."

He waves me off. "Nah. She's too much work."

Of course. That's why he's offered her to us. I get her dressed for him. Silas breaks her in. Levi works on her flaws. It's too late to argue about this—how could I? I'd be dealing with years of ingrained entitlement. I don't have that time—and honestly, it's not my place.

"Come on," I say, "I don't care what you do with her when you get home—just *go* home. You promised."

He relents, but not before finishing his drink. It's then that I notice how wasted he is and it's probably a good thing I showed up when I did. Rex may be Teflon inside Serendee, but outside? Things are different. People are watching and one false move could be a problem for everyone.

46

I mogene

THE SMELL INFILTRATES my dreams at the same time the bed shifts underneath me, jarring me from sleep. Before I can react a heavy hand weighs on my hip, then pins me by the arms. I blink, looking up at the figure in the dark. I can smell him; the spicy scent of alcohol on his breath, the leather from the bracelet I tied to his wrist. Rex straddles me, thighs on each side of my body, my arms caught in his grip.

"You're here," Rex says, running his hand over the side of my breast, "just like I told you to be, just like a good Little Lamb."

"You're drunk." My voice is raspy from sleep. I squirm but he clamps his thighs tighter, holding me in.

He laughs. "And a little high." His fingers reach between us, bunching up the silk and fingers the lace waistband of my panties. I stiffen and he says, "Calm down. I'm not going to hurt you."

The hard press of his erection against my lower belly says otherwise. At least he was true to this word and came home.

My mouth dries as I watch him lift slightly freeing himself from the confines of his pants. He's long and engorged, tip slippery already. The twist of fear and want wars in my blood. Pulse racing, heat building. Silas showed me it didn't have to hurt, but there's also something dark in me that knows I like pain. I think he likes it that way, too, and I brace myself.

He moves up my body, planting my arms under his knees, freeing his hands. He makes quick work of the silk top, tossing it on the floor. His hands move to my breasts, kneading them roughly. I swallow back a cry, knowing it will only encourage him.

"Remind me to thank Levi," he says, fingers circling my nipple and sharply tugging the peak.

"What?" Does he know about the Corrections? How pain turns to pleasure? "Why?"

"I know he encourages you eat more," he pushes my breasts together, enhancing the valley between them. "The results are worth it. Your tits are definitely bigger."

He bends, licking a hot trail between my breasts and then lathing his tongue over my nipple. I shiver from the feel of it, back arching. Rex laughs, his warm breath coating the wet skin. And he moves again, settling higher, pushing the tip of his cock between my breasts.

"What are you doing?"

"There's more than one way to fuck, you know that, Little Lamb?" His hands gather my flesh, and he slides his erection into the tight space. "It's not just the pussy, or even the mouth. Now that they're big enough, I can fuck your tits."

He thrusts into me again, sticky fluid coating the way. His hands hurt and his I fight for air. He bends over and whispers in my ear. "Just wait until I spread your cheeks and fuck you in the ass."

His words elicit the rush of warmth between my legs, I squirm beneath him. It seems to excite him, too, and he finds a rhythm, pushing and pulling his cock between my breasts. He's so dirty, so terribly bad, and this is not what I expect from my Mate. It's certainly not what I expect from the heir of Serendee.

His breath grows ragged, and I look up at his face; jaw clenched and tilted back. He's beautiful like this, with red cheeks and a slick sheen of sweat. His hair is pale, always catching light and giving off the hint of a halo. He's no angel. He's anything but. I should loathe him, but I've learned that my body and mind are not always in synch. Or maybe they are, and I just don't know what to do about it.

But that's why he picked me. I'm bad, too.

The soft flesh of my breasts feels numb from his rough handling and abuse, but I still feel it when he makes his final, lurching, groan, pinching his fingers deep into the skin. I cry out and close my eyes, feeling thick seed spill across my chest.

I lay under him like that, soiled and used, aware when he shifts back, releasing me from his weight. Without moving, I wait for the sound of him leaving, the gathering of his things and the slow exit. Instead, I sense the rustling of sheets and a soft cloth wiping off my chest. I open my eyes just in time to see him toss the cloth on the floor and kick off his pants. A moment later he's lying next to me. He's staying? He did say this was *our* bedroom. I curl up and away, facing the wall, pretending my heart isn't still pounding and that there's not a dull ache between my legs.

I shift my eyes away and stare at the wall next to the bed. There's a spider building a web in the corner of the windowsill, an insect trapped in the sticky threads. I watch its tiny legs spinning, faster and faster, as it approaches its prey. Rex curls behind me, his chest still rising and falling.

"Who told you to wear that outfit? My father?"

God. Gross. "No."

"Silas?"

Maybe he'll go away if I answer. "Elon."

"Did he now?" I don't have to see him to know the expression on his face. That his lips curve into a mix of cruel and amused. His arm slides around my waist, pulling me against his body. I don't trust the intimacy. I don't trust him.

"Yes. He took me shopping and brought me clothes that he thought you would like."

His fingers tug at the lace of my panties, thumb dipping underneath. I suck in a breath of air. "I bet he liked them, too. Did he touch you?"

I swallow and stare at the spider.

"He did, didn't he? You know, we've always liked the same things. The same cars, the same guns, the same women." He inches down between my legs, brushing against my clit. My reaction is a deep shudder and he chuckles in my ear. "Did he touch you here?"

"No."

His movement is so different from before, it's gentle and seductive. "You're so wet," he says, fingers slipping against my nerves. "I bet Silas gave you your first orgasm." He withdraws his hand, teasing. "Am I right?"

My hips rock forward, seeking friction. "Yes."

"He made it good for you, didn't he?"

He pushes a finger inside, curving it against the side. I sink into the feel of it, and he withdraws again. His voice hot against my ear. "Tell me what my brothers did to you, Little Lamb."

The demand is clear. Tell him and he'll get me off. I shouldn't want it, but the flame has been stoked. "Silas showed me TV shows. Movies. Elon kissed me and handled me a little rough, that's all."

He plunges his fingers into me again, applying pressure against my walls. His thumb holds against my clit, and I curl against him. Again, he withdraws. This time I cry out in frustration.

"And Levi?"

Do I tell him how Levi Corrects me? How he stole my panties after telling me to take them off and he spanked me until my flesh blistered? Levi told me Rex wouldn't like the levels of this kind of Correction. It's the kind of dedication to Serendee and The Way that he doesn't approve of.

His fingers hover over my entrance, slight pressure but not enough. He's mean enough that I know he'll walk out of here if I don't give him what he wants, and I'm desperate enough that I don't want him to. Still, I swallow the truth. "Levi is devout. He would never cross those lines, even if your father asked." I keep my eye on the busy spider, its tiny legs furiously spinning the web. Anything not to focus on the throbbing want between my legs.

"Thank you," he says, scraping the edge of my ear with his teeth. His fingers enter me again, this time with deliberate intent. He works me inside and out, drawing the orgasm out of me, in slow, incremental, waves. I push my face into the pillow as it rolls over me, the shudders wracking through my limps, stars bursting behind my eyelids.

Even after he withdraws his fingers for the last time, and the only sound in the room is my pulse pounding in my ears, he doesn't move, body close to mine. I tell him what I think he wants to hear.

"I won't let any of them touch me again."

He pushes the hair off my neck. "I wouldn't go that far."

For the first time, I turn to look at him. "What does that mean?"

He shrugs. "I've shared everything with them since we were kids. My house, my family, my *toys*." He touches my chin. "Why would I stop now?"

"But—"

"You belong to them as much as you belong to me. They're the ones that broke you in, eased you into being ready for me. It's not fair for me to take you for myself." He shifts his leg, his penis resting casually against his thigh. "Not that I told them that. They wouldn't accept it. I told them to continue their training."

"What are you talking about?" I know Rex is prone to extreme thoughts. Paranoia and maybe delusions but this seems insane. "You want to *share* me, with your best friends?"

"Brothers' really," he mumbles. "My father will never give them a mate of their own. He's got them right where he wants them—dependent on him and him alone. He'll keep pimping Silas out, he'll fuck and twist Levi's mind until he's the ultimate disciple, and he'll continue to harden Elon until there's nothing left but an angry shell." He wraps his arm around my waist and cinches it tight, pulling me into him. "They like you, Little Lamb, and I think you like them or at least how they make you feel."

My body blazes with heat. I feel called out—*seen*. But not in a good way. What he's suggesting and the simple fact I consider it for the tiniest moment is shameful. Indulgent. It's very, very bad.

I try to turn and face him, to tell him that he's lost his mind or maybe it's just another trick—a trap, but he's already asleep, eyes shut, lips slightly parted. His arm tightens around me, trapping me against his warm heat. I sigh and give up, my eyes returning to the spider, the only witness to what Rex is proposing. I thought when he claimed me at the ceremony that maybe things would make more sense. Now, I realize that I never left the web. If anything, it just grows bigger, stickier, and the more I struggle, the harder it is to escape.

WHEN I WAKE up the second time, it's lights out and I'm alone.

I don't know when Rex left or if he'll even remember coming in here. What I do know is that everything that he said last night confused me even more. He wants to share me with his friends, not just so they'll train me, but because he knows his father won't give them mates of their own.

He was drunk and despite what he said, *more* than a little high. If anything, it was a test of loyalty, to see if I'll betray him like my mother betrayed Serendee. What man would willingly share his wife with three other men?

I climb out of bed and go to the closet, pulling out a dress for work, ignoring the swirl of emotions which just thinking about it intensifies. I skip breakfast, feeling the need to withhold. Everything in my life has been consumed with Indulgence lately. Sex. Clothing. Food. I take a minute to reflect in my journal, horrified at how I let things slip lately. I can't let Rex derail my path to Enlightenment.

The Center is busy, thankfully, with a steady stream of new students coming in for classes. It allows me to focus on something other than myself. I see Levi once or twice. He has back-to-back sessions, instructing new recruits—most from the University. We don't speak, but the last time I was with him, Silas was burying himself inside of me while Levi held me in his arms. My cheeks burn when I think of the way he came against my back, breath ragged and warm.

After his class leaves, I pass him in the hallway. "Can we talk?"

His jaw tenses. "I have another class coming in, and I need to prepare."

"Right. I just..." I look over my shoulder to make sure we're alone. "I would like to schedule some time with you. Privately."

His eyebrow raises. "For Correction?"

I nod.

"Is this about the other night? Things got out of hand. I never should have—"

"It's not that." I pause, recalling our night together with Silas in the tent. Levi held me while Silas showed me what making love was really all about, instead of the harsh brutality Rex had shown me. "Well, not specifically. It's just everything going on over the weekend, the Bonding ceremony, and our new living situation, I feel very off balance."

"I'm not sure we should continue meeting now that you are Bonded."

Panic flares in my chest. Sheer, unbridled anxiety. I reach out and grab him by the arm. "Levi, I need this. I need something normal in my life." His expression doesn't change. "Rex told me last night he's okay with me continuing my training with each of you."

"He's expressed the same to us, but," his forehead furrows, "I'm not sure that means he's okay with me being your Guide? You know how he feels about Anex's procedures."

"I know that Rex doesn't believe in The Way. Not like you do. I know that you and I are caught between two warring men. Father and Son." My words are a whisper—inappropriate to be said aloud. Levi nods in understanding. "I've agreed to balance both and I need your Guidance to do that."

His hesitation is brief. As it should be. Rex may be his best friend, but he is loyal to our beliefs.

"Okay. We can schedule something," he looks at his watch, "but not today. Tomorrow?"

Relief rushes through me. "Yes, thank you."

His smile is tight. "You're welcome, Imogene."

I watch Levi walk away, thinking that if Rex thinks this man likes me he is very confused. I'm pretty sure I am nothing but an albatross around all of their necks. A naïve, little lamb that needs constant education and attention. I'm sure they have much better things to do with their time.

When I get back to my desk, an envelope is propped up against the phone with my name on it. The lobby is empty, but someone must have come in while I was in the back. I open it and see a typed invitation.

The time has come.
For you to embrace your Enlightenment.
If you're ready, wait by the oak tree at dusk.
Prepare for the future.

INSTANTLY, I know this is the invitation to the women's group Margaret, one of Anex's spiritual wives, told me about. A smile spreads across my face. I'd wondered, after so much uncertainty with Rex, if I would still be considered. But here it is. These women want me to be part of their group. Hell yes, I'm ready.

47

S ilas

"You're late," Elon says, shifting over on the sofa to give me some room. His nose wrinkles. "Jesus, you smell like pussy."

I sniff my fingers. "It's vanilla." To be fair, the guys are used to the oily scents following my massage sessions with recruits. To them vanilla probably does smell like pussy. "And Kayla is demanding a lot of my time. I need Anex to decide what he wants to do about her."

Kayla is one of the recruits from outside of Serendee. She is the heir to a trillion-dollar company and seeking meaning in her life. Anex is willing to allow outsiders into Serendee for a price: loyalty, dedication, commitment, and cash. My job is to make them comfortable, to show them a taste of Enlightenment. His is to lock them, and their bank accounts, in for life.

"Do you know what this is about?" Levi asks, his knee bounces up and down. "Is Rex coming?"

"Rex is down in the barn prepping a batch for delivery," Elon says, "so whatever we're doing here, it's probably about him."

We'd been called to the little sitting room up in Anex's quarters. This isn't the first time we've been here. He often uses this room for instruction and personal meetings, but with everything going on with Rex and Imogene, I can't help but be a little apprehensive. I'd shown Rex the rooms where the Fallen are kept and told him that this is where Imogene would go if he rejected her. It seems more and more obvious that Anex's interest in her go far beyond being Rex's mate.

He wants her. I'm just not sure if it's to enact revenge on her mother's Regression, or if it's for something different. Either way, the desire to keep her safe is strong. I suspect the same from Elon and Levi.

The interior door opens and Anex walks in. He's alone, which is unusual, and makes me even more apprehensive. Elon is stiff as a rod next to me, and Levi's knee doesn't stop bouncing until we stand in unison, touching our foreheads and giving him a slight, respectful bow. We may be in the inner circle here, but everything we've done lately is uncharted territory. Like everyone else in Serendee, we're not immune to Correction

"Boys," Anex says, smiling warmly. "Thank you for coming to see me on such short notice."

Opting out of a meeting with Anex is unheard of. Most people in Serendee would love this opportunity of a private audience with our leader, but most people don't know what he's capable of. Who he is in private.

There's a soft knock on the door and a woman enters, carrying a tray of tea. She's young. She keeps her head down, not making eye contact with Anex. I catch a glimpse of her profile and recognize her. Her name is Bethany and she is being punished for kissing a boy before she came of age and received her Order. She's one of the Fallen, and this is the first time I've seen her out of the locked room.

Anex waits as she serves the tea, her hands shaking as she pours the steaming liquid into the china. The cuff of her sleeve draws up, and I can't help but notice the red welt circling her wrist. He watches her closely, observing her every move. When she's finished, he says, "You can go back to your room now, Bethany."

"Yes, sir," she replies, shuffling back out the door.

Anex shakes his head when she is gone and says, "That one has a dark streak of Regression inside of her. Born and raised here, but the darkness still crept inside. It's a problem, one that I'm creating a solution to, but in the meantime, I'm working with her—individually. I'm confident she'll progress." He takes a sip of tea and then smiles. "Now, I know you're not interested in the mundane aspects of my responsibilities and are wondering why I brought you up here today?"

Levi and I nod, while Elon mutters an affirmative.

"Now that Rex and Imogene are settled, I want to talk to you about a program Margaret has started. It's a women's group, a place for them to support and encourage one another as they follow The Way."

"A women's group?" Levi says. He teaches many of the men's classes down at the center. Viri Regum Sunt: Men Are Kings. "Like VRS."

"Similar," he says, "but obviously not the same. As you're aware, the needs of a woman are uniquely different from a man. They desire to belong. They need constant approval and have an absolute weakness for Indulgence." He lists these flaws with confidence and authority, adding, "While our masculine predisposition is to conquer and dominate. It's what sets us apart."

Elon frowns. "Why do you want to talk to us about a women's group. Isn't that... um, for women to handle?"

"You'd think," Anex says, "but no. Even in the biblical myths, Eve was created from Adam's rib. There is no Eve without Adam. No female without the male. Our ancestors knew this truth. Biology understands these facts. But like the participants in VRS, these women need to feel the support of other women, the confidentiality of their gender. As with everything else, we will provide the structure." He holds his teacup between his long, thin fingers. "And you three, specifically, will see to Imogene's journey in the group."

"Imogene," Levi blurts. "She's joining?"

"She's been invited, and she's eager to get to know the other women, but as you know she's different. Like the Regressive that just left here," he glances toward the door, "there's a virus that burns under her skin. I can't let her infect the others."

"What do you want us to do?" I ask, feeling uneasy.

"I want her monitored every step of the way." He nods at Levi. "She'll come to you for Correction. She'll feel guilty for keeping secrets from Rex, for being different, for her sexual urges." He gives him a knowing look, and Levi's cheeks turn pink. "Continue to help her find Enlightenment and keep her in check."

"Y-yes. I can do that."

"Silas."

I jerk my chin up. "Yes?"

"There's going to come a time when you'll be needed to provide what only you can offer. Prepare her for that day and for the aftermath."

I have no idea what this means or what he wants from me, but I nod. What else is there for me to do? I've taught her how to pleasure herself and others. I've shown her love and compassion. I've healed her wounds.

"And me?" Elon asks.

"Your role is always the same, son," Anex gives him a stern look. "Protect Serendee and the leadership inside. These women will be required to provide collateral. I need you to collect and assess the threat of their confessions."

Elon and Anex hold one another's eyes for a long beat, and although my friend nods in agreement, assuring Anex that he will do what is needed of him, I get the distinct feeling these two are no longer on the same side. I'm not sure any of us are, things have shifted so dramatically lately, but to protect our lives—and Imogene's —we have no choice but to submit to our leader's commands.

"What about Rex?" Elon asks. "Does he know about this group?"

He leans back in his seat, expression grave. "In order for the females to fully immerse themselves in this movement, mates will not know that their partners are participating. The women will be told specifically to keep their involvement a secret. Rex can't know that it is anything beyond a standard support group. You three, outside of myself, are the only men aware that this group exists."

Another secret, like the one where he asked us to train Imogene for Rex. That didn't go over well. He'd lashed out at her and threatened to leave. We'd barely been able to keep him from going. I busy myself with my tea, not wanting to look at Anex or the others. There is no way this ends in anything other than hurt and betrayal.

Which, I think, may be exactly what Anex wants.

48

I mogene

THE OAK TREE stands by the edge of the forest, on a hill that allows for a magnificent view of Serendee. It's a significant marker in the community—the place where Anex realized the potential of the space. He stopped at this tree and declared the land the perfect spot to build his vision of utopia. My mother was there that day, notebook in hand, jotting down details for what would later become the blueprint for designing our self-sustaining home.

Now, as I approach the tree, I wonder what she would think about me being Bonded to Rex and joining this secret women's group—being a part of the Chosen. As much as I'd like to think she'd be happy for me, that I'd overcome the dark legacy she'd left me with, I know that isn't true. She would be horrified to know I'm tied to Anex—the man who was forced to banish her from her home and family.

There's a basket under the tree and a stack of white handkerchiefs. Attached is a note that says, "Cover your eyes and wait."

I look around, wondering if anyone is watching, but, other than the sound of nature, it's quiet. Carefully, I fold the bandanna and wrap it around my eyes, tying at the back of my head. I lean my backside against the tree and wait. I have no concept how long I wait, but eventually the snap of a stick alerts me that someone is nearby.

"Are you ready to start your journey?" the female voice asks.

"Yes." I'm both nervous and excited as I try to orient myself to her voice. A strong hand clasps around my wrist and leads me off the path. Even blindfolded, I can tell we've entered the forest. My skirt drags against the low growing shrubs, and my escort quietly guides me over roots and rough terrain.

"Can you tell me where we're going?" I ask once we're deep in the woods.

"You'll find out soon enough."

Sweat beads on my back by the time she slows, the hike leveling out and into a field. I smell the smoke before I hear movement—the shuffling and squish of soft dirt underfoot—and feel the warm heat and crackle of a fire. When the blindfold is removed, I blink, taking in the scene.

There are five others like me, all positioned around a large fire pit dug into the soft dirt. I recognize a few of them. Most are older than I am, their mates in the higher rungs of Anex's circle. Although, one woman catches my eye—she's someone Silas has recruited. Kayla is her name. I've seen her name in the files at The Center. Her family is wealthy, and she came here seeking something more than her family's power. I'm surprised to see a recruit here, but it's not my place to question, and I focus on the other women, the ones draped in green robes, their faces obscured by a large, draping hood.

"Welcome kindred souls, we're honored you've come to join us in our quest of empowerment," Margaret's voice rings out from the cluster of robed women. "What you're about to experience will tap into Anex's wise lesson and help you become a fuller, more Integrated being."

The sun drops behind the trees, dropping the temperature. One of the other robed women steps forward and commands us to undress.

Having grown up in the Domum, I'm accustomed to disrobing in front of other females. I quickly unfasten the buttons on my dress and allow it to drop over my narrow shoulders and waist. The only self-consciousness that I feel is from the weight gain over the last few weeks. Rex wants a woman with curvier hips and plumper breasts. I've been allotted more food than normal, but I hope the other women don't notice my Indulgence.

A cool breeze rustles in the trees, pushing past the heat of the fire.

"You're laid bare," Margaret says, "as a sign of rebirth. Coming into this group the same way you came into this world, naked, innocent, unbiased—but most of all vulnerable. Females do not like to be vulnerable, to show the weakness that lies in the essence of our being. This group is here to show you that embracing these traits makes you stronger."

She walks around the circle, assessing each of us as she goes. There's a firm kindness in her expression, a knowledge that I crave to possess. This isn't a woman that allows her insecurities to rule her life. She accepts who she is.

"Like a babe fresh from the womb, you will start at the bottom. Latched to the breast of another, wiser woman who will guide you through this journey. When you ascend again, you will not be the same person you are today. You're getting a second chance to grow into a fully Integrated female, attuned to The Way."

Her words inspire a surge of giddiness through me. Who doesn't want a chance to start over, to be absolved of your sins and embrace The Way? Through this emotion I try to absorb everything Margaret says: we will report to a "Main," who will guide us in our journey. She'll push us to our limits; exploring everything from pain to shocking self-awareness. Our renewal will be affirmed with a "birthmark," pressed into our skin as a symbol of starting new. We will be required to submit Collateral, because joining this group is an honor, a gift, and we must sacrifice something of our own in order to embrace what's being given. And at the end, when we are already to ascend into a fully formed, new being, The Way will test us, physically and emotionally, to confirm that we are worthy.

The leaders fan out, approaching each of us with a white robe. Margaret steps behind me, draping the robe over my shoulders.

"Put this on," Margaret says, in my ear but also loud enough for everyone to hear. "Feel the swaddling of the soft cotton, as if you're being wrapped for the first time." Her hands are gentle, but firm and I relax, truly feeling the gravity of the moment. "Thank Anex for allowing us this opportunity to be better."

As a group, we verbally thank our leader for his wisdom.

"One last thing," she says, going back to stand in front of the fire with the others. "This is a group for women, by women, you may not tell anyone outside of the group about what happens here. Not your Mate, not your family. This is a private journey that you must take alone. Your support comes from your Main." She holds up her hands. "Come, clasp hands and join me around the fire."

As the others rush forward, I find myself hesitating, feeling a twinge of doubt. Secrets don't go over well with Rex—especially when they come from the directive of his father's spiritual mate. It's also hard to keep anything from the others. Elon is naturally suspicious. Levi is well connected to the inner circle, and Silas has a way of getting me to share my private thoughts. Unlike the other women attending this ceremony, I have four men I must keep in the dark.

I think back to that day, so long ago, when Rex and I sat on top of the cliff as children. He'd hated me even then. I'd always been tainted in his eyes, and I always will be. Perhaps this cleansing, this rebirth, will be what I need to do to make him love and accept me as something other than a body to abuse, or a way to get back at his father.

I glance at the fire and then back at Margaret, the flames giving her hair a wild glow. Our eyes meet and her lips curve into an encouraging smile, her hand waving me to come closer, and the worries fade away.

49

Imogene

I WAKE up the next morning feeling giddy for the first time in... well maybe ever. *Renewed* is the word I'm looking for. I feel like a different woman, empowered and ready to take on the challenges of my household. If that's the power the women hoped to impart, I'm feeling it.

The sound of a low snore draws my attention to the other side of the bed. Rex is asleep. He must have come in after I did and for once didn't wake me to fill me with his seed. I prop up on my elbow, taking in the man next to me. He's on his side, facing the closet, shirtless, his skin a warm tan from his time in the sun. His hair is darker now, not the white blond from his childhood but still golden. His features sharp and appealing—the cut of his jaw darkened by stubble. He's got the body of a man—they all do—and it's one thing I find so jarring. I never experienced boys past the age of twelve. We were segregated and now that I'm confronted with it, even passively, every-thing about his physique seems different and strange.

I peer over him, eyes roaming over his hard abdomen. The trail of golden hair that vanishes under the white sheet. Emboldened by the gathering the night before, and my resolve to better things between me and my mate, I push the sheet down and rest a hand on his hip.

He shifts, not waking, but twisting toward me. My hand travels the slope of his hip until it's resting more on the hard muscle of his lower abdomen. My cheeks burn even though no one is looking at me. No one knows my Indulgent thoughts.

Carefully, I unpeel the sheet, revealing the darker thatch of hair and his cock resting against his thigh. What startles me is the fact it is already thick, hard from erection. Silas taught me about this, 'morning wood' is the slang for it. I get it.

I want to touch it.

Gathering my courage, I move my hand to his thigh, muscular and strong. I run my finger over the tip and instantly clear fluid builds. Rex shifts, but I'm focused on his body. The hard elegance —a body I know can be turned into a weapon in a blink. I remember how he's used it on me. In my mouth at the club that night, forcing me to swallow. On the dock when he took my inno-cence. The cold way he Bonded with me and the way he came on my tits.

I pull my hand back, reconsidering when—

"What are you doing, Little Lamb?" His voice is rough. Gritty from sleep.

I freeze and tilt my head. "I-I—" All that comes out is a stutter.

He reaches out, warm fingers tilting my chin upward. "Use your words. Why are you touching my dick?"

"I-I—" I swallow. "You looked so peaceful. Quiet. And you graciously let me sleep last night. I thought maybe I could show you my appreciation the way a mate would."

He shifts around, propping on his elbow so he's facing me. From this angle his erection looks impossibly larger. Or maybe it *is* larger. My heart pounds and a sense of inadequacy fills me. As though he knows, a small smile lingers on his mouth. "How exactly would you do that?"

"I could, uh, touch it?" The heat in my face quadruples. "Until you reach completion."

His eyebrows raise in a way that makes me feel foolish. "You want to give me an orgasm?"

"Yes. A handjob—that's what Silas called it right?" I'm so flustered, so out of my element that my palms start to sweat. "Unless you would rather me not."

His forehead creases at Silas' name, but a moment later it smooths back out. "Let me tell you one thing, Little Lamb, no man is ever going to decline an orgasm first thing in the morning." He stretches on his back, arms behind his head, elbows bent. Although he's the picture of calm, his cock rises between his legs, eager with anticipation. "Ready when you are."

I try to remember everything Silas taught me: *Act confident. Men love to have their cocks touched. Don't act nervous. Enjoy it. You're giving someone pleasure—that's a good thing, especially if he's someone you care about.*

Do I care about Rex? I ask myself, building up the nerve to take him in my hand. His lower belly dips when I finally do, caving inward. A surge of pride runs through me. *I* did that. I do have control here. I can give this man—my mate—what he wants.

I stroke gently at first and Rex hums with approval. "Don't be scared, Imogene. I won't break."

I tighten my grip, stroking up and down, feeling the velvet covering the hard shaft. His breathing changes, deeper—louder. His fingers on one hand twist in the blanket, but his other hand finds the back of my neck, the nape, and he tugs at my hair.

"That's good, baby," he grunts. "God, your hands are so soft."

My stomach flip flops, burning desire building at my core. If he touched me right now, I think I'd let him. Let him draw me to the edge and fulfill my own needs. He doesn't, he just watches me with those piercing blue eyes, jaw tensing as I grip him harder, tugging until there's nothing but blistering hard heat.

"Fuck," he grunts, body growing rigid. "Fuck, I'm gonna—"

White semen spills from the tip, hot and drippy over my fist. As he seizes, pulling hard at my hair, I remember the taste, the salty fluid. There's a craving to taste it again, but I focus now on not making a mess. On making sure he's fulfilled. I hold firm, not releasing him until I've milked every last drop.

He falls back against the pillow, releasing my hair. His chest covered in a thin sheen of sweat.

"Damn," he sighs, hand running through his hair. "Guess I should thank Silas for that, huh?"

Or me, I think, but bite it back. No. It's not about me. It's about him. And if anyone should be thanked, it's the women from the gathering last night. They are the ones that gave me the courage to take this step.

"I hope that was good enough," I say, grabbing a section of the sheet to clean up. I wait to see if he's going to say more, but when I look up from the mess, his eyes have fluttered shut and his chest has the rise and fall of a sleeping, satisfied man.

I'm on the way to the Center when I notice the construction. I'd taken a different route, stopping by the butcher to request an order for dinner that night. The small shop is two blocks over from the community center and there's a scenic route I sometimes like to take to the gate out of Serendee. The land is unused and a bit isolated, spotted with pines. Now it's been cleared, the ground has been churned up and flattened into a smooth surface of red clay. Large dirt moving machines are scattered across the field—community members on the construction team are busy at work.

I pause, staring at the space, wondering if I missed some announcement or news. Usually, construction or buildings are presented during one of Anex's talks. Was I too distracted by my circumstances to notice? Did it come out during the lecture when I sat in Rex's lap, and he pushed his hands between my legs?

It's after I've walked away that I see a familiar face. Clarissa, the woman that supervised my Domum, is coming down the road. Her expression brightens when she sees me and we rush together in greeting.

"Imogene," she says, "you look well."

"Thank you, as do you."

Clarissa looks the same as always. Modest blue dress, hair swept behind her head in a tight bun. She's single—and revealed to me that Anex never gave her an Order. She's wise and understands Serendee in a way I don't think I fully comprehended when we shared a home.

The sound of a machine moving draws my attention back down the hill. "I didn't know they were building," I say, admitting my possible Lapse. "Do you know what it is?"

"Anex hasn't officially announced it yet," she says, giving me relief that I'm not completely clueless. "But," she lowers her voice even though no one is around, "it's going to be a new childcare center."

"A childcare center?"

"Yes, for infants and toddlers. An opportunity to reach the youngest members of our community—sharing The Way as early as possible."

This is new. Children born into Serendee stay at home with their mothers or fathers or maybe are watched by a relative or neighbor. It's one of the foundations of the community—slowing down, making time to raise children in The Way. There has never been any kind of formal care for the smallest members of the community. But I can see the need. As the community grows, so do our obligations and time commitment.

"Anex asked me to help set it up." Clarissa beams, clearly proud of the assignment. "He recognized the success I've had with the girls living in the Domum."

I grin back. "That's an honor, but not a surprise, not with your years of service to the community." She blushes, something I'm not sure I've ever seen her do before. "I can't wait to see what you come up with."

"It's become his number one priority," she says. "I think that's why he hasn't announced it yet publicly. He's just moving fast, but you know how he is when he's excited about a new project."

She's right. Anex gets a vibration about him when he's in the middle of something new—something *great*—for the community.

We part, my heart feeling even lighter than before. Progress is being made in Serendee. Our leader is expanding and focused on the future. It's a wonderful time to live here.

That's the attitude I take with me back to the Center. A hum of excitement running through my blood. It's time for me to do my part. To ready myself for Enlightenment.

It's time for Correction.

50

____

L evi

"SHE CAME TO YOU AGAIN, didn't she?" Anex asks. There's no question about who 'she' is. There's only one she. "Seeking Correction?"

I didn't tell him when he called us in for the meeting, unsure of how to handle Imogene's need for discipline and the information about the women's group. He figured it out anyway. I guess there was a part of me that had hoped she would come to my room again and let me meter out punishment there in the privacy of my bedroom. I should've known Anex was aware. He's always aware.

"Yes. Just like you said, despite all the conflict and Rex filling her mind with questions, she's on the path. She craves discipline."

He gestures to the door in the back hallway of The Center, and I follow him down to the basement. We stop in the small area adjacent to the main room. Imogene should be here any minute for our scheduled session.

"Good." He walks over to a cabinet hanging from the wall. "I know this has been challenging for your Levi. Rex is testing your loyalty to both him and The Way. It's a hard place to exist—harder on you than it is on Elon or Silas. You've always been so devoted and followed my teachings as closely as possible. I know what I'm asking of you has been hard."

"I understand," I tell him. "I trust your judgment. The number one goal is to keep Rex in Serendee, and so far, we've accomplished that."

"We have." He smiles and I can't help the surge of pride in my chest. Praise and favor from Anex are all I've ever longed for. Even now, caught in this web between him and his son, the feeling emerges. "As long as we keep him and Imogene moving forward, I have faith Rex will come to his senses."

"And Imogene?" I ask, not meaning to. "What happens to her in the end?"

He looks thoughtful for a moment, but says, "Imogene has always been on a unique path—almost like she's been on a special journey. One that has led her to this point. What happens to her next is up to her, Rex and all of you assisting her."

Ah. There it is. The subtle threat that underlines all of Anex's directives. Do as I say. Follow the rules. Make me happy. And if you do those things, everything will be okay. If not?

Well, it's not a risk I'm willing to take.

He opens up the cabinet door and attached to the wall are a variety of instruments—all used during Correction. I've been trained to use many of these and watch as he removes a brown leather strap off of one of the hooks.

My heart skips a beat when I see it, but I keep my emotions close. I learned a long time ago that if Anex sees a reaction, he files it away for later. He holds it up. "I think she's ready."

I'm not so sure about that.

A knock on the outer door cuts our conversation short, and I enter the basement, leaving him. I keep my eyes away from the framed artwork on the wall—the image of Serendee. A sun moon and crown combination. Nearly every room in Serendee is monitored. This one is no different.

I rest the strap on the table in the center of the room and then open the door. Imogene stands on the other side, her expression innocent, but I see the spark of fire in her eyes. She craves these sessions, the feeling of surrendering herself to pain while seeking the pathway to redemption. A flicker of energy thrums between us that neither of us acknowledges. She steps into the room, the scent of her shampoo wafting behind her, and I try not to think about what it was like to have my nose buried into it while she leaned against me, and Silas buried himself between her legs.

I shut the door, making sure it's secure. "Do you want to tell me why you're here today?"

She stops in front of the table centered in the room and stares at the strap. Her skin pales and her fingers twist together. I see the long swallow in her throat and the way she forces her eyes away from the instrument, to look at me. "I stole and ate half a cake during Anex's birthday celebration," she starts, as if the Lapses can't help but fall from her tongue. "I tried not to eat today, but I felt lightheaded."

"You've been given permission to expand your caloric intake," I remind her. "And I suspect stealing that cake was more Rex's idea that yours."

"It's my job to keep him on the path."

"It's your job to keep him in Serendee. Focused. You did that." I cross my arms over my chest. "If that's all you're coming to me with, you probably should leave."

It's a ploy, of course, a way to get her to tell me more—confess to deeper Lapses. I wonder if she'll tell me about the women's meeting, if she'll betray the secret she promised to uphold?

"You're going to make me say it?" Her accusation is thick. "Even though you were there?"

I hold her eye. "Part of the process is admitting the Lapse. No one can own that but you."

"Fine," she says defiantly. "I had sex with a man that is not my future mate. I kissed another man. I received pleasure from a third."

The look she gives me is pointed—accusing. "And then when my Ordered came to claim me I fought him off." Her chin lifts. "Is that enough?"

"It should be." I cross my arms over my chest. "But even with those Lapses, I'm not sure I should be correcting you now that you and Rex have bonded. Things have changed."

A small tremor runs through her. She wants the Correction. Even if she hasn't done anything to deserve it—she *needs* it. "Rex has given his explicit permission for us to continue our... relationships. Approved or not, it's wrong. I know it in my soul."

And there it is. That's what sent her here. Rex uses her for his own needs and then tosses her to the wolves like scraps of meat.

"Please, Levi." Her voice is soft, barely audible. "I need this."

The truth is that I was always going to give her what she wanted. It's my job to make her work for it—to suffer through the moment. Enlightenment doesn't come easy. Not for any of us.

I give her a small nod and command, "Lift your skirt and bend over the desk."

Relief rushes out of her, and she reaches under her skirt. Hopping on one foot, she removes a pair of white, lace, panties and rests them on the table. Her hands shake as she gathers the fabric, balling it around her waist. She knows the position: bent over, hands flat on the table, backside propped up and exposed. I'm hard before she bares herself, the smooth, pale, flesh healed from our last session. I know she's already warm between her legs and soon she'll be slippery and wet.

This is as much of a test for me as it is to her. I reach around her, grabbing the strap. The leather is cool and smooth in my hand, similar to her pale backside. I run my hand over the skin, gentle, getting a feel for her supple flesh. My heart pounds as I grip the strap in my fingers, knowing this girl has done nothing to deserve this type of punishment, yet also very aware that she's been conditioned to want it.

Just as I've been conditioned to give it.

I swing my arm back and strike her against her backside, my teeth grinding from the force. The power surges her forward and a small cry escapes her mouth. Hearing that sound brings up a swell of desire, but I swallow it back. This session is about training Imogene, not fulfilling my needs, and although we crossed that line once, it was in the dark hours of the night, in our home. Not here.

Not with Anex watching.

51

I mogene

THE FINAL STING of the strap barely filters through the fog that has
lowered over my brain. The first jolt was severe, a sensation I've never
experienced. I felt like my skin had been cracked open by a shock of
lightening. Tears streamed down my cheeks, and I fought a wave of
nausea. I almost begged him to stop.

Almost.

I asked for this. Wanted it, and despite the fact that my backside
became numb after the fifth slap of leather, the warm familiar spread
of heat built in my stomach, desperate and hungry. Levi is diligent
with his Correction. The strikes coming in a consistent measure. He
throws his whole body into it, and I feel the force all the way down to
my toes. My body surges forward with each hit, knees shaking, until
I'm nearly flat on the table, unable to move.

I take it, knowing I deserve it, but there's a tingle under my skin
because what I truly want comes next. I wait for the escalation, the

heavy breathing, the touch of his hands between my legs, the sound of Levi's zipper lowering, and the final rush of transcendent euphoria.

It never comes and neither, to my surprise, does he.

I glance over my shoulder and see Levi's sweaty, pinched, face. He looks disgusted. With me? With himself? As I struggle to an upright position he walks toward the door. "You're leaving?" I ask, feeling more exposed than during my Correction. I grip the table with one hand and squeeze my thighs together in a futile attempt to quell the urges.

"We're done here." He shifts with discomfort, the bulge of his erection obvious. "Clean up and leave when you've composed yourself."

My brain is still a fog, caught up in the blistering numbness of my backside and the ache between my legs and I watch as he exits. The door shutting with a click behind him.

I don't know if I should be angry or hurt. Maybe neither? What I know is that I'm flustered and in pain. Throbbing, inside and out. I do know that if he's left the room, then so should I.

I lower my skirt and smooth the wrinkled fabric with shaking hands. My panties, which were on the table, are gone now. That makes two pairs Levi has taken. I can't help but wonder what he does with them.

When I get myself to point of control, I take a hesitant step outside. The summer sky is bright, the birds are flittering in the nearby trees. Things are normal out here, the direct opposite of the room I just left. My skin feels raw and my senses are still numb, I'm distracted—deep in my thoughts—when a figure steps in my path.

"Oh." I blink. "Elon? What are you—"

There's no reason to finish the question. I know why he's here and he knows why I'm here.

"Do you need something?" I ask. "I was just on my way—"

"No, Little Lamb, I don't need anything," his eyes skim my body, like he can see through the fabric of my dress, "but I think you do."

"Excuse me?" I look around. This is not a topic for a public area. "I don't know what you're talking about."

He grabs my hand. "You're shaking."

"Because I shouldn't be seen with a man that isn't my betrothed." I try to twist away from him, but his grip is firm. "Let me go before we both get in trouble."

"Why? The more trouble you get in, the more Corrections you can have. Isn't that what you want?"

His presence is powerful and intimidating, but his knowledge is worse. It's wrong for me to push back and question him, but my heart is still racing from the emotional and physical overload of the Correction, and I'm not sure I can handle this. Not now. Not with him.

"I want what I always want—to seek Enlightenment. To squash indulgence. To do better."

"I think you want something else, Imogene." My real name coming off his tongue feels even more threatening—more intimate. His hand runs down my back. I brace myself and when he touches my raw backside, I hiss. He bends down and whispers in my ear, "A little sore?"

"I'm fine." In a fast movement he grabs me under the legs and picks me up. "What are you doing! What if someone sees!"

"No one will see," he assures me.

A six-foot-four man, carrying another man's future mate around Serendee like a bag of flour. Someone *will* notice. I fight against him, but it's useless. My energy is zapped, my backside screams in pain, and he's just too big.

"Are you taking me to Silas again?" I ask, hopefully.

"No, his salves won't fix this." He turns back to the door and props me against his knee while he presses the code into the door. The lock unlatches, and he steps inside where he drops me in front of the table I'd just been bending over. The strap lies where Levi left it. He stares at it for long moment and then says, "I'm here to finish what Levi started."

My heart leaps from my chest to my throat. "You're going to punish me more?"

Levi's strikes had been strong and powerful, but Elon... he'd break me.

"No. This isn't about punishment. It's about giving you what you really want." He yanks up my skirt, exposing my blistering behind. The cool air feels good on the raw skin and against the searing heat between my legs. His voice is low in my ear, "This pain... it's just an excuse to take you where you want to go. I don't like to see you hurt like this." His finger gently runs over the welts. I flinch, but he holds me still. "I know what you need and how you need it."

I have no time to think about what Elon is demanding of me, because he grabs my waist and spins me around, pushing my hips into the table. The legs scrape against the cement floor, but all I hear is the sound of his zipper lowering.

My belly bottoms out when I feel his erection slide between my legs, sending a shiver of relief down my spine. "Tell me this isn't exactly what you came here for, Little Lamb, and I'll stop."

All arguments die on my tongue because the feel of him next to me, slippery and wet, *is* exactly what I want. It's all I think about. It's all I crave. Levi lit a fire in me and left it smoldering. Elon's stoked it back to life and as his hand presses into the curve of my lower back, I beg, "Don't."

"Don't what?"

"Don't stop." Then I add, "Make it hurt."

His fingers twist in my hair, and I cry out when he yanks against my scalp. "Like this?"

"Yes." The answer turns into a hiss when his hand brushes against my swollen, sore backside, but it just adds to the intensity of the moment. The sheer, uncontrollable want that surges through me.

"All of those other sessions have built up to this." His cock rubs against me, the tip pushing and prodding at my folds. "Levi is too good, too righteous to take it where it needs to go. Where *you* need it to go." He grabs me by the neck and twists my mouth up to his. His lips are scorching, his tongue demanding. I pant into his mouth, and he says, "But I'm not. I'm just the kind of man to give you what you deserve."

He drops my head and grips my hip, pushing into me with a hard thrust. I slam forward, caught by surprise by the feel of the force of him inside of me. He's big, thick, and he pushes against my sides. He's intrusive, invading, and although he gives me a second to catch my breath the second punch is just as forceful—if not more. He slams into me, fingers pinching into my hips. Every time he does it, pushing to the hilt, my backside sings from the contact—a constant reminder of my Lapses. With every thrust, I just keep adding them.

"Tell the truth," he says, voice tight, "you want this. You want it dirty and hard and primal."

"N-no." I stutter, the word thrust out of me. "I want Enlightenment."

My head snaps back with a sharp yank of my hair. "You want to be fucked. You want your pussy so full of my cum that it'll be dripping down your legs when it's over."

I fight back—trying to stay focused, even as he thrusts into me, nerves frayed. "I seek pain to fight the Indulgence of an easy path."

The phrases come so easily. They're rote. Ingrained in me since childhood.

"Bullshit," he growls, jerking me up and pinching my nipples roughly. A shock of desire travels straight between my legs, and his hands follow the current, stopping at my core. "It's okay to want it because you like it. You like it when I touch you here and fuck you at the same time."

I swallow an affirmation. It's wrong. Nothing in my life is about what I want. I've been taught that from the beginning. I didn't grow up in the same world as Elon, where gluttony is rewarded with rolled up money and fast cars. Where women give sex freely without consequences and guilt.

"I want you to come for me, Little Lamb. For *me*. Not for Anex. Not for The Way. Not for Rex." He leans over me, bodies pressed together. He's moving deliciously slow now, dragging his cock in and out. My legs wobble, and he holds me up. "I want you to do it for me because you like how it feels when I'm buried deep inside you. When you can't tell where you begin, and I end."

God, he feels so good. So sinfully good. A tremor rolls through me and I fight it. "It's wrong."

"Is it?" His breath is hot on the back of my neck, his body slick with sweat. I feel the cascade building, intensifying with every press of his fingertips, every stab of his cock. He's right. I don't know where I begin, and he ends. I don't know anything other than it hurts so good. "Come for me," he urges. "Just for me."

"I can't."

"You can and you will."

He's right, of course, my body has a will of its own and all it wants is release. His fingers rub circles against my clit, and I groan, over-whelmed by so much stimulation. The first twinges come quick, and the orgasm rushes over me, down my arms and legs, spreading from my core up my spine. My body grows numb, lost in the luxury of euphoria, and Elon picks up his pace, flattening me on the table. Every thrust sends another shockwave across my body. Part pain, part desire, all of it lost to the feeling of him thrusting so deep.

"That's right," he mutters, voice rough and caught between ragged breaths. "Clench around me. Hold on tight." I don't know how long he'll go, and I feel a second wave of want tickling at the base of my spine. Abruptly, he comes to a halt, jerking into me with a groan as his cock swells thick. We stay like this for a long moment, his seed spilling into me, my muscles milking every last drop. Slowly, I float back down into my body, and he pulls out. I push up on my elbows and stand, feeling his cum drip down my inner thigh.

I panic, looking for something to clean up with, but he drops to his knees and pulls a handkerchief out of his back pocket. Before I can stop him, he gently wipes away the evidence of his transgressions.

He stands and looks at me, eyes less rageful than I've ever seen. I almost thank him, but for what? Cleaning me up? Nearly forcing himself on me? Pushing me to my limits?

The words falter on my tongue because I'm not entirely convinced that what just transpired between us wasn't the biggest Lapse of my life, or if it was exactly the level of Enlightenment I've been seeking.

"From now on you either tell Levi what you really want from

these sessions, or you come to me. Or if you're that desperate," he grins, zipping up his pants, "come to us both. Understand?"

Both? That idea shocks me to move, and despite my wrinkled dress and messy hair, I rush out the door. Thank God, no one is around as I limp back toward Serendee. I pretend I'm a normal woman, going back to my normal home, with my normal mate waiting for me. I pretend that Elon's fluids aren't wet between my legs, and Levi's strap marks aren't blistered on my backside and that I haven't just willingly participated in something I don't fully understand.

The only thing I do know is that for the first time in days I feel satisfied, physically and emotionally, which either means I'm on the right path, or headed down a very, very, wrong one.

52

R^{ex}

THE EXCHANGE TAKES place in the back entrance of the Lambda fraternity house. The crates lined with bricks of weed, then covered in soft packing material. On top is an assortment of fresh fruit and vegetables. The truck I'm driving today is rusted out and looks like something that belongs on a farm, the faded Serendee logo on the side. It's all part of the image: organic and wholesome, yet pull back a few layers, and the truth is exposed.

"Thanks, man," Mac says, handing me the envelope of cash. "We've got a big party coming up this weekend. We need to *feed* a lot of people."

Mac's a big guy—looks like he spends more time in the gym than in class—but what do I know? My father limited my education to the classes available on Serendee plus his own lectures. I guess he did give me a big dose of economics, too: supply and demand. There's a reason he picked weed as his primary product. Our community is adjacent to a notorious party school.

"Happy to do business with you," I say, opening the creaky, rusty door. "I think you'll be very happy with our... produce."

"Hey," he calls as I step inside. "You should come by the party this weekend. Bring some friends."

"Thanks, I'll swing by if I have time."

I get in the truck and crank the engine. This is how it works. Serendee grows the product, I deliver it, posing like I'm just a regular guy, and I get an invite. Then I start recruiting for more sales and yeah, marks for my dad.

He only wants the rich ones—preferably women, but he'll take a few men. He needs able bodies to do the grunt work down at the farm or around the community. Turning out of the frat house driveway, I take a left, riding through campus. I check the time. The hand off went pretty quickly, which gives me time for another stop.

I find a spot to park on the street and head up the big set of stairs toward the University library. Inside I go straight to the bank of computers, passing clusters of students on their laptops or at tables surrounded by books. It's not hard to fit in. I'm the right age and know how to acclimate—another one of my father's traits that I inherited. Most of it is about confidence, just *thinking* you belong. Knowing it. I pass a group of chairs where a girl in a short skirt looks up and gives me a flirty smile. I return it, but keep walking, sliding into one of the privacy corrals. I take one more discrete look around, before getting online. I never can be sure, but I don't think Anex has any spies in here.

I have an entire series of accounts that I only use when my father can't see them. Although the rest of Serendee shuns electronics, the Chosen have access to pretty much whatever we want. He talks a big game about not rotting your mind with secular devices, but he knows how the world works. You can't rule it without high-speed fiber and access to offshore banking.

I start how I always do, pulling up the file I've collected on my mother, Beatrice Wray. Sometimes her maiden surname, Holt. Nothing much comes up, a few articles about the beginning of Serendee. I bring up one article that I've read a dozen times. It's from the University paper, talking about a group of students with an inspiring project; the development of a self-sustaining community. It's mostly my father's early ramblings, about fresh air and food, equality and getting back to basics. It's long before he took on his iconic role of the leader in the community. Back when his name was Tim Wray, before he took the title of Anex.

There's one quote from my mother. "I look forward to living in a safe, supportive community, free of the disparity and corruption of society."

"Safe," I mutter, shaking my head. "You married a sociopath. There's not much safe about that."

I flip over to the medical examiner's report—Beatrice died at home, a blood clot exploding in her brain. I've skimmed this paper a hundred times, but I don't believe it. I was fourteen when she died, and I felt the change in her long before that. I saw her nervous smile and heard the whispered arguments between her and my father. He'd started implementing the Domums. He'd changed his name. All eyes were on him—not the community as a whole. Guards were placed around the borders, and the barn was under construction. He had plans for Serendee and my mother didn't agree with them.

How lucky for him that she died during this tension and turmoil. And, I think, looking at the bottom of the report at the medical examiner's signature—Virginia Bloom. How lucky is it for him to have the doctor that signed this paper to now be a member and his personal healer in Serendee?

I pull up the internet browser, taking the steps to open my social media accounts. They're under false names—as much to hide them from my father as from anyone looking into our business dealings. I like friend contacts in the secular world—the frat boys and people I meet at the club. I've also found my mother's long defunct account. I can see her profile, but it's limited. The photos are old—she'd stopped using it when they moved to Serendee, back when it was more of a campground than a commune. Just the fact she kept it up feels like an act of defiance to my father—something that makes me feel closer to her. It's useless to me though. What I need is to get into the actual account, but I have no idea what email she used or her password.

I stare at the computer for a long time, frustration building. This is where I always hit a brick wall. How can I prove what my father did if everyone believes his lies? If the medical examiner is covering his tracks? On her page, I click on the different tabs. Photos: just old profile pictures. Information: blank. Friends: the list is short, but it pops up. I scan down the page.

A face pops out at me, and I pause, feeling a hollowing out in my stomach. The name, Camille Sanders means nothing to me, but the face... I know it. I've seen those lips pull back in a nervous smile and the eyes widen with fear.

That face—or a younger version of it—belongs to Imogene. My mate.

IMOGENE WASN'T at The Center when I stopped to look for her. Another girl sat behind the desk, gawking at me and mumbling about how she wasn't feeling well and went home. I drive back to Serendee. In general vehicles aren't allowed outside of the garage and work areas, but I'm too impatient to stop, pulling the old truck in front of our cottage.

I've just closed the front door when Silas walks out of the downstairs bathroom, holding something in his hands.

"Where is she?" I ask.

"Upstairs, but—"

I don't wait for an answer and take the stairs two at a time. I've always known about Imogene's mother—the Regressive. She'd been removed years before for her destructive thoughts and attitude. I've never really thought about where she is now, or the fact she knew my mother. Maybe she can tell me more about what I'm looking for.

I enter our bedroom without knocking, prepared to rouse Imogene to tell me what knows. She's asleep. Flat on her stomach. I move to wake her when I hear, "Don't. She needs her rest."

I spin and see Silas in the doorway. "What gives you the right to tell me how to handle my mate?"

"The fact she stumbled in here, barely able to walk two hours ago."

"What are you talking about?" I frown and look down at her. Nothing about her looks unusual other than her position. Every other time I've seen her asleep, she's been curled up on her side. "What's wrong with her?"

I don't wait for an answer, yanking back the quilt covering her body. She's wearing a cotton nightgown, but it's pushed up to her waist. Her ass is blistered, flaming red.

"She went for Correction," Silas says. "Things got... a little rough. I gave her a pill and applied some salve. It worked last time, but the wounds weren't so severe."

"Last time? Who did this?" Wild rage burns in my chest. I spin and look at Silas. "Was it my father?"

"No," he replies, but I see the flicker of apprehension in his eyes. "She chose this, Rex. It's part of the philosophy. You know that."

"This," I say, turning to look back at the bloody welts and bruises, "is my father's fucked up mind games. It's how he controls." I step toward him. "I'll ask again and I expect an answer. Who did this?"

Silas isn't as tall as I am but he's broad shouldered and not intimidated by me. He glances over at Imogene before grabbing me by the shirt and drags me into the hall.

"You're right. She's a creation of your father's just like the rest of us. Correction is part of her life—it's how she copes. You can't blame her Guide. It's not like you're around Serene to take care of her."

My hands ball into fists, but I don't hit him, I just push past him down the hall and fling open Elon and Levi's doors. Neither are inside, but just seeing Levi's room, the books and journals tells me everything I need to know. Levi will do *anything* my father asks, including damaging my property.

"Where is he?"

He swallows. "Don't make this harder than it already is", he says.

I run my hands through my hair, tugging at the ends. "Where the fuck is he?"

The door slams downstairs and rage fuels me down the stairs. Levi stands in the hallway, hanging his satchel on a hook on the wall. I rush him, plowing my hands into his chest and smashing him into the wooden door.

"What the hell?" he shouts, eyes wide with shock. He struggles against me, but I leverage my forearm against his chest to keep him pinned.

"I saw what you did to her. She's torn up and bloody!"

"I'm her Guide," he says, without an inch of remorse. "She asked for Correction."

"And you beat her black and blue?"

"She—"

"No! No excuses. I've given a lot of leniency when it comes to her and you three, but destroying my property isn't one of them."

The backdoor flings open and Elon walks in. He takes in the two of us and exhales. "What is this?"

"Levi Corrected Imogene," Silas says. "Rex has suddenly decided he's the only one that can play with his toy."

I spin around. "Shut up."

The distraction is enough for Levi to shove me off and get around me. He stands next to Elon and rubs his chest. "Tell him," Levi says, looking at Elon. "Tell him about his Ordered."

There's something about Elon's expression I can't read. Something conflicted yet knowledgeable. "Tell me what?"

"She wants it like that," he says. "Needs it. Rough and painful. Anex has gotten in her head. She's so fucked up and twisted she can't tell pleasure from pain. So, when she's confused or feels guilty she goes to him."

My eyes dart to Levi. "And you what? Fuck her?"

"I *Correct* her. That's all." But I see it in his eyes. That's not all he does to her.

"He's telling the truth," Elon says, crossing his arms over his chest. "I saw her after. She could barely function."

"Because he tore the skin off her ass."

"Because he left her hanging. She was sloppy wet, cunt swollen and aching. She couldn't see straight."

"So what? You brought her home and let Silas put her to bed?"

"No," he shakes his head, without a trace of remorse. "I gave her what she needed. I fucked the guilt and pain out of her. I fucked her pussy so hard that all of this bullshit was gone—your rejection, your father's manipulation, her worry about Lapses." I start to argue but he holds up his hand. "Before you start about how you're not like your father, just stop. You're not any better. Taking her virginity like that. Going in at night and showing up when you feel like it. She'll do anything to please you. Take any abuse."

"Don't you dare compare us."

"He's not," Silas says, jumping in, "but you need to pay attention, brother. She's lost. Confused. Caught up in a world we've dragged her into. One that you keep threatening to leave, and one in which your father will then remain, ready to snatch her up when you go.

"I'm here, aren't I?"

But the statement falls flat. I'm here because I needed something from *her*. I wasn't there when she needed guidance. When she needed a cock buried deep inside to relieve the pain. Or later when she needed someone to soothe her wounds.

I take, I don't give. Fucking hell, I am like my goddam father.

"I don't know how to give her what she needs. That's not who I am," I admit.

"See, that's the thing," Silas says, clapping me on the back, "we do. We need to build her up, keep her strong, and show her that we can take care of her."

"And my father? Let's not pretend you aren't all working directly for him."

"We do this like we do everything," Elon says, "one foot in and one out of the system. He taught us this world, Rex, but he also gave us something he didn't anticipate."

I raise an eyebrow. "What's that?"

"Power."

53

I mogene

I WAKE to the bed shifting, the weight of a person next to me. I'm still on my stomach, backside aching, but turn my head to see the person next to me. Silas.

"Good morning," he says, pushing the hair off my neck. "How did you sleep?"

"Okay, I guess. I tried rolling over a few times." I make a face. "Didn't work so well."

He holds up a small pot. "I brought some salve. It'll help heal the wounds and swelling. May I?"

I nod, eager for some relief. Things got a little extreme with Levi the day before. Something intense came over me. Like a craving for water on a hot day. I didn't just want him to Correct me like that, I needed it to survive. That doesn't even include what happened with Elon afterward.

Silas gently lowers the blanket and pushes up my nightdress

allowing the cool air to hit my backside. I watch his face as he does it, the wrinkle in his nose at the sight of the injury.

"Is it bad?" I ask.

"I've seen worse."

That surprises me. Almost as much as the sensation I feel when his fingers make contact with my flesh, rubbing the cool, icy feeling salve over my blistered skin. "Oh! That's nice."

"Good." He smiles. "I made it last night. I knew you needed something a little more potent than my normal cream."

I relax into the massage, enough that I build the courage to ask, "What did you mean when you said you've seen worse?"

He dips his fingers in the pot, scooping out a glob. "Part of my job is to treat wounds like this. I'm not a healer—well not the medical kind—I'm more about treating the soul, the sexual one, and sometimes that pent up frustration results in physical injury. Like yours."

He continues to massage, moving away from the blisters, down over the curve of my backside, until he dips his fingers between the crack. My belly flutters, twisting with that familiar desire. This one is less conflicted though. It's nice. Wanting. Relaxing.

"Do you think I'm crazy for letting Levi do this to me?" I ask when his fingers travel up my back.

"I think you're seeking The Way—Enlightenment. That doesn't come without sacrifice."

"Have you ever done something like this?" I watch his face when I ask. "To yourself or others?"

"I've experienced the strap," he says, the corners of his mouth tugging down. "But it's not my thing. I love skin and flesh. I like it soft and whole. I want to taste it, lick it, kiss it, treasure it." His eyes meet mine. "I'm not judging. But I prefer to push myself and the people I work with to the edge in a different manner. Less painful. More transcendent."

As he explains this, his hands wander, gently stroking my skin. He explores every inch, the soft parts under my arms, or the slight curve along the side of my breasts. It tickles and nags, pulling at a string coiled tightly at my belly. Heat builds on my skin, a contrast from the cool salve Silas coated over my wounds.

"There's more than one way to reach Enlightenment," he says, pushing my cheeks apart and running his finger down to the tight ring. "Do you want to experience it?"

My body jerks in surprise, but that is followed by a spreading warmth under my skin. It pulses in my veins. I have no idea what he's asking of me, but I trust this man. He's done nothing but keep me safe and healthy. "Please," I breathe. "It's all I want."

He removes his hands and retrieves a different bottle. He wipes the salve off his fingertips and coats them in a slippery oil. He returns to his work, massaging the underside of my butt cheeks. The pressure is deep, assuring, and by the time he returns to the puckered ring my body is wracked with desire. Silas teases around the edge and whispers in my ear, "Relax, Imogene, you'll feel a little pressure at first, but I'll go slow."

I take a deep breath and just as I release it, he pushes his finger inside. My belly twists and my muscles tighten.

"Ease up, or it'll hurt."

What Silas doesn't know is that pain doesn't scare me, but even I can sense my tension is keeping him out. I inhale again and he pushes inside, stretching me as he goes. "How does that feel?"

"Strange?" He curves his finger a little and a shiver runs down my spine. "Good. Oh, yes, good."

He settles into a gentle rhythm, stretching me from the inside out. There's discomfort, but it's different. It's not tied up in conflict. It's just my body acclimating to something new—something exciting.

Silas's free hand shifts, and I feel the flutter of his fingertips along the nerves at the front of my body. They're slippery and slick, coating the hot bundle at the crux of my body. I suck in a gasp, bucking forward and back. To feel Silas inside and out like this, it sends shockwaves through my body, each one escalating as it builds toward the strong force that overtakes me.

"That's it," Silas says, bending to kiss me. "Ride it out."

The orgasm wracks through me, and I close my eyes, panting

through the experience. It's not until my body stills, and Silas has removed his fingers, that I open my eyes and realize we're not alone. I jolt up, fearful. "I—"

Rex's eyes are blazing, his mouth set in a thin line. "Clean yourself up and get dressed. We need to talk."

He walks out before I can react, and I look to Silas who is still beside me. "Is he upset?"

"It's hard to know lately. He's on edge."

"Will he be upset that you did that to me? That I allowed you to do it?"

"He gave us permission, remember?" Silas brushes my hair off my face and helps me to an upright position. The pain in my backside feels better. "And I doubt he's mad. Probably jealous."

I snort. "I doubt that."

He shrugs and kisses me gently on the mouth. "It's good that he's here and wants to see you. Get ready. I'll tell him you'll be out soon."

I take my time, washing up and braiding my hair. I pull on one of my every day dresses, the fabric made from hemp cultivated on site and dyed with natural colorings. By the time I go to the living room, walking gingerly, he's there alone. His eyes sweep over me, most likely resentful of my choice in clothing.

"Sorry I took so long. Can I get you something to eat or drink?"

He nods at the chair. "Sit."

I ease into the chair, trying not to grimace as the pain swells. I place my hands in my lap and wait for what's coming; punishment, admonishment, abuse. With Rex it could be anything.

"I want to talk to you about your mother."

I blink, trying to process his words. "My mother?"

He nods. "Yes. I know she and my mother were friends."

Heat prickles at my neck. Speaking of my mother... it's not completely forbidden but it's frowned upon. It puts a target on my back by making people remember what happened when she rejected Serendee and Anex's ways. She's Regressive and was banished from the community.

"I'm sure that was before my mother made her thoughts and feelings known. I doubt Beatrice would have allowed herself to be tarnished by someone so—"

"Stop." He says. I gape for a moment, then swallow. "You shouldn't feel shame about your mother. God, she's probably the only person that lived here that I respect."

"Excuse me?"

"She had the guts to stand up to my father. She fought for her beliefs." He sets his eyes on me. "The only thing I blame her for is leaving you here."

I stare at him, my heart thudding in my chest. No one has said anything positive about my mother in years. Her name is uttered as a curse—a warning, but here is the second most powerful man in Serendee telling me that he respects her. As much as he can respect any female.

As much as I'd like to bask in it, paranoia creeps up my spine. "We shouldn't talk about this."

"See," he runs his hand through his fair hair, "that's what they tell you to keep us from developing our own ideas. To keep us from the truth. If topics are forbidden then we won't ask questions and look for answers."

"What answer do you want?" I ask, feeling the edge of anxiety building. "What possibly can you want to know that involves my mother?"

He leans forward and I catch a hint of his warm, clean scent. It's alluring and disarming. "I want to find her, Little Lamb, and I want you to help me."

54

I mogene

REX'S REQUEST hangs over me like a cloak of paranoia as I go about my work. Part of living in Serendee is never feeling alone. We're a community. We live together, eat together, work together. Eyes are always on us, but it's for our own good. It's how we work to Be Better, knowing someone else is keeping us accountable.

The other things: the training, the extra calories, the bras and panties I wear under my standard dresses, those happen behind closed doors. But looking for my mother's contact information? That requires stealth and sneakiness.

Rex doesn't tell me where to look, but I have a good idea of a place to start: The Center.

I arrive early. The only other business open is the coffee shop two doors down. I keep my chin level, forcing myself not to look at the ground or appear suspicious in any way. It's silly, because no one notices me, but my heart still rattles in my chest as I open the front door and disengage the alarm.

I lock the door behind me, but don't turn on the light, then carry my belongings to my desk, putting everything away like normal.

I'm obeying my husband, I remind myself.

I am acting at his request.

I am fulfilling my duties as a mate.

This is what I tell myself as I walk down the back hallway to the records room. This room isn't a secret—the words are written on a plaque outside the door. Records. About every person that walks into this facility. Every person that lives in Serendee.

If there's information about Beatrice or my mother, it'll be in this room.

The problem is that no one is allowed in here without permission. I've only been in here twice, under the guidance of a male instructor who is tight in Anex's inner circle. I watched him punch in the code that day, and I stand before the keypad now, hoping it hasn't changed. Terrified that a slip up will alert someone to my presence.

I am fulfilling my duties as a mate.

I punch in the string of numbers I memorized. Why did I memorize them? Because that is who I am on a basic level, right? Tip toeing in the edge of Regressive. Defiant. Rebellious.

Inhaling sharply, I enter the last number and the keypad lights up, flashing green before the sound of the lock echoes in the empty hall. I enter before I can talk myself out of it and step into the room. It's the size of a classroom, each wall filled with file cabinets and four rows in between. I walk to the nearest one and pull out the drawer. Just as I remembered it is filled with file folders. Some thicker than others, but each with a name typed across the tab.

I pull out one and see the name Maribel Ashwood. Inside is a single sheet that has her age (19) Residence (Wittmore University) and the date she came in the Center. She took two classes but never returned. There's a picture of her stapled to the top, along with a few other details like her father's occupation, net worth and notes jotted by her instructor.

Looks like standard follow up methods were taken, but no one could get her to return. Right before I put her file away, I notice that her first meetings were two years ago. The last documentation on her though was three weeks ago. People are keeping tabs on her long after she lost interest.

The truth is that most people that walk into the Center don't join our ranks. They take a few classes, learn about Enlightenment but either can't afford to continue classes, or it's not a good fit. Not everyone is ready for this lifestyle.

I shut the cabinet door and move down the row, stopping at 'M.' I pull the drawer open and pick through the files. My stomach feels like a stampede of elephants is running through it, nausea rolling over me in waves. Once I open this wound, there's no going back. Not for Rex, not for me.

I am fulfilling my duties as a mate.

I stop at her name. Montgomery. There are three of us, my dad, my mom and me. My father's file is average for a man who has lived here his whole life. A history of his classes, job service, dedication. I don't waste time looking into it. Not now. My file is thick—twice the size of my father's which would have been surprising to me before my Ordering but not now. Anex would have documented every moment of my life once he found out his son wanted me for his mate.

It's tempting to see what it says about me, but a flash of the appointment with Anex's healer rushes to my mind, and I don't want to know. I'm barely able to make it through one day at a time now. To see it written on paper? I can't.

So I focus on the thinnest file of the three. Camille Sanders Montgomery. My heart sinks before I flip back the cover. It's too thin. Sure enough, there's a single sheet and a photo of my mother—young— right after college. The paperwork is succinct. Name, age, history, and a big red stamp across the page: Regressive.

The elephants in my belly vanish and are replaced with something else. Something I didn't know I was carrying until I saw the file.

Curiosity.

Real, genuine, curiosity.

Who is Camille Montgomery? Where is she? And why has Anex scrubbed her history?

~

I REALIZE LATER there is one person I can ask.

During my lunch break, I take the gravel road to the cluster of single person residences near the gym. Anex was an early adopter of small, environmentally sustaining homes. His theory is that people don't need to spend so much time isolated, not if they live in a strong community. Bathrooms and kitchens are part of a shared space in the center. My father has lived in one of these homes since my mother left, and I moved into the Domum.

I knock on the door knowing he should be home. I checked his work schedule before I left the office. I have access to everyone's daily schedule, and his said he was off today. As expected, it only takes him a moment to open the door. "Imogene," he says, his voice conveying his surprise. He recovers quickly, spreading his arms wide and giving me a hug. "How are you?"

"Good," I reply, allowing the gentle hug. My relationship with my father is superficial. The people of Serendee are my family. Anex my leader. Rex my mate. We both understand this. "How are you?"

"Wonderful." He gestures to the small front porch and we both take a seat on the ledge. "It's been a long time since you've visited," he says. "But I know you've been busy with your Order and the excitement of joining Anex's family."

He beams. It's a rare honor to become part of the inner circle. It reflects on him as well—just like it reflected on us when my mother was forced to leave. My current status elevates us both, which is why my coming here—and the reason behind it—is such a risk.

"It's definitely been a change," I say, smoothing out my dress. "Getting used to living with Rex has been eye opening." I give him a smile. "I'm sure you and mom went through your own challenges when you got married."

His grin slightly wavers. "That was a long time ago. It's hard to remember."

"I'm sure." I take a deep breath. "I need to ask you something."

"Anything, sweetheart. I owe you a betrothal gift."

"That isn't necessary." I look around, checking to make sure we're truly alone. All I hear is the birds chirping and the sounds of a tractor off in the distance. "Do you have a way to contact her?"

His head tilts. "Her?"

I hold his eye and a deep line forms on his forehead. "I don't know what you're talking about."

"Yes, you do, and I know it's an inappropriate topic, but I need to know."

He shakes his head, and I don't miss how his hands tremble. "Imogene, you've come farther than I ever expected with the mark of your mother's betrayal following you around. Why would you dig this up now?"

"It's important," I say, feeling the lump build in the pit of my stomach. "To me."

"No. Someone else is behind this." His voice is barely a whisper. I say nothing, just give him a hard look and he replies. "Anex? He wants this information? Is this a test? Is he questioning my loyalty?"

"No!" I say, too forcefully. A crow takes flight off the top of the community building. "No, daddy," I say, using the name from my childhood. "It isn't a test. Anex will never know. This is just between the two of us. I…" I swallow. "I'm about to mate with a powerful man and honestly, there are times in a woman's life where only one person can help her. I need my mother."

He takes my hand and squeezes it. The skin rougher than what I remember. "I can't help you, Imogene. And if you're smart you won't ask anyone else. If," he looks around, "if anyone hears of this, the consequences will be swift. Not even Rex will be able to help you."

It was a long shot, a stupid idea to come here. My mother wouldn't contact him anyway. My father is too weak. He doesn't carry the streak of defiance that runs through my blood—that clearly came from her.

"I understand," I say, rising. "I'm sorry if I upset you."

His blue eyes hold mine. "I'm sorry I couldn't give you what you wanted, but it's for your own good, sweetheart, I promise you."

I nod, taking a step away from the man I used to call my father. I realize now that whatever bond we shared back then is truly dissolved. Anex probably knew that the day he sent my mother away.

It's probably safer for both of us this way.

"It was good to see you, Imogene," he says, watching me walk away. "Be safe."

The last part is a warning, one that never would have been a problem—not until the day I was Ordered to marry Rex. I exit the housing area, headed back to the office, already trying to figure out the next step in fulfilling my mate's demands, no matter how risky they are.

WHEN I RETURNED to the office an envelope was leaning against my pencil cup. Inside are directions about the next women's meeting. Again, I'm to come alone, but this time not to the woods, but to Beatrice' house.

The house is dark, but the soft glow of candlelight flickers in the window. I enter and a note on the foyer table tells me to go to the second floor. The house is eerie like this, quiet and empty, but curiosity takes hold. This isn't just a house. It's Rex's childhood home. A shrine to his dead mother and family.

The instructions, set next to a lantern with a handle on top, say to go to the third door on the right, but I disobey, opening two others before I find the one I'm looking for. Rex's childhood bedroom. It, too, is set up like a museum: everything, from toys to photographs to the sports themed bedding, frozen in time.

I stop to look at a photograph of the family and hold up the light. Anex, Bea, and Rex, probably about six, posed outside on a beautiful fall day. Anex, who went by Tim before his wife died, is handsome, with warm sun-kissed skin and a wide smile. Beatrice is pretty—and I can see shades of both of them in their son. Rex stands between his parents on a brick wall, arms around their shoulders. I try to find hints of the man he is now, the man that spends his time tormenting me, but all I see is a sweet little boy.

I feel a tug of sorrow for the loss of him.

"There you are," a voice says, dragging me from my thoughts.

"Margaret." She's not hooded this time, although she's in dark clothes. I guess we're not hiding this time.

"Did you get turned around?" her question has a tone, one that implies that she knows I didn't misread the directions.

"Yes," I lie. "I was just so nervous; I didn't pay attention."

She takes my hand. "Don't be nervous. Tonight is about Enlightenment. When you walk out this door, you'll have the weight of womanhood lifted from your shoulders."

The weight of womanhood. Is that the cause for the noose around my neck? I follow Margaret to the room next door. It's the master bedroom. My spine goes rigid when I look behind the headboard. There's a painting—a portrait—of Anex. It's huge, framed in gold. He's sitting in on his lecture chair, legs crossed, body casual. I've seen this position a million times. At celebrations, at midnight meetings, at any event where he's speaking. Now he looks down at us, his blue eyes painted an unnaturally bright color blue.

I'm so caught up on this painting—disturbed by it, I don't even notice that at the foot of the bed, a circle has been drawn and single candle, surrounded by various stones, marks the middle.

Margaret looks up at the painting and says, "A reminder that this ceremony is blessed by Anex and all he wants is for you to find your true self." She squeezes my shoulder and moves to stands over the circle. "This is the circle of confession. A place where you will release the burdens that hold you back from your true self."

"Isn't that what Correction is about?"

She smiles, her lips looking elongated in the shadowy light. "This is different. It's about sharing your burdens to another woman. Someone who can help carry the weight." Her hands thrust over the circle and reach for mine. "It will be a journey; one we will take together. Are you ready?"

My heart thuds, a month ago this would have been a dream. Spending time with Anex's spiritual wife, would have fulfilled all of my wishes, but now... it's not just scary, it's terrifying. I have secrets. Big ones, ones that could hurt so many people.

But she doesn't wait for my response, stepping into the circle and drawing me in with her. We both sit, her on one side and me on the other. With my hands still in hers, and our knees parallel. Her smile is kind, and I remember who I am, how I was raised and what I believe.

The Way will always carry me through. Margaret is just another guide.

"I'm ready," I say, a few minutes too late.

"Good. Did you prepare like you were told?"

The folded-up paper burns in my pocket. I retrieve it, but don't hand it over. Not yet.

"Is that your collateral?" she asks.

"Yes," I say, my stomach rolling with uneasiness. "I wasn't exactly sure what you wanted."

Although, that's not entirely true. They want secrets. Dirt. Skeletons in the closet. The directions were clear, I was to write down a confession about something in my life, a secret no one else knew about, that if I told anyone about the woman's group or ever betrayed anyone else involved, that secret, or collateral, would be used against me.

For me, it wasn't a matter of if I had a secret that could be used for collateral, but which one I should share.

I'd thought hard about it. Channeled The Way. Searched for the right answer. There wasn't one. I could just as easily write down that Rex wants to destroy his father, that our Ordering is a sham, or that he's searching for the truth about my mother and his. I could tell them about the intensity of my Corrections: how it's moved beyond seeking Enlightenment for my Lapses and down a dark, seductive, rabbit hole I can't escape. I could confess to the panties in my drawer, the porn on Silas' computer... there are too many infractions to count.

But most of those were approved of by Anex. And the stuff about Rex? That's a betrayal with deep consequences. So, I wrote down the only thing that felt like it was big enough, but also everyone involved knew about.

"Just read me what you wrote down," Margaret says.

My hands shake, making the paper tremble. I look up at her and she nods. "Since my Ordering, I've been intimate with other men than Rex. A man of his stature has particular needs and wants. I was instructed to receive training from Rex's friends, preparing me for my future mate's unconventional needs and desires."

As I say the words, I'm sure that Margaret already knows this. She's been mentoring me for a while and is wise and Anex's closest confidant. But still, admitting it out loud, feels wrong and shameful.

"Did you enjoy this intimacy?" she asks.

"Sometimes," I confess. "They're difficult men. Not always nice. Demanding but..."

"But what?"

"But they know women and their bodies. They know what Rex wants in a mate and that is always my priority."

Margaret squeezes my hand and takes the paper from me. "You're a strong woman, Imogene."

"I don't feel strong." God, that's the most honest thing I've said in days. "I feel weak and lost and confused. I'm overrun with emotions and desires. It's like I'm a slave to my body, to these feelings I've never experienced before."

"You are doing the work of Serendee," Margaret says, "following The Way. If Anex wants you to explore your sexuality with other men, then what you're doing must be right."

Because Anex is never wrong.

I take a deep breath. "Was that enough? Collateral?"

"More than enough," she says, leaning across the candle and tucking my hair behind my ear. "You've unloaded your burden, and I'm here to carry the weight. Are you sure there's nothing else?"

Loads, I almost say, but I just shake my head.

"And you don't think I'm a bad person for what I just told you?"

"Imogene, you're a beautiful, sexy woman. I know you were taught modesty and faithfulness to the man you were Ordered with, but not everyone is meant to follow the same path. You're part of the Chosen, mated with a powerful man, and that means different demands will be placed on you. We've talked about this before."

I know her relationship with Anex is different. He has many spiritual wives, but he's also special. I'm not special. I was chosen because Rex needed something from me, something I didn't fully understand until he asked me to contact my mother.

"Thank you for sharing this burden," I say, feeling the slightest weight off my shoulders. "Rex is torn between two worlds, and I'm determined to be the anchor that ties him to Serendee. I'll do anything for him."

I realize as soon as I say it that, the words are not only true, but they're the kind that get a person in trouble. I search Margaret's expression, but I don't see anything that implies she noticed. The unease doesn't subside as my mentor chants a mantra of healing and then extinguishes the candle. The hairs on the back of my neck stand on end as I pass Rex's childhood bedroom and descend the stairs.

It's not until I'm outside that I take a breath.

I *will* do anything for this man, which is startling and concerning. My duty as a member of Serendee isn't to devote myself to my mate.

It's to devote myself to our leader, his father.

55

———————

E^{lon}

She doesn't notice me as she walks down the steps of the bungalow and up the road. Imogene is lost in a world of her own, and I can't help but wonder what transpires between her and the other women in the group. Knowing Anex, it's transactional and involves secrets, lies and manipulation. Other than money, those are the currencies he trades in.

I follow her, keeping an eye on her as she walks in the dark. Her blonde braid swings across her back. Unlike the women in the secular world, she's fearless. Those other women have a wariness about them. They've been conditioned to keep an eye over their shoulder, to be aware that bad men are out there. Men that hurt.

Imogene? Well, she's been conditioned to think that bad men are good. That hurt is love and that pain means you're following The Way.

It's not just her poor little brain that's fucked up. It's her body, too. I've never seen a woman crave hurt so much.

As she walks down our street, my phone vibrates in my pocket. I pull it out and look at the message.

Silas: Can you grab my kit.

Elon: Yes. What's up?

Silas: Meet me at the Main House. I'll explain then.

I hadn't planned on approaching her, but now that Silas needs his kit, I catch up as she opens the front door.

"Hold the door," I say, announcing myself. She turns at the sound of my feet pounding on the porch steps.

"Oh, sure," she says, cheeks flushing slightly. "I was just—"

"I need to grab something for Silas," I say, cutting her off before she is forced to tell a lie about where she's been. A lie that'll send her back down to that dungeon with Levi for Corrections. I step in the house and search the cubbies by the door. "Ah, there." I spot the blue case on the top shelf and pull it down. "Silas asked me to bring it to him."

"His First-Aid kit?" she asks, frowning. "Is he hurt?"

"No, I don't think so." I curl the handle in my fingers. "He said to bring it to the Main House."

"Someone is hurt," she says, eyes narrowing as she tries to piece it together. "Someone that can't see a healer?"

I hadn't even thought about it. Silas' job... it's not something I ask about. The things he is asked to do, the tasks Anex makes him perform... I'd rather not know.

Imogene and I share a look and I realize she understands this as well. She should. He's healed her wounds more than once. "I'm coming with you," she says suddenly.

I laugh. "No, you're not."

"Why?"

"Because Silas didn't call you."

"Call me? I don't have a phone, Elon. No one in this community has a phone but the four of you."

True. "I don't know what we're getting into, Little Lamb, and the farther you stay from the Main House, the better. Rex wouldn't want you up there."

"Well, Rex isn't home, and since when are you afraid to show me the under belly of Serendee?" Her arms cross under her breasts, drawing my eyes down. When I drag them back up her expression has softened, her eyes pleading. "Let me help."

It's then that I realize I can't tell this woman no. Not when she looks at me with those clear blue eyes and pink pouty lips. I run my hand through my hair and grunt, "Fine, but you stick by my side. No wandering off and if anything out of control happens, you get the fuck out of there, understood?"

"What could—" she starts to question, but I shoot her a look and she amends, "understood."

～

SILAS WAITS for us by the backdoor, forehead creasing when he sees Imogene. His eyes dart to mine. "What is she doing here?"

"I wanted to come," she says, answering for herself. I shrug and hand him his kit.

I can tell he wants to argue, but there's also a current of urgency vibrating off of him. He just jerks his head toward the door and punches in the code to disable the lock. Once we're inside he takes a staircase that leads downstairs, then continues down a long hallway.

"What is this?" Imogene asks. I'm not sure myself, but a bad feeling inches up my spine. Silas has told us about The Fallen and how they live separately, in small rooms under the mansion. I'd never had an opportunity to see it for myself. No, I'd never wanted the opportunity. Sometimes it's better to live in the dark.

"I heard from one of the girls that Charlotte is struggling."

"Charlotte?" I vaguely recall the name.

"She's the girl Anex reprimanded the day we went shopping," Imogene says. "Anex punished her."

The memory clicks. "For contacting her sister?"

"Yes." Her hand reaches out to Silas' and she links their fingers. "What's wrong with her?"

He stops at another door and uses another code to get past the lock. On the other side is a long hallway, rows of closed doors, each with locks, on both sides. A small window looks into each room.

"This is where he keeps them." Silas says, walking past several doors. Imogene makes an effort to look inside, but I push her along. I'm not exactly sure what happens behind these doors, but I don't think it's anything she needs to see. "Charlotte was sent down here to consider her Lapses. Why she feels the need to reach outside of Serendee for affirmation from her family." Neither Imogene or I argue this, it's a standard rule of the community. No outsiders unless they're approved. "She's a strong female," Silas says, eyes sliding from Imogene to me. "But she wants to please Anex."

He enters the code, and the door opens. The sour scent of body odor greets us.

The room is tiny, barely big enough for a small, single, bed and a desk. Log books sit on the top, along with three pencils, all worn down to the nub. On the bed is a skinny girl. I barely recognize her from that day in Anex's room. Her hair is stringy. Her arms bone thin. Her skin pale and ashy.

Imogene sucks in a gasp, her fingers dropping from Silas' hand to move to her mouth.

"Hey," he says, getting her attention. She shifts her head slightly, eyes trying to focus.

"I filled out my logs. Every calorie. Every Lapse. Every negative thought." She moves to sit up, but she doesn't get far. It's obvious why. Her hand is cuffed to the bed.

"It's fine," Silas says, gesturing for her to lie back down. "I'm not here to check on your progress. I'm here to make sure you're okay."

"Is this a test?" she asks, eyes narrowing. "Are you here to test me? To make sure I'm worthy?"

"No. I know you're worthy." He runs his fingers over the purple bruises on her wrists.

"I'm not." It's almost a whisper. "I'm not worthy of Anex's grace. I broke the rules. I made this happen."

"Sweetheart, let me check you out. Can I do that?"

Her eyes slide from Silas to Imogene and then over to me. She visibly flinches when she sees me. "Are you going to tell?"

I blink. "Tell?"

"Anex. I know you're one of the Chosen. You're impossible to miss." She tries to sit up again but falls back. "Are you going to tell him about me?" Her voice trembles. "Tell him I won't cry. Not this time. I promise."

"No one is telling Anex anything," Imogene says, turns to me. "I think you should step outside."

"Excuse me?"

Silas looks over his shoulder. "She's right. Just stand outside the door. I think you make her uncomfortable."

"Why? I don't even know the girl."

"Elon," Imogene says, "this girl is hurt. She needs help, and you're very intimidating." My eyes skim over her again, noticing the purple bruises on her wrists. "Just wait outside. We can take care of this."

We?

Since when is she part of this? Any of this?

But I do step back, giving them some space. The room is small, and I'm a big man. Intimidating. I don't deny that. I watch as the two of them focus on her. Silas with his bag of first-aid ointments and salves he mixes himself. Small packets of medications he carries as part of his job. He's not a healer, not in the traditional sense, but he is a caregiver. One that specializes in the broken females of Serendee.

"Charlotte," Silas says, sitting on the edge of the bed. "I know this is uncomfortable, but I'm going to examine you. Make sure you're okay."

There is no world in which this girl is okay. Imogene picks up one of the logs on the table. Her finger runs down the pencil marks. "This is all you're eating?" she asks.

"They bring me food. I only eat half. I'm not Indulgent."

Imogene's eyes flick to mine. Worried. "He likes me this way. The less I eat, the more he comes to... visit."

"He...?" Imogene asks.

"Anex."

While Imogene keeps her talking, Silas checks her skin for bruises, his fingers lingering over her inner thighs. From the door I see the purpling flesh—the imprint of a thumbprint. Charlotte pulls down her shirt, trying to cover them.

"How often does he come?" Silas asks, removing a protein bar from the kit and opening it. She stares at it like it's poison but he doesn't relent until she takes a bite.

"If I'm good he blesses me with multiple visits and oversees my re-education himself. Sometimes it's just once a day. Unless I cry. Then he makes me go through Corrections before he comes back." She gives a wobbly smile. "I almost never cry anymore."

Imogene picks up the second log and studies it. She moves closer to me, and I realize she's showing me the book—a calendar. Each day is filled with a series of X's. "Charlotte," she says, stepping toward the girl. "What do those marks mean?"

Her pale cheeks turn red, but her eyes shine with a dark glint. "That's when he comes. When he blesses me. I mark each time so I don't forget. Sometimes the days get confusing in here."

"He blesses you?" Imogene repeats. "Re-educates?"

"It's how I regain my status. Only Anex can work me though the levels of re-education." I didn't know for sure what Anex did with the Fallen. I didn't really care but seeing this girl—seeing Imogene's reaction to her—it stirs something in my chest. Charlotte looks up at her. "You're part of his family, aren't you? His son's mate." Imogene nods. "Will you tell him I won't be a bad girl anymore? I won't call my family. I can get the money. I'm here for him, always. I'm devoted."

Clutching the calendar against her chest, Imogene nods and turns abruptly, pushing past me to exit the room. Silas and I share a look and I follow her out. In the hall she's frantically peering into each window. I grab her. "Hey, I need you to settle down."

"Settle down?" she shouts. I drag her down the hall to the door and push her outside of the wing. The door slams behind us. "You want me to settle down after I saw that?"

"It was a lot," I admit, cupping the back of my neck. "What's happening down there—"

"He threatened to send me there," she says, cutting me off. "He said if my Bonding with Rex isn't real, he'll send me down with the Fallen, in the 'room I saved for your mother.'"

"Jesus," I mutter. "He's not going to do that."

"How do you know?" Her eyes are wild, full of uncertainty.

I grab her and pull her to me. "I know because he has to get through me to do that. He has to get through Silas and Levi and most of all Rex, who is more than willing to have an excuse to kill his father."

"Those 'blessings?' That's just him having sex with her, Elon," she says, as if I hadn't just spoken. She thrusts the calendar at me. "Multiple times a day all under the guise of 're-education.' All under the concept of being 'Better.'" Her voice rises. "He locks her up and uses her for his personal needs all day and night. Did you know about this?"

"This?" I ask, looking at the calendar—at the dark pencil marks documenting each and every time. "No. No more than you did."

"What does that mean?"

"It means, Anex uses the people of Serendee, Imogene. You know that. You've experienced it first-hand. You were raised in it just like the rest of us. We are at his mercy," I tell her. "He is our path to Enlightenment, isn't that how it goes?"

"What do you believe, Elon?" she asks. The tremble in her voice implies she knows how risky that question is. I answer it anyway.

"I don't know how I feel," I admit. "I'm caught somewhere between Rex and Levi. I know there is a bigger world out there, but unlike Rex, I don't believe I deserve it. I'm in Serendee because this is where I belong. I work for Anex because he is better than I am. If I deserved more, I would be given more. Until then, I have a job, and I'm thankful for that."

"And what exactly is that job?" she asks.

"Right now, it's training you to be a better mate for my best friend." I swallow, knowing it goes deeper than that. The secrets and lies. "Tomorrow it may be something different, but until I'm given different orders, my job is protecting the future of Serendee."

"And if that means leaving that girl in there to be," she swallows, "'blessed' by Anex every day for the rest of her life, then you'll do it."

I will. She knows it and so do I, but there's something else she's not admitting.

She doesn't have what it takes to save that girl either.

56

———————

I mogene

WHEN WE RETURN HOME, Rex and Levi are waiting.

"Where have you been?" Rex asks, eyes darting between me and Elon. Neither of us spoke on the way back to the house. The disgust and guilt over what I'd witnessed is too much to bear.

"Silas needed help," Elon says. "I took Imogene with me rather than her be here all alone."

"Anex has called a late-night basketball game for the men," Levi says, "Mandatory."

"Son of a—" Elon mutters. "Tell him I'm sick. Or running a job. I'm not in the mood."

"Who is?" Rex says. "You're going. I can't afford having him look into any of our activities right now."

Elon glances at me, jaw hard. Rex is right. Anex doesn't need to ask questions about where I'd been earlier, at the women's meeting, or then up at the house. It puts us all at risk for being defiant.

"Fine." He walks over to the refrigerator and opens the cabinet above. He pulls out a bottle of clear liquor, unscrews the cap and takes a swig. "But if I'm going, I'm going drunk."

Levi grabs his notebooks and shakes his head. He stops by me and says quietly, "Everything okay?"

"Just tired that's all." I give him a tight grin. "It was a busy day."

"Get some rest." He runs his fingers gently down my neck. "When Anex calls the men like this, it's viewed as a moment of respite for the women. Take the opportunity to recharge and reflect."

The last thing I want to do is reflect on what I saw up in the Main House.

"I will," I say, watching him step out the door. Elon follows with his bottle of liquor, barely looking me in the eye. Rex follows, but I grab his wrist and tug him back. His eyebrow raises.

"I spent some time today looking for answers to your question."

"Any luck?"

I shake my head. "Not yet, but I'll keep trying."

"Thank you," he says, resting his large hand on my hip, thumb rubbing tiny circles. "I guess you get a night off from our arrangement."

"Levi said it was an opportunity to recharge and reflect."

He snorts. "Like my father gives anyone a night off from anything."

"Try not to get in a fist fight with your father, okay?"

"Is that a request?"

"I just..." I think about Charlotte, her broken mind and body. Rex is the only thing keeping me out of a room like that. "I just want you to remember that you have a bigger plan."

His crystal blue eyes hold mine, and I have no idea what this man is thinking. But his hand rises to my chin, and he tilts my mouth towards his and he kisses me. For once it's not forceful, but his jaw is strong, tongue sweeping against mine. I feel the rush of our connectivity surge through me. Me and Rex... we've had this chemistry from the start, all the way back to that day we stumbled onto one another at the overlook when we were kids, bonded by our mothers.

Here we are again, literally 'bonded' by that and more.

"Good night, Imogene," he says, after he pulls away. My lips feel hot as does my skin, warming me after such a traumatizing night.

I'm still processing it, when Silas comes in, worn and exhausted looking. He returns his kit to the cubby by the door and barely looks up when I enter the foyer.

"Hey, can I get you something to eat? Drink?"

He shakes his head and walks past me, going to his room. A moment later I hear the water running in the shower. I stand in the doorway, caught in confusion. Should I do something? When I learned about caring for the man in my life, it centered around food and keeping the house orderly. Silas taught me more about how to make a man feel good, but that doesn't seem right, not now. He's also not my man.

I tap my fingers on my thigh. Or is he? Aren't they all? Isn't that what Rex told me he wanted? A woman for his friends who Anex would never give one of their own.

The urge to comfort Silas, the way he has comforted and soothed me through my own pain overwhelms me and without hesitation I stride into his room and enter the bathroom. The glass is fogged from the steam, but I see the shadowy outline of his naked body behind it. I peel off my dress, goosebumps rising on my flesh from the cool air, and open the shower door. Silas has his face lifted to the running shower, as if he's trying to wash away everything he'd seen, but he turns when he hears the door open.

"Hey," I say, sliding in the shower behind him. He doesn't move, and I wrap my arms around his waist, leaning into him. "Do you want to talk about it? We don't have to. I just..." I press my cheek against his warm, strong, back, "I didn't know you had to do things like that."

He reaches for my hand and pulls it tight against his toned belly. "I don't, and Anex will be pissed to find out I interfered, but I feel an obligation to these women."

I hear his heartbeat under my ear and feel his muscles tense at my touch. He's a strong man but filled with emotion and compassion. So different from the other guys.

"You aren't the one that hurt her, Silas. Anex did that."

He turns to face me. Our belly's touching. His cock half-erect and pressing between my thighs. "I played my part. Rex gets them in the door, Levi into classes and I... well, I strip away their inhibition. I confuse their mind and their bodies. I show them what feels good, so that they forget the bad." His forehead drops to my shoulder. "I own my guilt in this, Imogene. The least I can do is try to relieve a little of the pain."

I force his head up until I can see his face. "Did you give her the comfort she needed?"

"I gave her some medication." His mouth forms a frown. "She has an infection—from too much sex and inappropriate hygiene."

"Why would he allow that?" I ask, so confused by the actions of our leader.

"Because he can?" Hot water runs between us, but he shivers anyway, and I press my chest to his, trying to give him warmth. "He takes, Little Lamb, and when he notices you enough to give you something in return, it's never good."

His words hit my heart like a hammer, and the smallest piece chips away. I don't know what it means, or what any of us can do, but I have to act in some way. I look up at this man, so handsome and kind, so talented and skilled. I grab the soap and lather it in my hands, then gently scrub his skin.

He watches me as I work, coating his shoulders and then down to his chest, my fingers gliding down his hard flesh. His muscles tense, and his abdomen caves, quivering under my touch. His hands reach out for me, fingering my nipple, and watching it rise to a hard peak.

"You don't need to—" I start, wanting to focus on him, make him feel better, but he cups my breasts in his large hands and pushes them together, then drops his mouth to latch on.

The sensation runs through me, electric shocks that run straight between my legs. He moves to the other breast, and licks and sucks just as greedily, eliciting a moan that echoes off the bathroom tiles.

Silas looks up at me, eyes dark with heat. His mouth crashes against mine, kissing me with intensity. I've never felt him like this—

so raw and feral. I didn't know he had this side to him. I hold onto him tight, wanting him to pour all of that into me.

I shift backwards, searching for the wall. I find it and drag him to me, hiking a leg over his hip, feeling his length between my thighs.

"Fuck me," I tell him, finding the words he taught me. "Fuck me and make this all go away."

His eyes meet mine and a dark glint shines back. "You're just another one of my sins, Imogene. Another victim to add to the list."

"No," I tell him. "I'm not one of your victims. I'm one of *you*. One of us. Born and raised for this moment."

His hands move under me, lifting me off the floor. My back is pressed against the tile and the tip of his cock probes urgently at my entrance. I rock my hips, desperate to feel him inside of me. Somehow, he holds back. "You don't belong to me, Imogene."

"Is that what you think?"

"It's what I know. Anex wants me for his own use. He'll never give me an Order."

"Fuck his Orders, Silas." I kiss away the shock of my Regression, licking his lips, his tongue. "Rex owns me, and he has opened our life to you. All of you. He loves you that much and I—" I swallow the word. Love is complicated in Serendee. I rock my hips against him again and this time his cock inches in, stretching me slowly. "This is between us, the five of us, not *him*." I bite down on my bottom lip and then whisper, "Don't make me beg, not tonight."

Something in him breaks, like a dam crumbling under the pressure. His hips rear back, and he eases in, filling me with his length. The air knocks out of me, and he does it again, with deep sweeping thrusts. Even in all of this, Silas is a man of skills, a man that knows how to make a woman feel good. My tits bounce against his chest, grazing my nipples over the hard muscles, sending shockwaves through my nerves. He spreads my ass cheeks, and massages in the spot he'd explored before, eliciting shuddering quivers from back to front. He isn't hard and fast, or lost to his own demons like Rex. He doesn't pound into me like Rex, trying to bruise every inch of my soul. With Silas, every movement is intentional, delicious, and by the time the orgasm rolls over me, my entire body begs for release.

"Keep doing that," I cry, and he captures my mouth once again. I taste his tongue, swallow his hot breath, as the orgasm comes hard, a bright blinding light, in a sea of darkness. Silas doesn't stop until his body tenses, muscles undulating, hips rocking, until his seed fills me —our bodies tight and loose at the same time.

His mouth releases me at the same time he unsheathes himself, gently lowering me back to the floor. He takes the next few minutes to clean me up, washing away his cum with the cooling water.

Wrapped in warm towels, we stand just outside the shower, soaking the floor mat beneath our feet.

"Thank you," he says, pushing the wet hair off my shoulder. "No one's ever done that for me before."

I frown. "Done what?"

What he says next doesn't just break my heart, it shatters my soul. "Take care of me like that."

"Because you're always taking care of everyone else?" I ask, trying to understand. Silas has a position of authority in Serendee. He's chosen, but tonight showed me he's responsible for the most bruised and broken of us all. "It doesn't have to be that way. I'm here for you. The guys are here for you. We can shoulder some of the burden."

"No," he says, voice firm. "It's my place. Not yours. My duty to Serendee."

I blink, the truth of it all crashing down. "This is wrong, Silas. This is not what The Way is about. Our bodies are temples. We keep them clean and pure so we can become Enlightened."

He laughs, it's dark and lacking humor. "No number of lectures, Corrections or showers will make me clean enough for Enlightenment, Imogene."

I grab his hand, still damp. "What do you mean? Everyone can earn their way back. Even the Fallen."

"I wish that were true," he says. "I mean, I wish I could believe it. I used to, during those early days, when I was being trained. I thought I was working toward the greater good, that I was blessed with this face and this body, my persuasive nature by The Way, to help build Serendee into a place of wonder." His fingers thread through mine. "But now I'm not so sure." He drops his forehead to mine. "I just feel so dirty. No matter how many showers I take."

"But—"

He kisses me gently. "Thank you. For being you and giving me this moment."

With a squeeze of my hand he exits the bathroom. I'm struck by the simplicity of what he said, how even though this man is one of the Chosen and integral to the stability and growth of Serendee, he is just as lost as the rest of us. Rex may be right. I may need to be the anchor for all of these men. The question is will they let me?

57

———————

Imogene

I STARE at the dinner on the table... baked chicken, roasted vegetables, fresh from the Serendee garden, and mashed potatoes. A bowl of fruit and a homemade pie sit on the counter. All of it is cold now , having come out of the oven hours ago.

I look at my watch. Eleven PM.

Not one of them told me they wouldn't be here. And one in particular promised he'd come home at night. I guess that lasted all of two days.

I didn't just cook. I changed after work into one of the outfits Elon picked out for me, trying to be obedient to my mate's desires when he got home.

I'm *trying,* but I don't see how this works if he doesn't hold up to his end of the deal.

Twenty more minutes go by when I hear the front door open. Levi steps in eyes darting from the table full of food to me, sitting alone.

"Hey," he says, shrugging off his coat. "This looks amazing."

"It's cold," I announce. "I thought you'd all be home hours ago."

"Oh." He frowns and pushes his fiery red hair out of his eyes. "I had a late class at the Center, and Elon got called in to make a delivery." He picks a blueberry out of the bowl. "Silas went with him."

My jaw tightens and I will myself not to ask, "And Rex?" but it comes out anyway, bitter and harsh.

"I, uh," his hand swipes through his hair again, "I think he had some business to attend to on campus."

My eyebrow raises. "Business?"

"At the fraternity house," he admits. "It's good for him to be seen while his product is in use and, well, a good place to recruit."

"Women."

"Mostly, yes." His head tilts. "Are you questioning his service to Serendee?"

I snort. "He's at a party, Levi, not conducting a business meeting, and I'm aware of how Rex 'recruits' women. Will he sweet talk them back? Who does he hand them over to next? You or Silas?"

His forehead creases and he crosses over to me. "What's this about?"

Shame fills me. I'm being Indulgent, thinking only of myself and my desires. I drop my eyes from Levi's gaze. "Nothing. I just went to all this trouble to make dinner, and it would be nice if someone had told me none of you were going to be here."

"Well, I'm here now." He takes my hand and kisses the back of it. "Let me go shower and clean up. Then we can eat together."

I give him a tight smile and hold it until he's in his room, door shut behind him. All I can think of is Rex being at a party. Surrounded by secular women. I've witnessed this before, the way they hang on him in their tight clothes. He's handsome. Charismatic. He is his father's son after all.

Knowing he's out there, with them, creates a twist in my belly that is unfamiliar. An urge to find him and force him home. I stare at the food on the table and make a split moment decision.

I leave.

I can hear the sound of the shower running as I slip through the dark streets. I stick to the shadows, knowing that if I'm caught out late like this, alone, there will be consequences. Most of the other houses are dark. It's late. People work early and have long days. You never know when Anex will send out the signal and call us all to a lecture. The awareness of these facts only makes me angrier and more upset that Rex has pushed me to this point.

My hands tremble as I push open the gate, stepping over the line that divides Serendee from the Secular world, leaving the quiet behind. The world seems loud when I go outside the walls. Noisy and disruptive. There are so many people. So many eyes and cars and glowing devices. Sometimes the people barely notice me—so focused on their phones. But when they do it's like a wolf stumbling upon a single lamb... "Little Lamb," they call me. I understand it when I'm out here.

Tonight though, no one takes much notice. Not when I pass the bar or the late-night café. I realize it's because of my outfit. Jeans and a fitted shirt. A girl stares at me, and I realize it's the braid. I tug it out as I walk, letting it fall over my shoulders in waves.

I head toward campus, walking quickly past The Center on the way. I know where the fraternity row is located and I turn down the path that leads toward the street made of big blocky houses. These buildings make sense to me. A group of young people all sharing a home? A domun? I've lived this life—just in another world.

The party isn't hard to find. I just follow the people walking down the street. I watch them. Study the way the girls' hips move so easily, how the boys touch them without care. It's like the TV shows Silas had me watch. There's so much freedom here, while also, tension and stress.

I reach the house—three stories, red brick with columns. Greek letters hang over the door, Zeta Sigma. I'm shocked they don't fall off from the vibration of the music inside. From the sidewalk, I can feel it bouncing in my chest. People cluster on the porch. Men, women, dressed in a variety of ways. All clutching red cups in their grip.

Rex is inside there. I know it. Sense it, but another awareness comes slamming home; this is not my world. What was I thinking coming down here? I wasn't. I was being Indulgent. Lapsing. Everything I've strived not to be.

"I'm not sure what's going on in that pretty little head of yours, but it must be intense."

It takes me a moment to realize those words were meant for me.

"Excuse me?" I ask, taking a look at the man in front of me. He's tall. Lanky but broad. Shoulders wide and powerful. He's wearing a hoodie with a 'W' on the chest. An X underneath it made out of two oars. 'Wittmore Rowing' is embroidered in white thread.

"You just look a little lost and confused, although I don't know why," he grins. "You're exactly the kind of girl we love to see at our parties." He offers me his hand. "I'm Knox."

I stare at his hand. I've never touched a man outside of Serendee. Never had a conversation this long. He tilts his head, line creasing his forehead and I snap out of it, thrusting my hand into his. "I'm Imogene. I'm uh, new here."

"Imogene." He rolls the word on his tongue. "Unique, but I like it." He looks over my shoulder. "Hey Miller," he calls. I turn and see another man. This one is also tall, blue-eyed with a devilish-purely Indulgent glint in his eye. "Meet Imogene. She's new."

His smirk spreads into a wide grin. "Well, then, we need to give Imogene the Zeta Sigma new student treatment, don't you think?"

Knox nods, winking over my head. He throws his arm over my shoulder, and the two of them usher me past the guy standing at the door, through a crowd of mostly women, toward the kitchen. I search the house for Rex, but it's too thick with students and an ever-present cloud of smoke, that I don't see him. Maybe he's not even here? Miller grabs me one of the red cups and hands it to me.

"Welcome to Wittmore and Zeta Sig." Miller holds his own cup to mine, except his is black, not red. "May tonight be a night you won't soon forget."

I sniff the drink. It smells fruity, not sour like the heavy wine Elon forced me to drink a few weeks ago. I'm trying to think of a nice way to decline, when I spot a familiar blond head across the room. His jawline is unmistakable, as is his smile.

I rarely see it, but he's not holding back here, gracing some girl in short shorts and a tank top with its full intensity. Jealousy, dark and angry flares in the pit of my stomach and I tip the cup to my lips and swallow. The sweetness is followed by a burn. I cough and feel a warm hand on my shoulder.

"You okay?"

"I'm fine." I smile and take another, smaller sip. "Thank you."

"No, sweetheart," Miller says, "thank you for gracing us with your beauty tonight. We like to have the most beautiful girls on campus at our party. You just notched it up to a ten."

After weeks of battling the men in my life, of living on the edge of pain and humiliation, Corrections and Lapses and Regression, his words untangle something in my chest. Just hearing kind words, not laced inside twisted manipulations... I feel a rush of relief.

"Drink up," Knox says, "and let us show you a good time and forget about whatever put that frown on your face."

"Okay," I say, eyeing Rex and his plaything across the room. "Yes. Please show me a good time."

His fingers link with mine, warm and firm. Miller's hand lands on my lower back, guiding me to follow. Soon we're in the middle of the room, dancing in a throng of people. The music is loud, my blood hums. It's weird and wild and kind of reminds me of the late-night celebrations back at Serendee, except here there's no watchful eye following and judging our moves. No Anex pulling the strings.

"God you're beautiful," Knox says, running his fingers through my hair.

"You're pretty, too," I say back. The room grows a little fuzzy. I laugh and both boys laugh with me. I lift my cup and take another sip of my drink. Someone bumps into me and the liquid sloshes, sending a wave cascading down my chin.

"Oh," I say, trying to catch it. Miller steps forward and lifts the hem of his shirt, using it to wipe off the mess. I eye his abdomen, ripped with a ladder of hard muscle. "Thank you."

"Come on," he says, taking my hand. "Let's go clean you up."

Again, I'm led through the party, passing people that no longer take full shape. Miller pulls me into a room. It's a pantry of sorts, with a counter and small sink. He shuts the door behind us and turns on the faucet, then grabs a cloth out of a cabinet. He wets the cloth and wipes my chin and neck, smiling as he does it. I sigh and lean against the counter. "That feels good," I say, as he gently wipes my chest. "It was hot in there."

"No baby, that's all you." His fingers graze my neck. "Smokin'. I can't believe you just wandered in here off the street. Like a goddamn vision." I reach for the cup to take another sip. He grabs it from me and sets it on the counter. "You may want to slow down on that."

I look up at his chiseled jaw and say, "I wish I grew up in a world like this, with boys like you."

His forehead creases. "What kind of boy am I?"

"Sweet," she says, "Nice."

He chuckles and pushes the hair off my neck. "Exactly what world did you grow up in?"

"Serendee," I say, the word sliding off my tongue. "I'm from Serendee."

He pulls back. "The cult?"

"It's not a cult," I respond. My fingers feel weird. Numb. "It's utopia."

He shrugs. "I knew you were different. Special." His hand slips under the hem of my shirt. "I've heard about you girls. You look all innocent and sweet, but it's really all about sex, right?"

The statement echoes in my head. I've heard something like it before—out on the street when I was accosted by men before my Ordering. Rex, Elon, Silas and Levi protected me. At the time I thought the accusations were gross. Completely off base, but maybe... god, maybe they aren't. Sex has become the focus of my life.

I open my mouth to respond but the door swings open behind Miller. He's yanked back by his collar.

"Get your fucking hands off my woman." Rex looms in the doorway, a murderous glint in his eye. He tosses Miller into the hallway, back slamming against the wall.

"Hey, man, I didn't do anything to her. She spilled her drink, and I just helped her clean up."

"Bullshit. I saw you out on the dance floor, pawing at her like an animal." He steps forward and grabs him by the front of his shirt. Miller isn't small, but Rex? He's honed and sharp. I realize it now; deadly.

My heart pounds, and I curl against the counter terrified of what Rex will do. We don't abide by secular laws in Serendee. Touching another man's mate? Rex could skin him alive and Anex would give him the blade, but even I know the rules are different here.

"Stop!" I shout, lunging at Rex. I grab his bicep, tense and bulging. "Don't."

"Not now, Imogene." He attempts to shrug me off, but I hold on with both hands. "I don't know what the fuck you're doing here, but no one touches you without my permission." His hand balls into a fist. "Not even this pretty, entitled frat boy."

"Woah," a voice says from the hall. Knox appears, holding his hands up. "What's going on."

"Your *brother* brought my woman back here."

He looks around Rex and spots me. He's quiet for a moment then says, "Imogene, right?"

"Yes."

"Yeah, she told us she came here looking for you, didn't you?"

I don't know who this guy is, or what kind of game he's playing, or how he knew, but we're not in Serendee. There are laws out here and Rex can't just beat a man to death because he took me in a pantry. Especially since I went willingly. "Yes," I say. "I came here for you."

His shoulders relax minimally and he looks down. "Why?"

"You didn't come home like you promised."

He stares at me long and hard then turns back to Miller. He tightens his grip on his shirt, cutting off his air, before shoving him back, "Get the fuck out of my face and stay the hell away from women that don't belong to you."

"Dude," Miller says, rubbing his neck and inching down the hall, "you're in *our* house."

"Yeah, and everyone in this place is high on the weed I supplied." Rex shrugs. "I can take my business elsewhere."

Knox grabs Miller by the shoulder and pulls him down the hallway. "Just leave it dude. Royer's gonna kick your ass when he finds out about all this."

"Shut up," he says, shrugging Knox away. He starts down the hall and turns back and gives me a wink. "Just a tip, you've got about another thirty minutes with her before she's completely incoherent."

A growl rips through Rex's chest, but instead of going after Miller he pushes me back inside the pantry and slams the door shut. His eyes dart to the cup. "You drank from that?"

"It's just a punch," I tell him.

"Yeah, made with a hundred proof and laced with GHB."

I don't know what either of those things are. He lifts me off the floor and sets me on the counter, grabbing my chin and tilts my face upward, thumbing under my eyes and peering into each one. "What are you doing?"

"How much did you have?"

"Not that much," I say. He continues to inspect me, fingers sliding down my throat and stopping over my pulse. "A couple sips. It burned my throat and I spilled half of it." I look toward the door. "Miller actually made me stop drinking it."

"Yeah, he probably wanted you coherent when he fucked you."

My jaw drops. "He wasn't going to—"

"Yeah, Little Lamb, that's exactly what he planned to do." His fingers drop from my neck, down my arm. "You walked right into the slaughterhouse; you know that? And for what? To drag me home?"

"You promised." I have nowhere to put my hands, and my brain is a little fuzzy, so I rest them on his stomach. His muscles tense. "You said you'd come home, every night."

"This is work."

I roll my eyes. "That girl you were talking to was work?"

"Recruitment," he says simply. "I have a quota. You know that, Imogene."

I do, but it doesn't lessen the sting. "You defy your father all the time, but not when it comes to other women. That's about you, not him."

"That's about me doing what I'm told so that he doesn't get suspicious and start sniffing around more than he already is." He tilts his head. "Did anyone see you leave?"

"No. Elon and Silas are doing a job. Levi was in the shower."

He snorts. "He's probably panicking right now."

"Probably," I say feeling a little guilty.

"You can't walk the streets alone, Imogene."

"I was dressed like a secular girl. No one noticed me."

"Oh, they noticed you," he says, running his finger over the collar of my shirt. "Those two assholes were on you the second they saw you."

"They were just—"

"Men." He pushes his fingers under my shirt. "Men are aware of you, Little Lamb. They see your beauty. Smell your innocence. They want to be the ones to break you in, claim a little piece of you."

"That's not true," I say, squirming against his touch. My skin warms and my nipples tighten. He notices and brushes the pad of his thumb over the peak. I suck in a breath and shiver. "I just looked lost, and they were being—"

"Don't you fucking dare say nice." I swallow back the excuse and lean into him. "If another man touched you—violated you—without my permission, I'd have to kill him."

"You wouldn't."

He shoots me a look, one that tells me I don't understand the lengths he'd go to protect his possessions. "You're mine, Imogene, inside the walls of Serendee *and* out. No one has the right to touch you, speak to you or be near you without my consent."

"You don't believe in the rules of The Way," I say, pretending his words don't send a pool of heat between my legs.

"I don't," he agrees, leaning forward and running his nose along the shell of my ear. "This has nothing to do with Serendee, and everything to do with you and me."

His lips capture mine, not gentle. Not demanding. Owning. He kisses me. Hard. Jaw working against mine at the same time his fingers push up my shirt and his hands massage my breasts.

He licks my chin, my neck and along the path where the liquor spilled earlier. He doesn't stop until he's removed my shirt and has my tits pressed together, mouth consuming both of my nipples at once. I slam my head back, knocking it against the cabinet, and he lifts me cleverly unbuttoning my jeans and dragging them over my hips.

He pulls back and looks at me, eyes grazing over my body, one hand shifting up and down the bulge in his pants. My soul sets on fire.

I wait for him to release himself, to free that weapon cloaked in cotton, but he gives it one last long stroke and focuses back on me. He kisses the inside of one knee, then the other, then spreads apart my shaking thighs. His lips are warm, but the kisses leave a wet patch that cools, sending shivers across my flesh.

"You don—"

"Yes, Imogene, I do."

His tongue swipes over the hot patch of skin and my hips rise. I grip his shoulders for stability. "Rex," I start, trying to maintain composure. He inhales my scent, then parts my folds, pushing his tongue inside. It's wet and warm and— "Yes. Oh—"

His tongue dips in and out, circling. I drop my hands to the counter, curling them over the edge, and snap my thighs shut, the sensation too much, too overwhelming—

"Don't come," he says. "Not yet."

"But—" isn't that the point? Isn't that why he's doing this? To show me how he can make me feel? How much control he has over me?

"Not yet. Hold onto it, Little Lamb." He lifts his eyes to meet mine. "Hold onto me."

I pry my fingers from the edge of the counter and skim them over those hard biceps, up to his shoulders. He dives back in, tongue working against my clit. I shut my eyes and dig my nails into his rock-hard shoulders.

"Jesus, you taste so fucking good."

That's what does it. That's what unbinds me from my body, unravels the tight coils in the pit of my stomach. I rise off the counter, and he grabs my ass with both hands, stuffing his face with my pussy. His movements are slow, dragging licks across my frayed nerves. It's good. It's amazing. It's too, *too* much. It's heat and fire and boiling liquid and— "Rex," I push against his forehead, unable to bear it anymore. "Please..."

I feel one last touch, one faint press, a kiss between my legs before he rises. I stare at him through glazed eyes, taking in his red mouth and flushed cheeks. He's always handsome, but right now he looks boyish, like he'd been caught stealing cake.

He shifts himself, grimacing, and I wait for him to take out his cock, to grab me, to pin me to the counter and fuck me hard.

He doesn't. He opens the cabinet next to my head and pulls out a clean cloth. How he knew they were there is beyond me, but he runs the cloth under the water and carefully cleans between my legs. Without another word, he helps me off the counter and back into my jeans.

"Are you not going to..." I start. He pauses, looking at me. "You know... fuck me?"

"Definitely," he says, lip quirking. "But not now. Not when you're drugged," he says simply. "And not when I'm feeling," he pauses, "so territorial."

"But you just—" I shake my head. He's so confusing. He's never worried about consent before.

He rests a hand on my shoulder. "It won't happen again."

Wait, what? What won't happen again? Because that... I really want it to happen again. "Rex—"

"Staying out late." He interrupts me. "It won't happen again. I made a promise to you. I'll stick to it, but don't forget, you made one to me, too."

I do everything he says. *Everything.*

I nod, and he takes my hand, leading me out of the pantry, down the hall and out into the warm night. Rex has claimed me, inside and out of Serendee. Whatever arrangement we've made, I realize that reaches beyond the bond we made in front of his father and the community as a whole.

I have no idea what that means.

58

———————

E ^{lon}

Facing the mirror, I swipe the razor down my chin, removing the last strip of stubble. Twisting my neck, I check to make sure I got everything. I don't see anything I missed, but what I do see is how fucking tired I look.

Last night had been long.

Anex is determined to expand our territory—pushing for us to make contacts outside of Wittmore University and local buyers. No one inside Serendee knows it, but the rumors about what's going on behind our walls are starting to gain steam. The word cult is tossed around a lot, as well as scam, con-artist, and charlatan. None of these are good for business or recruitment.

I dry off, patting my face with a towel, then my chest where a few droplets landed during my shave. I unwrap the towel around my waist and hang it on the hook behind the bathroom door and replace it with black pants. In the bedroom, I open the closet and notice a shadow under the bedroom door. I pause, waiting to see if someone is going to knock, but nothing comes. The shadow doesn't move.

I stride over and open the door. Imogene is frozen in her spot, fist poised to knock. Her eyes stare straight ahead—at my chest, then travel downward. She swallows thickly.

"What?" I ask, pressing my hand to the doorjamb.

"Never mind," she says, turning to leave. I snatch her wrist before she's too far out of reach and yank her back.

"I don't have time for your dramatics today," I snap. "What do you want, Imogene?"

Her eyes drop to the ground. "I'm sure you're busy—I can ask Silas."

"You can ask me," I reply, not releasing her. Her arm is narrow as a reed down by the lake. "What do you want?"

"I need someone—you—to take me outside of Serendee."

I drop my hand and cross both arms over my chest. Her eyes lift, taking in my muscles and my dick twitches. I ignore it. "Take you where?"

"Well, that's the thing. I'm not exactly sure. It's for, um," she looks over her shoulder, although we're home alone, "for something Rex asked me to do. I don't exactly understand everything he told me to do, but I figured you would."

Why does hearing this make my stomach clench uncomfortably? She came to me because I'm the kind of guy that will break the rules of Serendee. The shade of gray in this otherwise black and white world. "What does he want?"

"I'd rather not talk about it here." Her hands twist in the fabric of her dress. "Can you take me into town?"

The answer should be no. The response should be for me to go straight to Anex and tell him that a member of his community is behaving with Regressive intent. But that isn't who I am, which is exactly why she came to me for help. "I'll do you one better. I've got business two towns over. Whatever you need to do, we can do it there —away from any potential complications."

Complications means, Anex or any of his people.

"Should I change?" she asks.

I look down at her pale blue dress and the little embroidered flowers. Growing up in Serendee, seeing the girls covered up and revered, gave me intense fantasies about what happened underneath the soft cotton. Then we started going outside of the community, finding women who dressed provocatively and were willing to let us do all the things we were told we couldn't do inside the walls. Indulgent things. Regressive acts because we were not waiting until Anex gave his Order. But these dresses, the thin cotton, and high collars, the godforsaken buttons. It never failed to make me hard, and those fantasies, they never went away, even after I'd had my fill of secular flesh and pussy. My cock tightens in my pants, desperate and ready to be unleashed. And the way Imogene looks at me, I know she wouldn't fight if I bent her over the nearest surface and claimed her like a beast.

Like I've done before.

I swallow all that back. Now isn't the time, and this isn't the girl that deserves such treatment. She's trying so hard to be good, to serve her mate, and she ought to have someone much worthier than a man like me.

"Yes," I say, looking away from her. "You should change in to something more secular. I'll meet you out front in ten minutes."

"Thank you, Elon. I really appreciate it."

I reply with a grunt and step back in my room. Ten minutes, I think, heading straight to the bathroom. I open the drawer under the sink and pull out a bottle of lube with one hand while unbuttoning my pants with the other. Ten minutes to get rid of this boner so I can spend the rest of the day without acting like a feral animal in heat.

I pour the lube in my hand and oil up my cock, making it good and slippery. With one hand on the counter and the other stripping my cock, I close my eyes, not wanting to see my face as I think of the way I'd defile my best friend's mate. I know he doesn't care, but I do. She's too good for me. Too pure, and the way I jerk myself off while thinking about her like this is further proof.

Stroke.

I'm disgusting.

Stroke.

A degenerate.

Stroke.

I'm a man unworthy of his own mate and Anex knows it.

Stroke.

Imogene is too good for me. Too Enlightened. Too—*I think of her, bent over, ass bloody from the strap, begging me to go harder—*

Groan

I lurch, fingers curling around the edge of the sink as cum spills into the basin. I milk my cock, pushing out every last drop and take a deep breath, hopeful, that this will make the trip with Imogene a little bit more bearable.

Hopeful, but not confident.

~

"Wait," she says, looking at the ramshackle building on the side of the road. "Exactly what are we doing here?"

"Business," I reply, shifting over my jacket to check the gun I tucked into my pants. When I look over again her jaw is loose.

"This is where you have business?" she asks, looking at the organized piles of tomatoes and cucumbers. "I'm confused. We have our own produce. And why do you need a gun?"

I frown and glance out the window of the truck. I drove the F-450. Completely inappropriate for a road trip, but I like how powerful it feels in my hands. There's one customer picking through a stack of melons and it strikes me that bringing Imogene with me was a bad idea. The average female resident of Serendee has no idea about the collection of fire power Anex has accumulated in this armory. Imogene would know that there are guns for hunting and general security, but this goes beyond that. Me, Rex, Levi, Silas and any other male in the inner circle have been trained extensively for a breach of the walls—to defend the property and our business.

"Elon, why do you need a gun?" she repeats.

I watch the customer reach for her wallet and scratch my forehead with my thumb. "Because I'm not here to buy organic fruit. I'm here to collect on an outstanding payment. It's a pretty standard situation, but since you're with me, I'm not taking any chances."

The customer finally leaves, and I exit the cab. Walking around the back to grab the basket of green beans I brought with us from the farm, I do a quick check for the two kilos of hard-packed marijuana underneath. With the basket in one hand, I wrench open Imogene's door and offer her my hand to get down. A warm buzz passes between us during the few seconds we touch. She's in a cute striped T-shirt and navy-blue shorts that reveal her long legs. Very college co-ed. Very innocent but sexy.

Fuck. Now is not the time to get hard.

Walking into the open-air stand, I move slightly in front of Imogene. It smells of hay and fresh food, dirt and greenery. A man in overalls and a wide brimmed hat arranges husks of corn in a large pile, while a female in a heavy jumper and bonnet cuts up a cantaloupe by the counter. Soft strains of guitar music waft through the breezy shed.

"Morning, Jeb," I say, eyes combing the area for anything out of place. Everything is quiet, quaint and normal. Well, as normal as can be.

"Elon," he says with a nod, eyes flicking to Imogene. "Wasn't expecting you today."

"Well, I had some extra time, and it turns out you and I have some unfinished business."

Jeb's eyebrow arches. He plays like he's a small-town, innocent farmer, and not a shrewd businessman. He and Anex are cut from the same cloth. It's not a surprise that they found one another, or that one is trying to get one over the other.

"Honey, offer this young woman a piece of that cantaloupe, while the men handle our affairs," he says, smiling over at Imogene. "So sweet you wouldn't believe it."

Imogene looks to me for approval. I nod, keeping an eye on her.

"Thought your women dressed more modestly in Serendee."

"Who said she was from Serendee?" I say, not liking the way he's looking at her.

He grunts and darkness flickers in his eye. I should've made her wear her normal clothes. Why did I bring her? Deep in my chest the truth threatens to reveal itself. My Indulgency will be my undoing. My desire to see her skin, to have her close, to pretend like she could be mine.

I follow him behind a sheet of burlap that acts as a barrier between the 'shop' and the back. Keeping an eye on Imogene through the sliver of space, I say, "It's my understanding that my runners shorted you last time. I apologize" I hold up the basket. "Two kilos of our best batch."

He takes the basket and pushes aside the beans, finding the drugs underneath. He must like what he sees, because he reaches behind his bib overall and pulls out a packet of money. He starts to hand it over but then draws back. "I don't know," he says, voice hesitant. "I've put a lot of faith into this arrangement with Anex and to just accept this... well that means I'm accepting bad practices."

"It shouldn't happen again." It *shouldn't*, but I'm not convinced. Anex is expanding too fast. Moving to territories where we don't understand the culture or know the people. He's brought in more of young men in the community—giving them access and jobs they aren't prepared for. That's how this mistake happened. One of our men, Malen, fucked up.

I glance into the shop front and see Imogene holding a piece of melon in her fingertips and quietly speaking to the woman. "I'll personally make sure of that."

The man chuckles. "That's not as comforting as you think it is son."

My jaw tightens. "Then what would smooth this over? This partnership is important to Anex and to the community of Serendee. Tell me, what's it going to take to make this right."

He reaches up and rubs the tip of his chin with two fingers. His beard is thick, long. His nails dirty. "Rumor has it there's other merchandise for sale in your community."

I blink trying to follow. There's the herbal trade, the salves Silas makes and uses. A group of women harvest honey and wax, along with other products from the hives. There's dairy and of course, the produce, which he already seems to have in supply. I frown. "What merchandise are you speaking of."

He pulls back the burlap curtain and nods inside. "Property like that little thing in there."

"Women?" I blurt.

"Girls. Females." He says it with zero emotion, completely business-like. "The community I belong to... we've recently changed our decrees to include polygamy and we have too many men. We need more females."

"You want to buy her." It's a statement. One I manage to keep controlled despite the rage building inside. "From me."

"From Serendee. Anex has made it known this is a service he plans on providing soon." He tilts his head toward Imogene. "If you want to make things right between us, you'll give me that one as a peace offering."

I'm not sure how to describe the sensation that runs through me. It's white hot, searing straight from my soul. I only know one thing and it's that I will slaughter anyone that dares touch—to possess—Imogene other than me and my brothers.

My gun is out of the waistband of my pants before Jeb even blinks. The barrel two inches from his forehead.

"Woah," he says, holding up his hands, one still holding the packet of money. "Settle down, big boy, if that one is your toy, let me know. I'll pick another one."

I take a step in the small doorway and say, "Little Lamb, get in the truck."

"What?" she says, but then I hear a small gasp. She must've seen the gun. "Elon what—"

"Get in the truck, *now*."

I hear more than see her leave the rickety building. Her feet shuffle across the hay floor and the heavy truck door opens and shuts with a slam. Once she's safe, I cock the trigger. "I don't know what you heard or have been told about the women in Serendee but you've been given the wrong impression." Jeb swallows, his scraggly beard dipping to touch his chest. "Our women are sacred, prized possessions to be honored and worshipped." The words are what I've been told a thousand times sitting at Anex's feet, listening to hours of his lectures. But they taste bitter on my tongue. It's what we preach, but not what we practice. "Take your product," I say, shoving the basket at him and then snatching the money out of his hand. I'd leave it, but then I'd have to tell Anex why I came home empty handed. "And be thankful I'm not blowing your brains out." Jeb's eyes close when I unlatch the trigger, the click loud in both of our ears. "If I find out you're buying women from anyone else, I'll be back. Understand?"

He nods slowly, and I step away, keeping my gun trained on him and then the woman at the counter. She's hunched down, tears running down her face. I wonder if she knows how disgusting this man is.

Quickly, I get to the car, slamming the door and cranking up the engine with a deafening roar. I'm backed out and a mile away before I start breathing again.

"What happened?" Imogene asks.

"It was just a reminder that people aren't always what they seem." I grab her hand, threading my fingers with hers, and lift it, kissing the back.

She stares at me with a million questions in her eyes. I have no idea how to answer them because I have too many of my own.

59

I mogene

I CAN'T GET anything out of Elon as he speeds away from the farm stand and drives to a nearby town. He hasn't let go of my hand, steering the car one handed, the muscle at the back of his jaw ticking. All I know is whatever happened back there shook him up. As the miles pass, I can't help but look at the packet he left on the seat between us. It's thick with money—money that goes back to Anex.

He'd looked so different back there. Sure, he was strong and powerful. Commanding. Seeing him with the gun in his hand sent a thrill down my spine. Fear. Awe.

But it was the way he told me to run—the plea for my safety— that felt different. The look in his eye wasn't hard and angry. It was soft and kind. Elon cares about me. And not just because I belong to his best friend. A strange feeling swirls in my belly as we drive over a bridge marked with a sign announcing that we're entering Thistle Cove, home of the Vikings, the state football champions.

"Have you been here before?" I ask, desperate to break the silence.

"A couple times. There are just a few small dealers in the area. We keep them supplied."

My whole life has been nothing but inside the walls of Serendee and the short trip to the Center once I got a job. Seeing all of these other places, it's like visiting another world.

The town is small but cute and Elon quickly finds the public library. He parks the truck and says, "Just stick close to me, okay?"

I nod and wait as he exits the driver's side and walks around to open my door, helping me down from the oversized truck. Our skin sparks when it touches, and his fingers linger, tangled with mine.

He looks down at our hands and pulls away, allowing mine to fall. Clearing his throat, he asks, "You said you needed to check social media sites?"

"Yes." I follow him up the sidewalk to the library door. "Well, that's what Rex called it. I kind of know what it is from my training sessions with Silas—the entertainment he showed me, but I don't know how to navigate it at all."

Social media, or how I understand it, is places on the computer where people can talk and meet each other.

"Who is he looking for that he couldn't do it himself?" he asks as we walk into the cool, quiet building. A librarian observes us walk in, probably aware that we're not from around here. A row of computer sits along one wall. Elon presses a hand into my lower back and directs me toward them and pulls out a chair for me. I sit and he grabs another chair, setting it close to mine.

My palms sweat at his question. What I'm asking him to participate in... well, it's going to make whatever happened back at the farm stand seem minor.

"He wants me to find my mother."

Just saying those words are enough to have me labeled as Regressive and sent down with the Fallen—after intense Corrections and public reprimand. It's a testimony of how much I trust Elon that I would ask him to help me with something like this.

"I assume this is really about *his* mother?" He asks. I nod and he just sighs, running his hand through his thick, dark hair. "And this is the rabbit hole he's going down. Fucking great."

He pulls the keyboard toward him and starts typing. A screen pops up that says, 'Facebook' and I watch as he types in a familiar, forbidden name, Camille Sanders.

Before I can breathe, a photo pops up. It's both familiar and not. The eyes are the same, and the mouth, but the hair is short and graying. There are wrinkles and a lift to her chin—a confidence.

I grab the machine and twist it in my direction, touching the screen with my fingers.

"That's—"

"Her. Yes. I remember what she looked like."

I squint trying to absorb everything. I push his hand off the mouse and frantically try to make it comply. It spins out of control. "I just want to make it bigger!"

"Shhhh!" the librarian shushes from across the room. Elon's hand closes over mine, warm and heavy. He helps orient the mouse and clicks on her picture. It takes us to a page with limited information.

"Is that it?" I ask, speaking over the lump in my throat. "Is there nothing else?"

"It's a private account, which, frankly, is smart." He clicks around a little more but doesn't make much progress. "If you want to speak to her directly, you'll have to make an account and engage her."

The suggestion hits my chest like a battering ram. "Everything you just said is a violation."

He nods. "It is."

My hands shake and I put them in my lap. Again, he clamps his over mine and a feeling of calm follows. "If you do this, Imogene, you can't Correct this out of your system. You'll be crossing a line that comes from being part of Anex's inner circle. One you can't come back from, and one," he lowers his voice, "you can't have Levi take out of your hide with a strap."

"What do you mean?"

"I mean, you make a decision. You're either a sweet little lamb that follows The Way, or you're one of us."

I look up at his handsome, intimidating face. "Who are you?"

"The Chosen. We're not exactly *above* the rules and Corrections, but there's a gray area. That's where the four of us exist."

"I don't know if I can do that." Give up everything I know—the rules and belief system—The Way.

He squeezes my hand. "It's okay if you can't, but I need you to understand your limits. Because you can't keep punishing yourself for our Lapses."

"I don't know if I can separate the two."

He watches me closely, his dark eyes drinking me in, like he's trying to see inside my mind, how it works. "How about this," he says. "I'll do the research. Take down the information. If you want it, I can tell you, but it's my burden. My Lapse. Not yours." His eyes flick down to my mouth and back up. "And if you need me to, I'll go to Corrections to make it right."

It's a generous offer, and one that, like he said, wades into the gray water of our world. But at this point I don't any other option. It's a lifeline.

I take it.

"Okay, let's try that."

He takes the keyboard back and types quickly, faster than I would've thought possible. He enters in my mother's name. "Grab that flyer," he says, nodding to a stack on a nearby table. He pulls a pen out of his pocket. I watch as he jots down addresses and strings of phone numbers. He's quiet, but thorough, sliding the paper over to me when he's finished.

"I think she lives or works at one of these addresses. It's hard to tell—she's good at covering her tracks."

I stare at the information, trying to reconcile it with the years of her absence.

"You okay?" he asks, knee nudging mine.

"My mom, Camille, has been gone so long. I guess I didn't think it would exist." I lift up the paper. "But here it is and I guess I just don't know what to do with this?"

"Give it to Rex?"

"Do you think I should?"

"Wasn't that the plan?" he asks.

"Yes, but... I guess I didn't think it would be this easy or maybe even possible. Or..."

"Or what?"

"Or maybe I hoped she was dead and that's why she never came back for me."

"Anex wouldn't have let her come back, you know that."

I do know that, right?

"He would've put her in with the Fallen," he continues. "She would have been punished severely for her betrayal. Banishment was a mercy."

I take a deep breath, trying to steady myself. "Is there anything else we can find out first? Like does she have a job. Or," I swallow, "a family or something."

He looks at me for a long moment. My cheeks burn. "Sure, let me see what I can find."

His fingers move fast, entering in different variations of my mother's name and certain words. 'Keywords.' He pauses over something, and I sense his shoulders tense. "What?" I ask leaning over.

"There's a link to a group." He clears his throat. "It's for survivors of cults."

Cult.

Serendee is not a cult.

The people who say that do not understand who and what we are. They can't comprehend the community we've created. They view us as a threat. The self-sustainability, the progress and Enlightenment. Anex has always said that people who think we are a cult are missing out on the truth of The Way.

Yet...

I stare at my mother's face in a photo on the website. It's a picture of her smiling, her hair short, and wearing secular clothing.

Under her photo is a caption. I close my eyes and say, "Read it. What does it say?"

Again, he clears his throat, his foot bouncing on the floor. *"Camille*

Sanders spent decades in a cult that she not only willingly joined but helped create. She brings that unique perspective to others when they are seeking freedom from a controlling group..."

"Stop."

Elon pauses. "Imogene."

"I can't do this." I stand, leaving the paper on the table and walk toward the door. "Rex will be upset." Furious. "But I can't do this. If he wants to dig around in this blasphemy, he has to do it on his own."

I step outside, letting the warm afternoon sun hit my face. I stand there until Elon is behind me, leading me back to the car. My chest is tight all the way back to Serendee, where I expect to finally breathe easy until we're back home, safe behind the walls.

For the first time in my life, there is no comfort.

I TRY my best to pretend like everything is normal.

Normal.

As residents of Serendee we've spent our lives pushing back on that word. Rebelling against the status quo. We're Better. More Enlightened. But the more I learn about the outside world, the less 'normal' make sense.

Is it normal to live in a community that sells illegal drugs?

Is it normal to have young girls kept in seclusion for re-education?

Is it normal to maintain your diet, clothing, hygiene all by the order of one man?

Everything I'm taught says yes.

Which is why the slip of paper Elon wrote my mother's information on burns where I've hidden it under my clothing, against my chest.

I haven't given it to Rex yet. He wasn't home last night when we returned. He'd left a note about working late down at the farm. It was dawn when he came in, undressed and crawled into the bed next to me, asleep in seconds.

I've been at work for three hours—greeting new recruits. Handing out paperwork and scheduling appointments. Normal stuff. A normal day.

I pretend the paper isn't there.

"How much did you say the next level costs?"

I smile at the girl across from my desk. She's a thin brunette that Rex recruited from the Wittmore campus. Over the last three months she's depledged from her sorority, come to three different workshops and is ready to commit to more. One of my jobs is to help the recruits level-up, paying for the courses that help them transition to Enlightenment. Once they pass through all the levels, they are slowly transitioned into potential community members. That's where Silas' skills come in—then Anex.

This girl, Brianna, is months away from that place—years even—but I can already see the gleam in her eye. She's hooked—high on the coursework and potential. She wants to Be Better, so much she can taste it.

"Five thousand," I tell her. The fee is part of other commitment. Anex only wants the most devoted to get to the higher levels. It's an important phase of the system. I look down at her paperwork. She's a college student with no income of her own but her mother is an architect. A quick skim of her financials, which we run after the second session, and it's obvious that her family has the type of resources Anex prefers.

"That's a lot," she says, twisting her fingers. There's a tan line on her ring finger. She'd been engaged when she first started coming. Is that over now? "I can probably swing some of it. Do you have a payment plan?"

"There are some options," I say, knowing this woman ticks all the boxes of the potential recruit Anex is interested in. "You know, I think you have the kind of energy Anex is looking for. Let me show him your file and see what he says about finding you a way into the next levels."

Her eyes brighten. "That would be amazing. I'm getting so much out of the courses, I'd hate to stop now."

"I understand," I say, giving her an assuring smile. I can't help but wonder what Rex did to get her in the door. Did he flirt with her? More?

I shake that off and tell her to come back the following day—that I'd let her know about funding. Gathering the file, including a recent photo of Brianna, I take it to the back. There's a small area outside of Anex's office, prepared to leave it in the mail slot for important papers. I've just slid the papers inside when the office door opens.

"I thought I heard someone out here." His eyes rake down my body, eliciting a chill that runs down my spine. "I didn't expect it to be my son's beautiful future mate."

"Anex," I say, bowing and touching my forehead. "I didn't know you were in the office."

"I snuck in the back," he says holding his finger up to his lips. "Shhh, don't tell anyone."

It's that kind of informality that makes Anex such a compelling leader. He's easy—approachable. It's also why I'm conflicted by imaginary weight on my chest. That note could destroy me and the guys. I laugh, hoping it doesn't sound nervous. "I was just leaving a file for you. A potential recruit, level three, that doesn't have the funds to proceed. She fit the criteria you requested for review."

"Thank you, Imogene. You're so thorough." His smile wavers. "I wish some of your diligence and dedication would rub off on Rex."

I still, not sure how to respond to the statement. Do I agree and criticize both my mate and his son? Or do I laugh it off, pretending it's a joke. The glint in his eye, the same blue eyes that Rex has tells me it wasn't in humor.

Before I dwell too much on it, I say, "I wanted to thank you for Ordering us together. Although it's been a challenge working through our differences, lately things have been good."

His eyebrow raises. "Really?"

"Yes. He seems more focused land efficient. He comes home at night instead of spending time outside of Serendee." In clubs and parties. All of that is true. "I feel good about the match."

"I like hearing that."

"You chose wisely," I tell him, hoping the flattery works.

"I've been wanting to speak to you," he says, "Do you have time now?"

It's a question but there's no possible way to say no. Not to Anex.

"Of course. Melody is up front. She can handle anyone that comes in."

He gestures for me to enter his office. I've been here before—but just for a few moments. Before I was Ordered to Rex my interaction with Anex was rare—I probably saw him a little more since I work at the Center but even then, it's not as if he mingles with us. He's busy. I didn't understand the enormity of the businesses being run out of Serendee until Elon showed me. What we really sell and trade to keep the community running.

I enter the room and although I expect him to sit behind his desk he doesn't, leaning against the edge and crossing his legs in front of him. I watch as he reaches for a box on the table and pulls out a small hand wrapped cigarette. He doesn't speak as he strikes a match, the smell of sulfur hitting my nostrils. He lights the end and takes a drag.

"Have you ever?" he asks.

"Um..." Me? I glance over my shoulder—waiting for something. But what? I'm with Anex. Nothing can happen to me here. "No. It wasn't allowed in the Domum."

"I'm shocked my son and his friends haven't introduced you."

They haven't. And for a moment it makes me wonder why? Do they not trust me?

He tilts his head. "Your mind is running wild, isn't it?" He laughs. "So like your mother. Always thinking. Scheming."

The sensation of something creeping up my spine keeps me rigid, that and the fact that I have the notes about my mother under two thin layers of cotton. Is this meeting more than it seems?

God.

Does he know?

It's insane to think, but Anex has his ways.

It's the paranoia of any kind of resistance that makes me admit,

"It's hard for me to turn my brain off sometimes. I don't know why. I think it's all those years of worrying—of being considered different."

"Because of Camille." He nods. "I can imagine. She was a powerful person."

Was.

She no longer exists in this world. We may as well be speaking of the dead, but the paper against my chest, the evidence on the computer last night. My mother isn't dead. She's alive and actively working against Serendee.

"Don't worry, Imogene. Other than that, you're nothing like her." He reaches out, brushing his fingers down my cheek and tucking a strand of hair over my ear. "You don't think I'd let a female with a true Regressive streak mate with my son, would you?" His hand lingers for a moment, trailing down my neck, before he steps back and takes another hit, before offering it to me. "You should try it. Take the edge off."

The pressure is intense. I reach for the tiny twist of paper.

"Ah," he says, withdrawing it a little. "Let me."

He holds it to my mouth, leaving just an inch for me to press between my lips. Awkwardly, I bend forward, inhaling the sweet herbal grass. As the smoke drags into my lungs it burns, spreading across my chest. I try to hold it in, but I cough, my throat raw.

"I'm sorry," I say, sputtering.

"It happens," he says. "Just takes a little practice." He leans forward again, pressing the joint to my lips. I have no choice but to inhale. When I pull away, he looks at me, eyebrow lifted. "You've been practicing, right?"

"Practicing?"

"With Elon, Silas, and Levi. Practicing to be an appropriate mate for my complicated son."

Anex is fit—mostly from the hours of nightly basketball games and his healthy lifestyle. He's vegan, meditates, practices yoga. His personal healer is always on call. Like Rex, his frame is imposing, muscular, and no matter how friendly his tone, there's something intimidating about him—always.

"I, uh..." Be it the question or the cannabis running through my system, it's hard to formulate words.

"I know all of this is new for you, Imogene. Exposing yourself like this—after the years of modesty and decorum." He sits on the edge of the desk. "I know it doesn't seem fair, but the males...we allow them more freedom so that when it's time for you to enter your mating, someone understands how things work. My son is more aware than most. He's experienced the decay and desperation of the outside world. It has left him hollow. I should have protected him more—especially without a mother." He smiles gently. "That's one reason I thought maybe you two would connect—the lack of a mother."

"It has," I say, tongue feeling looser. "It's been an adjustment for both of us.

"What kind of things do they ask you to do... they do ask you? Or do they force you?"

My stomach twists. The look in his eye conveys something darker, deeper—hunger.

"Do they hurt you, Imogene? Or do you only like to be hurt during your Corrections?"

The question shocks me—I'm aware that Anex has access to our logs and journals. That Levi reports to him, but has he told him about that? About my desires? How the pain and pleasure turn into one?

"You're such a good girl," he says, words thick. Or are my ears thick? "You've always been a good girl, Imogene, even when you're feeling bad."

"I—"

He rests his hand on my shoulder, the weight heavy, pressing me down.

"Ask me."

"For what?" I whisper.

"For a blessing."

I've done this before. Everyone in Serendee has been blessed by Anex—it's an honor—one we usually receive at ceremonies. I bend my knees, resting them on the hard floor. He stands above me, my eyes level with the seam of his crotch. Never before has it been like this—with his erection bulging against the fabric. Or if it was, I didn't know what I was looking at.

God, I was so naïve.

No one touches you without my permission.

I hear Rex's voice as his father's hand comes down on my head. He murmurs, words I can't fully make out: *girl, Enlightenment, The Way, peace and succumb.* Rambling on as his hand moves, cupping my cheek and lifting my chin.

"Is there anything you need to confess to me?" he asks. "Anything weighing on you?"

He knows. He knows about Elon and the computer. The search for my mother. The information we have. He knows and he'll use it against me and I open my mouth to tell him everything. I close my eyes, listening to the thrum of my pulse in my ears, my chest, feeling his thumb graze over my bottom lip.

This is wrong—he is wrong. I do not belong to him. I belong to Rex. To Elon, Silas, and Levi.

I understand that more than ever.

But this man is my leader, he has been my entire life, and no matter how scared I am, or how wrong this feels, I'm frozen under his power. He tilts my face upward and I look into his eyes—wincing at the similarity with his son. Except there's something missing—the deep intensity that Rex and I share. The connection.

What I see in Anex's face is disturbing want—the same kind that sent the blood rushing to his erection. I know that look now. I understand it from my training. Anex doesn't view me as a member of the community—or his son's mate. He sees me as something he wants *physically*.

My breath catches and his other hand shifts, moving to the front of his pants. It's in those mere moments I see my future flash before me. Anex forcing himself on me. Rex discovering it. The fallout. Bloodshed. Loss. Destruction.

Footsteps echo in the hallway outside the door, breaking me from the spell. What I can only describe as The Way, surges through me and I jolt to my feet.

"Thank you," I mumble, cheeks hot. Anex doesn't move, doesn't react as I race from the room, ignoring Melody dropping paperwork into his mail slot.

I run, passing my desk, out into the streets. I don't stop until I'm at the path that leads back home and only then do I stop to retch, the contents of my stomach, of my *soul*, trying to flee my insides. Nothing about me is good, or better, and soon the whole of Serendee will find out, and what will I do then?

60

____

L^{evi}

The creak of the door wakes me, followed by the sliver of light that vanishes with the sound of the latch sliding in place. I sit up and blink, "Who's there?"

"It's me." Her voice is quiet. Small.

"Imogene." I rub my eyes, trying to rouse myself. "What are you doing? What time is it?"

"Late," she replies, her voice closer. "I couldn't sleep."

"How come?" I'm groggy. The day had been long—filled with courses and a game of basketball that lasted past 3 AM.

"I can't stop thinking about all of the Lapses I've accumulated over the last few days. All of the Indulgences. The Regress—" The violations rush from her, like a dam breaking under pressure.

"Stop." I sit all the way up, the mattress squeaking under my weight. In the dark I feel for her, fumble for her hand, and pull her to the bed. "Sit."

The bed sinks, warmth brushes against my leg. I pull back, cock already hardening. What man hasn't had fantasies of a beautiful woman coming to him at night. My blood pumps through my extremities, but there's a hard truth mixed with it. She doesn't want me—she wants what I dole out—punishments.

"Talk to me," I say, my eyes finally acclimating to the moonlight coming through my window. "Tell me what's going on."

She shifts, hands clasped in her lap. She's not wearing a cotton, Serendee approved nightgown, but a Rex approved nightie, lace and satin. The soft brush of light highlights the swell of her breast and holy—my balls clench.

"It started when Rex asked me to do some research for him." She tells me about what Rex wants. Information on her mother, Camille, so that he can search for the truth about Beatrice. Like a breeched dam, the information pours out of her, the revelations spoken in whispers, only revealed in the dark.

I understand why. If anyone is going to report her back to Anex, it will be me. And admittedly, the impulse is strong. The urge to run to the Main House and tell our leader all of the darkness, all of the deceit screams in my veins. I was raised to be an informant.

But the woman sitting on the bed, hands fisted in her flimsy skirt, tugs at something deep in my chest. "I haven't told Rex yet. I've barely seen him, but today I had the information on me at the Center and Anex called me in." Her voice wobbles. "He could have caught me, Levi. Then what?"

"He didn't," I say, terrified for her. If he'd found that information on her. Christ. She'd be with the Fallen right now. Or worse. Banished. "He didn't, that's all that matters."

"There's more," she adds. "He offered me cannabis. I took it. I had no choice."

"It's not against the rules of Serendee to smoke—especially with the leader."

Her eyes drop. "He was familiar with me. He touched me—"

"Where?" My tone is sharp. Harsh.

"Nothing inappropriate." She glances up, eyes wary. "Not really. It felt inappropriate. I *know* Rex would be angry."

I take a deep breath. She's right. Anex's interest in Imogene has surpassed appropriateness. But what is considered appropriate where he's concerned. He establishes the rules—the boundaries. I reach out and touch her cheek and hear myself say, "It's okay, Imogene. It's going to be okay."

"It's not," she says, through a quiet, shuddering sob. "Asking Elon to take me there, looking it up on the computer, reading all the blasphemous, Regressive thoughts my mother is spewing. Maybe I do need to be Re-Educated." She looks up at me, eyes shining. "Maybe I should be with the Fallen."

Maybe she should.

No. *No.* That's years of conditioning saying that. Not The Way.

"She called Serendee a cult," she continues, the words are barely a whisper. More breath than voice. "Please, Levi. I'm trying to be a good mate to Rex and give him what he needs, but it's tearing me apart." She presses against me, her the fullness of her breast against my arm. "Please help me become whole again. Show me The Way. Help me seek Enlightenment."

If I give her what she wants, then we can both be saved. Her from her Lapses and me from having the knowledge. But every time Imogene comes to me like this, my motives become convoluted. Slippery like sand. My brain doesn't rule my decisions, but the hard, throbbing want in between my legs. Imogene isn't the only one drowning, being pulled between what's Right and what Feels Good.

But that's not all. Anger courses through me. Hot and dangerous. How could Rex put her in this position. Put Elon and then me? What the hell is he thinking?

And Anex... would he dare covet his son's mate? Would he cross that line by getting her high and loose? The answer rises faster than I want to admit. *Yes.* Yes, he would.

Rage born of confusion and conflict flickers and my fists tighten. It would be so easy to take this out on another—on Imogene. I could tear her skin apart, use her to quell the storm building in my soul.

So easy to hurt her.

So easy to ruin her.

Her fingers touch my chin and force my eyes to hers. "Levi?"

"I won't."

"Won't what?"

"Can't." My limbs tremble. "This is how he destroys us. It's how he pits us against one another and allows evil to worm further under our skin."

"Who are you talking about."

I stare at her, unable to say his name, fearful of being struck down by some greater force, but I see the understanding flicker in her eyes. She knows. Anex.

"He's the one that wants me to... Correct you like this. The escalation. The strap. He wants you fearful and weak." I swallow. "It's why he invited you into his office today. He doesn't know about the information. If he did, the recourse would be swift and public. He wouldn't play games." I shift on the mattress, getting closer to her. "He may suspect something, but he was fishing."

"Are you sure?"

No. "Yes."

"That doesn't take away everything else," she says, although she looks relieved. "The need for Correction. It's The Way and despite everything, I still believe."

I shake my head. There's a part of me that wonders if this isn't part of Anex's plan. To make her uncomfortable. To have her Lapse, and then come to me to start this cycle over again. It sucks us both in, keeps us both complicit, hungry. Horny.

"I'm worried we're going too far—that Anex wants us to go too far. Everyone logs in their journals. Confesses and shows some penance, but where this has gone..." I swallow. "It's eating away at me. Inside and out."

"You don't like it? You don't want to do it?"

I brush her hair off her cheek. "No, Imogene, I want it too much. So much it scares me. The things I want to do to you. How I fantasize about treating you. It can't be right."

My brain hurts. My arms and legs ache. My stomach churns.

'She called Serendee a cult.'

Camille Sanders Montgomery is notorious for being a lot of things, but I've seen the records, the history and foundation of her work building Serendee. At one point she was a believer and hearing that she has used that term to describe us rocks my foundation. If someone like that can change her mind, what does that mean for the rest of us?

Imogene shifts next to me, lifting up the covers and sliding her legs in next to mine. It's an act of softness, tenderness and it's in direct opposition of how we treat one another. She must know it, because her limbs remain tense as our bodies draw together, like two magnets. She tucks against my side, pulling my arm around her shoulders. Unsure of what else to do, I rest my other hand on her belly.

"What if she's right?" I ask. "What if we're just being manipulated and controlled?"

It's the thing Rex has fought with his father about for years, but even he's too under his thumb to really leave.

"Then our whole lives are a lie," Imogene says, pressing her lips against my collarbone. "But what's worse? Living the lie or breaking free?" She sits up. "What would you rather do? Pretend nothing is wrong and keep living this life or go out there? Live in the secular world with their noise and dirty streets and crime? Maybe it's just the price we have to pay?"

She leans toward me, her tits round and full. I cup one with my hand, running my thumb over the nipple. I've only touched her like this once without inflicting Correction—pain. And there's a disconnect between my mind and body. She grabs my hand and places it over her breast, applying pressure.

"Make me pay, Levi," she says, grinding against my thigh. My cock swells. "Help me reconcile my actions."

She wants it hard. She wants pain with her pleasure. It's mixed up and confusing, but in the darkness of this room, it doesn't have to belong to anyone but us. Anex may have made this monster, but I'm the one releasing it from its cage.

"Are you sure?" I ask, because I feel the same pull.

"Yes." She nods, taking my hand and pushing it between her legs. It's hot. Wet. Ready. "I've been a very bad girl."

I rise up, shifting from the unsure, insecure man who doesn't know what to do with a woman in a bed, to the one that understand this specific language. This desire.

I already know what I want to do to her. I've been waiting for her to return. I knew she would. It was a matter of *when*, not *if*.

"Lay back," I tell her, and she arranges herself on the bed, head on the pillow. Opening the drawer on the bedside table, I pull out the hard, heavy object. The handle nestles in my palm. Imogene watches me with wide, worried eyes, a line creasing her forehead. I lick my bottom lip.

"What's that for?" she asks, a tremble in her voice when she sees the knife.

"Are you sure you want to know?"

She nods. "Yes."

In all the times we've been together I've never fully exposed myself to Imogene. I've kept on my clothes unless I've caved, spilling my cum on her back. She's been so honest with me, that I feel compelled. I hook my thumbs in my shorts and lower them, revealing myself.

I show her what I've been hiding all this time.

Her eyes dart my erection first, taking in my manhood, but then they slide to the side, to the flesh next to my hip. I don't look, ashamed of the wrath I've taken out on myself. She sits up, her fingers darting out. They touch the scarred skin, gentle and cool.

"You did this?" she asks, eyes darting to the blade in my hand. "With that?"

"Yes." Something feral unwinds in my chest, years of secret punishments. The only person that knows is Anex. "I'm allowed to do my own Corrections, as long as I log them in my journal."

She runs her thumb over the puckered skin, some scars run over time and time again. There are dozens, one for every Lapse, for every Regressive thought, for each Indulgence and every time I could Be Better and wasn't.

For every urge of pleasure, every ejaculation, every lingering desire I have after giving Imogene Corrections.

She's speechless, but I see the worry in her eyes. The pity. I swallow back my emotions and ask, "Do you trust me?"

Her nod is hesitant, but she doesn't run. Too bad, that's a game for another day.

"The normal way we'd do this is for me to give you a Correction for every Lapse." I unsheathe the blade, the silver glinting in the moonlight. "But this is about us. About release. I want you to tell me when you've had enough. When you're close... okay?"

"Okay."

Roughly, I spread her thighs, running my fingers over the creamy smooth skin. I know Imogene has a history of self-Correcting by cutting her flesh. This is another level of that. Pushing her panties aside, I rub my fingers around the wet heat, watching her tremble, then I take the tip of the blade and press it into her inner thigh. I make the cut quick, guiding the blade down her inner thigh. Her legs quiver and I duck, lapping up the trail of blood with my tongue.

Her body is still, tense, frozen, and I wonder if I've gone too far, revealed too much of my darkness, but she drops her fingers to my head, curling them into my hair. "More."

I'm happy to oblige.

Again, I cut her, the thinnest of marks, the most delicious taste, coppery blood with the scent of her dripping pussy. When I lick her, her hips rise—seeking. I glance up her body, at her tits, and I see her nipples are hard, her free hand moves to it, tugging at the sharp peaks.

"How does that feel?" I ask her, the words a low grunt. My cock is blindingly hard, my mind delirious with lust. "Close?"

"Not yet," she says, spreading her legs wider. This time I don't cut her thigh but run the blade through the crotch of her panties. She gasps, eyes wide. I climb over her and flip the blade, nudging her pussy with the handle.

"You need more, don't you?"

"Yes." She nods, biting down on her bottom lip. I bend and capture her mouth, her tongue and press the handle of the knife into her. Her jaw drops and a small breath catches in her throat. Her hand lands on my forearm, the one holding the blade, and she squeezes the muscle as her hips rock forward. I plunge the handle in, knowing she wants it rough—raw—and give her what she needs.

"Oh!" I kiss her to swallow the cry. I thrust the handle in, fist dragging against her clit with every motion. "Harder," she begs against my mouth. "Fuck me harder, Levi."

I only wish I could do it with my cock, bury myself into her, pounding out every ounce of grief and rage and regret, but I don't deserve a woman like Imogene. She isn't *mine*. But I can give her what she needs, something Rex doesn't understand.

"Come for me, Imogene," I tell her, feeling her rising to the edge. "Let it go. Let go of the shame built up inside of you. Release all the pain." I keep away from the language of The Way, not wanting that to be what this is about. It's not about Lapses or Regression.

"I'm close," she says, and I slow my motion, dragging the handle in and out slowly, brushing my thumb over her clit. I bend, licking the trails of sticky blood off her inner thigh. It's that way, with my face between her legs and the knife pushed to the hilt that she finally comes, a deep guttural groan releasing all of the pent-up emotions she's been carrying.

I fist my cock, rock hard and a few strokes away from exploding and get to my knees. Imogene looks up at me, eyes glazed, fingers grazing my hipbone. "Let me—"

"No," I grunt. It's too late. I'm too far gone. I seize, back arching, jaw clenching, and come, thick ropey spurts of semen spilling on her thighs.

Our breathing slows and I look at us, truly look at the mess on the bed, the broken-down girl, the ripped panties and the blood and the semen. I don't know if I helped her or harmed her. Or what is up or down, if Anex is right or if we're all wrong.

One thing I'm pretty certain of, is that the two of us are fucking ruined, raw like a scabbed over wound I can't stop picking at.

Neither of us know how to stop making it worse.

~

"He's going to be mad when he sees these," she says, looking down at the wounds. "I don't know who he'll be angrier with, you or me?"

I grunt, fishing through the bedside table for a pot of Silas' salve. I find it, spinning open the top. She stopped bleeding a while ago, the cuts aren't that deep. I've learned the balance, how to manage the weight of the tip.

"I'll deal with Rex," I say, dipping my finger in the pot and scooping out a thick glob.

"It's okay. I can please him other ways."

I glance up at her mouth, imagining Rex's cock buried inside. Imagining *my* cock buried inside. I coat the cut with the salve and cover it with a bandage. "Keep it clean," I tell her. "But the knife is disinfected. It should heal okay."

Her hand rests on my hip, thumb rubbing the scars underneath my shorts. Regret washes over me. I shouldn't have shown her. It's my burden to carry, not hers.

"You know you can come to me, too," she says softly. "When you feel the urge to Correct."

I snort. "That's not how it's done."

Females do not Correct men. They don't have the disposition for it. They're too fair. It's the male's job to inflict, which is why Anex trusts us to do it to ourselves.

"I know it's not how it's done, Levi," she says, "but nothing we do here is by the book. We're all wandering through this together." Her voice lowers. "I'm worried about you. Those scars..."

"I shouldn't have shown you."

I move to stand, but her hand grabs my forearm. "Thank you for trusting me."

Trust.

I'd asked her to trust me, and I made her bleed and fucked her with a knife, yet here she is, pleading with me to let her in. Let her close.

I nod, but it's without conviction. There's no room for Imogene in my life. There is me, my faith and Anex.

Nothing else.

61

R ^{ex}

IT'S BEEN a week since I've seen my father, and it's not a surprise when I'm called to his rooms. I'd like to say there was some consistency, planned little meetings where my father checks in on the progress I'm making with the business or you know, just to check in on his son.

But no. Consistency isn't what makes Serendee tick. Not really. It looks like a well-oiled machine on the outside but under the surface, like the drugs and money, and sex and gluttony, is well-designed chaos.

It's how I've managed to keep Imogene so spun-out, so conflicted and confused. So willing to wear lace panties and go on birth control, to beg me to be in her bed at night. I've got her right where I want her and have no intention of stopping any time soon.

I step into the cool entryway of the Main House and start for the stairs.

"Rex."

Elon is standing right off the front hall.

"Hey," I say. "Going up to see, Anex."

He jerks his chin, indicating I should follow him. Huh. Curiously gets the best of me and when I get to the hallway he's nowhere around, but I stop, counting the wooden panels that make up the wall. I glance around, making sure no one is watching and tap on the top corner of one. It pushes back, revealing a small room.

"Wow," I say, looking around the cramped space. "It's been a while since we've been in here."

When my father built this house, he added in several secret rooms and passages, 'just in case.' No one in Serendee knows about them other than the closest of the inner circle. The guys and I used to use them for elaborate games of hide and seek or a spot to duck into when Anex was looking for us. Now, I look at my best friend and ask, "What's going on?"

"I don't even know where to start," he says, annoyance flickering across his face. "I got caught up in some bad shit yesterday making a delivery. Anex has us dealing with some shady people involved in even shadier shit."

I look at Elon closer. He's rattled. "What kind of shady shit?"

His lips purse together. "Imogene was with me, and the dirty old bastard tried to buy her from me."

Heat licks up my spine. "Jesus, Elon! Why the hell was she even with you?"

"Because I was taking her to run an errand for you." His finger jabs in my chest. He's a second from snapping but I don't give a shit. I am, too. "I thought it was a basic drop with some hippies or something. They were pissed Anex screwed him on the last drop off and wanted payment—in flesh."

"Son of a bitch." I rub my forehead, trying to wrap my head around everything he's saying. The fucked-up drug deal, I can get. Some of Anex's new recruits are sloppy and the business is growing too fast. But offering to buy my woman? Fuck no. "How did you leave it?"

"Without anyone getting killed, that's how. But it was fucking close."

"Why the hell would he presume Imogene was for sale?" I ask, trying to keep my anger in check. I know Elon would never knowingly put Imogene in harm's way, but every day living and working for my father is a dangerous pursuit.

"Yeah, that was my question, too. It was heavily implied that Serendee had expanded its services beyond selling weed. Apparently, he was under the impression we're trafficking women now."

Sex trafficking. I've spent enough time in the secular world to know we bend a lot of conventions in Serendee, but even that one doesn't sit well with me. Elon and I share a look, one that doesn't need to be spoken. There's no doubt who my father is using to build this trade, the ones he's already broken: The Fallen.

My chest is tight, caught up in the sheer insanity of what Elon is describing. I force myself to exhale, an attempt to control my rage. "She's okay?"

"Yes. I didn't tell her about the old guy trying to buy her, and she didn't see much of the altercation." His eyebrow rises. "She didn't tell you any of this?"

I shake my head. "No."

I'd come to bed last night as promised and passed out—hard. She was already out of the bed when I got up this morning.

"Then I guess she also hasn't told you about the dirt we dug up on her mother?" he asks.

I blink, again, trying to catch up. "That was the errand? You took her to find information about her mother?"

"Yes, asshole." His grim expression is back. "What the fuck are *you* thinking?"

"I'm thinking that woman may be the key to everything." I lean against the wall. "What did you find out?"

"She's hard to find, unless you dig deep enough, but the main takeaway is that Camille Sanders is very involved in an anti-cult group. One specifically focused on Serendee and your father."

Anti-cult.

The word rings in my ears. Cult. My father is many things, but a cult leader? Bullshit. That's just a word to discredit him and everyone in the community.

"There's more," he says. "And she doesn't know about it. I read all of the websites. Her mother has spent the last few years trying to get Imogene out of Serendee but has been unsuccessful."

"Trying how?"

Elon just shakes his head. "I don't know."

Possessiveness grips me. Get her out? As in remove her? Away from me? Fuck no. But I realize something else. I'm not the only one that won't let this girl get away from me. Neither would my father and the lengths he would go to in order to keep her here would far exceed my own.

"Thank you for coming to me, brother," I say, pressing my fingers into the wooden panel and open the door.

"What are you going to do?" Elon asks. He came to me for a reason, so that I could take care of this.

"I'm going to find out exactly what my father is up to."

I WALK past the guard and open the door leading to my father's rooms. My rank keeps anyone from stopping me or questioning my movements. There are no rooms, no sections of this community that are off limits to me.

I step inside the outer room of my father's luxurious suite and find the room empty. I make my way across the room, stopping at the bar to pour myself a drink. I need one after everything Elon told me. A loud bang from an adjacent room draws my attention, or rather a series of them, the thudding falling into a distinct rhythm, the unmistakable sound of fucking on the other side.

Guess I'll wait then.

I swallow the drink whole and am halfway through another when my father emerges from the bedroom, casually tying his linen robe. "Ah, son," he says, leaving the door ajar. I see three women in the bed, naked and looking well-fucked. Two I recognize from recruiting into Serendee myself. If my memory serves, she gives amazing head. "Sorry to keep you waiting, but my mates were in need of Enlightenment, and it's my duty to show them The Way."

I wonder if they truly are here on their own volition. The tactics I use during recruitment are heavy handed and determined. I don't take 'no' easily, and I'm as skilled at the art of persistence as Silas is with eating pussy. These thoughts piss me off, and I finish off my liquor.

"We're both here now," I say, lowering into one of the white chairs. "What did you call me up here for?"

He sits across from me and picks up a pipe on the coffee table. Carefully he packs the bowl, filling it with the strong-smelling herb piled in a ceramic pot. "Just catching up. We haven't spoken since the ceremony." He presses his thumb to the center of the bowl. "How is your mate?"

"She's fine," I say, leaning back, pretending I don't care that he's mentioning her. "Although a little rattled after the ambush she and Elon got into yesterday."

He hesitates, *slightly*, before resuming his task. "I don't know what you're referring to. Ambush?"

He probably doesn't, but I don't trust this man or his motives.

"One of our buyers was under the impression that we don't just deal weed, but that we also trade in flesh." I watch him closely. "And they tried to purchase Imogene."

Anex scratches a match across the side of a box and lights the pipe, taking a few short puffs before a long drag. He holds his breath, eyes watering, and then holds it out to me. I wave it off, controlling the urge of stabbing his eyes out with the mouthpiece.

"Did you hear me?" I ask.

"Yes, I heard you, and this sounds more like a matter of why Elon was parading your young, beautiful mate in front of non-community members. If you don't want people coveting your property, son, don't let it out of the gates."

"No," I say, shifting to lean closer, "that is not what happened.

What happened is you're expanding our trade to people we don't know and cannot trust. *And* they are under the idea we sell women." Anex takes another long drag. "And I suspect there's truth to that, isn't there?"

He rests the pipe on the tray. "What are you implying?"

I glance toward the bedroom door where the women are still cuddled together on the bed. I don't hold back. "The women we bring in here. The ones you don't keep." I lift my chin. "The ones you lock up in the basement. The Fallen. You're selling them, aren't you?"

"Those women are in a re-education program that they've agreed to participate in. They're consumed by their Weakness, and I am simply trying to help them get back on the right path."

"To The Way," I state. I never noticed how my father spoke before he sent me out to recruit and deal to the frats in the University. How his words and terminology are specific to our community. I always felt like that elevated me, made me special. Better, but at some point, I realized it was just more mind games and manipulations.

I've heard this same tired rhetoric over and over again. My life has been filled with lectures and sermons and bullshit terminology, all of which leads back to him being in control, taking what he wants, *removing* the people that are a problem.

Like my mother. Like Imogene's.

The events of the last week come crashing down on me. The altercation with that prick, Miller, at the Zeta Sig house the other night—how he almost had his way with Imogene. And the situation with Elon, and later the details about her mother... how she's been trying to get her out. I'm bone tired and my patience has worn thin.

My father isn't a cult leader—he's a conman.

"If you're asking if I'm expanding our business opportunities, the answer is yes. Our crops are booming, our reputation and product is stellar, and it's time to venture outside of Wittmore frat boys for buyers."

"And the women?"

He lifts his pipe and takes another drag. "The women are willing to do what it takes to attain Enlightenment."

"By whoring themselves."

Anex shrugs. "It's their nature, Rex. If you took the time to attend the men's group lessons, you would understand that." He leans back and regards me. "But I don't think you need a class to teach you about women. You inherited that trait from me, and even if you didn't, I think the actions of your betrothed should be enough evidence of what a woman will do if allowed sexual freedom with more than one man."

"This isn't about Imogene."

His head tilts. "Isn't it? Your mate can't keep her legs shut, son, and her darkness, it runs deeper than I could have ever anticipated. I knew she was a risk; her mother caused enough chaos when she lived here, but Imogene struggles on a different level."

I think about the lashes and the Correction she craves so much— the way she goes to Levi to inflict it. She's devoted, but strong-willed. She's lost—but claimed. Years of living under my father's control has left her with a mind so fucked up that she's barely any different than the women downstairs, locked in those tiny cells.

"She is mine to deal with," I say, voice low and even. "And what happens in my house, with my woman, is not your business. You keep your mind and thoughts and manipulations away from her."

My father doesn't move, doesn't tense, or shift a muscle but I see the dark glint in his pupils, the flash of warning. "I'd watch your tone, son. Everything in Serendee is under my leadership. *Including* your mate. I gave her to you and just as quickly, I can take her away."

There's a menace under his words. An unspoken threat. *'Like your mother.'*

I stand, hands clenched tight at my sides. If they weren't, they'd be wrapped around his throat, choking the life out of him. The way he looks at me, with his chin lifted and his lips twisted smugly... it's almost a dare.

I walk away before I do something irreparable.

"Rex," he calls when I'm almost clear. I pause. "Tell your men the expansion is on. That'll mean longer hours and increased production, but that's a necessary sacrifice."

I turn slightly. "And the women?"

"That will be more discrete. I'll continue to prepare them for their next phase of Enlightenment and notify you and your friends when it's time."

"Fine," I say, swallowing back the thick bile rising in the back of my throat, but I don't let him see my disgust or horror. This is what my father does, who he is. He pushes us one step further, deeper, farther away from who we are as a community. As a people.

I'm afraid he'll push us so far one day we'll lose who we are entirely.

62

I mogene

I'm WALKING BACK from the Center when I see Elon go into the gym. I'm not sure why I follow him, but something urges me to follow.

The community gym is a hub in Serendee. Mostly for Anex's basketball games, but even when I lived in the Domum we would go for calisthenics and fitness class.

Today is the first time I've seen the soft flat mat in the middle. It's blue, with a red edging creating the impression of a box. I peer across the room at Elon as he drops his bag on a bench and pulls off his shirt, revealing his toned upper body. He reaches into his bag and pulls out a roll of something—tape, I realize as he wraps his knuckles.

Boxing. Or fighting. That's what this is.

There are other guys in the gym, but my focus is on Elon. His shoulders are wide, tapering down to his muscular chest and ripped abdomen that vanishes into a deep cut 'V' that travels under the waistband of his shorts. I didn't know men like this existed—or maybe I just never thought about it. We were kept so separate, so segregated.

My neck warms as I think about how this man has bent me over a table like a rag doll and pounded into me—releasing the buildup of pressure buried in my core. I wonder what it would be like to have him over me, all that muscle and deep-rooted anger.

I take a step back and let the fresh air just outside the gym, cool me off.

Elon doesn't want me like that. We've never had the intimacy that Rex and I have managed, or Silas with his sweet, caring nature. Even the connection I have with Levi is different... it's violent and all-consuming, but emotional.

At best I feel like Elon tolerates me. A means to an end. Another part of his job in Serendee. An obligation.

Thinking of it that way quells my urges and I step back inside, curious about the fight.

Two men are on the mat now. Elon and one I recognize from around the community, Malen. He's leveled up lately, working closer to Anex. Wearing the all black clothing of members of his security.

He's also punching Elon in the face.

Shock ripples through me. Elon. Powerful, commanding and sure is getting his butt kicked by this other guy. He strikes him with his fist, his foot, his elbow and knee. Elon takes it, over and over, righting himself after each hit and gesturing for Malen to come at him again.

I step inside, closer, compelled to understand. There are others watching—all men—engrossed by the annihilation of one of Serendee's strongest.

Malen wipes the sweat from his forehead. "Had enough?"

"Nope," Elon says, spitting blood on the ground. "Another round." He looks at one of the guys waiting by the edge. "You, too."

Malen shrugs and bounces on his toes, waiting for the other man to walk into the ring. What I'm seeing feels unbelievable. Watching Elon take on two men—while seemingly not fighting back.

Malen's elbow jerks back for another punch.

"What is happening?" I ask—out loud—although I mean to say it in my head. One of the other men looks back, eyebrows raised, surprised to see me.

"You're not supposed to be here," he says, but his tone isn't bossy. I see from his expression he recognizes me.

"What is this?" I ask, flinching when Elon takes another hit.

"None of your business, I imagine." The guy approaches me, putting his body between me and the ring.

I push him aside. "Stop!"

Elon's eyes jerk to the side at the sound of my voice. Just in time to snap away from Malen's fist slamming into his jaw.

"Stop!" I shout again. I rush past the guy blocking me and enter the ring. Malen's eyes widen when he sees me, his fists dropping.

"What is this?"

Elon's hands are on his knees, and blood drips to the mat. I can't tell if it's from his mouth or his eye. Maybe his nose.

"Stop," I breathe. "This has to stop."

"Go away, Little Lamb." Elon's voice is gruff, hard.

"No." I jerk my chin at Malen. "Go. Get out of here."

His lips curve. "Not sure it's your job to tell me what to do."

"You can do as I say, or I can go get my mate. Who would you rather deal with?" The way his spine straightens tells me he knows exactly who my mate is. "I thought so. Go." I look at the others. "You, too. Get out of here."

I drop down beside him and tentatively touch his shoulder. Once I hear the door slam, and I know we're alone, I ask, "Want to tell me what this is all about?"

"No." He rises up, shrugging me off. I don't back away though, worried about his face and head. His ribs. His mouth tugs down in a grimace and he limps off the mat.

"Elon! What is this? What are you doing?"

He turns. It's slow and looks painful. "I'm doing what I said I would." His eyes dart to the mat, now covered in blood. "Those were my Corrections."

I blink, remembering how he'd promised me he would take

Corrections for finding the information on my mother. He was assuming my guilt—my Lapse.

I had no idea he'd do it this way.

"Are you crazy? You could get seriously hurt!"

"Me?" He's shoulders shift back and he strides toward me. "I'm trained. I spent years learning how to fight and defend myself. But what about you? About the beatings you take from Levi to assuage your guilt? The assault you call Enlightenment?"

"It's not the same. You weren't fighting back."

"Neither do you." His eyes narrow—or they try. The left one is swollen and puffy. He looks unsteady on his feet. I don't think, I just wrap my arm around his waist.

"I'm fine."

"Okay, sure." He doesn't resist when I help him over to the bench, although to be fair, he outweighs me by at least a hundred and twenty pounds. "Sit."

For once in his life, he follows directions, sighing heavily as he eases to the hard seat.

"Wait here."

I head to the back room—a small kitchen, I've been in while serving refreshments at the basketball games. There's an ice machine and a stack of clean towels. I fill the towel with ice and wet a few others in the sink. When I come back out, he's on his back, the hard bench aligned with his spine. I bend down to my knees, pressing the ice to his swollen eye. "Hold this."

"You're awfully bossy today," he says, keeping the ice in place.

"Well, I think Malen knocked your good sense out around the third punch."

He laughs, but it's lacking any real levity. He winces and groans.

"How often do you do this?" I ask, wiping the blood off his chin.

His eyes meet mine. "Not often. Corrections are something I gave up a long time ago."

"So, why now?"

"Because I promised." He looks away. "And because I put you in harm's way and that deserved some consequences." It may be the most honest thing he's ever said to me and my heart aches because I'm the one that drove him to this.

I stand, leaving the cloth on the bench. Bending, I grab the hem of my skirt and lift it. His eyes widen as I reveal myself. If he questions it, he never speaks. This isn't about sex or lust or anything else. It's about showing my scars, the way he just showed his. I know when he sees them. His eyes widen, lips turn down. His hand shoots out and he grabs me by the back of the thigh, pulling me close.

"Who did this?" His thumb grazes under the red, scabbing wound. It's ugly, like I feel inside.

I swallow, heat burning my cheeks. "Levi, but only because I asked him to."

Begged.

He rises up, spinning his legs until he's sitting up and facing me. His hand fists in my skirt, and he pulls me close.

"I don't like it," he grunts.

I touch the side of his face, grazing his puffy eye, the result of his own Correction. "Are you sure?"

"That's different. I don't like it when you hurt yourself." He kisses the healing cuts. Each one. Slow and gentle. "Your skin is perfect. Soft. You're perfect."

I thread my fingers in his hair, lifting his face to mine. "I'm anything but."

"I guess that's why we like you then, because neither are we."

His hands slide up my skirt, hiking my foot up on the bench. He kisses the scar again, but pushes his fingers underneath my panties. He rubs against my clit, sending shockwaves deep to my core. "You like it?" he asks.

"Mmhmm."

"You're getting wet for me, aren't you?"

I nod, biting down on my bottom lip. My pussy is inches from his face, my foot is planted on the bench. He rubs tiny circles against my nub, until my breath is labored and if he doesn't stop I'll come like this, right on his hand.

"Elon," I warn. "I'm going to—"

He drops his hand and drags me onto his lap. I feel him beneath me—hard and eager. He shudders, and I think it's from pain, but when his eyes meet mine, I sense it's something deeper.

Maybe Elon and I have a connection after all.

I kiss him gently, taking care not to bruise his already busted lip, he doesn't seem to care, coming at me hard, fingers digging into my skin like he's trying to claw his way inside. Between my legs, he yanks my panties to the side, brushing his fingers over the sensitive, pooling heat. I shiver and confess, "That feels so good."

"Everything about you feels good, Imogene." He kisses my throat. "*Everything.* Your skin. Your body. Your pussy." His finger sinks in when he says it, eliciting a cry. "So tight and wet. I just want to bury myself inside of you, fill you up until you can't take it anymore."

"Do it," I say, it's less of a challenge than a plea. "I want to feel you, too."

My heart hammers and my skin grows hot. Beneath the folds of my dress, he pulls out his erection. I can't see it, but I feel it, hot and steel-hard against my inner thigh, probing at my entrance. I wrap my hands around his neck and hold on as he impales me with his length, sinking down to take him as deep as I can.

He groans when our bodies connect, my forehead is dropped against my shoulder.

"You feel so good," he says, licking my collarbone. "So fucking good, Imogene."

I like the sound of my name on his tongue and lift his head so I can kiss him. Tongues tangled, his hips rock back and then forward, his hand sliding down my back to settle above my ass. He holds me there, thrusting into me. Channeling all that anger he had in the ring into me.

"I've told you before—stop hurting yourself. Come to me, I'll fuck that Lapse right out of your body." He jerks into me, pulling me with every thrust. I hold onto him, loving the feel of him inside—he's thick and stretches me with every invasion. I want him deeper, as deep as he can go and I raise my heels onto the bench next to him, "Oh," I say, as he grabs my ankles, pushing them behind his back. "Oh, that's it. *That's* it."

My clit rubs against him and what crests over me is unfamiliar— it's not laced with anger or regret. It's want and desire and true confession. It's something I've held inside of me for weeks, my real feelings for this real man, hard muscled and pounding into me. The orgasm comes at me like an impact, hard and dizzying, my breath caught in my throat and my nerves screaming from exposure.

"That's it, baby," he says, breath hot on my ear. "Come for me. Clench around me. Milk my cock. *Own* me."

He rises up with his final thrust, holding me against his body. His fingers dig into the flesh of my backside, his cock buried deep. Elon's orgasm comes with a roar, bouncing off the high ceilings, rattling deep in my chest. "Fuck, fuck, fuck, Imogene," he chants, each word accentuated with a punch, my pussy holding onto him like I never want to let go, because in this moment, it's us. There's no pain. Just feeling good. Feeling right.

Feeling a million miles away from this made-up world and the controls they have over us, I kiss him, wanting the feel of him linked to me last a little longer. The kisses are slower, longer, our chests rising and falling together as we come back to center.

"Promise me," he says, pulling back and cupping my cheek. He's still inside of me. I'm not ready to let go. "The next time you want to hurt yourself, let me try that first."

"Only if you do the same."

He nods, but there's something guarded in his eyes. A wariness, like he knows he can't keep his promise, even if he wants to. I don't push on because with the foundations of our upbringing and Anex's watchful eye, I can't either.

63

I mogene

I'VE JUST COME in from work and am hanging my bag from the hook in the foyer when the door opens and Rex strides in. His shoulders are tight, his jaw set, and my stomach flip flops in worry about what he's upset about now. How much he'll make me pay for whatever has made him angry.

"We need to talk," he says, walking past me to the living room.

I follow him, nearly tripping over the hem of my skirt in the process. When I catch up I say, "You must be hungry—"going for the age-old lesson of feeding your man. They taught us this in the Domum. Keep your man fed, and he'll be happy. Back then I didn't realize part of the care and feeding of men was allowing them free reign of your body.

"I'm not hungry, Imogene." His eyes dart to the couch. "Sit."

I swallow and do as I'm told, sitting on the edge of the chair, eyes cast down. "Have I done something to upset you?"

His hand shoots out, fingers rough on my chin, and he lifts my gaze to his. "Fuck no, Little Lamb. It's not you I'm angry with, it's..." His whole body stiffens further. "Elon told me what happened on the delivery—how you could have been hurt." His touch lightens, fingers trailing down my neck. "I'm furious at my father for allowing this to go so far." The hand by his side clenches tight. "I'm furious that anyone would think they could have you without my permission."

"It was okay," I say, taking that fist into my hands and loosening his fingers. "Elon was there. He protected me."

His blue eyes meet mine. "It's *my* job to protect you."

"Apparently, it requires more than one man to keep me safe." I smile up at him. "I'm just thankful you allow the others to be there, too."

"You like them, don't you?"

"They're growing on me," I admit. "Even Elon."

"I'm glad. I know it's unconventional, even in Serendee, to belong to more than one mate, but you're right. To protect you, to keep you safe, to keep you ours, it has to be all of us."

We sit like this for a long beat, me holding his hand, him grazing his fingertips along the column of my neck. My heart flutters, the fear having vanished. Having this man's attention—in a good way—is almost more than I can handle. His eyes dart down to my mouth, and he tilts his head, drawing me in for a kiss.

For once he's not angry or punishing—there's no manipulation, and I sink into him, the warmth of his tongue and the feel of his strong jaw. My body buzzes, humming the strains of an invisible music, and God, this is what I've been wanting from this man. This kind of tenderness and care.

Apparently, all it took was my life being threatened to bring him to surface.

His hand drops to the buttons at my neckline, working each one out of its hole. It's painfully tedious, my heart threatening to rip from my chest. I barely hear the front door open and close, although I'm aware of Elon the moment he walks in.

His presence is undeniable.

"Go away," Rex says, also aware of his friend standing five feet away. He never stops unbuttoning my dress.

"Rex," Elon says.

He kisses me, deep and long before pulling back to say, "Fuck off. Whatever it is, it can wait."

His casual but determined banter catches me off guard. Does he want me that much? My body warms and I catch the way his lips quirk, coy and sexy. I can't help but smile back.

Elon, determined as ever, doesn't leave. "We have a job."

Rex sighs and gives me a look that says, '*don't move,*' and stands up. "Fuck the job. I need some time with my mate."

Elon's eyes meet mine, and I see a dark urgency behind them. As much as I want Rex, this sweet, protective mate to stay at home with me, I squeeze his hand and say, "Go with him. He wouldn't come in here if it wasn't important."

The two men stare at one another for a long moment, but I know that Elon's going to win when Rex runs a hand through his hair and grunts, "Fine." He turns to me, grabbing my hand and lifting me from the couch. His hands circle my waist. "We're not done, Little Lamb."

I nod and push up on my toes, kissing him on the jaw. His face turns and his lips meet mine, drawing me in for another kiss.

"Be careful," I say as his hand eases off my hip. I'm spurred to go to Elon. He watches me closely as I take his hand. "You, too. Don't do anything dangerous."

He brushes the hair off my cheek and skims his fingers down the side of my face, to my chin. He tilts it up and kisses me. Like everything else about him, it's hard and full of deep intensity. When he pulls away, I feel wobbly on my feet.

Rex gets his jacket and I notice as he shrugs it on there's a black gun nestled against the small of his back. He lifts his chin. "Tell Levi and Silas we'll be back as soon as possible."

Feeling a chill from seeing the gun, I wrap my arms around my upper body, seeking warmth or assurance. An anxious feeling builds inside of me, and I'm aware that it's not new, that it's been growing for days.

Things are about to change and I'm not sure if I'm ready.

WHEN I HEAR a sound at the door, I think it's Levi or Silas returning home for the night. Neither man emerges and then I realize it's a knock—soft—barely a tap. I push back the curtain on the window and see a young boy—maybe eight or nine.

"Hello," I say, opening the door.

"Are you Imogene?"

"Yes."

He holds out a square envelope—my name scrawled across the front. "This is for you."

I recognize the script—it's the same as the ones to all the other women's meetings—and it sets my heart racing. While looking over his shoulder, making sure no one sees me, I take it from him.

"Thank you."

He nods, and jumps down the porch steps, vanishing down the road. I don't go back inside before I run a finger under the flap and open it. More instructions. The meeting is tonight. Eleven PM. Dress in ceremonial white.

There's a tug at my heart this time—less excitement—more worry. Rex and I were on the precipice of something. A more honest, real relationship. I know him well enough now, that if he finds out that I've been attending this women's group, becoming more bonded to the women in Serendee, he'll be furious.

Betrayed.

Things are changing so quickly for me. It's confusing and over-whelming. Rex and the guys have shown me this other side of life: sex, lust, and every temptation in the outside world. The information about my mother and Beatrice. The Fallen. But then the women's group... it's the kind of acceptance I've always wanted in the community.

It's an honor I never expected to receive.

Being part of this bonded group of women is important to me, but

I also feel like I'm losing another piece of myself with each meeting. Telling Margaret about sleeping with men other than my mate, well, it's all twisted and confusing.

Regardless of my mixed feelings, there's no real way I can decline the invitation. I've already committed. I've given them my collateral. I've taken the oaths.

As always, I do as I'm instructed, changing into my white dress, slipping on my sandals. Like a ghost, I slip into the night, traveling up the hill to the meeting spot—Beatrice' house. Margaret is waiting with a wide, welcoming smile.

"Sorry it was so last minute," she says. "Did you make it out okay."

"Rex and Elon were called away to an assignment. Silas and Levi didn't make it home."

"Good. I set it up for them to not be home, but juggling four men is a challenge."

I laugh and say, "Tell me about it," even though the knowledge that she orchestrated their assignments fills my belly with worry. This woman has so much power.

"Tonight is going to be so special, Imogene." She thrusts both hands out, fingers wiggling for me to grasp. "But before we go, there's something I want to share with you—since we're family."

"Oh," I say, "is something wrong?"

"No, the opposite really." She pulls my hand to her stomach. The move startles me, but not as much as the feel of a bump under the loose, flowing dress. *A bump.* I blink and look at her face. She's beaming. "I'm pregnant."

The news hits me—hard like an impact. Shock? Surprise. Maybe both.

"Rex is going to be a big brother and you're going to be a sister-in-law." She laughs, possibly knowing how crazy it sounds. Or, hopefully she does. He'll be over twenty years older than the baby.

"I'm just..." I suck in a breath. "Congratulations. That's amazing news."

"Isn't it?" She looks down, rubbing her hand over the swell of her stomach. She looks to be a few months—although Margaret is so thin, she may be further along. "It just makes tonight even more special."

I tilt my head to the side. "How so?"

"Tonight is when we truly become sisters." She squeezes my hand. "Now that you've released your collateral and have committed to the women's group, there's one last step." She lowers her voice. "Tonight, in a special ceremony, you'll get your birthmark."

The birthmark. She'd told us about this the first night in the woods. The final step of our initiation. I shiver, unable to discern if it's nerves or excitement. No, what Anex would tell me is that it's fear. Fear of embracing Enlightenment. Fear of handing myself over to a trusted spiritual leader.

I squeeze Margaret's fingers in mine and say with complete honesty, "I can't wait."

64

E^{lon}

I SHIFT the car into gear, pushing the speed limit, as we exit the county. The road is familiar. I'd driven it two days before. This time I know what I'm getting into.

"Is someone going to tell me where we're going?" Silas asks from the back seat. I'd picked him up on the way to the garage, telling him we needed him. Which we didn't. Not for the easy drop off over at the Phi Kappa house.

It was the second, unofficial job I had planned. One I detailed to Rex after we left Imogene at the house. Our kind of work isn't exactly in Silas' wheelhouse, but he can use a gun. Every male in Serendee knows how to wield a weapon and defend the community. It's a concept ingrained in us since childhood. If shit goes sideways tonight, and it may, I want backup.

"Anex has communicated to some of the people we do business

with, that members of our community are for sale," I say. "We're going to send a message that not everyone in Serendee agrees."

"Especially," Rex says, inspecting one of the guns he brought with him. The silver metal glints in a passing headlight, "When they're trying to buy my mate."

"Say that again?" Silas says, moving into the gap between the seats.

"I went on a sales trip yesterday, trying to fix a prior delivery error," I say, catching his eye in the mirror. His expression is hard, eyes tense. We're used to bending to the rules of our home—to our leader—but this is one step too far. "My apology and money weren't enough. The bastard wanted Imogene as part of the deal."

"Son of a bitch," Silas swears. "And let me guess... the people Anex has for sale are the Fallen."

It's not a question. "Yep."

"Fuck," he says, followed by a string of curse words. "I knew something was off."

I agree. The way those women looked in those tiny, filthy cells... it's been gnawing at me for days. One moment those people were productive members of the community. The next they'd crossed Anex in some unforgivable way, and their lives were over.

"My father just keeps pushing and pushing the boundaries of what our community is supposed to be about. Weapons, drugs, re-education, and now sex trafficking? This is way outside of the founda-tion of Serendee."

I know it's hard for Rex to admit it. Even if he's harbored suspi-cions about his mother's death, and dislikes his father, he's spent years reaping the rewards of Anex's control and command of the community, but he's right. We can't allow this to continue.

Risking Imogene's safety was the final straw.

"So what's the plan?" Silas asks, as I turn off the highway and down a long, dark road.

"We're going to give Jeb a little visit." I ground my jaw. "That bastard almost killed me."

I explain to them both exactly what went down, how Jeb and his wife pulled guns and are fighters. "They're extremists of some kind," I add. "Living off the grid, dealing to backwoods communities, heavily armed…"

"So you mean like Serendee?" Rex asks, the sarcasm thick.

If it didn't rankle every belief, every foundation of my entire identity I'd agree, but it does, so I don't.

"That's it," I say, instead, gesturing to the little shack by the road. "His file noted that they live in a house at the back of the property."

Anex keeps dossiers on everyone we work with, from frat boys to isolated extremists.

"Jesus," Silas mutters, eyeing the run-down stand. "I fucking hate hillbillies."

"Anyone else lives with them?" Rex asks.

"Just the wife as far as I know." I didn't see any other occupants in the house, but with a guy like Jeb, you never know.

We park down at the end of the road, car tucked in near the farm stand, checking weapons and securing them before we head down the long driveway. Sure enough, there's a small house up ahead, lights warming the windows in an otherwise pitch black night. It's quiet and Silas picks up a rock, tossing it toward the house, trying to rouse a dog or anyone else watching. When no one responds, I nod to Rex to take the back door. He vanishes around the side, a stick snapping under his foot. I hold my breath, waiting for all hell to break loose, but the same stillness fills the night air. When Silas finally exhales next to me, I realize he is, too.

"*On three*," I mouth, holding my gun at level. I count down and rear back, kicking my foot into the door. It splinters in a loud slap, voices shouting from the interior. We move so fast that the scream Jeb's wife is about to let loose is caught in her throat.

"Don't you dare," I tell her, pointing the gun at her. Jeb has his hand under the couch, and I see the black steel at his fingertips. "Touch that weapon and I'll blow her head off, Jeb." I jerk my chin at Silas, who is a foot behind Jeb with his gun cocked and ready. "And then he'll blow yours off, too."

Unbelievably, I can tell he's considering it, unphased by his wife's panicked whimpers. Finally, he relents, drawing his hand back. I bend and remove the shot gun, positioning it behind me.

"There," Jeb says, once he's lost his weapon. "I don't know what the fuck you're doing on my property like this, but I can tell you that you've lost your goddamn mind." His eyes narrow. "Your guru knows you're here?"

"He's not a guru," I reply, not even sure what that word means. "He made an error and we're here to rectify it."

"By what? Killing me and the wife? That's not rectifying anything —that's triggering a war." He grins, revealing crooked and yellow teeth. "Once Anex's buyers find out about this, everything he's built up will crash."

"You think you're that important?" Silas asks, hand shaking. He's still furious that this man tried to take Imogene. I can see the darkness in his eyes. "You're nothing."

"I may live out here alone, minding my own business, son, but your leader is a dangerous man. There are protocols put in place in case he," he glances at me, "or his minions, decide to overstep." He laughs. "You kill me and a tremor will travel across Anex's enterprises, and you'll be the one to feel the aftershocks."

I lunge, grabbing him by the shirt, and lifting him off the couch. My nose is less than an inch from his when I hear the trigger cock. Somehow, somewhere he had another gun and I feel the hard press in my gut.

The two of us are in a stand-off, my gun pressed against his throat. His to my gut. Silas covers the wife and fuck it all, we're screwed.

"You may want to lower the gun." Rex's voice amplifies the tension. My eyes are locked with Jeb's, and he doesn't take his eyes off me, but a panicked whimper from his wife forces me to break contact. Rex is standing at the entrance to the hallway, a young teenage girl in his grip. Sweat drips down my back. Fuck, shit just got worse, way worse.

"Jeb," the woman cries.

"Not now, Doreen," he snaps.

"Daddy?"

That's when it clicks—the pieces falling into place for Jeb. He turns, and the distraction is all I need to grab the pistol, turning it back on him with sweaty hands.

Rex grins at the man, smile wide and evil. "The woman you tried to purchase yesterday is my mate," he growls. "How about I take your daughter back to Serendee with me, sell her to the highest bidder.

The girl shakes her head, fat tears running down her cheeks. I want to feel bad for her, but her father needs a lesson. *And* we need to get out of here alive.

"I thought we were making a deal," Jeb says, voice less sure. "You owed me."

"Bullshit," Rex strides forward, dragging the girl with him. "You wanted my woman. You wanted to put your filthy hands on her." He pushes the girl toward Silas who catches her, holding onto her tight. Rex grabs Jeb's arm and drags him over to the fireplace, pushing him to his knees and slamming his forearm against the stone surface. "You wanted to *use* her."

Seamlessly, Rex, pulls a knife out of his boot. Doreen and the daughter scream.

"Don't hurt him," the girl cries, turning her face into Silas' chest. As angry as he is, I see his hand curl around her shoulder. It's just his nature to provide comfort even while he has a gun to her temple.

Rex ignores her pleas and presses down on his wrist. "Maybe if you don't know how to keep your fucking hands to yourself, I should just remove the temptation. "

"No! Please! Don't! I didn't know she belonged to you! I thought that's why you brought her!"

Rex, lays the blade of the knife across Jeb's wrist, pressing gently. One move and I know he's got the strength to cut his hand clean off. I'm only a few feet away but I can barely hear him command, "Tell me everything."

"I-I got a message." Jeb's body trembles, head to toe. "Word about a new product. Women mostly, but a few boys if that's what's desired. Cash only. I seriously thought that since there was the product screw up, you'd brought me a bonus." He lifts his gaze to me. "No one has ever brought a woman to a drop before. Especially not one that looked like her."

The statement stings and the accusation is clear. I'm the one that put her in danger. He's not wrong.

"Let me make something clear," Rex says. "The people of Serendee are not for sale."

"You may want to tell your Daddy that, but between us, it's understood."

"That's not all," Rex says, pressing down. Blood beads and drips down his wrist. "Since you're so fucking connected, you notify everyone you know that we do not sell people." Jeb nods, but Rex continues. "If someone, including my father, tries to traffic any member of our community, or any other community, I'll hold you personally responsible."

"Yes. I understand," Jeb says, eyes pleading. Rex doesn't move, considering Jeb's commitment, but finally releases him. I nod at Silas, and he lets the girl go, too. She runs to her mother, folding into her side.

"This ends today," Rex says. "Your relationship with Serendee is over. Find another distributor." He looks over at Doreen and the girl. "And learn to treat women better. They aren't objects or possessions to buy and sell."

Those words haunt me as we leave, striding away in the dark, worming their way into my brain.

Serendee does sell people. Maybe not for money but good behavior. Loyalty. Devotion. Service. Girls are separated and trained. Arranged with a mate. There's no other option. It's all at Anex's choosing. And with Imogene? The four of us came along and made her our possession.

Fuck.

"We're going to pay for that," Silas says from the backseat. More than anyone he understands the consequences for defiant behavior. "He's going to find out and when he hears you cut him off as a buyer..."

There's no need to say anything else. We all know.

Ahead I see a junction, the split in the highway. One leads back to Serendee. The other to a little town I've never visited, but the address is stamped in my brain. Memorized just in case.

I take the unfamiliar road.

"Where are you going?" Rex asks.

"Silas is right, there will be consequences, but we're not going to be the one to suffer it."

"Shit," Silas says from the back seat. "Imogene."

I nod. "We're going to make sure that she's safe, even if that means letting her go."

65

L evi

"JUST REMEMBER," I tell the class, "you are called to lead for a reason. You were born with the temperament to handle things the females in your life can't."

A hand raises in the back—Kenneth. Born and raised in Serendee. He's on the fast track with Anex and that's why he was invited to my class. I nod for him to ask his question.

He fidgets, shifting nervously in his seat. I raise an eyebrow and say, "This is a safe place to express yourself, Ken. Nothing said here, leaves here, right guys?"

The small group concurs, eager to help a fellow member.

He takes a breath. "What happens if your mate questions your authority. Calls you sexist or demeaning?"

"Ah," I say, ignoring the pink ruddiness on his cheeks. "I get it. Describing your flaws to the group is hard. Not being in control of your household is humiliating, but that's why we're here. To learn from one another." I sit on the stool in the font of the classroom. A method I learned from Anex about presenting myself as understanding and compassionate. "Taking care of you family isn't sexist. It's not demeaning. It's empowering. The Way shows us that time and time again, we revert to these roles, when we embrace our masculinity—and our positions of authority, the women in our lives feel safer. More secure." I grin. "More intimate and loving."

There's a chuckle at my insinuation. I mean, what do I know about love and mates? Yet Anex said The Way was calling me to teach this men's group. At least now I can draw on my experiences with Imogene.

She's not my mate and God knows if I love her—but there's something intense transpiring between us—something I can't describe, but I try to use that now to educate the men in the group.

"Part of my role in Serendee is to guide and implement Correction. Currently I have one female that I am guiding through this process." I exhale. "It hasn't been easy, but what I've come to learn is that I give her what she needs—and sometimes that pushes me to my limits."

Like the night with the knife. We pushed that so far, the boundary line snapped.

"Is it uncomfortable sometimes? Yes. But no one said following this way of life, following The Way, would be a cakewalk. We are given these roles as a challenge to ourselves and to those we guide—in Corrections, in Bonding, in any part of our lives in Serendee."

"She doesn't hate you for it?" Jacob, another member asks.

"No," I reply. "Actually, now she comes to me—willingly—we even discuss how far things should go." I look at Kenneth. "Show your mate your control, don't just tell her. Be there for her. Help her though her Lapses. Those actions are what define us."

He nods, seeming a little more confident and I use that as the opportunity to wrap up the class.

"Make sure you complete the worksheets for our next meeting." I slide off the stool. "I'll see you all next week."

I straighten up while the men file out of the room, handing me their guide books on the way out. The building grows quiet. It's evening and I should be the only one left, but I hear movement in the hallway and look up. To my surprise Anex stands in the doorway.

"Good evening, Levi."

"Oh." I stop what I'm doing, resting the stack of books on top of the shelf, and bow, touching my forehead. "I didn't know anyone else was here."

"Just doing a little last-minute work," he says, entering the room. "Whenever we're in a building phase, I tend to have more to check of my list."

"The childcare center?" I ask. "I saw the construction the other day. Looks like it's coming along."

"Nicely," he agrees. "That's actually what I came here to talk to you about."

I frown. "The childcare center?"

"Well, not exactly," he says, walking over to the stool. He eases up and nods to a chair in the front row. "Take a seat, Levi."

I walk over to the chairs and sit. It's a strange vantage point, I'm used to being the one at the front of the class, but at the same time, Anex is my teacher. I should be honored he's taken the time to address me personally. "What is it you need me to do?"

"This is actually about Imogene."

"Imogene?" A flicker of worry fills my chest. "What about her?"

"My family is growing, Levi. Margaret is with child. Rex has brought Imogene into our lives. After years of only having a son, I now have a family." The declaration seems harsh—seeing as how we thought *we* were his family, but I understand. It's why I crave a mate of my own. "The Way has spoken to me about how to integrate Imogene into the future of our family. After much meditation and thought, I've decided to move her out of her position here, at the Center and to the Childcare facility once it opens."

"That sounds like a wonderful opportunity," I say. Working in the Center is an honor, but so will a position at his new project. Anex choses positions carefully. "I know she loves her work here, she's very devoted, but working on a new project... I can only imagine she'll be excited."

"Change is hard for women like Imogene. Her defiant streak runs hot, but yes, I think she'll come around to it." He looks down at me. "It's out of necessity. Some recent activities, mostly outside of Serendee, have made me reassess. As a member of my direct family, the risks are too high for her to be outside of the community."

I nod. "That makes sense to keep Rex's mate safe."

I notice the slight twitch in his eye when I say Rex's name. I press forward. "I'm ready for whatever task you need me to do. I'm glad to help her transition if necessary. She's taken to me as her Guide, and I think I will be able to—"

"You will no longer be in charge of Imogene's Corrections."

The news hits me hard—like my anchor has been lifted and I'm suddenly unmoored. "I—" I clear my throat, trying to compose myself. "Can I ask why?"

"As you just said, you've done remarkable work guiding Imogene during the transition of her Order. It was no easy feat, not with her temperament, and Rex's determination to muddy her mind about Serendee with his toxic beliefs." His voice is calm, collected, even though I know Rex's Regression bothers him deeply. "Tonight, she will complete her initiation with the women's group. Despite the distractions by my son, she has taken the steps toward higher Enlightenment. She's ready for more and I applaud you for your role in that—it's just no longer needed."

"Anex—if I may," I say, trying to soothe the panic building in my chest, "Imogene will still require Corrections. Like you said, she has a defiant streak and the only thing to keep her in line is by addressing her Lapses."

"I agree," he says, "which is why I, as the leading male in her family, will take over her Corrections."

"You?" I whisper.

"Of course. It's my duty." He looks over my head, around the room. "Is that what you've been teaching in your course?"

"I—" I swallow. "Yes."

He smiles, kind and empathetic. "Don't worry, I'm not demoting you or anything. With the growth of my family and obligations to Serendee, I will need you to take over some of my obligations." My back straightens. This is... a surprise. An honor. "I would like you to take over the re-education of the Fallen."

The Fallen. I'm aware of who they are, and where they live. They have not been part of my duties—but Silas'. He has told me about the women kept there and how just visiting drains him. I have seen Bethany with my own eyes as she serves us during our private meetings with Anex.

I know what re-education means. These people are the dregs of Serendee. No matter what he says, it's a demotion. Or at the very least a punishment. My mind races, what have I done to deserve this and then it hits me.

I'm too close to the one person he wants the most: Imogene.

I swallow the lump in my throat. "Thank you for the consideration," I say, "but I am not sure I'm comfortable with that position."

Anex's eyes narrow. "Are you trying to decline the opportunity I just offered you?"

"I think it would be of better use here—teaching this class. Instructing the men on how to manage themselves and their households." I'm aware that what I am doing is unheard of—saying no to Anex. I have never done it before. Not once. But he's just taken the one thing I've ever wanted—ever had—away from me and now... he's giving me the rejects? The worst of our kind? "I'm sorry, I just don't think that this is the best use of my skills and gifts given to me by The Way."

He stares at me, unmoving, for a long moment. Enough time for sweat to bead on the back of my neck. Finally, he slides off the stool and says, "I understand."

I rise from my seat. "I'm sorry."

"No, don't be." He steps forward, thrusting out his hand. I give him mine and he clasps them together. "You've always been my most devoted son," he says. "If you feel called to decline this opportunity, then I must consider that."

I exhale. "Thank you."

He cups my cheek with his hand. "Thank *you* for your honestly, Levi. I wish more of the people close to me were."

The smile he gives me before he walks out of the room doesn't quite reach his eyes and it fills me with an uneasiness. It could be from the shock of everything I just learned.

One thing I know for certain, things are changing in Serendee and I suspect it's going to impact us all.

66

Imogene

I'M BLINDFOLDED AGAIN and forced to trust Margaret as she guides me through Serendee in the dark. She's careful, and although we take circular route, I can tell when we enter the main house. It has a certain scent—less earthy than the rest of the homes, where air conditioning units are frowned upon, and solar panels provide much of our energy.

I almost ask why we're going to Anex's home—Margaret had assured me this group was disconnected from him outside of his blessing and approval. Something about being here makes me feel uneasy. I can't help but think about the women in the cells below, the Fallen.

"You'll wait here," Margaret says, nudging me into a room. Her hand clamps down on my forearm and squeezes. "After tonight, I won't be just your Main but your sister, too."

I hear others. Their shifting feet and a few other sounds of anxiety. We shouldn't be afraid to have our vision blocked. We're Enlightened and our other senses should take over. At least that's what I remind myself once the door closes and Margret leaves, and my pulse starts to race.

"Keep your blindfolds on," a voice calls, breaking the quiet. "But remove your clothing."

"All of it?" a soft voice asks.

"Strip completely. Tonight isn't about material bindings. It's about spiritual ones. Connecting to the other women in the group. There's no reason to hide your true selves. Not your body, nor your mind, or your secrets."

Something nags at me as I obey, unbuttoning the tiny pearl buttons on the front of my dress. Maybe it's because for once I do belong to someone else—more than one person. We're in a relationship. Committed, even if by arrangement. My agreement with Rex is deeper than the one I made during the ceremonies. We've made promises to one another. My body belongs to him and the other men in our home. Something tells me he wouldn't like the fact I'm revealing myself to others.

Still, I do as I'm told. How can I not? My dress slips from my shoulders, and I remove my Serendee approved undergarments. Fabric rustles around me as the other women do the same.

Little Lamb.

The nickname echoes in my head, but it feels wrong. I'm not a lamb. I'm nothing more than a sheep.

"We're ready," that same voice says, light and full of joy. "Grab the hand of the person next to you and follow me."

I'm trying to reconcile my thoughts, my emotions, the thrumming in my chest, when a hand grabs mine and pulls, dragging me along with the others. My steps are clumsy, and our bare bodies run into one another. Nervous laughter bubbles from somewhere ahead. I sense when we cross the threshold. It's the scent that hits me. The smell of antiseptic. The blast of cold, sterile air. My nipples, already hard, tighten painfully. Goosebumps spread across my flesh. The pit of my stomach clenches, turning over. And I know before our host says, "You can remove your blindfolds," exactly where we are.

The healer's room.

Anex's healer's room.

I peel back the blindfold and see that I'm one of four other women. There had been more initially. Had they not made it to this part of the process? That thought sends a jolt of pride to my chest, but it's tempered when I look away from the other women and take in the room—I've been here before. The medical table in the middle of the room, where I was studied and tested, twice on the command of our leader. The table is covered in a white sheet, the symbol of innocence and purity, but that weird, distressed feeling in my belly only intensifies.

Margaret, in a white cloak, steps forward, a serene smile on her mouth.

"Welcome," she says, spreading her arms. "This is the night you've been waiting for. You've completed your steps. Your commitment to the women in Serendee. You've given your collateral and been deemed worthy. Anex has given me full control over this group and through that power, I am able to tell you that you've been chosen for the final step that will make us sisters."

Her words set me on edge. I'm reminded of the fallen, the girl babbling about the sacrifices she was making to attain Anex's approval. Are Margaret's words any different?

"Tonight you'll take the mark of our group—a birthmark. This is a rebirth. One not tied to your parents or anyone else. You'll be tied to Serendee. To The Way." She makes a symbol with her fingers, that looks like a sideways 'W.' "We're women. We're Enlightened."

Those words send a shiver down my spine. Enlightened? That's the ultimate goal. And this ceremony is the final step? There's an immediate shift in the nervous energy that filled the room when we walked in. Now it's anticipation. Our nudity and sacrifice make sense: we must shed everything to reach this state. Our fears. Our pride. Our modesty.

We've been chosen.

"Let me prepare you," Margaret adds, "this won't be easy. It will hurt, but from pain comes empowerment. And if you violate the sanctity of your sisterhood, your collateral will be exposed to your loved ones, your community, and Anex." She taps on the door, and it opens, another woman in white joining us. "Healer Bloom has been anointed to assist in the process. I'm grateful for her strength and skills."

The woman crosses the room and stops at a rolling cart arranged with instruments. A square box fills most of the space. She rolls it over to the exam table and presses several buttons before lifting something that looks like a wand.

"Kayla." Margaret nods to the woman next to me. "You're first."

Kayla steps forward and Margaret meets her, pulling her into a hug. She whispers something in her ear and gives her a hand as she climbs onto the table.

"We'll need your assistance," Margaret says. "Come hold your sister through her experience. She may fight due to the intensity, but remember, she chose to be here, she was *chosen* to be here. Help her get through to the other side."

The three other women and I surround Kayla, two by her arms and two by her legs. I am at her upper body, where I can see her face. I smile down at her, hoping to be reassuring, but all I feel is my own anxiety. "You're strong," I tell her. "Worthy."

"I'm scared of needles," she whispers, assuming the mark is a tattoo.

"Face that fear. Own it."

She nods and adds, "Thank you."

Margaret lays a square of paper on the flesh below her hip and dabs a cloth on top. When she pulls the paper back, the symbol is there. A sideways 'W' with a small slash over the left side. It's elegant with thin lines. My fears dissipate, knowing I'll be carrying something with such meaning on my person.

Kayla watches as Healer Bloom holds up the wand, the metal tip, shining in the overhead light. Holding it like a pencil, she lowers it to the template and presses down.

I expect a buzz, the sound of needles inking the skin, but the room fills with Kayla's screams. In the chaos, Margaret is louder.

"Hold her down! Hold her down! Don't let her move! It's for the greater good! It's the pain that leads to empowerment!"

My eyes flick to the woman across from me. Her name is Dorothy. I don't know her well other than she's a few years older than me and works at the farm. Her eyes well with tears but she never falters, holding onto Kayla's arm with all her strength.

I look down at the woman I know Silas' recruited into the community. She chose to be here, to leave her family and join this way of life. It's harder, I think, than growing up in Serendee. But now as she fights to sit up our eyes meet, hers are pleading. Filled with betrayal.

A fleeting thought runs through my head.

What would my mother do?

As if reading my mind, Margaret shouts, "If you allow your sister to fail, you all fail." Her eyes meet mine. "You don't want to fail. I can promise you that."

In the heat of the room, the sweat and panic, naked and fearful, I look down at Kayla and say, "I'm sorry," and tighten my grip. Someone shoves a strap in her mouth, her teeth bearing down on the leather. A moment later the room is filled with the scent of burning flesh.

Kayla never stops looking at me and I see the hate. It's deep in the green of her eyes, or maybe it's just my reflection. Either one I know I'm no one's sister.

I'm just a sheep.

THE SUN RISES to the east on our return home. The ceremony took hours, and after the screams the quiet of the streets only amplifies the numb sensation overtaking my brain and body. The only exception is my lower hip, where the pain is searing. God, it hurts. Deep and painful, like they branded me all the way to the bone.

"I know that was a lot," Margaret says, keeping close. We were each escorted out of the mansion, sweaty and exhausted. She rests a hand on her belly, as if she's comforting the fetus inside. "But doesn't it feel amazing now?"

I want to tell her it hurts like hell, and not in the good way. I feel sick. Confused. Betrayed. I'm no innocent to pain, but this... it was otherworldly. No one screamed after Kayla. They didn't have the opportunity. Healer Bloom made sure the strap was placed in all our mouths before she started.

I still taste the leather on my tongue, the burnt skin in my nostrils, Kayla's screams in my ears.

"Imogene?" she prompts, forcing me to a stop.

My house is a few feet away. Lights blazing in the windows. They'll be waiting for me. I know it and I have no idea what I'm going to say about what's been done to me. What I allowed to be done.

"I'm fine," I lie. "Just tired. Like you said, it was overwhelming."

"You're special," Margaret says, pulling me into a hug. I fight a hiss when her lower body brushes against the wound on my hip. "More than the other women. You were chosen for a reason, don't forget that."

A month ago, those words would have given me a sense of validation, but now, I can't escape the uneasiness coursing through my veins. I give her a tight smile, hoping it comes off as exhaustion and tell her goodnight.

I step into the house, into the bright light of the foyer. I'm not surprised when Levi meets me there a moment later. "Where have you been?" he asks, rubbing at the heavy bags under his eyes. It's obvious he hasn't slept.

"A meeting," is all I get out before he strides toward me, grabbing my hand and pushing up my sleeve. A dark bruise mottles the skin from where I'd been restrained.

"What kind of meeting?" His voice is low. Dangerous. "Who did this to you?"

I don't get the chance to answer before the door opens and heavy footsteps enter the house. Levi's eyes dart over my shoulder and I turn. Rex, Elon and Silas appear, looking as worn out as I feel.

"What's going on?" Silas asks, taking us in.

"I just got home. There was a…" I search for an excuse but simply say. "I met some of the other women." I swallow. "Margaret invited me."

A flicker passes through Levi's eyes. Something I can't discern. "Is that where you got the bruises from?"

"What bruises?" Rex asks, closing the space between us. His picks up my other hand and reveals the marks on the other arm. He swears when he sees them.

"Were you restrained?" he asks. His voice takes on that tone—the one I can't quite identify. Anger? Distrust? Suspicion?

I pull my hand away, but in the process hit my hip. I yelp and soon all four of them are on me. "You're hurt," Silas says, eyes meeting mine. "Where?"

Elon reaches for the hem of my dress. I try to step away but land against the hard muscle of Rex's stomach and chest. He holds onto me, while Elon lifts the fabric up, looking for whatever caused my pain.

"I'm fine," I tell them, but tears well in my eyes from the burn. From the betrayal. I know what I've done is wrong. Even if it's unspoken, the branding is a violation to my commitment to Rex. I can feel it. I know it.

Elon lifts my dress until he spots the bandaged wound. Silas steps forward and slowly removes the tape, revealing the branding.

"Christ," Elon mutters. "What the hell is that?"

Rex leans over my shoulder, trying to get a better look. He must see it because he growls in my ear. "*Who* the hell did that to you?"

"I'm getting my kit," Silas says, staring at the wound long and hard before running down the hall.

A million questions run across Levi's expression as he stares at the brand, but he doesn't ask one of them. He just looks at the wound, like he can't figure out how it got there.

I shake my head so forcefully, tears fall. "I can't tell," I say to all of them, although Rex is the one that asked.

"Yes, you can, Imogene," he says. "You can and will."

"No," I try to pull away, but Elon's hand is clamped tight around my unbranded hip. "I can't. Not without endangering all of you."

Rex has grown eerily still and I turn, forcing myself to look at him. He's staring at the branding, head tilted, eyes slightly glazed. I wait for the rage, the accusation, but he shudders an exhale and says, "Fucking hell. Goddamn him."

Him.

"It wasn't your father," I say. Silas returns, his kit already open and he eases me away from Rex and Elon, down on the couch. Levi takes the seat next to me and together they sort through his salves and creams.

"No?" Rex asks, unphased by the men caring for me. "Who else would brand my father's initials in your skin?"

"It's not his initials. There's no 'A.'"

He reaches out, finger pointed. I brace myself for the pain of his touch, but he simply traces in the air. "T. W—Timothy Wray. My father had someone brand you with his fucking initials."

I look down, past the image I'd been told was being branded on me. The 'E' for Empowerment and Enlightenment. A sideways 'W' for Women and The Way. And see it for what it really is.

Anex branded me and four other women with his initials, like we were nothing but livestock down in the barn.

The rush of bile rises in the back of my throat, and I hold onto my stomach, trying to keep it down. Levi looks stricken by the knowledge and Elon storms out of the room. A moment later, something big and breakable crashes against the floor, followed by the sound of fists slamming into the plaster.

"Rex," I say, wanting to explain, but, how can I? The collateral. The threats. And now this? Anex must have been behind it the whole time. This was no exclusive group. It was another manipulation. Another level of control.

I walked straight into it like a lamb to slaughter.

I look to Rex and see his handsome face, twisted into furious rage. "Who was it?! Who the fuck branded my father's initials into your skin? Margaret?"

"If I tell—"

"I don't give a shit what they threatened you with, Imogene. There is nothing my father can do to me, Elon, Silas, or Levi that justifies this." Our eyes lock. "Tell me."

"A-a while back I was invited to join a women's group. I was told it was exclusive to women—blessed by your father, but that he was not involved." Silas wipes the branding with a damp cloth, and I hiss at the pain. "Oh god... I thought it was just women—like the men's group. A way to Empower and work on our Indulgences in a safe space. The meetings felt sacred—special, because only a few other women were invited. Things were secretive and, yes, there were times I wasn't comfortable with what they wanted me to do. But isn't that what we're taught? Enlightenment is uncomfortable." Fresh tears build in my eyes. "By the time I realized what was happening, it was too late. I was committed."

"What did they want you to do?" Elon asks, he's returned, uncaring about the blood dripping from his knuckles.

"I had to give them collateral—something personal about myself that they could then reveal to the community if I broke any of the rules." I look at each of them. "Including telling you."

"What kind of collateral did you give them?" Rex asks.

"I didn't tell him about looking for your mother or mine. I didn't tell them anything about how much you hate this place or how you think Anex killed your mother, but," I stare down at the branding, wincing as Silas uses a Q-tip to apply salve, "I did tell them about us. I told them about our relationship—about how all of us—together. I had to write it down and hand it over."

Silas' movements stop. The other men grow still. I force myself to look at them.

"I had to say something, you understand that, right?"

Although Anex gave his approval for the men to train me for Rex, this is not something the rest of the community will find acceptable.

Anex Orders us to another member of the community. We Bond. We Mate. If he denies that he requested me to do this, and I have no doubt he will, we will be shunned.

I've put us all at terrible risk all because I wanted to feel special —accepted.

"I had no idea it would go this far," Levi says, voice panicked. "When he told us about the group, I didn't know he would use it to manipulate it—"

"What did you say?" Rex asks.

Silas curses and stands. "Look, man. We knew about the women's group. Anex told us it was for Imogene's good."

"And you just went along with it?" Rex asks. His eyes dart to Elon. "You knew about this?"

"Yes, but—"

Rex slams his hand in the air, palm out, shutting him off. "You hid this from me? All of you? About my mate? When you know my father had had nefarious intentions toward her the whole time?"

"What are we supposed to do? We have no other choice. This is our home. Our livelihood." Elon's voice cracks. He sounds scared. Something I've never heard from him before. "He's our leader."

Rex stills in the middle of the room, hands shoved in his pockets. The dark smudges under his eyes look more pronounced. He's exhausted, like we all are. No one is thinking clearly. We're all in pain.

"Can we just —" I start, hoping we can sleep on it and think clearly in the morning, but Rex straightens his shoulders and waves me off.

"I can't do this anymore," he says, "I cannot allow him to control my life. Not anymore." He walks down the hallway and out the front door, slamming it behind him. The four of us sit in silence, before Elon turns to go after him.

"Wait." Levi stands. "Let me go."

When the two look at one another, something passes between them. Elon nods, stepping aside to allow Levi to pass him in the hallway. It's in that moment that Elon stops and grabs him by the forearm. "Don't let him do anything stupid."

"I won't." Levi glances back, eye locking with mine. "I'll get him back."

The door closes softer this time and I exhale, staring down at the branding, the T and the W so obvious now.

Everything seems obvious.

Except for the way out.

67

———————

L^{evi}

THE STREET IS empty when I get out to the porch, and I scan both directions. At the end of the street, I see a shadowy figure slip around the corner. It's the way to the Main House.

Jumping down the steps, I race after him, quickly getting to the corner. It's morning and a few people are up, headed to the farm or other early-day jobs.

"Morning," I say to one of the men I know works at the dairy barn. He tips his hat in greeting but I sense the judgment in his eyes as they skim over my rumpled clothes and unshaven face.

I don't owe that man any explanation. I'm one of the Chosen. Our ways aren't questioned the same way it would be if the roles were reversed.

"Rex," I call, jogging after him. "Hold up."

He doesn't stop, in fact, I'm pretty sure he widens his stride. He may be bigger than I am, but I'm fit, and I jog to catch up. When I finally fall into step, I realize that, like me, in the light of day, he looks rough.

"Listen, we shouldn't have kept the information about the women's meeting from you."

His eyes cut my way. "No, you shouldn't have."

"We don't have the ability to rebel against Anex the way you do. He's our leader—"

"Jesus." He stops, running his hand through his hair. "I'm tired of the excuses. He told you do to something. To lie to me, and all three of you fell into line. I get it," he says, "your loyalty is to him, not me."

"It's not that—"

But it is and we both know it. Anex has us by the balls. Our livelihoods, our shelter, food, clothing, *everything* is controlled by that man. Rex stares at me. "That's not the problem, Levi."

"Then what is?"

"You knew, and you didn't keep her safe."

That one lands—harder than a punch—because he's right.

"I'm sorry."

His jaw sets. "I'm not the one you should apologize to." He sets off again, striding up the hill, the big white house looming on the hill.

I follow, keeping up with his long legs. "It'll just get worse if you confront him."

"I'm not going to Anex," he says, still walking.

"Then what are you doing?"

He spins, stopping a few feet up the hill from me. "To get money. Supplies. A vehicle. I've got it all stashed for the right time."

"You're running?"

It wouldn't be the first time he's threatened it.

"I'm not running," he says, voice tight, "I'm getting her the fuck out of here. For good."

Imogene. He wants to save her.

I'm at a loss for words, but he's not finished. "My father's business is out of control. He's stepping into dangerous territory, and I don't want to be here when it implodes. I also don't want him to have any reason to use my mate as leverage. That branding was about ownership. Control. He put it there because, like the cows down at the barn, he views her as his property. *His.* Not mine." His eyes hold mine. "Not *ours.*"

"Where will you take her?" I ask. "Because he'll find you. He'll send his men out to bring her back."

Rex's expression changes, to something wary and worn. His arms cross over his chest and, even though he's my friend, I understand it's meant to be intimidating. "If I tell you, can I trust you not to take this back to my father?"

It's a fair question. Of all of us, my loyalty to Anex is the strongest, but things have shifted since Imogene came into our lives. Rex is right. His father branded her for a reason. A visible, painful reminder of who she belongs to.

The pieces of my conversation with him at the Center fall into place. He told me that tonight was a big deal. He's changing her job, taking over her Corrections.

God, Rex needs to get her out of here *now.*

"I won't tell him anything, I promise."

The look he gives me is skeptical.

I dig my nails into the wood of the fence. "You're right. I haven't been protecting her. Not the way I should. I will not risk hurting her even more by telling your father any of this." I lift my chin. "I stood up to him tonight. He asked me to do something and I said no."

Rex's eyebrows raise. "How did that go?"

"I don't know."

But deep down I know I fucked up. Big. "If you tell me what your plan is, I can help you."

Our friendship runs deep. Different from him and Elon, who have bonded over their jobs outside this world, or with Silas with who he shares the guiltiest of pleasures. But we've always been friends—tight —and I hope he can still trust me.

"My plan is to take her to someone who is willing to fight for her more than anyone else." His eyes dart around. "Her mother."

My chest tightens. This is real. He's not fucking around this time. Panic burns. "You found her?"

"Yes. Well, Elon found her. But tonight, after we handled the Jeb situation, we went to locate her."

Blood rushes to my ears as I listen to my friend describe what happened that night. Rex, Elon, and Silas went to the address they found on the internet. It's a meeting space, for people that have escaped a cult or for family members wanting to help their family and loved ones out of a cult.

"She was there," he says, 'closing up after a meeting."

"And?"

"She recognized me," he admits. "I look a lot like my father did at my age—when they were friends. It took me a few minutes—mostly Silas—to convince her we weren't there for trouble, but to talk to her about Imogene."

I grab ahold of the picket fence just off the side of the road, bracing myself.

"And?"

"And she wants her. She's always wanted her. My father was the obstacle in the way."

A wave of emotion rolls over me. Panic. Curiosity. Fear. When it settles, one bubbles to the surface: Anger. "So what? You pack her up and just drop her off at her mother's house? To a woman she hasn't seen in years? Stealing her from the only home she's known her entire life and tossing her into the secular world?"

"I want to get her somewhere safe, Levi, and this is my only option."

"There's nowhere safer than Serendee."

"Do you really believe that? After seeing that brand on her? After seeing the marks you've given her?"

It's a low blow, but one I maybe deserve. Still, I deflect. "She asks for the Corrections, Rex, begs for Enlightenment."

"Why?" Rex's voice trembles. "Why do you think she wants you to Correct her like that?"

When I don't answer he turns away, but I hear him clearly when he says, "She's as bad as The Fallen. As compliant and confused, you know that right? For every effort I made to break that out of her, it was pointless. Imogene is *already* broken. I don't know if there's a way to fix her."

"So that's what this is about? You're throwing her away? Tossing her aside like a broken toy?" The rage builds in my chest. "Angry because your father marked her first?

"Shut up," Rex says, arms dropping to his sides, while his chest puffs out.

"No, because someone has to talk some sense into you." My voice rises and I'm aware of a couple walking within earshot. I lower it. "He will find you, and when he does, it will be a hundred times worse."

"Maybe that's just what he wants us to think." His chest rises and falls, like he's barely containing his own anger. "She needs to get away from the darkness of this place. I've spent most of my life being a selfish prick, Levi. For once, just let me do the right thing."

His eyebrows raise, like he's offering me the chance to challenge him one last time. I don't. He's right. We may not be able to save ourselves, but we can do the right thing for her.

"Go," I tell him. "Get everything ready and let me know what you need me to do."

"Thank you," he says, thrusting out his hand.

I look at it, prepared to shake it, but instead step forward, dragging him into a hug. "Just make sure she's safe," I say. "For real safe."

"You got it, brother."

We separate, and as he walks toward the house, I don't know why it feels like a goodbye. Maybe it's just the reality of what comes next, or the sensation of separating the past and the future. No matter what it is, whatever comes next will change life for all of us.

I'VE JUST STEPPED into the house when the music starts.

Clair de Lune. The solemn strains rise from the speakers situated through the community. Serendee is being called to the community center by Anex.

Despite my complete exhaustion, I stop by the living room where

I find everyone asleep. Elon has sprawled out on the couch. Silas is across from him in an armchair, his feet propped on the coffee table and Imogene is curled up on the love seat. I shake her awake first.

"Did you find him?" she asks, rubbing her eyes.

"Yes," I tilt my head. "But there's no time to talk about it now. We're being summoned."

Her eyes widen as the music processes and she nods, standing quickly. She winces at the pain blow her hip.

"You okay?" I ask, worried about the wound. It's deep and ugly.

"I'm fine," she says, reaching to smooth her hair. "We need to hurry."

I wake the others, jostling them from sleep. "Come on, there's a meeting."

Silas groans, rubbing his face while Elon stretches his arms over his head. I don't miss the lines of worry on his forehead when he asks, "Is this about Rex?"

"I don't see how, I just left him a few minutes ago and he wasn't going to see his father."

Elon and Silas exchange a look, both skeptical. I don't blame them, but I feel confidant Rex was telling me the truth.

"I guess we'll find out soon enough," Silas says, slipping on his shoes. The music grows louder—that's what happens. It starts off low and gentle, but then grows with volume and aggression as the minutes pass.

The four of us quickly get to the community center, funneling in with the rest of the residents. It takes longer during the day with people scattered all over Serendee and in town. As usual, Anex's chair is positioned in the middle of the stage—what's different is the lack of other seats—the ones for the inner circle. Our seats.

They've been removed.

"What the..." Elon mutters. Imogene tugs his hand and pulls him over where there's an empty section on the floor.

"Weird," Silas says, still a little groggy, but not enough to miss the strange vibe in the room. "Do you see him?"

Him—Rex. I scan the crowd.

"No," I say. Anxiety inches across my skin. Something feels off—wrong. Did he get caught preparing to escape? Did he leave without Imogene?

I look over at her. Her pale hair catching the overhead lights and creating a soft glow—that along with her white ceremonial dress makes her look even more innocent. But I know that's not entirely true. I know what's hidden under the cotton. Not just the wounds I've given her but the fresh one as well.

People spill through the door part, and Rex's massive frame emerges. I watch as his eyes dart to the stage, from his father's chair to the lack of our own. His jaw ticks, clocking everything in the room.

A bad feeling builds in my gut, that itchy feeling that I would normally rely on my beliefs to combat, but all of that is confused. Muddled by recent events. By my feelings for Imogene and the changes happening in Serendee.

"There he is," Silas says with relief. He turns to Imogene. "How's your wound?"

"Sore," she says, but her pale complexion suggests worse. "I'll be fine."

Is this the compliance we've trained her for? Take the pain and abuse and suffer through it? Ask for more? I know in my heart that it is—and I'm one of the worst.

My confusion turns to nausea. Rex is right. We have to get her out of here.

Rex works his way through the crowd and squeezes between me and Imogene. I grab his arm. "Did you do it?" I whisper—meaning the money and supplies.

He gives me a short nod. "I tried to catch you before you came in here. This would have been a good cover." He glances around. "Any way we can get out of here before it starts?"

The meetings can go on for hours, but I don't think he's right. Anex would definitely notice their absence. That's confirmed when our leader walks across the stage, eyes going straight to his son and mate.

He's dressed in all black and several of his spiritual wives follow him in, bowing and leading the community to do the same. Margaret stands close, wearing a stomach revealing midriff and a low-slung skirt. Her belly protrudes, the pregnancy obvious. As I follow the motions, touching my forehead in reverence, Rex stands unmoving, staring at Margaret.

"Did you know about this?" he asks. When I don't answer he scowls. He looks to Imogene. "Did you?"

"I just found out tonight," she says. "I didn't get a chance to tell you."

He may forgive her, but it's just another secret I've kept from him, another chink in the bond between us. I want to heal it, solve the rift between us, but he's staring at the stage, at his father, and ultimately, I yank him by the arm after his wives sit at his feet, forcing him to the floor with everyone else.

"I know you're mad, but now isn't the time to get caught up in your anger," I whisper. "We sit through this and then follow your plan. Get Imogene out of here. We'll deal with the rest."

On the stage, Margaret sits on the arm of Anex's chair, positioned for the entire community to see. Her hand strokes the swell of her belly, her bare skin pale and smooth. I wonder if Anex branded her as well.

I realize then that everyone has been removed from the stage, not just us, his other spiritual wives as well. I'm not used to looking at the community from this perspective—on the floor with the others. It's intentional. Everything Anex does is with intention.

"Fuck," Elon mutters, "She's pregnant."

His eyes dart to Rex, waiting for some kind of reaction but it doesn't come. The Rex sitting next to me is the one that is made of stone. Elon looks away, not exactly worried, but he doesn't know about Rex's plan to escape tonight. Or Anex's plans to move Imogene to the childcare center—to take over her Corrections. There are so many changes happening but none compare to what Anex's brought us here for.

"Good morning," Anex says, raising his hand to tug at the short beard on his chin. "Thank you for setting aside your business and work and obligations in order to bask in the glory of The Way." He grins. "I dislike distracting you from the work of the community—it requires many hands and much diligence to keep our Utopia running, but the words that have come to me... well, they can't be held back any longer."

He reaches out and places a hand on Margaret's belly. "As you can see my mate is carrying my child." A series of shouts fill the room, claps and cheers of congratulations. I glance at Rex and see his skin has turned pale. "Thank you. Thank you so much." He holds his hands in a manner to calm and quiet the crowed.

"Becoming a father for the second time, has spurred something in me. The desire to usher Serendee into a new phase. A new birth, as it would seem. I'm sure you've all noticed the construction down on the south field. It's no secret that we're building a childcare center, a place for the infants and toddlers of Serendee to be blessed with the way from the very beginning. It's not just a place of nurturing and care. It will be a birthing center, with midwives and doulas. It will be a place where the women of Serendee can bond over their young, their bodies and practice of The Way and raising devoted children. It will be the finest addition to the community, the one that will lead us into the future, and the first child to be born there, will be my own."

He pauses, and Margaret nods at the wives on the floor, the signal for them to clap, praising Anex for his decision. Next to me Rex mutters, "What the fuck?"

"But I didn't just call you here to spread the good." The room stills at that. "There are some challenges we've been facing. I've been shielding you from this for as long as I could—trying my best to protect the community from Indulgent, Regressive behavior of those that live among us—but that is no longer possible. Not when the people committing the largest indiscretions are part of our leadership and have used their positions to undermine The Way."

Hushed murmurs ripple through those around us, and despite the claustrophobic heat in the room, the hair on the back of my neck stands on end and an uneasy chill climbs my spine.

"It is rare for me to handle something like this so publicly. I prefer smaller, more intimate, meetings when a member of our community has gone astray. But this…" he trails off, his eyes gliding over the crowd, like any one of us could be the offender, "this is too personal. I need witnesses. What better than the whole of Serendee?" His arms lift and he holds up his hands. "Because, brothers and sisters, what has transpired in our quaint, private utopia is blasphemy against the entire community. A mark against everything we do and everything we are."

"What the fuck is he going on about?" Elon whispers. Rex shakes his head, his eyes focused squarely on his father. I see the way his fingers ball into a tight fist. The restraint he uses just to be in Anex's presence.

"We're careful," Anex continues. "So careful about who we allow into Serendee. As you know there is a process, a way to weed out the unworthy and undedicated. Because of that the people we invite into our world help it to flourish and grow." His lips form a thin line. "But sometimes it's not the new blooms that cause the problems. It's the roots, the foundation, which, over the years, without proper attention, rots. It becomes unstable." His eyes flick to our section. "Toxic. My hope is that with early guidance the childcare center will eliminate this problem, but that's the future. Not the presence. To keep our community strong, we must purge the diseased parts and nurture what remains."

The room has grown painfully quiet as we cling to his every word. As fear builds in our hearts. I can sense the shift in the room. The questions in everyone's minds. *Who. Who is he talking about?*

Anex is never one to leave his followers wanting.

"I need the following people to stand." He clears his throat, eyes flicking down. "Elon, Silas, Levi."

My movements are instinctive. I stand on command, following his words like he has me connected to puppet strings. Elon and Silas do the same and when I steal a look, their expressions are blank. I have no idea what they're thinking. Will he have us remove the offender? Is he separating us from Rex and Imogene before he focuses his attention on them?

"Boys," he says, and my eyes snap to his. "I raised you like my own. I provided you with education, access, skills, and positions of leadership." His eyebrow raises. "And what have you done in return?"

None of us speak. Not even Elon, who I assume is one second from unleashing. What have we given? Our lives. Our souls. Our everything.

I'm not stupid enough to answer. Either are they.

Anex shifts his gaze to Margaret and holds out his hand. She dips her fingers into the collar of her blouse, deep into the crevasse of her swollen breasts, and pulls out a square of paper.

"This is a testimony brought to me from one of our members." He slowly unfolds the paper and takes a long moment to read over the contents. When he looks up, his eyes go directly to Imogene. "Please stand, Imogene."

She quickly gets to her feet, fighting to hide the grimace of pain. Her awkward movements make her trip, stepping on the long hem of her dress. Silas' hand shoots out to catch her. "Careful," he says quietly.

She nods and regains composure, but nothing feels right.

Once she's on her feet, Anex says, "Come stand next to me."

"You don't have to," Rex says, grabbing her wrist.

"Yes, I do," Imogene replies, easing herself from his grip.

Anex, all of us, watch as Imogene walks to the staircase and climbs them. No one else can see the way her nose wrinkles in pain from every step. How the brand sends a jolt of pain through her. I can tell. *We* can tell. All I want to do is chase after her, drag her away from this place—this moment—but she's stronger than I am, crossing the stage and moving next to him.

She bows and honors him again. Thick bile rises to the back of my throat when he speaks, "As you all know, I gave my son and Order this spring, to the lovely Imogene."

She searches for Rex in the crowd and smiles when she finds him. It lights up her entire face, although there's no mistaking the fear in her eyes.

"It was a risky move," Anex says. "The daughter of a Regressive with a powerful man like my son." Rex remains on the floor now. The only one of the five of us. There's no doubt it's with intention. "But my son requested this female and I felt inclined to give him what he wanted. He is the heir, after all." My muscles tighten with every word, and I fight the urge to run up there and pluck her off the stage. "I gave her every opportunity. Access to my wives, invitations to select groups, leeway on the rule surrounding secular society, because of my son's business outside of Serendee." Imogene's face reddens and her fingers twist in the fabric of her dress. "Unfortunately, as I feared, she's like her mother. A betrayer."

Rex bolts to his feet and propelled by rage, pushes past us, rushing to the base of the stage. "She's my mate," he hisses at his father. "Not a betrayer or Regressive."

"Oh, dear boy, you let the allure of what lies between her legs trick you." Anex holds up the paper. "This is a confession—in her own handwriting, isn't that true, Imogene?"

He shows the paper to her and although you can feel the hesitation in her movements, she nods and says, "Yes."

"Good girl," he says, but his tone is flat. Hard. "I'll read the confession to you now, so that you understand the decision I've had to make." He clears his throat. "*I have spent the days since my Ordering in an intimate relationship with my mate's best friends. I've used them to explore my sexuality—to understand Rex's needs and desires.*" A small curve tugs at Anex's mouth. I don't dare look around me to see the reactions of the other people in the room. My stomach churns. I knew Imogene was forced to tell secrets but this will ruin all of us, and it seems Anex has no plans of stopping. "*I know it's wrong to be with other men but—*"

With a roar, Rex leaps up the stage, lunging at his father. "You did this!" he shouts. "You did this to her! You gave her to my friends. Encouraged them to play with her—break her in."

Anex steps out of the way, but his son is too big, too fast, *too angry*, and tackles him to the ground. It only takes a moment before he has his father pinned. Elon is on the stage within a second, standing over the two men. He grabs the paper from Anex's hand and shreds it, tossing the pieces to the ground like confetti.

"Elon!" Silas shouts. Their eyes meet and he jerks his head to the side. It's too late. Anex's guards, heavily armed, charge at the two of them. The room falls into chaos, shouts and screams. The wives fleeing from the stage. Black automatic weapons point and aim. "Get down! Get down! Get down or I'll blow your fucking head off!"

The nose of a rifle presses into Rex's back and he reluctantly releases his father. He lays flat on his stomach, and holds his hands up in an uneasy surrender. Next to him, Elon is shoved to his knees, arms jerked back by the guards, and he's restrained. Neither Silas nor I have moved, but two guards stand by each of us, weapons poised. Anex jerks his head and the guards next to me and Silas, nudge us toward the stairs. Bright lights shine in my eyes as I step on the stage, the audience shrouded in the shadows. The guards stop us by the edge and Elon joins us by force. Rex is still on his stomach, eyes trained on Imogene.

She stands alone on the stage, frozen other than tears streaking down her face, watching in fear. The urge to go to her, to take her hand and run, is strong, but it's nothing compared to the dark sensation in my chest. The one that tells us that we're trapped.

There's no getting out of this.

I wait for Anex to tell the members to leave. To go home while he deals with us, but he stands, giving the signal for quiet. The room falls into a nervous hush, although all I can hear is my heart pounding and the taste of bile in the back of my throat.

"As you see," he says, "I've allowed too much leniency in my son's house. I've allowed too much autonomy between Rex and the boys I called my sons. The young men I placed in my inner circle. There has been too much freedom between the outside world and our community. They've grown weak and Indulgent." He wipes a drop of blood from his mouth where Rex got in a solid hit. He looks down at me and Silas, then over to Elon. "The three of you are no longer welcome in Serendee."

"What?" Imogene cries. She's not the only one, the people around me surge with panic. "You can't—"

"I can and I will!" Anex shouts, the volume of his voice unusual. He's always calm and collected, but today he's rattled. The fight, the letter, using his guards. It's a side of Anex I knew existed, but in private, not public. "This is not open for discussion. You are no longer members of this community. You may not have contact with anyone that lives inside these walls." He looks into the crowd. "Any communication with the Regressive will be banished as well."

Banished.

I understand the word, but in all my time of working with Anex, of being one of his instructors has this only been an option. He Re-educates. He Enlightens. He pushes people to Be Better... but Banishment?

Me?

I've only done what he's asked of me. Followed his directions. I've only ever given my life to this community and our leader. I look over to Silas, who has given just as much, if not more. His face has paled and his body trembles. Elon has retreated into himself, expression blank, eyes cold. He may not look panicked, but I know he is. This is all we've known. It's our home, our family, our community.

I vaguely take in that he's dismissed the room, the residents quietly making their way out the door. They must be confused. *I'm* confused, and once the audience leaves I take a deep breath, and say, "Anex—"

"Do not speak," he snaps, voice low, "not if you want to make it outside these walls without a bullet in the back of your head."

"You did this," Rex shouts as the guards lift him from the ground. "You told them to train my mate. You encouraged it. She never sought this out."

"Did I?" he asks, his tone innocent. "Imogene confessed to her Indulgences. Those were her words, not mine."

"That confession is gone," Elon says. "I tore it up."

Anex laughs and tilts his head to the rafters where a red light blinks menacingly. "If you think I don't have backed up evidence, you truly do not understand me."

That's the thing. I don't understand. This is not the man I loved and respected. He's something dark and nefarious.

"Why are you doing this?" I ask. "Why are you destroying us?"

He walks over and stands before me. He reaches out and I flinch, but he just rests his hand on my shoulder. "Levi, you have been loyal and true, and I tried to give you the opportunity to change with us, but you declined my offer." He grins. "Your response was Indulgent. Selfish. And there's one thing I've learned during my time building this community, it's that if you are not going to fulfill the needs of this community, then Serendee no longer has a place for you. That goes for all of you."

"You don't have a place for us?" I ask. "What does that mean?"

"It means you've become an obstacle to what I want and it's time for you to leave."

"What you want?" Silas asks. "What do you want?"

Anex's gaze swings to Imogene. "Her."

I'm shocked he says it. I think everyone is, but Rex who shouts, "What did you say?"

Anex removes his hand from my shoulder and turns to face his son.

"I know you think you're the one that discovered this little lamb?" He chuckles. "Yes, I know your pet name for her. It's fitting. I've had my eye on her for a long time—first to make sure she didn't inherit any of her mother's Regressive traits. But as I waited on her to work her way through the Domum, as she came of age, I saw the wild beauty of this precious female." He walks over to Imogene. He touches her cheek, and a shudder rolls down her spine. "I was ready to set her aside, train her for myself, but then you requested her for the Ordering. It pained me, but I figured it was a passing whim. I know the kind of women you like, Rex. The slutty whores of the secular world. I understand—I find them appealing, too—but I figured you'd break her in and cast her aside and if you didn't..."

"You'd have my friends do it."

"Exactly." Anex tucks a loose piece of hair behind Imogene's ear. "At first it worked. You hated her, hurt her, happily handing her over to your friends, who," he looks over at us, "taught her well. Easing her morals. Heightening her desires." His eyes land on mine. "Pushing her to her limits."

"We didn't train her for Rex," Silas says, the pieces clicking into place, "we trained her for *you*."

"You, along with Margaret, and a few other well positioned members of the community. Last night, when she took my brand, things solidified. But really, you did an outstanding job preparing her for this day." He turns away from Imogene. "Unfortunately, I haven't been as satisfied with your other work. The run-in with Jeb was a setback. The refusal to adjust to our new product—"

"You mean sex trafficking," Elon says.

"See... this is the problem. You seem to think that this is a democracy. That you get an opinion in how things operate—how I operate." He walks over to one of the guards and yanks the gun out of his hand, lowering it and pressing the barrel under Elon's chin. "This is a dictatorship and I'm the one in charge. You do as I say, or you suffer the consequences."

"Like being banished," Elon says, ignoring the press of the gun.

"Only two of you are truly being banished," he says, lowering the gun and turning to Silas. "Since Elon decided to destroy my new venture, you'll be the one to explore the feasibility of this trade."

The reality of his statement hits hard. Exploring. Does that mean manage or work. Is he going to traffic Silas or force Silas into trafficking members of the community? It doesn't matter. Either will be enough to destroy him.

"And Rex." He turns to his son. "You're my son. You'll remain here. Frankly, you know too much and are too easy of a target for my enemies. You'll enter re-education training."

"Fuck you and your deranged mind games," Rex growls. "You don't control me and your reeducation is bullshit."

"See?" Anex says with a sigh. "That's the kind of attitude we need to work on. Don't worry. I've been honing my methods."

He nods at one of the guards. He walks over and without warning, shocks Rex with a taser, sending a jolt of energy through his muscular frame.

"Rex!" Imogene cries, watching her mate's body spasm with the shock. "He's your son! What's wrong with you?"

"Nothing, dear girl. I'm just trying to keep my family—my newly upgraded family together." He shifts his gaze to me. "Levi."

"Yes?" A desperate, last flicker of hope fills my chest. It's shameful and corrupt, but it's all I know. This is all I know. "I shouldn't have said no to your offer. I'll take it. Do whatever you want—"

"You and Elon will leave Serendee tonight." His tone is cold and authoritative. "If you attempt to return or contact anyone inside the walls, you'll be shot on sight."

My stomach drops, but there's no time to process it before strong hands grab me from behind. I look to Rex, then Imogene. Both seem frozen. Numb. The same sensation spreads through my limbs.

"Take them," Anex says, waving them off. "I never want to see your faces again."

He waves his hand and the guards snap into action, dragging us toward the side entrance. No one goes easily but the fight isn't fair. The weapons they have are greater than any resistance we can put forth.

Elon and I are pulled one direction. Silas and Rex another, and before he goes out of view I hear Rex shout, "What about my mate? What are you doing with her?"

"Ah, the Little Lamb," Anex says, nodding at the guard to bring her close to him. She fights, but it's pointless, the guard too strong. His fingers grip her chin, forcing her to look at him. All traces of respect and honor for the man are gone—it's replaced with fear and anger. "I've already told you about your new position. You'll work and live at the childcare center. While you take care of my wife and her unborn child, she'll teach you how to be a proper spiritual wife. How to cater to my needs and demands."

"I won't," she spits out.

His hand shoots down and he drags up the hem of her skirt,

revealing the cotton of her undergarments. He hooks a thumb in the top and drags it down, exposing the angry brand. "You agreed to this. You handed yourself over." He loosens his grip, allowing the skirt to fall. His voice softens. "You've spent your whole life waiting for this moment—for true acceptance. Well, the day has come. From now on you'll have the most important job in Serendee." He kisses her forehead. "To fulfill each and every one of my needs and desires."

Horror cascades down her face, recoiling through her body. Anex jerks his head, and the guards descend, pulling all of us in a different directions. I open my mouth and shout, "Anex! Please!" but the sound is muffled when a hood is yanked over my head. The last thing I hear is Rex's voice echoing off the high walls, but it's followed with the sound of electricity crackling.

The barrel of a gun leads me down the stairs—away from my family, my friends, my leader—and Imogene. The girl that changed me in ways I'm only realizing now.

I'm thrust toward a new life.

A life away from Serendee.

68

I mogene

"Twelve pounds."

As I stare at the number on the scale, Healer Bloom's disappointment is obvious. The weight that Rex wanted me to gain, to become more like the women he found appealing, is no longer acceptable.

She sighs and jots the number down on my chart. "At least you lost three."

We're in the exam room at the new childcare center. The center is also my new home. I eat, sleep, work, and attend these appointments, ordered by Anex, weekly. I come in, strip, get weighed and checked for any changes in my body. Healer Bloom's eyes always linger on the pale white scars crisscrossing my wrists, or the newer pink ones on my inner thigh. I lied when she asked how I got it—saying it was an accident. I know better than to tell her Levi gave them to me—that I asked him to. That memory is mine, and I refuse to give it up. Especially now that he's gone.

"I've cut back on my portions and have maintained my caloric logs." I swallow. "The rest of the weight should come off."

She grunts, clearly not impressed with my results. "Menstruation?"

"No, not yet." Anex discontinued my birth control the day I moved into the facility, but my period hasn't returned, despite the fact it's been a full month.

"No spotting?"

"No." I shake my head and fight the chill that ripples across my bare skin. I've learned not to complain, or she'll drag the process out longer.

She sets the clipboard on the counter and approaches. Her eyes are focused on my hip—or rather the spot just below. The brand is healing—still red, but the scab is almost gone. "Are you picking at it?"

"No." I pretend it isn't there. That I haven't been marked with Anex's initials. That things are like they used to be when we were all together, before he exiled my lovers, and forced my mate into submission.

I didn't realize how good we had it—even if it was just for a short time. It all feels like a trick now. Anex's way of fucking with our minds, our bodies, our souls. He dangled something in front of us—hope, love, companionship—and snatched it away. The way the pieces fell into place, I have to think he planned it all from the start.

He wanted me like this from the beginning: marked, isolated, controlled.

Broken.

"You need to lose the remaining twelve pounds," Healer Bloom says. She reaches into a cabinet and pulls out a bottle. I recognize the sticker on the side. It was made at the Serendee Apothecary. "Mix this into your tea. It should stimulate your hormones."

"My hormones?" I ask.

She nods at my clothing—permission to dress. I don't hesitate, pulling on the approved undergarments and dress quickly. I have no idea where the clothes Elon bought for me are. Burned probably. Maybe in effigy in front of the whole town as an example.

I'm the example of who you don't want to become.

"I'll be honest with you, Imogene," she says. "You need to become fertile. Preferably before the winter equinox."

My heart lunges at her reference to the winter equinox. That's the date when Rex and I were to be truly mated. Where we'd be "married" in the eyes of Serendee.

Or it was until I was sent here, while Rex was sent to Re-education. It's foolish, but hope swells in my chest. Maybe all of this was a different kind of test. I've done everything Anex has asked. Maybe Rex is doing that as well. Maybe our leader understands we are fated to be together—and he wants me fertile so that I can give him a grandchild.

"Has Anex changed his mind? Is he going to let Rex and I have our Mating Ceremony?" I'm already planning what I can do to earn his favor. Eat less. Work harder. Study more. Submit to Corrections...

"Our leader needs you strong and fertile for the Mating Ceremony, but not for his blasphemous son." When she looks at me, I spot the small smirk on her mouth—the dark glint in her eye. "He has plans for you, Imogene, and they don't involve any of the men you've been fornicating with for the last six months."

My jaw drops, shocked at her tone—at her condemnation. She hands me the bottle.

"Take your medicine," she says, gathering her clipboard and walking to the door. "And don't forget, we're watching."

As much as they're watching me, I'm watching back.

I keep an eye on Margaret as her stomach swells, growing bigger every day with Anex's child. I assess the other pregnant women that come in the center with their luggage, kissing their spouse's goodbye, so that they can immerse themselves and the fetuses they carry with the purest form of The Way.

I watch the big window that looks out over the fields, gaze trained for broad shoulders and a halo of hair. Sometimes I see him, dirty after a hard day's work. His hair darkened, damp with sweat. The hands that were so harsh on my body, so deliberate, are now coated in grime. He's almost unrecognizable, except for the fact that I'd know him anywhere. My Ordered. My Bonded. My first, callous and violent. Shining and bright.

Rex.

Now he's a shell, broken down by his father for Regressive intent, for daring to choose me.

I watch the door, praying that Elon will kick it down, the hinges cracking under the force. Levi will follow him through it, all traces of pain and betrayal clear from his face. Silas will be there too, scooping me into his arms, tell me everything is okay, kiss me—

"Imogene."

I blink, looking up from the cutting board and the sweet potato diced in a pile. I'm chopping air. Margaret stands in the doorway, hand on her belly. "Sorry." I brush my hands together and hope she doesn't see the flush on my cheeks. "Did you say something?"

"There's a new addition in the waiting room."

"Oh," I say, coming back to myself. "Yes, of course."

She smiles gently. Despite everything that happened with Anex the night he banished Elon and Levi from the community and punished the rest of us, she's remained true to our bond. "Sisters" is what she calls us. But like everything, there's a power imbalance, and like always, I seem to be at the bottom.

"I think you'll be excited to greet our new housemate," she says, walking down the hallway.

I'm not sure why she says that, not until I walk into the registration office and see her. Maria, my best friend from the Domum. My eyes drop to her stomach and under her cotton dress is the smallest swell. Pregnant women are required to report to the child center once they reach the second trimester.

"You're pregnant," I blurt, unable to present the happy façade I give to every expectant mother that walks in the door.

"Three months," she says, not quite making eye contact. No one does. The whole community is aware that I'm being punished for sleeping with men other than my mate. What they don't know, or believe, is that Anex commanded them to train me. He set me up.

"Welcome." I force a grin. "We're here to celebrate the growth of our community and ensure the future by nourishing the body, mind, and soul of the mothers and children born here."

The words come on command, memorized from my training with Healer Bloom. Margaret watches me carefully, probably aware of my history with Maria. How we'd been so close when we were teenagers—before we were Ordered. I don't reveal my true feelings, how I mourn for who Maria was before she walked into this facility.

It's not a place of care and support.

It's a noose tightening around our necks, and like everything else in Serendee, Anex is holding the rope.

69

____

R^{ex}

Every part of my body aches.

My back, my legs, my cracked and bleeding knuckles. Manual labor sucks, and I'll be the first to admit it, I had no fucking clue how shitty most of the jobs in Serendee were before I was forced to do them myself. The farm work I've been assigned to isn't just back breaking. It's soul crushing.

Never think my father doesn't know exactly what he's doing.

At the end of the day, I'm too exhausted to think about running. I'm too hungry to worry about anything but my next meal. My brain feels fuzzy. My reaction time is slow. Every symptom is intentional—a way to make me complacent.

"Pick up the pace, Rex."

I don't look back to see who's speaking to me. It's a guard, assigned specifically to follow me around all day. They rotate, and I know them. Grew up with them. The one following five steps behind me right now, Erik, lived in my Donum. Another one of my father's games.

God, I want to kill him.

Hence the guard.

I take a small amount of pride in knowing that despite how run down I've become in the last month, Anex still views me as a threat. More than the others. I know Elon and Levi, wherever they are, won't be able to see it, but my father gave them a gift. Freedom. He's kept me a prisoner because he knows this is the worst punishment he can give.

He took my money, my cars, my ability to move in and out of Serendee. He took away my job of recruiting rich, attractive women into the community. All those privileges I didn't fully understand until they were gone.

And none of them are even the most important.

"Seriously, man," Erik says, nudging me along with a hard shove. "You do this every day."

He's right, I think, glancing over at the building as we pass. Wide glass windows make up the walls of the Child Care facility. I drag my feet when I'm passing the building—a route my father surely chose with intention. I don't care about his conniving, or how I'm sure he thinks parading me in front of her facility every day is a punishment. I've caught a glimpse of her once or twice. Her blonde hair is hard to miss—her gorgeous face.

That's all I need. A glimpse. Something to tell me she's okay.

"Why are you doing this to yourself?" he asks, voice low and close. It comes with the sensation of hard metal pressed into my back. "She's not yours, and the longer it takes for you to understand that, the longer he'll keep you here."

Erik probably believes there is a way out of Reeducation. That Anex's pathway from the Fallen back to the fold is possible. It's not. There are no second chances. No test we can pass, and I'm paraded through the community like this, every day, as a reminder to everyone of what happens when you cross our great and infallible leader.

My eyes linger on the building, but the windows are clear. I push aside the nagging worry of what could happen to her without my protection—without the others.

Even if I couldn't have her, I'd be okay if he left her with one of my friends. But no, that wouldn't have been painful enough. It's also not what he wants. I see it now. My father has wanted Imogene from the start. Probably as revenge against her mother for leaving, but I know it's more than that. Imogene is special. Beautiful. So fucking strong.

The men in our family clearly have a type.

The walkie-talkie on Erik's belt crackles as we continue down the path. There's no speed in my step. Once work is complete, I'm forced to stay in my room until the next morning. Room is an exaggeration. Closet? Cell? My food is delivered to me. My toilet is two feet from my bed. There's no window. But I do hear the cries at night. The Fallen as they go through Corrections. As they're tested and fail.

Some nights I even hear his voice and I know he's down there, looking to see who he can break next. Who he can use, abuse, and worst of all, sell.

Erik pauses, turning his head to speak into the device. His eyes flick to mine, then away, but not before I see a shift in them.

"Understood. We're on the way." He clips the walkie-talkie back to his belt, his movements hurried.

"Everything okay?" I ask, the smallest hope that the day I've been waiting for has come. This underlying hope that my brothers will return for us. Elon and Levi are out there, and I know they'll fight for us. It's just taking longer than I'd hoped.

"Everything's fine," he says, lifting his chin to the east. Toward the Main House. "You're not going to your room... not yet."

My hope sinks, but I'm curious. My days have been a strict routine since my father put me to work. Rise at dawn. Work 'til dusk. Locked up overnight.

"Where are we going?"

His jaw tightens and his hand rests on the weapon attached to his side. Like he's afraid he'll have to use it. "To see your father."

～

Anex sits in his chair—what the hell, let's call it what it really is—his *throne*, as if we've seen one another since he took my mate from me and banished my friends from Serendee.

He's got that same smug expression on his face, his hair slightly disheveled, and a knowing glint in his eye. It's all a con. I know it well. He's the one that taught me the methods of persuasion. While other dads were teaching their kids how to play ball, he was refining my skills in manipulation. In seduction.

I can get just about anyone to hand over their money, their clothes, their *pussy*, but most of all, their integrity. Just like my father.

He waits patiently, Erik bowing before him and touching his forehead in reverence. Anex's crystal blue eyes, another matching trait passed down, dart from the guard to me. He wants me to honor and respect him? Fuck no.

Finally, he says, "I see your attitude hasn't adjusted."

"By plowing fields? Is that the outcome you expected?"

"I thought maybe some manual labor would set you straight. Show you how entitled I've let you become."

I sigh. Every muscle in my body screams with exhaustion. I just want to go to my room, eat dinner, and sleep until the day repeats itself. I'm too tired to even jerk off. "What do you want?"

"A father can't check up on his son?" he asks, waving over one of the girls standing by the wall. I scanned their faces the instant we walked in, both hopeful and horrified that Imogene may be one of them. She's not. These girls are young. Probably underage. Children, I assume, of members of our community, unless he's started recruiting at the local high school.

The girl that steps forward is waif thin, dark circles under her eyes. She carries over a tray of fresh fruit, her arms shaking from lack of strength. Disgust builds in the back of my throat. No, this one has been here for a while, probably grew up in Serendee, but somehow managed to offend my father.

How did this happen to my community? When?

Serendee—my father—he wasn't always like this.

Or has it? Has *he?*

"I'm sure you have your methods of keeping track of me." I tilt my head toward Erik, who shadows me most of the day. "It's not like you trust me."

"You're right about that." He grabs a handful of grapes and pops one in his mouth. "You haven't earned back my trust." He reaches out, tucking a strand of hair behind the girl's ear. "At least not yet."

Ah, here it is. The big play. Dangle hope in front of me—an opportunity—see if I take the bait.

"I'm not interested in regaining your trust or anything else." I take a step back, as if to leave, but Erik's hand comes down on my shoulder. Hard. "I'm done with you."

Anex waves the girl off and leans forward. "I'm trying to be patient here, Rex. Rebellion is normal in a man your age. You want to spread your wings—your seed." He grins knowingly. "And I gave you a lot of leeway. Much more than anyone else in Serendee, because I knew for you to step into your rightful role, you had to experience what we are keeping the community safe from." He adjusts the gold watch on his wrist. "But things changed when you infected our circle with Secularism. When you pushed your Regressive, blasphemous views on the weak minded. I had no choice but to step in."

For the last month, hell, the last few years, there's been this dark ball in the center of my chest. Most of the time, I keep it still, smothering it down, but at night, alone in my room, I see it for what it is: a ticking bomb. *Tick, tick, tick.*

"By stepping in, do you mean branding my mate?" I ask, fingers twitching.

A beat of silence runs between us, dark and feral, the bomb in me ready to explode, but Anex is more calculating than that. He ignores me and gets to the point of this sham of a meeting.

"As much as I'd like to keep you toiling in the fields, your skill set is better used elsewhere." My skill set. Conning women into taking classes at the Center, handing over their personal details, bank accounts, bodies... "One of your recruits, Jasmine, is insisting on working with you." He snorts. "Apparently, her pussy and Daddy's pocketbook only open for you."

Tick, tick, tick.

"So, you're willing to pull me off grunt work, so I can seduce a heiress."

He shrugs. "Under supervision."

"You can force me to work in the fields, but what? You are going to make Erik stand over me with a gun while I fuck this girl?" I shake my head. "I don't think she'll be into it."

A line creases between his eyes. It's his tell. He's pissed. The first time I noticed it was when me and the guys came home late one night, rolling on molly and rummaging through the kitchen in the Main House. We'd trashed one of the cars, wrapping it around the mailbox of a professor's house just off Wittmore's campus. He didn't lose control then, and I don't expect him to now.

But that doesn't mean I won't pay.

"I think you've forgotten your roots. The Why of this community. How we are One and work together for The Way. How your petty, rebellious actions affect everyone."

His tone drops at the word everyone. Even if I'm isolated here, I know I'm not alone. Imogene and Silas are both bound to me. From the quirk on Anex's lips, I know where this is leading.

"You're upset about Imogene," he suggests.

"*Don't* say her name."

He stands, slowly walking toward me. When he speaks his voice is low. "You seem to be confused about how Serendee operates. This is my community, and these are my people. I *gave* you Imogene, which means I can, and have taken her away. The fact she kept the women's group and their actions a secret from you, fucked your friends on *my* command, and subjects herself to intense sessions of Corrections, means she never belonged to you. That's why I branded her. She's *mine*." His voice shakes, anger pushing through. "By the equinox she will be claimed," he smirks, "intimately."

My hand shoots out, clamping around his throat. His eyes bulge, jaw parts, fingers grabbing for release. "Not if I kill you first."

My fingers squeeze, tightening, but around me the guards, Erik, in particular, have sprung into action.

"Get off! Get him off!" a voice shouts. Hands grab at me, weapons are drawn. I have Anex too close for them to shoot me and I take advantage of the chaos swirling around us.

Another trick he taught me.

I don't stop, gritting my teeth as I try to snuff the life out of my father. "You will die for this. I will wring the life from you before I allow you to defile Imogene."

I grin down at him, he's losing strength—air—just a few more seconds and—

Slam!

A hard weight crashes down on the back of my head, I stumble back, dragging Anex with me, but my brain is fuzzy, consumed by distant echoing clicks. I blink, looking up at the barrel of Erik's gun, wishing for him to end it. To take me out.

Finish this for good, because the pain in my head, in my limbs, in my fucking gut is too damn much.

Our eyes meet, and he rears back, dropping the gun and the last thing I see is his fist slamming into my face.

Then I black out.

70

———

I've got one last person to visit when I see the burly guards drag Rex into his room. He's unconscious—he has to be. Otherwise, I can't envision any scenario where he's manhandled like this without a fight.

"Jesus, he's heavy," one of the guards says. I duck around the corner, hoping they didn't notice me. I may not be on lockdown, or outright banished like Levi and Elon, but I'm being closely monitored.

"Get him in there before he wakes up," the other replies. "I saw what he did to his father. I'm sure he'd have no problem taking us out too."

Rex did something to Anex?

"Do you blame him?" I hear one say. "Look at him, his father is the leader and he's locked in here like the rest of the Fallen."

"What did you say?" The voice is curt, tone hard. "You're questioning Anex's decisions?"

"N-no." He clears his voice. "No. That's not what I said. I just—

nothing." I hear them back in the hall, door closing behind them. "Let's get out of here. It creeps me out."

They move quickly, exiting the locked door down on the end of the corridor. I understand their haste. There's an underlying fear in Serendee that Regressive thoughts are contagious.

I wonder where they got that idea?

As the days pass, I'm learning more and more that the people down here have done little to deserve their fate. I sensed it before, the punishments seemed too swift, too severe, the conditions the Fallen are held in, demoralizing and dangerous. The younger women are used as a receptacle for Anex's hypersexual needs. The young men? An example to the rest of us about what can happen if you disobey.

Which is why, even though I'm worried, I don't go straight to check on Rex. It's too risky. Instead, I punch in the code to the room next door, pausing for a moment after the lock disengages. I've been avoiding this visit all day.

Charlotte is curled up on her bed, eyes darting to mine when I walk in.

"Silas," she says, rising. Her eyes brighten a little and it just makes me feel worse. "I hoped you were coming today."

I shut the door behind me. Charlotte is one of the Fallen I supervise now—a role given to me by Anex the night all hell broke loose. Charlotte, and the others down in this ward think they are being Reeducated to reenter Serendee. The truth is that Anex has bigger plans for them. They're being groomed for sale, and I've been assigned to prepare them.

"How are you?" I ask, noticing her dinner plate is empty. Stacks of Anex's books are on the small desk, pages dog eared and well-read. A food log is open. I stop by it and run my finger down. She's counted every calorie and every bodily function. "You ate all your dinner."

"I did," she says beaming. When I came down here before, with Elon and Imogene, Charlotte was in bad shape. Her weight was tragically low and she had an infection. She was bruised, her hair a stringy nest. She was desperate for Anex's approval, which was deranged. He was the one hurting her.

But as it became clear he wants to put her up for trade, he's allowed me to increase her caloric intake, provide her extra grooming time, and a few additional rewards. She looks better, eyes brighter, hair cleaner, although there's no mistaking her exhaustion. Anex is all about product, be it his classes or produce from the farm, or weed grown under the barn. He wants a superior product and Charlotte is nothing more than that.

An object to sell.

The craziest thing is that he managed to break her down to the point that she was afraid to eat the extra food at first. Terrified of accepting new things. Her brain was so twisted up, so wired to meeting Anex's insane demands, that she felt better starving herself than being healthy.

"Good," I say, and her smile widens, encouraged by my praise. I walk over and sit on the edge of the bed, taking her arm to assess her skin. The rash on her wrist from the shackles is finally healing. "I'm glad to see that it's better." It took a while, but I finally convinced Anex that the chains were unnecessary. Unfortunately, Charlotte is as passive as they come. "How are you sleeping?"

"Better. The meditation techniques you showed me help." She grins but ducks her head. "Do you think he'll come tonight?"

She asks me that every time I come—sometimes they are the first words out of her mouth. He's fully convinced her that the only way to reach Enlightenment is through his approval. She'll do anything to attain his favor. Even with extra calories and hygiene, her devotion to Anex is no less intense. Again, our leader knows how to manufacture the perfect product. Docile. Submissive.

"I'm not sure." I think about what the guards said, how they said Rex injured his father. "I think he may have other obligations."

"Oh." Her expression falls. "It's been a few days."

According to her journals, Anex used to visit her regularly—enacting Corrections personally as part of her Reeducation. Being in his presence is considered a gift, and for the Fallen, it was like being visited by God himself. What Charlotte doesn't understand is that she is no longer of interest to him outside the amount of money she can add to his coffers. He's done his work, broken her down, stoked her insecurities and lack of self-esteem. She's putty, primed and ready for trade.

"You seem tense," she says. "Everything okay?"

No, I want to say. Nothing is okay. My best friend was just dragged, unconscious, into the room down the hall. My other friends have been banished from the only home they've ever known, and the woman I love is being locked up in a fortress created to house and control the women of Serendee even more than before.

And the woman in front of me—girl really—is being expertly groomed for trade.

Nothing is fucking okay.

"I'm fine," I say, instead. "Just a long day."

"Maybe you want to hang around for a while?" Her hand rests on my thigh, falling into the role she's been taught so well. "I can help you out for once."

Bile rolls in my stomach, squelching any possible desire. Even though she's completely out of reach, the only woman I think about like that is Imogene.

I miss her so much. Her innocent smile, her kindness and compassion, the way she instinctively knows how to take care of those around her. It's what I thought I was doing all those years, but I was really just another layer in the system of abuse.

Still am.

Despite Imogene, the idea of having sex with Charlotte makes me physically ill. In a few days she'll be sent off to her new owner.

And I'll be the one making the trade.

Her hand drags upward, toward my crotch, while she leans forward, pressing a soft kiss against my neck. I swallow, trying to still my stomach, and ease Charlotte's hand off my leg. "I don't think so, sweetheart. I have a few other people to check up on tonight."

"Oh," she pulls back, but takes my rejection in stride. I don't sleep with the Fallen, even though Anex would approve. Someone needs to be there for them, look out for their health and needs. I know it's not much, but it's all I can do, at least while they're still here.

"Any update on my Rising?"

"Soon," I tell her, standing to create some distance.

Rising. That's what he—we—are calling it. Rising back into society. The first step out of the status of Fallen. From the ashes, blah blah blah. Anex has waxed poetically about it to me for the last month. It's just a shiny word for an ugly, terrifying thing. Sex-trafficking.

"I hope I've passed all my tests."

She has. Medically, psychologically, physically. Charlotte is the perfect fit for our first trade. She's pretty, docile, compliant, and willing to do anything Anex asks of her.

"You're going to do great," I tell her, hating myself for every word. Hating myself more for what I do next. My hand dips into my pocket and I pull out the green pill. "Here you go."

Her eyes light up. She gets one every morning and every night. A special blend of narcotics created here in Serendee. It's to keep the Fallen complacent, enough not to fight back while regaining enough strength not to look like shit for the buyers.

She happily takes it, swallowing it as fast as she can, then curls back on the bed, like she was when I came in. "Thanks, Silas."

I don't respond, I don't even breathe again until I'm out of the room, door locked tight. What I'm doing is so fucking wrong, but what other choice do I have?

I hear footsteps coming down the hallway and tense, but it's just the food delivery person. I watch as he stops at each door. I don't miss the taser on his hip, and he does his job expertly, no engagement, no conversation, just dropping off one plate and retrieving the one from the prior meal. The heavy doors click into place as he walks to the next room.

He nods as he passes, popping into Charlotte's room. I start to make my way down the hall, but then he pauses in front of Rex's room, and I stop.

I don't have access to his room. Anex didn't give me the passcode, which is understandable. Keeping us apart is just another nail in our punishment. I watch as he hesitantly approaches Rex's room, free hand shifting to the taser. This is also understandable. There's no fucking way Rex makes anything easy on anyone in here. He visibly braces himself and punches in the code. This time he doesn't go in, just slides the food across the floor and jumps back out.

Like Rex is a wild animal or something.

He scurries off, and on instinct I dart forward, shoving my foot in the empty space before the door catches. I know it's possible I'm being watched, but fuck it. My friend is hurt and I'm going to check on him.

I duck inside, wedging a handkerchief between the jamb and the door to keep it from locking.

Rex is flat on his back, the skin under his eye swelling and discolored. Blood oozes from a split lip. From my vantage, I see his chest rise and fall, confirming he's at least breathing.

"Hey," I say, nudging his shoulder. "Rex."

He shifts, a groan caught in his throat, and relief washes over me. It's been weeks since I've seen him and it's clear the time has been hard on him, at least physically. Although he's still big—tall and broad shouldered—his muscle mass is waning, his cheeks gaunt and under the forming bruises I see dark shadows under his eyes.

"Brother, wake up," I say, trying to push his frame closer to the wall. It takes both hands to move him over enough for me to sit next to him.

He blinks and our eyes meet. "Silas?"

"Yeah, it's me. You look like shit." He grunts, eyes fluttering shut. "Stay with me, okay? You definitely have a head injury, and you need to stay awake. Tell me what happened."

"Anex happened," he says as I unzip my bag, rummaging through for the scissors I carry with me. The blades are short, surgical, and I use them to cut the front of his shirt, ripping off a strip of fabric. I reach for the cup on his tray of food and dunk the fabric in the water. Balling it, I shove it in his hand and lift it to his mouth. "Apply pressure if you can."

I fall into routine, finding the package of bandages, rubbing alcohol, and salve I carry with me. Pretending the ache in my chest isn't one of revenge and anger. This is my friend, my best friend, and his father is the one that hurt him like this. It's wrong. Everything about this hell of the Fallen is wrong, but there's nothing I can do about it but tend to his wounds.

"Do you want to tell me what happened?" I ask, cleaning his knuckles with the alcohol.

He winces at the sting. "You know what happened."

Imogene.

My heart leaps in my throat. "Did he do or say something specific?"

His eyes open and his crystal blue gaze holds mine. "He wants her."

There's no mistaking what he means. I see it every day down here, the girls Anex keeps for his own services. "I think he made that clear when he branded her with his initials."

"No, Silas," he pushes up on his elbows, a struggled huff of air escaping his lungs. "He *wants* her, for his own. For his pleasure and under his control." He hisses when I swipe the ointment over the scraps on his hand. "He's going to claim her on the equinox."

"What?" I ask, a tremor rolling up my spine. "The equinox?" There's no mistaking what that means. It's a ceremony. It was to be Rex and Imogene's ceremony before everything fell apart. "He wants to mate with her."

"He's going to, Silas." There's an undeniable pain in his voice. "He will unless..."

"Unless we save her."

We fall into silence, both of us well aware that the other would have done something if we could. We have no freedom. No money. No confidence we can get her to safety.

Rex sighs. "Any word from the guys?"

"Nothing." I gesture for him to turn. "Let me check your head."

The contusion is about the size of my fist—but there's a clear outline—the butt of a gun. I gingerly press my thumb against the spot, and he shouts, "Son of a bitch, Silas!"

"Sorry, I was just testing it."

"Well, it hurts like a motherfucker."

I stand, walking across the room to lean against the small metal desk. "It's a bad injury. Like I said, you probably have a concussion, but this isn't my area of expertise."

"Yeah, you're better at massaging vaginas and soothing psychic trauma."

His tone is snide—dismissive, but I know he's just upset. I'm upset. "You're right. The damage your father does to the Fallen down here—it's not as violent, but it's also no less brutal."

"So, he still plans on selling them?"

"Any day now, I suspect."

"And you?" There's no mistaking his concern. "What's he going to do with you?"

"I don't know." I push off the table and start to collect my supplies. "But I'm pretty sure if he found out I'm in here helping you, he'd put me out there with them."

"You're right." Something in his eyes is clear, like he's struggling through the fog. "You being here is dangerous. Not just for me and you but—"

"For Imogene." I straighten and grab my bag. Not wanting to leave my friend, not hurt, not ever. I start for the door, pausing with my hand on the knob. "I'll get to her," I tell him. "I'll make sure she's okay."

"No," Rex snaps.

"You don't want me to check on her?"

"I want you to make sure she's safe," he says, expression turning hard—looking more like his father than I've ever seen him. "But what I need you to do is make sure she gets away from here—from him." He holds my eye, understanding passing between us. Still, he asks unnecessarily, "Got it?"

"Rex," I say, shaking my head.

"Silas, I'm serious. Promise me."

I swallow past the knot in my throat, a wave of nausea not far behind. Rex isn't just my best friend, he's also the leader's son. The heir. My loyalty to him is greater than it is to anyone else, including Anex. That's the reason I nod and accept his directive, even though it goes against every instinct I have.

Rex wants me to do whatever it takes to get Imogene out of here. Even if that means leaving him behind.

71

E^{lon}

"Make it a double this time," I say, gesturing to my empty glass. The bartender, a woman named Shelly, eyes both me and the glass before grabbing the bottle from the shelf and pouring the amber liquid to the rim.

"You're a big guy," she says, gently pushing it my way, "but even big guys have limits. I think you've about reached yours."

"Sweetheart," I say, pulling the glass close, "you have no fucking idea about my limits."

Trust me, I've been testing them. Day after day. Night after night. Just trying to see if I can reach them—reach the point where I can feel something other than the all-consuming rage that festers in my chest. The alcohol, well, it's an attempt to numb it a little bit.

There's only one thing—one person—that can quell the dark anger coursing through me, and she's locked away, out of reach. She's lost to me.

Who am I kidding? She was never mine to begin with.

I swallow the liquid in one gulp, letting the burn take over for a brief moment.

"You come in here, night after night, looking like hell and then head down to the ring," the bartender says, dark ponytail swinging against the column of her neck. She takes my empty glass and drops it into the sink. The message is clear. She's done serving me. "What's your deal?"

I catch my reflection in the mirror behind the bar—my dark hair messy, a thick beard covers my cheeks and chin—as well as the gauntness of my cheekbones. It does nothing to hide the dark circles visible under my eyes that give me a look of worn-out desperation. The dried blood on my split lip I received during last night's fight only accentuates it. I look homeless, which is apt.

I'm without a home.

Without my community.

Without my leader.

Banished.

"Don't people come to these places to get lost?" I ask, reaching for the cash in my pocket—cash I earned downstairs—and peel off a few bills. "Isn't it your job to make your patrons feel at home? Or at the very least, not ask a lot of intrusive questions?"

She leans over the bar, tits pressed against the thin fabric of her tank. She's not wearing a bra, she never does, and her nipples seem perpetually hard. She's the kind of girl Anex warned us about, tempting like a sweet, delicious, fruit, but she's not the kind of secular girl we pursue. Too independent. Too confident. Trouble.

"You're right. That was rude of me, but let me make it up to you." She looks at the clock over the bar. "How about you come find me after your match."

The bar is on the other side of the Whittmore campus, a shit-hole frequented by students trying to pretend they're something more than entitled frat boys. It's not the usual haunt Rex and I would frequent while working the University. This place doesn't have the right clientele for Anex's recruitment. That's why I'm here. Well, that and the fact that downstairs is a fighting ring, a place for petty grudge matches and high stakes bets. I've spent most of my nights drinking and then going down to blow off some steam and earn a little cash. It's not like Anex is funding my life outside Serendee.

"You in?" Shelly asks.

Fighting makes sense. Fucking, not so much, but I hold her eye, wondering how it would feel to lose myself in her—in someone. To find a reprieve from the anger and ache.

"Don't embarrass yourself, doll," a voice says from next seat over. "You're not his type."

Shelly's gaze flicks to him. "Mind your own business, Royer."

"He likes his women a little more subservient," he grins over at me with a crooked and clearly drunk smile. "Isn't that, right?"

My eyes shift to study the asshole's face in the mirror reflection and realize I've seen him before. He's one of the frat presidents over at Whittmore. We've done business—which means he may know more about me than I realize.

Shelly's eyebrow rises. "What's he's going on about?"

"Nothing." I stand. My history isn't anyone's business, especially these two. "Night."

"He's one of those wackos," Royer says, apparently not ready to give this up. His voice lifts over the music and crowd. "From that cult."

My spine tenses at the word, my heart racing. Instinct is hard to alter, and a lifetime of defending Serendee is second nature. My fingers curl into a fist.

"You know, where the girls wear those creepy dresses and act all pure and innocent." He snorts. "I heard a rumor that they can't actually leave —the girls in particular. That the freak leader has more than one wife."

I turn on him. "You're really going to talk to me about subjecting women? I know what your parties are like, how you treat the women let in the door. They're nothing but glorified whores."

Behind the bar Shelly's eyes are wide. "You're in a sex cult?"

The weird thing is that she doesn't seem entirely disinterested. Maybe she's a better target than I realized. The kind of girl I can introduce to Rex, and he can—

Fuck. I rub my hand over my face.

I keep doing it. I fall back into the routine over and over. That life is over. Rex and Silas are trapped behind the walls, suffering God knows what kind of punishment. Imogene is—I can't even think of what could be happening to her.

And Levi.

Shit.

There's no doubt he's taking the banishment harder than I am. His entire life was wrapped up in Anex and The Way. His entire identity. Where Rex, Silas, and I succumbed to the temptations of the secular world, Levi... he held firm to his faith.

And now he truly has nothing but me, a Regressive, with no path to Enlightenment.

"Is that true?" Shelly asks again. "Is the leader a polygamist?"

The argument that Serendee isn't a cult—isn't a sex cult—is on the tip of my tongue, but for the first time in my life I'm too tired to say it. Or maybe, for the first time I don't believe it, which is why the following falls from my lips.

"Why?" I ask. "Do you want an introduction? Do you want to go in and see if he'll take you?" I look her up and down, at the outline of her nipples, at all the flesh and exposed skin. "You can try, but before you even get in the door he'll break you down, bleed your bank account, isolate you from your family, and force you to submit to his whims." She swallows, my bluntness shaking her confidence. "Is that what you want? Someone to demean you? Control you?" I snap my arm out and grab her wrist, leaning over the bar until we're inches apart. "If that's what you want, you and I can go to the back, and I can give you a taste of what it's like personally."

A tremor runs down her spine, spreading goosebumps across her skin, tightening those nipples into hard peaks.

"Don't hurt me," she says in a quiet voice. "Please."

Royer's hand comes down on my shoulder. "Let her go, asshole, or lose the hand."

I release her, dropping her wrist like her skin is made of fire. I need to get out of the bar. Get away from these people. Fuck the money from the fight. We'll make due or maybe we can try to—

No. I shake the thought from my head for the millionth time since we were tossed outside the gates. We can't go back. Not just because Anex is a fraud, but because he won't let us. I'm certain of that.

And that, I think, exiting the bar and heading into the night, is the worst part of it all.

If he let me come back, I'd probably go.

Because without Serendee, without Anex, I not only don't know who I am, but I'm not sure I'm anything at all.

"Hey," Royer calls, grabbing me by the shoulder and spinning me around. "Don't think you can manhandle her and walk out of here."

I snort, head swimming from the night of drinking. "And you're going to stop me?"

"Someone needs to."

Gazing down at the guy, it's easy to see that I'm not just taller than him, but I probably have him by thirty pounds. It's when I meet his eyes that I see there's something wicked lurking in there—a wildness I've seen before. Rex gets that look when he wants to cause trouble and that's what this guy wants—trouble.

Maybe I'm the one that should give it to him.

I look over at Shelly, her hand rubbing the spot on her wrist where I had hold of her and the reality hits me harder—I'm not any better than Anex. I hurt. I take. I abuse.

"You want to fight me?" I ask.

"More than anything," he says, pushing up his sleeves.

I jerk my chin toward the stairs. Someone should have stopped Anex a long time ago. And even though I doubt this kid can take me, I should at least give him a shot.

Someone needs to stop me, too.

～

"You've got to stop doing this." The bag of frozen corn lands on my stomach. I jump, as much from the cold as the aching pain in my side.

"I was made for this," is my short reply. Born for it. Cultivated like the weed growing under Anex's barn. Wincing, I lean over and shove my hand in my pocket, pulling out the wad of cash and tossing it at Levi. He lets it fall to the floor, like it's too dirty for him to touch.

"You're welcome." I lift the bag and press it against my temple. That Royer prick may be a dumbass, but he's got a solid right hook. Too bad for him, all those years of corrections make taking a few hits seem like a cake walk. More than that, I enjoy it—*deserve* it.

"There are other ways to make money," Levi says, sitting on the chair across from mine. With his red hair in disarray, and slumped in his seat, he looks as beat up as I feel.

"Name one that I'm qualified for other than drug dealer or fighter."

After Anex banished us, we were forcibly removed from the property. Tossed in the back of a van and driven miles from town. Dumped by Anex's guards in a park with nothing but a bag of generic clothing and supplies. He'd given us both a hundred dollars in cash, along with our ID's, but we had no idea what to do with it. Sure, I'd spent time outside the walls of Serendee, but due to my position as one of the Chosen, I had stacks of cash, nice cars, clothes, and access to clubs and restaurants. Living a life of secular poverty was an unknown.

We didn't go quietly. At least I didn't. I had one goal, get back to Serendee, breach the walls and find Imogene, Silas, and Rex. But as the hours passed, and Levi managed to get us a ride back to town, my plot altered. I knew getting inside the walls would be impossible, especially unarmed. We'd need supplies. Weapons. A plan. Intelligence.

I wanted my woman back in one piece and I wanted Anex dead.

To his credit, while I wallowed, Levi stepped up and found this crappy little apartment two miles from campus. It's an efficiency. With a double bed, a scratchy couch, and an ancient, avocado green refrigerator that rattles all day and night. We at least had shelter. But we needed money. I'd heard rumors about the bar that held nightly fights and decided to check it out.

"There are legitimate jobs," Levi continues.

I switch the bag to my swollen knuckles. "Have you had any success finding one of these magical jobs?"

He shoots me a resigned look. We both know he hasn't. Why? Because we were raised with no real skills. Anex hamstrung us for living a life outside of Serendee. For living a life *inside* Serendee.

"So, you're struggling to find a job where you can lecture people in the glory of basking in the glow of Anex's genius? Or no one will allow you to dole out Corrections for personal failures?"

"Elon…"

"Fuck, Levi, at least he taught Silas how to be a whore! He could survive out here! We're just…."

"Fucked. We're fucked, I know!" He shouts, the last thread of his patience snapping. "You don't have to keep reminding me!"

If I thought rattling Levi would make me feel better, I was wrong.

Now I just feel like shit. Faith is all he has. It's all he's ever had and watching those beliefs slip away is like watching a man drown.

I sigh. "You know what I think about when I'm in the ring, letting those assholes get in a few punches?"

"What?"

"How much of our world was orchestrated by Anex. Did he sense who we are, who we could be, from childhood? I don't misunderstand that he used us to build Serendee. At what point did he realize my body, my strength and power, could be honed to pressure and compel? To enforce? That Silas's was nothing more than a vessel to be exploited, his body used to manipulate and convert?" Levi's face pales, his hands gripping the arms of the chair, knuckles white. I continue, "Or when did he recognize that your mind, your faith and loyalty, would keep the rest of us on the path to Enlightenment even when we knew better."

"Don't—"

I'm not finished. I lean forward, feeling the burn against my rib—

relishing the pain. "And what about Rex? The heir. Gifted and power-ful. He always had the ability, and freedom, to become the greatest of us all. But was there ever any real freedom? Were we really friends? Were any of us more than pawns?"

"I don't know the answer to any of those things." His eyes are cast down and my heart sinks, because Levi always knows the answer to these questions. He's always a rock, reliant on faith even when the rest of us aren't. And if he can no longer draw on that, then what are we supposed to do? "I don't know who I am outside those walls, outside the classroom and literature and books." His gaze meets mine. "Outside of Anex's approval."

I haven't told Levi about my plan. About the lists I keep in my head. The number of guns. The knives and explosives. How I will get Imogene first. Then Rex and Silas. And after they are safe, I will find Timothy Wray, the man that started all of this, the man that destroyed our lives, and I will end him.

72

I mogene

"I understand it's hard for you to be away from your mates and your homes right now, but starting your child's life in our new Childcare Center will allow them to be one step closer to Enlightenment and The Way. Their entire foundation will come from a place of hope and love—from a compounded energy passed from each of you, from me, and my wives. We're no longer just members of a community, we're a family. I will be the father to all of your children, just as you will mother each other's children."

Anex's words create a cold ball in my belly, a reaction to the lies and manipulation. Even though I can see it so clearly now, how he uses his gifted tongue to draw people to his will, there's part of me that is surprised I'm no longer influenced by his lectures. I know better now. He isn't a good man.

I stand just outside the room, uninvited to the meeting as I am both Fallen and not pregnant, waiting to clean up when he dismisses them. I can see the women, including my former friend, Maria, whose face is bright with Anex's declaration of a shared family unit.

"Before I go," he uses his hands to gesture to the women, "come forward, and I will bless each of you and your unborn child."

Bile rises to the back of my throat, nausea from watching these women so easily manipulated. Margaret goes first, her belly exposed, in one of her unconventional outfits. Clothing forbidden by other women in Serendee. Her skirt is long, but her top cinches under her swollen breasts, revealing the exposed skin of her protruding belly. The top is cut low, and it's the kind of clothing we'd always been warned against, but rules don't seem to apply to Anex's favored wife. Still, she goes through the motions, touching her forehead and bowing before our leader. When she stands, Anex rests his hands on her stomach and he bends, kissing the stretched skin softly. It's an intimate act between a man and his mate—she's carrying his child, after all. Margaret smiles and steps to the side, and the next woman is waved forward. She goes through the same motions of honoring Anex.

"Sweet Doris," he says to the woman. She was Ordered and Mated a few years ago. "It's no secret you've struggled with conception. And you went through the process to discern what you were doing to block this gift from your life. You spent your time in Reflection and Correction. You've studied and meditated over The Way. You've searched for Enlightenment and ultimately, you allowed your body to accept the seed of life. A seed we shall cultivate and foster in our family garden."

His words are a twist of confusion—a blessing and a condemnation at the same time.

"Lift your skirts," he commands. Without hesitation, Doris does as she's asked, lifting the fabric and revealing herself to the room—to him. Anex's hands splay across her stomach, a gentle caress, similar to the one he gave his wife. "This baby shall be a gift to Serendee—the future of our community. The hope for alignment and peace." He bends, kissing the pale skin. A sick feeling heats my throat as I watch the scene unfold. The way Doris smiles down at him. The way Margaret looks at them with such loving confidence.

Everything in this room is wrong—so wrong. I look up to my

friend Maria, waiting for her blessing, aware of the shiny glaze in her eye. It's awe and respect. Devotion.

I stumble back, away from the intensity of the room, struck with my own emotion. Grief. Jealousy. Abandonment. It's too much to comprehend and I turn away, escaping down the hall. I enter the first door I come to. Inside, the room is dark other than a small lamp over the exam table. Pressing my back to the door I shudder out an exhale.

"Imogene?"

My heart lurches and I turn to the dark corner I heard the voice.

The *familiar* voice.

"Silas?"

The instant his name is out of my mouth, I wish it back. It's foolish. Ridiculous. I'm losing my mind. This place, the isolation, is making me crazy. Silas isn't welcome here.

"Imogene, it's me." I don't believe it until I feel his hands on me, one on my hip, the other sliding behind my neck. His eyes dart from my face across my body, assessing. "God, tell me you're okay."

I nod, unable to speak past the lump in my throat. Fear that this isn't real. A tear slides down my cheek, and he catches it with the warm pad of his thumb. "Baby, it's okay. Take a deep breath."

I inhale, allowing the air into my lungs and when I exhale, I ask, "What are you doing here? How did you get in?"

"The apothecary." He nods over to the corner he'd come from. A box sits on the counter, stamped with Serendee Apothecary on the side. "The Center requested a delivery and I volunteered to bring it."

"Anex is here," I warn him, pressing my body to his. "Talking to the mothers. If he finds you—"

"I don't care." His hands roam my face, like he's searching for something. "I needed to see you—make sure you were okay." He swallows, Adam's apple bobbing in his throat. "Has he hurt you?"

I shake my head. "No."

His hand runs along my side. "You've lost weight."

"He... he prefers me this way."

Silas swears, a secular, forbidden word. "You don't belong to him."

"Do I not? Do I not wear his brand? Live with his wife? Do his bidding?" I whisper, looking into his darkening eyes. "Are you not under his thumb, too?"

"Let me see it."

My head tilts. "What?"

"The brand."

Heat prickles my skin. "No."

He grabs my wrist, but it's not harsh. It's warm. Strong. Touch I've craved for weeks now. "*Yes*. Let me make sure it's healing correctly."

"It's humiliating," I confess. "It's embarrassing to wear his mark like this."

Silas' sharp, angular, jaw clenches tight. "You think it's not degrading to do the work he forces on me? Preparing the Fallen to be whored out to the depraved and perverted?"

"Silas—"

"We were raised to protect one another, Imogene. Community at all costs, but I spend my days and nights doing the opposite. I am a traitor to my brothers and sisters, and that has left me as marked as you are, mine is just under the flesh, burned into my soul." His skin pales. "What he's asked me to do to the Fallen—"

"And Banished," I interject. He stops, worry drawing his eyebrows together. I see he's afraid to say their names too. Elon. Levi. Rex.

"So," he says, licking his lips, hand firm on my hip, just above the branding, "let me see it."

I don't fight as Silas reaches for the hem, lifting the gray jumper to my waist. He hooks a finger at the waist of my underclothes and pulls them down.

Again, I flinch, moving to cover it.

His hand stops mine, and when our eyes meet his are hard with determination. "Don't hide yourself from me, Imogene."

I relent and lean back against the hard door as his fingers gently explore the wound. I refuse to look at it, hating the damaged, burned skin, the red, never healing sore. Silas drops to his knees, and a low curse cuts through the quiet of the room. His fingers explore the edges of the brand.

"It's fine," I tell him, wincing as he touches a sensitive spot. "Hardly any pain left. The scabs are healing—"

"I'll kill him for this." I hear the promise in his words.

If only.

If only Anex wasn't surrounded by armed followers. If only he didn't have Rex guarded twenty-four hours a day. If only we knew how to find Levi and Elon. If only we'd left when we'd had the chance—when Rex asked us to. He knew. He knew and we fought him.

I touch Silas' chin, lifting his gaze upward. "You're not a killer."

His jaw sets. "You don't know what I've done or what I'm capable of, Imogene, especially when a man harms something so important to me."

I see it now, that even in this short time, Silas has changed. That I've changed. We're raw. Lost. Broken.

Desperate.

"I know you're strong, but I also know you're a good man. You care for people, and you can't let him take that away, or allow him to use it against you." I press my hand against his cheek. "We're here to make a difference. To help those who can't help themselves. The Fallen—the pregnant women out there. Someone has to, and if it's not us, then who?"

"You're too good for Serendee," he says, still on his knees. "You're too good for *him*."

He takes my hand, kissing my fingers before moving back to the brand. He kisses the skin around it gently, so soft I barely feel it, except for the siren of goosebumps rising across my flesh. My head falls back, sinking into the touch of the man that showed me a whole new way to view my body—opening me up to something besides what I'd been taught. That it's okay to seek pleasure, to fulfill my desires.

Silas's kisses move from the wound, down my legs, and to my inner thighs. His tongue lathes over the scars put there that forbidden night by Levi. His touch is feather light, soft sucking that sends sparks of heated want between my legs. It's wrong to want this, to risk this, but it's been weeks since I've seen my men—felt their touch. I crave something other than the cold sterility of this place.

The threat of what's to come.

I crave him.

"Silas," I whisper, tugging at his thick hair. "Please."

"Please what?" he asks, breath hot on my pussy. A tremor runs up my spine.

"I want you inside of me." His tongue drags across my core, and I buck against his mouth. "Silas, give me this."

He rises, taking more time than he should, more time than we have, kissing a trail along my neck. I push at the buckle on his pants, reaching for him with needy hands. The feel of him, hot and hard, sends a rush of sticky warmth between my legs. He doesn't hesitate, hooking my leg around his waist and entering me with a thrust.

"Oh," I breathe, loving the invasion—the feel of him thick and wide—pushing at my walls as they clench around him. "I've missed this."

"I missed you." He rocks back, punching in, and I wrap my other leg around him, wanting him deeper. "I dream of you at night. Of this. Being with you, being safe."

My reply comes in a rush of air, panting from the way he makes me feel. Silas is a skilled lover—trained—and the way he touches me, strokes me, guides his cock into my body, sets every nerve on edge.

But none of that is what sends me to the precipice. It's the look in his eye, the way his tongue licks hot against my lips, is the way he sees me—the way no one else in this place can. Silas and I are bonded in this moment, in the fear of being caught, in the struggle of being alone—our closest confidants ostracized.

His thumb grazes over my clit, making my walls clench around him. "Fuck, baby, you feel so good."

Silas stifles his pleasure by biting down on my shoulder, teeth bared, hard and painful against my skin. That pain, so delicious and raw, triggers a shuddering orgasm. Warm and deep, a hard final thrust. We stay this way for a long moment—him inside of me—my body clinging to him inside and out.

He looks down at my shoulder. "I'm sorry—"

"Don't be." That pain is a sharp reminder I can carry with me long after he's gone. I kiss his jaw. "You have to go."

My statement comes out abrupt, but we both know it. Every minute he's here is a risk we're discovered.

Even with the pressure, Silas moves with care, making sure to wipe between my legs, removing any trace he'd claimed me.

"Have you seen him?" I ask, finally speaking his name. It feels even more dangerous than what we just did. "I only get glimpses from the window."

"I saw him." His eyes shift, not meeting mine.

"Is he okay?" A dark laugh rushes out. "Of course not. Anex wouldn't allow it, and Rex—"

"He's still stubborn. Defiant. He took a pretty severe beating. Thankfully, I was able to sneak in and treat him."

"A beating? Why?"

This time his eyes meet mine and there's no mistake. *Me.* He took a beating because of me.

I reach for Silas's shirt, curling the cotton in my fingertips. "Tell him to stop. Tell him that there's nothing he can do to save me. He shouldn't sacrifice himself—"

"Imogene." He smooths down my skirt. "You belong to him. To us. Telling any of us not to sacrifice for you is like asking for our hearts to stop beating. It's impossible."

Warmth fills my chest, but it's also tinged with fear. "No, what's impossible is Anex allowing it. The best thing for all of you, is to forget me."

This was a mistake. Seeing him like this, feeling him, when I know that a future together is impossible. "He's planning on me becoming his mate at the equinox. There will be a ceremony, and he's waiting for me to begin menstruating again so that after the ceremony..."

I can't say it, but I don't need to, Silas knows. What I don't expect is for him to say, "You're not going to have a period, Imogene. Not if I can help it."

A door slams in the hallway, followed by footsteps and voices. Our time is up.

"What are you talking about?"

His voice is barely a whisper. "I've been swapping your supplements. The ones he hopes will make you fertile for a compound that does the opposite. It's not a guarantee, but the herbalists say the mixture will keep you from ovulating."

I blink. "You're why my period hasn't returned?"

He cups my face in his hands, voice a whisper. "I mixed it myself. Something to buy us time."

"Time for what? For them to come for us?" Uneasiness blooms in my chest just thinking about my men on the outside. "They can't, and they shouldn't."

He presses his lips to mine and steps back, moving to the door that leads away from the hallway. "Never underestimate what the four of us can do. Especially when it comes to you."

He slips out, my heart hammering from his kiss and the threat of being caught. I scramble to the counter where he left the delivery, picking up a bottle just as the door opens. Healer Bloom narrows her eyes at me.

"What are you doing in here?"

I keep my hand steady, hoping she can't see the red of my cheeks in the dim light. "There was a delivery from the apothecary. I figured since everyone was busy with Anex's visit..."

Her lips set in a frown. "Make sure you check everything off the list. And put everything in the correct place."

"Yes, ma'am."

She gives me one last glare and exits the room. I exhale, but don't fully breathe until hours later, long after Anex has left, and it's clear that Silas escaped undetected.

73

Levi

Elon never sleeps until the sun rises, and today is no different. He finally succumbs, still drunk, but exhausted. And if the pattern he's kept up the past few weeks maintains, he'll stay this way, until he goes back tonight and repeats the cycle.

He pretends he does it for money, but we both know the truth. It's self-punishment. Correction. Why? It's how they were raised. Those lessons are impossible to break—inside or outside of Serendee.

Probably even more so now that we're out, which is exactly why Anex banished us. He knew how bad it would hurt. How devastating. It's exactly what I would have done, if I'd been the leader.

I shrug on my jacket and step into the hall, quietly locking the door behind me. The hallway smells damp, like mildew and moisture. Like the stale cooking odors behind residents' closed doors. The stairwell is worse, reeking of piss and beer. I hold my breath as I take the steps, not inhaling until I reach outside. The air is better, but clogged with the gust of the idling bus. I long for the clean air of my home, the fresh homegrown food, and my classroom.

I need a purpose, and over the last few days, while Elon succumbs to his demons, I've come up with a plan.

A plan to earn our way back into Anex's good will and Serendee.

A way back to Enlightenment.

Using a few of the dollars Elon won in the fight, I step onto the bus and pay the fare. I take a seat and watch the buildings change from deteriorating, to the crisp, clean façade of Whittmore University. The passengers change, the bus filling up with students on their way to class—on to learning about the secular world. Greed and destruction. Wars and wealth. Science for profit. I shift, leaning forward, squashing the nerves as we approach the long strip of businesses where The Center is located.

For a heartbeat, I consider aborting the plan. Passing by and heading back home, but that lick of desperation tickles my spine and I stand, yanking the cord for the driver to stop. The bus lurches forward, and I stumble down the stairs, expelled into the street. The bus hisses and drives off, leaving me in a cloud of exhaust. Two blocks away, I see two women, wearing pale blue long dresses, their hair long and twisted into tight braids.

Turning quickly, I duck into the alley next to the building and make my way to the back. As much as I'd like to walk in the front door of The Center and demand an audience with Anex, I know I wouldn't make it past the threshold.

But I'm not just any member of Serendee—I'm one of the inner circle. I know the workings of this building and many of the others. I step behind the building and search for the brick with Serendee's logo stamped in the side. I pause, considering the last time I saw this design it was branded into Imogene's flesh. Property. His intention was clear. Imogene belongs to him, the same way this building does.

Using the tips of my fingers, I work the edge of the brick out and peer inside. A flat key rests against the back. I remove it and replace the brick. Standing before the door, I have a brief fear that maybe he changed the locks, but it's quickly replaced with the knowledge that no, Anex wouldn't change his locks. It would never cross his mind that I would return without his blessing. That I would ever go against his will.

Anex may understand me, but he doesn't understand this emotion coursing through my veins—this desperation.

As expected, the key slips in, and I turn it, releasing the bolts. A moment later, I'm inside.

The room is the same as the last time I was here. The table in the center of the room where Imogene bent over and I lashed her backside with a leather strap. Where I became so angry, so lost in my own desires, that I left and Elon came in to finish the job.

Well, this time I will finish what has been started.

I approach the wall and stare at the point where I know a camera is placed and speak aloud, "I know you never want to see me again, and you can send your guards to toss me out, but I think it's in your best interest to come talk to me." I swallow back the fear rising in my throat. "Alone. I'm pretty sure I have something you want."

FIVE MINUTES LATER, my stomach drops when the door opens and a guard walks in. His hand is on the butt of his pistol, chin jerking toward the table. "Face the table. Legs spread."

My mind blanks, wondering if this is the end, a bullet to the back of the head. A quick and quiet removal. No one would ever know. Not Elon, who I left without a note or any indicator of where I was going. Not Silas or Rex... not Imogene, who I wanted to see more than anything.

I do as I'm told, placing my hands on the table, legs slightly spread. The guard shifts behind me, hands running down my sides, patting my hips and legs. "He's clear," he says, and it dawns on me that he's just looking for weapons.

Anex thought I came to kill him.

No, this man doesn't know me at all.

Turning, I see Anex in the doorway. He gestures for his guard to leave. Once the door shuts, he looks at me with expectation. The movement is instinctive, I touch my forehead and bow. "Thank you for meeting me."

"I'm not used to taking demands," he says, walking around the table and settling in the only chair. "Especially from the Banished."

All of this is expected. Anex, for all his power and control, can be petty. Especially if he doesn't have the upper hand. Knowing I'm treading on thin ice, I get to the point.

"Things... things did not go as planned," I admit. "You asked us to train Imogene for Rex, in an effort to prepare your son for his position as heir and although we tried..."

His blue eyes watch me carefully. "You became Indulgent."

"Yes."

A smile quirks the corner of his lips. "As much as I want to say that you should have been stronger, that The Way should have provided you with the strength to resist temptation, I believe I unintentionally set the three of you up for failure."

I blink, trying to process his words. "Excuse me?"

This time he laughs. "I knew the Regressive streak was strong with her, but I didn't realize Imogene is a siren. She beckons men into foolish, emotional, *physical* reactions. She is impossible to resist. You fell for it. Elon. Silas. Even Rex, who, to his credit, noticed it sooner than I did. He requested her. My son, who has spent his life in Indulgences, teaching himself how to resist the depravities of the outside world, succumbed to her seduction."

Imogene. Of course, he would blame her for all of this. Not himself, not truly, just her. The Regressive in our midst.

"Then why not Banish her instead of us?"

He leans back in the chair, fingers tented in a contemplative pose. "You were my brightest teacher, Levi. Why do you think so?"

"Because she is a lesson. An example."

"As were you, yes." His eyes hold mine. Swirling anxiety fills the cavity of my chest. "Imogene is the worst kind of Regressive. She came by it naturally—born into it from her mother's betrayal, but she plays the part so well. A lion in sheep's clothing. A toxin in our water. A poison among our innocents. She is dangerous inside these walls and out. Banishing her is an impossibility. Reeducation is a risk, but at least a warning to the other women she may have tainted with her ideas."

"Then what?" I ask, fearful for the woman that opened up my soul.

"Only one person can eradicate the evil inside of her."

His smile tells all.

"You."

"Yes, Levi, me." He licks his bottom lip. "In a few short weeks she will become my mate. I will reclaim her. Filling her with my seed—giving her my blessing and light. She will become whole again. I will save her and bring her personally to Enlightenment."

His plan... It sounds righteous and true. It sounds like the perfect embodiment of The Way. There is nothing I can do but nod, because if I open my mouth, I may scream. But I am here for a purpose. I have a plan, and Anex may have just given me the path back in.

I swallow back the sour taste rising in my throat. "I want back in. I want Elon back in."

"And why would I allow that?"

"Like you said, we fell victim to a powerful and dangerous woman. We were weak. Confused. We lost our Way."

"I didn't come down here to listen to your groveling," he shifts, the metal chair creaking under the movement, "tell me what it is that you think I want to hear."

"You and I both know there is no Redemption for the Fallen. You kept Silas here to train them for your next endeavors. Yes, you need an example for your followers, but not just an example of punishment—you need an example of Redemption. Elon and I can come back as proof that the Fallen can emerge and regain their rightful position." When he doesn't respond, I add, "Hope is a much better motivator than fear.

"Possibly, but who are you to come to me with demands."

"Well, that is where I can get the one thing you've been desiring and is out of your reach. The person you truly want to punish."

His eyebrow raises. "And who is that?"

"Imogene's mother."

74

Imogene

Serendee is, at times, a strange mix of past and present. Anex discusses this in his lectures, how taking from both creates a perfect community. We don't drive cars inside the walls—we walk, or occasionally use horses or wagons. But there is still use for the innovations of the outside world—trucks for delivering product from the farm. Solar powered electricity to keep the buildings running day and night. And thankfully, he believes in washing machines because the amount of laundry we go through at The Center is getting out of hand.

Our detergents and soaps are locally made, and we hang everything on the line. That is my task for today, but when I walk into the laundry room, I stop short. Maria is already there, pulling white sheets from the machine. It's not so much that she's in the room that causes my pause, it's the way her hands flutter up to her belly—her bare belly. She's in a top and skirt similar to the one Margaret wears.

"What—" I clear my throat, drawing my eyes away from the deep v of her cleavage. "What are you doing in here?"

The women do help around the house, but nothing physical.

Mostly sewing or cooking. She shrugs, hands still splayed over her pale stomach. I've known Maria my entire life. The skin on her abdomen has never seen the light of day before.

When she doesn't, I step forward and thrust out my hands. "Let me do that."

"I'm fine."

"You don't need to do such strenuous work." I bend, taking over the chore. "I've got this, you go..."

"Go what?" she snaps, stepping back with the swish of her skirt. "Imogene, you know I need something to do. Sitting around isn't my thing."

She's right. Maria is a hard worker. She was always busy with something in our Domun. And now Anex has taken that away from her too. He's taken her home, her mate, and now her clothes.

Maybe Maria and I aren't so different after all.

I pick up the loaded basket and nod to the container of clothes pins. "You can carry those and hand them to me while I hang the wash."

"Seriously?"

I shoot her a look. "Do you want Healer Bloom lecturing you about overworking?" She shakes her head. "Then take what you can get, Maria. That's all any of us can do."

We walk out the back door, to the grassy area set up with clothes lines. The weather is a perfect pre-fall day. It's a reminder that the clock is ticking—the equinox is coming. The idea makes me tense and I get to work, lifting the first sheet.

Maria stands behind me, one hand trying to hide her stomach, the other holding the clothes pins. I can't help but notice her discomfort with showing so much skin outdoors. I pick up the next sheet and pause. "Here," I hand it to her, "hold that to cover yourself."

She takes the sheet and pulls it to her belly, holding it loosely. "Thank you."

I go back to my chore. "You shouldn't be put in this position in the first place."

A gust of wind blows, whipping my hair around my head. I grab for it, pushing my collar aside in the movement.

Maria gasps. "What happened?"

I frown, fingers brushing over the spot where my neck and shoulder meet. The skin is tender, and my nose wrinkles at the sensitivity. "Oh, nothing," I say quickly, adjusting my collar back. "Just a bruise I got from being clumsy."

She eyes me warily, and I refocus on the laundry and keeping it off the ground. Maria knows me—well, knew me—better than anyone. If anyone can see through my lies it's her.

"Looks painful."

"It's nothing." Just a love bite from my forbidden lover, that's all. "I'd forgotten all about it."

She hums and hands me a clothes pin, watching as I struggle with attaching the corner to the line.

"You're different," Maria says.

I glance down at her belly. "I'm not the only one that's changed." She blanches and clutches the sheet like a shield. "What's with the clothes?"

"Anex decided that Margaret's dress elevated the importance of the womb. That for the baby to experience the most love, it should always be forefront."

"You're pregnant. Exposing your skin doesn't make it more noticeable." My eyes dart to her chest where the real feature is her tits. "And it's not just your belly you're revealing."

"Anex said—"

"Do you hear yourself!" I twist the cotton sheet in my hands, trying to control my annoyance. "Anex said. Anex thinks. Anex wants to see how far he can push you outside your comfort zone and see your tits, Maria. Trust me, that's all."

She blinks. Cheeks red, horrified at my words. Women in Serendee don't talk like this. We don't use words like this, but all I do is smirk and say, "I'm Regressive, remember?"

"This is what I mean." She shakes her head. "You're not the same person I knew—that I grew up with and studied and learned with."

"You're wrong," I say, but then reconsider. "But also right. I am that same girl but... things happened to me after the Ordering. Before really." The examination by Healer Bloom comes to mind, the truth that I know we weren't alone in the room. I think about how much Anex loathes my mother, how betrayed he felt, and how that anger has festered into something deep and complicated.

I think about my training. My men, and how they opened up the world to me.

But I never speak those things, not to Maria, not to anyone.

"You were Chosen. How could you give that up?"

"That word doesn't mean what you think it does," I tell her. "I know it is impossible for you to understand, but I did everything asked of me." Like a beacon, the brand itches below my hip, and I fight to scratch it. It's a constant reminder of who I belong to. How far I was willing to go for approval, for *Enlightenment*.

"Anex builds mazes," I continue. "Complicated labyrinths with only one way out. Every turn leads to the same ending—the one he has determined for you." I look around the grounds, out in the distance to the massive red barn. So peaceful on the outside. Danger and trouble buried underneath. "This is your maze, Maria. It's only going to end up where he decides."

Maria watches me closely, the white sheet pulled to her belly. "You think I don't know that?" she says. "That I don't accept that his decisions will be the best for me and my baby? He is our *leader*, Imogene. Are you saying you don't trust him? That he doesn't know best?"

Maria doesn't know the truth about what he asked me to do, the way he looks at me—touches me—the plans he has that I can't fully comprehend. She hasn't seen the Fallen or known about the people Anex plans to trade to men like chattel. All Maria can see is the path he has created for her. One she—and everyone in Serendee—thinks will lead to Enlightenment.

But in reality, it's a path of doom.

A path none of us can veer off. The walls are too high. Too

narrow. I look at my friend and say, "Whatever you think of me, understand I am here for you and your child."

She nods. "Anex wouldn't have put you here if he thought you a danger to us."

I fight a laugh. Anex put me here for monitoring—for Healer Bloom to make me fertile. For whatever perverse plan he has next. He put me here to keep me away from *them*.

"I'm glad you see that," I say, because even though it's foolish, it does feel comforting for my oldest friend to trust me.

75

R^{ex} The rattle of the doorknob startles me from a restless sleep. The door opens before I can swing my legs over the side of the bed, the bright light from the hallway, a glare in my eyes.

"What the fuck," I mutter, rubbing my eyes. There are no windows in here, no way to tell what time of day it is down in my father's hidden home for The Fallen. I blink, trying to acclimate to the light and sense movement in the door.

"Jesus, Erik, what happened to knocking?"

"I don't knock in my house; you know that, Son."

I turn my head and see my father standing in the doorway, head nodding to the guard outside to shut the door.

"Of course you don't." I reach for the bottle of water by the side of the bed and take a gulp. "What did I do to earn the honor of a personal visit?"

Anex has something draped over his arm, clothing from the looks of the way it hangs. He tosses it to the end of the bed. One glance, and I can tell it's not for work—at least not the manual labor

I've been doing lately. It's the kind of clothing I wore when I was still the heir.

"Get dressed."

I could fight it. Fight him, especially without the guard here, but my father isn't weak. He's a strong man who could snap my neck if it came down to it. But I'm barely healed from last time, and I know Erik is right outside the door waiting for a reason to come in. I take a deep breath and think of the conversation I had with Silas. Getting the shit beat out of me, staying locked in this cell, none of that is helping Imogene. If anything, it's probably making it worse.

It just makes me so fucking angry.

I step to the corner, to the small toilet installed in the wall. I yank my pajama bottoms down and handle my dick. The stream is loud, filling the tiny room, but not loud enough to cover as my father huffs at the human display.

"Sorry, there's no privacy. The room came this way." God he's such a prick.

I finish up and flush, then kick off the cotton pants, followed by the shirt. I feel Anex's eyes on me as I pull on the pants first—black linen. They gape around the waist, an indicator of how much weight I've lost. My muscle seems more pronounced, but not in a healthy way. Like I'm eating myself from the inside. I grab the shirt and slip my hands in the sleeves, hating how right the expensive linen feels next to my skin. I'm spoiled. Entitled. Chosen.

Or, rather, I was.

I look down at my cracked, raw, hands. They tell the story of the weeks of Banishment. I glance up and catch him watching me.

"You're too thin and your hands..." His nose wrinkles in disgust.

I hold them up, tanned from the sun. "Have a distaste for the working man all of the sudden? The backbone of Serendee?"

He shakes his head, but he barely meets my eye. I wish it was shame he felt, but this man has no humility. No conscious. Not even when it comes to blood.

"What's this about?" I ask, like I don't already know. My father made it clear the day of our fight. He needs my services. He's spent years relying on me bringing in the big fish—the big *bank accounts*—he needs to live his extravagant lifestyle. He needs me to seduce someone.

He's well aware that I know so he doesn't waste time.

"I've got Jasmine West upstairs, the princess of Cobra Tequila. She needs a little nudge. I've got her committed. She's been taking classes down at the center. A week ago, she moved into one of the guest suites. Everything is going according to plan, but she keeps asking for you—making it clear that your involvement is a deal-breaker."

"There has to be someone else that can handle Jasmine."

"Sorry, Son. Whatever you did to her over at Whittmore has her focused on you and, I suspect, your dick. She wants you and only you. Otherwise, there's no way we're getting into her trust fund."

There was a time my father wasn't so blunt about it. So crass. Everything was for the Greater Good, but I guess the scales have fallen and we're not pretending anymore. At least not father and son.

I start to tell him that Jasmine doesn't want my dick. She wants the pretty pictures from the brochures. What the classes and certificates and courses push. Extravagance, plus meaning, plus sex, with an added dash of rebellion against her family. She wants more. *Everything.* And my father and myself have sold her on Serendee truly being utopia.

I start to tell him this, but I don't. My father has forgotten the true product of Serendee. The fantasy. Which means I finally have something: leverage.

"I'll do it—for a price."

"Ah, there he is. My son, the negotiator." He leans against the metal edge of the bed and crosses his arms over his chest. Pride lights his eyes. "What do you want?"

Without hesitation, I make my demand. "I want to see Imogene. In person. Face to face."

Conflict crosses his expression, but it quickly fades. "I can do that, but you have seal this deal for me. I need a million dollars transferred from her trust to our account today."

I run my hands through my hair. "Done."

"You're that confident?"

With Jasmine? "Absolutely."

"You make that happen and then you get to see Imogene." He pushes off the bed and then adds, "On my terms."

He offers his hand, but before I shake it, I say, "Don't try to get something over on me with this. A deal is a deal. I want to see her. Talk to her. No fucking around."

"I'm a man of my word, Rex, you know that." Our eyes lock. "But no fucking around on me either. You do whatever it takes to lock Jasmine in. Understand?"

My father never just wants one thing. Sure, Jasmine's trust fund is the priority, but if he can degrade me in the process? Get me to betray Imogene by being with another woman? Icing on the cake. I should tell him to fuck off, but I reach for his hand and shake it, confirming the arrangement.

Anex has what I want, and I'll do what it takes to make it happen. Even if that means doing what he's taught me to do best: selling myself.

Erik escorts me from my basement cell, through the maze of staircases and hallways in the Main House, to the French doors that lead outside. Jasmine is sprawled on a lounge chair, catching the last rays of warm sun by the pool. From this vantage point, Serendee appears to be a luxurious retreat. Sure, by the time a recruit gets to here, sitting by the edge of the sparkling infinity pool, they have taken the classes and learned the lessons of being part of our community. But the classes are not equal. What the natural born residents of Serendee experience is a different world than that of the chosen plucked from outside the walls—the women and occasional men attached to wealthy portfolios and trust funds.

These people get special treatment from my father and will continue to do so until they no longer suit his needs.

"Don't do anything stupid," Erik says, easing into a position near a massive white column. His gun is hidden, but I have no doubt he can access it quickly. "I'll be watching."

The only stupid thing I did was not forcing Imogene and the others to leave this godforsaken place when we had the chance. I descend the stairs, eyes sweeping over the pool. Jasmine isn't out here alone. My father has other guests, recruits, people he has in various states of fleecing. My gaze lands on two people floating in the far corner of the pool. Two men. One familiar. One not. Silas.

His eyes flit past mine, not making any kind of lingering contact, before locking back on the man he's entertaining. The man is a little older. Hair graying at the temples. He's not bad looking, nearly as handsome as Silas, in a more distinguished way. Men like this... they're usually in some kind of mid-life crisis, seeking meaning in their lives, and my father snaps them up.

My stomach twists as the guy places his hand on my friend's muscular shoulder, fingers spreading over his warm skin. It only coils tighter when Silas gives him a coy, flirty grin in return. I recognize the move. I have a dozen of my own, but the things my father has Silas do... it's different from me fucking a sexy blond.

I don't miss the dark shadows under his eyes. The exhaustion in his limbs. The weight of what he is forced to do for my father is weighing on him. All the grooming and manipulation. What strikes me is that my father has us both out here, selling, trading, degrading ourselves to fill the coffers of Serendee.

Does he need money?

"Rex!" I snap my eyes away from Silas and his target, shifting them over to Jasmine. She's blonde, young, and beautiful. Exactly my father's type. She's in college, so somewhat educated, but barely hanging on, with abysmally low grades. Like many girls at this point in their lives, she's trying to find herself—separate herself from her family identity and make her own. It's so much easier when daddy's bank account is funding the process. Girls like Jasmine are at a crossroads. Finish school and live up to family expectations or take her own path.

Serendee is the latter.

Jasmine stands, revealing her lithe, taunting body in a barely-there bikini. It's not exceptionally warm—and a rush of goosebumps rises across her flesh, hardening her nipples into sharp peaks.

"They said you've been busy." Her lips twist into a pout.

I take her in, the blond, bottled hair. The expensive swimsuit that fits like a second skin, the flashy gold jewelry around her neck and fingers. The skin. The nipples. The mouth.

Six months ago, if I met up with Jasmine or any woman that looked like her, I'd be calculating how fast I could get my dick in her. How hard I could use her before getting access to her bank account. What those lips would look like circling my dick. But now?

Disinterest settles over me.

All I want is my mate back. I want her shy, clear expression. Her fair, natural hair that curls by her ears. I want to bask in nervous movements. Her eagerness to learn. Her loyalty. I want her nipples. Her mouth. Her *everything*.

But most of all, I want the woman who can see Serendee and my father for exactly who he is and still want me.

I push all that want, all the need, deep down to that black ball in my chest and slip into the man my father made me and flash a smile at Jasmine.

Doing this, whatever it takes, is the only shot I may get.

"Sorry, babe," I say, striding over and giving her a kiss on the cheek. "My father has had me occupied."

"The fact he relies on you is proof of how good you are at your job."

Word must not have gotten out to the potential recruits that I've been Banished. It makes more sense why Anex kept me here. He still has use for me beyond backbreaking work. He needs me, just like Silas, to be his whore.

Jasmine pushes up on her tip-toes and presses her lips against my neck. Her tongue darts out, lathing the flesh and it strikes me. I can't do this. I won't betray my mate. I made a promise, and I plan to keep it.

To both her and my father.

I glance across the pool where I see the target resting his chin on his elbows while Silas rubs his shoulders. Our eyes meet over Jasmine's head, and I lift my chin toward the pool house.

"Babe," I say, tilting her chin toward my face. "How about we take this somewhere a little more private?"

She leans into me. "That would be great."

Sliding my hand down her backside, I lead her across the pool deck to the small cottage. Inside, Jasmine gushes, "This is freaking adorable," as she takes in the space. A soft, circular rug fills the main room. The rug is dotted with fuzzy pillows. Twinkling lights hang from the ceiling casting the room in a hazy light. Unlit candles sit on mounted shelves, their lingering scent earthy and warm. I don't know who decorated it, but I suspect Margaret had a hand.

This isn't just a pool house; it's a trap.

Against the back wall is a bar, stocked with wine and alcohol. A box of premium weed is tucked behind the glassware, but I don't want anyone stoned. Not for a decision like this. I need everyone clear—their decisions firm. I flip on the stereo and soft music spills from the hidden speakers, then walk over to the wine rack. "Grab a few glasses out of that cabinet, will you?"

She skips across the tiles, the ties on her bikini bottoms swaying with every step. I select a bottle and Jasmine locates the glasses quickly, bringing them over to me while I turn the corkscrew. "Are you trying to get me drunk?"

"No, but it's been a few long weeks, and I'm happy to see you." The cork gives, and I fill the two glasses, handing her one. I hold up my glass, and she does the same. "To catching up and new beginnings."

The glasses meet, emitting a chime in the small space. She takes a gulp and while I lift the glass to my lips, I barely take a sip. The wine is sweet, but it does nothing to take the bitterness off my tongue.

"Come," I say, linking her fingers with mine and lead her over to the rug. "Tell me what's going on. How did you end up here? The last time we were together, you hadn't made any decisions about Serendee."

To be fair, the last time I saw her there was no talking involved. I didn't really give a shit if she joined up or not. Most of the potential recruits don't, and once my father gets them to the Main House, he hands them over to someone more skilled in this area, like Silas.

Jasmine curls against a pillow, wine in one hand, and beams up at me. "I don't even know where to start. The last few months have been incredible. I've really immersed myself in the programs down at The Center. There's just something about it that feels so right." She reaches out and rests her hand on my thigh. "But you know that, right? I mean, you'd have to when you have someone as smart and powerful as Anex for a father."

I reach for the wine, needing something to do with my mouth other than tell the truth about the man she idolizes. I swallow it down and do the job I promised to do.

"I hear you're trying to decide if this is the life you want or not—long term."

Her fingers play with the linen covering my thigh. "I know it's what I want... it's just that my family doesn't approve. My father and I have been fighting about it. He thinks I'm tossing my life away to join some 'hippie commune.'"

Her eyes roll as she mocks the word with air quotes.

"Well, he's not entirely wrong. I mean, my father loves a drum circle." I flash a grin. "But not everyone understands what it's like to have a higher calling. To have the tug of something bigger than what you're used to. Where we don't worship chasing money, but seek a different way. It's a life away from all the secular nonsense—all the traffic and non-stop connection. Phones and laptops and constant input."

"Yes!" She jerks up, tits threatening to spill out of the top. "It's so much more than just a group of people living together. It's a revolution. It's something I want to be part of."

I reach out and push a lock of hair behind her ear. "You want Enlightenment."

Her eyes lower to my mouth. "More than I've wanted anything before."

I clear my throat. "Let me guess. Your father doesn't like the idea of you relinquishing your secular connection?"

Money.

She smiles, impressed by my bluntness. "No. He thinks it's a scam —a way to steal the Cobra empire." She snorts. "As if my trust fund even makes a dent in his billions."

"My father has no need for another's empire, but what he does demand is absolute commitment. Loyalty and dedication. You're a guest here, but out there—" I jerk my thumb to the land behind the Main House, "—that is where the real Serendee lies. Where the real value is in giving everything up to live this life. The sustainability, the organic food, the fresh air, and peaceful life. Access to that, to Anex's teaching, to the lifestyle afforded to residents, it's expensive. You're not buying in with dollars—you're trading an old life for a new one."

I see the wheels turning in Jasmine's head. She wants this, but she has to give up everything to take it. Her family, her money, her future. That part she understands. What she doesn't know is everything else Anex will take.

The door of the cottage opens, and Silas appears in the gap. He's shirtless, wearing a pair of obscenely tight swim trunks. "Oh sorry, I didn't know the room was occupied."

A shadow moves behind him: his target.

"There's room for everyone," I say, ignoring Jasmine's questioning expression. I rest my hand on top of hers and give it a squeeze, before hopping up. "I just opened a bottle of wine—let me get you a glass."

Silas enters and gestures to the man following him, "This is Robert."

"Jasmine." Her eyes take him in. These two have more in common than looks. Their wealth wafts off of them like a perfume. There's no need for an introduction with me and Silas. We're inner circle. We're known. It's what allows me to do what comes next.

"We were just talking about taking the next step toward Enlightenment. What it's like to be part of this community." I allow my eyes to slide from Silas to Robert. "Anex doesn't believe in coincidences. He calls those opportunities. I have to think you showing up means that you were both sent by The Way."

"Very perceptive," Silas says. "So, you're saying you'd like us to join you?"

"Please." I open a drawer and pull out a box of matches. "How about lighting the candles?"

Robert takes them and the scent of sulfur fills the air as he strikes the match against the graphite. I grab the bottle of wine and turn my back to Jasmine and Robert.

Silas leans toward me. "I can't believe he let you out."

"He needed something from me," I whisper, glancing over my shoulder. Robert smiles at something Jasmine says. Good, they're distracted. "And I made a deal."

His eyebrows rise. "For?"

I hold his gaze, but don't speak her name. Understanding lights in his eyes.

"I have to lock Jasmine in. But if we play this right, we can kill two birds with one stone." I fill the glass. "I can't cheat on her, Silas. She's my mate. I made a promise, and I won't let him destroy that."

He nods, pushing the second glass closer. "I understand." He inhales. "Remember that weekend your father sent us to the hotel for my sixteenth birthday?"

God yes. That weekend taught me a lot about myself. About all four of us. It bonded us forever. It's what made me able to trust them with Imogene, to train her to be my optimum mate. That weekend allowed me to open myself to the possibility of more.

"We play it like that."

He rests his hand on my forearm, squeezing it with his strong hand. To get out of this—*with her*—we have no choice, but to work together.

76

Silas

"The path to Enlightenment is about releasing Resistance," I say, handing the glass of wine to Robert. He takes a sip before setting it off the rug, on the tile floor. Like Rex, mine is left mostly untouched. It may be counterintuitive, but we both need to be stone cold sober for what comes next.

My best friend and I join the tight, intimate circle. I'm only wearing swim shorts, but the room is warm. But before he sits, Rex unbuttons his shirt and tosses it on one of the pillows. His thinness shocks me—weeks of deprivation—but it doesn't take away from his overt masculinity. Rex is a big man, not as bulky as Elon, but a commanding presence. I understand why women and men are attracted to him. It's not just looks, although that's part of it. It's his charisma. His dominance. Even after the degradation Anex has put him through, he hasn't lost it.

While he leans back on the pillows, stretching his legs to the middle of the space, I cross my legs and sit where I can see everyone.

One thing I've learned in all my training, eye contact is important.

Robert and Jasmine relax, although I can feel the spark of energy running through them. Once we're settled, the candles are flickering warmth around us, I continue, "You both seem to be at the same point in your journey, standing on a cliff trying to decide if you're going to jump or turn back around."

Jasmine nods, licking her lips, and glances at Robert, whose eyes slide down to the swell of her breasts.

"To make that jump, you have to release all of those hang ups from the secular world. The conventions and norms that keep people from taking those first steps toward understanding The Way." I reach out and take Rex's hand, stroking along his thumb. "Here's the thing. The people that were raised here, who live here, they do not go through this process. They were born into this world pure, unburdened by the sins of the outside world. To take this step toward enlightenment, you must shed it. All of it. You must rid yourself of everything tying you to that world. Everything." I lean over and kiss Rex. His mouth warm and receptive. I pull back and look at Jasmine and Robert. "Are you ready?"

"Yes," Jasmine says, without hesitation.

"Me too," Robert says. I'd had him locked in for a while. It's different for him. He's handing over his own money. Sure, his family may get suspicious, but he's an adult. And right now, I can tell he wants to dive in head—or dick—first.

Jasmine rises to her knees, inching closer. "I want it. All of it. Show me."

I sense Rex tensing next to me as she reaches for him. This is where things get complicated. I understand his desire to stay true to Imogene, and I'll help him achieve that. I intercept Jasmine's hand, and I give her a soft look and an even softer kiss on her shoulder. "You and Robert need to experience this together. Take this journey as one." I turn back to Rex, licking open his mouth, begging for his tongue. "Jump off the cliff."

They need a little nudge, so I run my hand down the front of my too tight swim shorts and stroke my cock. Every eye in the room watches me do it, watches me swell in my hand. It doesn't take much. I'm already turned on by the heat of Rex's body next to mine. Jasmine responds by facing Robert and tugging at the strings behind her neck. Her top falls, revealing her tits, and Robert's eyes lock on. He's a fucking goner and doesn't skip a beat, dipping his head and capturing one of Jasmine's nipples in his mouth.

The room fills with her moan, and Rex's hand slides behind the back of my neck, drawing me closer. Our bodies meet, and it's familiar. I love this man, and he loves me. We love the same woman, and this is how we get her.

With my tongue in his mouth and his warm skin pressed against mine, I flash back to the first time we kissed. Anex set us up in a fancy hotel suite for Rex's birthday. He'd just started introducing us to the secular world. It was overwhelming. Bright and shiny. Decadent.

The suite was awesome. Cable. Booze. Greasy pizza and piles of junk food. All the stuff off limits at home. The first night was just for fun. We were all alone, living it up, but Anex had told us about the surprise for the next night. The *entertainment*. He'd hired prostitutes from a nearby brothel to pop each one of us off. He explained that we were men, and we couldn't lose our virginity in Serendee. The girls and boys were kept completely separate. He left us with an all-access pass to the porn channels and a stack of condoms.

It was a night of experimentation. Learning what our bodies like —what they respond to. Although I understand now that it was something else. It was the start of our training—in truth, Anex was already breaking down our boundaries. It's the night that opened Elon and Rex up to using their charm and sexuality to lure recruits into the Center. It confused and conflicted Levi into devout dedication—something Anex manipulated. And it was the test Anex needed to use my looks, my body, and my nature to keep the community in line.

We never spoke of that night, but it bonded us. In every aspect of our lives. And I understand exactly why he needs me to take the lead now.

I glance over at Jasmine and Robert. She has her hand wrapped around his cock, and they look fully engrossed in one another. It's the charm of the cottage, the music and candles, the soft lighting and comfort. It's warm in here, making our skin damp with sweat, enticing. The room is designed to draw out our senses, and it seems to be doing its job.

I turn back to Rex, and I know we could probably end this here, but if Anex found out, if he's *watching*, it'll give him the excuse to back out of the deal.

I rest my hand on his abdomen, feeling the hard muscle dip. There's no mistaking his erection pushing at those thin linen pants. He's gone weeks without release. His body not used for pleasure, but for service and solitude. His skin still carries the faded tint of healing bruises. I dip my fingers underneath the waistband, brushing over the soft hair that trails under his navel. Before I get far, his hand stills mine.

"No?" I ask, looking up at him.

He caresses my cheek and says quietly, "You give too much of yourself to everyone here, Silas. And everyone takes too fucking much." He holds my gaze, fingers moving under my chin, not allowing me to drop it. "For once, let me take care of you."

I'm stunned by the sincerity of it. In the sincerity in *him*. Rex is my best friend, but I know he's a spoiled, entitled, brat. This is part of the change in him. The change Imogene has created. When I don't respond with anything other than a nod, he takes charge, pushing me to my back. He positions himself between my knees, his Adam's apple bobbing roughly. I watch him as he hooks his fingers in my shorts, freeing my erection. His eyes never leave me as he abruptly stands, dropping his pants, and climbing back on top of me.

"I'll make this good for both of us," he says, licking my ear. The heat of his breath on my skin elicits a shiver but then he slides his hand between our bodies and grips both of our cocks in one of his large hands.

"Fucking hell," I choke out, feeling warmth spiral down to my balls.

Slowly, he jacks us together, applying friction with every stroke. His mouth finds mine, his stubble rough, kissing me hard. I feel the need behind his movements. This isn't just a means to an end; we're both desperate for affection from someone that actually understands who and what we are. We're desperate for someone that cares.

With the next upstroke, I feel the pre-cum slide down my tip, mingling with his own slippery fluid. It eases the friction into something sweeter, slicker. My balls tingle and my breath comes in jerky bursts. I've sucked a lot of cock in my life. Eaten pussy. Groomed and manipulated, but no one has ever taken care of me like this.

My hand covers his. "I'm gonna come."

"Not yet," he says, eyes shifting over to Jasmine and Robert. She's sitting on his face while he eats her with abandon. Her head hangs lazily to the side, and she pinches her nipples. Our work here is done, I know it. He knows it. But one look into his crystal blue eyes, tells me he's not finished.

He releases us, our cocks springing apart. A moment later he's working his way down my body, fingers skimming my overheated flesh. He stops with his mouth inches away from my cock. Lower down, he's gripping his shaft, rubbing slowly.

I swallow and ask, "Have you—"

"No." He cuts me off, cheeks a faint pink. "How hard can it be? Dicks aren't complicated."

I laugh and he smiles, cutting through a little of the tension—mostly from the sound of Robert's grunts from the other side of the rug. I focus on Rex, on his mouth, on the pink of his tongue and block out everything else.

It's not hard to do once his lips graze my cockhead.

Fuck.

It feels so good when he closes his lips around me. Skin prickling, balls aching, blood thumping in my veins. He wraps his hand around the base and takes me in, warm and hot, then sucks.

My cock pulses, and he groans, signaling that he's not hating this at all. He's still working his cock, jerking his length with controlled strokes. His eyes fog over, and he focuses all of his attention on me. My hips rise, fucking upward, he never flinches, taking everything I give him—all the way to the back of his throat.

That's when I feel the climax seize my balls, and I push him back.

His broad shoulders tense and a heartbeat later, the rush of cum spurts between us—his and mine—as we both grunt through the release. It pools hot and sticky on my abs and chest.

I blink at him hovering over me, chest heaving, at the mess spilled on my body and feel the first sense of calm in weeks. He grabs his shirt and wipes us down.

"Thank you," I say, rising up on my elbows. I know it took a lot for him to do this for me. For us. For *Imogene.*

"God, that was hot." We both look over and see Jasmine slick in sheen of sweat. Robert lies spread eagle on the floor, cock flaccid against his thigh. He's lost in some kind of post orgasmic haze. "That," she says, pointing at the two of us, "is all I want. That. I can just feel it rolling off of you."

"Feel what?" I ask.

She grins. "Enlightenment."

77

———————

E lon

"I'm not sure about this." I stare at the small brick house. The bungalow is tucked in a transitional space between commercial and residential property in the small town of Thistle Cove. There's nothing interesting about it. The awning over the front porch is rusted and needs a fresh coat of paint. There are no signs announcing what goes on inside. If it's a residence or a business. Just big numbers with the street address—the nine hung askew. The only sign of life is the wreath made of sunflowers on the door.

I didn't go in last time we were here. Silas and Rex went in. I stayed outside to keep watch. It wasn't my idea to come today. That's on Levi. He's the one pushing us to meet Camille Montgomery. Imogene's mother.

"We have to do something," Levi says.

"*This* seems extreme."

He looks from me to the house. Camille works in that house, helping former cult members move on with their lives. It's the word cult that trips me up. I'm not dumb, I know Anex is up to shady and nefarious shit. I know he uses his charm and charisma to manipulate, but cult? I'm not even sure what that word means. It was never in our vocabulary other than defensively. We were told our entire lives that Serendee is a community. Not a cult. And the people who say so are trying to destroy what we've worked so hard to build.

People like Camille.

It's been an hour since the bus dropped us off at the stop across the street from the house. I look over at Levi, taking in how tired and lost he seems. Even so, I don't hold back. "I'll tell you what I told her," I say, remembering the day I took her to the library, and we covertly tracked her mother down on the internet. Imogene had been conflicted—scared. Levi glances at me. "I told her by searching for her mother we were crossing a line. That it would change everything."

I'd been right, more tragically right than I'd even realized.

"Everything's already changed, Elon," he says, running his hand through his red hair. His eyes never leave the house. "We're broke. Basically homeless."

"I make money."

"Getting the shit beat out of you," he snaps, but there's not much energy to it. "We need help."

He's right. We can't keep going on like this. My body aches. I probably have a concussion. Levi has an edge—a nervous energy that I've never witnessed before. He needs *something*, a focus, and maybe this is it. What I don't admit to him—to myself, is that I feel wrong coming to Camille empty handed. Without her daughter.

Fuck. I need to man up.

"Let's do it." I rise to my feet. Levi follows, hands shoved in his pockets. We wait for a truck to pass, then cross the street. I've just stepped on the brick pathway leading to the porch when the front door opens.

"Hold up." I pause, grabbing Levi's elbow, and jerk my chin to the door.

A figure steps out, shadowed by the awning on the porch. It's not until they step out into the daylight that I see that it's a woman.

And she's holding a shotgun.

Her voice carries, calm and collected, across the yard. "You have fifteen seconds to explain why you're on my property."

"Whoa." I hold up both hands. "We don't mean harm—"

"I know who you are and who sent you." She's far enough out now that I see her short blond hair. Her eyes, her bone structure, the tight, sassy, set of her jaw. This has to be Camille Montgomery. Imogene's mother. "You need to turn around and go back to your master. Tell him that if he keeps sending his boys around, I will retaliate."

Boys. Rex and Silas.

Next to me, Levi swallows. "No one sent us. We came on our own."

Her gun falters, half an inch before she levels it again. "Where's my daughter?"

"Rex was going to bring her to you." I take a breath and slowly lower my hands. "But Anex..."

"Timothy stopped it, didn't he?"

I blink at the use of Anex's name. "Yes."

"And what? You're here to finish me off?" Her eyes are wild and that gun, it's still pointed at us. "Shut me down? Teach me a lesson?"

Hearing the pain in this woman's voice, the *anger*, it shakes me to my bones. Why? Because I feel the same way. Levi and I look at one another and the grimace on his face says he does too.

"We're here," I say, hating the clench in my chest, "because we need your help."

Camille checks us for weapons before allowing us inside, forcing us to grip the railing of the porch while she pats us down. Her hands are firm—diligent, checking inside our boots. We must pass her inspection, because she grunts, and opens the screen door with a screech.

I'm anxiously following her in. Not because I'm afraid, but because I get the sense that she is. And scared people do impulsive things.

The inside of the house is much nicer than the outside, although it's clear it isn't used for a home. The front living room has a defined reception area, with a small desk. A rack on the wall is filled with pamphlets that have titles like, "*What Makes a Cult?*" or "*Releasing Your Mind.*" I avert my eyes, not liking the way the titles make me feel, but I notice Levi lingers, gaze glued to the literature.

I turn, and see that the adjacent dining room has chairs in a circle —like it's set up for a meeting. Still, it's got a warm feel to it, welcoming—you know when you're not being held at gunpoint.

As I assess our surroundings, I keep one eye on Camille. The shotgun is in her hand, but at least she now has the barrel directed down to the floor. I take the opportunity to introduce myself.

"Ms. Montgomery," I say, thrusting out my hand, "my name is—"

"Elon. And you're Levi. I remember you, and your parents." Her eyes roam over us. "Although you've grown since the last time I saw you."

I rub my chin, feeling my beard. "Yeah, I guess we have."

She taps the barrel of the gun on the hardwoods. "I need you to understand that I will protect myself and this program." Her jaw tightens. "I will not allow him to enter this world. Is that clear?"

Him.

Anex.

"Yes, ma'am," Levi says. "We're not here to hurt you."

"Maybe not intentionally," she says, but gestures for us to follow her. We walk down the hallway toward the back of the house. We pass the kitchen and enter a sitting room.

She points to a couch, and Levi and I take a seat. She leans the gun against the fireplace, and it's not until she's sitting across from us, pushing her hair out of her eyes, that I have a striking memory of this woman in Serendee. She'd been on the stage with Anex during one of his talks, and her expression had been clear and pure. Enlightened.

What and how had everything gone so wrong between her and Anex?

"What happened?" she asks. "Rex told me that he was going to convince her to leave Serendee. I said I would take her. Happily." She looks down at her hands. "To be honest, when she never showed, I assumed she changed her mind, or that Rex was probably sent here on a recon mission for his father. Are you telling me something else happened?"

"She didn't choose Anex. He, unfortunately, has chosen her," I admit. It's hard to know where to begin. I'm not sure exactly what Rex and Silas told her—or what she assumes about Imogene's life. It's clear Camille is a smart woman, and it's probably better not to withhold information. "Things escalated over the last few weeks—months really. Ever since Imogene and Rex were Ordered."

"To marry," she says, then clarifies with an eyeroll, "to *mate.*"

"Yes," I reply. "She was instantly in over her head. Being Ordered to Rex wasn't like being paired with an ordinary resident of Serendee."

"He's 'Chosen' and that put Imogene in the spotlight—again." She uses finger quotes around the word chosen. "I'm well aware of Timothy's bullshit hierarchy."

A laugh bubbles from my chest. Levi frowns at me, but I don't care. I raise an eyebrow at the woman. "You're ballsy."

"Yeah, well Timothy tried his hardest to break me down, and he almost did it." She frowns. "He's punishing Imogene for my betrayal, isn't he?"

"Partially," Levi admits. "He definitely is focused on her. He's convinced that she's got bad blood—Regressive."

"God, these stupid terms." She looks between us. "You know he made all of these up one night after too many tequila shots, right? Regressive. The Way. Enlightenment. He added to them as needed—when someone stepped out of his ever-changing line."

"Fallen," I add, the word making me feel dirty.

"Correction," Levi whispers.

She studies him for a long moment, then says, "Exactly."

I lean forward, resting my elbows on my knees. "Rex has been disillusioned with Serendee and his father's methods for a while. He's suspicious of his mother's death. Judgmental of the hypocrisy between the Chosen and the rest of the community. Falling for Imogene has only amplified that."

Camille straightens. "What do you mean 'falling' for her?"

Levi and I share a look, we're not about to admit to the unconventional relationship we have, not when we've just gotten our foot in the door. But she can know the truth about Rex.

"Rex loves her," Levi says. "He wants to protect her—at any cost."

"Then why isn't she here? Why didn't he get her out?"

It's Levi that answers. "The truth is that Imogene wasn't ready to leave on her own. She was committed to Serendee, to following The Way and finding Enlightenment. She'd been chosen for a special group and was very excited about it."

"What kind of group?" Camille asks, warily.

"A women's group, run by Anex's spiritual wife—"

"You're fucking with me."

"No," I say. "Anex has additional wives now. One in particular, Margaret, has the most sway. She invited Imogene to an exclusive group that involved offering damaging collateral."

Her eyebrow rises. "You mean leverage. Blackmail."

Levi nods. "Yes."

"The final part was a ritual." Bile rises in my throat. "A branding."

Camille's face pales. "He branded my daughter?"

"With his initials," I admit. Then, knowing she needs to hear the rest. I place my hand on my body, pointing to the location. "Right here."

A tremor wracks through her body, so violent that I start to reach for her. She jerks back, giving me a cold look of warning, and I give her space. "This is on me. I never should have left her with that monster."

"You couldn't have known he was going to go this far," Levi says. Of course, the problem is that I did know. Anex told me his plans for

Imogene, and he didn't warn me about this. "His focus on Imogene is... it's different."

"The night we found out about the branding, is the night Rex decided she would leave. He was livid. He knew why his father marked his mate. He was claiming her as his own," I explain, aware that every word I say is making it worse. "He was going to force her to leave—to come to you. But Anex called a last-minute meeting—it was late, the music sounded, and we knew that not showing up would tip him off. It felt safer to go and leave after."

Camille's eyes are ringed in red when she guesses, "But that never happened."

"He called us out in front of the entire community. He read Imogene's collateral, proof that she'd been Regressive. That we had broken rules. He banished me and Levi—tossing us out of Serendee, and forced Imogene, Rex, and Silas into Re-education."

"That's not all he wants from her, is it?" she asks.

"Anex wants her to be his next spiritual wife," Levi says quietly. "They'll be mated at the equinox."

"If I could get her out, I would've done it years ago." Her hands fist at her sides. "Why are you here? Just to hurt me? To pick at old wounds? To show me how, after all this time, he still has control over me?"

"We're here because we have nowhere else to go. No one else understands what we've been through." But it's more than that. "You understand Anex—Timothy Wray—what he is capable of. We need someone as desperate to get Imogene out as we are."

"You care for her?" she asks, blinking as though she's seeing us for the first time.

"Rex and Silas are our brothers," Levi says. "Imogene... she's important to us. We won't leave them behind."

"How? How do we get them out?"

"First," Levi says, running his hands over his thighs, "we have to get inside Serendee."

"That's not going to happen," she snaps.

Levi tilts his head. "It will if Anex thinks we've got something he wants."

I frown. His eyes shift to Camille and recognition hits the two of us at the same time.

"Camille—" I whisper, but she cuts me off.

"Me." Her expression is impassive as she repeats, "He wants me."

"You're the one that got away. The only thing he wants. The failure he needs to redeem." His voice seems steadier. More confident and I realize Levi had this plan all along. It's why we're here. "The only way we're getting them out is if we trade them for you."

78

———————

I mogene

"Imogene."

"Shoot." The sound of my name makes me skip a stitch and the needle stabs in my finger.

"Sorry to startle you," Margaret says. She's standing in the doorway of the common room where me and several of the pregnant women have spent the afternoon sewing baby clothes. "But I need you to come with me."

Her voice is light—unassuming—but my chest clenches regardless. I feel like all I do is try to keep a low profile, stay off the radar of anyone with connections to Anex. I should know better. This is his world, and I'm nothing but a planet caught in his orbit.

"Of course," I say, trying to keep the blood beading at the tip of my finger from spilling on the white cotton dress I'd been working on. Maria, who is sitting next to me, takes it without a word.

"Thank you." I stand, giving her an appreciative grin.

I'm met with silence and a blank expression. We've spoken very little since hanging laundry together. There's nothing much to say. She thinks I'm Regressive.

She's not wrong.

The other women watch this exchange closely, and I ignore them as I walk past them to Margaret. When I reach her, I ask, "Do I need to change?"

Her eyes flick down to my basic gray dress. It's in sharp contrast to her and the other pregnant women, with their growing bellies, and swollen breasts, bared for all to see. I've been trying to acclimate to this change—to the revelation of skin and intimacy—but it's so far removed from the way we were raised, that it's impossible.

How is this okay, but my behavior is deemed Regressive?

"You're fine." She takes a step back. "We shouldn't waste time anyway. He's waiting."

He.

My pulse beats, the urge to run overwhelming. But just over her shoulder, standing by the exit, is one of Anex's guards. There is no running.

"Do you know what this is about?" I ask as we exit the center and start up the road toward the Main House. As much as I dread this, the fresh air feels nice, and the stretch in my legs. I've been trapped in that building for weeks.

"Nothing bad." She gives me a small smile. "In fact, I think you're going to be pleasantly surprised."

That information does nothing to allay my fears, instead sending a chill of warning up my spine. The feeling doesn't decrease as we walk up the steps and wind through the maze of staircases and hall-ways. It's hard to believe that this was my home a few months ago.

"You know," she says, pausing in the hallway I know leads to Anex's private rooms, "you're caught in the darkness of this journey right now, Imogene. The bad days leading to the good. The narrow part of the path. You've already been accepted. Chosen and Marked. Anex isn't the bad guy here. He's waiting for you to see the way out, but only you can do that." She takes my hand. "Stop fighting him. It'll make everything fall into alignment."

Margaret didn't grow up here. She wasn't raised in a Donum or told to conform. Her dress and autonomy prove this. She probably thinks that she convinced him to let her wear these clothes. To plaster on makeup and become sexually free. But no one manipulates Anex. She's just the vehicle he's using to change our world.

"You realize," the words spill from me impulsively, "that you think you're different. That his affection for you will be enough to protect you. But it won't. He'll turn on you just as fast as he turned on his own son. On Elon, Levi, and Rex." Her eyes narrow as I speak the truth. "On his real wife, Beatrice."

"Beatrice was a fool," she snaps, her façade slipping. "Just like your mother."

"No. You're a fool. The rest of us were born into this disaster. You chose it, Margaret. You're the one who is blinded by the man behind that door."

"That man is a god. He is the only one that can bring any of us peace. As you're about to find out now." Without another word, she squares her shoulders and opens the door.

My eyes go straight to Anex's chair, but it's empty. The space next to it isn't. My stomach caves, and my breath catches in my throat.

Rex.

His eyes pin to mine when he sees me, raking down my body in a long, assessing gaze.

"What..." I ask, unable to finish the thought. It's good to see him. Even though he looks thin and tired, that same commanding presence defines him. I glance at Margaret. "What's going on?"

"He earned it," she says, stepping back.

When I look back at Rex he's striding forward. The gap vanishes, and he scoops me against him. I sink against him. The man I once feared, that took everything from me, is now one of the few things to bring me solace.

I feel the difference in his body. The thinning of his arms and the lost bulk in his body.

He earned it.

I pull back, getting a good look at his face. His cheeks are hollow, and there's faint bruising near his temple. "What did you do?" I ask quietly.

"What I had to," he admits, but there's no shadow of guilt in his piercing eyes. "I needed to see you. To make sure you're okay."

"I'm fine." It's not entirely true, but physically, yes, I'm solid. For now.

His hand runs up my neck, settling on my jaw. "I should've—"

"Stop. Whatever time we have together, it's not enough to go into should'ves."

He frowns, gaze darting between my eyes and my mouth. Fingers on one hand digging into my hip. There's a hesitation there, but that is not who my mate is—he takes what he wants, and I know for certain he wants me. I push up on my toes and brush my lips against his, reminding him of who we are.

That's all it takes, that one small, heated brush, flesh against flesh for him to snap back into himself. His tongue seeks mine, strong and coaxing. Rex roughly pulls me against him, and for the first time, the balance between us is even. He needs me as much as I need him.

That's the moment our armor falls away and I know for absolute certain that this man is different than the one I was Ordered to. There's no façade here. No farce. No mind games or manipulation.

There's only us.

Until, there isn't.

"Ah, the lover's reunion." Anex's voice carries from across the room. My spine tenses, habit and self-preservation propelling me to bow and honor my leader. Rex doesn't allow it, hands cupping my cheeks as he continues to kiss me. He groans regretfully against my mouth, before stepping back. "Don't stop on my account, Son."

Rex turns, his hand dropping to hold mine. "You told me we'd have time—*alone*."

"That was when I was under the assumption that everyone was playing by the rules." Rex's fingers twitch against mine, and his shoulders stiffen, the armor setting back in place. "I've allowed this meeting because Rex fulfilled a promise to me. Which," he addresses his son with his eyebrow raised, impressed, "well done. I've never had someone hand over her entire fortune to me so quickly. Whatever you did to her must have been magnificent."

There's an implication in his words—that Rex had done something to convince a recruit to hand over her fortune. I'm not stupid. I'm well aware of what Rex and the others are required to do to fill the coffers of Serendee. He'd made a promise to me, that he wouldn't sleep with another woman, but none of us have autonomy right now. It's nothing but a constant state of survival.

If Anex wanted a reaction from me, he doesn't get one, and continues, shifting his blue eyes to me. "Unfortunately, I can't say the same for Imogene who continues her Regressive ways."

"I—" I swallow past the lump in my throat, "I don't know what you're talking about."

Anex crosses the room, passing us, and approaching Margaret who is standing near the door. He kisses her on the cheek, lifting a hand to her full breast, and squeezing it gently. He then bends, pressing another soft kiss to her belly. Once I would have thought this was sweet—a loving father expressing his delight for a new child, but now I know better. It's a display of power. That Margaret, her body and the child inside, belongs to him. Just like we all do.

He faces us and says, "Security caught Silas going into the Childcare center—entering the back door carrying a box from the apothecary. Once this was confirmed, Healer Bloom conducted a complete inventory of our supplies and discovered you'd been taking supplements not prescribed to you. In fact, they have the opposite, desired effect."

The blood rushes down my body, leaving my head woozy and light. As if he can tell, Rex's hand drops mine and circles my waist.

"That's Silas' issue," he says, pulling me to his side. "Not Imogene's. She couldn't have known."

Anex shakes his head. "You think I'm stupid."

"No," I blurt. All that does is turn his gaze from his son onto me. My knees shake at his attention, increasing as he walks over.

"Oh, Imogene. I'd like to say my son and his friends corrupted you, but we both know it's the other way around." His hands snap out, one grabbing for my collar, the other clasping my skull.

"Get your filthy hands off her!" Rex lunges, but the tell-tale sound of a gun racking forces him still. Erik, the guard is across the room, the gun leveled at him, a hair's breath away from shooting.

"Rex," I whisper, terror squeezing my vocal chords. "Don't."

He grimaces and swears under his breath. Anex cuts his eyes between us, then wrenches my head and neck apart. "Care to tell me where you got this little bruise?" His eyes narrow. "Careful, Imogene, I'll know if you're lying."

"It was an accident," I reply quietly. "While I was doing chores."

"It looks like a love bite." He releases me, fingers trailing down my neck. "If you haven't seen Silas, been intimate with him, then where did you get this? Are there other men trying to claim you?"

That last question is a trick. He knows there are no other men that can get access to me. He wants me to report Silas for breaking the rules. I can't—*won't*.

"I understand. You don't want to betray one of your lovers." The corners of his mouth turn down. "Well, I'll save you, Imogene. One of your housemates saw the mark directly after his intrusion."

It had to be Maria. The hurt from knowing she went to Anex about me... it burns in my gut.

"Do you deny it?"

I can't speak, but I manage to shake my head.

"For the violation of meeting with another member of the Fallen, for going against medical policy, and most of all," his jaw tenses, "betraying my trust, you'll receive Correction."

"Hell no, she won't." Rex moves toward his father, uncaring that the gun tracks his every move. "That's not happening."

"There is no alternative, Son. She willingly violated the rules of Serendee."

"*Your* rules! No one voted on these. There were no agreements. It's your unilateral command."

"Do you think you're shocking when you say things like that? That you've revealed a dark secret of this place?" he asks. He walks over to the mahogany chest pushed against the wall, opens a drawer, and removes something. He turns. "Serendee is under my will, Rex. It has been since the day I purchased the land. Since I created the bylaws that we adhere to. The residents of this community have chosen to follow my path. My way." He walks back over, the dark object clenched in his hand. I can't see what it is. "It pains me that you are choosing the opposite. That you, your friend, and this girl have all decided to work against me."

"We will never be on your side, Anex," Rex declares. "Never again. Just let us go. We don't need money, or anything more than the clothes on our back. Banish us—all three of us—and you'll never have to worry about us again."

"I would if I could." His father stops before us. "But letting you go would be the easy way out, and finding Enlightenment isn't easy. It's arduous. Exhausting. Painstaking. I will not release you from finding your way."

His eyes are on me as he says this, and as it is every time Anex has blessed me with his attention, I'm caught in his vortex. Except this time, I don't feel the desire to appease him. I feel the urge to run, because the way he looks at me, the small curl to his lips, it's the look of a predator and I'm nothing but prey.

"Sit," he says simply, nodding at a hardback chair.

"Anex." My voice is a whisper.

His hand rises and I see the object. A paddle. Slightly larger than a hairbrush, with silver rivets embedded across the back. "Come here, Imogene, and prepare to receive your Correction."

Rex vibrates next to me. "If you touch a hair on my mate's body, I will end you."

Anex sighs, deep and exasperated. "I appreciate your bravado, Son, but you don't have the upper hand here. You never do. When will you learn that?" He waves over the guard. "I'd have you remove him, but he needs to see this. See what happens when they break the rules." His eyes go to the gun. "Keep him in line."

"Yes, sir." Erik's eyes never leave Rex, as if he knows that all my mate needs is a split second.

"Imogene, come," Anex commands. "Or I'll be forced to make you." His head tilts. "Or is that what you want? Is that what gets you wet? Binding you up? Forcing you?"

"Stop!" Rex roars. "I swear to God."

Anex snorts. "There is only one God here, and I've already made up my mind. Imogene will be punished, and you'll watch." He jerks his head to another guard stationed at the door. "As will a selected audience."

"Punish me instead," Rex blurts. "Leave her alone."

Annex's eyes narrow. "I'm sure you'd like that, but no. That's not how this works."

The guard opens the door and a small group files in. I know the majority of them—the women, at least. They were all part of the secret group I'd joined. My eyes meet Kayla's—the woman I'd person-ally held down while she was branded, talking her through the pain. The scent of burning flesh, singed into my nostrils. The scent I will always associate with guilt and regret.

But she doesn't look regretful. No. She and the others surrounded Anex like a harem in their flowy dresses and painted eyes. I would have been one of those women—should've been.

The urge to run across the room, grab Kayla by the shoulders and shout, *'Can you see how easy it is for him to turn on you?'* That the brand doesn't protect you, it makes you a target? They're Collateral. I know for certain it will be used against them. Not if, but when.

"Fuck," Rex swears, and my eyes are drawn back to the door.

One last person walks through. His hands are bound in front of him, tied at the wrist. A watchful black-clad guard stands nearby. My heart cracks in two, because I'd hoped he would leave him out of this and focus his punishment on me alone, but no, Anex is always two steps ahead.

Silas.

"Everyone, take a seat," Anex says, gesturing to the area around his chair. They file in, curious looks on every face—everyone but Silas, whose skin is pale.

Rex's eyes dart around the room, at the guards and the new witnesses. To Silas and then to me. They finally land on his father. The tension trembles between them, or maybe that's just the fear spiking up my spine.

"May I approach?" Rex asks.

"With caution." That simply means Erik never lowers his weapon.

Rex moves toward his father, and he speaks, voice so low that no one in the room can hear. No one but me. "You can't Correct her like this. Not when you want her for your own." He swallows painfully at the admission his father plans on keeping me for himself. "You'll see those scars every time you're with her, a constant reminder of this event. The humiliation and defeat."

"Marks of her journey," he counters. "That she deserves."

Rex continues as if his father hasn't spoken. "More than that, she'll hate you. She'll poison any future children you have with her into hating you too—and she'll have the proof she needs to convince them."

The thought of losing more children seems to make Anex consider the argument. He rests a hand on Rex's shoulder. "You make a good point. I've trained you so well, Son. I can sense the leadership that runs through you. My blood. My power." He presses the paddle into Rex's hand. "You do it."

"What?" The device falls to the ground like it's made of fire. "No."

Rex has done many things to me. Hurt me in many ways, but he's never Corrected me. Levi, of course. Elon, when I needed it, but not Rex. This kind of behavior goes against his values—the ones that make him such a threat to his father.

"Do it," Anex says, eyes darting to the paddle on the carpet. "That way, when I see these scars on her body, I'll remember the strife and trouble it took to get her to a place of Redemption. And I'll remember that you helped."

"You're fucking deranged, you know that, right?"

He shrugs, the gesture small and innocent. "There's a long history of people calling genius insanity. I'm willing to join their club."

They stare at one another for a long beat, a power struggle that ends with one of them Correcting me. In a slow, sweeping movement, Rex bends, swiping the paddle off the floor.

I witness the whole thing, the entire exchange where it becomes strikingly clear that I *will* be Corrected. I have no choice in that. My mate has just managed to negotiate who inflicts the pain.

Anex crosses the room, heading over to his chair to surround himself with the small group of spectators.

"I'm sorry," Rex says quietly as he turns to me.

I lift my chin and clear the tremble from my throat. "Let's get this over with."

79

———

R^{ex}

I hate everything about this.

The knowing, smug expression on my father's face. He has me right where he wants me—controlled, demeaned, and inflicting pain on my mate.

I loathe the guilt deep in Silas' eyes as he watches this scene unfold.

I hate the fact that Jasmine and Robert have been brought in the room to watch this sideshow. Can they tell this is all part of the same manipulation tactic I used on them? Trading bodies and souls? Exploiting intimacy. Bile rises to the back of my throat from awareness. I deserve this for what I've done, but Imogene...

She looks at me with those wide doe eyes, and my heart skips a beat.

I may deserve all of it, but she doesn't.

She's a pawn in this game between me and my father. A prized toy we're squabbling over like two boys on the playground. It's wrong, so fucking wrong, but there's no out for either of us. I cursed her the moment I picked her for my mate, but she was doomed long before that because of her mother's betrayal.

"I know some of you may find this excessive, or even barbaric," Anex says, from his throne. "But such is the resolve of The Way. It doesn't adhere to the laws of man—the moralistic and ethical. It's harsh and unyielding." His tone has shifted, lowering to that mesmerizing tenor that lulls the most Regressive into compliance. "Enlightenment comes in many forms. Imogene has expressed in her logs that she feels closest to her higher self when in a state of Correction. What Rex is giving her is a gift."

His justifications—his lies—they make the hard ball of rage inside of me send a spark of energy through my limbs.

Margaret is on one side of my father, Jasmine on the other. That's who he's addressing—Jasmine. He has plans for her now that her money is locked in place. From the corner of my eye, I see him stroke her hair, doling out affection and praise.

The look on Jasmine's face when our eyes meet? Pity.

I grip the paddle and take a deep breath.

Anex clears his throat and nods to the chair in the middle of the room. It has a high back, made of solid, carved wood. I remember it being in my childhood home—placed at the head of the dining room table. My father's first throne, back when he was only the leader of my family, not an entire community. Before he eliminated his biggest threat: my mother.

"Undress," he commands Imogene once we're positioned near the chair. Her hands move to the high neck of her dress, to the first of the long row of tiny buttons. A tremor runs through her fingertips, shaking uncontrollably.

"Here." I step forward, placing the paddle on the seat of the chair. "Let me help."

She nods, words seemingly caught in her throat. I keep my eyes on hers, finding a strength there to get through this moment. The tedious nature of the task, the small, slippery buttons, the slow reveal of her pale skin underneath.

Soft.

Perfect.

Mine.

"We'll get through this, okay?" I tell her once her dress sags from her shoulders. "You and me, no one else."

It's a dumb thing to say. We're in a room full of spectators. Captives, like Silas. My father. His followers. But when I look at her, at her beautiful face, I feel it: me and her. Us.

The dress drops, sliding down her narrow hips, hitting the floor. Reaching for the hem of undergarments, I lift her top, exposing her to the room. My eyes fall to her nipples, watching as they harden. I run my fingers down her sides, resting them on the waistband of her shorts. I pause, unable to push them off—unwilling to show her perfect body to these vultures lying in wait.

Her hands cover mine, urging me to finish what we've started. She shimmies the shorts over her hips, and they fall with the dress, pooled around her feet. My gaze falls to the brand, still scabby after all this time. Painful and slow-healing. Every act from my father sends a message, and that brand is the loudest. His initials, bold but hidden. His ownership.

I press my thumb into the soft skin just above it and clarity strikes. He had to brand her because he knows that deep down, she'll never belong to him. Not like she belongs to me. To Silas, Elon, and Levi.

That thought allows the anger and rage, all the frustration and dark thoughts to vanish for a moment, another emotion taking hold. It's unfamiliar and pure. It's pure instinct—maybe, fuck, maybe it's the ever elusive Enlightenment. Whatever it is, it propels me to take her face in my hands and brush my thumb over her full lips, whispering, "I love you."

The smallest, brightest, most life-affirming smile tugs at her lips. "I love you too."

Before I can process it, act on it, she inhales deeply and then turns to face the chair, bending, hands flat on the arms. She's offering her body to me, under duress, but offering it all the same. It's wrong, but my cock twitches at the sight of her soft, supple flesh and all I want to do is—

"I love your initiative, Imogene, but you won't be bent over for this. Sit in the chair, sweetheart."

I blink, my father's voice snapping me back to the moment.

She rights herself, hands moving to cover her breasts and pussy. Her forehead creased in confusion. I feel the same.

"What are you asking me to do?" A thought flickers in my mind. "You want me to beat her face? That's foolish even for you."

"Of course not." He waves this off as if it's a ridiculous thought. As if I'm the sadistic lunatic. "Her breasts. A lash for every Regressive act."

Next to me, Imogene's arm flattens across her tits.

I start to ask why, but I know the answer. Imogene does get a thrill from spanking. She and Levi have been experimenting with that more and more. My father isn't willing to go over existing territory. He wants to push her further. Degrade her more. Expose her to the room—face and body.

"How many is that?" I try my hardest to keep my voice even.

Anex licks his lips and holds up a hand. One finger ticking off at a time. "*Meeting* with Silas. *Altering* her supplements. *Spreading* Regressive thoughts to the other women in the Center. *Lying* about it when given the opportunity to confess. *Defying* her leader."

Five. There are five in all.

"Rex," he says. "Do it right."

The threat is implied. Do it right, or the consequences will be far worse. Reaching around Imogene, I grab the paddle off the chair. Schooling my face in the hard, controlled expression my father raised me to wear in situations like this, I command, "Sit." She does, dropping her arm, revealing her breasts without being told. I brush a strand of hair off her cheek. "Good girl."

In our world, women's bodies are hidden under thick cotton, high collars, and complicated buttons. In the secular world, I've had my share of tits. I've sucked, fucked, bitten, and come on many. But

Imogene's are the first I've revered; that I've wanted to cherish. I take them in now, full and round, nipples a dark peaked pink.

I say a silent prayer that she doesn't hate me when this is over.

The first slap comes without warning. A hard strike to the soft side of her breast, driving it into the other. She cries out, eyes instantly watering, cheeks turning red.

Her hands grip the arms of the chair.

"One," Anex says from his throne. "Don't hold back."

I switch hands, elbow back, slamming the paddle against the other breast. Welts rise from the raised surface. Her teeth bear down on her bottom lip and a fat tear slides down her cheek. The sight of it triggers something inside of me, and I lower the paddle. "Imogene—"

"Keep going." She cuts me off, her eyes forged of steel. Lifting her chin she whispers, "That's two."

Again, I paddle her, my grip wavering, catching her nipple with the rivets. She yelps but swallows it quickly, pale throat bobbing dramatically. It's after that third strike that I see it. My eyes draw up to hers, then back down. Her hips shift, the slightest squirm.

My balls twitch in response.

Licking my bottom lip, I slap her again, just the tips and hitting both of her nipples at the same time. Imogene groans, head falling back. Her fingers tighten around the arm of the chair, but I realize now it's not out of the urge to run—it's to stop from touching herself.

Sweat gathers on the back of my neck and my cock thickens, the urge to bury myself in this girl—my mate—dire. But I know better than to let my father see what is transpiring between us.

I grip the paddle, thinking of how I want to do this, how I want to please my mate. How far I can take this—how far can I push her? Because that's the truth about Imogene, she's looking for that line and she hasn't found it yet.

I reach out, rearing back, striking her hard, twice. She screams, unable to hold it back, but I drop the paddle, my hands snatching out for her nipples. Her eyes widen at my forcefulness—at going off script—and I twist them, sharp and hard, driving another scream from her. Her legs fall apart, and I see the slick wetness between them.

I grab her by the throat and lift her from the chair like a goddamn rag doll.

A slow clap fills the room, followed by my father's voice. "Bravo, Son. Gave her exactly what she deserved—and a little more." He chuckles. "You pretend you're different from me, but we know the truth, don't we?"

I don't take the bait. I just say, "I'm going with her."

He doesn't fight me, just waves us off. The show is over. He's moving on, and when I grab Imogene by the waist, holding her up as we pass by him and his shiny group, I see Jasmine's hand on his lap, stroking an obvious erection.

Well, I guess she will fit in here perfectly, after all.

Silas is the last person we pass, still bound and guarded. Our eyes lock, his red-rimmed and worried. Something deep transpires between us. Something I'm not ready to accept.

In a small sitting room. One where Anex entertains members of the inner circle. Female members. There's only one way out and I shut it behind us.

"Rex." My name comes out as a moan, and she sags against my side, body rubbing against mine.

"Hold on, baby," I say, kissing her neck. "I'll take care of it."

She's impatient—grinding her pussy against my thigh. I feel the warmth through my pants. Her fingers twist in my shirt and she looks up at me, tears streaming down her face.

Not out of fear or humiliation. Out of want.

Reaching between her legs, I groan at the slippery heat. "God, Imogene."

She bucks against my palm, her pussy seeking friction. Something primal comes over me, the urge to satisfy my mate. I slam her into the wall, using the surface to hold upright. Crashing into her body, tongue thrusting inside her mouth, two fingers sinking deep in her pussy.

She cries out, teeth rattling. I fuck into her, seeking the quick release she so desperately needs. The walls of her pussy are tight, clamping around my fingers. I add in a third, stretching her.

"Let go, Imogene," I tell her, licking her tongue. "You're safe here. You're a good girl. You're such a good, good, girl."

Her eyes open, meeting mine. I grab her thigh, lifting her leg, and hook it over my waist. The shift in angle is what triggers the release. I feel every wave of it, in her straightening spine, the clench of her pussy, the vibrating groan deep in her chest. Her head falls to the side, the tension finally easing. I hold her up, hold her *to* me, and lift her in my arms. Crossing the room, my hand thrusts out to brace us as I lower us to the couch and settle her in my lap.

"I don't know what's wrong with me," she says quietly. With the urgency past, I take a moment to assess her wounds. Her tits look rough, with red welts rising, nipples looking raw and sore. "The more it hurts, the more I want."

"It's a kink, baby." I press a gentle kiss against the swell of her breast. "Silas taught you about that?"

She nods, chest slowly rising and falling at the feel of my lips. "He told me, but that in there... it went somewhere different."

"Exhibitionism. Punishment. Degradation." I ghost my palms over her nipples, barely touching them. "My father primed you for this kind of desire, Imogene. The corrections and deprivation. The need for approval. He's a goddamn son of a bitch."

"That makes it worse. He's everywhere, Rex. In my mind and body."

My heart feels heavy, weighed down by the trauma of what we just went through. How sex and intimacy is always part of a game—a manipulation.

"I went too far," I tell her. "I lost myself in the moment. It was wrong."

She shifts in my lap, her crotch heavy against my cock. "You gave me what I wanted."

"You only want it because he's created that desire in you." I grab her face, forcing her to look at me. "He may have created this, but you get to own it." My thumb catches a tear. I fucking hate seeing her cry. "I get to be the one that helps you through it. Not him."

Her lips blaze across my cheek. "And I get to help you."

She rises to her knees, hands grabbing at my waist, creating room to push down my pants. My shirt goes next and then she's back on me, pussy warming my swollen dick. Her pale hair curtains around us and I take her tits in my hands, carefully squeezing them together, lathing my tongue over her nipples. I want her to feel the good in my touch—not just the pain. There's a place for both of those but right now, in this brief respite from my father's insanity, I want her to feel cared for.

She looks up, eyebrows furrowed.

"What?" I ask.

"Why are you being so sweet?"

Fair. We've had our share of hostile encounters. I'd forced my cock in her mouth. The way I took her virginity. My drunken late-night fucks.

"You deserve to be cherished," I confess. "Treated like a queen. It's okay to want it hard, but it's also okay to let someone take care of you." I slide my hand behind her neck, pulling our foreheads together. "Let me take care of my mate."

"Can I take care of you, too?" she asks.

"Fuck yes."

Imogene's hand falls between us, gripping my cock. I feel huge against the spread of her fingers, desperate because I fight the urge to come the second she touches me. She jacks me, thumb grazing over the sticky tip, and it becomes hard to breathe.

"Baby, that feels so good." My eyes are cast down, watching her work me, watching those perfect tits sway between us. I look up and capture her mouth with mine. "I want to be inside. Feel you around me. It's been so fucking long."

Lifting again, she rests a hand on my shoulder and angles herself with the tip of my cock, pressing me to her entrance. My balls quiver, it's been so long since I've had this woman. Felt her skin, smelled her scent, had her this close and I don't want it to go too fast, but I also know that door is going to open at any minute and reality's going to come rushing back in.

Imogene sets the pace, lowering herself, taking me in, inch by inch. With my eyes closed, my hands hold onto her hips, reveling in the feel of her, how her walls hug me tight. We sit like that for a long moment, just feeling one another. I open my eyes and find her watching me.

"What's wrong?"

"Did you mean it?" she asks. "What you said in there."

That I love her.

"I meant it." Fuck yes, I meant it.

"How do you know? Are you sure it wasn't just the moment? The stress of the situation?" She frowns. "It's okay if that's what happened. I won't get upset."

I rest my hand on her lower back, pulling her as close as possible, which is pretty fucking close since my cock is buried inside of her. "We're connected, Imogene. Physically and emotionally. Hard against soft, lost against broken." I move my hips, barely, softly. "He can drive us apart, force us to hurt one another, banish and abuse." Moving faster now, but with restraint, I kiss her breast, licking a hot trail to her neck. "He can do whatever he wants, but ultimately, we're bonded. We're mates. We've probably been so since that day on the cliff, two messed up kids, traumatized from losing our mothers."

She shifts against me, arms linked around my neck. Nose to nose, I stare into her eyes, willing her to believe me. I didn't agree to a mate because I wanted love. But I found it anyway. In this beautiful girl writhing on top of me.

The room fills with the sound of our breath, the slip-slide of our bodies, the whisper of our voices. I tell her again. "I love you," warm on her ear, for only her to hear. And when I fill her with my seed, hot cum, buried deep inside, I vow anew to get her out of here.

Sagging onto me, bodies still connected, she looks up and says, "Silas..."

I shake my head. There's only one reason my father left us alone.

He had business to attend to. Silas is already gone. My father will not abide by his betrayal.

Next, he'll come for me. This time together? It's another game, a way to lull me into thinking I have the slightest thread of control. That if I work with him, we can come to an agreement, but I know my father. He's biding his time before he banishes me for good. All that will be left is the prize he truly wants.

I'm selfish enough not to let him have her.

80

L evi

The squeal and hiss of the city bus outside jolts me awake—but it's not like I was sleeping very deeply. The noises are different here. Mechanical. Loud. *Secular.* The bus came by several times overnight, along with the constant passing of cars. The lights flashing in the window a constant reminder that I'm not home. That I've been Banished.

It's more than the distractions though. My brain won't shut off, not with so much at stake. I keep going over my plan again and again, looking for loopholes. Mistakes.

The springs in the bed next to mine creak, straining from Elon's weight. The upstairs of Camille's bungalow has spare rooms. Twin beds in each bland, nondescript room. The drawers are filled with extra clothing—clearly for people with no possessions—people on the run.

We're refugees.

Dressing in a worn T-shirt and loose sweatpants that I find in the drawer, I leave Elon to get more rest. It's the first full night's sleep he's had since being Banished. The first night without a fight down at the bar, trying to scrounge together enough money for us to survive. I wonder if they noticed. I wonder if the people in Serendee notice us being gone. Are we missed? Or are we just a reminder of what could happen to anyone that breaks the rules.

Halfway down the stairs, I hear a voice—two voices. Camille and another woman. I pause, unsure if I should interrupt. Slowly, I take one more step and peer around the corner.

"I feel so helpless. Like, if I could just talk to her—get her out of that place—and make her listen, she'd see how crazy all of this is."

The two women are in the former dining room, sitting on two of the chairs that form the circle. A teapot and two cups sit on the coffee table. Camille's forehead has a deep, concerned crease slashed through the normally smooth skin. "I'm not going to tell you that you shouldn't feel this way. You should. Your sister has been behind the walls of Serendee for months now. She's in a dangerous position."

"We've just always been so close. How could she push me away like this?"

I study the woman, trying to get a better view. She looks to be in her mid-thirties. Dressed in secular clothes, a V-neck sweater and jeans. Gold bracelets wrist and a smart watch circle her wrist. Her eyes are red-rimmed, tears building in the corners. There's something vaguely familiar about them. I've probably met her sister, perhaps taught her in my courses.

"Gabi," Camille says, reaching behind her to a box of tissues. She snatches out a few and hands them to the other woman. "You have to understand, none of this is about you. Or anyone else. Her erratic behavior is the result of the methods conducted in that place. The residents of Serendee are under deep control. Sleep, diet, and sensory deprivation are part of the tactics. Fear that they may lose favor with the leader of the group."

"I've watched some of his videos. Early on, Kayla was trying to talk me into taking courses with her." She dabs at the corner of her eyes with the tissue. "How is this guy appealing? I mean, he's attractive, but otherwise I don't get it. Listening to him talk about all this stuff, Enlightenment and The Way and all that bullshit just... well, it sounds like bullshit."

Camille laughs. "It *is* bullshit, and Timothy slings it with perfection." The way she uses Anex's birth name so casually is unnerving. No one calls him that. He's said over and over that he is no longer that person. Calling him Timothy Wray is with intention—one Camille wields like a sword. "You're right though. He's handsome. That gets people in the door, especially women. But he has this knack for finding a weak spot. A hollow place inside of people that they desperately want filled." She takes a sip of her tea. "What is Kayla's weak spot?"

Kayla. My thoughts sort, flipping through the files in my mind, ultimately landing on the right one. Kayla Montclair. Priority recruit due to her status of being the heir to a publishing empire. She's a newer recruit. Heir to the Montclair Publishing fortune.

"She was engaged," Gabi says, "and was in the middle of planning a very extravagant wedding. Then she found out he was cheating on her. The entire situation was very public and humiliating. After that she started immersing herself into a lot of self-help programs, which we had access to because of the publishing house. Yoga retreats. Health and wellness workshops. At first it seemed good that she was throwing herself into the business. My father was ecstatic. She was able to test products, go to seminars, get free courses. It was obvious she was really seeking 'something,' you know."

"That's the kind of thing Timothy is good at. Spotting that 'something' no one else can."

"Slowly she just drifted away. Her language sounded like nonsense. All these fake terms. She started losing weight and looked like she hadn't slept in a month. Then, one day I went by her apartment, and it was clear she'd abandoned it. Left all her clothes and possessions." Her eyebrows rise. "Everything, but the bank accounts."

Camille doesn't seem surprised by any of this and confirms that by saying, "As horrifying as it sounds, all of this is right out of the Serendee playbook. She's not the first to be taken in by this man. He's good. Very, very good. And once he has them locked behind the walls there's little chance of them leaving, especially on their own."

"So, what do we do? How do we save Kayla?"

Camille squares her shoulders. "We gather evidence. Keep trying to make contact. Don't push. Play by her rules. I'll connect you to our private investigator who has been helping us gather information for years."

"Okay, I can do that."

"Most of all though, you have something different from the others that have come through here. Influence. Your family is connected. For the first time, we may be able to get people to listen."

"I've tried. The police couldn't do anything. Said she was there on her own free-will."

"We have to go higher than the local police and see if we can find someone else in a similar situation. Politicians. The county prosecutor. Maybe the attorney general. Whoever your family knows that can dig into the dirty secrets of Serendee."

A strange feeling spreads across my chest at the idea of really exposing the innerworkings of Serendee. I watch as Gabi frowns. "What kind of dirty secrets are you talking about?"

"You and I know the real focus is getting the victims of this con man out of his control, but, as you know, that's nearly impossible to prove." Camille grabs a file from the seat next to hers. She opens it and starts flipping through papers. "The way we're going to take him down isn't about kidnapping or holding people against their will. It's through boring, stupid stuff like tax fraud, embezzlement, running illegal businesses." She pauses, eyes flicking from the paper to Gabi's face. "Then we expose him for the monster he really is: Human trafficking."

The words linger in the air. The real dark and dirty secret of Serendee. The Fallen. Those sent to Re-education. Corrections.

I look down at my hands, clean and smooth. The scars, the *blood*, from the pain I inflicted are still there even if you can't see them.

"I get the feeling Timothy is going after bigger and bigger marks —people with extreme wealth, like your sister. The government may not care about people, but they sure as fuck care about money. Especially money they want to get their grubby hands on—taxes."

"But why? Isn't the whole point of Serendee that it's self-sustaining?"

"Once upon a time, maybe. But those days are long gone. Serendee is there to feed Timothy's insatiable ego, and he's going to need money and influence to do it." She reaches out and takes the woman's hand. "We're close, Gabi. I've been trying to find a way to bring this man down for years, and for the first time I'm hopeful."

"I just want my sister back."

"That's all I want, too."

I step back up the staircase as the women say goodbye, considering the exchange. Camille's program is more than just helping victims and families of so-called cults. She's not just focused on saving individuals. She's determined to bring Anex and Serendee down. I don't even fully understand all of the terms she just used. *Tax fraud, embezzlement, illegal businesses.* Taxes are something Anex taught us is an absurd government overreach, something we were Better than. The people of Serendee shun the ideas of the outside world, the laws, and regulations.

The other ones... Anex has the right to manage, control, and determine the use of all monies coming in and out for the betterment of the community. It's part of our fundamental beliefs not to get tied down in these secular rules. We don't abide by any philosophy but our own.

Camille knows that. She helped define it. And the fact she's willing to use this against Anex means she's more dangerous than I anticipated.

⌇

Holding the key in my hand, I pause when I notice the apartment door is ajar. I'd left Camille's house an hour before, prepared to clean out the few things we'd left. It isn't much, but when you have nothing, it matters.

Turns out I may be too late and that the manager beat me to it when we didn't pay next week's rent—due yesterday.

It only takes a heartbeat to realize it isn't the manager.

I see the guard first, standing stiffly next to the refrigerator. Unmoving, his eyes sweep over me. Across the room, Anex ligers by the window, fingers parting the metal blinds as he looks down on the street below.

"Anex," I say, already bowing. When he turns, he waits for me to go through the motions, touching my forehead, giving him honor. "I didn't know you were coming." I didn't know I was coming. "How…"

The question trails off.

"I followed you from the house."

Ah, right. Has he been watching us the entire time?

My neck warms. "I can explain."

"No need." He waves his hand and assesses the chairs, nose wrinkled, trying to determine which is cleaner. He picks the one at the small kitchen table. "Camille's been working out of that little dump for years now. I figured you'd end up there." He looks around at the cobwebby corners of the room. "Even if it's a dump, it's less dumpy than this."

The criticism of my temporary home rankles me. He kicked us out with nothing. Literally nothing to make our way and he's judging where we landed? I swallow my ire and circle back.

"You've known about Camille's program."

"Of course. I've been tracking her since the day she left." He gestures to the chair opposite of his and I sit, back rigid against the hard seat. "I knew she wouldn't go far—not with Imogene still with us. She's a betrayer, but it hurt leaving her daughter behind." He crosses his legs, resting his hands on his thighs. "To be honest, I thought she'd get over her silly tantrum and return. She was weaker than I realized, so Regressive it ate away at her very soul."

Weak isn't how I would describe Camille, but I wisely keep my mouth shut. Anex isn't finished. "What did you tell her when you and Elon showed up on her doorstep?"

"The truth," I respond without hesitation. "Anything less would have made her suspicious. She was suspicious, but our story smoothed that out. She's happy to help two fellow outcasts."

I try to keep the pain out of my voice. Speaking of this so lightly— it digs deep under my flesh. Serendee is my home. Anex my leader, but things are different now. I am on uneven ground. I have to do everything I can to level the field.

I must answer correctly because Anex simply nods and asks, "How is Camille?"

"She hates you." I flash him a grin. "And you're right, she's completely lost to The Way. But she's also conniving. She's aware that there's no way to get to you—at least by normal means."

"She's never had the power to touch me."

So arrogant. How had I never seen that before? That his confidence and false sense of identity will be what brings him ruin. Yet here I am, telling him. "You need to know she's rallying the families of the people you've brought in recently—the *wealthy* families."

"Interesting." His eyes flick over to the guard, and he scratches his chin. "Did she say how?"

I shake my head. "She's hoping to use their influence."

"Bad press? Politicians? Government bureaucracy. How pathetic." His voice rises an octave as he stands. "She's going to use the system to take *me* down? What? Uncle Fucking Sam? What a goddamn hypocrite."

My hands grip the edge of my seat, body frozen as he rants. I've seen many sides of Anex. Thoughtful. Wise. Intelligent. All powerful and judicious. But this anger, it comes in a flash and sets my nerves on edge.

"She's culpable, you know that? Her name is on so many things— all of the early ideals of Serendee. She made promises to me. Oaths. I wonder how she'd like me to expose her to the world for being a lying, betraying, cock-teasing bitch?" He swings his arm around, catching the top of the chair and slinging it across the room. It clatters against the floor before toppling into the wall. "Fuck!" He spins. "No, fuck *her*."

The outburst is intense. Wild and erratic. I slide my eyes in the direction of the guard, but he hasn't moved an inch. I take a deep breath and swallow past the lump in my throat. "Although she wants revenge, I think the one thing she wants more than that, is to see her daughter."

"That," he snaps, head whipping around, "will never happen."

"No, I would assume not, but," I weigh my words carefully, "what if there's another way to handle all of this?"

"I would have killed her already if that was an option."

The lightness in the way he says it chills me to the core. "Although that's one way to do it, I'm not talking about killing Camille."

Anex snaps his fingers and the guard bolts forward, picking up the chair and placing it back at the table. He sits, running his hands through his hair, regaining composure. "Explain."

"Serendee operates quietly. We keep to ourselves, living in our small, walled-in community. We're self-sustaining. We don't need outsiders, but that's one of the things that makes people uncomfortable. It seems like we're keeping secrets." I run my hand down my thigh. "We do have secrets, but they're locked up and hidden under barns. We may need to open the doors a little to ease some suspicion."

"Impossible. We can't have the secular world gawking at us. At our women. I've always promised they would be safe, and I'm not going back on that because of a threat."

"How about we open the doors to one person. To one event."

"What are you talking about, Levi?"

"I think, no, I feel," I touch my chest, "The Way is speaking to me, telling me that you should invite Camille to the equinox."

"The equinox."

"To her daughter's mating ceremony."

"To *our* mating ceremony." He grins. "As a gift, to Imogene."

"Yes. No secrets. No hiding. Fully transparent."

"I like it. I like it a lot." His eyebrow rises. "And you actually think you can get Camille to come?"

"I do."

"If you pull this off, I'll grant you and Elon status back in Serendee."

"As part of the inner circle," I include, feeling the sweat spread across my lower back. "Full standing."

His smile never falters, but the corner of his eye twitches, and I think maybe I've pushed it too far. Overplayed my hand. But I've spent a lifetime studying under this man. I know his strengths and weaknesses. I know his ego. And right now, I know he'll do anything to get Camille Montgomery under his thumb. Even reinstating me and Elon back in the fold.

"I'll accept your proposal," he says, leaning forward. "I can see now that when I assigned you, Elon, and Silas to train Imogene you weren't as strong as I'd hoped. You were taken by the allure of that girl's innocent, tight, pussy." He laughs, as if he deeply understands where things went sideways. "But, understand, once Camille is behind the walls, once she's come voluntarily, she and her daughter are mine to deal with."

81

E lon

Camille looks over her shoulder when I walk into the kitchen, giving me a tight smile. "I hate tea," she says without any context, then dumps two cups into the sink. "But it seems to put people at ease." She opens a cabinet door, revealing rows of mugs. "Coffee?"

"Sure." I don't miss the way her forehead rises as she pours me a cup and slides it across the island. "What?"

"I thought drinks like coffee were off limits. You know, anything addictive." She pours herself a large cup and takes a large gulp, as if making a point. "Or did he change those rules?"

"I wasn't raised like normal people in Serendee—one of the perks of being best friends with Anex's son."

She glances down at my scabbed knuckles. One had torn overnight, leaving a spot of blood on the sheets. "Where'd you get that?"

"There's a bar on the other side of Whittmore's campus. They have paid fights in the basement." I sip my coffee, feeling burn on my tongue. "We had to earn money somehow."

"Right. Limited education. No real job experience. No paper-work." Hearing it sounds so pathetic. She looks me up and down. "You're a big guy. What did you do for Timothy?"

I try not to squirm. It's been a long time since I've been around a woman like Camille. A mother. I left my own home at twelve and moved into the Donum like everyone else. At least until Anex brought us to the Main House to be with Rex. "He saw my size and ability. I worked in security. Protected Rex, mostly."

"He decided," she says. "You had no choice."

I open my mouth to reprimand her. To remind her that it isn't just Anex that makes these decisions, but it's The Way, the gut feeling he gets about the people in our community. But I stop myself. Those beliefs are lies.

"No," I confess, probably for the first time, "I didn't have a choice."

"Who are you, Elon?" She rests her elbows on the countertop, leaning forward slightly. It's unnerving looking at her—so similar to Imogene. My heart contracts. "If Anex wasn't there to decide for you, who would you be?"

"I don't know." I stare down at the hand holding my coffee mug, looking at those worn, torn, knuckles and think. I try to remember who I was, who I wanted to be, but there's little space between who I am, who Anex created me to be, and any organic truth. I close my eyes, and a memory returns. I'm back to when I was a kid—bigger than the rest—and I'd spin the others on the merry-go-round at the playground. That was the first time I saw Imogene, wide-eyed and bossy.

I'd told her about this memory after she was Ordered to Rex and later, I kissed her for the first time.

Those moments unearth something in me, something long buried, away from Anex and his greedy control.

Across the table Camille watches me, and a flood of emotion runs through me. It's her daughter I'm thinking of. Her daughter that tech-nically belongs to another man—my best friend. Camille has been tolerant of us, but knowing how we share Imogene?

There's no way she'd accept that.

Except the truth is on my tongue and heat builds in my cheeks. Approval from this woman suddenly means everything. I open my mouth to speak, but the front door opens, and my courage slams shut, just like the door.

"There's no reason to talk about 'what if's.'" I rise, carrying my cup to the sink. I wash it quickly, feeling my hands burn under the hot water. "All we can do is accept reality."

82

I mogene

Just when I thought this mansion of horrors couldn't get any more disturbing, Rex and I were taken to a room in Anex's wing that made the rest of the Main House seem like high level accommodations—*including* the basement cells.

The guard came for us not long after Rex and I dressed. He gave me his shirt, eyes worrying over my tender and swollen breasts, while he pulled on his pants. By gunpoint we were led back through Anex's room. It was empty. No Anex. No Inner Circle. No Silas.

I wanted to ask about him, but I knew better than to express concern. Anex was determined to destroy the things I loved. I wouldn't give him more ammunition.

"What the hell is this?" Rex had asked, feet planted to the floor. The room in front of us is divided into two, a clear, thick wall separating the space. Everything was pure white. White walls, white bed, white chair, white carpet. Two white toilets and sinks sat in each corner. Rex's eyes grew wide. "Hell no!"

Erik shoved Rex into one side and secured the door. He jerked his gun at me, and I entered on my own volition. The instant the door closed I felt the air grow thin. I slammed my palms against the glass door. "Is there enough oxygen in here? Is this how it ends? With Anex suffocating us."

"Please, Imogene. Acting out isn't going to make this better for anyone."

I turned and saw Margaret standing outside the door, hand cradling her belly. "Let us out!"

"This is your room for the foreseeable future." I looked over and saw Rex sitting on the end of the bed, eyes vacant. "Your father designed this room knowing that one day he may need to keep you close, the both of you."

"He built this room a year ago," Rex said, forehead creasing. "Before the Order."

"Your father is all knowing, Rex. Led by The Way," Margaret says. "I don't know why you're surprised."

"He planned this," Rex said, pieces clicking into place. "From the beginning. He never was going to let me have you as a mate. He set up the training with Elon, Levi, and Silas. He got me to fall for you. Got us to *all fall* for you so that we'd make mistakes. He knew I'd get possessive, blind with obsession and want. And that would make me, and the guys, trip up and fall right in his trap." He ran his hands through his hair and looked up at Margaret. "The whole plan was to keep Imogene for himself, but he couldn't just pluck a girl out of Serendee and make her his mate. That would raise questions, so he had me do it instead. The catch is that he didn't expect her to be so goddamn stubborn. So defiant." He laughs darkly. "So *Regressive*."

"You'll stay here," Margaret repeated, ignoring Rex's moment of clarity. "Where your every movement can be watched. Every piece of food you consume. Every supplement. Every bodily function will be monitored."

"Everything?" I asked, eyes shifting to the toilets.

"Everything, Imogene. You've lost the right to privacy, to autonomy, to everything. Anex is fully in control now. It's how it has to be. It's The Way."

"For how long?"

Her expression softened, and there was a flicker of something in her eyes that chilled me to the bone. Something dark and lost. "Until the equinox, of course."

Fear climbed up my spine. "The equinox?"

"The day you will finally be mated."

That conversation had been days ago, at least three, I assume, but the days are getting shorter. The sunlight fading sooner. I can measure this through our window. It's high, out of reach, but it does provide some awareness of the time of day. This is especially true in the morning because the window faces east, and the bright stream of sunlight makes it hard to sleep.

Which stinks, because sleeping the day away, dreaming of being somewhere else, would make everything more bearable. The light has been glaring in my eyes for at least an hour when I give up and swing my legs over the side of the bed. Across from me, on the other side of that clear divider, Rex is already up. Well, up and down. Rex is in the middle of one of his impressively long sets of push-ups.

My eyes follow the taut muscles that run the length of his back, the way they pull against his skin as he rises and falls. There's a brutality to his movements, the distinct impression he's punishing himself.

He does this every morning. Push-ups. Sit ups. Balancing exercises. At first, I thought it was just his regular routine, but then I realized that there was something else going on.

He's distracting himself from my visits from Margaret.

The unlocking of the door draws my attention away from his muscular form. Like clockwork, Margaret arrives, holding two trays of food in her hands. "Rise and shine, sweet Imogene." She says this every day, cheerful and unrelenting. The exact opposite of how I feel.

Rex flips on his back and begins the sit-up phase of his routine, eyes focused on the wall. Margaret slides his tray through the small opening at the base of the wall, then carries mine into my section.

The food smells good. Eggs and bacon, homemade biscuits. Everything sourced from Serendee. Anex hasn't been limiting either of our meals. A quick glance tells me Rex has an appropriately larger portion than I do, but one thing is for certain, our leader is allowing me more calories. Margaret explained that the first day she delivered food.

"Anex is a genius, but like all men, the female body is something of a mystery. I explained that by reducing your intake he could be inadvertently stopping your menstruation."

So, right. He's letting me eat again so I can be fertile. For the equinox.

"Here's your supplements," she says, resting the tray on the end of the bed and handing me a small cup of pills, followed by a cup of water. She watches as I take each one, swallowing and showing her the inside of my mouth to confirm. "Good girl. Now, time to check."

Every time she mentions the "check" my cheeks burn hot. "There's no need. Nothing has changed."

Margaret shakes her head. "We go through this every morning, Imogene. You know I need to look for myself."

"Why? So you can humiliate me?" My eyes snap over to Rex who hasn't missed a crunch. "I'm not bleeding. I promise, I'll let you know if and when it happens."

She frowns, a flicker of empathy crossing her face. "Is that what this is about? Your feelings of insecurity, like you're less of a woman because you're not having your period?"

"What?" I stare at her like she's lost her mind. For the record, she has. She lost it the second she stepped into Serendee and fell into Anex's trap. Again, I glance across the room at the man who made me realize I'm more than the parameters that Serendee has placed around me. Rex. Silas. Levi. Elon. They taught me to be a real woman. Rex never stops his movements but his head tilts slightly, and I know he's listening. "Unlike you, I don't feel less female without falling into Anex's antiquated version of womanhood. I don't need to bleed to feel complete."

I yank up the hem of my dress and pull down my pristine white panties. I toss them at her and she catches them in her hand. If my rant affected her, she shows no sign of it, not when she checks the crotch of the panties for signs of menstruation, or when she fishes a clean pair out of her skirt pocket and hands them to me.

"It'll be best for you," her eyes flick to Rex's back, "for all of us, Imogene, if you stop being a petty bitch and remember your place."

"I'm a captive no matter what I do, so if I want to be a petty bitch, I will." I cross my arms over my chest. "What happens if my period doesn't start before the equinox? What if it doesn't happen at all? Does he keep me locked away forever?"

"It will happen because Anex wills it. It is The Way, Imogene. When will you realize this is out of your hands?"

I refuse to answer, and she stares at me, unblinking. I do the same, refusing to back down. I know I can't beat Anex. I know my life is fucked. But holding my own against this woman, this manipulator, feels good.

At least for a minute.

~

The rest of the morning falls into a routine. Rex has the grace to look away as I tug on the clean panties and use the toilet. I do the same for him, although it's futile. When Rex urinates, I'm reminded of horses at the stable. Does a man's bladder always hold so much? Is that what I sound like?

We've each been given two sets of clothes. Mine are thin dresses. While Rex floods the earth with his heavy stream, I start to lift my dress over my head when I notice he quiets. I sense something, turning my head. He's watching.

"Will you show me?"

It's an ask. Not a demand. He's careful with his words, careful not to sound like Margaret. It's a subtle change. I know what he wants. He's asked me every day. Always my decision. I turn around fully and remove the dress.

"It looks better." I know he's lying because his forehead stretches upward when he sees my breasts.

I glance down at the mottled flesh, a mixture of yellow and purple. I make a face. "Thank you for saying so, but you and I both know I look awful."

He shakes his head and presses his hand flat against the clear divider. "You're beautiful."

"Stop." I reach for my dress. "I'm not beautiful."

"Don't cover yourself. Not yet." His voice is deep, impossible to say no to, and I find myself standing in front of him, exposed. His gaze rakes over me. "Jesus, Imogene. I know you don't believe me, but you're the prettiest, sexiest, thing I've seen." His other hand shifts to the front of his pants and I see his erection straining at the fabric. "I'd tear down this wall to get to you, if I could, to kiss those bruises away and make new ones if you'd let me."

My heart pounds and I press my palm against his, the plastic in between. "I'd let you," I confess. "I'd let you do anything you wanted to me."

The muscle in the back of his jaw tenses and releases. "He's doing this to dehumanize us to one another. To force us to see one another in our most base moments, so we're unattractive and unappealing. And maybe with anyone else it would work, but every moment with you just makes me want you more." Below his waist, his hand moves, tugging down his pants and exposing his hard erection. His hand wraps around his shaft and he tugs upward, Adam's apple bobbing as he reaches the tip. "All I ever fucking want with you, Imogene, is more."

Heat unspools in my belly, a hot coil wound inside. The warmth flickers out from there spreading first to my arms and legs, then to my nipples and between my thighs. I understand what Rex is saying because I feel it too. After the time here together, I only love him more.

"Touch yourself, baby," he says, leaning his forehead against the surface. I run my hand down my body, over my tender breasts and stomach, down between my legs. He licks his lips and nods. "That's it. That's my girl."

His words spur me on, fingers sliding between my slippery folds. My breath hitches and I press against the glass. Our bodies are separated, but our movements fall into sync. The push-pull, the shuddering want. Keeping my eyes wide, I take in the long line of muscle on his forearm, that tenses as it draws up and down his cock.

Rex's shoulders quiver, his eyes meeting mine. "I love you."

"I love you, too," I say back, feeling it bloom in my chest, feeling it *explode* between my legs. I'm all alone in that room when the orgasm comes. Alone as Rex's guttural groan bounces off the cold, oppressive, walls. Alone when we're both finished, nothing left but the greasy print of our bodies on the glass.

We spend the day that way. Eating our now cold breakfast. Telling small stories to pass the time. Fall asleep. Alone, but together, satiated but sacrificed, until the streaming light from the window wakes me the next day. A twinge in my belly draws me to my side, and my eyes meet Rex's as he lowers himself to the floor to start his workout. His mouth lifts in the smallest smile.

I rise, tossing my legs over the side of the bed, feet on the cold floor, warmth between my legs. Blinking, I look down and see the spread, dark and red, like a flower blooming across the bottom half of my night dress.

Movement across the room draws my gaze, and I see Rex, pressed against the divider, eyes wide and focused on the red.

My period.

The Way has spoken.

～

Rex is mid-pushup when Margaret arrives. He hasn't spoken since he saw my bloody panties, the closeness of the day before gone. Just like any hope I'd had of getting out of this.

"Rise and Shine," Margaret calls, giving me the worst sort of déjà vu. I've already changed. My soiled panties are wadded in a ball. I don't hesitate to hand them to her without a word.

She sets the trays down and looks at the balled-up cotton. Her lips are turned down, but she unfolds them, revealing the dark stain. "I knew it would come. Just in time."

Up and down. Up and down. Rex never stops, even though his muscles are quivering from exhaustion.

"What now?" I ask, bracing myself for the sharp pain of another cramp. I haven't missed these.

"You'll go into Preparations."

"Already?" Every Ordered female goes into Preparations three days before the Mating Ceremony. It's a secret, mystical time. I used to crave knowing what happened, to be one of those women elevated to the next step, but after everything I've been through, after the branding, the idea sends a tremor of fear along my nerves.

Nothing good comes from being Chosen in this world.

"I told you, Imogene, your bleeding came just in time. It's a sign from The Way. The equinox is in three days."

It takes everything in me not to slap the grin off her face.

I'm using every ounce of energy trying not to cry.

Her hand stretches out. "We should go."

"Wait." I glance at Rex. Sweat drips down his temple. He stares forward, never glancing my way. Why won't he look at me? I just need to see his eyes. To feel their warmth. To know he still loves me.

Otherwise, how do I survive?

"Imogene, everything changes now. All of this," her hand waves around the cell, "all of this vanishes. Your bleeding is proof that you're worthy. That Anex was right to have persevered. It means you are no longer Fallen. The Reeducation worked."

I drag my eyes away from Rex and look at this woman, wondering if I ever sounded this delusional.

"Everything," she continues, "goes back to the way it was supposed to be."

"How was it supposed to be?"

She grins. "We'll be true sisters. Spiritual sisters, bonded together with Anex in union."

Warm, prickly heat coats my body. My armpits and neck. Bile thrusts up my throat and I bend, arm across my stomach, trying to hold back the gag.

"I know it's a lot to take in," she says, placing a hand on my back, "but it's right. You have to understand that."

I understand nothing, other than the fact that my fate was sealed long before my awareness kicked in. Nothing will change the course of Anex's will. My mind slips away, along with the urge to fight or rebel. It's done nothing but make things worse all along.

Maybe Margaret is right.

This is The Way.

And there's nothing I can do about it.

83

E lon

The envelope arrives on a Monday. Tucked between the stack of mail Camille carries into the kitchen. I recognize the paper right away. Handmade from recycled materials.

"Stop." The words are harsh. Blunt. "Give me that."

Camille's eyebrow raises. "What are you talking about?"

"It's from Serendee," Levi says, striding into the room. "The paper. It's unique."

Every muscle in Camille's body tenses, but she doesn't relinquish the envelope. She just stares at it, long and hard, until she asks, "Did you give them this address?"

Levi shakes his head.

"No," I reply. "But it's not unlikely that he's had an eye on you this whole time, you know that, right?"

I've felt his eyes on us since we arrived. Nothing I can confirm. Just a sense. It could just be paranoia from years of living under his rule, but it feels like more.

"There have been threats over the years from a variety of groups that don't like us helping the families of their victims." My jaw tics at the word "victim." "You realize Serendee isn't the only cult out there? It's not even the only one in this region." She grabs a knife and wedges the tip into the corner of the flap. The sound of tearing paper fills the kitchen. Levi and I watch as she pulls out a single card. It's handwritten, the curling cursive writing printed across the paper. Camille's eyes flick over the words and she says, "It's an invitation."

"To what?" I ask, heart thudding in my chest. Something is off. Weird. Wrong.

"To a ceremony." She tosses the card on the table, turned so we can read it. I see, not only her name listed, but mine and Levi's as well. My eyes jump to read what it says, but Camille beats me to it. "In two days, Anex is Mating with my daughter and he wants all of us to come."

~

Camille doesn't say much after reading the invitation. Just excusing herself and taking the stairs to the second floor. A moment later a door clicks shut.

I, too, feel the need to move. And I run upstairs, grabbing the bag Levi picked up at the apartment, and head back to the front door.

"Where are you going?" Levi asks, hot on my heels.

"Out." I clear the steps, but stop when I feel his hand on my shoulder.

"Elon, wait."

I spin, glaring at my friend. "I can't sit around here and just do fucking nothing while all of this is going on, Levi. I can't log all my feelings into a journal, or meditate to the fucking Way, hoping everything will work out."

"So what then?" I don't miss the hurt in his eyes at every jab I make about his values. "What the hell are you going to do?"

"Not what I want," I say, hitching the bag over my shoulder. "But the only thing I can. I'm going to go hit something."

Or someone. Hopefully one of those frat boy pricks down at the bar. It always feels nice to hear the smack of my fist against their pretty faces.

I pass the bus stop and head north. It's not the best part of town. Seedy hotels and abandoned buildings. Drug dealers lurk in the shadows. I'm familiar with the area because of Serendee's drug trade. It's not the neighborhood anyone chooses to live in, not anymore.

"You're not taking the bus?"

"I need to blow off some steam first." Goddamn Anex. Goddamn him. It's bad enough that he's doing this to Imogene. To *our* girl. But to invite Camille? Us? He's relentless and evil. The absolute worst. And if I know him as well as I think I do, it's a fucking trap.

That thought lingers and I stop short, turning to face Levi who is still only a few feet away. He stops too, wariness in his narrowed gaze.

"What?"

"You set this up, didn't you?" I ask, slowly walking toward him. "The invitation?"

"We agreed to use Camille as bait. I just cast the line. Anex bit, just like we thought."

"Using Camille to get Anex to work with us is one thing. Walking into the lion's den," I shake my head, "to witness that—you went too far."

"I did what I had to do, Elon. You knew it would have to be drastic."

I search his face. His body language. Look at the way he's standing. His shoulders and hands. His feet. All the tells I'd been taught to assess someone on the spot. But Levi is also trained, and he gives me nothing. Finally, I go with the truth. "You've handled all of this well. Too well, Levi. The Banishment. The Shunning." I start walking again, to the corner, I wait for the light to change, letting him catch up. "Your entire life was wrapped up in Serendee. In achieving Enlightenment and Anex's approval. Way more than me and Rex."

Something's off and I've felt it for days. I was just too preoccupied with my own pain to address it.

The light changes and I cross the road, passing an old boarded up building. People lurk in the old alcoves, men and women—*girls*—slumped against the walls, in skirts too short for this kind of weather. I keep my eyes open, instincts on point. The last thing we need is to get caught up in trouble down here.

"How many times have you talked to him?" I ask, terrified of the answer.

"Twice," he answers quickly. "Once at the center, hoping to establish contact. Then again at the apartment. He was waiting for me."

This time when I stop, my arm snaps out and I grab him by the collar, twisting until my knuckles bear against his throat. "And what? You just offered the three of us up on a platter? Happy witnesses to the abomination of the century?"

He doesn't fight me, just swallows thickly. "I had to do something. We need a way back in."

"I don't want back in!" My fingers twist. I'm hurting him and I don't care.

"For them," he wheezes. "For *her*."

My grip loosens. "What are you talking about?"

"I've gone over it a million times. All night. All day. While you were out beating the shit out of college boys, I was coming up with a plan. A plan that gets us back into Serendee. That's why we needed Camille—the one thing Anex is willing to compromise for."

"We take one step on that property, and he'll never let us go again." I drop him entirely. Disgusted. "He definitely won't let Camille leave again. That's not a compromise, that's a goddamn trap."

"It'll work. I convinced him that this will make him look good—transparent. That there are people investigating him, and he needs to look above board. If he has nothing to hide, then don't hide it. He's going to let us walk in, and then when it's over, we're walking away with our family."

I want to think this is a good idea, but I can't. There are too many obstacles. Too many guards and guns and hidden, secret cells underneath that mansion. But I also know that he's right. This may be our only chance. Walking in on his terms.

"If you're lying to me, Levi, I swear I will end you. I don't care if we've been friends for twenty years, or everything we've gone through. I will destroy you if this is just another way to fuck with my head."

His eyes dart over my shoulder. "Elon."

"Don't talk to me unless you're going to tell me every step of your plan. All of it. Up front. No secrets."

"Elon," he says again, eyes shifting from mine to behind me. I exhale and turn, prepared to fend off a junkie or a hooker. I'm not wrong. There's a prostitute in the alley behind us, with a man. His hand is wrapped tight around her arm and she's fighting him as he drags her farther away from the main road.

"Let go," she hisses, stumbling over her heels. "I can't just—"

"You'll do what I want," he barks, shoving her against the brick wall. "And if it's good enough, then I'll think about paying."

I don't get there before he yanks at her top, the strap snapping in two, but I do get a hand around his throat before he takes it farther.

"She said she didn't want to go with you."

He fights against me. "Fuck you."

"Get her out of here," I grunt at Levi.

I hear her heels on the pavement, the sound fading as she gets further away. I laugh. "You got me on the wrong day, brother. I've been looking for someone's ass to kick."

"You're going to kick my ass over a whore?" He scoffs. "Trust me dude. No piece of ass is worth it."

Once, I'd felt the same way. Women were objects to be toyed with. To be used. But then Imogene came into our lives, and fuck, I treated her exactly the same and now all I have is regrets and the pain of losing her.

"Women should be treated with honor," I growl, my fist balled and elbow lifted. I slam my fist into his jaw, hearing the snap I'd been craving all day. I go for another—

"Elon!" My name echoes off the brick.

I ignore him, knowing he's going to try to make me stop.

"Elon, you need to see something," he says, voice firm. "Then you can finish kicking this guy's ass."

I shift my gaze long enough to see Levi and the girl at the end of the alley. He's removed his jacket and slung it over her bare shoulder. The way she looks at him is... familiar. Slowly, I release the guy and say, "Beat it and don't you fucking come down here again."

He doesn't ask why, just scrambles away, running the opposite direction down the alley.

The scabs tore off my knuckles and I wipe them on my pants. Getting closer I narrow my eyes at the girl. I remember her from the cells under the Main House. How Anex groomed her to work out on the streets. Silas and Imogene had taken care of her. Her name pushes past the adrenaline. "Charlotte, right?"

She nods, hands are trembling like a leaf as she wipes away a line of mascara dripping down her cheek. "I was on the way back from the store and that guy just came out of nowhere and grabbed me."

"So he wasn't a client?"

Her mouth turns down. "I don't have clients. We *recruit* from there."

Her wet eyes slide over to a building that isn't boarded up. The windows are still intact, the front steps clean. An uneasy feeling rolls over me. "Recruit?"

"It's Anex's new program." Her expression brightens when she says his name. Fuck.

"Is he up there now?"

"No. He only comes once a week." Her hands twist together. "Please don't tell him this happened. I know it's my fault. That I should do better, but I just... I want to see him."

"And he won't if he finds out about any problems." Understanding flickers across Levi's face. He mutters, "Jesus."

"I'm trying so hard to follow The Way. To be the good girl he wants." She grabs my forearm. "But you can go up and explain. Explain that it wasn't my fault, right?"

My gaze meets Levi's. "Yeah, we're happy to clear things up."

And find out exactly who's running this sex trafficking business. Maybe I'll still get to beat the crap out of someone today after all.

We enter the building—an old hotel—and it's cleaner than

expected. We pass a reception desk, manned by another vaguely familiar face, and follow Charlotte into a spotless elevator. The doors open on the top floor, and she steps out, heels sinking into a new emerald green carpet. She stops at a door.

"Thank you so much," she says, turning to us. "I've been working so hard, and The Way must have sensed my need."

Levi nods. "Because it sent us to protect you."

"Yes!" She smiles. "And because you're the only two that he'll listen to."

She opens the door and before we even cross the threshold, we see him, her handler:

Silas.

84

S ilas

"Charlotte." Her cheeks are stained, makeup a mess. I'm already off the couch when I realize that underneath the unfamiliar, too-large, jacket the strap of her dress is torn. "What the hell happened?"

"It's okay," she says, letting me inspect her. There are no real injuries, just some irritated skin near her shoulder. And the tears. "Some guy got rough with me, but they were there."

"They?" I tilt my head, realizing that we're not alone. Instinct propels me to reach for the gun at my back, fingers coiled around the handle. I shove Charlotte behind me, extending the weapon.

Except, the men in the doorway aren't a threat. At first, I think I'm hallucinating. It wouldn't be the first time since I got here. Whatever is in the pills Anex makes me take every day sends me on fucked-up trips until they work their way through my system. But my hallucinations don't touch me and right now the figure closest to me grabs me, pushes the gun aside like a gnat, and pulls me into a tight hug.

"Elon?" I ask, but I feel him. Smell him. An anchor in the storm.

"Yeah man. It's us."

Us. I see Levi over his shoulder, and he tugs Elon back, pulling me into an embrace. I squeeze him tight, wanting to feel his warmth and strength. His existence.

He releases me, and I turn, setting the gun on the table. Tears burn at my eyes, relief at seeing them. I wipe them away and ignore the way Elon's studying me when I turn back around. "Charlotte, honey, why don't you go clean up? Take a shower. Eat something."

"Okay." She turns to the guys. "Thank you, again."

Elon looks like he wants to say a million things. Throw her over his shoulder and drag her out of here to safety, but he must realize how precarious this situation is, and lets her go with a nod.

Once the door shuts behind her and the lock engages, I return to the couch and sit, sinking into the cushion like a thousand-pound weight rests on my shoulders. The guys don't wait for an invitation, they each take an armchair.

"Fuck," I start, pushing my fingers through my hair, "it's good to see you. I've been worried."

Worried is an understatement.

"We're okay," Levi says. "Managing."

Elon runs his thumb over his knuckles. They're raw, bloodied recently, but I also note the yellowing bruise by his eye. I've spent years taking care of his post-fight wounds. I know a fresh injury when I see it. I can't help but ask, "You sure about that?"

"Yeah," Elon replies, noticing my attention. He drops his hands to his sides, out of view. "Tell us what's going on?"

"What is this place?" Levi adds.

I rub my eyes. They burn from exhaustion. Sleep is elusive. Ever since I was forced to watch Rex Correct Imogene. Watching him punish her for *my* crimes.

"*This* is what Anex has been preparing me for my whole life." I laugh, although it comes out more of a choke. "I think he always knew that the four of us weren't enough to build the membership of Serendee the way he wanted. Our process was too slow." I look at Elon. "You and Rex flirting your way into rich girl's pants, giving them just enough to draw them down to The Center. Once there Levi would educate—indoctrinate. And then once they're good and hooked, I'd seal the deal by providing them with the best orgasms of their life." I'm not telling them anything they don't know. "Anex needed something more streamlined. Faster. A broader approach and he created this: a new kind of recruitment center."

"A whorehouse," Elon clarifies.

"Anex knows that the way to a man's wallet is through a woman's pussy. Or a man's cock. Whichever applies." I wave my hands. "And apparently my fate is to orchestrate it all."

Levi's eyebrows raise. "You're a pimp."

It hurts to hear him say it. I sag back against the cushion. "Basically. I mean, haven't I always been to a degree? Haven't we all?"

"Well, I don't—" Levi starts.

Holding up my hand I cut him off. "We all are, Levi. We all use our bodies one way or the other. Elon's brawn. Rex's charm. Your brain. And yeah, my... everything."

Levi frowns, but for once doesn't argue. He looks around the room. "So, this is why he's needed to lock in the bigger fish lately. He needed money to expand."

"Yes, and that's also what made him realize that he could be making more money, smaller, but more consistent. And he's been cultivating his workers for a while: the Fallen."

Elon shares a look with Levi. "This setup also eliminates nosy family coming around wondering where their family and bank accounts went."

Levi nods thoughtfully. "I knew he had big ideas, but this is more than I imagined."

"This place has thirty-six rooms. Right now, only twelve are finished. I'm responsible for four females and three males that are working their way through Re-education by fucking prospective recruits that come in looking for a little Enlightenment."

"Jesus," Elon mutters. "And if they don't want it?"

"We keep their 'introductory fee' and they can come back as often as they want—each time a little pricier."

"And if they do want more than sex?" Levi asks. "Then what happens?"

"They're given one-on-one time with an educator." I look him up and down. "Basically, someone like you."

"And everyone is just going along with this?" Elon's jaw tenses. "No one has pushed back?"

The accusation makes a direct hit. No matter, I have one of my own to toss back. "I did what I had to do because my number one priority was Imogene. Rex was locked up, and while my movements were limited, I did what I could."

Unfortunately, while I was busy doing everything I could to protect her—Anex was planning this.

Elon's eyes soften at her name. "Did you? Protect her?"

"I tried." Guilt hardens in my gut. "I tried. She was held in a secure location, but I managed to get in once and see her. I was able to adjust some of her supplements to push things off as long as possible, but in the end my defiance only made it worse on her and Rex."

"What does that mean?" Levi asks.

"It means Anex is a monster, does it have to be more than that? You know it. I know it, but that's about it. He's got everyone wrapped around his finger." I stand, gesturing to the door Charlotte walked out of. "And if not that, wrapped around his goddamn dick. These people are a herd of lost sheep, and he assigned me to be their fucking shepherd."

The more I speak, the more rattled I become. Every word out of my mouth is Regressive. Every word could get me in more trouble, but what's worse than this? I cross the room, reaching for the bottle of pills on the counter. I open the top and shake out two. Hallucinating is better than this. I control the accusations there. The dark, accusing looks in my friends' eyes.

"Whatever those are," Elon says, "put them the fuck down. You're coming with us."

"No." I close my hand around the pills, making a fist. "Didn't you hear what I said? I'm their shepherd. I'm the only one watching out for these people. I make sure they eat. I force them to sleep. I clean their wounds and keep them as healthy as possible. I'm not leaving them."

"We have a plan, Silas," Levi says. That statement elicits a frown from Elon. "Come with us, and we'll come back for them. Every one. I promise."

"How far do you think we'd actually get, brother?" I lift the cuff of my pants, revealing the black band around my ankle. "He'll track me and whatever plan you've got worked up will be over before it's started."

Elon rises, shooting Levi a look loaded with meaning. I don't know what, but he runs his hand through his hair, a sign of agitation. "We're going to take him down, Silas. Levi has a plan and it's coming up fast. Two days."

We're conditioned to know the big dates in Serendee. There's no mistaking which one is coming up. "The equinox."

"We're not letting him have her." Elon's words are calm but forceful. "She doesn't belong to him. She belongs to us. And we'll do whatever it takes to get her out."

"Good," I reply. "Once you have her out and safe, then you can come back for us."

Levi thrusts out his hand, and I shake it. Followed by Elon and something unwinds in my chest. I have no idea if they'll be successful, but I'm doubtful. What I know is that if they make a move, nothing will ever be the same. One way or the other, there's no coming back.

No matter the consequences, I'm ready for the end.

85

———————

Imogene

After leaving the cell I shared with Rex, I'm taken to a different wing in the Main House, this one on the ground floor. Panic shadows me with every step. Margaret says she's taking me to Preparations, but she's also the one that lured me out into the dead of night, marking me with Anex's brand. She took my Collateral and handed it over to be revealed to the whole community.

She's complicit, and I don't trust her.

Down the hall, I see the black clad guards that are stationed at the double doors leading to the wing, these men—boys from the hunch of their shoulders—are new. "Are there more guards now?" I ask, the question slipping out.

"Recent events have made Anex increase his measures of security."

I'd never even noticed the guards until I became one of the Chosen. I'd lived a blissful, ignorant life of what really made Serendee prosper. But the veil has been removed and now it's all I can see.

"They seem young," I note.

"A special group selected from the donums."

Okay, that *is* new.

Halfway down the hall, Margaret touches my arm, drawing me to a stop. "Imogene, I know the last few weeks have been a challenge."

I snort. "That's an understatement."

"I know it's been a challenge," she repeats, "but now that Anex has accepted your Reeducation, it's time to release the anger and hostility you've been carrying." Her thumb runs gently over my arm. "This is your second chance. Make the most of it."

She doesn't wait for a response, heading for the doors. The guards open them and step aside, allowing us to enter. I cross the threshold, but stop instantly, taking in the wing. It's not like the rest of the house, a maze of hallways and closed doors. This area is large with glass walls and ceilings. The air is humid, and green leafy trees grow in every corner. A circular clear pool is in the center of the space.

"What is this?" I ask, stunned at the sight. How can Serendee have so many unknown rooms? Every day it's like a new layer of this place is stripped away and something new is revealed.

"Anex calls it the Cleansing Room. It's to be used before important ceremonies, or in times of transition."

Laughter across the room catches my attention, and I see a group I knew in the donum—the other girls Ordered the same day I was. They're all wearing white robes embroidered with flowers along the hem.

Maria is among them, her pregnancy now showing and pushing against the fabric of her robe. It hurts to look at her, knowing she's the one that betrayed me to Anex by telling him about the love mark Silas left on my neck.

I hesitate. "I don't think they'll want to be with me."

"Everyone that enters this room comes at Anex's request. This is a place of repurification. Where Regressions are washed away, and your body and soul are realigned for Enlightenment." She touches my face gently. "You are Chosen, Imogene. You are special. They will accept you because it is Anex's will."

Not one word of that makes me feel better.

"Come," Margaret says. "It's time to start your Preparation and I have a surprise."

She gestures toward a small room off the solarium and a line of women in dark gray dresses file out. I spot Clarissa, my house mother from the donum. She gives me a small smile when she sees me and walks over.

"Clarissa will attend to your needs during your Preparations." Margaret smiles warmly. "I thought it may be nice to have a familiar face during this."

I relax, marginally. At least she's not Healer Bloom, or Margaret herself. Clarissa may believe in The Way and everything that comes from the journey to Enlightenment, but at least she's not a monster.

At least, I don't think she is.

～

"We lift these women to The Way. Asking for cleansing and purification of every cell in their bodies, their spirit, and nature. Return them to completeness in preparation for their service to Serendee."

Margaret stands at the end of a narrow, tiled, passage—shower heads mounted to the ceiling. Quickly, I learn that the cleansing part of this is literal. We'd stripped and had our foreheads anointed with oil. Then we filed into the shower room, where we receive Margaret's blessing, bare as the day we were born, skin gooseflesh from the cool air.

With her hand on a lever, her words echo off the floors and walls.

"May the powers that guide us to Enlightenment be with each and every one of these women as they prepare themselves for their mate."

She flips the handle and a hard, hot, stream falls from the shower-heads, pounding painfully into our skin as if it's trying to strip off a layer of flesh.

Then we're scrubbed down by our attendant. I can't help but notice the way Clarissa's eyes linger on the brand, her touch careful as she makes sure not to tug on the last few scabs.

She's not the only one that notices the mark, curious eyes watching as my skin turns pink. As abruptly as it started, the water stops, and we're shuffled out of the shower and wrapped in thick towels.

From there it's mostly hair removal—trimming, plucking, shaving, waxing. By the time it's over I'd almost wish for another branding. At least that was fast.

It's dark when we're brought to an outdoor patio. There's a firepit in the middle, the heat of the blaze hot on my overworked and sensitive skin. Scrubbed, plucked, and robbed, we take a seat on one of the soft pillows and receive a cup of tea. Everyone looks relaxed and at peace. Holding the warm cup between my fingers, I feel nothing but anxiety. The last time I was with a group of women like this, I was held down and branded.

A woman, Nadine, who was one of our health and body teachers in school draws our attention. She's in her educator's dress, dark blue with cream trim.

"Seeing you all here today is like coming full circle," she says, the flames dancing across her face. "I remember teaching you the fundamentals of hygiene and how to manage your cycles and document your caloric intake for your food logs. Together we learned how to care for your bodies while honoring The Way. All the pieces of developing into a young woman in Serendee." I remember other lessons too—about graciously receiving Corrections for any transgressions. "And now you are about to be mated, and you need to learn about that, too."

Every girl leans forward, eager to learn the secrets of men from this woman.

"Men are simple," she begins. "They have the ability to be brilliant—Enlightened—but they are easily distracted by needs and desires woven into their biological nature. They are ruled by their bodies. It's what's kept them alive and evolving since the beginning of time. That instinct, that drive for creation, is what built Serendee. But it must be harnessed. Regressive thoughts are always seeking to take over. That's why Anex leads these men. He is there to keep them on the path. To help them follow The Way. But Anex cannot do it alone."

"He needs us," a girl near me murmurs.

"Yes," Nadine says with a serious expression. "Our leader needs you to do your part to keep your men healthy, happy, and productive. For the Betterment of Serendee." She walks around the fire pit, making eye contact with each one of us. I remember her doing this in school. Back then it always felt personal. Now it just feels intimidating. "They will need to be fed, which I assume you are already doing. They will need you to use your ears—to *listen*. Communication is good, but our roles are specific in Serendee. Anex's commands are what keeps our community running smoothly. He doesn't need your input on duties and jobs. He needs you to run interference with those needs and desires."

Everyone here has lived with their Ordered for months now. It's doubtful that anyone is unclear about what she is speaking of. It's not forbidden to lay with your Ordered, not after the ceremony declaring intentions. My fingers reach instinctively for the leather bracelet that I'd worn after Rex and I went through the process. It's gone. Stripped from me like everything else.

A girl across the firepit named Deena looks at Maria, eyes darting down to her belly. "What was it like?"

Maria blushes, but she's unable to pretend otherwise, the evidence of fornication pressing at her abdomen.

"It was fast," she admits with a shy smile. "Hurt a little, but you get used to it."

"Did it feel good?" one of the girls asks.

"It didn't feel bad."

"Then it sounds like he didn't do it right," someone whispers, loud. Too loud.

Nadine shoots her a glare. "Maria's pleasure isn't a priority."

"Why are you asking me?" Maria says cheeks dark red. "Imogene is the one with experience of having been with *four* men."

Every eye in the room swings to me, and I busy myself by taking a sip of tea. It's bitter, but warm, and I take another drink. Maria's outburst about me isn't new information. They were all there when my Collateral was exposed for the entire community to hear. When Anex lied about instructing me to train with Rex's friends to prepare myself to be a better mate. He hadn't been specific though, just that what I'd done had been enough to send me to Reeducation.

Nadine's eyes narrow. "Stories from the Fallen shouldn't be used as an example."

"Telling her story is part of the purification process. She must purge her past Regressions," Margaret says, eyes twinkling in the firelight. "Tell us, Imogene, what was it like to allow four Regressive men to have their way with you? To let them defile you in any way they want outside the sanctity of Anex's Order."

My gaze holds Margaret's, fully aware of what she's trying to do to me. She's always trying to break me down. Tear me to nothing so that I'll relent and become the passive mate Anex wants so badly. She wants me to tarnish the memory of my men, betray them in front of the masses to belittle what we had.

I lift my chin. "No."

"No?"

"No. I'm not going to tell you about my relationships."

Margaret's eyebrow raises. "I remember you coming to me, eyes red from crying all night after being forced to your knees by Rex."

I remember that day, too. Clear as crystal. Rex had forced me to suck his cock at the club. I'd been humiliated. Naïve. Margaret had been an ally then—or pretended to be. She'd soothed my sore eyes and talked me through the pain. She gave me advice. Clearly all of that was a set up. Everything is a set up—probably including this.

"Rex is—*was*—my Ordered. I was only pleasing my future mate."

"What about the desires you have during Corrections? When you found pleasure while being strapped by Levi? Or when Levi couldn't finish the job, he sent Elon in to finish it."

I see the jaw drop on a girl across from me, and the person sitting closest to me shifts away. I inhale in an attempt to steady myself. I look around the room at the innocent, naïve women who have no idea what they are getting into. No more than I did.

"Fine, you want to know? I'll tell you." I straighten my back. My tongue feels loose and I'm tired of hiding who I've become. "At first, it was a challenge, because the men assigned to train me were raised as the Chosen. Part of Serendee led by a man who believes all this nonsense Nadine is spewing. About serving men and meeting their needs and desires to keep their Regressive thoughts in line." I roll my eyes. "Men are horny, plain and simple. They want to get their cocks into something warm all the time. They want to get their cock into *you* all the time."

"Imogene!" Maria gasps, but I'm too busy thinking about Rex hurting me that first time. And how Silas took the time to take care of me and educate me about all of this confusing stuff. How to enjoy it. I think about that first kiss with Elon and the relief he gave me after Corrections with Levi. And Levi... well, he showed me a side I didn't know existed.

"Having a man worship you is fantastic. Having *four* men worship me was fucking outstanding." Around the fire, wide eyed girls listen to my every word. Even though I know I should stop, I can't seem to do it. "For the record, that is what it's called. Fucking. They fuck you with their cocks, burying it deep into your pussy. If you're lucky it's big and thick and yeah, it hurts like hell the first time, but after that..." God, I miss them. We didn't get enough time together before we'd been torn apart. "...it's good. Complicated and really, really good."

"*Imogene*," Nadine says, "I think that's enough."

"Agreed." I stand, done with this little circle of truth. "I hope your men treat you right." Blood rushes to my head as I step forward and my eyes swim. The teacup falls to the floor, shattering into a million pieces. "Wha—?" I ask, but the words get lost. The faces around me blur, and the last thing I remember is reaching out to steady myself and the world turning black.

Open your eyes.

My brain sends the message, but my eyes won't open.

Open your eyes.

I follow the command, but I'm too tired. I just want to sleep—longer—deeper. I try to curl into myself, snuggle against the soft sheets, but nothing gives.

Open your eyes, Imogene.

Struggling, I get my eyes open into small slits. Warm light makes flickering shadows against the walls. My eyelids drop shut, as if they're pulled down by weights, but I'm more awake now.

"Where am I?"

I open my eyes again, taking in the room. I'm no longer in the solarium. This place is small. The ceiling is low. I crane my neck, spotting a portrait over the bed. The light shimmers off the ornate, gold frame. Slowly my brain starts to work, the image coming into focus. Anex sitting in his lecture chair.

Suddenly, I know exactly where I am: Beatrice House. This is where I took my oath for the women's group. I'm in Anex's former bedroom that he shared with his wife—Rex's mother.

Fear jolts up my spine, igniting my body to move. I jerk up. Or try. Nothing moves but my neck. I know instinctively it's not from sleep or drowsiness. From the sharp digging in my wrist and ankles, I know I've been bound.

"Careful." The voice comes from beside me. A hand brushes the hair off my forehead. Anex comes into view. "You don't want to hurt yourself."

"What is this?" I ask, voice gravely.

"This is for your own protection," he says. His hand is still on my face, thumb grazing my cheek. "You're a danger to yourself, Imogene. Physically and spiritually."

"So you tied me up? You..." I try to think back. I was sitting around the fire. Ranting about fucking men. My teacup shattering and the bitter taste on my tongue. "You drugged me."

"There was little chance you wouldn't act out at the preparation ceremony, but it was important for the other women to believe you'd been Reeducated. The plan, all along, was to slip you a sedative in your tea, to keep you from any outbursts. Unfortunately, it must not have been enough because the reaction was delayed."

My head swims. From the drugs and the deep sleep. From the horror of my life.

He sighs, fingers trailing down my neck. "I hated doing it, but it's the only way. The regression streak is so strong in you. Every attempt has made it worse. Corrections. Training. Reeducation... defiance runs deep in your soul."

"Then let me go. I'll never come back." I swallow as his fingers inch lower, down to the plane of my chest. "I promise."

He smiles sympathetically. "I wish I could, but The Way won't allow it. I've been led to you. Originally, I thought you were for Rex, but I realized quickly that I'd made a terrible mistake by allowing those boys to take your virtue. It should have been mine."

Tears spring to my eyes. Anger and fear. Hatred for this monster standing over me.

"Anex—" His fingers push at the collar of my robe, spreading it apart, exposing my skin to the cool air of the room. "Please don't..."

"Your Preparation is almost complete. There's just one more layer of purification we must complete." I wince as his hands ghost over my breasts, barely touching. It's almost worse than if he'd touched me. "Once this process is over, you'll be ready for the ceremony, and ready to be mine. *Forever*."

My body turns rigid as he unties the knot of my robe, arms and legs paralyzed. My stomach rolls as he touches the brand on my lower hip.

"You look perfect wearing my mark." His fingers drag downward, and I push through the fear, clamping my thighs together. "Don't be afraid. All of this is part of a larger plan."

He makes a gesture, and it's then I realize we're not alone. Two figures move from the shadowy corners of the room. They're cloaked, hoods pulled low over their heads. The same cloaks we wear at our women's group. These are two of my *sisters*. I look to the one on my right.

"Don't let him do this to me! Help!"

One hands him a rectangular, carved wooden box. Anex ignores my protests and opens the lid, lifting an object from inside. Holding it up, the candlelight passes through the thick crystal. It's large, cylindrical in shape, honed and rounded at the top. There's no doubt what the object is for and where he's planning on using it.

"Anex, no." Again, I look to the cloaked women. "Please help me."

"Bless this crystal of purification. Accept this as the call to release all negative and Regressive energies bound inside Imogene. Penetrate the dark rebellion and replace it with the path to Enlightenment."

One of the women pours a clear, thick liquid into Anex's open palm. He coats the sides and tip of the crystal, leaving it in a thick sheen.

Sweat rises on my skin and whatever he says next is covered by the hard beating of my pulse. He runs the tip of the crystal between my breasts, across the tips of my nipples and down my lower body. My thighs press tighter, as far as my bound legs will allow it, and fear ratchets through my body. The women's hands pull apart my thighs.

"I'm still having my cycle," I argue, neck straining.

"It's good that you're bleeding. It's like your body knew that you needed to purge the foul toxins." He nods and one of his partners reaches between my legs and pulls out the tampon holding back my flow. Anex stands at the end of the bed, staring down at me, eyes fixed between my legs.

"Perfect," he says, licking his lips. "Absolutely perfect."

He presses the tip against my entrance.

"You don't have to do this," I tell him. "I'll be with you. I'll go through the ceremony. I won't fight. I'll forget about Rex and Levi and Elon and Silas. I'll be the spiritual wife you want."

"I know you will." My body fights against him, muscles tight and resistant. "Relax, or it'll tear you apart. Don't make me hurt you, because I will. Nothing can stop the path of The Way, especially not a dirty little whore that I can just as easily toss on the streets as welcome into my bed." He wedges the tip in a bit more, lips turned up in a small, l twisted smile. "Nothing will stop me from getting what I want."

Our gazes lock and something in me slips away. This is my leader. My guide. He's raised me and now he's Chosen me—yet here I am, fighting him every step, instead of embracing the honor.

To what end? The abuse of the other men in my life? The Banishment and Shunning? The loss of my friends from the donum? My educators and mentors?

This is not just my second chance. It's my *only* chance.

I exhale, forcing my muscles to release—allowing the crystal to enter my body. Allowing the final step of purification to begin. Allowing Anex what rightfully belongs to him.

Everything.

86

———————

L evi

"Are either of you expecting a package?"

Camille stands in the doorway of the kitchen. She hasn't said more than three sentences to us since the invitation came in the mail. Not while Elon and I discussed plans for getting Imogene away from Anex. Or how to get out in one piece ourselves.

"No," I answer for the two of us.

She carries the large box to the table, setting it down. Leaning over I see that it's addressed to the *'Residents of 238 Arbor Street.'*

The Serendee logo is stamped in the top corner.

Camille opens a drawer and pulls out a knife. Elon's shoulders tense. This woman... we still don't know her well. And we know for certain that she doesn't trust us. We watch as she presses the point of the knife to the center of the package, slicing through the tape.

Elon leans closer, looking into the box with a wary eye, like he's expecting a snake to jump out or something. She pushes past the tissue paper and frowns.

"Un-freaking-believable," Camille mutters, pushing the box toward me.

It's not a snake. It's clothing.

"There's a note," Elon says, reaching inside. It's a simple card, again stamped with Serendee's logo—the same logo branded into Imogene's hip. *"A little something to make you feel more comfortable at tomorrow's ceremony. A car will arrive to pick you up at 11 AM."*

I dole out the items. Basic black for me and Elon; a shirt and pants. Camille's is a dress, made from a bright blue fabric. She stares down at it and says, "He has to control everything, doesn't he?"

"To be fair," I say, folding my shirt into a square, "we would have looked very out of place in Secular clothing."

Her eyes cut to me, and I expect anger. Instead, I see sadness.

"I don't know if I can do this."

"Do what?" Elon asks.

"Go through with this plan. Put on this dress and play puppet to an evil man."

Elon stares at our host, jaw set. "It's a little late to back out now, but if you can't, I guess we—"

"This may be your only chance," I cut in. We need her to attend, or Elon and I won't make it past the gates. "Do you want to wait another eight years for an opportunity to get her out?"

I leave the rest unspoken. If Imogene stays in Serendee for another eight years she'll spend that either locked up with the Fallen or as Anex's mate. She'll never get away from him, which also means, we'll never get to see her again.

Camille has proven herself to be resilient and tough. Determined. But now she stands in front of us, twisting her fingers in the dress.

She looks nervous.

"Are you worried about Anex?" I ask. "Because other than petty control methods like the clothing, he won't try anything on a day like this. He'll want everything to go over perfectly."

"It's not Anex I'm worried about," she admits. "I'm kind of eager to face him again after all this time."

Elon glances at me and says, "If you're concerned about seeing Imogene, don't be. She'll be happy to see you."

"Are you sure?" she asks. "Don't pretend that Anex hasn't tainted her view of me."

"I won't." He meets her eye to eye. "He did do that. You were an example to all of us—"

"Which is why his invitation is a big deal," I cut in. "He's trying to prove he's not keeping your child from you or holding grudges."

Camille sighs and sits at the table. "You know, I tried to get her to come with me, but she wouldn't, and maybe that makes me a bad mother for leaving anyway."

"I don't think he gave you much of a choice," Elon says.

"I had a choice. Be his new wife, take the place of his dead wife— my best friend—or run. I chose to run—even if that meant leaving Imogene behind." She looks up, eyes shiny, looking more vulnerable than I've seen her before. "She has to resent me for that."

"I was with Imogene when we located the information about your whereabouts and this program. She wasn't angry. She was scared. She knew that if Anex found out that she'd found you—how she'd found you—there would be severe consequences," Elon explains. "I got the information for her, because I knew then that she was going to need you one day. I just didn't know when or under what circumstances. She's not going to resent you—she's going to be thankful that you're here."

She sniffs quietly, then stands, grabbing her dress out of the box. "It's going to be a long day tomorrow. I think I need some time to prepare myself." She looks between us. "Is there anything you need me to do?"

"Just be ready," Elon says. "It's going to be a long day."

Neither of us speak until she's upstairs, then Elon turns to me and asks, "Do you think we can really pull this off? Get Imogene and Rex out while saving ourselves?"

I want to tell him with confidence that we will, but there are a lot of balls in the air with this one. My plan with Elon. My plan with Anex. Our plans with Camille. It's ever evolving—constantly moving —but my goal is singularly focused:

Getting back to Imogene.

~

THE CAR RIDE to Serendee is quiet. There's something about an armed guard that makes conversation seem prohibited. Add in the fact that there are no pockets in our clothes, no way to discreetly hide a weapon. We're managed, contained, restrained, all without putting a finger on us.

Anex is always one step ahead.

Unfortunately, for him, he kicked out one of the more powerful people in his inner circle. Due to Elon's position in security he's aware of hidden weapon caches all over Serendee. "Anex's paranoia will be his doom," he'd told me, when we started laying out the idea. "He was terrified of an ambush or raid by the feds. Expected it, really. So unless he moved them—"

"He may have," I countered. One step ahead. "He should have."

"I agree," he admitted, "but he didn't monitor where the caches were located. Not all of them."

Then he drew a map.

From there the plan is vague. Get to the weapons. Get to Imogene and Rex. Get everyone out alive. I don't like it, but we're walking into a familiar world that follows only their own rules. Rules that change on the whim of a narcissistic leader.

"Look," Elon says, breaking the silence. The car drives toward the front gate—a driveway never used. Residents either walk to town on the path or vehicles are taken out the back entrance, carrying products. The gate has always been purely ornamental. But today it's wide open and not flanked by guards. Instead, two young women and two men stand at the entrance, each dressed in fall colors, holding a basket of flowers. They wave as we pass. "What the fuck?"

Anex agreed to transparency, at least a sense of it, and I guess this welcome group is part of it.

The car stops near a field near the front of the property, and we're escorted down the drive. There are no vehicles inside Serendee—it's one of the primary tenants. Elon instantly shifts into security mode—eyes peeled, looking for threats. Between us Camille's breath comes out short and uneven.

"Are you okay?" I ask, reaching out to steady her arm when she stumbles over an uneven spot in the road.

"It's just super weird being back here." Her hand presses against her chest. "So many memories."

"Take a deep breath," I say, trying to channel Silas. "I'm nervous too, but what we're doing here is the right thing." She nods, following my instructions and inhaling. Silas would distract her, and I point to the Main House in the distance. "Anex has expanded a lot since you left. That's his house."

"A mansion?" She snorts. "God, if Timothy isn't a predictable, pretentious, asshole, I don't know what he is."

The open way she slanders Anex still feels alarming—blasphemous—but there's no time to process my emotions on this. The conversation between us doesn't really ease the tension, but it gets her moving. We pass the donums, the housing area, the community center, and the new childcare facility. In the distance are the fields and barn. On the open field is where the ceremony will be held. A small tent is set to the side and that is where our escort guides us.

I realize then we aren't the only guests from outside Serendee.

Everyone is wearing identical clothing—they must have been sent outfits as well. I scan the area and recognize a woman. She'd been at Camille's house that morning—Kayla's sister: Gabi.

She and Camille do not acknowledge one another. Maybe they don't see one another but my skin starts to itch. Something feels off—like maybe I'm not the only one with a plan today.

"Anyone know what's supposed to happen here?" This comes from an older man. Probably someone's father. Did he really allow in family members? The ones pushing for contact with their loved ones?

"Some kind of ceremony," Gabi says. "Celebrating the equinox, I guess?"

Her voice is even. Calm. Too calm for someone so desperate to see her sister.

"Yes, the residents of Serendee celebrate each of the seasons." Every eye in the tent swings in my direction. "It's a way to thank the earth for a bountiful harvest." Elon shifts next to me. "Part of the event will be what people outside the community refer to as a wedding. Couples will be bound and blessed."

"A group wedding?" the guy asks.

I shrug. "It's just a way for everyone to celebrate efficiently. Everything in Serendee is shared resources. We already have the music, food, and guests." I point to the small group in the tent. "Why not knock out more than one celebration at once."

Camille gives me a curious look—probably wondering why I'm defending the ceremony. I'm just trying to keep things moving forward. The last thing we—or these people—need is to get kicked out before it even begins.

The flaps open, held out by two other smiling residents. These I recognize. They're Anex's guards. They've just dropped the black clothing for the day and their weapons are obscured by the loose fabric. Elon's eyes narrow, and his hand taps his lower back, confirming that, yes, they're armed. No way Anex allows visitors in without protection.

Before I can react further, he walks in the room, Margaret a step behind.

Bowing on instinct, I elbow Elon halfway down. We're here to grovel. To prove we want back in. That we can be trusted. Anex has to know we mean it, even if Camille thinks we don't. The truth is that in my soul, I'm still conflicted. When Anex's eyes drift over me that aching need for approval surges in my chest.

But he's not interested in me or Elon. He briefly nods and greets the outsiders, but then leaves Margaret to entertain the guests. Anex doesn't stop moving until he's a foot from Camille. He smiles warmly, offering his hand. "Camille."

Her throat bobs with a thick swallow, but she doesn't reach out to touch him. "Timothy."

His name rings in the quiet tent—Margaret's eyes darting over. Even Elon stiffens, but Anex, ever charming, just clasps his hands in front of his body and says, "I've always thought you looked lovely in blue."

Hence him picking it out for her to wear. Not for her—for *him*.

"Margaret, dear," he calls, beckoning her with his hand. She comes dutifully. Camille is focused on Margaret's stomach. "I'd like you to meet my old friend—"

"And partner," Camille adds.

"Yes, and partner, Camille Montgomery. Imogene's mother."

Margaret leans against Anex, belly jutting out. She grins wide, showing her perfect, straight teeth. "It's wonderful to meet you. Imogene has become such a dear friend of mine—more like a sister."

Something dark washes over Camille's face, but she pulls it back, ignores Margaret, and turns her attention back to Anex.

"Can I see her?"

Although she's addressing Anex, she asks the question loud enough for the others to hear. The slight tensing in his jaw reveals that he's aware of the entire room watching. All the other guests, the families there to check up on their loved ones, the people noticing their bank accounts dwindling.

"Of course," his teeth grit. "After the ceremony. There's not enough time now."

"I'm her mother, and I'd like to wish her good luck on this special day." She reaches under the collar of her dress and pulls a necklace. "I'd like to give her this—it was my grandmother's."

"I love that," Gabi says from across the room. "My mother gave me something similar and it means so much to me."

A grin is plastered to Anex's mouth. "It's a lovely gesture but—"

"Unfortunately," Margaret interjects, accentuating. "Our time is limited. We must go."

Camille's eyebrow raises, her gaze affixed to Anex's. An energy flickers in the room. Margaret may be his spiritual wife, but Camille... she's something more.

"Please, Timothy," Camille says quietly. "I'd be in your debt."

This time he doesn't bristle at the use of his given name and a spark appears in his eyes. The connection between these two is unmistakable. I'm not the only one that notices, and their gaze breaks contact, and he looks around the room at the watching crowd.

"I'm sure we can spare five minutes so a mother and daughter can reconnect." His head tilts slightly toward Margaret. "Don't you think, sweetheart?

There's no other answer than "yes" and Margaret knows it. This woman thought she understood how to be with this man, and her time on the outside gave her the impression she could be his equal. There is no equal to Anex.

Except maybe the woman standing next to me.

"Thank you," Camille says, doing her best to be gracious.

He gestures and one guard steps forward while the other opens the flaps. Fresh air breezes in and I realize how warm and stuffy it is in here. Anex pauses before leaving. "Levi, I'd like you to escort Camille to Imogene's Preparation tent."

Me, I almost ask, but I catch myself and see the command for what it is. A loyalty test.

"I would be honored."

"Elon and Richard," he points to one of the guards at the flap, "will escort the rest of you to the ceremony. There's music, drinks, and delicious food; all grown and prepared right here in Serendee. Take time to enjoy everything our community has to offer and maybe a little more understanding of why your family has embraced our lifestyle."

"And afterwards I'll get to see my sister?" Gabi asks.

"She'll be eager to see you," Anex replies before dipping outside.

My gaze meets Elon's. Separating isn't part of the plan, but we knew there was no way to control the variables once we got here. Richard ushers the group out of the tent toward the main festivities. Elon hesitates at the entry and turns to me. "Get to her. No matter what."

"No matter what," I repeat.

Camille looks up at me. "What does that mean?"

"It means the task we came to accomplish—it's started." I lead her into the crowd, heart pounding as loud as the drums in the distance. "All we can do now is focus on getting Imogene safely out of Serendee."

She asks no more questions, just sticks close to my side. To the untrained eye, it would seem like Anex let us loose in the community alone, but I know better. I take her hand and drag her around a group of children playing a game, moving quickly.

Stumbling at our pace, she looks down at our hands. "What are you doing?"

"Getting away from the guard."

"Guard?" she asks, frowning.

"He's armed." I nod at a man searching for us. "So are half of these other men, and they're watching us closely."

"I shouldn't be surprised, but I always am."

Leading her toward the large Preparation tent, I take her to the backside of the structure. I stop before going further.

"Would you like me to go first?" I can tell by her expression that her anxiety has returned. "It should be okay, but me going through that door might be less of a surprise than your sudden appearance."

Camille takes hold of my arm and gives it a soft squeeze. "Thank you, Levi."

"I haven't done anything yet."

"You got me this far, and that's more than I've been able to do in years of trying."

I lift the bottom of the tent, and duck under, entering a room filled with women. They're all dressed in sheer, embroidered dresses, but not one of them interests me. I scan the room, passing a blur of faces until my eyes settle on her.

My heart nearly cracks in two.

A ripple runs though the space, the women spotting me. Imogene looks up, eyes glassy. I frown, wondering if she's sick.

"Is she drugged?" Camille asks from behind me.

Her cheeks are hollow. Her skin is paler than before. Her hair is clean but limp. Every effort has been made to make this girl beautiful for her Mating, but something is wrong. I stride across the room, not caring who sees me and kneel at her feet. "Imogene, what has he done to you?"

"Levi?" she asks, blinking away the fog. "Is that you?"

"Yes." I drop to my knees. "I'm here."

Her hands cup my face, soft and cool. She pinches my skin. "For real?"

"Definitely real."

"But why? Why are you here? How?"

I kiss her fingers. "You know why, Little Lamb."

"You shouldn't have come back," her gaze drops. "It's too late. I've already been through the Preparations."

Preparations. Even I don't know exactly what that means other than they spend time together before the ceremony. But knowing what I know now and the lost look on her face, fear blooms in my chest.

"It's not too late." I force her eyes to mine. "Whatever oil they've anointed you with, or blessings they've given—those things don't matter outside these walls."

Suddenly it hits me—why she's so lost. He got to her. The Reeducation, the punishments, the isolation and whatever else he threw at her—he got to her. Her mind is muddled. I understand this. I feel the tug to embrace the familiar. It's nearly impossible to ignore. But the sadness coming off of her is real. As is the unsettling, distant, look on her face.

This isn't the Imogene I've come to love, the spitfire, rebellious, fierce woman.

This is the Imogene Anex has created, and it'll take work to draw her back out again.

Brushing back a stand of hair, I ask, "Imogene, where's Rex?"

"I don't know. I haven't seen him since we were in the white room together."

The white room.

"I don't know where Silas is either," she continues, "but I don't think it's good. He tried to help me, and we were punished."

"It's okay, Silas is—"

I sense the movement of a body behind me, and her eyes lift over my shoulder. Imogene's jaw drops, words lost on her tongue. She looks back to me and whispers, "Levi, who is that?"

I stand, giving Camille room.

"Imogene." The strong confident woman that escaped this place stands tall beside me. "Oh, honey, it's me."

Her head tilts, like she's trying to process everything going on. "Mom?"

The reunion is interrupted, a high-pitched sound pierces the air outside the tent. Our eyes meet in confusion. "What was that?" she asks.

Faint pops sound in the distance, then grow louder and closer, until a large explosion shakes the ground around us.

Without thinking, the name escapes my lips. "Elon."

87

Imogene

I'd been lost since the night before. My mind is slipping somewhere safe—away from the madness and hurt. Somewhere I had to reconcile my truth.

Anex was never letting me go.

I was going to become his Mate.

And I would be required to perform all duties demanded of that position.

My life had always been leading to this—I realize that now. My mother's betrayal, Anex's hurt and obsession, my objectification. I can still feel the intrusion deep in my core—the promise of what's to come.

What I didn't expect was Levi. My mother *or* the bombs.

"Imogene!" Levi's arm comes around my shoulder, lifting me up. "It's time."

"Time?" I ask, feeling two steps behind. "Time for what?"

"To get you out of here." Another explosion rocks the ground. Cries come from the other women in the tent. Some have already run. A few are curled on the floor. Panic seizes the room in everyone but the man holding me.

"You did this?" I ask, my eyes shifting to my mother, who doesn't seem startled by the explosions. "And you?"

"We'll talk about it later," Camille says. "Right now, we need to get out of here while we can."

Levi pulls me out of the tent. The air is thick with sulfur and the sound of screams. Fear ripples through the crowd, releasing in panicked screams and feral cries. Whatever celebrations have been going on have stopped, everything altered by the attack.

"This is Elon?" I ask, gripping Levi's fingers as someone tries to wedge between us, stepping on the hem of my dress. His answer is lost in the sound of screams, but I believe it. Elon isn't the kind of man that just stops. He'll fight to get to his family—to me and Rex.

I jerk Levi to a stop. "We need to find Rex."

Levi turns, looking down at me. "You're the priority."

I yank my hand from his. "I won't leave without him."

"Do you even know where he is?" A woman, blood dripping down her temple, slams into me. Before I can react, she's gone, leaving a smear across the bodice of my gown. "What the hell is the white room?"

I tell him what I can, fear choking my throat. A room in Anex's private quarters, the last place I saw him three days ago. "How do you know he's still there?"

"We have to try, Levi."

Camille stands nearby, shifting on her feet. Smoke rises behind her, the stage on fire. My *world* on fire.

"We have to go," she says. "This is about to get nasty."

"Take her," Levi tells my mother. "Get her to safety. I'll go find Rex."

"Alone?" I ask. "No—"

"It's the only way it's happening, Imogene." He jerks his chin. "Go with your mother."

"But—"

He grabs for me. "Go with her. You can trust her. She got Elon and

I in here today." He lifts my hand to his mouth and kisses the back. "I love you, Imogene."

My heart swells. "I love you, too."

He's swallowed by the chaos, and I feel like my heart goes with him. Lifting my skirt, I start toward the path, the easiest way out of the walls, but Camille's hand comes down on my arm. "I know another way."

"There is no other way!"

The fact that I say this during this type of crisis means everything. Anex had us trapped. No way out.

"There is. Follow me."

I don't know this woman. I don't trust her. I barely remember her, but the set of her jaw is familiar. A mirror to my own when I'm determined. We head the opposite way, up an incline on the backside of Serendee. A screech cuts through the madness and a loud voice echoes over the crowd, amplified by a megaphone.

"Everyone, remain calm! Get to the ground! Follow orders, and no one will be hurt!"

That's when I see them. Men and women pouring into the field. They're wearing black vests, letters imprinted across the chest. Helmets and guns held in the air.

Thwap, thwap, thwap... I look up and see a helicopter circling above. The sound of the wings competes with my thudding heartbeat.

"We have you surrounded! Get to the ground!"

"What is this?" I ask, paralyzed. "Who are these people?"

Gunfire blazes across the field, and I see people fall, one after the other, tumbling down. Fear grips me, my spine rigid and unmoving. I want to run to help while also wanting to run away.

Camille grabs me and drags me away to a wall covered in thick ivy. She drops my hand, frantically pushing through the foliage. She stops suddenly, hand clasped around something hidden and yanks back. An old creaky, wooden, door falls open.

On the other side is a vehicle. Black and shiny. A man in a blue tie and mirrored sunglasses opens the car door and roughly pushes us inside. We're moving before the door even shuts.

"Did Elon do this?" I ask, trying to reconcile everything I saw. Everything I heard and smelled.

"No," she says, looking out the back window as Serendee fades away. "I did."

~

UNLIKE MANY IN SERENDEE, I've spent time outside the walls. I worked in the Center recruiting new members. Elon took me clothes shopping in an upscale boutique. I've eaten in expensive restaurants and met up with Rex in a bar. I've even gone to a fraternity party, drank too much, and had sex in a closet. But I've never been here: The police station.

"You're not in trouble, Imogene." The woman that repeatedly tells me this has short reddish hair and thick glasses that make her eyes look too large. Her badge says Agent McNair, and I don't like her. "We just need you to talk to us about Timothy Wray."

Timothy Wray. Anex. The man who groomed me, branded me, violated me. My leader. I can't bring myself to say any of this. One thing he instilled in all of us is that the government is not to be trusted.

"I just want to go home."

"There is no home," Agent McNair replies. "Not until this shakes out. The entire compound is considered a crime scene."

"She means with me." I look up at Camille—my mother—who hasn't left my side. She's the one that did this, invited these people into our home. "Imogene is my daughter, she'll come home with me."

I wish that statement brought me something other than fear.

"Where is Levi?" I ask. "Rex and Elon? Where are they?"

We're in a small room with a window covered with blinds. The bottom left side is askew, giving me a small view of the outside room. It's been nothing but a steady stream of people since I arrived. Each person is dressed in the clothing of Serendee. Each one as lost as I feel. Unmoored by the events of the night.

"I'm not at liberty to discuss the whereabouts of anyone from the compound."

"Stop calling it that!" I hiss. "It's not a compound—it's a community." I narrow my eyes at Camille. "It's not fair to all those people, and you know that."

I wanted to escape Anex—to live my life in peace—but I never wanted to hurt the people that lived there. Whatever happened tonight isn't what any of us wanted.

"What I know is that you're tired, traumatized, and need rest." She gives the agent a hard look. "Can we leave, or should I call my attorney?"

"Look," the agent says, sighing as if she feels as exhausted as I do. Doubtful. "Although the majority of your friends aren't in jail. They're being held in a safe space until we can work this out."

"I don't care about the majority of my friends. I want to know about three in particular. Elon, Levi, and Rex."

She flips through a pad of paper on the table. "You just listed three of Wray's highest confidants."

"You don't know anything," I bite.

"Which is why I need your help, Imogene. I just need you to answer a few more questions. Did you see evidence of illegal drug sales in and out of Serendee? What about sex trafficking?" She looks down at my dirty white gown. "Were you a witness to Timothy Wray's involvement in either of these activities?"

"She's a victim," Camille says, slamming her fist on the table so hard the agent's phone skips across the surface. "And she needs rest, food, and possibly medical care. We'll come back when she's had all of those, with our attorney. In the meantime, I think you have plenty of others to interrogate."

I blink up at this woman—my mother. I have never heard anyone speak with such clear conviction. Especially not a woman. There's no twisting of words or manipulations.

"We're leaving."

"One last thing—" She looks to me. "Do you know if Timothy Wray had other property outside the compound? Like another house? Business property? Close connections in another city?"

"Just the Center in town. Otherwise, we never left." I frown. "Why?"

"Because Timothy Wray and a few others in his circle managed to escape tonight. If you have any idea where they are, you need to tell us now."

I shake my head. "I have no idea."

Camille gestures for me to rise, and I follow, because I want to be anywhere but here. Also, Levi told me to go with her.

The outer room is filled with men and women in uniform, and I feel foolish in my gown—as if it marks me for being one of Anex's loyal followers. I only raise my head when I sense someone's approach. My heart stops. A cop leads three men, all of their hands bound at the wrists. Levi's red hair jumps out at me first, followed by Elon's broad shoulders, and then Rex's ice blue eyes.

They turn without seeing me, down another hall.

"Where are they taking them? Why are they handcuffed?" I ask, turning to Camille in a panic.

"You heard Agent McNair. They're Timothy's closet allies. They'll be questioned extensively."

"And then?"

"I don't know, but it's not your concern. You're away from them now. You never have to see any of those monsters again."

Monsters.

I start to argue, to tell her that they aren't monsters. They're *my* men. I love them, but it feels dangerous to say. Numb all over, I follow Camille out of the police station wondering if I've traded one nightmare for the other.

88

———

I mogene

We don't actually go to Camille's. Apologizing, she makes a detour, swinging into the hospital parking lot.

"Do we have to do this now?" I ask, arms crossed over my chest. "There's nothing wrong with me."

"I know," Camille says, "but the police want to gather as much evidence as possible."

"So you're saying my body is evidence?"

She frowns. "No. I just..." She looks out the window of the car, unable to meet my eye. "I just want to make sure we get him, Imogene, and that means we can't cut corners."

A social worker meets us inside, along with another female agent. My head spins. It's been hours since I'd slept or eaten. I'm worried about the guys—how long would they be at the station? Are they really in trouble. No one has answers. Just demands.

"Imogene, when you're comfortable, I need you to remove your dress."

I stiffen at the request. I know what my body looks like under the fabric. Bruised and scarred, some self-inflicted, others not. I hesitate, glancing over at Camille, both wanting her to see what she left me to endure and not wanting her to know.

"A little help?" I ask, gesturing to the row of buttons down the back of my dress. It's filthy, covered in dirt and grime from my escape —the hem frayed and torn. Camille moves to assist me, her fingers shaking as she works. This is awkward for her, too, but she's not the one who everyone's eyes pin to as the fabric drops revealing my Anex approved undergarments.

Freak.

The insults thrown at me walking from the Center to Serendee come rushing back. I'd always fought it. I never believed it but now, as I remove the tank and shorts, exposing myself to the room, I know it's true.

We *are* freaks.

It's in the clothes, the conformity, the secrets. It's in the lingering bruises inside and out. It's in the scars etched into my body.

It's in the brand.

"Jesus," the social worker utters when she sees it. Her eyes widen after the words slip out, aware of her error. She swallows. "Did they do that to you?"

"Yes." I ghost my fingers over it. It's mostly healed now, the scabs are gone, but the raised new skin looks angry and sensitive. "It was part of an initiation."

"So you just let them do this to you."

Let them.

"I wasn't aware that they would be burning my flesh. I just thought it was a place for the women in the community to support one another."

The officer circles me, taking photos of every mark, gesturing to the nurse to use a ruler to measure each one. She lowers the camera and nods to my chest. "What happened?"

For the first time heat rises on my skin. *What happened?* Something I can't explain. Something personal.

"Anex ordered that I receive a punishment."

Her eyebrow rises. "For?"

I shake my head, hands trembling. I won't tell them what for. Or who. Or anything else. Camille seems to sense my limit and steps forward. "Take the evidence. Do your tests, but she's not answering anymore questions."

I give her a small, thankful smile, but she doesn't notice. Her eyes are also roaming my body. At the marks on my wrists. On my inner thighs. On my ribs pressing against my skin. When she finally meets my gaze she says quietly, "I'm sorry, Imogene. I had no idea."

"Of course, you didn't," I say, loathing the guilt I hear in her tone. What I can't say is that every mark, bruise, and scar is evidence of my worth. Of my journey. Of my attempts at Enlightenment.

And right now, I can't decide if I'm proud of them or not.

The knock is firm, three raps followed by, "Imogene, dinner's ready."

Three times a day Camille knocks on my door, announcing a meal. Breakfast, lunch, and dinner. I haven't come down yet. The thought of food is like ash on my tongue.

I call out the same words I've repeated over and over, "I'm not hungry."

Usually she leaves, her heavy footsteps on the hardwoods going down the hall, but today I sense her loitering outside the door, her shadow shifting back and forth. There are only four people I care about entering this room, and so far, I've heard nothing about them.

This time she doesn't leave, instead turning the knob and stepping inside. I want to be embarrassed that she finds me curled up in a ball, wearing the same outfit I changed into when I arrived four days ago. I should be humiliated about my dirty hair, and dry skin, and the fact I haven't moved from this bed other than to use the bathroom.

I mean, I *am*, but... I also can't muster the energy to care.

"Do you have any news?" I ask, looking over my shoulder.

"They still haven't found Timothy." A tray of food is clutched between her hands. There are two bowls, both steaming with the scent of something spicy. My stomach clenches, but I push the feeling aside. "They think he may have fled the country with a few of his guards and his pregnant wife."

Margaret.

"I'm not interested in Anex." I swallow back the bitterness on my tongue. "Have they released Rex, Elon, and Levi?"

"Not yet."

"Silas?"

"No." She clears her throat and adds, "But even if they did, I don't think it's wise for you to see them again."

I roll over, facing her. "What did you say?"

"Imogene," she rests the tray on the desk and pulls out the chair. "I know it is difficult to be away from the people you considered your friends—"

"They're my family."

"Of course." Her voice is calm, annoyingly soothing, like one of the bulls down in the pasture you don't want to spook. "This family... it isn't real. The people you think you care for; they are either manipulating you or have been manipulated themselves."

"I know what's real, Camille. And what I feel for those men isn't manipulation."

Her lips make a tight, thin, line. "You were arranged to marry Rex, correct?"

"Yes but—"

"A decision made by Anex—not on your own?"

"That's not—"

"What it *isn't* is love. Taking away your freedom to choose. Destroying your autonomy. All of that is manipulation and coercion. It's brainwashing and look how much danger it put you in!"

I swing my legs over the side of the bed, planting my feet on the floor for the first time all day. Swaying, dizzy from a headrush and low blood sugar, I grip the headboard. "Those men are the ones that opened my eyes to the truth of Serendee and Anex's devious ways.

They brought me into the light—showed me what existed outside those walls. Don't you dare question their motives."

"They hurt you, Imogene!" Her eyes dart to my wrists. "I've seen the scars." She chokes on her next words. "I've seen your body. Love doesn't look like that."

I yank the shirt sleeve down. "My body is none of your business, but if you need to know the truth, I did that to myself. They... they saved me from him, and that's what made him turn on me—on *us*."

Her eyes meet mine, searching for something, then soften. "He felt threatened by you."

I nod. "Yes. He split us apart. Locked me and Rex away. Banished Elon and Levi. And I don't even know where Silas is." I inhale, holding back a sob. "I'm so scared for him."

Camille's hand grabs mine and I'm too tired to fight back. "I know, but you're safe now. I'm here for you."

I yank my hand back. "Are you? Because you left before. They didn't."

She recoils, stunned, like she's been slapped. Good. "I know I fucked up. Big time. Things were—"

"I know how they were. That's what I'm saying. Anex is the devil —he forces us into impossible decisions. *You* had to leave. I believe that. But if I'm not going to judge you then you need to realize that you can't judge us. Rex is not his father. Nor are the others. I love them. I *need* them, and until they're back with me, you and I have nothing to talk about."

A cold silence settles between us. I've been manipulated my whole life and I'm not going to let it happen again.

Camille sighs and says, "I'll talk to Agent McNair about Levi and Elon, tell them their part in helping me infiltrate the compound. But Rex... I'm not sure what I can do. He's Timothy's son—"

"And as much of a victim as any of us." I lift my chin. "He's also Beatrice's son. She was your best friend, wasn't she?"

She hesitates, her forehead creased like she's deep in thought. Finally, she says, "I'll do what I can for those boys—but if I do, you have to promise that you'll eat something." She slides the tray closer. "Just get your strength back."

I'd like to argue, but I'm exhausted, and I know she's right. Starving myself isn't helping anyone. I need to be strong for them.

"What can you do?" I ask, lifting the spoon.

"Maybe more than I realized."

The bed sinks next to me, familiar warmth sliding under the covers and against my skin. I sink into the dream, holding onto it like threads of gossamer. A hand slides across my stomach and warmth tickles the back of my neck. Silas always makes me feel safe. Loved.

"I've missed you," I tell him. Pressing against the curve of his body.

"I missed you, too. So much." It's the feel of a kiss on my neck, warm, then cool, that forces the thread to part. I'm awake, in the room at Camille's. Except I'm not alone—the body behind me is very real. I turn and find Silas curled into me.

"Oh my God." It's not the first time this week I'd been confused about reality. "This isn't a dream?"

His fingers trace the line of my jaw. "I fucking hope not."

Licking my lips apart until our tongues meet, he kisses me to prove it. I feel the heat of him through my limbs, electric and real.

Yeah, I think, definitely real.

"Where did you come from?" I ask, body glued to his. "How did you get here?"

"Your mom. I could have waited until morning, but—"

"No!" I kiss him. His mouth, his nose, his forehead. "Never wait." He laughs, but it sounds tired. His arms wind around my body. "So, my mom found you?"

He nods against my shoulder, chin scratchy with stubble. "Yes, me and the others were at the hotel. Anex sent us a message days ago that there had been some trouble and to lock the doors and wait. We had no idea about the raid at Serendee until your mom showed up with the FBI."

"She came with the FBI?"

"Yeah. She came in first and," he runs his hand through his hair, "honestly, I was kind of out of it. It was easier to stay fucked up than deal with everything going on. But she told me that you were here, and the guys are being detained. I thought she may have me arrested too, but she didn't. She actually made the Feds go easy on us."

I don't have to ask why. Even with my mother's bias about Serendee, she understands the circumstances Silas has been living in are not of his making. "Because you're victims."

Of sex trafficking, I don't add.

His eyes darken. "I don't know about that, Little Lamb."

"What he made you do—me do. That wasn't with our consent. Not really. That was stripped away from us a long time ago." I've seen Silas work and I've felt Silas' love. Although I know his mind is a mess over it all, these are two different things.

"I thought we would go to the police station but instead we spent the day in the hospital undergoing an exam and then the FBI came—asked a lot of questions."

"So many questions," I agree, laughing lightly. I touch his cheek. "Are you okay? Physically?"

He nods. "All my tests came back clean, but I wasn't working—not like that. Some of the girls... they've got infections. Hopefully nothing worse. The medications and supplements Anex had me give them... I don't know. I'm not a healer, but I don't think they're effective."

"Did Mom bring them back here?"

"A few stayed in the hospital overnight, and I think she has some other friends in her network that took the girls in." He exhales and tightens his arms around me. "I'm just happy to be with you."

He's skinny, but so am I. His eyes are tired, but so are mine. This is who we've become but we recognize it in one another.

"Does Camille know you're in here?" I ask.

"She didn't stop me." That's progress. Maybe I got through to her.

"I told the police everything I could to get the guys released. I don't know if it's going to work, but I tried."

"I know you did." I kiss him again and watch his eyes flutter shut. "Sleep and we'll figure out what we're going to do in the morning."

His breathing evens out and I find myself drifting off to the rise and fall of his chest. I've got one of my men back, but I won't rest until the other three are also home.

89

———————

Silas

I wake in the bed alone, daylight waning outside the window. I slept all day. Or more than one day? My brain is foggy. The sleep was so good.

The bed next to me is cool, making me wonder how long Imogene's been gone. Across the room I hear movement behind the bathroom door.

"Come in," she says when I tap on the door.

I walk in on her standing in front of the mirror, naked, hair long and wet, and dripping over her shoulders. Gorgeous, but battle worn. Her body showing the markings of a soldier.

For the first time in weeks, my cock thickens at the sight.

Stepping behind her, I press into her backside, I'm caught by her scent, by her soft skin and lick a trail up her neck. I've missed the way she tastes. Imogene exhales at my attention, then pins my eyes in the mirror.

"How did you sleep?" she asks.

"Like the dead." I brush aside her hair to kiss her shoulder. The move exposes her breast and my stomach drops. *Fuck*. It's been weeks, but the skin is still discolored from the punishment Rex was forced to dole out. Sliding my hand between her side and her arm, I ghost my fingers over the flesh. "I'm so sorry I couldn't save you that day. That punishment belonged to me."

"He did punish you. There was plenty to go around for all of us."

I touch her gently, running my knuckles over the side of her breast. "I hate this."

"I hate that I don't know the difference between what I like and what Anex has groomed me to like."

I nod, resting my chin on her shoulder. I understand. "It's so fucking hard."

"The lessons, and instruction, and Corrections, all the stuff he taught us muddles up the mind and body."

Because even though all I want to do is take care of her, seeing those bruises makes my dick hard. And taking care of women is what I do. I calm, I sooth, and yeah, I manipulate, usually resulting in my own pleasure along with whatever job Anex has me doing.

But it's not like that with Imogene. I know that. I want her because I love her. Because she's mine.

She takes my hand, placing my palm over her breast. Hers rests on top and she encourages me to squeeze. "I like it when it hurts. It feels right. Like I don't deserve something good without going through something painful to get it."

I press a kiss under her ear. "What if it's not about deserving and just what your body likes? Pain or pleasure."

There's something holding her back, a tension in her limbs, the shallow rise and fall of her chest. "Did he do something?"

"There was a cleansing."

I've heard this before—actually, I've applied some of the methods with the recruits as they come into Serendee, purifying them for their new life.

"Before the ceremony?" I ask, dropping my hands to wrap them around her waist.

"Yes. The Preparation. They said a blessing and anointed us with oil, then sprayed us in the showers." I nod at her description, but she isn't finished. "We were all sitting around the fire, getting a lesson on how to please our men."

I snort and that draws out a smile. "You probably could've taught that lesson."

"Oh, they wanted one, but... they put something in my tea, and I woke up the next day bound to Anex's bed."

My grip tightens around her waist, holding her tight. "They drugged you?"

"Yes." Tears build at the corner of her eyes, and she looks down. "Anex wanted a special cleansing for me because I'm so... dirty."

"Hey," I lift her chin and force her eyes to meet mine in the mirror. "You're not dirty. You're perfect."

She shakes her head. "What *he* did made me feel dirty. The way he used me as an example. The way he made the women hold me down when he forced—"

"Imogene," I ask quietly, "did he rape you?"

"I don't know. There was this crystal..." she doesn't finish, instead crumbles in front of me, sobs ratcheting though her body. It's all the answer I need. He may not have used his body, but still forced his will on her. I turn her, pull her into my chest and hold her. "It hurt."

"He'll never hurt you again," I assure her, holding back the mounting rage.

"You can't promise that."

She's right. A normal man couldn't, but this one? The one holding the woman he loves in her arms while she falls apart—so convinced she's damaged and dirty that she doesn't even recognize assault when it happens to her.

This man can make the promise. Because I know for certain that I'm going to kill him.

~

"What did you say this was?" I take another bite into the

rectangle. It's both hard and soft, the red fruit substance in the middle hot enough to burn my tongue.

Imogene holds up the colorful box. "It's called a Pop-Tart."

I glance at the toaster. "Because it pops up when it's ready."

"Right?" she says, picking hers apart with her fingers and eating it one small piece at a time. "I shouldn't like it but..."

"It's just so good."

Everything we ate at Serendee was grown there. Everything natural. We had all natural sweeteners, from fruits or honey, but nothing like the gritty substance in this tart. It feels luxuriously defiant, sitting in Camille's kitchen, eating foods that would make Anex's blood boil.

I take another bite.

"I think I should call Agent McNair," she says, resting her half-eaten tart on her plate. "Maybe if I talk to her directly again, I can get her to understand."

"Camille said we should let the lawyers handle it."

"I just think that maybe if I can explain everything, she'll let them go."

I shake my head. It may be my first time eating a Pop-tart, but I'm more familiar with the secular world than Imogene. "It's easy to say the wrong thing and make it worse."

Because of our positions in the community, we'd been instructed on how to talk to authorities outside of Serendee. Primarily—don't. And if you have to? Tell them nothing. Anex believes the government is filled with lying bureaucrats who will go to any length to keep ordinary citizens under their thumb. They want to control our lives, our health, and autonomy.

She runs her thumb over the edge of the table. "I don't want to make things worse."

I take her hand, linking our fingers together. "I know. It wouldn't be on purpose, but what we see as normal, they don't. Rex and Elon were involved in a lot of illegal activities. Especially the drugs—"

"They didn't have a choice," she argues. "No more than you had one to run the brothel, or I had in choosing my mate."

"You and I both know that, but to outsiders it's confusing. The police won't see it that way." I tug at her hand, and she stands, moving from her chair and into my lap. I circle my arms around her and hold her against my chest.

"Camille said she'd try to do something," she says.

It'd felt like a miracle when I'd woken up with Imogene that morning. Soft and warm. Just her scent was enough to evoke an emotion, something I'd been suppressing for weeks now—too afraid to hope we'd survive Anex's will.

Then she told me about what he'd done to her. The purification ritual. He's so full of shit. Always manipulating and trying to get the upper hand. There's nothing he loves more than demeaning women. Never again. Not with Imogene at least. Those days are over—she's free.

We changed into secular clothing. Soft yellow shorts for Imogene and an oversized T-shirt. She'd tossed me a shirt from the drawer. It had a worn lettering across the front, *Whittmore University 5k*. I tugged it on along with a pair of flannel pajamas and followed her to the kitchen.

Camille had been gone when we got down there. Leaving us a note and the box of Pop-Tarts to eat. There was an apology saying they were all she had and were normally for kids that came through the house. She didn't give a time for her return.

"Maybe if I go down there, it'll work. Barter with information. I worked in the Center. I know things—where he keeps his paperwork." Her finger traces the faded lettering on my shirt. "I could demand to see him."

"I want to bring them home as much as you do, but we have to be smart about this—safe." She frowns. "I don't think we should leave the house. He could be watching."

Imogene's eyes dart to the window. "Do you think?"

"I don't know, babe, but we have to be careful, and patient." I know for certain Anex isn't going to let us go this easily. Especially not her. He had plans for Imogene, dark and obsessive. There's no way he's going to give her up. She doesn't need to know that—not now. I just want her to feel safe. To feel loved and I'll do everything I can to make that happen.

"I'm pretty sure I'm not known for my patience," she says. "That's why my journal is filled with so many lapses."

Grabbing her thigh, I hitch her leg over my thigh until she's straddling me. Her hips rock into me and my cock responds immediately. I groan, and she laughs.

"Since you won't let me call Agent McNair, and we're trapped in the house, maybe you have some ideas about what we can do with our time?"

"Are you sure?" I ask. "I don't want to rush you after—"

After what he did to her. Us.

Her eyes meet mine, intense and determined. "He hurt both of us, Silas. Played games with our bodies and used us to advance himself." Her lips are a hair's breadth away. "I won't let him be part of this."

It's easier said than done. I know that. Anex has been in our brains for years. In the way we use our bodies, but he's gone and all I want is this woman. My heart nearly bursts when she adds, "I just want to feel something other than this aching fear."

I know it. I feel it. Our whole world has been turned upside down, it's scary as fuck. I want Elon here to protect us, and Rex to tell us what to do and Levi to make sure we're doing it right. They're not here, but we can comfort one another. Bending, I capture her mouth in mine, and glide my fingers between her legs until they brush against her clit.

She's sticky, ready, but I kiss her temple and ask, "How do you want it?"

Our eyes lock and I know she wants to tell me to decide for her—that she doesn't know—but my girl knows her body. What it can tolerate and what gives her the most pleasure.

"It doesn't matter. As long as you're with me."

I ruck up her shirt, lifting it over her head. I palm her tit with one hand, firm but not too much. I know they're tender. Then lick the nipple of the other, working it into a hard peek. When her back arches, I look up and ask, "That good?"

She nods, eyes closed and lifted to the ceiling. "So good."

I haven't fucked anyone since Imogene. That would've been too easy for me to lose myself into. Anex sent me there to pimp out the Fallen—force me to be the one that made the trades for their bodies. It would've hurt less to have done it myself.

But fuck, those weeks of celibacy have made my dick ridiculously hard and I lift her, setting her ass on the table. I drop my pants, kicking out of them and nudge her inner thigh. She spreads for me like the wings of a butterfly, and I hike one leg over my hip. A deep shudder rolls through me as her fingertips touch me for the first time in weeks, spreading precum over the head of my swollen cock. I don't wait for permission, I just kiss her, mouth crashing into hers as I push into her wet, tight, pussy. She gasps, followed by an exhale and she takes me in deeper.

"You okay?" I ask, searching her eyes. "You have to talk to me."

"I'm good," she says, fingers curling into the hair at the back of my neck. "You always make this good for me, Silas. Always."

I draw out, then punch back in again, wincing. "I hope you're ready, because I won't last long."

"You don't have to." Her jaw slacks and I ease my hand between us, reaching for the spot that makes her pant.

"Lean back," I tell her, reaching behind her to clear off the table. Plates and discarded Pop-Tarts push to the side. Leaning her back, it gives me space to trail my lips down her chest, to kiss those bruises, to suck her perfect nipples, to kiss my way down her flat, smooth, stomach.

"Silas," she hums. "Don't stop."

"I won't," I promise, flattening my tongue over her nipple. Her hips buck against me, fucking back in a frantic rhythm. I feel the sharp pain of her nails as they dig into my shoulders, legs spreading, allowing me in as deep as I can go. "I won't ever stop. I won't stop cherishing you. Protecting you." I lick her mouth. "Making love to you."

Because that's the difference. The depravity Anex encouraged wasn't about something good. It was about greed and lust. This—

what Imogene and I are doing is about love. That makes the pain worth bearing.

She pulls me close, until there's nothing between us, her body writhing against mine. I pound into her, wanting to feel every inch of her fall apart in my arms.

"Ah!" she cries, back arching, pussy clenching tight. Every muscle in her body tenses, rigid with release. I ride it out with her, thrusting everything I've been holding back for weeks, the fear, the rage, the disappointment, the loss. I pound into her body—into the woman that makes me feel real—the woman I am *never* letting go.

Hugging her to me, I come, the tight grip of her pussy milking my release. "Fuck," I grunt, her hair sticky on my face. I pull back and look at her red cheeks and shiny eyes. I close my fingers around her chin. "That was me and you," I tell her. "All of us. No one else. No one gets to claim that, especially not him. Do you understand?"

"I do." I don't know if she really does, but I plan to spend every day we have together proving it to her.

∼

After we redress, Imogene follows me to the toaster. I unwrap the pastries and she pops them in the slots. The door opens at the front of the house as I push down the lever. Turning, I see Camille. A tense line slashes across her forehead.

"Good, you're awake," she says, gripping the door jamb. "We need to go."

"Go?" Imogene asks. "What's wrong?"

She shifts her hips. "Agent McNair thinks it's best for you both to move somewhere more secure."

The hair on the back of my neck rises and I rest a hand on Imogene's hip. "Has he made a move?"

"She hasn't told me, but I'd assume something has changed." Her eyes dart to her daughter. "I don't want you to leave, but we know he's aware of this place. He sent the package."

"It's fine," Imogene says stiffly, then looks at me with soft eyes. "As long as we're together."

"Always." I grab her hand and kiss the back. "Go grab whatever we've got upstairs. I'll clean up."

She nods, and exits the room, leaving me and Camille alone.

"What aren't you telling her?" I ask.

Her eyes shift to where Imogene left, making sure she's out of earshot. "There was a threat. Down at the jail."

"What kind?"

"Explosives. Enough to level a city block."

"Shit."

"They discovered it in time," Camille adds, "which was probably intentional, but it's clear Timothy isn't going to give up easily. And even if he has left the country, he still has loyalists willing to do his dirty work."

I cross my arms over my chest. "He's not giving up." I nod at my girl. "Especially not when it comes to her."

"That's how I felt, too, and what I told the agents. The threat on the building that is holding his son... it's obvious that he's willing to go to any lengths to fight the government." She takes a step forward. "Silas, I'm trusting you to take care of her."

"That's not in question. Imogene is my priority."

"That's what I don't understand. Why are all of you so invested in my daughter?" She looks me in the eye. "The fact you don't think it's unusual for four men to be interested in one woman is a signal of how fucked up your understanding is of appropriate societal norms."

I lean against the counter, forcing myself not to be offended. "You're right. Societal norms are lost on us. We were raised differently. We didn't get to go to school or the university like you and Anex did. We weren't allowed to socialize with the opposite sex, past the age of twelve. We lived in the donums—raised by house monitors. We grew up under a rigid structure of documenting Lapses, receiving

Corrections, and forced to listen to hours and hours of Anex's lectures. We went through intensive training and ultimately were singularly focused on building the community Anex wanted. Then one day Anex decided we were different—we were brought into the inner circle and told the secrets of Serendee. The consequence of that is that we were removed even further from 'normal.'" I inhale deeply before immediately releasing it. "Imogene was given to us as a toy, another object for Anex to use to distract and control us. The difference is that over time, it became more than that. She became our reason to push back. We became her reason to challenge her beliefs."

"But don't you see that outside of Serendee, this type of relationship isn't sustainable?"

"That's not for you to decide."

We both look at the door leading from the dining room into the kitchen. Imogene stands there, a small travel bag clutched in her hand. Her words ring loud and clear.

"Honey, I—" Camille starts, but Imogene cuts her off.

"I've spent my entire life being controlled and manipulated." Imogene's voice is clear and convicted. "Everything from what I ate, to what I wore, to where I slept, and ultimately who I was mated with —and even that was taken from me." She moves to stand beside me, her small hand sliding against mine. "Silas is my choice. Rex and Elon and Levi are my choices. Just because you don't understand it, doesn't mean you're right. Not about this." She swallows. "I will not allow anyone to take this choice away from me."

She lifts her head to look at me, and I cup her behind the neck and say, "I love you," then brush my lips across hers.

"I love you, too," she says, pushing up on her toes to kiss me back. When we pull apart Camille's expression has softened, although the line of worry is still etched on her forehead.

"You're right. It's not my place to judge. And arguing about it isn't how I want to spend my last few minutes with my daughter."

"You're not coming?"

"They want me to stay here and pretend like everything is

normal." She jerks her hand toward the door. "There are two agents out there ready to take you to the safe house."

Imogene releases my hand and walks over to her mother. Next to one another it's striking how similar they look. There's no mistaking their connection. And when Imogene wraps her arms around her mother's shoulder and says, "Thank you for coming for us," something shifts between the two of them. Camille's arms cinch around her daughter and the two cling to one another like this may be their only chance.

If Anex has his way, it may be.

90

Imogene

Two agents were on the porch when we left and were ushered into a black SUV. My mother looked small and sad on the front porch, arms wrapped around her body, as we drove off.

"You'll see her again," Silas says, pulling me against his side.

I nod, but there's a knot of worry in the pit of my stomach. I don't know much about the police or federal agents, or the crimes Anex has committed, but I do know that none of these are things he likes—things he approves of—and every day that passes we've betrayed him more and more.

The bomb sets all of this in a new direction. It was a warning—a clear threat—that he's willing to take out his biggest assets. I lean forward between the seats.

"I need you to turn around."

The agent's eyes flick to mine in the rearview mirror. "Those aren't our orders."

"I don't give a fuck about your orders," I say, pulse quickening. With every word, I know this is the right move. "I need to talk to Agent McNair. Immediately."

He holds my gaze for a moment longer then jerks his chin at the man in the passenger seat. He pulls out a phone and presses a button. "Yeah." He says once she's picked up. "We're enroute. There's just a problem." He pauses, twisting to look at me. "I'm not sure. She can tell you herself."

He sticks his arm out between the seats and hands me the phone. I've never used a cell phone before and it feels strangely heavy. I hold it up to my ear like I've seen others do. "Hello."

"Imogene, Agent Kane tells me there's a problem?"

"I want to talk to you."

"We can arrange something when you get to the safe house."

I look at Silas. His expression is both concerned and curious. I take his hand in mine and link our fingers together. "We need to meet before the safehouse. I promise it'll be worth it."

She's quiet for a moment. "You're ready to talk?"

"I'm not only ready to talk, but I'm ready to give you everything you need to bring Anex down."

"I'm glad to hear that—"

"I'm not finished." I cut her off and draw a deep breath for courage. "I'll give you everything you need to bring down Anex but I want something in return."

"What are you requesting?"

"I want my men back."

I TELL Agent McNair that I need two things. One, for her to meet me at the Center. Two, to bring Rex, Elon, and Levi with her.

Our driver, Agent Mallory, makes a pass on Main Street, three times before bringing the SUV to a stop outside the building. Leaving us with Agent Kane, he exits the building, hand on the butt of his weapon, and checks everything out.

"Is this really necessary?" I ask, eyeing the way the front door has been barred with police tape crisscrossing the glass. Seeing the

Center shut down like this brings home the reality of everything: Anex is out of business.

At least this business.

"After that bomb threat," he asks, eyebrows raising, "hell yeah, it's necessary."

A crackle comes across the walkie talkie along with Agent Mallory's voice, "All clear."

"Stick close," he says.

"What about—" I start, worried she's not holding up to her end of the deal.

"Agent McNair will be here. I promise." He opens the passenger door and then my back door. "We're too exposed on the street. It's safer to wait for them inside."

I exit the car and Silas follows. People on the street watch us as we enter the building and I'm grateful to be in secular clothing, although if I've learned anything, outsiders can sense our differentness just like we can tell theirs. Inside, I'm struck by a wave of surrealness. Everything is exactly the same, but not. The Center is eerily quiet but has the lingering evidence of the Fed's raid. I walk over to my desk and see that it's rummaged through, desk drawers open. Pencil cup tipped to the side. Calendar removed. Mindlessly, I start to put things back in place.

"Don't touch anything," Agent Kane says, passing me.

I step back, unsure of what to do with my hands.

The doors swing open, bringing in a bright ray of afternoon sunlight. Agent McNair walks in, but my eyes skirt past her to the men that follow: Rex, Levi, and Elon.

Agent Mallory shuts the door behind them and stays outside.

"Thank god," I say, noticing their wrists are bound as I run over. I throw my arms around Rex and he plants a kiss in the crook of my neck. Reaching out, I squeeze Levi's hand. "Are you okay?"

"We're fine." Rex answers for all of them. "What is this?"

"I had her bring you to me," I say, looking to Levi. "A trade. Information for you."

Elon shakes his head. "You don't need to do this, Imogene, we can handle it."

I step in front of him, reaching up to cradle his face in my hand. "I know you think that, but this is bigger than our pride. This will be over soon."

He blinks, his tired eyes creased with worry. "What did you do?"

"What I should have from the beginning." I turn to the agents. "Do they have to be handcuffed?"

"Yes," Agent McNair says, gaze holding mine. "At least for now."

For now.

That means there's a chance *if* I can give her what she wants.

"I brought them with me just like you asked. As you can tell, we've already done a clean sweep of these offices and removed anything incriminating."

I turn and make eye contact with Levi. He and I worked most closely with Anex in this office—he as a teacher, me as his administrative assistant. "We need to show them," I say. "*Everything.*"

Awareness flickers on his exhausted face, and I sense his hesitation. I get it. What I'm about to show them will prove the enormity of Anex's crimes, but in the process, it'll show how twisted and depraved he really is. He grimaces. "Are you sure?"

It'll also show all of us, all of our friends and community members, in a compromising light. Him. Me. All of us.

"I need to do it," I tell him. "Or we'll never be free."

Levi nods. "Then do it."

I cross the room and enter the hallway, Agent Kane pushes in front of me, insisting on leading the way. Fair. I could be leading him to a room of booby traps. Instead, I point to a small storage room door, one that holds all the records. The lock is busted, and a quick look inside of the open, empty cabinets, I can see that the files have been removed.

"I told you," Agent McNair says, "We got everything."

"I don't think so. Anex recorded everything," I tell the agents. "Every meeting, every educational session, every midnight lecture, basketball game, ceremony." I swallow. "Every Correction."

"Correction?" Agent McNair asks. "What's a Correction?"

I inhale deeply. "You're about to find out."

I nod at the bank of floor-to-ceiling cabinets attached to the wall and open one of the middle drawers. I press my fingers against the back wall, feeling for the right spot, but can't find it. Panicked, I look back at Levi.

"Let me do it," Levi says, stepping forward. He brushes past me, his arm warm against mine, sending shivers down my spine. He holds up his bound hands. "It'd be easier if my hands were free."

Kane and McNair share a look, but ultimately, she nods. A moment later the ties are cut, and Levi rubs at his wrists. "That's better."

"Don't do anything stupid," Kane says, hand on his gun.

"It's just a lever," Levi says, reaching into the drawer. "I'm going to press it and it'll release a latch." A loud click follows, and he slowly withdraws his hand at the same time the cabinet detaches from the wall.

"What the hell?" Rex asks as Kane assists Levi in moving the cabinet. Next to him Elon shakes his head. Rex looks at me. "You knew about this?"

"Your father trusted me," I reply. "And Levi. We were his most devoted followers."

Just saying it makes me feel a pang—guilt maybe. There's no time to dwell on it. With his gun drawn, Kane steps through the small doorway and into the hidden room. "Holy shit," he mutters, then calls out, "It's clear. You can come in."

A moment later we're inside—all six of us in the narrow space. The room is filled with a variety of electronics. Nothing I understand how to use, but I'm aware of their importance. Against the back wall are computers and monitors.

"He's got everything," Kane says, pulling on a pair of latex gloves. "VHS, CDs, tapes, flash drives."

"He's been documenting everything for the last thirty-five years," Agent McNair says. She looks at Rex. "You really didn't know about this room?"

He shakes his head. "I knew he kept recordings, but nothing this extensive." He looks at the sheer size of the collection. "Imogene is right. He didn't trust me, Elon, and Silas the way he did her and Levi. They were devoted to him—and Serendee. He knew I had my issues with how he ran the community."

Agent McNair turns to face the shelves, eyes landing on a section titled 'Corrections.' Each recording marked with a name and a date. I pull one out and hold it out to her.

Imogene Montgomery.

The date is from two months ago, before the banishment and Reeducation. I know that she'll find sessions between me and Levi. Possibly the aftermath with me and Elon. She hands it over to Kane who pops it into one of the electronic devices.

"Stop," Elon says, lunging for the screen. Levi and Silas block him, holding him back. He shoves against them. "Get the fuck out of my way. No one has the right to see what is on those tapes—"

"It's okay, Elon." This is what I need to do to get my men back. Honesty and transparency. I look at the agents. "Watch it. You need to know the truth."

Kane presses play and an image comes on the screen. It's me and Levi standing in the middle of the room—talking. The table is next to me, the leather strap on the flat surface. My cheeks burn and I look to the floor as the recording progresses. The whole room watches as I bend over that table and take Levi's punishment.

An arm comes around my shoulder and Levi pulls me against his chest. I look up at his handsome face. "I'm sorry," he says. I'm not sure if it's about the Correction, or the fact this video is being exposed, or about everything that's transpired in the last few weeks.

"Don't apologize," I whisper, under the sound of leather snapping against my skin and my following screams. My body lights on fire. Humiliation. Desperation. Confliction.

I turn, pushing past everyone land leave the room. I stop in the hallway and press my shaking body against the wall, trying to remain upright. A person emerges from the file room. The shoes stop in front of me. Black. Feminine.

"Imogene," she says, her voice quiet. "I had no idea."

I look up at her, past the blur of tears in my eyes and ask, "Is it enough?"

She nods. "It's enough."

I sink to the floor, relief rushing through me.

I have my men back.

91

———

I mogene

The ride to the safe house is long, and my stomach aches with panic. Agent McNair had to handle release paperwork for the guys before they could come. I didn't like the idea of being separated from them, but there wasn't any other choice. They'd meet us there.

Wherever "there" is. All I know is that it's dark, and we turned off the highway and onto a dirt road fifteen minutes ago. Nothing about being surrounded by the thick forest of trees, tall pines that shoot straight up into the night sky, quells my nerves.

"Hey," Silas says, nodding out the front window, "looks like we're almost there."

"There" turns out to be a small cabin tucked away in a forest. The car slows with the crunch of gravel under the tires, easing to a stop next to an identical SUV. The two agents get out, doors slamming behind them. "You really think he won't find us here?" I ask, peering out the window.

"I think only a fool would underestimate Anex, and you're the smartest person I know."

"Although I appreciate the compliment, that's not very comforting." I roll my eyes and check out the other vehicle. "I wonder who that is?"

Neither Mallory or Kane seem concerned, and they open the back of the vehicle, removing the small amount of belongings we brought with us.

I climb out of the car just as the screen door whines and closes with a snap. Agent McNair steps out on the porch. My heart drops. "Did something happen?"

"Everything's fine." She gives me an unexpected smile. "Actually, I was able to handle everything over the phone. We just took a different route in case anyone had tracked us from the Center."

"We?" I ask, rushing up the steps. She jerks her thumb over her shoulder, and I run past her, wrenching open the door and bursting inside.

They're there. Hands free. Skinny and tired.

Mine.

"Oh my god." I want to go to them, but I'm just struck by deep and sudden exhaustion. My arm presses into my stomach and I bend, a deep, unrecognizable, wail coming from inside.

I turn and a figure falls in front of me. Elon, down on his knees. I meet him on the floor. "Babe," he says. I feel the press of his lips against my forehead. "What is it? What's happening?"

"I thought I'd lost you forever."

To Anex. To prison. To all the terrible things he said would come if we betrayed him.

"Never," he says, looking back as the guys come to stand behind him. His hands cup my face, and he thumbs away my tears. "We will never stop fighting for each other."

Silas' arms wrap around me, his body heat warm and comforting, and a moment later Levi's there, rubbing my back and pressing a kiss to my temple. Over Elon's shoulder, I feel Rex's intense gaze, his blue eyes sweeping over me, looking for wounds or injuries. Both of us know they're there–he just can't see them. I lift myself off the ground and go to him, brushing aside the tears on my cheek. "I've been so worried about you." He was inside the longest, left with nothing but his worries.

"Don't be," his thumb wipes away a tear. "I was fine."

That's impossible, but it'll take time.

He lifts his chin, some kind of silent signal, and Elon's got me in his arms, lifting me. He carries me across the room and up a flight of stairs, stopping when we enter a bedroom. He eases me to the floor and steps into the bathroom, turning on the faucet.

"What are you doing?" I look toward the door, to the sound of masculine voices downstairs.

"The guys are going to make dinner." He comes back to me, kissing my nose, then the underside of my jaw, my collarbone. A shiver runs across my skin. "And I'm going to run you a bath."

"You just got out of prison, I'm the one that should be cooking," I tell him, those old routines and behaviors falling into place. "You know I like to."

"I know you do, but tonight, let us take care of you, babe."

The idea sounds nice, and completely foreign. I'm also too tired to do anything but watch him run the bath, filling it with soapy, clean smelling bubbles. I haven't moved and he returns to me, hands pushing under my shirt, lifting it over my head. Kissing the center of my chest, he reaches behind my back and unhooks my bra, gently pushing it down my shoulders. His eyes go to the fading bruises, and he rubs a thumb over the side of my breast.

"Rex told me what happened." He tilts his head back, closes his eyes and swallows thickly. "I should've been there to protect you."

"You had no choice," I tell him, running my hands under his shirt to feel the hard muscle underneath. "None of us did, but we do now."

He looks down at me, eyes filled with dark intensity. His hand cups around the column of my throat and he draws me to him, kissing me on the mouth. A surge of warmth runs through me—the strength of his tongue, the taste of his lips. I allow myself to relax, to sink into him, knowing we're all home—and for the moment—safe.

Kisses down my body, reverently, taking his time. When his mouth closes over a taut nipple, lathing against the peak, I cry out, desperate for more. His breath is hot, spreading over my skin, down my belly as he licks and tastes. He stops at my hip and my hand falls to cover the brand, but he lifts it gently, kissing my fingers and the skin around the mark.

"He'll pay for this one day, love."

As much as I hate the brand, I appreciate that they don't ignore it—that they accept that it's part of me—just another scar left from Anex's domination.

There is no man more domineering than the one before me. The sight of him down on his knees spreads warmth between my legs. He's controlled and diligent as he explores every inch of my body.

He eases off the cotton pants I'd found in a drawer that morning. The drawstring is untied in a sharp yank. Exposed, he sets me on the edge of the tub, pushing my legs apart with his palms. He bends, teeth nipping at the delicate flesh of my inner thigh. The tease of pain makes me hotter, wetter. He looks up at me and says, "I've been dreaming of this for weeks."

"Me too."

"Hang on, babe," His tongue glides over my slick folds, delving into them, teasing and tasting. My fingers grip the sides of the tub, the steamy water curling up my spine. My breath is short, coming in hot, needy bursts, but It's when his tongue finds the bundle of nerves, the ones wound tight and desperate, waiting for him to discover, as I unspool, spinning toward ecstasy.

I cry his name out, the sound echoing off the bathroom tiles and buck against him.

"Elon," I say, again. "That was..."

"Just the beginning." He stands, pressing his hand against my back and easing me into the warm, steamy, tub. My limbs are jelly, my heart pounding like I've just finished a race. I watch him strip, then climb into the tub behind me. Water sloshes over the sides as he fits his massive frame in with me, cradling my back against his chest.

"Is this for real?" I ask, threading my fingers through his. "Me, you, this tub, the guys downstairs?"

He pushes the hair off my neck with wet fingertips and plants a kiss on my neck. "It's for real."

There's two words he's left off, but I allow it, not wanting to mar this moment with the world outside.

It's real—*for now.*

After what we've been through, I'll take what I can get.

"Did we really eat all that?"

I stare at the empty dishes on the table, the plates that are scraped clean. Levi and I offered to clean up after dinner while the others took showers and unpacked.

No, *dinner* isn't the right word. We had a feast. Agent McNair had arranged for a grocery delivery, apparently thinking it would last a while. Unfortunately, she didn't anticipate the appetite of my four men after subsisting on prison food and Serendee rations.

They ate a lot. *I* ate a lot, more than I should. Lately, I've found it hard to stop, even when I know I'm full, because there's this gnawing hunger in my belly all the time. I know in my heart that this is because of the limitations and restrictions we had on food in Serendee, but my brain hasn't been able to separate that yet.

"We did," Levi says, taking a stack of plates back to the kitchen. "I think I may have witnessed the definition of the word gluttony."

I grab two platters and carry them over to the sink. "If I keep this up, I'm going to gain more weight." Pressing my hand to my stomach, I feel the way it pooches out a little. I can't decide if I like it or not.

"You look good like this," he tells me. "Rex was always right about girls being a little meatier. More to hold onto."

"I keep reaching for my journal—like I should be documenting every lapse."

"It's okay to write things down," he says, as if he's reminding himself as much as me. "Just don't let it rule you."

I nod and head back to the dining room, bringing back another pile of dirty dishes. More than once, I glance over my shoulder, looking out the dark windows, searching the room for anything I or the agents missed.

"What are you doing?" he asks.

"I keep looking for cameras. I know they aren't here, but it's hard to shake."

Paranoia.

It was bad before but seeing that stash of recordings made it worse. Levi turns on the faucet, letting the water run until it turns hot. I don't miss how he keeps his hands under the water until it turns hot, turning his skin pink. He takes the first dish and rinses it off. "You were brave to show them the videos."

"I did what I had to. She wasn't going to let you go if I didn't."

"You don't have to justify it, Imogene. You did the right thing."

"Maybe." It still feels wrong, exposing not only myself but my friends and neighbors. My *lovers.* I scrape a pile of chicken bones into the trash. "I can't imagine what else they'll reveal."

"More than I'm willing to think about," he says quietly.

"There are so many shameful moments—some you may not even know about, like the exams in Healer Blooms clinic or how awful the branding was. How we turned on one another or how we treated one another to gain his favor. The farther away from it I get, the harder it is for me to reconcile."

"I know," he agrees. "I can't help but think about the way we bowed and doted on Anex every time we were in his presence. How quickly I did everything he asked." He glances at me. "How willing I was to hurt you for his bullshit belief system, when all he really wanted me to do was break you down."

It's an apology, one I'm not willing to take. "You weren't the only one seeking Enlightenment, Levi." I'd asked for that as much as he gave it. I wanted the pain. I still do, and that's something we have to figure out. "Do you ever feel like..." I start, then shake my head back and forth looking for the words. "Like we've been underwater?"

"Underwater?" he asks, eyebrow raising.

"I just feel like I have these moments where I'm clearing out the cobwebs, or running my hand over a fogged-up mirror, trying to see everything clearly."

"Yes," he says. "Absolutely, especially when we first got out. I could barely function. Elon was supporting us, and I was just... trying to figure out how to get back in." He glances at me. "Back to you."

"But you feel better now?" I ask.

"Food, sleep, getting away from the lectures and non-stop input seems to help."

"Sleep is good." Full nights. No music blaring through the grounds. No late-night basketball games or random work assignments. That doesn't mean I'm able to get a full night's rest, but it's better. More consistent.

He turns off the faucet and grabs a towel, drying his hands. Then he rests a hand on my hip. "You know, when he banished us, it gave me weeks to get ahead of where you are right now, maybe even more than that when you consider the other things you went through." He keeps his eyes pinned to mine. "The conditioning and control—over your body as well as your mind... it was a lot, Imogene."

I think about Rex at the dinner table, hungry but quiet. Elon's need to just be with me, to take care of me, to touch me under the dinner table with every opportunity. Silas' sleep, deep and long. "We're all going to have to heal in different ways, aren't we?"

"I think so." His hand drops down and squeezes my hip. "I've been reading a lot of the books and information Camille had at her house. It's overwhelming, but helpful. It makes me feel less crazy."

"I just want to feel normal."

He laughs. "I wouldn't even know what that looks like, would you?"

I push up on my toes and kiss him.

"What was that for? *Not* that I'm complaining."

"I like seeing you smile."

He grins wider. "I like seeing you smile, too."

"Are we going to be okay?" I ask. It's a big question. But Levi is my Guide. He's always been there to answer my questions and keep me on the path. It's just now we're on a different one than before. Before he can respond, I blurt out another one. "How long do you think will we have to hide?" Then another, "And where will we live when it's over? Do you think we'll have to testify against Anex?" My heart pounds, thudding hard against my chest. "What happens if no one believes us?"

He takes my face in his hands. "I want to answer all of those things for you, Imogene, but I can't. And for the first time, I won't lie or pretend that I can. That's what I would have done before. Just made up something to convince you that I knew better than you did or spewed a bunch of Anex's rhetoric to keep you in line." His thumb strokes my cheek. "But I'm not that person anymore—or I'm trying not to be. I can't tell you the future. I can't promise that by doing the right thing Enlightenment will follow. I can't do anything but tell you that I love you, and I'll stay with you, and we'll get through this together."

Fresh tears build in my eyes and press my cheek against his chest. "That's all I need, you know that, right?"

He nods and I hug him tight, maybe tighter than ever before and even not knowing what comes next, I feel more secure than I have in years.

I leave Levi and Silas downstairs reading and head to bed. I pause in the doorway of my darkened room, finding Rex under the covers, deep asleep. Even at rest, his face carries the weight of exhaustion.

"He's beat." I turn and see Elon coming down the hall. He's shirtless and in a pair of black sweatpants. "He barely slept at the jail."

An unease sits in my bones. Anex was relentless with him, mentally and physically. I want to go to him, make sure he's okay but I feel the barrier between us. "Are you sure he's okay?" *We're okay*, I want to add, but don't.

"All he wanted was to get back to you." His hand slides behind my neck, and he pulls me against his chest. His tongue licks at my lips, seeking entrance. It's easy to get lost in him, easy to want kisses and touches to last forever, but he pulls back and declares, "It's all any of us wanted."

"He made me a promise," I say, looking into the room. Rex's blond hair shines in the glow of the hallway light. "That he'd come home to me at night. No matter what." I step into the room. "Like it or not, I'm upholding it now." I reach out a hand. "Sleep with us?"

He looks between his best friend and me. "Are you sure? Because once you invite me in bed with the two of you, I'm not leaving."

My cheeks heat at the thought of Rex and Elon together. What that means for them and me. "Until I know for sure that Anex isn't going to come for me—for us—I want every minute I can get."

"I'll kill him first, Imogene." It's not a threat—it's a promise.

"Hopefully, it won't come to that," I say, leaving him in the doorway. "At least not until we're ready." I cross the room and stop at the edge of the bed, removing my clothes, before climbing into the bed and shifting to the middle, close to my Mate. I leave the covers down, an invitation. His hesitation slips away, and he follows, dropping his pants. His cock bobs between his legs and it takes everything in me not to reach out and stroke it.

Rex doesn't stir other than to wrap his arm around me, and I burrow against his warm skin, eyes pinned to Elon's.

"Thank you for saving us," he says quietly, hand gliding down my arm.

"Thank you for saving me," I reply. "You pulled the veil from my eyes, and as difficult as that has been, I owe you everything."

My own exhaustion supersedes the feel of want between my legs, and the way Elon struggles to keep his eyes open, I know he feels the same. I don't know if it's the sense of freedom, or the security of being between the two of them, but when sleep drags me under, I allow it to take me.

A tremor wakes me, running down my spine and between my legs. Hot breath at my neck, nipples pebbled and hard.

"Little Lamb, open up," I hear, before my legs are pulled apart, a hot tongue licking a hot path up my inner thigh.

I blink, seeing the shine of blond hair between my legs. I'm barely awake, but a jolt of energy rushes through me when Rex's warm tongue dives between my folds.

"God, you taste so good. Fuck I missed this." His words are quiet—a whisper. "I missed you."

My hips rise to meet him, a burst of desire shooting through me. My toes curl, fingers twisting into the bedsheets and a deep moan builds in my throat. With the gentlest of touches, he sucks at my clit and a cry rips from my throat.

"You like that?" he asks, lifting to his elbows. Rex's eyes meet mine, his blue eyes liquid heat. "I thought about you the whole time I was in that cell. How you taste, what you feel like." He palms my breast, lifting the nipple to his mouth. His tongue swirls around and around, building the heat between my legs, forcing my back to arch. "It's better than I remember. You're better." He shifts and looks over his shoulder. "Don't you think?"

It's then that I see Elon sprawled beside us, hand fisting his cock. He grunts his approval.

"Show him your pussy, Little Lamb. Elon wants to see." His hand grips my thigh, pushing my legs apart. The cool air meets the damp heat and Elon licks his bottom lip, focused between my legs. Rex rubs his fingers over my entrance, spreading me apart while his friend watches. My skin itches, like it's about to burst into flames, but I'd die first. All I want is for these men to make me come.

"One finger or two?" Rex asks, toying with my body, fingers dipping in and out.

"Two," I breathe.

"Three," Elon commands, chin lifting. "Take three, baby. Get ready for us."

A swirl of butterflies explodes in my belly, but I lean back on the pillow and let my thighs drop to the side. Rex's fingers, sticky from my excitement, push into me. One at first, gliding in and out. Then the second, adding more pressure. "That feel good?" he asks, brushing his thumb over my clit.

"Yes," I hiss, biting down on my bottom lip. "More."

He slides in the third finger, pumping in and out, the stretch feels good. He leans over and captures my mouth with his, kissing me hard. I want to curl into them, fuck them. I want them to claim me—make me their own. My whole body starts to shake, desperate for more.

He pulls back, eyebrows knitted together. "What's wrong?"

"Nothing," I say, although we both know it's a lie. "I want you in me."

Elon rises to his knees, cock thick and straining. "She needs us." A look transpires between them, and I know when understanding strikes Rex. He nods. Rex played games with my mind, not my body. He used me for his own whims, a battle with his father, but other than the strapping in Anex's room, he didn't take his emotions out on my body. Elon understands my desires better. He's helped me through the pain before. The unrelenting, *aching* need that can only be relieved by one thing.

"On your back," Elon tells Rex. He does as his friend demands, removing his fingers from inside me and stretching out on the bed, abs taut, erection hard and wet. I mourn the loss of him in me, but I lick my lips and bend to kiss him, licking the salty tip of his penis. He hisses and grabs for my breasts, tugging my nipples between his fingers. The sharp pain is exactly what I want, and I bob my head, taking his cock deep down my throat.

Elon moves behind me, grabbing my hips like I'm nothing but a rag doll. With his fingers digging into my flesh, his cock slides between my cheeks, rough and demanding, poking hard at my entrance. Rex's chest rises and falls as I suck him off, fingers twisting in my hair. He yanks at the scalp, and I cry out. His hips thrust up, his cock hitting the back of my throat.

God. *Yes.*

"Open for me, baby," Elon says from behind me, hips rearing back before he drives into me. He fills me, both deep and wide, pounding with deep slow strokes. The feel of him inside is better than anything in this world, that is until Rex removes his cock from my mouth, scooches down the bed and presses the tip against my already full entrance. "And now you're going to open for him, too."

I nod, my eyes meeting Rex's as he works his way slowly inside. This time the stretching hurts, God, it hurts, and I suck in a breath.

"Too much?" Rex, asks, hand cupping my cheek.

"No, just give me a second."

They do, Elon still behind me. Rex's jaw tenses. "Little Lamb, I gotta move."

The tendons in his neck strain, he's holding out for me. I nod, giving him the go ahead and he pushes in an inch more. This time the burn is better, slicker, and I breath deep and push down, taking him in the rest of the way.

I've never felt so full.

"Holy fuck," Elon mutters. "Christ. Do you know how good this feels?"

"So fucking good," Rex says, pulling my face down to his, our foreheads pressed together. "But if I don't move, I'm coming like this, just sitting inside of you."

I laugh, like that'd be the worst thing in the world, but I rock my hips, nudging them along. Both men groan, something deep and animalistic. After the first thrust, there's nothing gentle about it. The friction is too much—frantic and hungry—all I feel is them. It's all I *want* to feel—leaving the bad darkness of Serendee behind us. The manipulation and mind games. I just want my men, to feel them, to love them, to let them love me.

That hollow pit in my stomach, the one I can never seem to fill, vanishes.

Elon's thrusts send me into Rex, whose hands cup my breasts and squeeze them together. He mouths my nipples. My head falls back, resting on Elon's chest. His hand comes around my throat, and he twists my head, sweeping his tongue into my mouth.

"I'm gonna come," Elon says, teeth dragging down my jaw. He fucks into me, hard and furious, until he buries a strangled groan into my neck. His cock pulses into me and he drops his fingers, catching cum, and swiping the wet, slippery, fluid over my clit. I shudder, the start of my own orgasm rippling through me.

"Fuck. Fuck. Fuck," I chant, body going rigid.

Rex swears under his breath as my muscles clench around him. His cock slippery from Elon's slick cum. "Hold on, Little Lamb," he says, lurching to his knees. Both men lift me, fill me, holding me up as Rex drives into me with a final thrust.

"I love you," Rex says, breath heavy and hot on my ear. "I love you and you're mine, never forget that. You're Elon's and Silas' and Levi's. You belong to us, Imogene. Us and only us. And if we have to fuck you every goddamn day of your life to prove it to you, we will."

My body is numb, spine lax, as he whispers these things, and I barely feel it as they lower me back to the bed, body sticky and warm. And as we curl together, I'm struck by the awareness that even after they've pulled out, and are no longer in me, I still feel full.

92

E lon

Hack. Hack. Hack.

Chop.

Clunk.

I push aside the curtain and peer out the kitchen window at the continuous sound, day after day, since we got here. It's the sound of irritation. Restlessness. Distraction.

Hack. Hack. Hack.

Chop.

Clunk.

Rex heaves the axe over his head, biceps straining as he gains the momentum to chop the massive log. He'll split this it into smaller pieces before tossing it on the ever-growing pile. He's been out there since sunrise, his gray shirt two shades darker from sweat, showing no signs of slowing down anytime soon. Other than the night he and I shared with Imogene, he's been withdrawn. I know she's nervous about it. Insecure.

Hack. Hack. Hack.

Chop.

Clunk.

My eyes shift to the ridge behind him, scanning the narrow space between the trunks. Nothing but trees.

Nothing but the five of us settled into this close quartered, temporary situation—living, but not living—a different sort of life altogether.

It feels like we're still in exile.

It's not the life we expected and it's not easy. The cabin is small for a group of people that is used to living in an expansive, wide-spaced, nature-driven community. Our outdoor time is limited due to constant surveillance by the FBI, and as Levi continues to remind us, we're all struggling with our own trauma that we carried out of Serendee.

I'd argue with him, but I see it myself. How Imogene cooks, making elaborate, spice heavy, intricate meals, while barely taking a bite of it herself. She won't admit it, but I catch her counting calories, fingers twitching with the need to write each and every one down.

Levi's no better—having stationed himself at a desk that overlooks the yard with a wide window. He's surrounded by stacks of books that have spilled over to a pile on the floor. Each and every book is about a single topic: Cults. Surviving them, escaping them, defining them, rejecting them, recovering from them... His academic and intellectual drive has shifted from obsessing over Anex's doctrine, to analyzing cult behavior. I'm not sure the last time he slept, really ate a meal, or took a shower. I do know him well enough to understand that he won't stop until he considers himself an expert.

My eyes shift to the living room, where Silas has been sprawled on the large couch, eyes glued to the flat screen TV mounted to the wall for the last five days. The shows are mostly shiny things—plastic looking men and women parading around shirtless or in bikinis. They're called reality shows, but I don't get it. Everyone is playing a game. There's nothing realistic about it at all. I'm not sure what Silas is getting out of this, or if that's the point, it's nonsensical and mindless. Whatever it is, he's enraptured.

Me? Paranoia has settled in deep. I feel it in my bones, in every shadow and movement outside the window. I know in my soul Anex will never let us be free. We weren't just part of his inner circle—he believed he owned us—and that doesn't change just because he's on the run.

I keep track of the news. Looking for any information on Anex or his remaining circle that didn't get picked up during the raid. I find myself scrolling the tablet Agent Mallory gave us to use—one Anex's people shouldn't be able to track—searching to see if Margaret had the baby, or if any arrests have been made. I have alerts set up, dozens to chime if something comes up, but day after day it's nothing until...

I stare at the message that flits across the screen. "Silas, give me the remote."

"They're just about to decide who gets voted off the isla—"

I'm across the room in three strides. "Give me the fucking remote!" I snatch it out of his hands, the commotion bringing Imogene from the kitchen and forcing Levi to look up from his book.

"Can you keep it down?" he shouts from his corner.

"No," I reply, stabbing at the buttons. There are forty news channels, but I don't know how to get there. I throw it back at Silas, the plastic device hitting him in the chest. "Put it on the news. Now!"

He finds it quickly, and the press conference is already in progress. A tall black man stands behind a podium, a large set of columns behind him. At the bottom it says, *"State Attorney General, Michael Morris."*

"Shut up," I tell everyone, although the room is quiet.

"Today, Timothy Andrew Wray and co-conspirators were indicted for the crimes of sex trafficking, false imprisonment, money laundering, racketeering, and tax evasion."

"Oh my God," Imogene whispers beside me. Her fingers brush against mine and I hold onto them tight. Silas sits up, possibly for the first time in a week.

"Prior to this, Timothy was wanted for tax evasion and questioning, but due to the discovery of an enormous amount of irrefutable evidence by the FBI," the camera widens, revealing Agent McNair standing just to the side, "the state had no choice but to expand the scope of our investigation and alter the charges."

"Holy shit," Levi says, closing the book in his hand.

"As of right now, all four of the people indicted are unaccounted for. We are asking the community to report any sightings or information you may have on the following people to the tip line below." Photos appear on the screen, "Timothy Wray, who goes by the name Anex, and his followers Margaret Ackerman, Erik Heisman, and Jasmine West, heir to the Cobra Tequila empire."

"Fuck," Silas says, running his hand through his hair. "Rex and I," he looks back at me. "We recruited her."

"I remember her," I say. From the frat parties. She'd been on the hook for a while. I guess Rex and Silas locked her down.

"We caution you not to approach any of these people on your own. They are dangerous, their compound had extensive explosives and weaponry. We must assume they are armed and should be approached with caution."

We watch the rest of the press conference, but the attorney general declines to answer questions from the press.

"What they're saying," Levi rubs his chin, "is that they have no fucking clue where he is."

"Maybe it's a trick," Imogene argues. "Like, they're trying to pretend they don't have anything on him, making him more over-confident."

"I need some air," I say once it's over. I walk to the door and open it. Mallory is on the deck, watching the press conference on his phone.

"Where are you going?"

"For a walk," I reply.

"Not sure that's a good idea, Elon."

"Fuck good ideas!" My patience is hanging by a thread. "No one has a fucking clue where Anex is. We've been cooped up for a week. I need some goddamn air before I lose my mind."

Imogene steps out of the house and shuts the door behind her. She looks at Mallory. "I'll go with him."

"That doesn't make me feel more secure, Ms. Montgomery."

"We'll stay close. I promise."

He frowns and shakes his head, but says, "Fine, but I want you in sight of the house at all times. I'll be watching."

"Don't worry," she says, grabbing my hand, "we're used to that."

Gravel crunches under foot, and I try to steady my breathing as we walk farther away from the house. My skin itches knowing the agents are nearby but I suspect it's less about them and more like what Imogene said, we're used to having a lack of privacy.

"Talk to me," she says, tightening her grip on my hand.

"I just needed some air, that's all." I glance over at her, at the boots and fitted jeans. At the button-down plaid shirt with the sleeves rolled up to her elbows. "That press conference... it just feels like more games, you know?"

"I believe in Agent McNair," she says, leading me to an outcropping of rocks. They're mossy on the sides, but smooth on the top. I grab her hips and lift her to sit on top. She lets me fit in between her legs, linking her arms around my neck. "I believe she'll catch him."

"How?" I ask with complete sincerity. "How do you still believe?"

She shrugs and plays with the hair at the back of my neck. It's grown out, longer than I wore it at Serendee. "I grew up thinking the outside world was scary and dark. That people were conniving and ruined by the Secular world. That all they wanted was money and to exploit our bodies."

"When really Anex was already doing it," I add. "I know, but that betrayal, it should make you more pessimistic. If he could convince an entire community, he'll be able to talk his way out of all of this with that attorney general, or a jury in a courthouse."

"He may," she admits, "but until then I just want to live my best life."

I look around the woods, taking in the quiet, the cold. There are no leaves on the trees other than the pines. This far away from the house, other than the occasional bird, or snap of a twig, it feels like we're the only ones alive.

It's peaceful. Better than fighting or running drugs or living under Anex's omnipresent rule.

"What's your best life look like, Elon?" she asks suddenly.

I think about it, but the answer is elusive. Finally, I say, "I thought I'd live forever in Serendee. Working for Anex and Rex. There was no mate in the picture, not for us. Not until you came along, and I didn't think that would last either. I thought my Enlightenment would come from doing everything Anex asked of me, including what he asked me to do to you. But now I understand how so much of what he expected of me was wrong." My eyes flick to hers. "How could that not include you?"

"Because in the end we chose each other."

I shake my head, blinking back the emotion I can't seem to hold back. "I just want to be a good man for you, Imogene, and I don't know if I know how to do that."

She pulls back, removing her arms and gives me a glare. "You're fucking with me, right?"

I laugh. I can't help it. Swear words sound so weird coming out of her pretty mouth. "No."

"Baby, you've always been good to me," she says. "Even back when we were kids, playing on that merry-go-round, being the big older kid that watched out for the rest of us." She presses her hands to my cheeks. "You saved me on the street the night of my Ordering. Those guys wouldn't have stopped."

"That wasn't just me—"

"No, you were the one that walked me home, made sure I was safe." Her hands lower to my chest. "You taught me how to be Rex's ideal mate and lover, and you saved me from that backwoods farmer at his vegetable stand."

She doesn't know what happened after that—when we went back for him.

"And you came back to Serendee for me after being Banished. Nothing has stopped you from being good to me, from taking care of me no matter what obstacle."

"None of this was supposed to happen, Imogene. I think that's why I'm struggling. And what if he comes back? What then?"

She sighs, exasperated with my questions, but it doesn't stop her from answering. "If we peel apart what Anex taught us, that there's only one path, a path he laid for us, then the possibilities are endless. There is no supposed to be, it just is what it is. And what this is... well, I love you. So much. And I'm just grateful I don't have to hide it."

My heart thuds, from how beautiful and smart she is. How did that happen? We were supposed to educate and train her, but this girl didn't need it. She's always been leaps ahead of us. I press a kiss to her neck and whisper in her ear, "I'd show you right now how good I can be to you, but Mallory is watching."

"Then take me back to the cabin and show me there?'

I kiss her, capturing her mouth in mine, making sure she knows how much I love her—want her—but she knows. It's in my bones, the way I look at her, the way I get hard every time I'm near her.

I help her off the rock, wrapping her legs around my waist and carry her in the direction of the cabin.

"Is this necessary?" she asks, grinding into my waist.

"Your legs are too short." I can't wait to get the clothes off my woman. "And it makes you walk too slow."

I press another kiss to her neck too distracted to process the branch snapping in the distance. I do look up at the crack that follows, a zing cutting through the air by my ear. I drop Imogene to the ground, covering her body with my own as another bullet flew past.

"Mallory!" I shout, but I hear his footsteps pounding off the porch. I look down at her, "Baby are you okay?"

"Y-yes," she nods. "What was that?"

Kane appears from the opposite direction and I push Imogene at him, snagging the gun off his belt in the process. "Get her back in the house."

"Elon—" he starts, realizing what I've done.

"Elon, no!" Imogene shouts.

Rex runs across the yard, shirtless, body worn from chopping wood. I pin my gaze to his. "Get her inside. I'm going to deal with this."

He nods, pulling her back to the cabin and knowing she's safe with him, I load the chamber. Making a mad dash into the woods, I press my back into the nearest tree. Bullets land, spraying shards of bark everywhere.

I knew Anex would come for us—for *her*.

And there's no fucking way in hell I'm going to let him have her.

93

R ex

"Stay here." I pull the shirt over my head and fling open the closet door, looking for a coat. "I'm going to help Elon."

"Please don't," she says from the corner of the living room. It's a blind spot in case anyone tries to shoot at the house. Silas has his arm wrapped around her. "It's bad enough that Elon's out there."

Raking my fingers through my hair, I spin and look at her. My girl. My Mate. "He tried to kill you. I can't let that go."

"You don't have to." She looks to Levi and Silas. "Tell him not to go out there."

Levi's pressed to the wall, peeking out the window. "Looks like you won't have to."

"What does that mean?" I head to the window, not giving a fuck if someone sees me. I'm exhausted and burned out—past the end of my rope. If today is the day this ends, then I'm ready for it. But before I reach Levi, the front door kicks open. Elon enters, a dirty, bloody mess. Behind him, Mallory and Kane drag in a man wearing head-to-toe camouflage, fighting against the restraints cinched around his wrists.

It takes me a full heartbeat to realize who they caught.

Erik.

"You're fucking with me." Rage pumps through my veins like lava, and I lunge at him, grabbing him by the collar. "You came here to kill my Mate? My best friend?"

The crack of my fist hitting his chin comes before Mallory jerks him aside. When the agent looks up at me, I see the agent's split lip. Erik put up a hell of a fight.

"That," I tell Erik, "was for all the shit you put me through the last few months."

"Fuck you," he says, spitting blood next to my shoe. "You fucking traitor."

I lunge for him again, but this time Kane jumps between me and Erik.

"Damn it, Rex," he shouts. "We've got him under arrest. A team is coming to pick him up and take him to interrogation."

"Is he the only one?" I ask, heart thudding. "Did he come alone?"

"We didn't find anyone else on our sweep," Kane says, but he shifts on his heels, knowing it's not enough.

"Leave him here," I say. "We'll watch him."

He laughs. "You'll kill him."

"He won't," Levi says, "because if we kill him, we won't be able to find Anex." He gives me a hard look. "And that's our priority, right?"

I push the image of wrapping my hands around Erik's throat and watching the life drain out of his eyes. Reluctantly, I agree. "Right."

Kane nods at Mallory. "We'll check the perimeter. You stay here, out of sight, away from the windows."

Weapon drawn, he eases out the front door, taking caution that no one is out there. Mallory removes his gun from the holster on his side.

"Hey," I call before he follows Kane. "Can I interrogate him?"

Mallory touches his puffy lip. I notice his knuckles are bleeding, too. "As long as he's alive when we get back."

The door slams and the room is quiet. Silas brings a dining room chair into the middle of the room, his eyes more focused than they've been in days. Good. He needs to get off his ass and get pissed. Elon hands me a weapon, one I'm assuming he took off of Erik. I tuck it behind my back and help him hoist our hostage off the ground, then toss him in the chair. Levi moves to retie his binds behind his back, securing him to the chair.

"They're bad enough," Erik says, eyes focused on Levi, "but you're the worst, you know that? He thought you were a real believer. A teacher. Enlightened."

Levi stills, his expression blank, but there's no doubt a million emotions are running through him. His fingers curl into tight balls at his sides and I look to Silas. "Get him out of here." I jerk my chin at Imogene. "Her too. Upstairs until I'm finished."

"What?" Imogene cries, voice panicked. "I want to hear what he has to say."

Silas nudges Levi up the stairs, and I move to her, taking her face in my hands. "What I'm about to do? I don't want that to be how you see me. Elon either. There are tactics Anex taught us that you don't know about and that's a good thing."

"I'm not afraid of you, Rex."

She should be. After all the things I did to her. The pain I allowed her to suffer at my hands and my father's. "Please go. Don't fight with me on this."

"You don't even have to do this—you can wait for the agents to get back. Let them do their job." She looks past me to Elon. "I don't want you to lose yourself in all of this again—either of you."

"We won't." I shake my head and rub my thumbs along her cheeks. "But you know we're the only ones that can stop him, Little Lamb. We can't trust the Feds to do what really needs to be done."

She nods and I press a kiss to her forehead. Her hands squeeze mine. "I love you."

"I love you, too."

She goes on her own, heading up the stairs. I wait until I hear the door snap close before I pull the gun from where I'd tucked it in the back of my pants and face Erik.

"I should put a bullet through your head for how you treated me back in Serendee."

"You were Fallen. The dregs of our community. You deserved worse." He scoffs. "I held back on your pathetic, traitorous, ass because your father held out hope that maybe you could be redeemed."

Crack!

Elon beats me to the punch, slamming his fist into Erik's jaw before I even have a chance to swing. He winces, shaking out his knuckles, but the smug grin on Elon's mouth tells me it was worth it. "Shut the fuck up, asshole. You only got to that position because we were Banished. You gained from the bullshit, trumped-up charges Anex threw at us. Otherwise, you would have been a low-level lacky for the rest of your pathetic life."

I step forward, towering over him. "You think he won't turn on you the way he turned on us? Because he will. He's loyal to no one."

"You fucked up," he says, eyes shifting to Elon, then back to me. "Putting your carnal needs above your duty to Serendee. You betrayed your father, Rex. You still are by hiding out with his woman and working with the government."

"She's mine!" I lean forward, grabbing him by the collar. "And who do you think ordered us to do everything? For Elon to sleep with Imogene? For Silas to train her to become a proficient lover? To escalate her Corrections? Who invited her to the women's group and required her to write down the collateral that exposed us? It was a fucking set up, Erik, from the very beginning. It was a way to remove obstacles. To get me to kneel. To force Elon and Levi out because of his insecurities. To control Silas in order to increase his wealth." I release him, thrusting him back so hard the chair skids. "You think he won't do the same to you? You're not even blood."

The smug intention in his eye lawvers, flickering for a moment, but then snaps back in place. "You're the one that betrayed him with all your accusations and blasphemy. You started this, Rex."

There's only one accusation that means anything to me and I'm not afraid to say it out loud. "He killed my mother. I don't know how, but he did it, and one day I'll prove it."

He snorts, holding my gaze. "Even if you do, you'll never find him."

"Then I guess you'll have to be the one to tell me." I whip out the gun and press the nozzle to his head. "Where is he hiding? What are his plans?"

He lifts his chin defiantly, making the barrel dig deeper into his temple. "Do it. I don't give a fuck. But understand that this doesn't end with me. He'll send another. And another." He grins, teeth a pale pink from his bloody mouth. "His followers are wide and strong."

"His followers are in jail or scattered like the wind," Elon says, arms crossed over his chest. "You're delusional, Erik."

"You think so? Not everyone is a traitor like you." He looks around the cabin. "This is your life now. Running until he catches you and gets her back."

I let his words sink in. "You weren't shooting at her."

"Fuck no. I was shooting at him," looks at Elon. If it hurts my friend's feelings that my father wanted him killed, he doesn't let on. "Your father wants his property back. The smartest thing for you to do is to give her to me and let me go before anyone else gets hurt."

There's not a chance in the world Anex lets us go even if he has her.

"She'll never be his Mate," Elon says.

"Oh, he knows that, and he no longer wants her for a spiritual wife. He wants her to pay. To punish her. To make her beg and scream for mercy." He laughs, enjoying this. "He has plans for your Little lamb. Dirty and depraved things that'll make her wish I'd put a bullet in her head."

"Shut up," Elon roars, foot kicking out and flipping over an end table.

Erik doesn't heed, continuing, "He's already got it lined up. The house. The dungeon. The cameras." He smirks, although it's mangled from his puffy lip. "And if you're lucky you'll survive long enough to wat—"

He doesn't get the last word out before I shove the gun in my pants to free up my hands, wrapping them around his throat. My fingers squeeze tight enough to make his eyes flutter shut, his body jerking from the lack of air.

"Rex," Elon calls, but his voice is faint, a distraction lost in the years of pent-up anger. The grief over my mother. The rage at my father. "Anex set you on a fool's errand. If he wants to keep sending people after us, then go for it. We'll take you out one by one."

"Rex!"

A voice cuts through the fog.

Her voice.

"Rex, please."

I release him, and he makes a loud, choking, gasp for air. My hands shake and it takes everything in me not to finish him off. I want to. More than almost anything else in my life. Anything but her.

I turn and see her standing at the bottom of the stairs, expression worried. Silas and Levi stand behind her, watching me closely.

"She did this," I tell Erik. "She saved your ass. Remember that."

I storm off, pretending I don't hear Erik gasping for his life. Or feel the eyes of my friends as they witnessed me turn into a monster. I find myself in the hallway off the kitchen and open the only door—the room the agents are using, and slam the door behind me.

"Fuck," I mutter, running my hands through my hair.

The door opens behind me and then shuts. I don't have to look to know it's her. And as much as I want to push her away when she wraps her arms around my waist, for her own good, I don't.

"Hey," she says, "what happened?"

"I wanted to kill him," I reply simply, sinking to sit on the edge of the bed. "He threatened you and I just... snapped."

"It's understandable. He attacked us."

"It's not understandable." My skin feels hot and my stomach churns. "It's not okay to strangle the life out of another person. If I'd killed Erik, how would I be different from him? Or my father?"

She sighs and pushes her way closer, nudging my legs apart to stand between my thighs. "It's understandable that you reacted this way. You've been pushed to the edge, Rex. Tortured. Forced to torture others. Watching your friends get sent away. Watching me get carried off with the explicit intention of becoming your father's wife. You've sold yourself as much as Silas has. Demeaned yourself to keep others safe. Fought as much as Elon. All under the pressure of being your father's heir."

"I tried so hard not to turn into him. Everything I did was the opposite." I rub my eyes with the heel of my palm. "I pushed to live outside Serendee. I partied and drank and smoked. I fucked around, and lived hard, Imogene. All I wanted was to get away from the son of a bitch."

"But you stayed for me." She reaches for my fingers, linking them with her own.

I snort. "It wasn't a selfless act, little lamb."

"I begged you to stay. I'm the one that foolishly thought there was good in Serendee. That I could reach Enlightenment."

Her tone is filled with disappointment. In herself or in Serendee, I don't know. What I do know is none of this is her fault.

"I hurt you, Imogene. Not just that day in my father's chamber." I wince at the memory of beating her with that paddle, how I bruised and battered her tender flesh. "I hurt you the day of the Ordering. I hurt you when I forced you to your knees, humiliating and exploiting your innocence and naivety. I was cold and callused when I forced myself on you and took your virginity." I feel sick thinking about it but I can't stop. Not now. "So many times, I had the chance to treat you better and I didn't." I look down at where our fingers curve together like links on a chain. "I don't deserve you. Especially not out here in a world where women get to choose their fates."

"I don't blame you for those things."

"You should. You should never want to be around someone like me again. You have the opportunity to start new. Go live your life with someone that isn't a monster who is still fighting the urge to go back in that room and end that man's life."

"You know what I think?" she asks. When I don't look at her or answer, she continues. "I think that's why Anex sent him here. He wanted you to lose control and question everything. He does know us. He knows you, he programmed us to fall into line. He knew exactly how to get you to react and behave like he would." I swallow and look into her blue eyes. "Like a ruthless leader who will do anything to get what you want."

I let her word sink in, a bit of the fog and anger clearing. "You mean like how he killed my mother to ascend to the position of power that he couldn't while she was alive or while Camille lived in Serendee."

"Exactly."

I pull her hand to my mouth, kissing her knuckles. The adrenaline slowly starts to wane. "I don't deserve you."

"That's not for you to decide."

God, this woman. "He won't give up until he destroys us all, you know that right?"

"Then we find a way to stop him."

I shake my head. "How?"

"By giving him what he wants."

"He wants you, Lamb, and that's not going to fucking happen." She's quiet—staring at me—an intent in her silence. What she wants dawns on me. "No."

"Why not? My mom did it to get into Serendee, and that's how they got me out. Why can't we do it again."

"Because Anex isn't dumb enough to fall for that twice, and I'm not stupid enough to risk you." She gives me a look, determined yet pleading. "No, Imogene. It's not going to happen."

"It's the only way to end this."

I struggle to get air to my lungs. The thought of putting her in harm's way is too much to bear. "I won't risk losing you again."

"It's not about losing anything. It's about ending this for good."

Hopping up, I pace the floor. "No, you don't! This is the kind of crazy move he wants us to make! Something impulsive and dangerous." I eye her. "But that's what you want isn't it? The danger. The risk. The feel of adrenaline when you're doing something wrong."

"What?" The hurt is clear on her face. "Why would you say that?"

"Because we're fucked up and broken, Imogene. All of us, and we fall right into old patterns. Yours is to see how much pain you can handle." I stride to the door. "Mine is to be an entitled prick, but for once," I open the door and step into the hall, "I'm not going to let it happen to me or to you either."

94

I mogene

The house feels different that night, like we're in limbo, waiting for the next attack. Erik, neck ringed with red bruises, is taken away in a van with blacked out windows, still refusing to speak. Additional agents arrive, assigned to help Mallory and Kane until the FBI moves us to a new safe house.

The events of the day are enough to make me wired, but that's not why I can't sleep. It's memory of Rex's anger and accusation. In the past I would have deferred to him, pushed aside my nagging impulse to fix this once and for all. He's my Mate and I was raised to let him make the decisions. And what if he's right? What if I just want to feel that rush of danger? The temptation of being bad?

That tell-tale twist of defiance churns in my stomach and it's not long before I finally give up and get out of bed, already knowing where I'm going—who I'm looking for.

I pass Silas sleeping on the couch, the TV down low, light flickering in the dark room. At the desk, Levi sits in the leather chair, absorbed in a book. The title is visible, *Healing the Mind: The Psychology of High Control.*

He looks up when he notices me and swivels the chair to face me. "You're up late," he says, closing the book, but keeping his thumb in it to mark his place. "Everything okay?"

My heart rattles in my chest and my skin feels hot, prickly. Shifting on my feet I finally say, "I need you."

Levi's back straightens, his thumb slides out of the book, and it falls to his side. "What's wrong?"

My hands twist in front of me, twisting at the long T-shirt I'm wearing as a nightgown. Agent McNair left me soft shorts and pants, I can't wear them, not after so many years of wearing dresses. "I need you to Correct me."

"Why?"

"Because I'm having Regressive thoughts." I swallow. "I want to disobey my Mate."

He takes a deep breath. "First, you shouldn't use the words, Regressive and Corrections. They aren't real and are only give Anex power he doesn't deserve." He rises, standing tall in front of me. "Second, I'm not going to punish you for having free will, Imogene. You don't have to do everything Rex tells you to do. He doesn't control you out here."

"Do you really believe that?"

"I'm trying to." He takes my hand and tugs me toward him. "Why don't you tell me what's going on and we can try to work through this?"

He sits and I go with him, perching on his lap. It feels good to be close to him, but that desire to pay for my Lapse is still strong. A war of conflict wages inside of me.

"Talk to me. What's made you come to me like this?"

"Instinct," I blurt. "When I do something wrong. When I have a Laps—" He frowns, and I swallow the word. "When I feel like I've been *bad*, my instinct is to come to you and you Cor—*punish* me."

"What did you do that made you feel like you're bad? How are you disobeying Rex?"

"I want to go after Anex—to let Agent McNair use me as bait to draw him out."

He weighs this, ultimately admitting, "It's not a bad idea."

"Thank you."

A smile flickers on his lips and then vanishes. "But I understand his hesitation. We just got you back. The idea of putting you at any risk is terrifying."

"It wouldn't be dangerous. I'd talk to Agent McNair. Do it the right way."

"Honey, there is no right way when it comes to dangling you in front of Anex like a piece of meat. He's unpredictable—probably more now than ever before."

The rejection of my idea stings—more than it should. It's irrational, a deep-seated need that I can't shake. Maybe Rex was right. I want to feel pain and putting myself in harm's way is one way to get it.

"You just said I have free will—then you'd be okay with me going against your wishes too?"

"I'd want us to keep talking about it and come up with a solution we all can agree on."

Well, now his reasonableness is just pissing me off.

"What if I ran out that door right now and snuck past the agents? What if he has one of his men out there and they catch me? What if I finally lured him out—getting him to expose himself?"

His forehead creases. "You're trying to get a rise out of me."

Grinding down on him, I say, "I'm trying to get *something* on you to rise." He holds my hips, forcing me still. A dark laugh bubbles in my chest. "So this is how it is."

"How what is?"

He's going to make me say it. Fine. "Without the Corrections you don't want me."

"What are you talking about?" His eyebrows knit together. "I don't understand what you're saying."

It's a lie. He knows exactly what I'm saying, but if he wants me to, I'll spell it out. "I know what we did together was messed up. I know it was Anex manipulating and controlling us—forcing us to break down our boundaries so that he could exploit them later, but..."

"There's no but, Imogene, it was wrong," he swallows thickly. "Treating you like that wasn't right."

My heart sinks. I thought if anyone would understand it would be Levi. That what we did together in the dark of his room, or down in the basement of the Center, was more than just punishment. Humiliation rises to my cheeks. "I'm sorry," I say, scrambling to get off his lap. "This was stupid—I should go."

I turn to rush out of the room, to anywhere but here, but a figure steps in front of me and grabs onto my upper arms.

"Silas. You're awake," I breathe. "I was just going to bed."

"You were running away." He releases me and runs his hand through his hair and glances over at Levi, who is frozen in his chair. "So yeah, I heard all of that."

My cheeks burn even hotter. "Well, forget it. I made a fool out of myself."

"Babe, you didn't. Look, all this stuff is fucking confusing. I get it. I'm confused. Just so fucking confused. There's real and not real. Our desires mingled up with manipulation. Where our wants end and Anex's conniving begins." He scrubs his face. "Trust me, I know."

Silas' body has been used for Anex's whims and greed for years. It's fair for him to be conflicted. Me? I'm not so sure.

"Then what do we do?"

"We don't let him continue to control us."

I look to Levi and after days of reading and focusing on moving ahead with his life, it's clear he's struggling. With clenched hands, he admits, "I don't know if I can give Imogene what she wants without losing myself." His voice drops. "And I don't know if I can give her what I want without her losing herself."

"Go on," Silas says, crossing his arms over his chest.

"Every escalation of our Cor—" he fights the word—"*sessions* was at Anex's hand. He encouraged me, he gave me the strap, he pushed you to the brink so you'd come to me begging for absolution."

"Did you give her absolution?" Silas asks.

"There *is* no absolution," Levi says. "Not in Anex's world. It's all a façade."

Silas turns to me. "If he didn't give you absolution, what *did* he give you?"

I think about those sessions. The welts he left on my back side that left me dripping with want so intense that Elon had to fuck it out of me. The night Levi cut me with the knife and then fucked me with the handle, bringing me to one of my most intimate and intense orgasms. I didn't just take the Corrections because I deserved it. I took them because I craved it.

"Relief," I say. "Because I have this emptiness in the pit of my stomach all the time. A hollowness that is only filled by my love for all of you. Every time I'm with one of you I feel more complete. Steadier." I look at Levi. "And when you bring me to the edge like that, I feel like I can fly."

"Are you sure that's not just old habits making you say that?" Levi asks.

I shake my head. "Are *you* sure that by asking me all of these questions you aren't just falling into *your* old habits?" The question seems to stun him. Shock him on an innate level. "I think you're doing all of this because you don't want to accept how much you liked our sessions. You liked them, not because Anex told you to do it, but because you got off on it."

He rushes me, slamming me into the wall. The impact hurts, but it's the good kind of hurt. The only sound is my heaving breath when he says, "Why are you doing this to me? My brain is finally clearing, and you're trying to drag me back in!"

"I don't want to drag you anywhere, Levi." His hands have my wrists pinned and the look in his eye is dark and feral. "I just want to be us. The real us."

"I'm afraid of what I'll do to you if I'm allowed to go untethered."

"I trust you. Unequivocally, but Silas will keep you from going too far, won't you?" I look over at him and he looks more awake than he has been in days. Helping makes Silas feel good, like he has a purpose, and if anyone can get us through this, it's him.

"I will," he agrees. "If this is what you both want."

His promise makes the tension in Levi's shoulders unwind, but he doesn't release me.

"I don't want to punish you because you're a bad girl," Levi says, his green eyes darkening a shade, "I want to tease and taunt you because you're sexy as hell." His hand runs up my shirt, fingers splayed over my stomach. "I want to bring you to the edge, make you cry out in pain and desire because it makes me so fucking hard I can barely see."

My belly drops and warmth spreads between my legs. "Yes, please."

His mouth hovers barely an inch from mine. I can feel his breath and I'm dying to kiss him, to feel his tongue in my mouth, but he steps back, removing his hand, his warmth. Crushed, I think maybe he's not into this after all.

Then I look down and see the hard line of his erection pressing against the front of his pants.

"Strip," he says, matter of fact. I glance at Silas who does nothing but watch quietly. Dropping my hands to the hem of my shirt, I pull it over my head and stand before them in nothing, but my panties. The room is chilly. Exposed. My nipples tighten from both the air and anticipation. We're playing a dangerous game, one where an agent could walk out at any moment. The idea shoots adrenaline down my spine.

He sits back in his chair, hand shifting his erection. "Are you wet?"

"Yes."

He leans back. "Show me."

Hooking my fingers in the sides of my panties, I pull them down. The crotch is damp. He holds out his hand and I give him the panties. He runs his fingers over the wet spot and presses it to his nose.

"Fuck," Silas mutters, shifting next to me. Levi's eyes flick to his friend, a coy smirk toying at his lips.

"Touch her."

Silas follows his friend's direction, his hand gliding down my hip, fanning over my pussy, and dipping between my legs. He feels around and my hand grabs his shoulder, bracing myself. He holds up his fingers. "Soaked."

Levi nods. "Spread her legs. I want to see her scars."

Silas drops to his knees, grazing his knuckle against my clit as he parts my thighs. I suck in air and my knees instinctively try to slam together, but he keeps them apart. His thumb brushes gently over the pale scars on my inner thighs.

"How did it feel when I gave you those?" Levi asks.

"Good." My belly flutters at both the memory and Silas' face being so close to the hot pulsing nerves between my legs. "A rush. A release."

"Do you need a release now?

I nod, hopeful. "It's been so long."

"Is that why you're being defiant?"

"Maybe," I say, willing to agree to almost anything if one of these men will touch me the way I need them to.

He reaches into his pocket and pulls a long object. A pocketknife. A tremor works its way from my belly to between my legs. Fear. Panic. Need. He flips it open, exposing the blade. It's long. The handle thick.

"You can choose, Imogene. Do you want me to cut you, or to fuck you?"

"What if I want both?"

"Greedy." There's an old glint in his eye, like he's calculating the Lapse.

"You make me that way." I tell him, without the least bit of shame. "I want the rush. The feel of you." I look down at Silas, run my fingers along his cheek. "Of him."

"I can give you what you want." Levi stands, unzipping his pants, pulling his erect cock out of the flap. "So can he."

Silas, who has been holding on far longer than he'd like, plants a single, hot kiss on my pussy. He then works his way up my body, stopping for a sharp tug on my nipple. I hiss, "Oh, God," wanting him to do it again, but he steps aside. Levi stands before me, knife in hand.

"Is this where I ask either of you if this is going too far?" Silas asks, rubbing his palm down the front of his pants.

"We're good," Levi says, licking his bottom lip. "But you may want to brace her for this."

I don't mind the feel of Silas behind me, his hard erection pressing into my backside. But I don't know what Silas means until he gently presses the tip of the knife under my ear.

"You'd look lovely painted in red," he says, voice a whisper. Silas' hands clench on my hips, this scene unfamiliar, but in my bones it feels right. I know Levi won't hurt me—no more than I want it.

No more than I crave it.

He trails the blade down my body, circling my breasts, and slashing my abdomen with phantom cuts. The touch feels like a flutter, a whisper against my skin, toying and teasing, making goosebumps rise and my nipples tighten into hard peeks.

He settles the tip on my hip, just below Silas' fingers, above the brand.

"He doesn't deserve to be marked on your body," he says. "You don't belong to him."

I feel what he is saying, deep down, like a siren calling my soul. I grab the handle and his hand. Applying pressure, I force the blade into my flesh. Levi's eyes widen. "Imogene, no—"

At first, it's a prick, just a slice, but I press harder, slashing through the mangled flesh, pushing over the fresh, still healing scars. I hurts and I bite down on my bottom lip, keeping the scream inside. Silas must sense it, the way I'm about to unleash, and turns my head, kissing me, swallowing the scream into his mouth.

Blood coats my hands and the knife falls to the floor with a clatter.

"Shit," Levi's mutters, pulling off his shirt to cover the wound. But I lick Silas' tongue and face my redheaded partner.

"Let it bleed," I tell him, catching the slippery warmth in my fingertips. I laugh, feeling a rush—*the rush*—freedom.

I grab his length, fingers slick and greasy with blood. He pulls back, as if he wants to recoil, but his cock pulses thick in my hand.

"Fuck," he mutters, liking it. I stroke him, gliding the blood up and down.

"You're right," I say, pressing my ass into Silas' crotch, "he doesn't own me. You do. Claim me. Make me yours."

Silas' hand wraps around my body, palm bloodied and flat on my stomach. Behind me there's the rustle of fabric and the hard poke of his cock as it's freed from his pants. He drops into the chair and drags me with him, bringing me down.

"You ready for me?" he asks, rubbing my clit. I buck and the tip of his cock slots against my entrance, pressing into me until his hands steady my hips and he punches inside. He fills me, his cock deep inside and I exhale at the feel of him, stretching me wide.

Levi closes the gap, taunting me with his cock in my face. I grab it, pulling the tip to my mouth, licking the salty, warm blood off the head. His legs tense, and he groans, thrusting deep to the back of my throat.

"I take it back," Levi says, fingers tugging at my hair. "You are a bad girl. So fucking bad."

This. This is when I feel right. When my body is in motion, filled and stretched. I love the taste of Levi in my mouth and the feel of Silas deep in my core. Silas' teeth bare down on my shoulder, and he palms my tits. They're everywhere. Slippery and hot.

Mine.

The urge for more consumes me and I ease back from Levi's cock, sucking at the tip. I look up at him, skin pink, a swipe of blood across his hip. His fingers brush hair off my cheek and I say, "I want you in me when you come."

Silas kisses my neck and starts to lift me up, but I press back down. "No. Both of you." I know from Rex and Elon I can take both of them, and that need to feel full is overwhelming. My legs spread and Levi lowers himself. It's awkward, with limbs and dicks and fluid everywhere, but when he straddles the two of us and slides his cock next to Silas' my eyesight grows fuzzy, black spots clouding the edges. It feels so good. The stretch so intense—so right, that my orgasm rips through me on the first thrust.

"Oh!" I cry, struggling to stay coherent.

"That's it, baby," Silas says, grunting in my ear. His arm wraps around my waist and he holds me to him. I fall into the sound of his breathing, the little words whispered in my ear, the final hiss as he comes, spilling his hot seed inside.

The two of us are lax, slumped in the chair while Levi continues to pound into me with absolute abandon. This man. My partner. *My guide.* He led me here, to this moment, to this depravity of blood and sweat and semen. His hair flops over his forehead, the long line of his jaw clenched tight. He's an angel—fallen like the rest of us. A long groan building in his chest and he grips the base of his cock and I close my eyes as he makes his final thrust.

Then it's just the three of us, a pile of heavy breath, sticky skin, fused bodies.

"Jesus Christ," Silas says, shifting beneath me. "I knew you two had your thing, but fuck, it looks like a goddam massacre in here."

I open my eyes and all I see is blood, smeared across the three of us. Levi bends over and kisses me gently. "Are we okay?"

"We're perfect."

"You two are monsters," Silas says, easing me off him and stretching his legs. "I'm not sure if I'll ever be able to walk again."

Levi rolls his eyes, but helps me stand. He wraps his arms around me. "What are you going to do about Anex? Still determined to play bait?"

"I still want to do something. I mean, I plan on it, but you're right. It should be something we all agree on."

"Any ideas?" Silas asks, cleaning up with his T-shirt.

"Yeah," I say. "But to make it work, I think I'm going to need some help."

95

Silas

"Do you think we should go up there?" Rex asks, glancing at the staircase.

"No," Levi says, continuing to read and flipping the page of his book.

"I'm just not sure they should be alone."

"Rex," I say, "she's talking to her mother. I think she can handle it."

He runs his hands through his hair, a clear sign of agitation. It's not a surprise Rex is possessive of Imogene, he chose her after all, but this isn't jealousy that he's feeling. It's insecurity. For all their time estranged, Camille is still her mother. And mother's carry weight.

"She just may want some support—a little back up as she presents her idea," Rex continues, pacing in front of the fireplace. "What if Camille tells her it's shit? Or encourages her to do something different? Her idea is good, but Camille can be a little...."

"Controlling?" Elon says. He's holding a stick in one hand and a knife in the other. Somewhere along the way he decided to take up whittling. I suppose it's better than fighting for money.

"Bossy?" Levi tosses out.

I roll my eyes at both of them. "I'd say protective."

After talking it over as a group, Imogene had the idea to talk to her mother about ways to lure Anex out without putting herself at too much risk. At first, Camille didn't want to discuss it—any level of danger was too much. But after Imogene pled her case, they came up with a plan. They're in an upstairs bedroom on a call right now.

A call we weren't invited to participate in—hence Rex pulling his hair out.

"So what's this really about?" I ask. I've worked with enough anxious people to know we're talking about a bigger problem. "Why are you so stressed about her being alone with her mom?"

"I'm not—"

"Son of a—!" Elon curses, staring down at his thumb where the knife slipped. "Fuck."

I hop off the couch and rush over. "Are you okay?"

"It's fine," he glares down at the spot. "It's just a graze."

Looking him over, I agree. Not too deep, but still bleeding. I walk into the kitchen and grab a clean cloth, running it under the faucet. Back in the room, I hand it to him and glance up at Rex. "You were saying...?"

He sighs. "What if Imogene does this interview and like they said, the whole world learns about us—about Imogene. Once it's out, she may want more."

"You mean she may want normal," Levi says, finally looking up with his book.

"Fuck normal," Elon growls, applying pressure to his thumb. "None of us are ever going to be normal."

"We played in the Secular world a lot," I remind him, "or have you forgotten the frat parties?"

"Yeah, that's the thing," Rex says, dropping into an armchair. "We did frat parties. And clubs. We drove cars and got our licenses. We had money. All kinds of shit. Imogene, she didn't get to do any of that, and once this is over, once we leave this house, the whole world is going to open up for her."

And that's it. Rex is scared. Maybe for the first time in his life, he's scared.

Levi frowns. "You don't think she'll want us anymore?"

"Or," Elon points out, "maybe she'll only want one of us."

My stomach clenches. We haven't talked about this. About how we want to handle the future. I know she loves us and I'm pretty sure she wants to be with us—all of us—but Rex is right, there are a lot of unknowns.

"Living here made the transition seem possible," Elon says, toying with the cloth, "but we've been pretty isolated. No one knows we're here. We've been able to pick up where we left off."

"Rex may be right," Levi says, "From my reading, as her mind clears, and the further we get away from Anex's control, she's going to want to live a normal life."

"Fuck." Rex deflates in his chair, as if Levi's statement confirms all his fears. He thrusts his fingers into his hair and tugs at the root. "I don't know if I can live without her. I love her."

"She loves you too." My heart thuds anxiously at the thought of letting her go, but he's right. They may not be Ordered anymore, but Imogene is loyal and she clearly loves Rex. If she's choosing anyone, it's him.

"She may, but that's not the same as wanting to be with us," Rex says, then adds, "*all* of us."

"Wait," Elon straightens, "you'd want that? To let us be part of this?"

"Why not? I love you too. You're my family, the only one I've got left." He frowns. "You know, if that's what she wants too."

Hearing Rex put someone's desires above his own, especially a female's, is big enough. Big enough to make me wonder if maybe we can make this work.

Elon stands, blood seeping through the cloth wrapped around his finger. Rex rises to meet him, but before he catches his balance, Elon throws his massive arms around his best friend and gives him a tight hug.

Rex looks at me over his shoulder, eyebrows raised. I clear my throat and say, "What Elon is expressing is a thank you. For being our best friend, our brother, and allowing us the chance to be with the woman we love. You don't have to, even outside of Serendee, you could have coveted her and kept her for yourself."

"He's right," Levi says. "Anex was never going to let us have a mate, but you did, and that bonds us together."

Elon steps back, clapping Rex on the shoulder. "And if she doesn't want all of us?" he asks, wiping at his eyes.

"Then we fight for her," Rex says, looking calmer than he did moments before. "She could maybe say no to me, but all of us?" A grin tugs at his mouth. "She doesn't stand a chance."

96

I mogene

The lights are glaringly hot, and my armpits feel like the inside of a damp swamp, but I've just survived the first segment of my interview with Jane Morgan. Across the room, behind a crew managing cameras and microphones and the swamp lighting, my mother gives me a smile of encouragement.

This interview, it's the compromise to me playing bait. Turns out my mother had been fielding interview requests for weeks, buffering me from the hordes of journalists that had been vying for an exclusive.

Apparently, everyone was curious about the Sex Slaves of Serendee and due to statements I'd made to the police about my time in captivity, the branding, the secret women's club, and Timothy Wray's plan to make me his mate, my name was at the top of the list.

"Are you ready?" Jane asks. Her hair is perfect, a thick helmet framing her symmetrical face. Her eye makeup is thick, making her seem a little unreal. Can someone's eyes really be that color blue?

I think of Rex. Yes.

The weird thing is she's exactly how Anex would have described a member of the media: a superficial puppet whose only goal is to exploit the Enlightened out of jealousy.

Which is not how *I* view her. It's not, but those mental assumptions are hard to shake.

"You've already told us a little about your childhood and what it was like growing up in Serendee. We'll start with a few more easy questions before we build up to the heavy stuff, then we'll bring in your mother."

"Sounds good." I smooth out my black skirt and shift on the couch cushion, a lame attempt to hide my nerves. I don't think it works. "I'm ready when you are."

The camera man gives his cue, and around us the lights dim, other than the bright ones directed at us. My mother gives me a tight smile, and I'm reminded why I'm here.

Timothy Wray can hide, but we're going to expose him for his crimes. We're going to reveal the world to who he really is even if it means having to expose myself to do it. Camille and I were intentional when picking out which show to give an exclusive interview. Popular, with a big audience, and a reporter that would make me look strong but sympathetic.

Jane Morgan was the winner.

"Imogene," she starts, "for the majority of our audience... well, they're going to have a hard time believing you and the other residents didn't know about Timothy Wray's illegal activities." She looks down at a sheath of papers. "Tax evasion, money laundering, distribution of illegal substances and of course, the horrifying charges of sex trafficking and imprisonment. Is it possible for all of that to be going on and no one being aware of it?"

Way to start with an easy one, Jane.

"I won't justify our ignorance. And that is what we were, ignorant and naive about the truths of our home—in Serendee. We were very isolated from what we called the "secular world" and Anex controlled the access we had to information coming in and out of our community."

"Including media, right?"

"Correct. We had no televisions or radios. We relied on Anex to let us know what was important and to make the standards for how we lived and worked. He gave us skewed views of government and laws." I swallow, feeling the heat prick the back of my neck. "It feels foolish to say we just didn't know, but we didn't, and even if we did, what would we do about it?"

"You were afraid of him."

It's not a question but I answer it anyway. "Yes, very much so and the more I learned, the more I understood how much danger we were in."

She leans forward. "In what way?"

I take a deep breath and try to formulate my words. Camille, Levi, and I spent hours going over possible questions, but now that I'm here it's a struggle to articulate it accurately. "Timothy Wray controlled our minds and bodies. He managed what we ate, what we wore and when we slept. We spent hours listening to his lectures and absorbing his propaganda." I give her a small smile. "That's a word I just learned. It wasn't part of our vocabulary."

"Did he punish people?"

I'm not going to talk about the corrections. I'd already made that decision. I'm also not speaking about my relationship with my men. Anex already used that against me once, I won't allow it to happen again.

"In his own way. The biggest reward you could get from Anex was his attention. It was the most coveted thing in Serendee. He knew it, and he doled it out carefully and strategically. He didn't have to punish people often because all anyone wanted was his approval."

"Is it true you were arranged to marry his son?"

"Yes." *Mate.*

"And that allowed you to become part of what people refer to as his 'inner circle.'"

"It did."

"And being part of that inner circle allowed you more access to Timothy Wray and his activities?" she asks.

"I don't think it allowed me more access to him," I struggle to breathe just admitting it. "I think it allowed him more access to me."

Jane leans forward, hand covering mine. "What did Wray want from you, Imogene?"

I look to my mother, and she nods. We knew I'd have to tell the truth. Reveal to the world what kind of person he really is.

"I was flattered by his attention," I admit. "And I was asked to join a special group of women. To join we had to tell our deepest secrets." Collateral. "And we were marked—branded—with a symbol. One we thought represented Serendee."

"But it didn't represent Serendee, correct?"

"No. We were branded with Anex's initials." Tears burn in my eyes at the memory. The pain and humiliation. The utter mind control he had over me. "Anex wanted me to be one of his wives and the months leading up to my escape were spent either in isolation, being groomed, or being manipulated by him."

"Did you say wives? Plural?"

I nod.

She lets that sink in, then adds, "You understand that people will say that you could've left at any moment. You're eighteen. Your mother had left the group years before. But you stayed and willingly participated in these activities. People will say this isn't a cult, that he's just a con man who convinced the weak people in the community to believe in what he's selling."

"I would tell those people that I was born and raised in Serendee and that I was taught that even though there are times the community hurts, we believed it was less than the world outside. That our family and friends, that our rules and our leader, would keep us safe on our path to Enlightenment."

"Why are you here, Imogene? Why tell a story so many will find hard to believe?"

"Because it's time for Anex to practice what he preaches. He's always telling us obstacles are just another test we have to endure. That only the weak and fallen fall victim to outside interference." I straighten my spine. "I believe *this* is his test. One he needs to be present for. He taught us to believe in our convictions, in the truth of our community. If he has nothing to hide, and he did nothing wrong, then why is he on the run?"

Jane nods, her expression pleased with my response. She waves Camille to come over and my mom crosses the small space and sits on the couch next to me.

"Is it true you two have been estranged from one another for years?"

"Yes, since she was twelve," Camille says. "Leaving her was the hardest thing I ever had to do."

"Then why did you? Most parents wouldn't leave their children in that situation."

"I refused to go," I tell Jane. "She tried to get me and I refused. Serendee was my home."

Jane looks back at Camille. "Do you regret it?"

A tremor runs through my mother, and I reach for her hand. "Every day, but I also know how scared I was at the time and I did what I thought I had to. That I don't regret."

"Scared of Timothy Wray? You thought he was going to hurt you?"

"His first wife was my best friend. We all started Serendee together. Timothy changed over time, he started gaining power and control over the residents. He wanted an open marriage and his wife, my best friend, Beatrice, refused." She looks at me. "She was dead two months later and he wanted me to take her place. There was no way that was happening, but it became clear; fall in line, become his wife, let him continue his tyranny or my fate would be the same as Beatrice's."

My stomach rolls with queasiness. Back then I never would have believed Anex was capable of such things. Even a few months ago when Rex told me his suspicions, but now I know better.

"You think he hurt his wife?" Jane leans in slightly, eager for an answer.

My mother doesn't let her down. "I know he did. He took away my best friend, he stole my daughter's innocence, and he's ruined hundreds of lives."

"Wow, that's quite an accusation." Jane's expression softens and she looks between us. "What's it like having your daughter back?"

"I never gave up hope that one day we'd be reunited, but I also wasn't sure if it would happen." Mom looks at me and smiles. "It feels like a miracle."

"And now?" Jane asks, looking at me.

"Now it feels like we have a second chance," I say, holding back tears. Camille and I have a long way to go, but the fact that she's here, doing this my way, is a huge step. "One of the tactics Anex uses to control people is to separate families. He managed to get my mom away from me, but that's another one of his cycles of abuse we're ending."

I say this more to the camera than to Jane. I'm talking to him.

"Everyone in Serendee now has the opportunity for a second chance, but we won't experience true freedom until Timothy Wray and his associates are brought to justice. He needs to understand what it's like to feel the walls closing in, to have your choices taken away from you, to become isolated and removed from your loved ones." I squeeze my mother's hand. "But until then we will keep living —surviving—because that's who we are. Ironically, he's the one that taught us to be that way and ultimately, we will be his downfall."

97

———

Imogene

In the end Timothy Wray isn't found on the beach of some tropical island, or deep in a forest rebuilding his community. Because of the popularity of my interview with Jane Morgan the whole world started looking for Timothy Wray.

Ultimately, four days after the broadcast, they find him in Las Vegas. Photos are plastered all over the news—images of Anex sitting at a table in the middle of a smoke-filled casino. He's got a cigarette between his fingers, a drink at his fingertips and he's wearing a base-ball cap and jeans. Two women sit on either side of him, watching him gamble.

Jane Morgan announces from the TV that these are sex workers. Not his sex workers, but ones he hired in Vegas to be his companions.

"I mean..." Rex says from next to me. His arm is around my shoul-der, and the five of us have been glued to the TV since the reports started rolling in.

"Right?" Elon adds, not able to formulate a full sentence.

"It's just so—"

"Anticlimactic?" Levi offers.

"Yes," Silas nods. "Exactly. It's anticlimactic. Not to mention fucking hypocritical."

The entire scene is surreal. Our leader, the champion for health and clean living, is caught in a smoky bar wearing polyester clothing surrounded by bright lights and gluttony.

"You know what?" I say, dragging my eyes from the screen. "I fucking hate that guy."

Rex laughs, pulling me into his side and kissing my temple. "Me too, Little Lamb."

"Can we skip to the best part?" I ask.

"I've got it," Silas says, fast forwarding a little until he gets to the next part of the report. I snuggle into Rex's side as the images on the screen flip, shifting to the scenes of the police surrounding Anex in the parking lot. He's shoved to the ground, arms behind his back.

"After Timothy Wray was taken into custody his partner, Margaret Robinson, who is eight months pregnant, was found in their lavish penthouse suite at the Royale Casino," Jane says, voice short and clipped. She's not doing a person-to-person interview here. She's reporting the news and her persona changes like a chameleon. "She was found with Jasmine West, heir of the Cobra Tequila empire, and another one of Wray's followers, Robert Carrington. Carrington is reportedly a self-made millionaire from the tech industry who hasn't been seen by family or friends in months."

The three of them are escorted out of the hotel by police, the bright lights of photographers' cameras flashing in their faces. Margaret looks huge, like she could give birth at any moment. The screen shifts again, this time to a press conference with Attorney General Michael Morris.

"We're thrilled to learn of the capture of Timothy Wray, Margaret Robinson, Jasmine West and Robert Carrington. We look forward to extraditing them from Nevada and bringing them home where they will face the charges brought by the state." He looks directly at the camera. "Many people have asked about the remaining members of the Serendee community. We continue the process of determining the roles residents played in Wray's schemes. Many, including dozens of children, are victims. It will take time to figure this out. We ask for your patience and consideration." He rests his hands on the podium. "And last, due to new evidence, I'd like to announce that investigators are looking into the allegations of foul play in the suspicious death of Beatrice Wray, Timothy's wife. Thank you. That's all for today."

Shouts come from the media, their voices drowning one another out. Morris walks off the stage, clearly not planning on answering any questions. Next to me, Rex disentangles himself from me and stands. "I think I need some air."

He walks to the door, closing it with a sharp snap. I look at the guys. "Go," Silas says. Elon nods.

He's out on the porch, leaning against the railing. I wrap my arms around him. "I doubt anything will come from it, but it's nice to hear they're looking into it. Thank you for getting this started."

"Me? I didn't do this, Rex. You did."

He turns, facing me. "What are you talking about?"

"The day you picked me for the Ordering, that's the day all of this fell into line."

"Careful, you sound like my father." he snorts and gestures to the house. "Or like Levi."

"Anex's talk about The Way and Enlightenment may have been self-serving, but there's a reason people wanted to be part of his world. This connection between us—this need for something bigger than us." I place a hand on his chest. "We found that. Me, you, Elon, Silas, Levi—we're bigger than Anex."

"I worry about everyone left behind."

"Me too."

"I wonder if there's anything we can do for them."

"I know who we can ask." I smile. "I have you to thank for her, too. You opened that door for me."

"One of us should have a mother in their lives, don't you think?"

Sitting here like this reminds me of the day up on the cliff, the day we first spoke, when we'd both just lost everything. The difference now is that we're no longer divided by power. By Anex's rules, or the lure of The Way.

We've found one another. We're true.

We're mates.

I feel it in my chest, when he looks at me with those brilliant blue eyes or touches me with his strong, steady hands.

The veil that kept us separated has been torn down. We've learned the truth and have survived. We escaped and will flourish. We went against all our beliefs but for the first time in my life, I feel it.

Enlightened.

EPILOGUE

I mogene
Three Weeks Later

Music fills the darkened room and I lurch up, body moving like I'm pulled by strings. Anex. He's calling us for a lecture.

"Hello?" A low voice says. A light flashes, glaring in the dark and the weight of a hand on my hip draws me back to the present. We're not in Serendee. We're at Camille's house. Anex is in jail.

"You're safe," Silas says, drawing me to him. "That's just Rex's cell phone."

I exhale slowly as Rex speaks low into the phone. "Now? Okay. We'll be there."

Silas and I both sit up and Rex comes back to the bed, sitting on the edge. He's wearing nothing but a pair of shorts, his body filled out after months of starvation and abuse.

"Who was that?" Silas asks, stretching his arms over his head.

"The jail."

Panic grips me. "Is something wrong? Did Anex—"

"The *women's* jail. Margaret's in labor." He looks at me. "She asked for us—me and you—to come to the hospital."

"Oh." My heart still pounds. Two scares too close together. I push back the cover and swing my legs over the side of the bed. "Do you know what she wants?"

"Nope," he shakes his head and offers me a hand, "but I guess we'll find out."

⁓

The car is quiet as Rex drives us to the hospital in my mother's car. The streets are empty in a way I'm unfamiliar with. I'm still not used to being in this world, the freedom of picking up at 2 AM and getting in a car, wearing jeans and an oversized sweatshirt, hair still messy from sleep.

"They didn't say anything else?" I ask. "Just that she wants us at the hospital?"

"That's all," he says, hands tight on the steering wheel.

"Then I'm sure everything's okay." I settle back in the seat, willing that to be true. I have no fondness for Margaret, she's responsible for much of my hurt as Anex, but that baby is an innocent. I just want it to arrive in this world safe.

Rex grunts and it's like every muscle in his body is tense. I rest my hand on his thigh and squeeze. "Are you worried?"

A car's lights flash as it drives past, highlighting the tick in his jaw. "No."

He's been a little distant, but it seemed normal to me. He watched his father get arrested, our whole life crumble, we've had to move from the cabin back to my mother's house. There are hearings and trials coming up. Testimonies and depositions. It's been scary and unknown.

He pulls into the hospital driveway, easing the car into an empty spot in the visitor lot. Turning off the car he clutches the keys, unmoving. "Rex, what's going on?"

"We need to talk," he looks out the window, up at the bright hospital sign. "But I don't think now is the right time."

"Why not?" I ask. "We have no obligation to go in there just because Margaret wants us to. She can wait."

A smile tugs at the corner of his mouth. "So independent."

"I'm just making you a priority." I take his hand. "Tell me."

"The guys and I," he starts, and I feel the tremor in his hand, "we've been trying to give you space—room to make decisions about the future."

"The future? What does that mean?"

He inhales sharply. "We've never really talked about it since leaving. Back there everything was set in stone. You belonged to me. It was determined. But out here, those rules don't apply."

"That's what you're worried about?" I move my hand to his chest where his heart pounds erratically. "I'll always belong to you. I love you."

He exhales, a little of the tension easing. "Is that all you want? Just me or..." he swallows, "because I know it's not traditional and the guys are prepared. We're all prepared to do what you want. And everyone has just been following your lead."

At night we sleep together, taking turns in the king-sized bed. Tonight, it had been Silas and Rex. Before that, Elon and Levi. Night after night I get to spend it with the men I love. We cook together, watch stupid television shows, shop and explore the city with new eyes. They explain this world to me, help me understand it. They're healing me, one moment at a time.

"We're hanging by a thread here, Little Lamb," he says, breaking into my thoughts. "I need to hear you say it."

"I couldn't give any of you up for the world," I say, tears pricking at my eyes. "The four of you are the only good things I brought out of Serendee. I want you. All of you."

He moves suddenly, eyes lit with emotion. His hand traces my jaw, and he whispers, "I love you," against my lips, before his mouth claims mine. A slow burn spreads through me, like the glow of daylight, despite the dark surrounding us. Rex is my sun. Elon, Levi and Silas are the rays that keep me alive. "I'll tell them when we get home. I should have been clearer. I took you for granted."

"Never," he says, hand clasping my face and kissing me one last time. His forehead presses against mine. "I guess we should go inside."

He exits the car and walks around to open it for me, hand clasping mine. One thing is for certain; whatever is waiting for us inside, it seems easier knowing that we'll handle it together.

~

On a wing filled with soft mauve décor and teddy bears on the wall, a guard waits outside the hospital room door, a stark reminder of who we're here to visit. There hasn't been a trial yet—Anex, Margaret, and Erik are all in jail awaiting hearings. Jasmine and Robert, with the strength of their family connections, personal finances, and denials of involvement of the more serious charges, were able to get bail.

"Spread your legs," the guard says, insisting on patting us down. I went first, but her hands seem to linger on Rex's large frame. "She's still on security measures," the square shaped woman with blunt bangs says. "You're to keep your distance at all times. Do not offer or accept anything. There are cameras." Her hands pat Rex's butt and he frowns, eyes narrowed. "Understand?"

"Has she already had the baby?" I ask.

The guard nods, actually giving me a glimmer of a smile, and opens the door. The room is small, but Margaret looks tiny in the oversized hospital bed. Her left wrist is attached to the rail by a chain and handcuff. Her right arm holds a bundle—a blanket rolled up so tight that all I can see is a little, squished, pink face in the crook of her arm.

A flood of emotion rushes through me. I'd always assumed I'd be there for the birth of Margaret's baby—assist actually. I feel a strange sense of loss at not being here, but also understand that I have no right. Margret looks tired. Deep purple shadows hang under her eyes. Her cheeks are gaunt and her hair stringy. I'm not sure if it's from the delivery or from life in detention. Could be both.

"Are you okay?" I ask, eyes shifting to the bundle. "Is the baby okay?"

"As good as a woman can be after pushing a nine pounder out of my vagina." Margaret works to sit up a little, wincing from what I assume is pain. "But the birth was beautiful. Not what I wanted, obviously, but still."

"It's a…" Rex starts, peering at the baby and taking in the pink hat, "a girl?"

"Meet your baby sister." She lifts her arm, offering the baby to Rex. "Go on, take her."

Rex shakes his head, eyes glazing over. Shock? I step in, bend, taking the tiny newborn from Margaret. She's so lightweight and fragile, yet firm and compact. Her mother watches me closely as I settle her into my elbow. "She's beautiful." I peer at her face at those blue eyes. I look at Rex. "She has your eyes."

"What do you want, Margaret?" He asks, visibly distressed. "Why have us come down here because if you think that you can—"

"Do you remember the story I told you about meeting your father?" she asks, cutting him off.

"Yes. At a café in town. You were a student, and he wooed you with his intelligence to come down to the Center for classes."

Her lips quirk. "Well, that was a lie."

Rex stiffens next to me, snapping out of his fog. "Then what's the truth?"

"I met your father when I was fourteen. I was working at my father's restaurant and Serendee was one of his suppliers. Back then Anex used to make the deliveries himself. He'd show up in that old red truck, the back filled with crates of organic vegetables. He was handsome as sin. All blue eyes and a smile that made you feel like you were the only person in the world." Rex shifts next to me, and I reach out, taking his hand. "He'd drop off the food, come in for a meal. I'd serve him and we'd talk." She laughs. "Well, *he'd* talk."

"Ow." She hisses, and the movement from laughing makes her wrap her free arm over her belly, wincing. "Sorry. They said to be careful about that." She takes a slow, settling, breath. "Anyway, his visits lasted for years. Sometimes he'd take me around in his truck, making deliveries to all the other markets and restaurants on his route. He told me all about you—" she looks at Rex, "and your mother who had died. He said he liked having the company of someone who didn't know his trauma or past."

An uneasy feeling tickles my spine. I've learned over the last year that everything about Anex is a well well-designed façade. But Margaret... even in her darker moments she always seemed so true.

"When I was sixteen, I started running wild. Staying out all night. Going to parties. Drinking, smoking, nothing big, you know," she winks at Rex knowingly, "but my father was at his wits end. He was a single father—my mother had been gone for years—and he just had no idea what to do with me. Then Anex came by the restaurant one day with a delivery, and my father told him all about it. I guess Anex suggested that I could come live at Serendee, that he'd straighten me out with fresh air and a wholesome environment. When I was better, he'd send me back."

"Were you angry?" I ask, rocking my hip a little when the baby lets out a yawn.

"God, yes. Furious. I felt betrayed that my father would just send me away and to some stupid, boring commune. I wanted my internet and TV. My cell phone, weed and my boyfriend who was a drummer in a band. Twice I tried to jump out of the car. Once, I succeeded, but he chased me down and dragged me back. By the time we got to Serendee we were both dirty and worn out. He'd also convinced me to give it a shot. He's amazing at that, you know, convincing people into things they're skeptical about. It didn't hurt that he was so good looking. Charming and charismatic. I was half in love with him the first day we met. By the time we got to Serendee I was head-over-heels. The all-consuming kind that threatens to swallow you whole."

She tells this story in a faraway voice, like she's a million years away from being that girl. In truth, that's exactly what she is. The woman in front of me is the aftermath of a man like Timothy Wray.

"I don't remember you being in Serendee when you were sixteen." Rex regards her with suspicion—like this is just another game.

"That's because your father didn't allow me to join the regular population," she says. "Not at first. He put me in an empty house on the edge of town, this was before the Main House was finished, and kept me there."

"How long?" he asks.

"A few years."

My throat threatens to close off, but I manage to ask, "He locked you in a house for years? Alone?"

"He *educated* me in that house. I didn't have the privilege of growing up in Serendee, like you two did. There were a lot of things I needed to learn before I would be worthy of living among the other residents. Of being worthy of him."

My fingers tighten around Rex's, a chill settling in my spine. "You were one of the Fallen."

"I was the *first*." She says this with pride. "A success too. It took a lot of work. A lot of Corrections. One step forward and one back, all of that. He trained me, just like you. I was broken down and built back up. It was my own journey. My path to under-standing The Way." She smiles warmly at me. "It's why I had such an affinity for you, Imogene. I understood your spirit, and he felt the same connection to you that he had to me all those years ago."

Bile rises in my throat, bitter and overwhelming. Panicked, I hand the baby to Rex, pushing her into his chest, before bending over, fighting off a gag.

"I'm sorry my father did that to you," Rex says, a tremor in his voice. I take a deep breath, willing my stomach to settle. Looking up, I see that the bundle is so small against his broad chest. "You were a child and deserved better. I'm sure if you tell the DA your story, they'll reconsider, and possibly allow you to testify for the prosecution."

"You misunderstand." Her eyes widen. "Your father saved my life. He introduced me to the philosophies of The Way. He chose me and I will eternally choose him. I will never speak out against him. *Ever*."

Rex and I look at one another, neither sure of what to say. "Then why did you call us here? Just to see the baby?"

"I want you to take her."

I blink. "Excuse me?"

"I can't raise a child in jail, Imogene. And the judge isn't giving me bail. I believe Anex and I will ultimately be proven innocent, but someone needs to care for her while we're fighting for our freedom."

"You can't be serious," he says.

"Dead." She levels an intense look at Rex. "You're her family. She needs to be with you. Her big brother. Not tied up in some foster system with strangers."

The nausea of finding out the truth of Margaret's past is overwhelmed by the request she's making. I'm finding it hard to breathe. To think. "Please. Just consider it."

Before there's a chance to reply, the guard opens the door, allowing a nurse inside. "I need a few minutes with the new mommy." She takes the bundle from Rex and says, "How about you push this sweet angel down to the nursery?"

We step outside, the square bed on wheels in front of us. The guard points down a hall to the nursery.

"That..." Rex says, voice so low I almost can't hear him, "that was fucked up. Every day I think my father can't be worse than I already think he is and sure enough, I'm proven wrong."

"I know."

"And a baby? We can barely function ourselves much less take care of an infant."

"Life is chaotic," I agree. "We've just gotten on our feet."

Rex stops, pressing his back to the wall and dropping his head to his hands. "Why is this so fucking hard, Imogene? When does it stop being hard?"

I know what he's asking. As terrible as those last few months in Serendee were, the majority of our lives there seemed stable. Familiar. It would be easier to go back to what we knew than living this life of unknowns.

"We can't take her..." his forehead is creased, and he gazes at me and then back down to the little girl, "can we?"

I look down at her, at those same blue eyes that Rex has, and I want to say no. That we're moving forward and leaving all of this behind, but Margaret is right. She's family. She's Rex's only blood relative that he has left. We can't allow Anex to destroy this little one's life too.

"We can," I say, feeling it in my chest. "But we should talk it over with the guys first—"

"They'll say yes," he says with zero hesitation.

"And probably my mom," I add.

He reaches into the crib, running his finger down her pink cheek. "We'll need her help."

"But we can do this."

He smiles at me, handsome and strong. "We can definitely do this."

18 Months Later

A lot can happen in a year and a half.

A community, a family, can be torn apart.

A leader can be held accountable for the terrible things he's done.

A new, different kind of family can emerge from the ruin.

And something so precious can be born, a reminder of the true meaning of life.

"Mom," I say, trying to formulate a response. "This is isn't necessary."

"Honey, I don't need it anymore. I spend all of my time over at Beatrice House and there's plenty of room for me to stay there."

I stare at the key she's holding out. "But it's your house, and you know I can afford something on my own."

When the evidence of the Fallen was revealed in court; the imprisonment, sexual abuse and trafficking, the jury delivered a swift and decisive judgment. It only took them two hours to convict Timothy Wray on all charges. The following day the sentencing was issued, and the judge gave him a hundred-and-sixty-seven years in prison along with the ruling that he pay restitution to his victims. *Millions.*

Anex claimed to be broke, that he'd gambled away his stolen fortune, but the government seized the Serendee property. An arrangement was made for Anex's victims to have the option of receiving land as part of their restitution, which allowed families to be reunited in a safe space. The community center was transformed into a resource center with social workers and job counselors. They also gave Rex his family home, since the title was in his mother's name. He, in turn, donated it to Camille to use as a new center for cult survivors and their families.

During this transition, we'd been staying at my mothers' house and while we figured out what to do next. The idea of moving back to Serendee doesn't appeal to any of us, but we also don't know where to go. The world is big and intimidating.

Mom leans against the porch railing, arms crossed over her chest. "Have I told you about buying this house?"

The porch swing creaks when I sit down. "No."

"When I left Serendee, I had no credit to my name. No bank account or savings. Everything had been tied up in the community." She runs her hand over the painted wood rail. "I didn't have any family to come back to. No siblings. My father died when I was in college."

"What about your mother?"

She laughs. "Things were already tense when I dropped out of grad school and moved to the property. She called it then—outright —she said I was joining a cult and to snap out of it. I told her she was closed minded and didn't understand how we were going to change the world." She laughs, but it's lacking humor, just filled with a tinge of sadness. "It didn't help that I borrowed money for school and invested it in the vision of Serendee. And later, the fact that I left you behind... well, she never forgave me." She looks down at her feet, the only sound is the whine of the swing chains. "I came out of Serendee alone, scared, broke, but eventually I got a job, saved every dime I could, and had enough for the down payment on this place."

In a matter of minutes my mother had filled in the gaps about much of my family history that I never knew about.

"The lack of support is why I started this program in the first place. I wanted to make a place for people to go to that needed help. And for people like my mother who needed support when she lost her child into something like this." She smiles at me. "I knew I needed to make up for what I helped start—for leaving you."

"Thank you for telling me all of that, but you don't need to give me your house, it's too much."

"I should have given you everything, Imogene. I should have been there for your first dance, your first date, to help you apply for college, to get you ready for life. I failed at all of that, but this is something I can do for you." She stands upright. "I can give you a home. One to make your own."

"You know I'll be living here with all of them, right?"

"And Bea. Yes, they're your family, I understand that." She's fought me on this. Encouraged me into therapy, worried I'm stuck in old habits. But I'm not. And my therapist agrees. This is just who I am, and they are who I love. How we came together may be unconventional, but nothing is going to change how we feel about one another. "I was thinking you could use some of your money to tear down a few walls and make a big bedroom and a room for Bea next door." She grins. "Maybe add a family room to the back?"

As she talks, I can envision it. The six of us in the kitchen where Silas and I ate our first Pop Tarts. A freshly painted living room with a sectional and big TV. A room decorated just for Bea—the sunshine in our life.

A place for us to continue to heal, to grow, and figure out what to do with our lives.

Together.

"Please." Mom holds out the key. "Take it."

I hold out my hand and she drops the key into my palm. I rush over, engulfing her in a hug. This is what Anex took from me. My mom. My history. My truth. But in this house, I'll rebuild it, we'll rebuild it, one indulgence at a time.

.

.

AFTERWORD

First, don't forget to join Monarch's on Facebook for all the good stuff! If you enjoy dark romance, make sure you check out my books, including the Royals of Forsyth U, available on Amazon. You can also find me on instagram @lawsonwrites or TikTok @angellawsonauthor.

Readers,

Writing this series has been interesting. I started to develop the idea for Serendee during the early days of the pandemic when I was walking a lot. There is a "cult-ish" community in my neighborhood and it got me thinking deeper about the topic. Not that cults aren't something I'm curious about anyway. I first read Helter Skelter in high school and Jim Jones and the People's Temple sucked me in during college. I won't deny there are elements of many different cults in this series. Heaven's Gate, NXVIM, Scientology, The Children of God and various other extremist religious groups, and a few off-the-wall cults that no one has ever heard of.

The interesting thing I noticed during my research is that all of these high control groups behave the same way. They build, they flourish, and ultimately their downfall follows predictable patterns.

Anyway, I appreciate you all "indulging" me in this possibly made up trope, cult romance, that allowed me to deep dive into my personal obsession + my love for reverse harem + giving all the characters I traumatize a happy ending.

The time period of writing this series was tough. I wrote the first draft of The Order before Lords of Pain was released. Obviously, once that book was out there, Sam and I were focused on the Royals. I also had no idea how to market/cover/or categorize a "cult romance" because seriously, this is not a thing. It took me a year to come up with a cover design (this was right before discrete covers became popular. I should have waited another 6 months!) and I rewrote the first draft to be a little darker, something I was more comfortable with after working on Lords.

By the time I released The Order my husband had been diagnosed with cancer. During the last 18 months he's had chemo, surgery, radiation, another surgery, and is coming up on his final *fingers crossed* surgery next week—typically, the day before this releases. Sam and I have written 6 Royals Books, are midway through Princes, launched a kickstarter campaign and I had covid!

Y'all it's been a LONG two years. Thank you for sticking around during all of this and allowing me to play in this side sandbox of delicious, deranged darkness.

Angel